THE RETURN OF THE MARINES

TALES OF THE MARINES IN THE NEAR FUTURE

VOL 1: THE FEW
VOL 2: THE PROUD
VOL 3: THE MARINES

GLOSSARY

Colonel Jonathan P. Brazee, USMCR (Ret)

Semper Fi Press

The Few: Originally published by iUniverse, 2009
The Proud: Originally published by Semper Fi Press, 2012
The Marines: Originally published by Semper Fi Press, 2012

Acknowledgements:

I want to thank all those who took the time to pre-read these three books, catching my many mistakes in both content and typing. My old roommate, Allan Whiting, CDR, USNR (Ret), and merchant mariner extraordinaire (when he is not discovering comets and such, that is), gave invaluable insights as to the merchant fleets. From VFW Post 9951 in Bangkok, I need to thank Ricky Reece, MacAlan Thompson, and Bill Bernstrom for their proofreading and fact-checking. I need to thank Mike, a reader from Amazon who has left comments on my other books and gave me pre-publication comments on this one. Another reader was Ann Bunch, whose reviews and insights were extremely helpful. Then there are the Military Times Forums where the Naval Aviation members fixed a number of mistakes, and from ArmyRangers.com, I need to thank PocketKings and Worldweaver for their assistance in getting my Ranger facts and terminology correct. My editor, Dr. Bob Rich kept me on the straight and narrow. All remaining typos and inaccuracies are solely my fault.

THE FEW

Prologue

The Military Reform Act of 2018, which merged most of the Marine Corps into the Army, consolidated the various service intelligence agencies, and brought logistics and procurement under one joint agency, was primarily passed as a means to lower the federal budget.

Without the Islamic Renaissance, however, it is unlikely that there would have been support to pass the act. When the leaders of all major branches of Islam, inspired by the efforts of such men as Prince Ghazi bin Muhammad of Jordan and Sheik Ali Gomma of Egypt, announced an end to terrorism as a means to promote religious causes, the US military seemed at once too expensive of a luxury to maintain.

The prime directive of the fatwa was that no violence could be conducted against innocents. That meant no more indiscriminate bombings, no more indiscriminate attacks, no more kidnappings, torture, and executions. Suicide was announced as a sure step into hell, as expressed in the *Qur'an*. Any Muslim who ignored this fatwah would be hunted down and killed as being false followers of the Prophet.

There were other parts of the Renaissance as well, such as the re-establishment of the university at Timbuktu (once the greatest university in the world), equal (if separate) rights for women, and a movement to the non-aligned sector of world politics. The rest of the world wondered if this was merely fodder for public consumption or if it was for real. Some Islamic religious leaders decried the fatwa and issued their own, but the public had grown tired of the years of violence and continued poverty when the rest of the world improved its standard of living. Western forces in Iraq, Afghanistan, and the Sudan drew back to their bases. Navy ships off the coast of Iran and Malaysia withdrew. The world watched as small flurries of violence erupted and as stubborn imams and their small forces were overwhelmed by local military forces joined by farmers, businessmen, students and shopkeepers. A few weeks of spasms, and calm entered the scene. It seemed the Renaissance was for real.

Within a year, all US forces in the Muslim world were deployed back to the US and the final cost of the War on Terror was being tallied.

That cost was high: years of deploying forces abroad, years of expenditures in equipment; years of military men and women coming home in body bags; years of increased security on the homefront. Years of politicians trying to justify the sacrifices.

With the removal of Islamic Extremism as an enemy, there wasn't a strong, obvious reason to keep a large military to a public weary of years of fighting. Who was the enemy? Why keep such a large military? A resurgent Russia was not considered a military threat to the US, and China's "threat" was economical.

Now, some politicians saw their opportunity to make their mark on the nation. A triumvirate of three legislators, Congressman Thomas Eddy (D-NY), Senator Katherine Brooke (D-MO), and Senator Michael Eduardo (R-CA) felt this was their opportunity. Although coming from different directions, all three had the same goal—a drastic reduction in the military. Congressman Eddy had always felt that violence was not the answer to anything, and that the show of military force always damaged the interests of the nation showing the force. Although he toned down his rhetoric somewhat to get elected, he was still an opponent of militarism. Senators Brooks and Eduardo thought that the vast expenditures made on the military could be used either in other programs or to reduce the budget.

Together, these three fairly junior politicians, with behind-the-scenes support from politicians in greater positions of power, were able to ramrod through the act. Large numbers of servicemen would be de-mobilized. Units were to be disbanded. Weapons programs shut down. Bases closed. And the Marine Corps? The Marines would cease to be.

The Marines might not have been on the skyline to get disbanded had it not been for Senator Eduardo. The Senator published report after report on how much savings would be realized without a separate Marine Corps. He pointed out that in the War on Terror, Marines and Army units had been used interchangeably. One Army Division, one Marine Division. Same mission. With only a handful of former Marines still in public office, it seemed as if Eduardo would succeed where Harry Truman had failed.

Although not a former Marine himself, Secretary of State Zachary Dischner's father had been a Marine, and Zach remembered his father's pride at being part of the "Frozen Chosen." Truth be told, he also liked having his own military, in a sense, with the Marine Security Guards at his embassies. He approached then President Holt and suggested that they shouldn't let Eduardo gain too much traction with this. By keeping alive the Corps as the Presidential and Embassy Guards, they would seem in touch with the needs to reform the military, they would somewhat appease those who served in the Corps, and would be able to have their own praetorian guards, so-to-speak. President Holt liked the idea of special presidential guard, but he liked more the idea of throwing a fly in the ointment of Eduardo's rise.

When the Act was finally signed, the Corps was alive—barely. Reduced to a single regiment, one battalion was to serve as embassy guards around the world, one at the White House and Camp David. The Marines would keep Quantico and the museum at the Washington Navy Yard. The Marine reserves would be reduced to the staff at the museum and a very small IMA detachment. Of the 180,000 active duty and 120,000 Reservists, most would be either released or transferred to one of the other three services. A select few would be retained as Marines to man the regiment.

Chapter 1

Early Tuesday Morning, Marine House, New Delhi

Gunnery Sergeant Jacob McCardle, USMC, sat in his skivvies on his easy chair in his quarters and sipped his Thums Up Cola, savoring the sort of cough medicine aftertaste that so many other Americans detested, but he sort-of liked, weird spelling of "Thums" notwithstanding. The cool air from the wheezing air conditioner rendered his room bearable, but only just. He glanced at his watch, and with a sigh, he realized it was time to get dressed.

He checked his dress blues blouse one last time as it hung on the hanger. On his blouse were the dual "toilet bowls" of a Marine basic marksman, the Marines' lowest level of basic shooting competency. Twice, Gunny Mac had qualified sharpshooter, but both times, he had fallen back to marksman the next year on the range. Of the 16 Marines in the detachment, only the Gunny and PFC Ramon were "dual stool." Above his shooting badges were the ribbons denoting his good conduct medals (seven awards), his National Defense Service Medal, Global War on Terrorism Service Medal, Iraq Service Medal, and the ubiquitous Embassy Duty Service Ribbon. Not really that much for 22 years in service, he thought, but at least he kept the Marine uniform when so many others had not.

Satisfied with his blouse, he carefully took his trousers off the hanger, trying not to wrinkle them, and cautiously stepped into the legs and raised them up to his waist. He zipped them and fastened the belt, then slid into his shoes. Lifting his blouse off the hanger, he slowly put it on and fastened the buttons. The tightness of the fit around his belly was more evidence that he might be putting on a little weight. He wondered if he was going to have to finally give in and get the blouse re-fitted. Well within Marine weight standards, Gunny was none-the-less unhappy with the overall "softening" of his physique over the last couple of years.

Gunny Mac stepped to the mirror for one last check on his appearance. Getting ready for an inspection was always harder on the inspector. Each Marine getting inspected had one set of eyes checking him or her out--his. But he had each and every Marine checking him out as well. And for this inspection, the stakes were even higher. Although he had seen the former president many times while on White House duty, he had never seen this president, and he had never seen a president in another setting. Personally, Gunny Mac would never forgive the president for his part in the dismantling of the Corps while a senator, but the man was his commander-in-chief, and the office carried a solemn weight in its own right. And the fact that the company XO would be there as well only added to the pressure. Gunny Mac was up for one of the two E-8 slots open this year, and there were a lot of other gunnies seeking those same slots. If this didn't go off well, he could kiss E-8 goodbye forever.

He took one last swig of the Thums Up then walked out the hatch and into the passageway. He looked at his watch—two more minutes to go. Down the passageway and out the main entry of the Marine House, he could see the ceremonial honor guard easing into position. The detachment had gone on a port and starboard watch to get ready for the visit, and the ceremonial guard was merely the planned off duty watch plus LCpl Saad. Four Marines in the color guard itself, and four in the cordon. The rest of the detachment would be on post when the president arrived. Gunny had already inspected them and sent them off to relieve the honor guard so they could get ready. Normally, for a POTUS visit, the other detachments in neighboring countries would send augmentation, but there had been problems with the Indian government and entry visas, so the New Delhi detachment had to make do with the personnel on hand.

The honor guard had been practicing for a week. Every one of the actual guard had already served at the White House and had performed honor guard duties time and time again for visiting dignitaries and ceremonies. So this should have been no problem. However, no matter how much the Corps had changed, some things never did. So they were instructed to practice and practice for their thirty seconds when they might be in view of the president.

The hatch to the duty office swung open and Captain Leon-Guerro walked out. The Company C XO had been hovering around for three days, trying mightily to let the Gunny do his job but worried that some detail would slip through the cracks.

Gunny knew that Captain Leon-Guerro was a Guamanian, a third-generation Marine. His grandfather had been a general, and it was accepted among the other Marines that that had been a major factor in his getting into the Corps. Slots for junior officers after the dismemberment were very hard to get, and Captain Leon-Guerro hardly looked like a stereotypical 8th and I Marine. At 5'4", the captain was one of the shortest male Marines in the company. But he wasn't a small man. His chest and arms were huge, and his legs were like logs. No one who saw him doubted his raw animal strength. It was common knowledge that he had played for the American Eagles Rugby team as a loosehead prop while in school, and it wasn't hard for Gunny Mac to imagine him charging down the rugby pitch in search of a victim.

The company headquarters was located in Nicosia, so the captain (or any officer, for that matter) was not normally at the detachment. Due to the presidential visit, however, he had come to watch over things. Gunny thought the Captain was OK, if somewhat prone to worrying. And he appreciated that the captain stayed mostly out-of-the-way and let the Gunny do his job. Major Morrisroe, the company commander, might have come instead, but he had chosen to go to Amman to oversee that stop in the president's itinerary. Gunny rather preferred having the captain come, if I had to be anyone. Major Morrisroe was rather demanding and hard to please, and he just didn't want to have to deal with that particular stress-bomb along with the rest of the rigmarole.

Captain Leon-Guerro seemed to have a permanent warrior's scowl on his face, but he was actually quite soft-spoken. He had the habit of chewing his fingernails when under stress. As he spied the gunny and walked over to him, he was chewing away.

"Gunny Mac! I need to talk to you."

Gunny came to almost-attention and faced the captain.

"I just got a call from Major Ingersoll in Amman, You are not going to believe this. The advance team told him that the president did not want the Corps Colors in the color guard. Only the US Colors. They had to ditch the Corps Colors at the last second."

Gunny Mac's mouth dropped open. "You've got to be shitting me, sir?"

"No, It's true. LtCol Duhs told him to call us and give us the word. No Marine Colors today."

Gunny Mac felt as if he had been poleaxed. "That doesn't make sense, sir. We had the Marine Colors at the White House and Camp David. We've used them here. What's going on?"

"I don't know. But we have the word from CO. We've got to lose the Colors."

"So we go with three Marines? The US Colors and two honor guards?"

"That's what they want."

"Aye-aye, sir." Gunny Mac said as he came to full attention, performed a left face, then marched down the passageway to the awaiting team, scowling as he went.

Opening up the front hatch, Gunny walked out onto the parking lot where the Marines were in a semblance of a formation. Staff Sergeant Child brought them to attention.

"Guard, atten—HUT!"

Gunny Mac decided to inspect them first, then give them the news. He marched over to Staff Sergeant Child who saluted.

"Honor Guard formed and ready for inspection!"

"Very well."

Gunny Mac looked at Staff Sergeant Child. Joseph Child. A modern day Marine hero, of sorts. The only living Marine of the modern era to receive a silver star when he was the lone survivor in his detachment of the attack on the embassy in La Paz. At 6'3" and 220 pounds of muscle, it wasn't hard to imagine him dragging the ambassador into the crypto room and holding off the attackers with a chair until the Bolivian police arrived to restore order. Walnut-colored skin, square jaw, and now with a slight scar from the attack crossing his chin, he was the poster-book Marine. Literally. He was the Marine currently on the posters still used by recruiting. Enlisting weeks before the dismemberment, he was technically "Old Corps" even if he didn't hit the fleet until after the dismemberment. He was the only Marine in his San Diego boot camp class to keep the Marine uniform. Brighter and more intelligent than just about everyone else, his future looked promising. Many thought him to be on the track for Sergeant Major. Gunny Mac tended to agree with that thought.

As usual, Staff Sergeant Child was immaculate. Gunny Mac nodded at him and said "Precede me."

Stepping in front of Sergeant Tony Niimoto, Gunny felt a small misgiving. Sergeant Niimoto was to bear the Corps Colors today. Gunny Mac felt a little outclassed intellectually by Korea Joe (a nickname he had picked up in bootcamp by a drill instructor who obviously did not know the origins of his family name.) It wasn't that he showed off his intelligence. In fact, he seemed like any other Marine, if rather talkative and prone to break out in a loud, donkey-like laugh at the slightest provocation. But he was a graduate of Stanford, and that daunted the gunny a bit. He was also the best marksman in the detachment, if not the company. While at Camp David, he had been on the depleted Marine team which won the National Rifle Championship trophy at Camp Perry against all the other service and civilian teams. Now, on his chest, he had the gold-colored distinguished shooter medal.

Gunny Mac nodded at Sergeant Niimoto and moved on the next Marine, Corporal Samantha Ashley. Corporal Ashley was taller than Gunny Mac, slender and hard. In uniform, she seemed to have a runner's body, but in the weight room, she revealed corded muscles that could push a surprising amount of iron. Quietly competent, she did what was asked of her in a determined and thorough fashion. She rarely joined the rest for a beer or cards, but spent most of her time reading or working out. She went out in town to worship at a local Christian church, and she had been taking

Hindi lessons. Gunny Mac could never get a feel for her. Not overly attractive, she had pale blonde hair and piercing blue eyes. The rest of the detachment often speculated about her—her background, her goals, even her sexual orientation--but since she pulled more than her own weight, they let matters lie.

Next in line was the other rifle bearer, Corporal Seth Crocker. Corporal Crocker loved two things in life—the Red Sox and Sam Adams beer. He somehow convinced someone at the embassy to have his Sam Adams piggybacked in with the embassy's booze shipment, and he kept that as his private stash. Technically against regulations, the previous detachment commander had chosen to ignore it, and when the battalion commander joined Crocker for a brew on one of his visits, Gunny decided to let that dog lie. Corporal Crocker also had Lance Corporal Steptoe take his PDA and hack past the subscription firewalls for the Sox games. A good Marine, he still needed to be watched. He should have received office hours for listening to a game while on post, but he had gotten off with a warning. Gunny Mac still kept track of when the Sox were playing and checked up on Crocker if he was on post at the same time.

On a sudden impulse, Gunny Mac turned quickly, without warning, to see if he could catch Staff Sergeant Child unawares. Child smoothly executed his own right face as if physically connected to Mac. The gunny almost smiled, struggling to keep on his game face. He wasn't going to catch Child that easily.

Stepping in front of the first member of the cordon, Gunny wiped the hint of the smile from his face. Lance Corporal Saad had his usual nervous look on his face. This was his perpetual countenance. LCpl Mahmoud Saad was actually part of the other watch, but he was in the cordon to make the numbers right. A logistics specialist, he was a natural linguist. Speaking English, Spanish, Farsi, Arabic, Chinese, Hindi, and who knows what else, he was the duty dictionary. Now he was studying Bantu. He was also the detachment pool shark. Many modern era Marines were athletic and fit enough to max out the PFT, but Saad could crank out 120 situps in two minutes and do 50 dead-hang pull-ups. He had trouble maxing out the run, though. Saad would offer smirking encouragement to Gunny when he was struggling to get his 20 pull-ups, so Gunny took a perverse satisfaction on running him into the ground during detachment runs. He knew it wasn't professional, but driving Saad in the humid New Delhi heat until the guy literally puked gave Gunny a small degree of satisfaction. But he could find no fault with Lance Corporal Saad's uniform, so he moved on.

No one would take Lance Corporal Harrington Steptoe for the twisted genius that he was. Tall and big, he had a look of softness about him and a dull expression which might make some think he was the village idiot. The Marine Corps got it right when they gave him the 2802 MOS. Steptoe was a genius with anything electronics. In another era, he would have been a master hacker. Now, he merely invented ways to make his life and that of his peers easier.

An African American, he had a small splash of freckles across the bridge of his nose. This caused him no end of grief from other African American Marines who pulled his chain constantly about how that proved he wasn't really black. When he finally gave up defending himself and began his own jabs back, the teasing on that aspect faded away. However, one aspect did not fade away. Lance Corporal Steptoe had a serious case of hero worship. He looked in awe towards Staff Sergeant Child. His feelings were so obvious that the other Marines started calling him "Stepchild." He took it as a badge of honor.

Then there were the two newbies, Privates First Class Ramon and Van Slyke. Both on their first duty station. Both going to see the president for the first time.

Gunny Mac stepped in front of PFC Ivy Ramon, known as "Princess" by the detachment. Princess was short, about 5'2" with a cute, very young-looking face. But there was nothing child-like about her figure. Her Alphas seemed to strain to contain her rather large breasts. Gunny Mac did not know where to look when inspecting her. He looked down at her while she stared straight ahead into his chest. As he looked down, his eyes were drawn to the swell of her chest. He looked away quickly, but then felt his eyes being drawn back.

Truth be told, Gunny was rather attracted to PFC Ramon. From the second she marched into the duty office to report in, he felt something stirring inside him. He really hadn't had a serious girlfriend in years, and seeing this pert, smiling woman with an amazingly curvaceous frame brought to the surface longings he thought he had suppressed. But Gunny Mac was a professional, first and foremost. She was a PFC in his command, and he would not step over the boundaries set by years of tradition in the Corps. So no matter what he wished, he tried to treat her like any other Marine.

But Princess was not like any other Marine. How she made it through boot camp was a topic of much discussion. Princess always seemed to just get by. On her first PFT, she barely passed. She barely passed her marksmanship training. She barely passed her drill. She had been counseled about laughing when on post. She picked up her nickname because of her obsession with her appearance and living quarters. She lightheartedly complained about any training that messed up her nails or hair, then would rush back at the first opportunity to give herself a manicure. She shared a room with LCpl Wynn, but there was little doubt as to whose rack was whose. Princess had a stuffed pink dog, a frilly pillow, and a pink comforter on her rack and a poster of some young movie star-of-the-moment (Gunny didn't even begin to recognize who it might be) posted above her desk. She was like a high school girl suddenly transported into wearing the Marine uniform.

Gunny Mac looked down at Ramon. He was surprised to see that her marksmanship badge was off kilter. The surprise was that Staff Sergeant Child had not corrected it. He started to reach for it, but then stopped. He wasn't sure how he should fix it lying as it was on the platform of her left breast. He decided to ignore it for now and make sure it was fixed before the president's arrival.

Private First Class Peter Van Slyke stood awaiting inspection. A Maine Military Academy graduate, he was a legacy Marine. Five generations of Van Slykes had preceded him. His great-grandfather had been awarded the Medal of

Honor in Vietnam, and his father was killed in Iraq. Van Slyke wanted to be an officer, but family tradition required that he serve as an enlisted Marine first. Of average height and with flaming red hair, Van Slyke had an earnestness about him which made the other Marines back off of riding him about his desire of being an officer. He had been pretty impressive so far in his short time on station.

Gunny Mac stepped away from PFC Van Slyke and moved slowly to the front of the formation, giving Staff Sergeant Child enough time to get in position. He stepped up to Child.

"They look good. As always. I need to talk to them, though. Have them form up in a school circle."

"Aye-aye, sir! Detail. Fall out and form up round the Gunny."

The Marines each took a step backward, executed an about-face, then moved forward to gather round. Gunny Mac looked at each one before beginning.

"OK Marines, you look good. For most of you, this is not big deal. But for you newbies, this is your first time with POTUS. Remember what they taught you at Quantico, though. He is not here to see you. You don't exist. You don't look at him. You are a statue. Once it is over, you can e-mail home and say you were two feet from the President of the United States. But until then, just do exactly as we've rehearsed over the last week. Nothing more, nothing less." He paused a second. "And there is a change. We are not going to have the full Color Guard. Only the US Colors will be presented." He looked at Sergeant Niimoto.

"That's bullshit, Gunny!" cried out Corporal Crocker. "We always have a full guard. Always!"

The grumbling started up in echo of Crocker's outburst.

"First he fucks the Corps, then he fucks us. Spits on us." That was Saad. He understood just where the decision had been made.

"I say fuck this piece of shit. He can march in with his Secret Service. He doesn't need us."

Gunny knew he should have stopped it right away. But he wanted to vent, too, and he let them vent for him. After a few moments of this, he considered it to be time to stop the complaints.

"OK, zip it. I don't want to hear about it. The Battalion CO is over in Amman now, and he gave us the word, and that came right from the president himself. He doesn't want the Corps Colors. Period. We go with the National Colors and the two honor guards." Gunny glared at the Marines around him.

Sergeant Niimoto looked up. "What am I supposed to do, Gunny?"

"Well, you aren't going to be in the guard. Just make yourself scarce. I'm going to watch from the Cultural Affairs office. Why don't you join me there? Or go to Post 2 and hang out there." Gunny Mac looked around. "Any more questions?"

The Marines stirred, but no one spoke.

"Staff Sergeant Child. Take charge. I want everyone in place by 1400." With that, Gunny Mac wheeled around and walked back into the Marine House. He could hear Child speaking behind him as he entered the building. Captain Leon-Guerro stood in the passage waiting for him.

"How'd they take it?"

"Like shit, sir. How'd you think they'd take it?"

"Yeah, I know. I'm taking it the same way."

Gunny Mac didn't reply but walked past him and into his room.

Chapter 2

Tuesday Morning, Marine House, New Delhi

When Gunnery Sergeant Jacob McCardle enlisted into the Marines, he entered a Corps which was a full member of the US military. Three active duty divisions, three air wings, and three FSSGs formed the offensive power that had served the nation so well over the years. Another reserve division, wing, and FSSG augmented the active forces, and had been in combat in Iraq, Afghanistan, and the Sudan since the turn of the century. The Commandant was a full member of the Joint Chiefs of Staff. One Marine, General Pace, had even served as Chairman of the Joint Chiefs.

Jacob had been a cross-country star in high school in Billings, Montana, earning All-State honors. Looking ahead past graduation, he didn't see much of a future for guys who could merely run fast. When his cousin, a soldier in the 101st Airborne Division was killed in Afghanistan, Jacob decided that he needed to step up. So he marched down to the Army recruiting office.

The Army recruiter had stepped out of the office to use the latrine. With Jacob standing waiting, looking at posters of "An Army of One," he felt a tap on his shoulder. He looked to see a Marine Staff Sergeant standing there. Staff Sergeant Woleski smiled and escorted Jacob into the Marine recruiters' office. Thirty minutes later, Jacob was signed up as a Marine.

At the Marine Corps Recruit Depot, San Diego, recruit McCardle fared well. Being a natural runner gave him a certain degree of "cred." He performed well enough to be assigned as recruit squad leader, a position he held until marksmanship training at Camp Pendleton's Edson Range. Recruit McCardle just couldn't shoot well, and when he had to endure marksmanship extra instruction, he lost his billet.

What was strange about his shooting abilities, or lack thereof, was that he excelled in other weapons. During the mortar orientation, he found he could hit any target at will.

One spotting round, and he could call for fire for effect.

Recruit McCardle qualified with the rifle with his platoon—barely. During the Gauntlet, his recruit squad leader was injured, and Recruit McCardle was promoted back up. Standing on top of Mount Motherfucker, looking down at the mountain he had just humped, he felt a lump in his throat. Exhausted as he was, he had just become a Marine. He had joined a brotherhood.

With the War on Terror, most new Marines moved into combat MOS. Recruit Jacob hoped to become an artilleryman, or if going infantry, a mortarman. But he had also shown an ability to write. So the powers that be decided Recruit Jacobs would become a Public Affairs Marine.

All newly graduated recruits attended a four-week course at the School of Infantry. One precept of the Marines was that every Marine was a rifleman. That is the prime purpose of any Marine, be they aircraft mechanics, cooks, or computer jocks. All of that is secondary—being a rifleman is primary. So Private McCardle became a rifleman. He also became known just as "Mac."

Private "Mac" actually preferred to be called "Jake." He thought the name had power, an élan. "Mac" was so common. It seemed like every Marine with a "Mac" or Mc" before their name became known as "Mac." He told several fellow Marines to call him "Jake," but names either stick or they don't. "Mac" stuck. "Jake" did not.

Four weeks later, Private Mac was off to Fort McNair, Maryland for the Public Affairs Specialist School. This was an intense 20-week school, and Private Mac was the junior person in the class. Normally, most services, including the Marines, sent to the school students who had already served a tour of duty in another specialty first. Private Mac and Airman Cynthia Conners were the only two students right out of basic training. Other students ranged up to E-7. Understandably, both Mac and Conners got pretty much every shit detail.

But Mac liked the school. He learned structure to his writing. He learned how to look at things in the way others might view them. And the proximity of the school to Washington, DC made liberty enjoyable. A Marine sergeant,

John Willis was also a student. Newly back from Iraq, Sergeant Willis had a car. On their first liberty, Sergeant Willis ordered Private Mac to get in the car. Private Mac had never been east of Montana before, so he had no idea where they were going. When the car finally stopped near a small, heavily windowed apartment building surrounded by trees, Private Mac still didn't know where they were. Until he stepped out of the car and turned around. There, down a slight rise and across an open expanse of manicured lawn, stood a statue of five Marines and a Navy Corpsman raising the US flag: the Iwo Jima Memorial. Mac felt a lump in his throat. This was the Marine Corps. This was his history now. Sergeant Willis didn't say anything. He let the moment speak for itself.

An hour later, at Boomerangs in Georgetown, Private Mac bought a beer for Sergeant Willis. He figured it was a small price to pay for that gift. Boot camp, Mount Motherfucker, graduation—all hinted at what it was to become a Marine. The Iwo Jima Memorial cemented what it was. And Private Mac knew then he wanted to be a Marine for life.

After graduation from Public Affairs Specialist School, now Private First Class McCardle was given order to the Second Marine Expeditionary Force (Forward) at Camp Fallujah in Iraq. Assigned to the MEF newspaper, *The Globe*, PFC McCardle began penning articles. Some of his articles made it as far at *Leatherneck* and *The Stars and Stripes*. He began to make a small name for himself. As the junior Marine in the office, he had also been sent to driver's school during work-ups and had received his license. His extra duty was to drive Colonel Parks, the MEF PAO, or sometimes visiting dignitaries. Colonel Parks was an infantry officer who was now assigned to Public Affairs. A platoon sergeant in the First Gulf War, and a company commander in Iraq for the invasion, he was now back—but not as a regimental commander. PFC Mac knew the colonel would rather be holding the point of the spear, but he did his best shepherding VIPs around. Although technically in charge of the newspaper as well as the television station, Colonel Parks spent most of his time babysitting visiting politicians and public figures. He knew he didn't know the first thing about running a television station, but he also knew that he could shoulder the burden of every VIP Division threw at PA and let the PA experts do their jobs with the paper and television programs. PFC Mac rather admired the colonel for that.

It was after his tour in Iraq that the world according to the Marine Corps changed. The Muslim World rocked the planet, and the US military lost radical Islamic terrorists as a foe. Then the Military Reform Act of 2018 regulated what became known among the Corps as the "Dismemberment."

Much to his surprise, Corporal Mac was selected to remain a Marine. He didn't think he stood much of a chance, so he was already planning his transition to the 1st Civ Div. When his notice came in, his joy was tempered by an almost sense of guilt. No one else in the PA office was selected. In fact, upon his arrival at Quantico for school, he found out he was the only Marine with a Public Affairs MOS to remain.

Over the following years, Gunny Mac served at the embassies in Tokyo, Phnom Penh, Buenos Aries, Quito, Vienna, and Helsinki. He served tours at Camp David and the White House. Now, he was assigned as the detachment commander in New Delhi. And his detachment was on the skyline with the planned arrival of the 48th President of the United States, the former Senator Michael Eduardo: the man who had gutted the Corps.

Chapter 3

Late Tuesday Morning, US Embassy, New Delhi

Gunny Mac left the briefing room where Diplomatic Security Agent Thomas had given a last-minute briefing to the embassy Regional Security Officer and the Agent-in-Charge of the U.S. Secret Service detail. Now they wanted the cordon backed up to the main entrance to the embassy. The Secret Service had wanted to eliminate it altogether, but Major Defilice, the Army assistant attaché, had stepped in and mentioned that after all their preparation, it would hardly seem fair to deprive the young Marines of their chance to see the president. Agent Thomas relented and agreed, but only if the Marines were back off the courtyard (read—where they would not show up on photos of the president's arrival.)

Gunny Mac was pissed on principle. However, he did not envy Agent Thomas his job. Part of the State Department advance team, he was to get the president from the airport through the streets to the embassy in a nation where the US had been becoming increasingly unpopular. The Secret Service had wanted the president to helo onto the embassy's roof, but this was President Eduardo's second trip abroad, and he wanted to be seen. So this resulted in super headaches for the DSS, the Secret Service, and the RSO.

Gunny passed Post One on his way to the courtyard. Sergeant Patricia McAllister ("Little Mac" to the detachment upon the arrival of Gunny Mac) nodded. Private First Class Jesus Rodriguez was standing beside her, nervously adjusting his blues. Other than the Standard Operating Procedures doubling of the posts for a VIP visit of this magnitude, PFC Rodriguez's main mission was to open the hatch for the president and his entourage after Sergeant McAllister buzzed it open. From the look of him, this was akin to lining up on the 40 yard line to kick the winning field goal with 4 seconds left on the clock. He looked terrified.

Little Mac winked at the gunny. For a second, he had the perverse fear that Sergeant McAllister would take the advice of the other Marines who'd told her yesterday that she should ask the president for his ID, and if he didn't have it, refuse him entry. That would be something to see, but Gunny rather doubted that neither he nor Little Mac would be around much longer after that. Little Mac had a streak of the ornery. An Arizona honest-to-goodness cowgirl, she had no fear. So if anyone would do it, she would.

Gunny started to turn back to her. She winked again. With a sigh, he turned back around and walked out. He knew in his heart she was digging at him.

Walking out into the bright afternoon sunshine, Gunny had to admit that the new embassy really looked good. The front courtyard was paved in granite brought in from New Hampshire. Entering by vehicle or by foot through the front gate, the huge circular courtyard drew the eyes to the vast embassy itself. In reality, the embassy was nothing more than a squat, square building. However, the architect, in what Gunny felt to be a spasm of creativity, added awnings, mirrors and abutments so that the whole building looked like it was almost ethereal. There was a helicopter pad on the top of the building, but that fact would not be evident to a casual observer. Windows in the outer offices were also mirrored, and it was hard to tell where the windows actually were, where the windows began and the embassy walls ended.

Gunny glanced to the left. The consular building, on the other hand, looked like it belonged in another era. Over the fishpond at the edge of the courtyard, and over a lawn, it rose with columns like a Southern plantation house. Gunny wondered which government agency gave the OKs for the two buildings. It had to have been two different agencies, because no single source could possibly have approved both. They just clashed too much. Separate from the consulate, adjacent the embassy walls and near the street, was a communications tower, disguised poorly to look like a bell tower, or a *campanile*, as the embassy guide termed it. Oh, there was a bell in the belfry, but it wasn't fooling anyone. Under the bell, there was a platform which gave technicians access to the equipment in the tower's cupola, and there were several rooms below the cupola with more equipment in them. The Marines of the detachment liked to go up there and sit. This was probably not allowed, but since the view and breeze were nice, it fell under the don't ask for permission rule. And until someone said anything different, the Marines would continue to use it.

Post 2 was in the consular building. Staff Sergeant Harwood and Sergeant Chen were at the post right then. Harwood was the SOG and should actually be at the embassy checking Post 1, but Gunny Mac knew he was probably trying to stay away from the procession. In days gone by, he would be leading a react force, but the DSS and USSS now took over that function. Gunny would have to speak to him later about hiding out at Post 2. He didn't have time now.

One of the Secret Service agents went up to Crocker and Ashley, asking to see their weapons. Crocker rolled his eyes, but handed his M18 over. The agent checked to see that there were no magazines in the weapons, then checked the chamber. As the agent stepped away, Crocker held up four fingers and mouthed to Gunny Mac that this was the fourth time he had been checked. Gunny smiled back. He also had been checked three times so far, and although he had no round in the chamber, his three magazines were full. Regulations, he told both the Secret Service and the DSS. They chose not to make an issue of it.

Gunny Mac went up to the cordon and had them move back almost to the embassy's front entrance, under the awning. Two on one side of the walkway, two on the other. He checked out Princess. Her marksmanship badge was straight now. Someone had fixed it. Standing further back was cooler, at least. The overhead covering which provided protection from the elements kept the sun off of them. Staff Sergeant Child and the two honor guards were stuck standing out in the full brunt of the late morning sun's heat.

He walked down the red carpet that had been laid an hour ago, and approached Child. "Everything OK?"

"Sure Gunny. We're ready." Staff Sergeant Child didn't even look like he was sweating, unlike Crocker who had a dark patch forming between his shoulder blades.

Gunny looked out at the street through the Embassy's main gates. There were a couple hundred protesters milling about out there, listless without someone upon whom to focus their attention. Lance Corporal Shareetha Wynn was manning the front gate with a DSS agent. Although in reality the purview of the Indian security employees, Captain Leon-Guerro had suggested a Marine be at the gate when the president arrived, and since the detachment was on a temporary port/starboard watch, there was the manpower to do it. Lance Corporal Wynn had just reported for duty two weeks earlier, so she got the job with the easiest requirements—come to attention when the president drove through, salute, and go back to parade rest. Of course, coming from Camp David, this was old news to her, thought Gunny Mac.

Looking back at the protesters, Gunny remarked, "Well, I guess he isn't getting a popular reception."

"No, I guess he wouldn't," responded Child. "His campaigning on bringing jobs back to the US and his stance on the Kashmir issue sure wouldn't have won him any friends here."

Gunny looked up at Child. He really didn't know much about that issue. Oh sure, he was briefed about the decades-long problem in the Kashmir, but jobs? What was that all about? Child continually surprised him.

The shoulder mic of the Secret Service agent standing at the head of the red carpet came to life. "Grizzly turning onto Sadar Patel Marg. ETA 5 minutes."

Chapter 4

Late Tuesday Morning, US Embassy, New Delhi

"Grizzly turning onto Sadar Patel Marg. ETA 5 minutes."

Staff Sergeant Child looked at Gunny Mac. The Gunny obviously had not understood his comment about the president's popularity in India, or lack thereof. Gunny was a good Marine, a good guy. But for someone who had been a reporter, he really did not seem to follow the news or world events much.

Staff Sergeant Child straightened up. "Well, here we go."

"I guess I had better get out of the way. You've got it." Gunny turned and walked back up the red carpet and into the embassy.

"Crocker, Ashley, let's form up." It felt a little strange standing there without the Marine Colors to his left.

Staff Sergeant Child had been in more than a few Color Guards in his career. And, God willing, he would serve in many more. So standing there with only the National Colors and flanked by two riflemen felt disjointed. But he could adjust. He always did.

Joseph Child came from Detroit, from an area where, if pressed, he would admit was "perhaps not the best." That was an understatement. He lived with his mother and father in a small tenement, where electricity was seemingly out off more often than it was on. He walked to school past the corners, amongst pushers and hoodlums, past gangbangers and hookers. Yet even then, there was something about him that made him special. People knew he was going somewhere, he was going to be somebody, and they left him alone.

His teachers knew it, too, and they felt validation for long hard hours in trying conditions when they saw Joseph (never "Joe," always "Joseph") soak in the knowledge. By high school, he knew more about certain subjects than his teachers. They knew he was destined for college where he would shine.

So it took them all by surprise when he enlisted into the Corps. How could he waste such an opportunity to become a mere soldier? That was OK for other kids who needed to escape the ghetto, kids with no other choices. But not for Joseph.

But Joseph was more than a child of the classroom. He was more complex than that.

Joseph's father, Will Child, had served in the Navy as a young man. He hadn't seen combat, but he had participated in a humanitarian relief effort in Bangladesh. When his tour was up, he got out and returned to Detroit where he was never able to land a good steady job. He regretted leaving the Navy, and he let young Joseph know that. He also instilled in Joseph a love of the country. Even though Will never seemed to get the break he wanted, he never blamed anyone else for that. He insisted that the US was the land of opportunity, and it deserved the love and support of all of its citizens.

Joseph was a bright kid with a quest for answers, but he also loved to compete. A natural athlete, he ruled the b-ball courts for his age group, and he was able to play with the older guys. He found an old skateboard, and he loved to play tricks on it. The school had long dropped its wrestling program, but Joseph found a dojo where he learned taekwondo. It seemed whatever he wanted to try, he succeeded.

Truth be told, Joseph liked to fight. There was something so basic, so primeval about being able to vanquish your opponents. When he was 9 years old, walking home from school one day, a stoned fiend was mugging strange Old Lady Williams who refused to let her purse go. This was in broad daylight, but no one moved to stop it. Something came over Joseph, and he dropped his books and charged. The suddenness of his attack, his fury, (and the fact that the mugger was stoned, most likely) overcame his youth and undeveloped body, and he beat the mugger into unconsciousness. He then dragged the body up the steps of the crack house nearby and dropped him on the stoop, a warning to others.

The neighborhood gangbangers thought it was funny and called him Little Big Man. He became sort of a mascot, so the dope fiends left him alone for attacking one of their own. Later, as his body matured and he picked up taekwondo, he didn't need anyone else. He could take care of himself.

In the back of his mind, Joseph also had the beginnings of an interest to serve in government. He knew he would have to go to school for that. But serving in the Marines certainly would not hurt should he want to go into politics. And it would give him a chance to see more of the world. But most of all, it was a challenge he could not pass up. So he enlisted.

During boot camp at Parris Island, Recruit Child shone. It seemed he could do no wrong. Well, almost no wrong. Initially, he worried about himself, and his performance became a competition against the other recruits. During week 3, after a junk-on-the-bunk one evening where he excelled and his bunkmate failed miserably, Sergeant Parton, one of his junior DIs, took him aside for some "extra instruction." Five hours later, after some "patient explanations" and arms which could barely move any longer, Recruit Child realized that the Corps was a team. Individuals can shine, but they shine more when the team shines. A renewed Recruit Child became the driving force in the series. It was a foregone conclusion that he would be the series honor grad.

Then the dismemberment became a reality. The series was in flux. What was going to happen? Graduation was both joyous and somber joyous for making it through, somber because only one recruit would stay with the Marines, Private First Class Child. And for the graduation parade, Will Child, leaving Detroit for the first time in years, wiped away the tears as PFC Child led the entire company in the pass-in-review.

Going to Quantico, PFC Child was given odd jobs until the incoming Marines arrived for re-training at the Security Guard School. And despite being in class with Marines up to E-7, he was once again the honor grad. Marines looked at Child and knew he was going places.

PFC Child's first duty station was the White House where he served an uneventful tour. It was at his next duty station at the Embassy in Lima where Child became part of Marine Corps history.

One aspect of the dismemberment was that Marines on Embassy Duty would not carry firearms. Carrying firearms was deemed too "militaristic," and an insult to the security forces of the host country. Colonel Byrd, the new Marine Commandant, resigned over this in protest. But the Marines were disarmed. "Every Marine is a rifleman" became hard to defend anymore.

Then on April 26, 2022, in a coordinated attack, mobs overran the embassies at Lima and Caracas. The local "security forces" either disappeared or joined the mob. Without weapons, the Marines were overwhelmed. In Caracas all the Marines were killed along with the ambassador and all but 3 of the American staff. A large amount of classified material also disappeared into the hands of the mob.

At Lima, the mob hesitated for a few moments as the ambassador, Hank Stellars (a political appointee who had contributed heavily to the then president's election) confronted them and asked for their grievances. This gave the Marines time to destroy the classified materials. Coming back out, the Marines arrived just as the mob surged. The Marines, aided by some members of the staff, charged the mob and dragged back the ambassador who had been knocked to the ground and injured. In a running retreat, Lance Corporal Child and others brought the ambassador back to the crypto room. Down to Child, another Marine, the RSO, and a Navy ensign on temporary duty to the Naval Attaché, the three stood over the ambassador and beat members of the mob who tried to enter the door with pieces of broken furniture. By the time the Peruvian Army arrived to drive the mob back, only Child and the ambassador were alive.

Lance Corporal Child was meritoriously promoted to Corporal and was awarded the Silver Star for his actions. And the regulations were changed. Marines would be armed again. The doors to all the Army's armories were opened, and the new Marine Commandant could take what he wanted to arm his detachments.

Corporal Child could have left the Corps then. He was a minor celebrity with his 15 minutes of fame, and he could have gotten into any university, or possibly even skipped school to enter right into politics, if he really wanted. But he liked the Corps. He liked being around others like him. He had found a home.

He was observant, too. He was aware that others thought he could make Sergeant Major. Sergeant Major of the Marine Corps. It still had a nice ring to it.

Several years later, Staff Sergeant Child stood in the courtyard of the embassy in New Delhi waiting for the president to arrive. He was well-trained, and he was thoroughly capable. Nobody could throw anything at him that he couldn't handle.

Special Agent Freely, whose shoulder mic had just announced the president's imminent arrival, turned to Child and needlessly announced, "The president will be here shortly." Freely had been part of the advance team, and Child had formed a rapport with him. It was Freely who had told him that while the president's code name was "Grizzly," some members of the secret service had pushed for "Enchilada," as in "The Grand Enchilada." Given that the president was the first Hispanic to hold the office, cooler heads prevailed. Still, some agents privately referred to him as "TGE." Child thought it was rather funny in a lame sort of way.

Staff Sergeant Child gave Crocker and Ashley one more look. Crocker was sweating heavily now, but there was nothing to do about that. He took his place at the edge of the red carpet, flanked by the other two. He could see the new Marine, LCpl Wynn come to a more formal position of parade rest. Evidently the DSS service agent standing next to her had given her the heads up.

Over his left shoulder, he could see some of the higher ranking embassy officials and their spouses milling in loose order against the front of the building to the right of the main entrance. Most of the staff and guests from the diplomatic community were already over at the consulate for the reception, but these select few would be there to bask in the twenty seconds it took the president to walk from the vehicle down the red carpet to and into the embassy.

There began to be some motion outside the gate. The Indian police were moving the crowd further back off the road. Sensing something was about to happen, the crowd started chanting "Down with Eduardo, down with USA." They pronounced the president's name as "e-dar-do," instead of "ed-war-do." They seemed to lack the fervor he experienced before the attack in Lima, so Child was not too concerned. Demonstrations against Americans were common happenings.

The front gate began to open. The chanting grew louder, but the local police seemed to have things in hand. Staff Sergeant Child could glimpse the flashing lights of the motorcycle cops coming down the road. "Detail, atten— HUT!" Child brought the three of them to attention.

The motorcycle cops stopped at the sides of the gate, and the first black Suburban entered the courtyard. It drove past the red carpet, and several secret service agents hopped out. The next Suburban entered the courtyard, then pulled to the right. More agents got out along with some staff members holding briefcases or talking on phones.

The third Suburban came right up to the red carpet. An agent rushed over to open the door, and President Michael Eduardo stepped out. He turned and waved to the chanting crowd as the Ambassador and the Embassy Staff Secretary got out of the other side and hurried over to lead the president down the red carpet.

"Detail, present HARMS!" Child heard Crocker and Ashley bring their rifles up.

The final Suburban entered the courtyard. Child could hear the gate begin to close. Out of the corner of his eye, he could see Ambassador Tankersly place his hand in the small of the president's back and point down the red carpet. The president took a step down the carpet, not acknowledging the Color Guard. Staff Sergeant Child felt anger rise up within him. He knew the president did not like Marines. But this was the US flag he was holding.

On the other side of the red carpet, Special Agent

Freely was pacing alongside the president, eyes not looking at the commander-in-chief but rather glancing back-and-forth at just about everything else. He suddenly stopped and looked up.

Chapter 5

Late Tuesday Morning, US Embassy, New Delhi

"Grizzly turning onto Sadar Patel Marg. ETA 5 minutes." The Special Agent in the front passenger seat spoke into his shoulder mic.

Michael Antonio David Eduadro, 48th President of the United States, settled back into the soft leather of the Suburban. He ran his hands over the seat, taking in the texture. There were Suburbans, and then there were Suburbans. When he was a child, his father had had a Suburban, taking him to the ranches and tracks where he made his living as a farrier. A work truck, his father's Suburban rode like it, even with the heavy-duty suspension installed to handle the extra weight of the equipment. Now this, this was different. This was like riding a tank—a luxury tank, to-be-sure. Even sitting in the back, he could feel the vehicle's power. During one of his first briefings by the Secret Service in the time after the election leading up to his inauguration, he had seen a video of one of the Suburbans on a test range somewhere withstand a direct hit from a rocket-propelled grenade. He really didn't know much about military weapons, but that impressed him.

But this Suburban was hardly just a fortress on wheels. It was plush, from the roses in the sconces to the chilled Dr. Pepper (bottles, not cans, and flown in from Texas using the original recipe with cane sugar, not corn syrup), to the incredibly comfortable seats, this was riding in style. As a senator, he had ridden in many limos, but for a boy from California's Central Valley, this was it. This was the one thing which really brought home the fact that he was the most powerful man in the world. Not living at the White House, not addressing Congress, not attending G-10 Conferences. Just riding in one of the many Suburbans stashed around the world. Somehow, this was something to which he could relate. Deep in his heart, he felt that he had somehow lucked into the presidency, that he wasn't really up to the job, that someday the nation would wake up to that fact. But in the Suburban, with his Secret Service in tow, he felt like a president. He felt "presidential."

As they rode through the streets toward the embassy, he tuned out most of what Ambassador Tankersly was saying, nodding at times to make it seem as if he were listening. Tankersly was a political appointee, but not one of his. He hadn't been president long enough to put in his own supporters in positions like these. And Tankersly obviously was angling to keep his job. Approaching 60, Tankersly was into pulp timber in North Carolina. From the briefing the president had received on Air Force One, he reveled in the diplomatic social scene in New Delhi, but he also seemed to be holding his own navigating the tricky path between the US and India, where job loss, trade imbalances, and most of all, the Kashmir and the US's tacit support of Pakistan has caused some serious rifts between the two nations. Looking at Tankersly's round, florid face, the president would not guess him to be that capable, but then looks could be deceiving. The president had many favors to fill, and an ambassadorship was one of the accepted rewards for political and, more importantly, financial support. And it might be that a career diplomat would be a better choice for India given the current situation. But perhaps Tankersly had earned the chance to keep his position. The president hadn't really thought about it enough to make up his mind.

It still amazed him that this was even something on which he had to make up his mind. He had come a long, long way since his childhood in Modesto and Bakersfield. Driving down the sun-dappled streets in New Delhi, his thoughts went back to his childhood, to his dream of playing ball for the Giants. Well, he never made it that far, but baseball scholarship to UC Davis had gotten him his veterinarian degree and introduced him to Jennifer. He smiled at the thought.

He tried to listen to Ambassador Tankersly, but he really could not focus. He held up a hand to stop the Ambassador.

"Sorry, Ambassador, but can we hold that thought for a second?"

"Of course, Mr. President, of course."

"Thanks. Ron, can I have the phone? I want to speak with Jennifer," he asked his Staff Secretary.

Ron Neal took one of many phones out of a briefcase, hit a speed dial, and handed it to the president.

"Hello?" said a sleepy voice on the other end.

"Hi baby. Just thinking of you."

There was a contented sigh. "That's nice, darling."

"I miss you. I want you to know that. I was riding here, and I was remembering how this all started, getting into the school board, with you putting up campaign signs with the kids in tow. Anyway, I just wanted to let you know you and the kids are in my thoughts."

"I saw you on CNN giving that speech in Amman. Nice job."

"Thanks baby. Nick wrote it, of course, but I can take the credit," he said with a laugh. "Hey, next State trip, let's think about you coming with me. I know you've got your education initiatives, but I think it would be good. OK?"

"Sure, if you think it is a good idea. I would like that." She still sounded sleepy over the phone.

"OK baby, I'll let you get back to sleep. Give the kids my love, and I will see you the day after tomorrow. Kiss, kiss."

He heard a "kiss, kiss" in return as he handed back the phone.

Looking back at the Ambassador, he shrugged. "Family takes precedence, even to running the country. Got to keep the homefront happy."

"I understand, Mr. President, and I fully agree. I don't know if you have been briefed on this, but we have implemented a number of family-related initiatives for lower income Indian families. I would be happy to put together a short briefing on them." The ambassador looked anxious to please.

"That would be great," he said, trying to put some degree of sincerity into his voice. The ambassador droned on as the president thought about his last few days. This was only his second trip abroad as president. The first one was a G-10 conference in Halifax, hardly an exotic location. This trip started with a day in Amman, then he had planned to overnight in New Delhi before heading to Beijing and Tokyo. The president was somewhat surprised to learn that he would be the first serving president to visit New Delhi since Bill Clinton back in 2000. He realized that the US and India had a love-hate relationship (a little more hate over the last several years) but as the second largest country in the world population-wise, and as the world's largest democracy, he would have expected some more attention from the executive branch.

Ambassador Tankersly's voice caught his attention. "This is Chanakyapuri, Mr. President. Most of the embassies are located here." The president looked out of the heavily tinted windows as the ambassador played tour guide. They turned right down a wide, tree-lined road. The president was impressed by the amount of greenery. This looked nothing like what he expected the capital of a major nation to look like. With traffic moved off the route for the motorcade, it rather reminded him of a typical Ohio small town. "Our embassy is right ahead of us."

Up ahead, as they neared the embassy, he could see people lining the road. "I see we have a reception committee ahead?"

"Uh, yes sir. As I told you at the airport, there have been sporadic protests against your visit. Pakistan and jobs, sir."

The president had never really seen foreign protests aimed at him before. At Halifax, all protestors had been kept far way for the resort acting as the summit's headquarters, and most of them were protesting against the Chinese delegation anyway. And in Amman, there has only been a handful of environmental protestors, barely enough to be noticed. Here, there had to be hundreds, if not thousands lining the street around the embassy. He looked on with interest. As the Suburbans drove by, the people seemed energized, holding signs and shouting out. The Indian police kept them off the road proper, but they lined it on the broad sidewalks for several hundred yards from the traffic circle up to the embassy gates.

As they drove into the gates and up to a red carpet, the

ambassador needlessly said, "The building in front of you is the embassy itself." As if it could be anything else. "Over to the right is the consulate. That is where the reception will be."

The Suburban stopped and a secret service agent rushed over to get the door. The president stepped out. One of the Marine guards alongside the carpet shouted out "Detail, present "HARMS!" as they did their saluting thing with their guns. He ignored them as he wondered, as he had done since being sworn in, why they couldn't speak normal English. "HARMS?" What the heck was that? He turned to look at the protestors, then raised his arm to wave at them as if they were welcoming him.

The ambassador and his Staff Secretary hurried out of the other side of the Suburban. The ambassador pointed down the carpet. As the president started walking down, the secret service agent, (Special Agent Freeman? Freely?) began to pace him. Suddenly, the agent stopped and looked up.

Chapter 6

Late Tuesday Morning, US Embassy, New Delhi

Gunny walked down the red carpet back into the embassy. He motioned for PFC Rodriguez to leave Post 1 and take his position by the front entrance. Rodriguez licked his lips and came out, running his thumbs along the front of his dress blues, removing imaginary wrinkles. He patted Rodriguez on the shoulder and walked into the passageway to the left. As the detachment commander, he really didn't have a mission. His Marines were at their positions, but he wasn't important enough in the embassy hierarchy to stand outside or even to join the crowd at the consular building.

He walked down the passage to the Ambassador's office where LCpl Jeb Kramer waited at parade rest. "Head's up. The president is about two minutes away."

"OK Gunny."

He checked over Kramer. A former jock, Kramer was voted "Man for All Seasons" at his high school in Des Moines. Despite having heard this from Kramer about half a million times, Gunny still didn't know quite what it meant. Something akin to homecoming king, but having to be a multi-sport star. Regardless, Kramer was still athletic, and he always looked good in uniform.

Inside the ambassador's office, Gunny could see one of the local Indian staff , an older man named Dravid, laying out the antique Russian tea set. He guessed the president would get tea in the ambassador's office when he arrived, tea a few minutes later at the reception, and probably tea when he went to the head (which he would need after drinking so much tea in the first place). Gunny liked coffee better, but Ambassador Tankersly loved tea, and he thought drinking tea showed deference to India.

Gunny nodded to Kramer and walked back down the passage to the Cultural Affairs Section. This was a large office with windows overlooking the courtyard, so he felt this would give him a good view of the president's arrival. As he walked in, he was only somewhat surprised to see Major Defilice and the DSS Agent-in-Charge agent already standing at the window. Most of the embassy staff was at the consular building for the reception.

The major turned around. "Ah, Gunny! Coming to slum with the peons?"

"I thought you'd be at the reception, sir. There's food there, you know?"

"Ah, but half the diplomatic community is there, too. A mere major could never hope to fight off the Romanian Assistant to the Deputy Science Advisor when there is a buffet line in front of him."

Gunny laughed and turned toward the window. The DSS agent eyed the 9 mm at his hip but said nothing. Directly in front of the windows and below were various embassy staff and spouses waiting for the president to arrive. Although he could not hear them through the reinforced windows, he could see the crowd outside the gates starting to intensify its actions. Both the color guard and LCpl Wynn came to attention.

"Well, I guess it's showtime!" murmured the major. The gate swung open and a line of black Suburbans drove in. There was a flurry of people jumping out of the first two Suburbans while the third drove right up to the red carpet. A secret service agent moved to open the door, and the President of the United States stepped out. Gunny had never seen this president in person, but he thought he rather looked just like he did on television. Overall, a handsome man, he looked trustworthy. Hard to believe this was the man who'd destroyed the Corps.

SSgt Child brought the color guard to present arms, but the president did not acknowledge them. *"Bastard!"* thought Gunny. He did acknowledge the crowd, though, waving like he was on the campaign trail. Ambassador Tankersly came around form the other side of the Suburban and started to direct the president down the red carpet. One of the accompanying secret service agents suddenly stopped and looked up.

Gunny thought that rather odd, still odder when the agent suddenly flung himself at the president, knocking him to the ground. "Did you see that? He tackled the president!" He felt a jolt as the agent standing beside him swore an oath under his breath and pushed past him, bolting for the door. Out in the courtyard, SSgt Child faltered, slightly dipping the colors as he took a hesitant step toward the prone president lying at his feet with an agent on top of him.

The next few moments seemed to slow down to a standstill. They just couldn't register on his mind.

There was a blinding flash in the courtyard. Gunny stared dumbfoundedly as the color guard, the ambassador, and the staff secretary seemed to be pushed to the ground. In quick succession there were four more blasts, rocking the window. Small ticks sounded as shrapnel peppered it, but the window held. The group of people standing outside in front of the window, though, collapsed almost en masse where they stood.

Major Defilice grabbed Gunny Mac by the arm. "Let's go, come on, let's go!" They ran out the door and down the hall toward Post 1. Inside Post 1, Little Mac was standing up staring open-mouthed out the front and down to the courtyard.

Seeing him, she started shouting "Gunny, Gunny!"

LCpl Saad was lying alongside the steps leading up to the entrance. He was holding his right shoulder, and Gunny could see the blue fabric of his blouse turning red. His mouth was open, and he was panting. Princess and Stepchild were huddled behind a stone column flanking the left side of the entrance. LCpl Van Slyke started to follow the agent, who was now rushing toward the president with a small, lethal-looking automatic weapon in his hand.

Rodriguez had taken a step or two following Van Slyke and the secret service. The agent charged toward the president when there was a rattle of fire and a burst of rounds cut him down. He pitched forward with the boneless flop of someone dead before he even hit the ground. Van Slyke went down as well halfway between the entrance and the president.

Gunny grabbed Rodriguez and pulled him to ground, sliding in back of the other stone column flanking the entrance. There was a blast of answering fire from a secret service agent, and a shadowy figure on the other side of the front gate collapsed. A single shot rang out, and that agent fell.

Gunny glanced around the column. There were a number of prone bodies lying on the ground in the courtyard. A couple agents, whether DSS or USSS, he couldn't tell, were upright and returning fire. One agent rushed toward the president when he stumbled and fell to the ground. He tried to get back to his feet when another round struck him, and he fell back motionless.

Off to the left, Gunny saw movement coming from the consular building. It was Captain Leon-Guerro, running through the fish pond and into the courtyard. Several shots rang out from unseen sources, but they merely kicked up chips of brick and stone at the captain's feet. Gunny watched in awe as the captain ran, powerful legs pushing him along toward the red carpet. A round hit the captain's leg, instantly shredding his blue trousers, but he didn't let that stop him. Then, two rounds hit his chest. This wasn't Hollywood. Captain Leon-Guerro did not go flying backwards in the air. He just collapsed. His momentum kept his body sliding across the ground after he fell, past the president, shoving up the red carpet, and up against SSgt Child and Cpl Ashley. He looked up and lifted his arm toward the US flag and tugged on it, as if he wanted to take it away from the scene. Then his body stilled.

Within a few short moments, the remaining agents in the courtyard were down as well. The gunfire slowed and ceased.

Gunny had pulled his 9 mm and with fumbling hands, inserted a magazine and chambered a round. But he couldn't see a target. The crowd, which had rushed backward after the first blast and gunfire, was now crowding forward, looking inside the fence. Gunny could see Indian police joining them, taking in the carnage.

Then he saw three men push themselves through the crowd up to the gate and spray the courtyard with automatic fire, even though there was no obviously moving target. They started climbing the gate. Gunny tried to get in position for a shot, but that was a long shot for a handgun, especially when made by a piss-poor marksman.

Over at the gatehouse, LCpl Wynn picked herself up off the ground. Even from this distance, Gunny could see the blood streaming down her face and neck. She calmly walked up to the gate as if she were back at Quantico getting ready to qualify on the range. The three men saw her and started scrambling to get their rifles in position to fire, but Wynn coolly shot all three, one after the other, one shot apiece. The men fell back over the gate into the pressing crowd.. She turned around, holstered her 9 mm, took a few steps back towards the embassy, then fell face first to the ground.

Gunny had five Marines down. And the president, and the ambassador, and a shitload of secret service agents. In the momentary lull after Wynn's shots, he jumped up yelling for the Marines near him to follow. Rodriguez, Steptoe, and Ramon jumped up and ran with him. Major Defilice rushed down the red carpet as well.

Gunny reached down to Van Slyke, but the Marine was pushing himself up. His face was covered in blood and his upper lip seemed to be hanging off. "I'm OK Gunny, I'm OK," he managed to get out of his mangled face, blood spraying. Gunny kept going to the end of the carpet.

The closest person to him was Crocker. The right half of Crocker's face was gone, sheared off. His left eye was open, and looked completely normal, as if nothing had happened. But it would never see again. Crocker was gone.

Staff Sergeant Child was moving slightly, but he was obviously hurt pretty bad. Blood was soaking his blouse and trousers, and a pool of blood was forming on the courtyard stones. "Rodriguez! Help me here!" Rodriguez started to kneel next to Gunny Mac when LCpl Steptoe pushed him aside.

"I've got this, Gunny." He reached down and slung Child over his back, exactly as outlined in the Marine Handbook. He could have been demonstrating to a class. He stood up and started back down the red carpet to the embassy entrance.

Cpl Ashley was lying on her back. She didn't look obviously hurt. "Take her back, Rodriguez." Rodriguez grabbed her by the collar and started dragging her. As he dragged her past him, Gunny Mac could see a broad swath of red form under her, as if someone was using a paintbrush to paint the courtyard.

Major Defilice had gone right up to the president. Lying underneath the secret service agent, his left arm was outspread, and there was some blood on it. Defilice and the Princess rolled the agent off the president, who moaned and tried to sit up.

"Take it easy sir. We've got you." Defilice got his arms under the president's shoulders while Ramon picked up his legs. Together they carried the president back.

Gunny looked around. The agent who had covered the president was quite obviously dead. Ambassador Tankersly lay in a pool of blood, his right arm blown off and lying a few feet from his body. The man who he would later learn was the staff secretary lay on his back wheezing, blood pulsing out between his fingers which were pressed up against his neck. As Gunny moved toward him, the wheezing stopped, and his hand fell away. The pulsing blood slowed to a flow. One hand still clutched the handle of a badly mangled briefcase, broken electronic components falling out of it to lie scattered across the ground.

Van Slyke came staggering across the courtyard, Wynn over his shoulders. A shot rang out, and Gunny could see another man pushing himself through the crowd to fire into the embassy grounds. Gunny stepped behind the president's Suburban, then cranked off a few rounds at the man. He didn't know if he hit him or not, or if he hit someone else in the crowd for that matter, but the firing stopped long enough for Van Slyke to make it to the red carpet. Gunny's natural instinct was to help him with Wynn, but he stayed at the Suburban and scanned the crowd outside the gate for another shooter.

Looking back at the embassy, he could see Saad step up to help Van Slyke into the building. Feeling quite vulnerable out there alone, he decided it was time to get back himself. He turned to run and almost fell over the US flag, lying in the blood on the courtyard ground. Looking at Crocker's body, he mouthed a small apology for abandoning his body, picked up the flag, then sprinted for the entrance.

Little Mac waited until he got through before hitting the release to lower the emergency door.

Chapter 7

Late Tuesday Morning, US Embassy, New Delhi

Gunny Mac placed the flag up against the emergency doors and took in the scene. The President of the United States of America was sitting down, back against Post 1, with Major Defilice and PFC Ramon kneeling beside him. A few feet away, Corporal Samantha Ashley lay on her back. PFC Rodriguez was holding her hand in his. Gunny raised a questioning eyebrow. Rodriguez shook his head and looked back down.

Staff Sergeant Child was also on his back. His breathing was steady, but small bright red bubbles were forming at the corners of his mouth. LCpl Steptoe stood by him, as Child's skin took on a sickly, gray cast. Saad was sitting on the other side of the passage, hand pressed to his shoulder, an angry look on his face.

PFC Van Slyke had laid Wynn down next to Child. Mac could see blood in Wynn's hair, and what looked to be bits of brain matter. But the shallow rise and fall of her chest assured him she was still alive. Blood streamed down Van Slyke's face. Gunny wondered how he could have taken a shot to the face and be standing alertly, looking toward him for orders. They all were looking toward him now, even the major.

A sense of weariness crept over him, of hopelessness. This wasn't how it was supposed to happen. How could this happen with the president of the freaking United States? Where was the secret service? Who was going to take charge?

He looked to Major Defilice. "Sir?"

The major seemed to understand. "I'm an assistant attaché, a logistician by trade, not a line officer. I'm in no one's chain of command. You're in charge here. You know what to do. Tell me what you want, and I'll help. But you've got the training for this."

Gunny Mac knew the major was right. He had the training. And he had to do two things first. Find out who was where, and destroy the classified. When he had run back down the red carpet, the crowd was still outside the walls. But someone had planned this, and it was only a matter of time before they and/or the crowd took over the embassy grounds.

Falling into the steps drilled into him over and over was better. Let the routine take over. This was just like a drill. He wheeled to the glass of Post 1. "Sergeant McAllister. Hit the Mayday. Then pulse Battalion and let them know what happened. Tell them we need help right now."

"Rodriguez, go inside Post 1. Get a hold of Post 2 and get a sitrep from them. Let's find out where everybody is."

"Major, maybe we should get the president out of the passageway here." He looked around. "How about the Admin Section's office? It's an inside office, no windows." When the major nodded, he added, "OK, let's get everybody in the office."

Major Defilice and PFC Ramon helped up the groggy president. At least he seemed to be able to walk under his own power--sort of. Steptoe and Saad carried Child, and Gunny helped Van Slyke with Wynn. He glanced at Ashley's body, but decided to leave it there for the moment. Entering the office, he told Steptoe, Kramer, and Van Slyke to push the desks together and clear them off so they could lay Child and Wynn on them.

PFC Rodriguez came running in and said, "Gunny! Sergeant McAllister told me to get you. None of her circuits work." Gunny ran back out and up to Post 1 where Little Mac buzzed him in.

"What's going on?" he asked.

"Gunny, I can't contact anyone. And the pulse doesn't look like it went out."

Gunny Mac looked at the control screens in the booth. The video monitors seemed to work. He picked up the telephone. The line was dead. He pulled his cell out of his pocket and checked the screen. The "No Network Available" message flashed at the top of the display.

"What about the land line?" he asked.

This was a protected communications line connecting the embassy posts. This line did not use transmissions and was buried several feet below the embassy grounds as it ran to between the posts.

Sergeant McAllister picked it up and pressed the talk button. "I've got them Gunny!"

Gunny grabbed the handset. "Post 2, this is Post 1. Give me a sitrep."

He could hear Sergeant Chen's excited voice coming over the line. "We're OK Gunny. What the hell happened over there?"

"Chen, give me a sitrep. Who's there with you? Are you under attack?"

"No, we are not under attack. We saw the explosions, but nothing over here. Some secret service agent tried to run over to the embassy, but I think he got shot. He is over in the fishpond right now."

"Who's with you right now? Give me a head count."

"Uh, me and Staff Sergeant Harwood are here in the post. Niimoto and Fallgatter are in the garden with the civilians."

"OK. Get Niimoto and Fallgatter. Tell them to come here using the service tunnel. Do not let them cross the courtyard. Understand?"

"Sure Gunny. I'll get them over," the sergeant responded.

Gunny turned to Little Mac. "Keep trying to get out a pulse. And let me know if you see movement out there. Oh, and give me the first aid kit." She reached under the counter and handed it to him. He left the post and went back into the Admin Section's office.

Major Defilice walked over to the president, who was sitting at the Protocol Officer's desk. He took off his jacket, tore a large piece from the bottom of his t-shirt, and began to wrap the president's arm. The major had obviously torn the bandage from the bottom edge of the shirt. Above the torn strip, there was a silk screen saying "Money Can't Buy You Happiness But it Can Buy You Beer, Drugs, and Women!" Despite the situation, that struck him as pretty funny. All the more so as the most professional Major Defilice was wearing such a shirt under his uniform when the President of the United States was coming. He almost broke out into a laugh despite the present circumstances.

As he walked up, the president looked at him and said, "Sergeant, the major here tells me you are trying to find out what happened. What the hell is happening?"

"We don't know yet, Mr. President. We've been hit by some sort of attack. We've got you back in the embassy, and no one seems to be storming the grounds yet. We need to secure the embassy until the Indian authorities arrive. We have tried to call them as well as pulse Quantico to let them know what's happening, but we have no comms. Ambassador Tankersly is dead, but the foreign civilians and other Americans are in the consular garden and are OK for now."

"No communications? Where is Neal? He has my direct communications with the White House," the president said, and when Gunny looked at him blankly for a second, "Ron Neal, my Staff Secretary?"

"Sir, if that was the man with you and the ambassador, well, he's dead. And the briefcase he was carrying looked like it took a direct hit."

"Ron is dead?" he said, looking stunned, then swallowed hard. "Well, use your backups then. I want the White House, and I want it now."

"Gunny, Sergeant McAllister needs to open the emergency doors," Rodriguez's voice came in from the passageway.

"Excuse me sir, but I need to take care of this," the gunny told the president.

Gunny handed Major Defilice the first aid kit, turned from the president and went back into the passageway where Rodriguez was holding open the hatch into Post 1. Gunny went inside and up to Little Mac who was looking at the monitor which covered the front of the emergency doors. When Gunny Mac looked for himself, he could see an older woman, covered with blood, who had managed to crawl up the side of the steps and was knocking on the emergency doors. Gunny realized she had been one of the favored few who were allowed to wait in the courtyard for the president's arrival.

Gunny looked at the other monitors. He could see the bodies in the courtyard and the mass of people still outside the gates, but no one else seemed to be around the embassy entrance.

The emergency doors were two tons of reinforced derma steel, impervious to most anything. They were intended to slam shut at the onset of any emergency. Once closed, though, they could not be opened without a code. Gunny Mac was one of five people at the embassy who had that code. He walked up to the console to punch it in, shielding the touchpad with his body so no one could the numbers. Then he almost laughed. What was the use of keeping it secret now?

The door started inching up. "Rodriguez, help her in."

Rodriguez lay down on the deck and reached under the door as it continued its slow process up. "I've got you ma'am, Lie down and I'll get you in."

He kept reaching, sliding his head under the door, then started pulling back, half assisting, half dragging the woman under the door and into the embassy. There was a loud crack, and tile chipped on the floor. Gunny, who had taken a step forward, jumped back.

"Fuck, they're shooting at us. Slam the door, slam the door!" he shouted.

Sergeant McAllister hit the release, and the door slammed shut once again, barely missing the outstretched leg of the woman. She lay on the floor in Rodriguez's arms. She was about sixty-five years old and heavy set. Gunny had seen her before, but really didn't know who she was. Her obviously tailored suit was now bedraggled, with a large tear in the shoulder and blood seeping from her face and shoulder gave its cream color a pinkish, tie-dyed look. There were what looked to be globs of blood and flesh sprayed across her skirt. She was pale and breathing heavily, the signs of shock evident on her face. She looked up at Gunny, took a breath, and with a seemingly forced bravado, asked. "Are you going to help me up, or what?"

Gunny snapped out of his daze. "Yes ma'am!" He reached down to take her hand, which was cool and clammy, and the woman stood up. She had on a black lacy bra, which was visible through the tear in the shoulder of her suit. Blood was running down her shoulder and over the curve of her breast, which was also exposed, then soaking into that bra. Her face showed every wrinkle of her years, but her chest seemed somehow younger. Maybe it was the bright blood. Gunny wondered why the hell he even noticed that, given the circumstances.

"Gunny Mac, is there someplace a little more appropriate where I can go?" she asked.

She knew his name? Not impossible, he thought, but most at the embassy never addressed him by name, and those who did usually used his full last name, either as "Sergeant McCardle" or "Gunnery Sergeant McCardle." Gunny Mac thought he sort-of recognized the woman, having seen her at functions, but he could not place the name.

"Yes, ma'am. Let's go back to the Admin office. The president is there."

"Is he OK?"

"I think so, ma'am. Rodriguez, McAllister, stay here on post. No one comes in. No one." He assisted the woman down the passage to the office.

"In case you are wondering, I'm OK." She looked like she was forcing a stern appearance, but in back of it, her eyes were in somewhat of a daze.

Gunny looked back. "Uh, right. I'm sorry ma'am. Anyone else with you make it?"

She softened the look in her eye somewhat, and she almost seemed to break before she gathered herself. "I don't think so. I think I have a lot of the charge-de-affairs' blood on my skirt here."

They walked into the office. The president was still sitting on the desk, but he looked up, still obviously dazed, but somehow defiant at the same time.

"Where is my secret service?"

"I don't know Mr. President. Some were killed out there, but the others should be here soon, I hope," Gunny said.

The woman brushed past Gunny to hold out her hand. "Mr. President, I am Loralee Howard. I'm married to Stan Howard, the charge-de-affairs here."

Gunny looked at her sharply. Loralee Howard? Stan Howard? Yes, he was the charge-de-affairs, but didn't she just tell him that she had his blood on her skirt?

Despite the circumstances, ingrained political behavior kicked in. President Eduardo reached out and took the hand. "Pleased to meet you."

"Well Mr. President, we are up Shit River right now. I hope you have some sort of Secret Squirrel hotline which is going to get us out of this."

The president, still holding and shaking her hand, looked slack-jawed at her.

Chapter 8

Late Monday Night, Executive Office Building, Washington, DC

Vice-President Jennifer Wright was in her office with her chief-of-staff, discussing an upcoming trip to Dallas when she saw the attack live on CNN on the television hanging on her wall. She stopped dead, her mouth falling open. David Spears, her chief, had his back to the wall and kept talking, not noticing her expression.

"David, look!" she said.

He turned around and saw the images of bodies on the ground on the screen.

"What....?"

Right then, Special Agent Mel Greene rushed in and said, "Ma'am, we have a situation here. Will you please follow me?" He grasped her arm and lifted her to her feet, belying to his phrasing that he was asking her permission rather than giving her an order. Several secret service agents preceded them as they walked down the hall, others watching the intersections. He escorted her down the stairs and through the tunnel to the White House and into the Situation Room, the Marine Guard waving them inside.

The room was empty except for the duty officer, who stood wringing his hands and looking at the vice-president. "The key staff are being informed and instructed to come here. Most of them are home at this late hour," he said.

She didn't know the duty officer's name, so she just asked "What do we know? Do we have communications with them?"

"No, Madame Vice-President. We have no communications with the president. But it looks like the president is alive. We saw him on CNN being helped into the embassy building. He might be hurt, though."

She sat down in the President's chair. Well, it was up to her now. He certainly was not going to be sitting in the chair during this crisis. This was on her to fix.

Jennifer Wright had been in politics for a long, long time. If someone had told her while she was a Congressional page while in high school or when she was working as a young volunteer for Ronald Reagan's campaign that she would someday be vice-president, she would have been overjoyed. But now that she was vice-president, she wanted more. She wanted the Oval Office. Oh, she jumped at the offer of being Eduardo's running mate. She knew her credentials as chairman of the House Armed Forces Committee and then her subsequent executive experience as governor of Virginia shored up some perceived weaknesses in what Eduardo brought to the table in the election. But after getting to know the man, she was sure that she would make a better president. She didn't really have anything against him as a person, but she thought his idealism and adherence to budgetary issues made him less than the right man for the job. And while she realized that the vice-presidency could be the final boost she needed to make a run of her own for the presidency, finally putting a woman in the oval office, she was getting older. The voters were far more forgiving of older men running for office than older women. It was possible that after eight years of an Eduardo presidency, she might be considered too old for the job.

She didn't feel the slightest bit of guilt at the surge of excitement that flowed through her upon hearing the news. Could her chance at the Oval Office be coming sooner rather than later?

Chapter 9

Late Tuesday Morning, US Embassy, New Delhi

Sgt Niimoto and LCpl Fallgatter rushed into the room. They took in the scene in a split second and rushed up to Gunny Mac.

Gunny realized that everyone was looking at him. He took a deep breath and then let it out slowly, calming him down a hair.

"Sgt Niimoto, everything OK in the tunnel? Any problems?" he asked.

"It was fine, Gunny. No problem."

Niimoto was breathing hard, whether from excitement or from running, Gunny couldn't tell.

"OK, Niimoto, Fallgatter, Steptoe, Kramer, start a security sweep. Check for any classified, but do it quick. Meet me at the vault. Saad, you OK?"

"Sure Gunny."

Saad's dress blues blouse was off and someone had bandaged his shoulder.

"OK, go with them. Meet me at the vault."

Saad nodded, then rushed out of the room to join the others.

Gunny Mac looked at Van Slyke. It still looked like half of his face was a mess of blood and tissue.

"How about you?" he asked.

"I'm OK," he sputtered, drops of blood spraying as he spoke.

"Stay here with the president. You too, Ramon. Major, can I ask you to stay here as well?" Gunny Mac asked.

Major Defilice simply nodded.

"Sergeant, where are you going? Shouldn't you be staying here protecting us? Or calling for help?" the president asked.

Gunny looked up at the president, who was glowering at him.

"With all due respect sir, we have to destroy the

classified. This area is fairly secure right now, and the major, PFC Ramon, and LCpl Van Slyke will watch you and Ms. Howard. We'll work on getting us out of this once the classified is destroyed."

"You are leaving me here with a soldier who has had his face blown away, and two other soldiers who aren't even armed?" the president asked, sounding indignant.

"Private First Class Van Slyke and Private First Class Ramon are Marines, sir, not soldiers." He looked to Major Defilice. "Nothing derogatory intended, sir," he added. "And as far as arms, we'll take care of that shortly. "

He came to attention, did an about face, then marched out, ignoring the protests arising from the president. Actually, he felt embarrassed that the president had brought up the fact that only he was truly armed with both a weapon and ammunition, even if it was only an ancient 9 mm pistol. He should have thought of that himself. He ran to Post 1, barely glancing at the body of Sgt Ashley, which still lay up against the bulkhead.

"Rodriguez! Run down to the auxiliary weapons locker and get weapons and ammo for everyone. Everything you can carry."

He pulled out the electronic key for the weapons locker and gave it to Rodriguez.

"Do we have any battle gear left?" Gunny asked, already knowing the answer but asking anyway.

"No Gunny, me and Van Slyke helped SSgt Harwood and Cpl Ashley box all that up last week and got it ready for pick-up."

The Army was under contract to the Department of the Navy to provide body armor and weapons to the Marines. The new body armor was to be delivered the prior week and the old shipped back to the States. The problem was that the new armor was held up in Indian customs, something to do with it being shipped via DHL as normal supplies when the Indian customs agents thought they were "instruments of war." Gunny Mac had tried to keep possession of the old body armor until the new actually arrived, but the shipping arrangements had already been made, and the company First Sergeant in Nicosia had told him they didn't have the authority to stop an Army shipment. So the old body armor had been boxed and shipped.

He really wished he had that battle gear now. But there was no use stressing over it—it was what it was. He grabbed PFC Rodriguez by the shoulder and gave him a light push. "Well, get what you can and meet us down at the vault."

Gunny rushed back down the hallway, swiped his card at the hatch to the stairwell, then ran bounding down the steps three at a time. He turned the corner and sprinted to the end of the passage and swiped his card again. He ran down one more set of steps, then back up the corridor to the vault. Putting in his key, he waited, but nothing happened. Taking it back out, he carefully inserted it again. The five lights went one by one from red to green, then a voice prompted him to put his chin in the cradle. He did, and a puff of air blew on his right eye. The voice let him know he was who he should be, and the hatch to the vault opened. In front of him, the barred doors remained closed, but perversely, these doors would open to anyone with an embassy card. He swiped the card, and the bars slid back.

In front of him was a room about 20 feet deep and 10 feet wide. The shelves to the right held an assortment of ciphers and hard drives. The shelves to the left held files of paper. All were labeled, and all had individual RFID transmitters. Each time a piece of classified material left the vault, the radio transmission from the RFID let the tracking software know the classified material had left the secured area. All existing materials were tracked this way, and newly created materials were logged in when they were first taken to the vault. With the president's visit, almost all material should have been returned, but a quick look at the monitor showed Gunny that there was a hard drive from the Commercial Attaché's desk missing. Gunny hoped Niimoto would find that as well as anything else not yet logged in as classified.

Each shelf was covered with a piece of metallic-looking plastic. And on each shelf, there were folded-up bags. These bags looked like normal paper bags, but upon closer inspection, they had a series of wires embedded in them.

Gunny had never used the new Classified Neutralization System before except in training, but it sure beat the old system. Just put the classified material in the bag, be it paper, crypto gear, or hard drives, seal the bag, place it on the shelf, then flip the switch on the right hand side of each shelf. Without heat, the classified material was destroyed. Utterly. Gunny didn't really know how it worked, only that it did.

Starting on the lower right shelf, he began stuffing the paper in the bags and then sealing them. He was about half-way through when the rest of the Marines arrived. Saad had the missing hard drive, and Niimoto had some papers. Together, they were able to prep the rest of the materials in another two minutes or so.

Despite the fact that the destruction released no heat nor gases, the Marines stepped back.

"Everyone ready?" Gunny asked the others. There were nods all around. "OK, here goes."

Gunny flipped the master switch. There was an audible puff as each bag seemed to shudder. Even having done this in training, this still seemed anti-climatic. Sgt Niimoto opened one of the bags containing paper. Inside was what looked like grey ash. He opened one of the bags that had held hard drives. The drives inside had obviously fused. "Well, I guess that's that!"

Gunny set the vault controls to open access so he wouldn't have to go through the entire procedure again to open the hatch. This was normally only used for allowing large amounts of items to be brought in and out, but Gunny wanted instant access for any member of his detail. He would have to remember to reset the access though, as open access was limited to two hours before reverting to normal.

They backed out of the vault, and Gunny was surprised to see the Indian staff member he had seen earlier dutifully waiting for him.

Sgt Niimoto said, "This is Mr. Dravid. We found him in the Ambassador's office ready to serve tea."

"Sir, can you please tell me what is happening? Is Ambassador Tankersly well?" the man asked.

The man seemed genuinely worried. Gunny had a

moment of strong suspicion, which he suppressed.

"The ambassador is dead," Gunny said without hesitation.

Dravid stopped wringing his hands and his mouth dropped open. Gunny wondered what to do with the man. Well, he could decide that later.

"Follow us for now," Gunny told him.

They moved as a group back up the stairs to the upper deck. On the second deck up, they met PFC Rodriguez already there burdened with weapons. Rushing forward, they (except for Dravid) relieved him of the rifles, grenades, and magazines of ammunition.

"I left some of them in with Van Slyke and that Army major already," the PFC told him.

Gunny nodded, realizing he should have told Rodriguez to do that in the first place.

Feeling a little better for being armed, the six Marines retraced their steps and returned to the office with the president. Things did not look good, but having a weapon in hand with the ability to cause somebody, anybody, grievous bodily harm, did wonders for the Marine psyche.

Chapter 10

Late Tuesday Morning, US Embassy, New Delhi

Gunny led his Marines back into the office. Major Defilice, PFC Ramon, and LCpl Van Slyke jumped up, weapons at the ready. The president was still sitting on the desk, not looking like he had moved since he first sat down.

"Hey, you might want to take a look at this," Loralee Howard said from where she was in the back of the office.ess.

Gunny went over to find her watching a television. He looked at it for a second before realizing that it was a live shot of the embassy.

"CNN at work," Major Defilice said as he moved up in back of Gunny Mac and was looking over his shoulder at the TV.

The scene was evidently shot from one of CNN's ubiquitous satellites, and it clearly showed both the mobs outside the embassy and bodies still lying on the ground in the courtyard. The mob seemed to be all facing the same direction, listening to a man up on the roof of a parked car. An announcer kept saying that the fate of the president was unknown at this time, and that the vice-president was meeting with the cabinet in Washington to deal with the crisis.

"I bet she is," the president said sourly. The president had moved off the desk and joined the group at the TV. He seemed a little unsteady, but otherwise in control.

"Well, what now? Have you been able to contact anyone?" he asked.

"No sir." We seem to have been cut off," Gunny said, staring at the screen for a few seconds longer.

"Sgt Niimoto, do you think you can take the sniper rifle and climb the bell tower? Think it would do any good? It seems to me that a few well-placed shots could stop the mob from coming in."

Niimoto's face lit up as he said, "Sure Gunny, I imagine I can do that."

"Take Rodriguez with you."

"Gunny, you're going to need everyone you can here. I'll go it alone," Sgt Niimoto said.

Gunny Mac hesitated a second, then nodded and said, "OK, but hook up to the landline jack as soon as you get there. Call Post 1 and let me know when you're set up."

"Aye-aye, Gunny."

Sgt Niimoto turned around and walked out to go to the weapons locker to pick up the sniper rifle, then to wend his way through the service tunnels to the bell tower.

"Where are the Indian police?" asked Loralee Howard.

Gunny turned around to look at her as she watched the television.

"Shouldn't they be coming to disperse the mob? Doesn't look like they intend to do much," she said, pointing to the screen where men in uniform seemed to be simply watching the crowd.

"You are right ma'am," put in the major.

"Honey, I am no one's 'ma'am.' Call me Loralee. Seems to me getting out of this mess is a little more important than protocol."

She gave a measured glance at the president, who seemed not to notice.

"OK, ma'—, uh, I mean Loralee. But you're right. They should be blasting away the mob. But they aren't doing anything," the major noted.

The president seemed to pull himself together. "Sergeant, I need to contact Washington, now. I'm going to see an end to this."

"Sir, we don't have communications. Even our Mayday didn't get out. They've got to be jamming us somehow," Gunny told him.

"How can they be jamming us? Doesn't this place have our best, most secure equipment?"

"Well, yes sir, but we aren't getting anything out."

"This is bullshit! I am the President of the United States of America, still the most powerful nation in the world. How the hell am I stuck in an office in the US Embassy with eight soldiers and a diplomat's wife? Just how the hell does this happen?"

"One soldier, sir. One soldier and nine Marines," Gunny said quietly but with conviction, hooking his thumb to point at Childs and Wynn, lying on the desks.

The president looked perplexed for a moment before saying, "I don't care if you want to call yourselves Campfire girls, you are just soldiers. I have dealt with you Marines before, and you always thought you were special, but you are just soldiers, just public servants. Now get me some communications!"

Gunny Mac looked at the president, not knowing how to respond. He finally did a mental shrug, then simply said "Aye-aye sir."

He walked out of the office and back to Post 1. Sgt McAllister looked up as he came. And yes, she winked. Gunny snorted in disbelief. McAllister was some sort of crazy!

"Do you have any comms with anyone?" he asked her.

"Just with Post 2. They keep asking what they should be doing."

"Nothing with anyone outside the embassy?"

"Nope. Nobody wants to talk with us."

"Well, fuck. We've got to get somebody. Niimoto should be on the landline as well once he gets into the tower."

"Yeah, he told me. Korea Joe's got balls."

"So do you, McAllister, so do you," Gunny Mac told Little Mac.

He turned to walk back to the office, McAllister letting off a hearty laugh as he left.

"Big enough for the both of us, Gunny!" she shouted after him.

LCpl Steptoe was waiting for him at the hatch into the office. "I know how they are jamming us, Gunny. It's the software."

Gunny stared at him without comprehension before simply asking "What?"

"It's the software. Who does all our programming? The Indians. We send all of it to India."

"But this is not Windows. These are highly critical, highly secure programs."

"Doesn't really matter. They're great programmers, and they do probably all of our programs in our non-secure systems. It doesn't take a genius to hack into our system and jam us. They might have a hard time breaking into our comms, knowing what we are saying. But they don't have to do that. All they have to do is block our systems. Turn off a few switches. Walla! We can't talk."

Gunny stared hard at Steptoe. "Are you sure? Shouldn't it be harder than that?"

"I never said it'd be easy. But with an entry into the system, a talented programmer could shut us down."

"Can you fix it?" Gunny asked.

"Give me a couple weeks, maybe. But I think I have another way. You know Crocker likes the Sox? Dang, of course you know that. But do you know how he gets the games?" When Gunny shook his head, Steptoe went on. "I took his PDA, and I programmed it to work as a repeater for the very low frequency transmitter and receiver I built at the Marine House. Really low. Lower than anything we have here. It travels pretty long distances, even with the low power. I've got a buddy of mine in Katmandu. He works there for Oracle. He just hooks up a netcast of the game, then retransmits it to our receiver at the Marine House, then it goes to Crocker on his PDA. If I can get his PDA, I can probably reach my buddy. I don't think the Indians would be blocking anything that low from here."

Steptoe looked expectantly at Gunny Mac as he digested what he had been told. Gunny's eyes lit up. "

So we can get comm out!" Good job!" Then as a thought crossed his mind, his countenance fell. "But where's Crocker's PDA? Back at the Marine House?"

"Gunny, Crocker never went anywhere without his PDA. He probably had it on him when he was hit," Steptoe told him.

"He had his PDA in an honor guard? What was he thinking?"

Then realizing that Crocker would not be thinking anything else, ever, Gunny fell into silence. He also realized that Crocker now lay in the courtyard, in plain view of the mob.

"Well, I guess we'll just have to have to go get it. Meet me at Post 1. As soon as Niimoto is ready with some cover, we'll do it."

He returned to the office and walked up to the president, who looked up expectantly.

"Sir, I think we might have a way to re-establish communications. Sgt Crocker, one of the Marines who was killed out there, has a PDA which should work. We just need to get out there and get it."

"Well, what are you waiting for? Go get it," the president ordered.

Gunny felt a wave of revulsion sweep over him. That was a US Marine, out there, a person who was now dead. The president's cavalier attitude struck him as just plain wrong.

"Sir, there are still gunmen out there. Going out now would be suicide. Sgt Niimoto should be in position soon up on the bell tower, and he can give us cover. It should only be a few more minutes."

The president looked at him for a few seconds, then saying nothing, turned back to watch the television.

"Gunny, who's going to get Sgt Crocker?" PFC Ramon asked as she came up to stand in front of him.

Gunny Mac hadn't really thought of it. But now that he was thinking, he didn't want to send anyone else out where he or she could get killed. He certainly did not want to risk getting shot himself, but that was better than sending someone else to get hit.

"I am," he said with a surprisingly strong voice.

"Not disrespect intended, but that is not such a good idea. You're in command here, and we need you safe and sound. I'll do it." She looked at him assuredly.

Gunny's mind reeled. He looked up to see Major Defilice nodding in agreement. The rest of the Marines were also looking at him, waiting to hear his response. Even the president turned back around to look at him. But a leader led from the front, right? He would not order anyone to do something he wouldn't do himself, right?

Then he remembered a conversation he had with Col Parks back at Fallujah, one of many he had while driving him around base. Col Parks told him one of the hardest things he'd had to do was to send Marines into the line of fire. But he realized that a leader leads. Not necessarily from the front, leading a charge just to show his bravery. A leader leads where and how he can best accomplish the mission. Where he can have the most impact on the mission, keeping the most number of his Marines alive, where he can secure the objective.

He now understood Col Parks. He needed to be in the embassy. He was going to have to send someone else, and that hurt.

He looked at the still waiting Princess. If the PDA was right where it could be grabbed, then Princess could probably do the mission. But Crocker knew he wasn't supposed to have a PDA while in an honor guard, so it was probably hidden. Crocker was going to have to be brought back inside the embassy. And Princess just did not have the strength to pick Crocker up and carry him back inside. He looked at the rest of the Marines. Steptoe was needed to use the PDA. Van Slyke was missing half his face. Rodriguez was also on the slight side. Saad would be a good choice, but even if he said he was fine, he had still taken a hit. Fallgatter, possibly. He caught the eyes of Kramer, who nodded slightly. Kramer, the former jock.

"LCpl Kramer, you're up," he said, decision made.

PFC Ramon frowned, started to say something, then evidently thought better of it and said nothing.

"Kramer, Rodriguez, Fallgatter, Ramon—come with me. You two stay here with the president," he told Van Slyke and Saad.

He nodded to the president, then left the office to go back to Post 1.

"OK, once Niimoto is ready, we are going to have him provide cover from the bell tower. Kramer, you need to haul ass, grab Sgt Crocker, and get back here. The rest of us will provide cover as well. Sgt McAllister, any word from Sgt Niimoto yet?"

Little Mac shook her head.

"OK, now we wait."

Gunny put his back against the bulkhead and slowly slid down until he was sitting. He looked up to see Sgt

Ashley's slack face staring at nothing. She still did not seem to be dead, somehow. Hell, Van Slyke looked much worse. But the total lack of tension in her skin and muscles told the tale better than anything else.

"Rodriguez, Fallgatter, take Sgt Ashley into the ambassador's office. Put her on his couch. Then come on back."

He did not her want just lying there, like a discarded piece of rubbish.

They shouldered their weapons. Rodriguez put his arms under her shoulders, and Fallgatter grabbed her legs. As they lifted, there was a slightly ripping sound where her blood had congealed on the floor. Gunny felt his stomach lurch. They carried their burden down the passage, then turned into the ambassador's office. A few moments later, they re-emerged and made their way back to Post 1.

As they sat on the deck waiting for Sgt Niimoto, each in their own thoughts, the magnitude of what was going on hit Gunny Mac hard. This was tantamount to a declaration of war, wasn't it? The Indians had attacked sovereign US soil, they had attacked the President of the United States of America. Where would this end? What would they do next?

The hatch to Post 1 opened, and Sgt McAllister stuck out her head and yelled out, "Gunny, it's Korea Joe."

Gunny jumped up and grabbed the landline and asked, "You OK? You in the bell tower?"

"Yeah, Gunny. I've got good fields of fire, but man, there are a lot of targets out there. This place is packed!"

"Ok, listen up, this is what I want you to do . . ." Gunny briefed him on what was going to happen.

The hatch opened again. "Gunny, it is the Canadian Ambassador. He's at Post 2, and he wants to talk to someone in charge."

Gunny rolled his eyes and said, "Not now, McAllister. I'm kind of busy right at the moment!"

He motioned for his team to gather round to give his last minute orders.

"I want Ramon and Fallgatter to the right of me and Rodriguez to the left. We aren't going to be able to see much from here, but if they fire on Kramer, we fire back. Watch what you're shooting at, though. Kramer will be coming right back at us. Sgt Niimoto is in the bell tower giving covering fire, too. You ready Kramer?

LCpl Kramer licked his lips and nodded.

A thought struck Gunny Mac. "Hey, you better stretch first. You pull up in a cramp, and I'm going to have to send Ramon here out to haul in your ass."

There was a nervous chuckle from the group, but LCpl Kramer dutifully went into a sprinter's stretch. It seemed sort of surreal, the four of them (five counting Sgt McAllister) watching Hank Kramer stretch as if he was back in high school getting ready for the Friday night game. He finally got up and merely nodded his readiness.

"Nothing fancy. Just grab Crocker and get back inside. Let's get into position. Prone Fallgatter!" he shouted as the PFC stood up, weapon at his hip. "We're not John Wayning this. Get on your face!"

He started over to enter the code to open the doors, hesitated, then walked back to the post.

"Give me a piece of paper, McAllister."

She put a pen and paper into the slot and sent it out. Gunny grabbed them, wrote the code for the door on the paper, then put them back in the slot. He went back to the code-box, entered the code, then lay down beside Rodriguez.

As the door slowly started to rise, the bright sunshine almost blinded him. He could make out the tops of the Suburbans, but from his angle, he could not see any of the bodies. He could hear the chanting of the mob, though, very loud and very clear.

"OK Kramer, as soon as you can, go."

The door continued its slow climb up. As it reached about 18 inches, LCpl Kramer slid underneath it and was outside. Gathering his feet under him, he started off on a dash.

"Hold your fire. Let's see if anyone will notice him first," Gunny ordered.   LCpl Kramer sprinted down the front steps and looked to be almost to the Suburbans when the tone of the crowd changed.

"Ah shit," someone whispered from the left.

There was a very faint soft chuff, which could have

been the sniper rifle, then several cracks of rifle fire.

"Fire, fire!"

The four Marines opened up, but without specific targets. Gunny Mac could see Kramer's head and shoulders, then he disappeared. Had he been hit? Gunny started to get to his knees when Kramer stood up with Sgt Crocker on his shoulders. He started running back, bounding up the steps in one giant stride, then running down the entranceway. As he approached the door, now open by about three feet, he threw himself forward, shoving Sgt Crocker's body through the opening and sliding in after it.

"Close it, close it," shouted Gunny Mac, but Sgt McAllister had already hit the emergency release.

As it slammed shut, PFC Fallgatter still fired, sending a number of rounds zinging around the inside of the entrance.

PFC Ramon smacked Fallgatter on the shoulder while shouting, "Cease fire you moron!"

LCpl Kramer lay huffing on the deck. Sprawled in front of him was Sgt Crocker. He had been out in the hot sun for over an hour, and his body was already showing signs of deterioration. His skin looked pale but puffy, and his uniform unnaturally tight. Gunny walked over to him. Where would the PDA be? Where should he look?

PFC Fallgatter evidently knew already. He soberly reached over, pulled up Sgt Crocker's right trouser leg, and unstrapped the PDA attached to his ankle. Wordlessly, he handed it over to the gunny.

Gunny looked at it for a moment, then back at Sgt Crocker befoe saying "Take Sgt Crocker and put him in with Sgt Ashley."

He turned around and walked off to the Admin Office, not waiting to see them lift the body.

"Good job Marines," he shouted over his shoulder.

He should have faced them and told them so, but he really did not want to see more of Sgt Crocker's bloated body.

He walked into the office, handed LCpl Steptoe the PDA, and said, "OK, get to work."

Then he walked over to the coffee mess and threw up in the sink.

Chapter 11

Late Tuesday Morning, US Embassy, New Delhi

Sergeant Anthony Niimoto climbed the last few steps into the rotunda of the bell tower with a sigh of relief. After grabbing a sniper rifle from the weapons locker and a box of ammunition, he had checked in with Little Mac before going down the access to the service tunnels. He had been in the service tunnels many times, the last time just 30 minutes ago when he'd made his way to the embassy from the consulate. But he really did not like them, and now, with what had happened, he felt more stifled in them, more aware of how good of a location this would be for an ambush. He was relieved when he finally reached the access into the base of the bell tower and made his way up the ladder into the campanile's belfry.

Tony Niimoto had joined the Marines for no particular reason. He'd gone to Stanford, much to the joy of his parents, and majored in philosophy, much to their dismay. Tony liked to experience life, but he did not have much of a blueprint for his future.

After graduation, he went back south to his parents' home in Pacific Beach, or "PB" as it was known in the San Diego area, living in his old bedroom, surfing most days away. One dismal January day, cold and rainy, he was out surfing, hoping to catch some nice rides. Sitting on his board out in the water, he was drawn into a conversation with an old man. Sam was rather scrawny, but he was interesting and could hold his own in the water, so when the he offered to buy Tony a burger at Hodad's, he accepted. Sitting in the ancient burger joint, under all the license plates from around the world hanging on the walls, the old guy regaled Tony with stories, claiming to have been a Navy SEAL. His stories of death and mayhem were rather intriguing to someone recently out of the brick walls of Stanford, and his stories of whoring around in the Philippines, Kosovo, and Korea were even more fascinating. San Diego was a conservative community with not much in the way of adult nightlife, and the tales of Fire Empire and Jolos in the Philippines piqued his sense of adventure. Tony spent the afternoon alternating between open-mouthed astonishment and braying his donkey laugh at some of the Sam's stories.

It was almost 4:00 when he left Hodad's. Something made him go across the bay and into downtown San Diego. Acting subconsciously, he was soon standing outside the Federal Building. With a sudden sense of determination, he walked inside and turned to the left where the military recruiters had their offices. It was about quarter-to-five, but when he went up to the Navy recruiter's office, it was already closed, even though the sign on the door said it was open from 8:00 AM until 5:00 PM. He felt a sense of deflation, as if something, something he really could not put his finger on, had evaporated away.

"Can I help you son?"

Tony looked up, and standing in the next doorway was a Marine. Tony did not know it, but since the dismemberment, the Marines really did not have to recruit much. In fact, they had recruitment offices in only a few select locations, and these were primarily process centers for getting the recruits to Quantico for boot. There was something about Tony, though, that caught the attention of Staff Sergeant Mike Santiago, something that his instincts made him speak out.

Tony walked over to the Staff Sergeant, walked into the office, and 45 minutes later, had signed on the dotted line. Tony was going to be a Marine.

And Tony found out he liked being a Marine. The Corps gave him a purpose in life which Stanford never gave him. He liked doing "manly" things. He found out he could shoot. He found out he liked the camaraderie. He liked the uniforms. He liked being part of a team. And despite his initial objections to being called "Korea Joe," somehow, even that formed bonds with his fellow Marines. Although he may have joined because of an old man's tales of whoring, to be honest, he had found a home.

And Tony was now thinking of applying to be an officer. He had not mentioned that to anyone, else, of course.

But the thought of putting on gold bars was rather appealing.

Sgt Niimoto looked around the belfry. While it looked like a bell tower from the outside, from inside the cupola, it was obvious that the stacks of locked cabinets with large cables leaving from the bottom and disappearing into the floor were the real reason the tower was built. Yes, there was a bell hanging there, but it couldn't even ring. There wasn't a clapper.

The Marines often wondered as to the exact nature of the cabinets, or why they were not in a secure location. Sgt Chen seemed to think that since they weren't guarded, they were not important. But Sgt Niimoto felt they would not have built the tower unless there was a good reason. Regardless, the off-duty Marines often liked to come up and hang out, and no one ever told them they couldn't.

Sgt Niimoto eased over to the rail and looked down over the courtyard. He could see the Suburbans and the bodies lying there, which caused a small lump in his throat. And arrayed outside the wall, there were what seemed to be thousands of Indians packing the street. There was some chanting, but most seemed to be listening to several men speaking on microphones. Niimoto didn't speak any Hindi, so he couldn't understand what was being said.

Sgt Niimoto looked down at his M48A1 sniper rifle. He checked the baffles of the rifle, the most obvious change from the appearance of the M40A1 rifle on which he had initially been trained. The M48A1 still used the Remington 700 receiver group, but the baffles around the muzzle of the barrel, when used in conjunction with the special M124 ammunition, made the report of a shot quite subdued. He had to make sure the baffles were clear, though. They easily picked up dirt and bits of detritus. He then checked over his ammunition, the boat-tailed, 178 grain round, making sure there were no dents in any of them, that they were in good shape. Although an intelligent man, Sgt Niimoto was not quite sure how the baffles and new ammunition worked, but the rifle was essentially silent out past 100 or 150 meters, depending on the conditions. Closer to that, the rifle made a softer chuffing sound rather than the sharp crack of a normal rifle.

Taking a headset from his pocket, Sgt Niimoto hooked it up to the landline jack. He dialed Post 1.

"Post 1."

"Pat, this is Tony. Let the Gunny know I'm in position."

" 'Bout time. They're all here waiting for you. Hold on a second."

Sgt Niimoto could hear McAllister call out for the gunny, then a few moments later, the gunny came on line. "You OK? You in the bell tower?"

"Yeah, Gunny. I've got good fields of fire, but man, there are a lot of targets out there. This place is packed!" he said as he looked back out over the crowd.

"OK, listen up, this is what I want you to do. We've got to get Crocker's PDA, Without it, we can't talk to anyone. I've got four of us here at the front hatch, but we really won't be able to see much. I'm sending Kramer out to grab Crocker and bring him back in. You've got to provide cover. If you see anyone shoot, if you see anyone about to shoot, take him out. Don't hesitate, just take him out. You've got that?"

"Roger, gunny."

"OK, we're going in just a minute or so. You be ready. Out."

Sgt Niimoto felt a wave of emotion well up. He could look down on the courtyard and see Seth's body. That could have been him down there. It would have been if the president hadn't canc'ed the Marine Colors. He subconsciously stroked the seam of his dress blue trousers. And he could see Capt Leon-Guerro sprawled across the ground as well. Sgt Niimoto didn't really know the Captain that well, but he was still a Marine, and that was what mattered.

He knew he could shoot, but shooting at a range was different from shooting real people. Flesh and blood. He felt a little queasy. Then, looking at the two Marines, the ambassador, and the others lying dead in the courtyard, he felt a degree of hardening. They started this.

Looking through his scope, he picked out several men who were armed and watching the embassy, not paying attention to the speakers. These were his targets. He put his crosshairs on the chest of a gunman standing on a concrete block up against the embassy wall. Due his high angle, he adjusted his hold, putting the crosshairs a little lower on the man. Taking a couple deep breathes, he slowly exhaled.

He sensed more than saw the doors open. A moment later, his target looked startled, shouted something over his shoulder, and raised his weapon. Sgt Anthony Niimoto smoothly squeezed the trigger. They rifle kicked, the vents chuffed, and there was an explosion of blood on the man's chest as he fell back into the crowd.

Another man had an ancient AK leveled and was firing into the courtyard. Sgt Niimoto swung his weapon around as a burst of fire came out of the embassy. Squeezing the trigger again, Sgt Niimoto watched the round hit the man lower in the chest, but he, too, fell back. Through the scope, he could see one more man jumping onto the same concrete block the first man had been standing on. Taking a breath, he squeezed the trigger once more. Kick. Chuff. The man's face burst into a pink mist before he fell back into the now panicking crowd.

Taking a quick glance back, he could see Kramer disappearing under the awning, carrying Seth on his shoulders. A couple more steps and he would be safe. Tony scanned the crowd again, but no one stood out as a target. People rushed the wall and gate, pointing and gesturing, but none were an immediate threat.

Sgt Niimoto leaned back and took a deep breath. He had just killed three men. Yes, he was a Marine. Yes, every Marine is a rifleman. But he never thought he'd have to kill anyone. And right now, he felt elated. Maybe he would feel something later, feel some regret. But now, he felt like he had just caught the perfect curl, had just sunk a 40-foot buzzer beater. He felt great.

Admittedly, the distance involved was not that great. But he was shooting at a severe down angle and with increasing shadows, and he had shot quickly. He had done well. And it looked as if no one had realized they were taking fire from the bell tower.

Sgt Tony Niimoto edged back down some and went back to scanning the milling crowd.

Chapter 12

Tuesday Afternoon, US Embassy, New Delhi

Gunnery Sergeant McCardle rinsed his mouth with water, swishing it back and forth before spitting it out into the sink. He turned around and surveyed the office.

Ms. Howard, er, Loralee, had sat Van Slyke down and was dabbing at his face with some paper towels, first aid kit open and ready, a look of concern in her eyes as she surveyed the damage. Van Slyke's undamaged side of his face was away from the gunny, so he could not see how the PFC was taking this, but his body was still. Gunny shook his head in amazement.

Towards the left, SSgt Child and LCpl Wynn were still laid out on two desks. Saad was watching over Child, holding his hand. That hand, once so powerful and full of purpose, lay limply, with a pale, sickly, grayish cast. But Child's chest rose in a seemingly normal fashion, breathing life into the body. His blouse had been taken off, and bandages covered his chest and neck. Gunny wondered who had put them there, taking care of Child. He had been so busy, he hadn't even had time to see to the wounded. Lying next to Child, the rise and fall of Wynn's chest did not seem as strong. Blood seeped from under her, snaked its way to the edge of the desk, and dripped to the deck, pooling in a small puddle of red.

The president and Major Defilice were by the television, watching CNN and making quiet comments to each other. MAJ Defilice was still in his t-shirt, uniform trousers, and issue shoes. The president was in a very nice pair of navy trousers, a white shirt, and shoes that probably cost more than the gunny made in a month, yet they huddled together, circumstances putting them on an equal footing. The president's upper arm was bandaged over his shirt, but he didn't seem to be in too much distress. Behind them, Mr. Dravid stood, trying to remain unobtrusive but watching the television as well.

LCpl Steptoe was hunched over the receptionist's

desk, working on the PDA. His concentration was evident, making him oblivious to the entire scene. The hatch to the office opened, and the remaining Marines trooped in. Ramon and Rodriguez looked somewhat subdued, but both Kramer and Fallgatter looked elated. Fallgatter had his M18 at the ready, his eyes darting around the room.

"Rodriguez, go back down to Post 1. Stand by and be a runner for Sgt McAllister. Let me know if anything comes up."

Rodriguez nodded and left the office.

Gunny walked over to Steptoe and asked "How's it going?"

LCpl Steptoe did not even look up, but replied, "Good, Gunny. Sgt Crocker has a password protect, but I think I can figure it out."

"OK. Good. Let me know as soon as you have something."

He made his way back to the president and Major Defilice. "Sir, we've got the PDA, and we should be able to talk to someone soon."

The president looked around over his shoulder at the gunny. "Good job, sergeant. Tell me, was anyone hurt getting it?"

He stared at the gunny with a look of concern on his face.

"No sir. Everyone got back fine."

"Good, good," he said before pausing. "Let me know when I can talk to Washington."

PFC Rodriquez came back into the office and said, "Gunny, Sgt Mac says the Canadian ambassador is back on the landline wanting to know what's going on. What should she tell him?"

"Ah, crap! OK, OK. I'll be there in a second."

Loralee stopped bandaging Van Slyke's face and said, "Don't tell him too much, Gunny."

"What do you mean, ma'am?"

"Do you really know who is over there? Most of the diplomatic community and half of the Indian government were waiting for the reception. Who over there had a hand in this?"

Gunny Mac gulped. That was a valid point. No sense making it easy for anyone who wanted to do them ill.

"I'll be careful, ma'am," he said as he left the office and made his way to Post 1.

"Buzz me in, Sgt McAllister."

He entered the post and picked up the landline.

"This is Gunnery Sergeant Jacob McCardle. Who am I speaking with?"

"I am Ambassador Tilden from Canada. What is happening out there? How is the president? How is Ambassador Tankersly? We have a lot of scared people over here, and we want to know what is going on."

"Sir, the president is secure, and we have initiated our emergency procedures. Please remain calm, and help will arrive. You've got the food and drink for the reception, so please make sure everyone is hydrated and ready for further instructions."

"I want to speak with the president," the ambassador told him.

"I am sorry sir, but that isn't possible now. The president is in a secure location. I am sure you can appreciate the situation."

There was a slight pause before the ambassador said, "Yes, I guess I do. But we are going to need some help here, and soon."

"Sir, you have SSgt Harwood there. He can assist you or get word back to us here as need be. I have to go now, but we'll be in touch."

He handed the phone back to Sgt McAllister who took it with a wry smile. Gunny Mac walked back into the office. The president looked up expectantly. Gunny started to walk over to him.

"Gunny! I'm through!" shouted LCpl Steptoe. Gunny hurried over. "He used the 'redsox2013' as his password."

"Redsox2013?"

"Yes, the last time the Sox won the series. I knew he had something like that. I'm dialing my friend now." All eyes turned toward him as he waited. "Dang, it's his answering service . . . Hey Trollbane, this is Elanadril. This is urgent. Call me back on Crocker's PDA. We've got big trouble, and we need your help."

"Elanadril?" asked Ramon, with a raised eyebrow.

Steptoe looked flustered as he said, "Don't ask. Hey, the good news is that the low freqs are not getting jammed. The bad news is that he isn't answering."

The president left the TV and walked over. "Can you call anyone else on that? Can you call the White House?"

"Uh, no sir. Not on Sgt Crocker's. I have it set up only for this call. If I had my PDA, I could do it."

"And where is your PDA?"

"Back at the Marine House. We aren't supposed to have extraneous gear for an honor guard or something big like this."

"But you have this PDA," the president went on.

"Yes sir. Sgt Crocker, well, uh, he didn't always follow the rules."

The president paused and actually smiled. "Well, thank God for small favors," he said as he swung around and went back to the television.

The PDA in Steptoe's hands buzzed. He grabbed it as everyone in the office crowded around. "Hello, hello! Is this Trollbane?"

The bored-sounding voice came over the small speaker in the device. "Yeah, Elanadril. What's so important that you have to call me when I'm taking a dump? The dragon's burning your fields again?"

"Have you seen the news? The Indians have stormed the embassy here, and we've got the president here, and we're stuck in the embassy!"

"What? What the hell are you talking about?"

The president leaned over to speak directly into the PDA. "Son, this is President Eduardo. I want you to listen up, because we need your help."

"Is this some sort of joke?"

"Trollbane, look at your news ticker. This is for real," Steptoe said.

There was a pause, then a "Holy shit! And this is you? That's really the president?"

"Yeah, it is."

"What do you want me to do, uh, sir?"

Gunny Mac picked up the PDA. "Mr. Trollbane, this is Gunnery Sergeant McCardle with the security detachment. We need you to make a call for us. You need to call the White House."

He suddenly realized he didn't have the number for the White House.

"Mr. President, what is the number?"

The president looked confused. "I don't know. I've never called the number. Someone else around me always has a phone."

"Mr. Trollbane –" began Gunny.

"Mike."

"What?"

"It's Mike. Mike Dupris. 'Trollbane' is for gaming."

"OK, Mike, I want you to search the net for the number for the White House. Don't hang up this connection, but use another phone to call it. Tell them we have the president here, and he needs to talk to them."

"OK, wait a minute while I go to another computer."

All nine conscious people in the room looked intently at the PDA while sounds of movement and low whispers too indistinct to make out came over the speaker. Finally, "I've got it!" broke out. "Let me see, uh, here . . . OK I've dialed." They hunched closer to the PDA, then the unmistakably brash tones of a busy signal could be heard. "It's busy."

"Keep trying son!" ordered the president.

And Mike, aka Trollbane, did keep trying. For 30 more minutes. The line remained busy. Not even a voice tree, much less an operator, was available.

"There has to be another number we can use. Sir, isn't there another high priority number?" asked Major Defilice.

"Of course there are numbers like that. But I don't know them. My military aide has some. My staff sec has some. My secret service agents have some. But none of them are here."

"Gunny, what about Col Lineau?" asked PFC Ramon. Col Jeff Lineau was the Commandant of the Corps, the top Marine. "He should be able to reach the White House."

"Yes, but our dedicated comm lines back to Quantico are down, and I really don't know his number."

"I can get through." She moved up to the PDA. "Mike, try dialing this number. 703 555 4543." She looked up at the rest. "In case I was going to be late from liberty," she said with a shrug.

There was a pause, then the wonderful sound of a connection.

"Private Smith, Headquarters Company duty. This is an unsecured line. How may I help you ma'am/sir?"

Gunny moved back up and spoke into the PDA, "Private Smith, this is Gunnery Sergeant McCardle in New Delhi. I've got the President of the United States with me. Listen carefully. I want you to go to the Commandant's office and get Col Lineau. Do not, I repeat do not hang up the phone. Just place the handset on the duty table there. Then, I want you to go to the Commandant's office and get Col Lineau. Bring him back to your post and put him on your phone. Do it now. Do you understand?"

There was dead silence on the other end. Gunny could almost imagine Private Smith wondering if the small chance that this was true outweighed the consequences of if this was some sort of prank.

"Aye-aye, Gunny!"

Gunny could hear the phone being placed on the table, then the sounds of footsteps running off into the distance.

Chapter 13

Early Tuesday Morning, HQMC, Quantico

Colonel Jeff Lineau, the 42nd Commandant of the Marine Corps, sat in his office with Sergeant Major Mike Huff and Lieutenant Colonel Tye Saunders, his XO. None of the men were saying much at the moment, but had their eyes glued to the television and the scenes from India.

As the satellite shot panned over the scene from above, the body of what had to be Capt Leon-Guerro could be seen lying on the deck along with the rest of the prone figures. The Marine Corps was small, and most Marines knew each other by sight. Truth be told, Col Lineau never had high hopes for Frank Leon-Guerro, but that really didn't matter now. He had proved the temper of his steel.

And now the question was the status of the rest of the detachment. Nothing much could be seen on the television screen, and attempts to reach the detachment via pulse and phone lines came up empty. There had been another Marine down, probably Sgt Crocker, but a short time ago, someone had dashed out and grabbed him. The angle and resolution weren't good enough to see just who had come out. And several Marines had earlier helped the president get inside as well. So at least a few Marines were alive and well. Hopefully more were, too.

Col Lineau looked around his office. Once the office of the Security Guard Battalion Commanding Officer, it was now the office of the Commandant. Of course, his duties were little more than the CO of old, but he was granted the somewhat honorary title of Commandant (or the "'Dant," as the Marines tended to refer to him). And now, he felt helpless as he watched what was unfolding on the screen.

Col Lineau had joined the Corps before the dismemberment. A Naval Academy graduate, he had intended on being a Navy pilot, but weak eyes and an admiration of the Marines sent to be company officers and instructors at the Academy impressed him, and he chose green instead of blue upon graduation. He had his goals though. Truth-be-told, he had harbored dreams of becoming Commandant while a second lieutenant back at The Basic School in Quantico, but he had never thought it would unfold this way. A tour as an infantry platoon commander with 3/5 at Pendleton, then as the recruiting station ops officer in Des Moines followed TBS and IOC. He then went to Amphibious Warfare School, finding time to meet and marry the former Alicia Hera, a student at William and Mary. He reported to 2/4 at Camp Lejeune, taking command of Golf Company, where he led the company into Iraq, earning himself a bronze star and making a small name for himself.

Additional staff jobs followed, along with a promotion to major. He received a Legion of Merit while serving in a joint billet with Joint Task Force Horn of Africa , something rare for his rank. When he made lieutenant colonel, he was given command of 1/8 "America's Battalion," which he led into the Sudan. It was here, while at the tip of the spear, that the Marine Corps was shattered. He brought his battalion back to Lejeune, decommissioned it, and waited along with everyone else to discover their individual fates. And Jeff was one of the lucky ones. He was offered one of the few O-5 positions left in the Corps, and became the S-3. Over the ensuing years, as retirement and one heart attack took those senior to him, he moved up and was promoted to Commandant four years ago. He was looking to retire in 53-days-and-a-wake-up, ready to go back to North Dakota with his wife and going south during the winter to spoil the grandkids.

He looked over at the other two Marines in the room. LtCol Saunders still wore the gold wings of a naval aviator on his chest, the only Marine left who rated them. An Osprey pilot before dismemberment, he'd asked to be retained in the Corps despite there being no aviation billets. Being a Marine meant more to him than flying. He was retained, and his tour as the commanding officer of Bravo Company in Europe proved to him that his decision was the right one.

Tall with deep chocolate skin, he made an imposing figure. But he was usually soft-spoken, a man whose faith was the prime mover in his life. If he were not a Marine, he could have been very happy as a missionary. Tye Saunders hid nothing from view. What you saw was what you got. And what you got was good.

Now he was hanging up the phone after yet one more try to contact the detachment. He looked at the colonel and quietly shook his head.

Sergeant Major Mike Huff was along slightly different lines. A radio operator in an infantry company whetted his appetite for adventure, and he followed that with tours in both battalion and force recon. He had combat experience with Force, and a silver star attested to his valor. Mike had confided in the colonel on a few occasions when they had shared a cold one after work that he never should have made it so far. He'd had a number of liberty-type incidents, about which he would only hint, which should have gotten him non-judicial punishment at the least, but he always had friends in high places who saw the potential in him, and his "punishments" for his transgressions were never official.

SgtMaj Huff still had the wild side to him, but he cared deeply for his Marines, and his ability to inspire their loyalty proved that those early benefactors had it right.

Admin had been undergoing an inspection, so the entire staff had stayed late. Otherwise, Colonel Lineau would already have been home asleep. When the news of the attack first broke, he had called his boss, Rear Admiral Chance Cates in N3. Chance had actually worked under him while at HOA, and, to be honest, there was not much love lost between them. He was told to stand by, and that was what they were now doing.

No one had said much for the last several minutes, each lost in thought on events taking place halfway around the world. Col Lineau sipped his coffee, wishing there was some sort of direct action, something he could be doing right now. But he was ordered to wait.

There was a thunder of feet coming down the passage, then a pounding knock on the door. Before Col Lineau could respond, the hatch burst open and Private Smith, one of the newest Marines, burst in, white duty belt around his waist, his face flushed. The three men, nerves taut, jumped to their feet.

"Sir, request permission to speak!" And before a

response, "I have the Marines in India and the president on my duty phone. And they want to speak with you!"

Lineau's mouth dropped open as his mind reeled. "How did you get that call?" He struggled for understanding.

"I don't know sir. My phone just rang, and then there was a gunny, then the president. They want you now!"

Unbelievable or not, a possible prank or not, Col Lineau snapped to and started running out the hatch, Huff, Saunders, and Smith right behind as they all sprinted down the passage, out the building, and over to the company office building. Staff Sergeant Felicia Boyles saw them through the window as they ran up, and tried to call the admin office to attention, her apprehension obvious on her face. The foursome never slowed, but ran down the passage to the duty office. They rushed in, and Col Lineau paused a second, catching his breath, before lifting the phone receiver from the desk.

"This is Col Lineau."

"Colonel! This is Gunny McCardle! We have been under attack, and we're trapped in the embassy. I've got President Eduardo with me. We've got no comms, and—"

"Let me have that, Sergeant," Colonel Lineau heard over the phone. "Colonel, this is President Eduardo. I'm going to give you a direct order as your Commander in Chief. I want you to get the White House on the line, and I want you to do it now. I want to speak with my chief of staff, and I want to speak with the vice-president. I want action taken to retake this embassy. Do you understand me?"

"Yes, sir!" He frantically mouthed to LtCol Saunders to get RADM Cates on the other line. "Uh, Mr. President, can I please speak with Gunnery Sergeant McCardle? I need to make sure we keep this connection."

There was a pause, then, "Gunny McCardle, sir."

"Gunny Mac! The news reported that all communications were cut, and we sure haven't been able to get through to you. How are you calling me? And why is the president calling us here?"

"Well sir, we sort of hacked to one of LCpl Steptoe's buds in Katmandu, and he's patching us through. And the duty was the only number any of us knew offhand."

"OK. Good thinking. I'm going to give this to SgtMaj Huff. Do not hang up!" He handed the phone to the Sergeant Major, then turned to LtCol Saunders. "You got him, Tye?"

Saunders shook his head and handed over the phone. Col Lineau put the handset to his ear and heard the cheery hold music.

"Mike, ask Mac for the name and the number of that contact in Katmandu."

"This is RADM Cates."

"Admiral, this is Colonel Lineau. I am in contact with our detachment in New Delhi. They have the president with them, and he wants his chief of staff and the vice-president on the line. If we can get a number, I can have them call, but frankly, I'm afraid to lose the connection. I'd like to patch them directly through this number here."

To his credit, Chance Cates didn't hesitate or question his subordinate. And less than two minutes later, there was a click as the White House communications technicians electronically hooked into the Headquarters Company duty phone. SgtMaj Huff caught the Commandant's eye, then hit the speaker button and the voices came over to fill the office.

"Mr. President, this is Arnie. Are you OK? Are you safe?"

"Just a second sir. This is Gunnery Sergeant McCardle. Let me hand you over to him."

Arnold Hatch was the president's chief of staff. He had never met the president before the Republican Party had essentially foisted him on nominee Eduardo, and at first glance, the older, overweight Arnie seemed the antithesis of the personable, charismatic nominee, but quickly the two had forged a true friendship based on respect and admiration. Arnie was the president's man.

"Arnie, is that you?"

"Sir, I can't tell you how good it is to hear your voice. We haven't had a clear picture of what is going on. Are you OK? Are you safe?"

"I'm a little dinged up, but I'm safe for the moment, I guess. I don't have any special agents with me, just a few Marines and an Army major, so I don't know how secure this is. What is going on back there? What are you doing?"

"The vice-president has the principles in the situation room, but no one knows just what is going on. She called in the Indian ambassador and has tried to call the prime minister."

"Has the military been given orders?"

"Well, sir, there has been some debate as to that. No one knows just what orders to give just yet."

"Arnie, get her on the phone. I want the military to move. We cannot be seen as weak."

"They're patching her in now, too. I told them to patch me in first. She should be here in a second."

"This situation is outrageous. Why hasn't the prime . . . wait a second." There was a muffled sound of someone talking, then the president came back on. "Arnie, one of the soldiers here tells me that this line is not secure. He doesn't think anyone is monitoring it, but that it could be monitored. I think it's a good idea if we speak with that in mind."

"Yes, Mr. President."

"I heard that too, Mr. President. Are you safe?" the vice-president said, joining the conversation.

"Vice-President Wright. For the moment, I'm safe Ambassador Tankersly is dead, and I don't know how many other people. We've got half the diplomatic community over at the consulate, and about a million Indians outside the gates. I'd say the situation is serious. What are you doing about it?"

"Mr. President, the Indian ambassador should be here within minutes. The prime minister has not accepted my call. I keep getting told that he is not available at the moment."

"What does the director say about this?"

The director of the CIA, Kaiyen Lin, was a trusted advisor to the president, and had been since his days in congress.

"They're in touch with their sources right now, but she thinks that there are indications that the government is at least passively supporting the mob. At least they helped organize the demonstration."

"She thinks that? I can't believe it. They're going to attack sovereign US soil over jobs? Just get the prime minister on the hook and patch me through to him. I want to talk to him face-to-face. We are going to resolve this, and now. What about the military? What are they doing?"

"They've been placed on alert, of course, but no specific orders have been given yet. This doesn't fall under any of our contingency plans, as you know," Vice-President Wright said.

"I don't care what plans there are or are not," the president said, almost in a shout. "I'm here on the ground, and this is an attack on US soil. I hope the Indian government gets things straightened out soon, but until then, I want our military moving, and I want them moving now. That is what we pay them for, to protect US citizens."

"Of course, Mr. President. General Litz reports that we have the Ronald Reagan Battle Group in Thailand right now, and we have our units in Guam and Japan, but nothing is really close."

"What about Diego Garcia? What's there?"

There was a pause and some mumbles voices as the vice-president asked someone a question. "There isn't much there, only some support forces, ours and the Brits."

"Well then, I guess you have some work to do, Vice-President Wright. I want you to keep this line open. Have someone report back to me in 15 minutes as to what's going on."

"Of course, Mr. President. We're working it."

As the speaker on the desk became quiet, the three Marines looked at each other. Col Lineau turned off the speaker.

"Mike, someone is going to think of this sooner or later, but send Gunny Cassel from the embassy in Katmandu to secure LCpl Steptoe's friend and his phone. You can be sure that State and the Secret Service and every other cat and dog will get there soon, and their priorities aren't going to be our Marines. I want one of ours there to let us know what's being passed on that line. And put someone else in here. I want a SNCO along with Private Smith to watch this phone. Tye, I want every swinging dick here in full battle rattle and ready to move in two hours."

"What is going on, sir? Where are we going?" his XO asked.

"Nowhere yet. I've got to make some calls first. I just want every possible body we've got here ready to go. Call Norm at Camp David and tell him the same. Every sickbay commando, every clerk, every possible Marine."

He turned the speaker back on, then turned and left the office. He had work to do.

Chapter 14

Early Tuesday Morning, The White House, Washington, DC

Vice-President Wright strode back into the situation room from the communications room where she had taken the call, Arnold following in her wake. She looked at the technicians who were feverishly connecting another phone. It was astounding, really, that in the heart of the White House, where decisions were made, they had not been able to simply transfer the call. Some problem with interoperability between the secure and non-secure lines, the communications chief had said.

"Well, I've spoken to him. He is safe for the moment, but rather agitated."

She looked at the gathered movers and shakers sitting around the edge of the table. There was a face she didn't recognize.

"Who are you?" she asked the young woman.

"Stacy Barnet, ma'am. Homeland Security. The secretary was on the Eastern Shore for the night and is on his way now. I'm here to take notes until he gets here."

The vice-president merely grunted. She looked around again. "Where is the Indian ambassador?" she asked no one in particular.

"He is pulling into the grounds now," replied a staffer, a communications bud in his ear.

"OK. When he arrives, get him to my office. I want to see him right away. General Litz, the president wants our military to move on this, in case things go south on us. With everyone else in the room here, please repeat what you told me about our options."

"Yes ma'am. Well, our options are limited, actually. We have the Reagan Battle Group on liberty in Thailand, and a few scattered ships in the Indian Ocean. We have our civil affairs units in the Horn of Africa, and our air and army assets in Guam and Japan. We could bomb the bejesus out of India if we wanted, but in a situation like this, I'm not sure we have the assets to take any effective action." The

Chairman of the Joint Chiefs, a former Air Force bomber pilot, looked uncomfortable and he glanced back down at his notes. "NORAD has just been placed on our highest alert posture, and the Quick Reaction Brigade in Korea has been placed on alert as well. They can be ready to move in 90 minutes, and we can get them to Thailand, Diego Garcia, or possibly even Sri Lanka, but we don't have any assets to get them all the way to New Delhi. Logistically, we could do an air drop with an airborne battalion, but even if the Indians just stood by for that, it'd be almost impossible to get them all to a landing at the embassy grounds."

"Surely you don't mean for us to physically invade India? That is ludicrous!" Simon Pitt, the Secretary of State, blurted out.

"No, Mr. Secretary, I do not. I'm just laying out our options."

"Well, that's one far-fetched option, doing a parachute invasion of India."

"Granted, Mr. Secretary. I don't think it can even be done if I thought it was a good idea, and I don't think that," the general said, looking annoyed.

Vice-President Wright interrupted, "Look, no one is advocating any sort of attack here. The Indian government will have to restore order, and we'll have to craft our response to this. Let's all keep cool heads, now."

The staffer with the comm earbuds moved forward and whispered into her ear, "Madame Vice-President, the Indian ambassador has arrived."

She nodded. "People, the ambassador is here. Mr. Lefever, if you will accompany me. General Litz, keep all our forces on alert as you deem fit. But get that carrier group out at sea and moving toward India."

"That could be seen as a provocative movement, Madam Vice-President," Secretary Pitt said.

"Storming our embassy, killing our ambassador, and keeping our president hostage are also provocative, Mr. Pitt."

She motioned to the Secretary of Defense to join her. They stepped out of the door and waited for the Secretary of State to move out of earshot.

Jennifer Wright and Paul Lefever had worked

together for years, he in various positions in the Department of Defense, and she as a congresswoman. He owed his current position to her, and they were as strong allies as anyone could be within the Beltway. Both disapproved of the way then Senator Eduardo had cut the military budget, and neither really had a high opinion of the man.

"Paul, we need to move on this," she said quietly. "But Pitt is right, as hard as it is to admit this. We really don't want a war with India. So let's move the *Reagan*. Let the world see that. But a few ships off the coast can't really do much. And if we don't have the forces to do anything, well, then that is the fault of those who did not want to pay for a strong military, and matters are just going to have to progress as they will."

She didn't say anything else. She didn't have to, and some things are better left unsaid.

Paul Lefever looked deeply into the vice-president's eyes and nodded. She knew he understood her.

The vice-president, secret service agents leading the way, walked back to her office. Her staff secretary was standing, waiting for her.

"Ma'am, the ambassador is waiting in your office."

Several men, obviously from the Indian embassy, were sitting on the couch in the reception area, and they came to their feet at her arrival.

"Thank you Ann. Please make sure no one disturbs us."

She caught sight of David hovering off to the side, his eyes asking if he could join her. She shook her head no and walked in. The ambassador was standing facing her desk, back to the door, arms clasped behind his back. He turned around at her entrance and stepped forward, offering his hand. She ignored it and moved around him to her desk and sat down. He held his hand out for a few moments then slowly lowered it.

She looked at him, seeing a man not quite sure of himself. From the contact notes given to her by her staff, she knew he was political appointee and had been ambassador in the US for over a year. With a masters from Brown University, his success in building a chemical empire and his financial support to his political party (well, perhaps that more than anything else) had gotten him the appointment. She had seen him at a few functions, but she had never really had any contact with him.

"Well, Mr. Ghosh, what is the Indian government doing about this unfortunate situation?"

"Madam Vice-President, first, accept my apologies for this incident. The people of India abhor violence, and the government is working feverishly to find a peaceful solution to the situation at your embassy."

"A peaceful solution? I don't see anything being done there. Does that look like anything is being done?" she asked, pointing to the televisions at the front of the office where CNN and Fox were broadcasting the scene.

He turned around, looked at the screen, then faced her again before saying, "Madam Vice-President. I just got off the phone with our office of external affairs. I've been assured that progress is being made with the people outside the embassy."

"Progress? I don't want to hear 'progress!' You have police, you have your army. The life of the president is in your hands along with half the diplomatic community of New Delhi, and you talk about progress?"

"Madam Vice-President. It is not that easy. Most of these people are peaceful protesters. They have a right to be there. And if we move in rashly to secure the area, they could erupt into violence," he said.

"Could erupt into violence? Mr. Ambassador, you don't think there has already been violence? Ambassador Tankersly has been killed, and the president is being held prisoner in his own embassy. And you tell me the 'people' have the right to 'protest.' What kind of unmitigated gall is that?"

On the defensive, the ambassador now seemed to grow a little bit of a spine.

"Madam Vice-President, we are the largest democracy in the world. Larger than the US, I might add. Despite the efforts of the US to keep India in thrall, we are an independent, democratic people. Our government is not going to go in shooting, massacring perhaps thousands of

Indian citizens and endangering the people in the embassy as well. We are going to do this right, with no further loss of life."

She saw the change in his demeanor and knew it was time to pull back. And while she almost would not admit it yet to herself, she really did not want a quick and safe solution. She had to couch what she said next in careful terms. History did not look kindly on leaders who let personal goals get in the way of what should be done, even if she fervently believed the nation would be better off with her at the helm rather than the current occupant of the White house.

"Mr. Ambassador, I realize that India is a great democracy. And no matter what happens, the US isn't about to do anything rash. India and the US are too close, and we are not going to let anything jeopardize our overall relations."

She hoped the message that the US would not take military action was coming through, and that there would be no serious retaliatory measures taken should the worst come to pass.

"This is happening in India, and we expect India to handle the situation. And we have full confidence in your government's abilities to take care of the situation."

She didn't mention that she knew there were Indian government agents in the mob, and that they probably had a hand in what was going on. Let the government have an out should things go downhill.

The ambassador seemed somewhat surprised at her response, but he recovered quickly.

"Thank you for your confidence, Madam Vice-President. We'll take care of this, peacefully, and without further bloodshed. The criminals who instigated this will be caught and prosecuted. And it is our fervent desire that our two great nations remain the close allies we are."

Vice-President Wright leaned over and punched her intercom button. "David, can you come in here, please."

She looked up at the ambassador and said, "Mr. Ambassador, I hate to cut this short, but you can imagine that I have a lot to do. And I imagine you do, too. Please give my regards to the prime minister and let him know the US trusts his abilities to manage this unfortunate incident."

David came in the door.

"David, please escort the ambassador back to his car. Make sure we get him all the assistance he needs. And make sure State has someone over at the Indian embassy to facilitate communications."

She held out her hand, and the ambassador took it. He looked closely into her eyes for a second as if trying to read her mind.

"Thank you, Madam Vice-President. I trust we'll have good news for you soon."

He turned around and walked out of her office.

She watched him leave. Hopefully, the Indian Office of External Affairs would read into her comments and understand that the US was not willing to risk direct action. Much hinged on whether Kaiyen Lin was right. If the Indian government was actively involved with this, or even passively supported it, then President Eduardo might pay the price. And if the Indian government was not involved, and if they successfully rescued the president, well, nothing much would change and it would be back to the status quo.

The president was not an evil man. Naive, maybe, misguided certainly, but not evil. Under normal circumstances, Vice-President Wright would never wish him harm. But she knew the nation would be safer and more secure if she was president, and if another nation helped that come to pass, then who was she to deny destiny?

Chapter 15

Tuesday Evening, Phuket, Thailand

Lieutenant David Littlehawk watched the sun finally disappear into the sea. There was no "green flash," just the last bit of orange winking out. An audible sigh arose from the several hundred Thais and *farang* vacationers at the Promthiep Cape lighthouse who gathered for the show each evening.

It had been a pretty good day, all told. His first day ashore in several weeks, and it was in Phuket, Thailand, one of the US Navy's favorite destinations. Good food, great weather, cheap cold beer, pretty and willing girls—what could be better? David had gotten a late start, renting a motorcycle in Phuket Town, then riding over to Patong Beach. Technically, he should have a liberty buddy, but no one else wanted to go exploring by bike, so he had left alone. He had gotten a good massage on a beach mat right on the water by an older, heavyset lady named Nok. It had felt so good, he had extended the massage from one hour to two, then had wandered over to one of the open-air restaurants for some lunch. Many of the restaurants offered American or European fare, but he wanted Thai. He had learned to like Thai food while a ROTC student at Oregon State, but this was different. The *Lard Na* was thick with sauce (looking sort of like flat noodles covered with snot), and the *Moo Ga Pow* was bitingly spicy. Good, more authentic perhaps, but not what he had gotten used to at the Thai Thai Kitchen in Corvallis.

He had gotten back on his bike, fought through the traffic in Patong town, then started up the long hill to ride over to Karon and the beaches to the south when he saw some elephants right at the side of the road. The elephants had benches on their backs, so he had stopped to look. These elephants, with no trees left to haul, made a living for themselves and their mahouts by giving rides. Then feeling like a million different levels of tourist, he had actually paid for a ride into the jungle. Surprisingly, a fighter pilot now used to being at sea, the animal's rolling gait had almost made him sick. As the elephant lurched up and down some washed-out jungle gullies, his stomach threatened to rebel, but the sun, the butterflies fluttering around, and the rubbery feel of the elephant's skin under the heels of his New Balances made the experience rather exotic. A man at the side of the road come out to take a photo of him on the back of the elephant, and after the ride, he was offered the photo for $10. Feeling even more like a tourist, he actually bought it. He knew it was kitschy, but still, he found out he really wanted it.

His guidebook had mentioned Rawai as a good place for seafood, (another taste he had acquired at school), so after getting lost only twice, he made it to the beach where open-air restaurants lined the shore. Walking into the closest one, he picked out fish and crabs by pointing at them, then he sat on the pillows scattered around some tables, which were offered instead of chairs. It surprised him that they did not offer beer. He ordered a cold Coke and looked out over the turquoise waters until his food came. He hadn't told them how he wanted his fish and crabs prepared, but he liked what turned up. He had no idea what it was, but the crab was in some sort of curry sauce with egg, and the fish was steamed with vegetables. He slowly ate his meal, smiling at the young Thai toddler who came up to stare at him. The toddler did not smile back, but just stared at him.

After the meal, he got back on his small bike and puttered up to Promthiep Cape to watch the sunset. While sitting on the stone wall around the lighthouse, waiting for the sun to dip into the water, two Thai teenage boys came up to him, mentioning "India" amidst a torrent of Thai, pointing at him and mimicking shooting rifles. This rather surprised him. He didn't really think his Native American features were that pronounced, and for non-Americans to recognize those features seemed rather far-fetched. And for them to act out what must be the cowboy role seemed somewhat rude, something out-of-character for Thais. Feeling uncomfortable, he merely ignored them and looked out over the Andaman Sea.

The sun got large and red as it slowly dipped into the sea. Young Thai lovers, no more than schoolchildren really, sat leaning against each other, watching the sun set. Tourists of all stripes wandered around, cameras in hand, or sat on the stone wall quietly watching. He had heard that there was an audible snap and a flash of light as the sun slipped over the horizon, but he never saw nor heard anything like that. The sun merely slipped away. The only sound was the communal sigh from the gathered throng.

As the crowd slowly dispersed after the sun set into the sea, LT Littlehawk got back on his bike and started up the coast for Patong, anxious to sample the infamous Thai nightlife. He had planned on hooking up with a few guys from the squadron at a bar they had picked out at random from the internet.

He made his way up the coast, past several small beach towns and up the hill, then down the long grade into Patong. He rode up the beach road and was surprised not to see several thousand sailors taking over the place. He felt odd parking his motorcycle at the beach side of the walking street before walking up towards Annabell's. The street was not deserted; just no sailors were in sight. There were the expected calls of "Welcome, sir," as the girls (and not a few guys looking like girls) gave their hopeful plugs to come in and sit down at the various bars lining the street.

Walking into Annabell's, he sat down and ordered a Singha from one of the short-skirted waitresses. As he waited, he scanned the bar for his compatriots. The bartender caught his eyes and motioned him over. She was an attractive woman, older than the average waitress, but with long black hair, a slender body, and a refined face. He shrugged and got up, walking over to her.

"You Loo tenna Little Hawk?" she asked pausing between the two parts of his name.

Somewhat surprised, he merely nodded. She reached under the bar and handed him a folded piece of paper.

Chickenhawk,

Get your ass back to the boat. We're pulling out at

2100. Look at the news and you can figure out where.

Gopher

He read the note twice. He automatically looked up at the television over the bar, but it had a soccer game on. He glanced down at his watch.

Shit! It was 2030!

He sprinted out the bar and down the street, knocking down one pot-bellied tourist who had already had a good start on the night's drinking. The man's challenges faded behind him as he ran to his bike. Fumbling with the key, he finally got the bike started and he tore down Beach Street, almost crashing head first into a taxi before he remembered that the Thais drove on the left side of the street.

Please let me make it on time!

He held the throttle wide open as the bike huffed its way up the mountain behind Patong, trying to will it to make some speed. Cresting the rise, he tore down the other side, cutting inside pick-ups and buses, passing wherever he could find a few inches to spare. Trying to follow the signs in to Phuket Town, he made one wrong turn and had to double back. Near a shopping mall, there was a line of cars waiting o at the light—he worked his way to the front, then scooted across the four-lane road in front of him against the red light.

Entering the town, he knew the port was off toward the right, but knowing that and navigating through the winding streets were two different things. Finally, he saw the bright lights of the port and drove up, blasting through the gate much to the consternation of the guard there who yelled Thai pleasantries as he sped through. Tearing around a group of warehouses, he looked up to see the *Reagan* moving out, several miles out to sea already.

His heart sank. Slowing down, he drove up to the landing where the liberty launches had been bringing in and taking back passengers. There was a knot of sailors there, perhaps ten or twelve, all in civvies. Two sailors in uniform, a lieutenant (jg) and a third class petty officer, were there as well, clipboards in hand.

He walked up to the two in uniform.

"Name?" the petty officer asked.

"LT David Littlehawk."

The sailor wrote it down before saying, "OK, if you can wait here, sir. We're gathering everyone who missed the ship. We'll get you put up for the night, then we'll get word on what's going to happen with you next."

"What is going on, anyway? Why the sudden departure?"

"You haven't heard, sir? The Indians have taken over our embassy, and they've got the president prisoner. We've got to get him back."

He turned away as another sailor asked him a question.

LT David Littlehawk, F-35C pilot, had missed movement when his training and skills might be needed. He stared at the *Reagan* and sat down on the edge of the pier, watching his future sail away.

Chapter 16

Tuesday Evening, US Embassy, New Delhi

"Gunny, something's happening!"

PFC Ramon stood with the major and the president, looking at the television. Gunny and Loralee rushed over to the screen to see for themselves. The satellite shot showed movement near the gate and what looked to be uniformed and armed men pushing back the crowd and then several of them climbing the wall.

"Finally, the Indian police. It's about time," the president said, sounding almost petulant.

They watched as about half a dozen men made it over the gate, collected themselves, then started walking, not toward the embassy, but approaching the consulate building. The CNN talking heads were giving all sorts of reasons they might be doing this, but the group in the embassy ignored most of the commentary. Gunny McCardle sprinted out of the room and down the passage to Post 1, arriving just as the call from Post 2 came in.

"Gunny, the Indian Army is here, and they want to get in the consulate. What do I do?" asked SSgt Harwood over the landline.

"Hold them off for a second and get Ambassador Tilden there. I don't know who is actually senior for the foreign ambassadors, but get him anyway. And get the senior US State guy there. See what they want. The consulate is still US soil, but if the Indian government is finally moving to help, then we don't want to piss them off."

"Roger that!"

Major Defilice and PFC Ramon came down the passage together. The major looked at the gunny, eyebrows raised.

"The Indian Army is here, but they want into the consulate. I don't know why they aren't coming here," Gunny Mac told him.

"Do you think we should meet them, Gunny? We've got the president here and our wounded."

"I don't think so, sir. You saw them on the screen. They walked right past the bodies in the courtyard. And they went right to the consulate. I told SSgt Norwood to get Ambassador Tilden there to find out what they want and what they're going to do."

He turned and sat down on the jutting shelf that served as the post's desk.   The group of them sat there staring at each other, wondering what was going on. The tension kept mounting. After five minutes or so, which seemed like an hour, the landline rang again.

"Gunny," came SSgt Harwood's hushed voice. "The Indians told Ambassador Tilden and Ms. Parker that they're going to evacuate the consulate. Ms. Parker told them they got to get rid of the mob, but the Indians say the situation is too delicate. Ms. Parker is pissed, and she asked about Ambassador Tankersly and the president, but the Indians keep telling them they need to evacuate first, then they can try to deal with the crowd. Oh, the Ambassador and Ms. Parker are going back inside now."

Gunny felt a sense of foreboding. He could see in his mind the photos of the Embassy takeover in Tehran in 1978, the photos of the blindfolded Marine security guard being led down the steps. The photos were part of a series of classes at Security Guard School, and all Marines had the images embedded into their psyche.

If the consulate was vacated, that meant the embassy grounds would be empty, and except for Sgt Niimoto, the only thing between the president and a hostile crowd was his group of Marines, an army major, an elderly woman, and an Indian servant of unknown loyalties. The doors to the embassy building were pretty solid, as were the lower floor windows. Then he thought of the access tunnel. If he knew about it, then certainly some Indians knew about it. Feeling paranoid, he got back on the landline.

"SSgt Harwood. They don't have a choice, and neither do you. They're going to have to evacuate. Everyone. And it won't be long. I need you and Chen to go down to the access tunnel and block it somehow. Jam the hatch, then put some furniture or something in front of it. No need advertising where the hatch is. Do it quick, because they're going to want you to evacuate, too. When they tell you to leave, do it. Help keep everyone calm."

"What about the post? We can't leave it unmanned," he protested.

"Mark, the situation has radically changed. You're going to have to leave the post anyway, so do it now. Flash the computer, then lock it up and leave."

"Roger that, Gunny. We're on it."

"Give me a report when you're done, then get out with the rest. Wherever you end up, there will be somebody in charge. Get word back to Quantico where you are, then wait for further orders."

Big Mac looked at Little Mac, gave a sigh, then turned around to go back down the passage and report to the president with Defilice and Ramon in tow.

Chapter 17

Tuesday Morning, HQMC, Quantico

Colonel Lineau looked at his S3, Lieutenant Colonel Stephanie Cable and asked, "You understand what I want, right?"

LtCol Cable hesitated a second before answering, "Yes sir, but are you sure you want to do this?"

LtCol Cable was a hard-as-nails triathlete and an outstanding operations officer, excelling at managing the training and operations of the far-flung Marines around the world. She was dual-hatted as the Staff Judge Advocate, and she was letting the conservative side of that billet make her urge caution.

"Yes, colonel, I am sure. It is my prerogative as the Commandant to place my Marines wherever I deem fit so they can best perform their duties. And I think that place right now is Thailand. And, if you can remember, we have dead Marines in India right now, and more in harm's way. You are to go to N3 and act as our liaison there. When I, or the XO, contact you and tell you to do something or cough up some assets, you are going to get it done. Period. I don't care how you get the Navy to play along, but that is what we pay you the big bucks for. Understood?"

"Yes sir."

"OK. Get going." As she turned around as started hurrying down the passage, he called out after her, "Stephanie, we are counting on you."

He turned to his S1, Captain Amir Mahmoud and asked, "How are we doing on personnel?"

Capt Mahmoud immediately replied with, "We have 63 Marines and Doc Hollister on their way to Andrews in POVs. Captain Krieg is in charge. We're the only ones left here, and we've got the duty van ready to take us."

Capt Mahmoud never seemed to use notes, but he always had figures at his beck and call, so Colonel Lineau took his words as gospel.

"The detachments at Bangkok, Phnom Penh, Hanoi,

Jakarta, Kuala Lumpur, Vientiane, and Singapore had been told to quietly get available Marines to U-Tapao, but we don't yet know how many that will be," the captain continued.

"Well, keep me informed as those numbers come in. Four, is everyone armed?"

Major Jesus Roberto, the S4 answered up, "Sir, everyone who has left is armed, and we've got three mount-out cases of ammo, grenades, C4, and some extra weapons. I've got a list here of what we have." He handed it to the commanding officer before continuing. "All those weapons are going in the POVs like you directed. I just hope nobody gets stopped for speeding on the way up to Andrews. This is a major, major breach of regs. I know why we're doing it, sir, but the Maryland Highway Patrol might not be so understanding."

"You've got that right. I hope Master Guns Chung put the fear of God in them before they took off. He's in the lead vehicle, right?" Col Lineau asked.

"Yes sir, and Captain Krieg is in the rear. Master Guns will probably blow out the tires of anyone who tries to pass him. When they get to Andrews, they'll go in Gate 4. I hope they've been cleared, sir."

Colonel Lineau glanced at the Sergeant Major who nodded slightly. "Yes, Four, they've been cleared."

Actually, Colonel Lineau seemed perhaps most surprised by this than by any other of the wheeling and dealing that had occurred over the last couple hours. From his experience, the Air Force tended way to the right on standard procedures. But somehow, the Sergeant Major, in that weird brotherhood/mafia of E9s, had paved the way for his Marines to get on the base with POVs and personal weapons, park next to the ball field, then get on a bus to the tarmac to meet the incoming C17 Col Lineau had managed to wangle from an Industrial College of the Armed Forces classmate who was now at TRANSCOM. There had been too much wheeling and dealing, too much going outside of channels. His career was almost certainly over after all of this, but he was due to get out in 52 days and a wake up anyway, so WTF? It was the right thing to do, even if he wasn't quite sure what they would do if they ever got that far.

The hatch opened and LtCol Saunders walked in. Col Lineau looked up at him expectantly and not without a little bit of dread. If Tye did not come through, then all the other rushed plans might turn out to be an exercise in futility.

A smile broke out on LtCol Saunders' broad face as he said, "Sir, I've got them. Four Ospreys on loan to the Indonesian government for piracy interdiction. Don't ask me how, but they are on the way to U-Tapao. I've got two Coast Guard pilots on their way who are qualified, and I've got an old squadron mate of mine who's now flying for the DEA heading to LAX to catch a flight to meet us there, too. The Indonesian pilots can't fly further than Thailand, so I am still trying to scare up some co-pilots. But we've got the birds."

A tremendous feeling of relief swept over him. Nothing was for certain yet, and he hoped the situation would resolve itself. But at least the Marine Corps was not standing by when its own were in trouble.

"Good job, Tye. Great job, I should say. OK, we've got to move. We've got less than an hour to wheels up, and I still have a call to make."

A chorus of "Aye-aye's" rang out as Marines started hurrying out of his office. Col Lineau picked up the secure phone and called a number that patched him through a series of comm links before ringing in the stateroom of RADM Joshua Conners, Commander, Carrier Battle Group 31, aboard the *USS Reagan*.

"Josh, it's me. We're on. We've got the Ospreys."

"OK Jeff. Then let's do it."

"We're wheels up at 1000 local. We should arrive at U-Tapao around 1600 on the 4th. Give us an hour to get on the Ospreys, then 4 hours out to your pos. So you need to be less than 1,500 miles from Thailand by then. Can you swing it?"

"Well, I just reported that we are having a little shaft problem which is slowing us down. I expect that we'll have it fixed in, say 23 hours or so?"

"Thanks Josh. You know, I really appreciate this."

"Yeah, I know." There was a pause, then, "Well, I guess it's been a good career."

"You were slated for your third star. You had better

places to go. I'm stuck at my terminal rank, and anyway, I'm out in 52 days and a wake-up. You're delaying a fucking carrier battle group for us. They could court martial you."

"Life's a bitch, then you die. So what? When we took an oath that July so many years ago at the Academy, we took an oath to the nation, but really also to our armed forces, and to each other." There was another pause. "Who would of thought it? Our Plebe Summer's two biggest shitbirds. You're the Commandant of the Marine Corps, and I've got two stars."

"Yeah, who would have thunk it. Well, I've got a bird to catch. See you in a few!"

"God speed , Jeff, God speed."

Colonel Lineau hung up the phone. He picked up his body armor and put it on, then his deuce gear. Strapping on his 9 mm, he took a look around the office before a thought struck him. Over 180 years before, another commandant was leaving Washington for battle.   He walked over to the computer and quickly typed, then printed out a page. He left his office and went to the front hatch where he could see the duty van waiting for him. He walked out, closed the hatch and locked it. Turning around, he taped the paper he had printed to the hatch. He turned again and hurried to the van.

On the paper was the simple message, word for word the same as that on the note left by Archibald Henderson:

Gone to fight the Indians.

Chapter 18

Tuesday Evening, US Embassy. New Delhi

Gunny McCardle sat in an overstuffed office chair, feeling he should be doing something, but not knowing right then just what that something was. He looked over at the president who was sitting with Major Defilice and Loralee, sipping the tea that Mr. Dravid had recovered from the ambassador's office, looking like British imperialists without a care in the world. Mr. Dravid stood attentively just behind the president.

LCpl Saad came up to the gunny and bent over to whisper, "What about him?" tilting his head towards Dravid.

Gunny knew what he meant, having some of the same thoughts himself. He looked over at Dravid, serving tea as if nothing had happened. A slight man in his early 50s, he had dark, smooth skin and a touch of gray coloring his hair. Gunny has seen him at various social functions serving the guests, and he knew that Dravid was a favorite of the ambassador, but other than that, he really knew nothing more about him. And now here he was, three feet from the president while a mob of his countrymen milled around outside having already killed and probably wanting to kill again.

He had considered restraining the man but hadn't decided it was necessary yet. But there was no use in taking chances.

"Just keep an eye on him, OK?" he said.

Saad nodded and moved around in back of the man and sat down.

"Steptoe, come here," Gunny called out. LCpl Steptoe got up and came to stand in front of him. "Great job with the PDA, by-the-way. Everything still OK with it?"

LCpl Steptoe hesitated before answering, "Uh, well, we are still connected. But I wonder how long the battery will last. The charge is half full now, but I don't have his charger here."

"Can we use anything else? Somebody has to have a

charger in one of these desks," Gunny asked.

"This is proprietary gear. It can only be charged with its designed charger. I can probably jury rig something to charge the battery, but I have to open this up and take out the battery to do that. And that means no comms while I'm doing it, and I might not get it back together right without the right tools here."

Gunny McCardle took a second to digest that. "OK, well, watch it and let me know when it starts getting low."

The president stood up and shouted, "Sergeant! What the hell is going on? I want Washington back on the phone, now!"

Gunny almost rolled his eyes but managed to stop the motion. He nodded to LCpl Steptoe who nodded back and went over the president to make the connection. Gunny chose not to listen in this time.

He called LCpl Kramer over and said, "Kramer, take Ramon . . ." before hesitating and looking around the office. "No, take Saad and stay in the Cultural Affairs office across the passage."

PFC Ramon had grabbed her weapon upon hearing her name, but when Gunny changed his mind, she sat back down with a scowl.

"Stay back from the window so no one can see you, but look out and watch. I think the people at the consulate will be moving out shortly, but let me know when that happens. I don't want to be relying on CNN for this."

Gunny sat back and half-listened to the president shouting angrily on the PDA. He was wondering just what he was missing, what he could be doing now. What he *should* be doing now. He was trained for this, but "this" was nothing he had really imagined would happen.

He looked over at SSgt Child lying on the desk and wondered for the umpteenth time if maybe Child would have been a better Marine for the situation. Well, there was no getting around it. He was in charge, and it was up to him to take care of things until someone else got there to relieve him.

PFC Rodriguez came into the office and said, "Gunny, it's SSgt Harwood. He wants to speak with you on the landline."

Gunny got up and followed Rodriguez back to Post 1.

He picked up the phone. "Yeah, Mark. What's your status?"

"We've got the hatch secured. And they are calling for me now. I've got to go. But you need to go and open your end of the tunnel."

"Why?" he asked his staff sergeant.

"Well, I thought we'd better secure the hatch from the inside, too. So Chen took this guy Drayton and did that, but now they need to get out of the tunnel, and that's up to you."

"Peyton?" he misheard. "Who the hell is that?"

"I gotta go, Gunny. The Indian Army guy is motioning me to put down the phone and get in line."

"But . . . well, OK. Get out of there. Don't do anything stupid and make sure you get word when you can back to Battalion."

There was no answer. SSgt Harwood had already hung up and left.

"Rodriguez, come with me."

They went the closed hatch to the tunnel. Gunny McCardle pulled out his 9 mm and knocked on the hatch. There was an immediate pounding back.

"Cover me," he told Rodriguez while he undid the locks and opened the hatch.

Sgt Greg Chen stepped up the last step and out into the passage followed by a thin young man in a suit coat with a red tie half-stuffed in the front breast pocket. Gunny had never seen the man before and instinctively kept his 9 mm at the ready.

The man handed Gunny a paper bag and stuck out his hand. Taking the bag, Gunny McCardle had to holster his 9 mm to take the proffered hand.

"Drayton Bajinski, USAID Dacca. Pleased to meet you. I thought you might want some of that, so I brought it along." He pointed, indicating the bag.

Gunny looked in the bag and saw a mishmash of what might have been at some time some very nice reception finger food. He looked back up.

"Sgt Chen, why is there a civilian with you?"

Sgt Chen replied, "Gunny, they were always asking for SSgt Harwood, so we knew he had to leave with the rest. But I might need help in the tunnel, and Drayton here had already been helping, so he sort of came along."

"Gunny," the man said with emphasis on the title as if he had just had the term explained to him, "don't blame Greg here. I bulled my way here, no doubt. I don't want to sit in some sort of detention center while they figure out what to do with us, and it sounded more exciting to be here with you. So here I am."

He positively beamed at Gunny McCardle.

"Exciting?"

"Yes, sir! I think so, and I can help. I'm pretty resourceful."

"Well, you're here now. No getting around it. OK, let's get back. Rodriguez, you go back to Sgt McAllister."

The gunny, Sgt Chen, and Drayton trooped back to the Admin Section's office.

Everyone else was gathered around the television when they entered, but Drayton immediately went up to the president and offered his hand. "Drayton Bajinksi, USAID Dacca. A pleasure to meet you sir."

Reflexes took over, and the president shook the offered hand. "Pleasure to meet you, too." He looked perplexed. "Where did you come from?"

"From the reception, Mr. President, or what would have been the reception, at least."

"Were any of my detail there? Did any of them make it?

Now it was Drayton's turn to look perplexed. "Your detail sir?"

"My secret service detail! Did any of them make it?"

Drayton looked over at Sgt Chen, who stepped up. "I think so, sir. I know a couple ran out, and I think they got hit. But another one, he was going to try and run out and get over here, but his boss, I think, held him back. Wouldn't let him go. I think the others had to leave when the Indians came and got everyone. "

A look of anger slowly spread over the President's face. He looked over at Sgt Chen and said, "I had secret service agents over there, and you didn't think of bringing them over here with you? These are trained professionals in this, not glorified security guards like you!"

Sgt Chen stepped back a pace and looked at Gunny Mac, arms splayed out with hands forward indicating confusion. "I . . . uh, sorry sir. Nobody told me nothing about bringing—"

Loralee interrupted while watching the television. "Looks like something is happening . . ."

LCpl Saad stuck his head in the door, announcing, "Gunny, they're on the move."

Everyone started for the door, but Gunny said, "Saad, stay here with SSgt Child and Wynn."

The rest moved across the hall and into the office.

"Sir, please stand back from the window. Without the lights on in here, no one should be able to see us, and the windows are supposed to be one way, but no use giving anyone any ideas," Gunny told the president, who nodded in agreement.

All of them stopped about ten feet back from the window and looked out across the courtyard. The darkness made it a little hard to make out, but a long line of people were being escorted by Indian soldiers along the front of the consulate and over to the front gate. Many of the diplomats glanced fearfully at the bodies still lying on the ground. Apparently the army did not want to tempt the crowd, because they kept the gate closed. They had leaned what looked like a garden-variety stepladder up the face of the gate, and those with Gunny could see the top of a ladder that was going down the reverse side. Slowly, each well-dressed member of the diplomatic community made his or her way up the ladder where a soldier helped them reverse and back down the other side.

This took a long time, considering the number of people to make it over the gate and the lack of physical prowess most of them had. It was almost dark when SSgt Harwood, the last person, got to the top of the gate. He turned around and made a quick salute in the direction of the embassy and disappeared over the other side.

About a dozen soldiers climbed back into the

compound and took down the ladder. They arrayed themselves along the edge of the fence, facing in towards the embassy with their backs to the crowd and coming to their best parade rest. They were on guard, but keeping the mob out or keeping the Americans in was the question.

"Well, I guess that is it," intoned the president. "Looks like we're here for the night."

He turned around and walked back to the Admin Section's office, the rest filing along behind him.

Chapter 19

Tuesday Evening, Phuket, Thailand

David Littlehawk sat on the couch in the suite at the Royal Phuket City Hotel, watching the BBC. He had been given a room, but he chose to sit in the suite which was serving as the Rear Party (or would the "Missing Movement Party" be more accurate?) headquarters. He and several other sailors were glued to the television, watching the same video clips over and over, listening to the commentators and the expert talking heads give their take on what was happening. Littlehawk was kind of partial to CNN, but the hotel did not carry it, so BBC it was.

Regardless of whatever legal trouble he might be in for missing movement, he had a hollow feeling in the pit of his stomach. He had trained extensively to be the best pilot he could be, and now that the nation might need his skills, he was sitting in a hotel suite in Phuket watching events unfold on the BBC. This was not supposed to be how things happened. He took a sip of his now-warm coke, then leaned back, hands behind his head, looking at the white ceiling.

The Rear Party OIC, LTJG Warren, hung up the phone. "Hey, listen up! It looks like we are going to get almost all of you back to the *Reagan.*"

LT Littlehawk felt a jolt of adrenaline surge through his body as he jumped up off the couch.

"We've got some Ospreys passing through, and the powers-that-be decided to order them to touch down and pick up you guys and get you back onboard. Grab your trash, 'cause they're going to get here in about 50 mikes, and we've got to get you back to the dock where the birds will touch down, Thai clearance willing. We've got, um, let me see, 96 boat spaces, so that's almost everybody."

"Petty Officer Kent, did we prioritize the list yet?" the j.g asked his assistant.

Kent shook his head.

"OK, well, then we have to do it on the run. I want the first bus to leave in five mikes, so let's try to get the highest priority folks on it, but just get it filled and off to the port. You three sailors," he said, pointing at them, "start pounding on hatches and getting people up out of the rack now and down to the lobby."

Littlehawk moved closer and grabbed the j.g. by the arm and asserted, "I am priority. I have to get on the flight."

"Sure lieutenant, sure. Just get down to the lobby and get Kent to manifest you."

Littlehawk rushed out of the room and pelted down the stairwell, ignoring the elevators. Bursting out into the lobby, he vaulted a couch in front of reception, thoroughly startling an elderly couple trying to check in as he rushed to get in position by the front door. By God he was going to be the first one manifested and the first one on the bird. As a fixed-wing jock, he had a fatalistic fascination with that whirly contraption that some people called an aircraft. That fascination did not extend to ever wanting to get onboard an Osprey, though. But at this stage of the game, he would strap a rocket to his butt if that was the only way to get back to the *Reagan*.

Down in the dumps five minutes ago, he was brimming with enthusiasm now. History was not going to pass him by. He was getting back to his ship.

Chapter 20

Tuesday Evening, US Embassy, New Delhi

PFC Ramon was pissed, plain and simple. She flounced to an empty desk and began to field strip her M18. Well, even if she couldn't shoot it very well, her weapon would be clean.

Everyone treated her with kid gloves, like she wasn't a real Marine. Gunny did it. The other Marines did it. She realized that she wasn't very strong and wasn't very tough, but that didn't mean she couldn't take her fair share of the load. Gunny wouldn't let her go get Cpl Crocker, and now he wouldn't even let her stand a simple watch. It just wasn't fair.

Ivy Ramon was born in East LA, the youngest of five children and the only girl. Her actual name was Haydee, but no one ever used that. As a toddler, she had a habit of holding tightly to her dad's leg, and he would even walk around the house with her clinging to his calf, sitting on his foot with her little legs wrapped around it. He would lift his leg for each step with exaggerated height and care, and she would shriek with laughter. He started calling her "Ivy," and the name stuck. Most people didn't even know her given name.

Her father had been a big jock in his day and had even played Double A ball before getting Ivy's mother pregnant with Arturo, her oldest brother. He quit playing ball, married her, and got a job in a local produce warehouse, but sports remained his passion. All four of Ivy's brothers were quite athletic, and both Arturo and Jorge, her number three brother, had received football scholarships to USC, and Jorge was now on the Seattle Seahawks practice squad (something she never told any of her fellow Marines).

Ivy, on the other hand, was not a jock, by any stretch of the imagination. Oh, she tried. As a small girl, she used to follow her brothers out to the vacant lots where they played ball and tried to get them to let her play. One of her undying memories was when she convinced Jorge to throw her a football. Her six-year-old hands could not close on the ball to catch it, and it hit her in the face. She broke out in tears and ran home, the boys' laughter chasing her. When she got home, her father pulled her in his lap and laughed, telling her that she was a girl. All she had to do was be pretty. She should not be trying to be a boy.

Later, she tried track and field, she tried softball. She couldn't make either high school team. Her mother had suggested that she do a nice "girls'" activity like cheerleading, so for three weeks she practiced that with abandon only to not make even the first cut at tryouts.

Ivy saw how much her father loved sports, and she felt this was the only way to get his approval. And not to get it gnawed at her.

But despite this, Ivy was a happy girl. Growing up, she loved her dolls and could spend hours upon hours dressing them up and playing make-believe. Her mother gave her a fashion cutout book, and she lost herself in it, imagining herself as a fashion diva. She pranced up and down her bed-turned catwalk. She loved ribbons and Barbie and Prancing Pony and all things little girl.

Ivy was a short girl with a slightly chunky body. Then, after her twelfth birthday, she started developing. Not in height, but in her chest. Her breasts started to swell, and they didn't seem to want to stop. She started to get noticed, and at first, she enjoyed the attention. But as her breasts got bigger and bigger, some of the attention started taking a nasty turn, so Ivy pulled away from people and spent more time at home.

Her mother kept telling her that this was a normal part of growing up, and she should use them for any advantage she could. Ivy's mother was also short and had rather large breasts. But she was also quite fat, and Ivy feared that she was going to follow her in that way, too. She put a mirror up in her room and daily stood in front of it naked, examining her body for any change. She thought her hips were getting too big, her belly too pronounced.

She thought about breast reduction surgery. It was not so much that she really thought they were too large, but rather that she did not like the suit-of-armor bras she had to wear to support them. She thought the frilly, lacey things she saw in the fashion magazines were so pretty, but it seemed they didn't make them in industrial sizes.

She often confided in Victor, a gay boy in class who was her sometimes confidant. When she expressed concern on her growing width, he told her that his brother, in a desperate and concerned "man-to-man, see-you-are-not-really-gay" talk, had told him a woman's body was fine if in the noon sun, her stomach was in the shadow of her tits. Ivy laughed out loud at this and took this as her personal boundary. As long as her belly was in the shadow, and it looked like it would be in the shadow for a quite some time yet, she was OK.

Ivy never really had a steady boyfriend. She played with Victor, teaching each other how to kiss, and she went to her junior and senior prom, but there was nothing too serious. Truth be told, her opinion of men was somewhat shaped by the men in her life. Her father and brothers were fit, well-muscled men, rather masculine, and rather appealing. None of the boys in high school fit that mold, so she never really felt a pull toward any of them.

After graduating from high school, her parents expected her to settle down and start producing grandkids to add to their growing count. But Ivy still wanted to do something more, to achieve something. When her friend Teresa needed to get a marriage license, she went down with her to the county building. Waiting on the bench, she looked up at a poster for the Marines. On it was a handsome black Marine, broad-shouldered and obviously fit. In other words, he was the kind of man who appealed to her sense of what a man was supposed to be.

She snuck off to the recruiting office where a Marine told her about the adventure of the Corps, all the while trying not to stare at her breasts pushing out against her designer t-shirt. Ivy listened and wondered if she could succeed in this man's game or not. She promised to bring her school records back, thought about it overnight, then came back on the next day when she signed on the dotted line.

Her mother cried when she left for boot camp, but her father gave her a crushing hug and told her how proud he was of her. As he let her go, Ivy could see a tear rolling down his face.

It was that tear that kept Ivy going in boot. As soon as she arrived, she thought she had made a huge mistake. The yelling, the shapeless cammies, the lack of proper skin care, the food. One DI, Sgt Contreras (known as the "Dragon Queen" to the other recruits) seemed to particularly take pleasure in tormenting her. Ivy, as in her attempts at sports, did not excel, and Sgt Contreras took great delight in pointing out all her faults, putting her through "extra instruction." Three times Ivy was called before a review board, the third time before the company commander. But each time, she squeaked through, the image of her father's tear pushing her forward.

The company commander seemed to take a personal interest in her progress. Ivy did not know exactly why, but she was willing to grab at any lifeline. And somehow, by some miracle, she made past all the obstacles thrown in her path. The O-course, the PFT, Range Week, all the hours of EI, even Mount Motherfucker. She defeated them all and graduated. Last in her class, to be sure, but she graduated.

She was amazed that before the graduation parade, the Dragon Queen came up and hugged her. Yes, physically hugged her. And said, "I knew you could make it *màna*, I knew you would." Ivy was flat-out astounded.

But more important than Sgt Contreras' opinion was that of her family. Her parents and all four of her brothers (and two of their families) flew to Quantico to see her graduate. This was the proudest moment in her life. She had made her father proud.

She went through the rest of her training without too much problem. She was certainly glad that she could wear regular clothes when not on duty, she could read *Seventeen*, and she was allowed to wear at least a little make-up again.

And when she reported for duty in New Delhi, she was surprised to see that the Marine on the poster, the one she saw in LA, was there, SSgt Child. He still was a pretty hot piece of man-meat, one who Ivy could really appreciate, but he was a Marine, and to Ivy, that now meant family. She didn't date her brothers.

She had caught MAJ Defilice checking her out, and during the day, they had spent time talking. He wasn't such a bad piece of man-meat himself, and she thought he was rather interesting. A bad boy with a heart. He was Army, so he wasn't a brother, was he now? But he was an officer. She would have to think about that.

Oh, she knew her fellow Marines looked at her and some were interested. She chuckled as she thought of tough SSgt Child not knowing where to look at the inspection early that morning (was in only this morning?), then she looked up guiltily at his prone body on the desk. Tears welled in her eyes.

She may not be the strongest or toughest Marine here, but she was going to give out some payback. Gunny Mac or not, she was going to whup some ass.

Chapter 21

Tuesday Evening, US Embassy, New Delhi

High in the bell tower, Sgt Niimoto watched the procession of diplomats climb over the fence. He kept his rifle at the ready, scanning the crowd, not having orders to fire, but knowing he would if the diplomats got into trouble.

Hungry and thirsty, he wished he had thought to bring some food with him. He had talked with Little Mac on the landline, and he knew the tunnels were secure now. So he was just going to have cope. He had gone through an extremely uncomfortable period when he thought his bladder was going to burst, so he had finally sidled over to the far side of the cupola and peed right there on the floor against the bulkhead. He had considered peeing over the side, but that might draw attention to him, so he was just putting up with the stench, even if it had since faded in the Indian heat. He was somewhat perversely fascinated with the ever-growing Rorschach-stain his urine made on the plaster of the wall of the tower. He wondered how much more the plaster was going to wick up the urine, and how much larger the stain would get. Oh well, thank God for small miracles that he hadn't had to take a crap yet.

Concerned about exposing his head and rifle barrel over the edge of the railing, he had taken out the cleaning rod for his rifle and tried to push it through the side of the wall. But once the plaster was removed, the wall proved to be some very heavy gauge steel or something that he didn't recognize. He couldn't even scratch it. Whatever this tower really was, that was more evidence that it wasn't a bell tower. Niimoto couldn't even guess as to what needed this kind of construction.

In the growing darkness, he felt more secure in peering over the wall and down to the antline of diplomats climbing over the ladders and down the other side. The Indian soldiers had a nice cordon going on the other side and up to the waiting buses, but the mob, while looking on with evident interest, did not seem to be agitated or trying to get at the diplomats. So Niimoto just watched, ready to take action if needed.

As the line finally started to peter out, Niimoto saw SSgt Harwood approach the ladder and hurry up. Once at the top of the wall, he turned and gave a salute back to the embassy. Niimoto started to laughed out loud before choking it off.

"Get some, Harwood!" he whispered.

SSgt Harwood climbed down the other side and sauntered over to a waiting bus, not even glancing at the mob. He looked like he didn't have a care in the world. He got onboard and an Indian soldier pounded on the side of the bus. The driver closed the door, and the bus pulled out and disappeared down the road. The mob slowly closed in on the space left by the bus until it was packed up against the embassy wall again. They seemed strangely subdued now somehow, without the chanting and gesturing that had been so evident before. Some soldiers climbed back into the compound and took positions along the wall, facing in toward the embassy building.

Still wishing he had something to drink, Sgt Niimoto settled back to watch. Just what he expected to see, he really didn't know.

Chapter 22

Tuesday Afternoon, The White House, Washington, DC

Vice-President Wright looked over her desk at the two men sitting there. She had briefly thought about taking over the Oval Office, but she knew that was pretty crass, and she was an astute politician, if nothing else.

David waited expectantly, and the vice-president could see him trying to maintain professionalism when excitement was trying to take over. General Litz was different, with a look of apprehension as he sat on the front third of his seat, back straight, hands in his lap.

The vice-president considered him. She had known the general for years as he climbed the general officer hierarchy. While not a close friend, her stand on military issues certainly put them in the same camp. He was known to be an efficient administrator with a prickly demeanor, and he was very concerned about how others perceived him. She decided the personal approach was the right choice here. David had given her the general's pilot nickname of "Coptic," but at the last second, she thought that would sound too patronizing.

"Hank, thank you for coming here. I wanted to talk to you privately to get a better feel for what's going on. Secretary Pitt is dedicated, but he can be a big distraction at a time like this."

The general's almost imperceptible easing of his back and the slight slide back into his seat confirmed her guess that this was the way to go.

"What is the situation now? Where do we stand?" she asked him.

The general cleared his throat. "Well, ma'am, as I briefed before, we have the Reagan Battle Group heading out from Thailand. There has been a slight delay as the *Reagan* is undergoing some repairs while underway, but it should be back up to full speed in about ten hours or so, and it should be off the coast of India by Thursday afternoon local. The *Honolulu*, though, a missile sub in the group, should be off the coast near Calcutta Wednesday night."

"Can the carrier really do anything about the situation?"

"No ma'am. Not really. It'll be there to show the flag. That's about it. Or, if—when—the president is released, it can serve as a receiving station. We also have various air assets arriving at Diego Garcia, and the Quick Reaction Brigade is still on alert in Korea. But once again, ma'am, we can bomb the hell out of New Delhi, pardon my French, but I'm not sure we can go in and secure the embassy safely and without collateral damage." He paused. "Do you want us to transport the Quick Reaction Brigade? We are just waiting for your OK on that."

She caught David's upraised eyebrows and short shake of his head. David was valuable to her, but goodness, he could be such a pain. She didn't need him to remind her of what was her own decision in the first place.

"Hank, don't move them. The situation is precarious in India now. Pitt is right about that, and moving the brigade might provoke the mob into rash action" (as if attacking the embassy wasn't already rash enough, she thought). "Keep the *Reagan* moving, but I want no action taken at all, none, that can be taken as offensive action. Keep everyone else out of the region. Understood?"

"Yes ma'am. Understood."

The vice-president smiled as she stood up and came around the desk, offering her hand. "I appreciate your efforts, Hank. I'm glad you are chairman during this crisis. We'll get through it."

"Thank you ma'am for your confidence. We're going to do our best."

The vice-president almost burst out laughing while he came to attention, saluted, then did a smart about face and strode out of the office. Once the door closed, she waited a second, then turned to look at David and did laugh.

"What a character!" she said, shaking her head. "Well, I think that went well."

"Yes ma'am. Great job playing both sides. Not sending the brigade will appease Pitt and be taken as judicious restraint. Sending the *Reagan* will show resolve and strength. And since the *Reagan* can't really do anything, we'll just let things—"

She quickly raised her hand stopping him. Some things were better left unsaid, even among the closest of confidants. Nixon had paid the price for not following that rule.

He looked awkwardly about for a second before pulling himself together. "Are you ready for Pitt now?"

"No, give me a few minutes. Then send him in."

He nodded and left. It had been a long night and morning, and the afternoon offered no relief. She walked back over to her desk and sat down, looking out the window through the leafy trees to the White House. Would that be her new address in the very near future?

Chapter 23

Late Tuesday Night, US Embassy, New Delhi

Gunny Mac woke with a start, wondering what he was doing and what he should be doing with a sense of panic until his brain came online. He looked around the room. The president was asleep on one couch. Major Defilice and the off-watch Marines were asleep either in chairs or on the floor. LCpl Saad was alert, watching SSgt Childs and LCpl Wynn. He had the PDA in front of him, which had been turned off to save power. A schedule had been made for it to be powered up and contact established. He nodded to Gunny.

It was fairly dark in the room with only the emergency lights on. These battery powered lights did well enough in enabling people to move back and forth and get along with what had to be done, but they weren't the same as regular lighting. When the power was cut off an hour after the diplomats from the consulate were evacuated, there had been a momentary panic setting in until the emergency lights kicked on. Now, at least they had some lighting.

Gunny Mac slowly got up and stretched. It seems a little surreal to be in the darkened room with people sleeping, considering the situation. He felt they should be doing something, but intellectually, he knew there wasn't much to do at the moment, and keeping everyone awake would only hinder their effectiveness later.

He only noticed then that Loralee Howard wasn't in the room. Maybe she had gone to the head, he thought. He got to his feet and walked out the door to go down to Post 1, but as he turned the corner into the passage, he almost stumbled on Loralee, sitting huddled on the floor, back against the bulkhead.

She gasped and sniffled, then pulled herself together. "Gunny Mac, joining the night owls here tonight?" she asked, rubbing her sleeve across her eyes.

Gunny looked down at her, feeling a lump form in his throat. He put his back to the wall and slid down until he was sitting alongside of her, their legs touching.

"I haven't said anything to you yet, Loralee, because I don't know what to say. And you seem so strong. But I am very, very sorry for your husband. He seemed like a real good man."

She was quiet for a moment, head back, staring up at the dim reaches of the passage. Suddenly, she put her head down in her arms, and Gunny could hear her quiet sobs. Not knowing what else to do, he put his arm around her shoulders. She tensed for a moment, then relaxed into his embrace, letting him support her while she finally let out the tears. They sat like that for several minutes, alone in the dark passage, her quietly crying and him just supporting her by being there. Finally, the sobs slowed, then stilled. She sniffed and rubbed her nose on her forearm.

"Yes, he was a good man, and I'm sure going to miss him." She paused for a few moments. "He was my second husband, you know? I married for the first time when I was 17, way, way too young. And when we lost our little girl, well, we were just kids ourselves, and we couldn't handle it. John, my ex, left me, and I just puttered along through life, not really caring about anything else. Then I met Stan, and he was so, well, so mature, so rock solid. I can be a little crazy sometimes, if you haven't noticed . . ."

"Oh no, never, not me ma'am," he responded with mock sincerity, and they both chuckled softly.

"Thanks for that, Gunny. You know how to sweet talk an old lady. But Stan, he was my governor, he kept me on an even keel. He was good for me, and I loved him for that. He wasn't the best looking man, the most exciting man, but he was right for me. And now, I am going to miss that man so much."

"You know, Loralee, it is OK to show your emotions. When we dragged you through the door today, well, I thought I must have heard wrong, that your husband wasn't even out there. You seemed so calm and collected."

"Oh, I am not one for much emotion. And I have to keep control now, do you understand? I can break down later, after we are out of here. But if I break down now, well, I'm not sure I can come back from that. And you don't need a hysterical old woman dragging everyone down. So, help me keep it together, OK? Help me keep strong. I will mourn my Stan later, when I can afford to do it right."

"Sure thing, but I kind of doubt that you really need me for that. You're an iron lady, Ms. Howard, if I may be so bold as to say that."

"Ah, once again, my dear Gunny, you sure know how to sweet talk a lady."

They sat like that in silence for several more minutes. Slowly, Loralee took a hold of Gunny's hand and removed his arm from around his shoulders and struggled to her feet.

"No more copping a free feel for you, and I think you have kept me from my beauty sleep long enough." She turned to stand over him, looking down.

"Thank you, Gunny Mac."

She leaned over, taking his face in her hands, and kissed his forehead, then turned and walked back into the Admin office. Gunny Mac sat there and watched her disappear inside the doors.

With a sigh, he stood up and walked down to down to Post 1. Sgt Chen was at the post along with PFC Van Slyke.

"Anything?"

"No Gunny. Quieter than a witch's tit out there."

"A what? And just how quiet is a witch's tit?"

"I don't know Gunny. Pretty quiet, I guess. I mean, who wants to go and grab a witch's tit. All ugly like that?" Chen said.

Listening in, Van Slyke laughed, then groaned and put his hand up to his face as the pain hit him.

"You OK?" He looked closely at the bandages on Van Slyke's face.

"Sure Gunny. It only hurts when I laugh."

"Well then—"

Both Chen and Van Slyke chorused in before Gunny Mac could finish, "DON'T LAUGH!"

Gunny Mac smiled and turned back, going to the Cultural Affairs office where Steptoe and the USAID guy, Drayton, were posted. Gunny had a problem with putting Drayton there, but the guy insisted, and he knew he should get his Marines as much rest as possible. There was no telling what was coming down the pike, and he wanted everyone in the best condition possible.

Drayton spun around nervously, weapon in hand, as Gunny Mac entered. He saw it was the Gunny, and he sheepishly lowered his M18. Gunny Mac almost said something about him having a weapon, then decided to ignore it.

"Anything at all out there? Any movement?" he asked instead.

"No Gunny," answered Steptoe. "It's been real quiet. After the Indian soldiers went back over the wall, there hasn't been much. We've seen a couple heads poke over the wall to take a look, and we can see people peering in through the gate, but nothing else."

"Well, OK. Let me know if you see anything. You've got another hour and Ramon and Kramer will relieve you. Try to get some sleep then."

"Aye-aye, Gunny," they both replied in unison. For a civilian, Drayton was picking up the Corps lingo pretty quickly.

Gunny Mac walked back to the Admin office and laid down on the newspapers with which he had staked out his claim on the floor. He tried to get some sleep, but it kept eluding him as his mind filled with thoughts on what he was missing, what he should be doing. He heard the ongoing watch get up and leave, then the off-going watch come back and lie down. Soon, snores were emanating from LCpl Steptoe, but Gunny Mac could not drift off himself. Finally, he gave up and went to join Ramon and Kramer where he watched the dawn slowly lighten up the embassy courtyard. He wondered what the day would bring.

Chapter 24

Wednesday Morning, U-Tapao Air Base, Thailand

LT Littlehawk stood anxiously in the old hangar at U-Tapao. He had flown up the night before with the rest of the *Reagan* stay-behinds aboard one of the four Ospreys, but now they were just in hurry-up-and-wait mode. He knew that with each passing moment, the *Reagan* was getting farther and farther away, and he wasn't sure about the legs on the Ospreys. The Indonesian crews had landed the birds, taxied them into the hangar, then drove away in two waiting vans, leaving them alone except for two Thai airmen guards who didn't seem to speak any English.

He stared across the runway to the nondescript terminal and the one commuter-sized plane parked there. The terminal seemed to shimmer through the heat waves radiating off the runway. The airport was obviously dual-purpose with both civilian and military aircraft, but the civilian side seemed a little light. A few old F16s with Thai markings were parked further down from the terminal near a couple of somewhat newer-looking buildings, and a number of helos were out on the aprons. On this side of the runway, however, there wasn't much. Three old hangars and a beat-up one-story building seemed to make up the bulk of the facilities. The sailors and Ospreys were obviously being kept as out-of-sight as possible.

The heat was getting a little oppressive as the sun beat down on the tarmac and radiated inside the hangar. Littlehawk looked back into the hangar where most of the sailors were sleeping wherever they could find a free space on the concrete deck. Another group was playing spades. No matter the situation, probably since time immemorial, sailor always seemed to find the will and the way for a game of spades.

An approaching van, coming from out of the dense jungle in back of the small facility, pulled in front of the hangar, and eight Marines in cammies and full battle gear got out. One, a staff sergeant, Littlehawk thought, came up to him.

"Can you tell me who is senior here?" the Marine asked.

"I am Lieutenant Littlehawk. I guess it might be me."

The Marine snapped off a salute, which Littlehawk instinctively returned despite not being in uniform. "Sir, Staff Sergeant Montrose here. I'm afraid there has been some mistake. We're from the embassy in Bangkok, and these Ospreys are for an incoming group of Marines. Someone doing the air schedules thought it would be perfect to get you back out to your ship, but he didn't know these birds will be full. So, I'm going to have to ask you to let your people know you're going to have to stay here until the JUSMAG can figure out what to do with you."

Littlehawk's heart dropped. He had thought he was going to get back onboard the *Reagan*, but now it looked like this was getting snatched away from him.

"What do you mean these birds are going to be full? Who's getting on them?"

"Sir, I am not at liberty to tell you that. Please, just inform your people and move them back out of the way. We'll be using the front of this hangar as an assembly point. Someone from the JUSMAG will get here soon and figure out what to do with you all."

He started to protest but realized this Marine was not in the position to change anything. He would wait until someone from the Joint US Military Assistance Group arrived, or whoever arrived to fly in these birds showed up. By hook or by crook, he was going to get onboard.

Chapter 25

Wednesday Morning, US Embassy, New Delhi

The president was antsy. He had barely eaten any of the somewhat smashed reception food or the fruit and crackers Mr. Dravid had gleaned from the ambassador's refrigerator. Now he was pacing while methodically cleaning each fingernail with the nail from the opposite hand's forefinger. He had just been briefed on the *Reagan's* movement and the progress (or lack thereof) on the diplomatic scene. Now the PDA had been turned back off, and the president had commenced pacing.

Gunny Mac understood the feeling. He knew he should be doing something, but he really could not determine exactly what he should be doing. Twenty-four hours ago, he was in his element, getting ready for a pain-in-the-ass presidential visit. He understood that. Pain-in-the-ass VIP visits were part of the Marine Corps' stock in trade. Now, he had dead Marines, Marines in his charge. And he had the President of the United States sitting in an office in a hostile, life-threatening situation. But it was jarringly quiet now. In fact, nothing much had happened since early in the morning when some Indian police had entered the courtyard and removed the bodies there. Gunny thought someone in the Indian government finally must have realized that the CNN satellite could easily see them, and those images were perhaps not in India's best interest. Still, no one had attempted to contact them in the embassy building itself, not even to ask as to the president's condition, which seemed more than strange.

He heard a quiet laugh and looked over to see PFC Ramon sitting alongside MAJ Defilice, while he grabbed her arm and tried to say something more. PFC Ramon threw her head back and laughed louder. Gunny felt a little pang of, of, well he wasn't sure what it was. It couldn't be jealousy, right? There was no reason for that. But it was a pang of something, never-the-less.

He heard steps and looked up to see LCpl Steptoe with

Mr. Dravid in tandem approach him.

"Um, Gunny? Mr. Dravid has been in the ambassador's office, and well, Cpl Crocker and Cpl Ashley, well, they aren't doing that well in the heat. Mr. Dravid wonders if we should put them in the reefer in the ambassador's pantry. We can take out the shelves, and they should fit. There's still ice in there, so it should stay cooler in there than out in the office."

Mr. Dravid stood behind Steptoe, looking over his shoulder at Gunny anxiously. Gunny felt the eyes of the others swing to him as well.

"Yes, I think that is a good idea. Go do it."

He felt a little guilty watching the two of them move off, but frankly, he didn't want to help move them, to see their dead bodies. The office returned to quiet.

"Sergeant, when do you think something is going to happen?" Gunny Mac looked over to see the president watching him expectantly.

"I don't know sir. It's been pretty quiet, but you know people are working on this."

"I know they are. I just got off the PDA with the vice-president. We've got the *Reagan* on the way, but it won't get offshore near Calcutta for another 14 or 16 hours. But what do *you* think? What does your gut tell you?"

The president was speaking normally to him, man-to-man, perhaps for the first time since his arrival. Gunny couldn't be sure, but the look in the president's eyes might have even been a little hopeful.

"Well sir, I don't know. I think this is going to break one way or the other before the *Reagan* gets offshore. Marines have been through this before. Tehran. Beirut. Nairobi. Caracas. Lima."

He gestured to SSgt Child, still prone on the desk, chest slowly rising and falling.

"I am surprised, to be honest, that the crowd didn't storm the place immediately, when they were riled up like that. I don't know why they didn't. Maybe it was Sgt Niimoto taking out those guys. Maybe they were as surprised as everyone else things escalated. What you told us about the government participation in all of this might mean the mob out there isn't really wired into all of this."

He paused for a moment before continuing, "But the fact that it has been so long, almost 24 hours now, well, that could be a good sign. That means if the government is involved, that they don't want something drastic to happen, or that our diplomatic efforts are doing some good. The longer this drags on the better, but that crowd out there, I don't think it's going to wait. Sgt Niimoto says there are guys with bullhorns taking turns speaking to them, and the crowd is agitated. Either they are going to get bored and go home, or they're going to come into the grounds."

The president walked over and sat down on an office chair, slowly rotating it back and forth. "If they come, can we do anything about it? Can we protect ourselves?"

"Well sir, to be honest, no. We can delay them, and we'll get you into the vault. But if they are here, given enough time, they can cut into even that. But I promise you sir, if they do that, it's going to cost those bastards."

The president leaned back, looked up at the overhead, and locked his hands behind his neck. He was quiet for a few moments.

"How long have you been a Marine?" he asked.

"I came in during Iraq, sir, before the drawdown. I was here for the Diss . . . for the reduction of the Corps' mission."

"Why did you stay in the Marines? The Army still needed good soldiers," the president asked him in a curious tone..

Gunny paused, then said, "With no disrespect to the Army, sir," he glanced over to where MAJ Defilice was still chatting up PFC Ramon, "the Army is a job. I mean, they're patriotic and everything, and they're good people. Their infantry is top-notch.   But being a soldier is doing a job, like truck mechanic, cook, office clerk—you know, like that. The Corps, well the Corps is a lifestyle. It is what we are. You can't change that. I'd just as soon cut off my balls and become a fucking eunuch before—" he stopped, face reddening after realizing what he has just said in front of his Commander-in-Chief.

The president seemed non-plussed. "So you'd rather

work as a member of a glorified security guard rather than be a member of the US Army? Or Navy or Air Force, for that matter?"

"Yes sir, I would. No 'bout a-doubt' it,'" he said forcefully.

His fervent feelings were undermining his normal this-is-how-you-speak-with-officers-and-bigwigs speech patterns.

The president took a longer pause, then asked, "Since it seems like it may certainly be a possibility, would you die for your country?"

Gunny hesitated, took a deep breath, and replied, "Don't take this wrong, sir, but I don't think I would willingly die for my country, as much as I love it. But I would die for my mission if that was necessary. I would die for Loralee over there, for Drayton, and for you." He seemed to consider that for a moment. "Yes, I'd die to protect you. But most of all, I would die for my fellow Marines. Without question, without hesitation." He gestured to Ramon. "I'd give my life for PFC Ramon, and you know what sir? I know she'd do the same for me. Maybe that's what it means to be a Marine. Whatever your background, whatever your situation, you are part of something bigger, something far greater than yourself. And so yes, I'd die for the Corps and my brother Marines."

The president looked down at his fingers splayed before them, absent-mindedly checking the nails.

"I've read my history. I know Marines have fought and bled for this country, and I know about Marines dying in combat. But so has the Army. When I was a kid, we were taught a song about a soldier named Roger Young, a nearsighted young soldier who willingly went to his death in the Solomons to take out a Japanese machine gun nest. Isn't that the same thing?"

"Well sir, I don't know this Roger Young guy, but there are plenty of brave men in the Army. Look at all the Army Air Corps bomber crews who died in that war. Hell, look at all the Navy sailors who died when their ships were kamikaze'd. The Army, the Navy, the Air Force, well, they all have good people, brave people. Even a Coastie was awarded the Medal of Honor, for getting Marines off a beach on Guadalcanal. And I respect all of them. But for most of them, especially now in peacetime, it seems to me that it's a job. It gives them a skill or money for college. And there's nothing wrong with that. But Marines? This is our life. Other Marines are our family. Marines are warriors, not people just looking for a way to pay for school."

"But there we go back to one of my original questions. The Marines are pretty much now glorified security guards. If you were a 'warrior,' why not join the Rangers, the SEALS? They fight, even now in this so-called peacetime?"

"Sir, you may have made our jobs into being guards," he replied, with a slight emphasis on the "you," "but every Marine in a rifleman. We are warriors, by a long tradition earned in blood. And I'm sorry, but with all due respect, no politician can change that."

Gunny was surprised and a little embarrassed to feel a small lump form in his throat while he said that.

"I am sorry sir, but I need to check on the watch." He turned away and walked out of the office.

The president just watched him go.

Chapter 26

Wednesday Afternoon, Ministry of External Affairs, New Delhi

Dr. Amarin Suphantarida, Thailand's ambassador to India, waited outside the office of the Indian External Affairs Minister. Dr. Amarin, or "Pui" as he was known by his friends, had been in Thailand for a family matter and was returning aboard the daily Thai Airways flight between Bangkok and New Delhi when the embassy was attacked. Given that he wasn't part of the diplomatic corps at the US embassy when it was taken over, given Thailand and India's close economic relationship, and given Thailand's good relations with the US, others, within ASEAN in particular, and the UN in general, thought he might be a good choice to try and jump start some action to rectify the situation.

Pui wondered now if he was such a good choice. Shortly before arriving, he had taken a call from Richard Case, the US ambassador to Thailand and a good friend. Pui and Rick had served with their respective missions at the same time in Cairo and London, and they had formed a close relationship based on mutual respect and a similar taste in sports, food, and movies. Now, both were ambassadors, and Rick was even assigned to Thailand. Rick's call was short and sweet and probably unauthorized. Rick told him that Thailand was being used as a staging area for a small number of US combat troops who may or may not be going to the region. Pui had known about the *Reagan* already. At a dinner with Rick and his wife two nights earlier, they had mentioned the carrier group and talked about 10,000 young men taking liberty in Phuket and the potential for incidents neither government wanted. But combat troops being transported via Thai soil? And why hadn't his own government informed him of this?

He made a sort of mental sigh, with nothing showing on his face as he sat on the hard seat. For perhaps the first time in years, he wondered if he had made the right choice in joining the Ministry of Foreign Affairs. It would have been so easy, as the eldest son, to take over his family's sprawling industrial complex in Chonburi, making auto parts for Toyota. But that fateful day upon his graduation from Chulalongkorn had sealed his fate.

Even now, so many years later, a feeling of awe flowed through him as he remembered that moment, that turning point in his life. Pui had sort of expected he would in fact take over the family business, and he had gone to Chulalongkorn without any different aspirations. As one of Thailand's "hisos," (short for "High Society"), he had his life mapped out for hard work and even harder play. He studied, managed to achieve passable grades, and was ready to move on. At his commencement, though, the King himself gave the commencement speech and presented the diplomas. The King spoke about the importance of serving society, serving Thailand, and not just serving oneself. Pui was pondering the King's message when he was in line, waiting to receive his diploma. As he walked down the stage, both excited and nervous on being so close to the King, he concentrated on not tripping or looking like a fool. He made it to the King and went into a deep wai. As he came up and reached for his diploma, he caught the King's eye. The King smiled and simply said "Thailand needs you." Taken aback at actually being addressed, he paused a moment, then deeply wai'ed again before hurriedly walking off the stage.

Oddly, he felt a sort of rapture, a sort of spiritual uplifting. Some casual questions with other graduates seemed to indicate that the King hadn't spoken directly with others. Pui wondered if he was somehow being singled out. The more he thought about it, the more he was sure this had to be the case. So right then and there, he dedicated himself to the public service.

With the typical Thai respect for education, he was able to convince his father that he needed to get some higher degrees. His father was willing to let him delay his entry into the world of business for that, so Pui earned his masters at Boston University and his doctorate at Oxford. It was after his doctorate that he told his father he was joining the government. And not only that, he was not joining one of the revolving parties of power and becoming a member of

Parliament or the Senate, but he was joining the Ministry of Foreign Affairs. His father at first actually forbade it, but when Pui told him about the King's words, he relented. He had two more sons, after all, who seemed more than eager to make money for the family.

So Pui, as a rich mid-level bureaucrat with an actual talent for the job, rose up through the ranks despite no real party affiliation. He earned a reputation as an honest broker. Now he wondered how honest he was going to be with the Minister. Should he or should he not mention the combat troops?

"Mr. Ambassador? The Minister will see you now," a young woman in a conservative brown suit said as she held open the door for him.

Pui sighed a little once more before standing up and walking into the Minister's office.

Chapter 27

Wednesday Afternoon, US Embassy, New Delhi

Sgt Niimoto was thirsty, real thirsty. He could smell the street stalls that some enterprising entrepreneurs had set up to feed the mob, and his stomach rumbled, but his thirst was becoming overpowering. He had once read where shipwrecked people sometimes drank their own urine, but he was not quite to that point yet. Give him time, he chuckled to himself, and he might be there.

Thinking back to his Psych 101 class and old Maslow and his *Hierarchy of Needs,* Niimoto now understood it on a more base level. Given the choice of Astral Humphrey, last year's Playmate of the Year, naked and willing, right there with him, or a tall, cold glass of water, he thought he might take the water, although maybe Astral would hang around a little, too, given the present situation. He sure wouldn't mind both.

The crowd's undercurrent of noise shifted some, so Niimoto peeked over the edge again. A group of civilians were coming over the ladder and into the courtyard. He grabbed the phone and rang up the embassy, getting Little Mac.

"Hey, we've got some activity here. It looks like 10 or 12 men are coming in. What do you want me to do?"

"Wait one. Let me get Gunny," she said.

Tony Niimoto could hear her tell someone to go get Gunny , then the sound of running footsteps fading away. He watched the men mill around for a few moments until Gunny Mac got on the phone.

"Sgt Niimoto, what do you got there?"

"Hey Gunny. There're about twelve guys over the wall. All civvies. None look armed, but wait, there's one soldier coming over now, too. What do you want me to do?"

"Hold off right now. Just watch them. I'm getting the rest ready."

There was a pause as Sgt Niimoto could hear him tell someone to get the rest of the Marines there ASAP before coming back on the phone.

"If they start shooting or something, or if you see us shooting, then take them out. Take the soldier out first, then anyone else. If they don't do anything, then you don't do anything," Gunny ordered.

"Aye-aye, Gunny."

Sgt Niimoto settled down to watch them. The group seemed to confer for a few moments, then most of them started for the embassy. Sgt Niimoto brought up his weapon and tracked them through the scope. The Indians walked up to the main hatch first and seemed to be inspecting it, touching it and obviously pacing its width. A few other men started walking alongside the walls of the embassy trying to look into windows. The soldier hung back, sort of covering the others, although his weapon was still at sling arms.

This took about fifteen minutes before one man called the others back together. They conferred for a few moments, gesturing at the hatch a few times, before they started to move back to the wall. One by one, they climbed the ladder up and over the wall and moved out into the crowd. The soldier was the last one over.

The phone's light flashed (he had disconnected the ringer).

"This is Gunny. Did they all leave?"

"Yes, Gunny. They've all left. They cased the place out pretty well. It looks to me like they are trying to see what it will take to blow the emergency doors."

"Yes, to me, too. I sent Kramer to the Cultural Affairs' office windows, but he couldn't see much from his angle. But that's what is seems like to him, too. Oh well, I guess we don't need a crystal ball to see what's happening." He paused, then asked, "How are you doing, Tony? You OK up there?"

"Well, I sure wouldn't mind some water here. Hell, I would even drink one of those Thums Up piss-water cola things you like so much," he said with a quiet laugh. "But I'm doing OK."

"OK, I'll run one up to you next chance I get. All you have to do is clear all those Indians away from the embassy. You want diet or regular?"

"Well, gaining weight might be the least of my worries now, so let's go with regular."

"You've got it, Tony. Take care up there, and keep your eyes on things. We can't see much from our vantage, so we're counting on you."

"Any word on some sort of rescue here?"

"I wouldn't bank on it. If the Indians are planning anything, I don't see how we can do anything about it in time."

"OK, then, it will just be up to us. Semper fi, Gunny."

"Semper fi, Tony, semper fi."

Chapter 28

Wednesday Afternoon, U-Tapao Air Base, Thailand

The C-17 slowly turned off the taxiway and onto the runway to leave U-Tapao. It had barely taken on enough fuel to reach Okinawa before starting its departure. Col Lineau shaded his eyes with his hand against the setting sun to watch it leave. The Globemaster had done its job in getting them there and could really do nothing else, but he still felt a small pang of abandonment. Well, he was pretty well committed now, so it was time to march forward.

He had spent the time aboard the C-17 with his principal staff trying to make contingency plans, which was difficult as they had no idea of what they might possibly face. But it seemed to make sense that the unit be broken into platoons and a headquarters section, sort of an old rifle company, albeit smaller. With the staff he had on hand, he decided that LtCol Norm Ricapito, the Camp David Det CO, would be the platoon commander of 1st, Maj Roberto the 2d, Capt Dave Kreig (the S-3 A) the 3d, Capt Mahmoud the 4th, and 1stLt Stacy Hoins the security force/reserve. Stacy was kind of a sports stud, an All-American at Princeton in field hockey and track, but she was so new and young! He thought about using Major Kristen Rogers, Norm's XO as a platoon commander, freeing up one of the other captains to take the security force, but he thought he would need someone of some rank to stay behind on the *Reagan* should something actually take place. Norm also had Captain Steve Kyser as his training officer, and Steve was one of the up-and-comers in the Corps. He would have given Steve a platoon without hesitation, but the young captain was off to Cancun on his honeymoon, so it was 1st Lt Hoins into the breach. He had assigned Master Guns Chung to be her platoon sergeant. He kept the sergeant major, Doc Hollister, LCpl Luc as a radio operator, and PFC McNair as a runner with him in the headquarters section.

If LtCol Tammy Dews, his Security Battalion CO, made it from Nairobi, he would put her in charge of the second team, sliding the other commanders over one and Stacy out of a position. But the commercial flight schedules didn't match up well, and as he stood here at U-Tapao, it didn't look like she was going to make it in time.

The Marines were lined up in sticks at the front of the hangar, getting used to their new organization. And the Ospreys, four of those beautiful birds, were sitting there, ready to go. Tye Saunders was there, going over a checklist with what looked to be two Coastguardsmen and a civilian, so he figured those must be the pilots. There were several groups of Marines from the regional embassies—he recognized Gunny Jasper from the Singapore embassy and Sgt Williams from the Malaysian embassy, among others. But there were also about a hundred or so military men in civvies lounging around, with a couple of them up and talking with his Marines. One seemed to be rather adamantly arguing with Capt Mahmoud who seemed to be equally as adamant in trying to ignore him. Col Lineau shouldered his pack and marched over the tarmac to see what was going on.

Capt Mahmoud was asking SSgt Boyles for a separate manifest for each bird, trying hard to ignore the tall gent who was attempting to get a word in edgewise. Col Lineau stepped up and grabbed the man by the upper arm.

"May I help you?"

The man spun around and took in the eagles on his collar. He came to attention. "LT David Littlehawk, sir. I am from the *Reagan*, with VFA 41. If you are going to her, I really need to get back on board."

He looked at the young man and could see the eager hope in his eyes, but also the fear of being left behind. Jeff could understand that, but he didn't see how he could help.

"I am sorry Lieutenant, but we are full on boat spaces. I'll have to leave some Marines behind as it is, so I don't think I can drop one of them so you can make it back to your ship."

"You don't understand sir, I'm a fighter pilot. I have to get back," he said, sounding desperate.

"And my Marines are riflemen. Your point is?"

He felt some sympathy for the young man, but to infer that fighter pilots were somehow more important than

137

others was something he had hated since his Academy days.

"You're a pilot?" Jeff turned to see Tye Saunders had walked up.

"Yes, sir!"

"What do you fly?" Tye asked.

"The Lighting II, sir."

"Have you ever flown an Osprey, by chance?"

The lieutenant's face fell as he said, "No sir. But I did fly the simulation at Pensacola in our platform orientation package."

He looked up hopefully.

"Any other pilots with you here?"

"One, sir. LT Shefield. He's a Viking pilot."

The XO looked to the CO and said, "Sir, we don't have any co-pilots. I sure would rather have someone in the right seat who has actually flown something than leave the seat empty."

Jeff turned back to the Navy lieutenant and said, "Well son, today is your lucky day it seems. Go get that other pilot, if you please, and report back to LtCol Saunders. We're leaving here in less than fifteen minutes, so make it snappy."

A huge smile broke out on LT Littlehawk's face as he came to an even straighter position of attention, then he shouted, "Aye-aye, sir!" before wheeling around and running off to the back of the hangar.

"Everything look OK, Tye?"

"Yes, sir. The birds look fine. Those Indonesians take care of their war toys. We are still short two co-pilots, but on a straight flight to the ship, I hope it won't matter."

Master Gunnery Sergeant Chung walked by with Sergeant Lipsz in tow.

"Master Guns, any confirmed location on the *Reagan* yet?"

The Master Guns gave his clipboard to Sgt Lipsz and pointed him toward the Ospreys.

"Yes sir. I just confirmed it with the Air Force major from JUSMAG there. The *Reagan* is more than halfway to India, about 900 miles from here. She's steaming at 25 knots with her 'mechanical problem.' " He raised his hands and used the double finger quotation hook as he said the words "mechanical problem."

"OK, that's good. That is what, about two-and-a-half hours from here?" He looked up at the XO.

"Maybe closer to three hours, sir."

"OK, three hours." He turned back to his Ops Chief. "Master Guns, please ask the JUSMAG major to see me."

Master Gunnery Sergeant Chung nodded and moved off, shouting, "What are you pussies waiting for? I told you to be on those goddamn birds in five minutes, what, seven minutes ago? What the fuck are you waiting for, a fucking invitation?"

The XO suppressed a smile. "That's our Master Guns!"

"Yes it is. I'm just glad he is on our side."

They both chuckled. "You better get to your birds. I really do want to be off the ground in ten minutes, if at all humanly possible."

"Aye-aye, sir," LtCol Saunders said as he came to attention and rendered a salute.

Col Lineau returned it just as smartly. Jeff watched the Marines start to file into the Ospreys as a major in Air Force fatigues walked up to him.

"Sir, I'm Maj Paulson with the JUSMAG."

He held out his hand. Jeff had automatically started the move for a salute, but he stopped it and took the proffered hand instead.

"Col Jeff Lineau."

"Uh, yes, sir, we know. Admiral Conners personally called our boss, COL Smith, and told us to help you as well as babysit his lost sailors. You're going to the *Reagan*, right?" he asked, positively beaming with excitement.

"Major, I hope you understand that I am not at a liberty to tell you anything right now."

"Oh I know sir, we can't tell anyone. But what with the president and everything, you are going over there, right?"

"Once again Major, while we appreciate your help here, I really can't say anything."

"OK, I understand, sir."

Then he gave Col Lineau a wink, an actual, drawn-out wink. Jeff didn't really know what to do, it was so out of his comfort zone. So he ignored it.

"I just wanted to ask you to help some of our Marines get back to their stations. Capt Mahmoud, my S1, he's the short guy over there by the first Osprey, has the list, but I think it's about twelve Marines who have to be left behind." He hesitated before adding "And Major, needless to say, this whole evolution is rather sensitive. This has all been done back channels, so-to-speak, so we would like to keep it quiet. I'm sure you understand."

"No problem with your Marines. We'll take care of them. Your captain has already given me the list. And we'll keep all of this hush hush. But you do know the ambassador knows all about this, right?"

Jeff's heart jumped. He really did not want anyone at State to know exactly what was going on. He did not want anyone to be able to counter any possible action. Better to act first and apologize later.

"How did he find out? I was to understand that Admiral Conners directed that as few people as possible be brought online for this, just the JUSMAG and whoever from the Thai military has to know to approve air clearance and landing rights?"

"Well, sure. We kept most people in the dark. But the ambassador, he is the head honcho here. COL Smith told him right away."

Well, there was no getting around that now. He hoped nothing would come of it.

"Col Lineau? We are waiting for you to get onboard now, sir."

He looked up to see Sgt Lipsz waiting expectantly by the first Osprey. He could see one of the Coast Guard pilots looking out the window at him, waiting for him to board.

"Well, thanks again, Major. I guess I've got to get going."

He shouldered his pack and loped over the tarmac and up the ramp of the waiting Osprey.

Chapter 29

Late Wednesday Afternoon, US Embassy, New Delhi

"You've got that all wired, Steptoe?"

"Yes, Gunny. We can talk to Post 1, Sgt Niimoto, and the post in the Cultural Affair's office," LCpl Steptoe said as he got off his knees where he had been jury-rigging a wire to one of the office phones. "It's connecting through the switchboard, so it'll act like a regular phone. I've assigned 2002 for bell tower, 2003 for the Cultural Affairs office. This one is 2000, and Post 1 is 2001. Just hit pound and dial the number."

"And the vault?" Gunny Mac asked.

"I'm getting to that now, Gunny. But you know, if anyone closes the hatch there, it's going to cut right through this wire, and phones won't work."

"Can't you hook it up to the intercom there?"

"Uh-uh," Steptoe said, shaking his head. "I'd have to drill a hole right through the vault, and that's pretty tough steel. I don't even have a drill here to try it."

He picked up the spool of wire he had scrounged and started out the hatch to connect the vault with the rest of the Marines.

Gunny Mac looked around the office. With the main power out, only the "green" lighting tube from the roof funneled enough light into the room to read. The emergency lights provided enough to move around and talk to each other, but they really weren't that bright. Loralee had found a magazine and was leafing through it, sitting directly under the tube's main dispersal globe. The president was sitting on one of the office chairs, head back, apparently sleeping. SSgt Child looked no different, but LCpl Wynn's breathing was becoming more labored. Mr. Dravid sat on the couch, watching him. Their eyes met, and Dravid gave a slight nod. MAJ Defilice was on one couch, head back and slightly snoring. It somewhat bothered Gunny that PFC Ramon was asleep as well, leaning up against the major's side. LCpl Saad was in the huge corner desk eating a very mushed what might have once been a finger sandwich. PFC Van Slyke had stripped his M18 and was cleaning it for the umpteenth time.

Gunny walked over to Van Slyke and put his hand on the young Marine's shoulder.

"You hanging in there Peter?"

Van Slyke looked up, and the damage to his face made Gunny Mac give an involuntary shudder. He looked like one of those zombies in a Hollywood gorefest.

"I'm OK," he managed to sputter out, the words garbled by the fact that half of his face was not functioning. "My face feels like shit, but what are you going to do?"

Gunny gave Van Slyke's shoulder a squeeze and said, "Good man. Put your weapon back together. I want you to go relieve Kramer. Give him a chance to hit the head and get some chow."

"You call this chow, Gunny?" Van Slyke laughed, then groaned as the pain intensified. "I've got to stop doing that."

"What are you complaining about? Good US embassy chow like this? It couldn't be better," Gunny said with a laugh of his own, gave Van Slyke's shoulder another squeeze, then turned around to scan the room.

He was pondering his next move when Loralee walked over.

"You kidding me, PFC Van Slyke? Good chow like this is heaven-sent. No Marine galley could match it," she said with a laugh.

Gunny looked at her for a moment before asking, "Loralee, I have to ask you, you certainly seem to know your way around the Corps. You were never a Marine, were you?"

She laughed again before saying, "Oh no, not me. I don't have enough discipline to last as a Marine. But my kid brother is a Marine. Ian Cannon. He lost his legs to an IED in Afghanistan as a Staff Sergeant and retired, and he lived with Stan and me while he was at Bethesda. I guess I spent enough time with him and with the Wounded Warrior Detachment to get a feel for the Corps."

"I thought you said he 'is' a Marine," the president said after walking over to listen in.

"Yes, I did."

"But then you said he retired," he said, looking

perplexed.

"Once a Marine, always a Marine, right Gunny?" Loralee responded.

Gunny nodded.

"Ian may not be on active duty anymore, but he is still a Marine. And president or not, he'd kick your butt if you tried to tell him different. His home is a homage to the Corps, like a Marine Corps Museum, and his buddies from the 'Stan drop in to see him all the time," she told the president.

"You know Gunny Pyle, from Camp David?" she asked, turning back to Gunny Mac.

It was a small Corps, especially within a pay-grade, so Gunny nodded. He knew Randy well.

"Well, Lance Corporal Pyle pulled Ian from the HUMVEE and helped hoof him to the aid station. Gunny Pyle stops in to see Ian whenever he can make it down Lejeune way.

"It was the saddest day in his life when his request to stay on active duty was denied," she said, looking thoughtful for a moment. "But he's a resilient old bastard, and he is doing fine."

Her face broke out into a smile.

"So being a Marine was that important to him?" the president asked, sitting down and looking up at Loralee.

"That's what you don't get yet, even after being with these Marines here. It is not that it 'was that important,' as you put it, but that it IS that important," she replied, with a heavy emphasis on the "is."

PFC Ramon nodded in silence behind Loralee from where she had woken up and listened in on the discussion.

The president started to respond when he was interrupted by the phone. Gunny pounced on it as everyone in the room swiveled his or her attention on it.

"Gunny, this is Fallgatter. We've got Indians inside again."

"I'll be right there."

Gunny rushed out and down the passage to the Cultural Affairs office, followed by the rest. He went up to Sgt Chen and LCpl Kramer who were mindful of their previous instructions and were hanging back about five feet from the windows. Everyone else rushed up as well, until there was a line abreast looking out into the courtyard. In the afternoon light, Gunny could see that about ten men had made it over the wall so far. The first of these started moving toward the consular building.

Gunny looked around to where PFC Fallgatter was still holding the phone, and said, "Hang up and then get me Niimoto."

Gunny walked over, took the handset, and heard Sgt Niimoto already on the line.

"Gunny, I've been trying to get you," Tony whispered loudly, "but the phone was busy."

Gunny took a second to glare at Fallgatter who looked back perplexed and shrugged his lack of understanding.

"We've got about a dozen guys inside now, and more are coming. What do you want me to do?" Niimoto asked.

Gunny Mac turned back around so he could see out the window and talk on the phone at the same time.

"Same thing as before. Hold your fire unless you or we are attacked. But keep an eye on things. We're almost one story high, so we can't see what's happening right below us. I'll keep this line open for now," Gunny said, handing the phone back to PFC Fallgatter.

"Keep this glued to your ear!" he ordered.

Fallgatter just nodded and took the handset.

Gunny rejoined the line of people looking out the window.

"What do you think is happening?" asked the president.

Several sets of eyes looked at Gunny Mac expectantly.

"Well sir, it is kind of hard to say. It looks like these people are checking out the consular building. We've got Sgt Niimoto in the bell tower watching them, too, and he can see a lot more than we can in here."

They all watched for a few more minutes.

"You know, this is bullshit!" the president said as he turned and folded his arms across his chest belligerently. "I'm sick and tired of this. The Indian government should have taken action long before this. What the hell are they waiting for?" He turned to Gunny Mac. "I want the vice-president on the phone again."

"Mr. President, I'm not sure that's a good idea. We are scheduled to contact them again in," he glanced at his watch, "uh, an hour and 36 minutes. The more often we call them, the sooner the PDA is going to be out of juice."

"I am not making a suggestion, sergeant. I am giving you an order. Get the vice-president," he said, with a glare in his eyes, almost daring any further comment.

Gunny didn't hesitate but said, "PFC Ramon, go get LCpl Steptoe. He's down in the vault." As Princess ran off, he turned back to the president. "It'll be just a moment, sir."

They stared at each other for a moment, the president still glaring, Gunny Mac keeping as neutral an expression as possible.

"Uh, Gunny? It's Sgt Niimoto. He wants to talk to you," PFC Fallgatter said nervously looking at the two men and holding out the phone to the Gunny.

"Yeah, this is Gunny," he said into the phone's mic.

"Gunny, most of the Indians are in the consular affairs building, but about four are back at the security doors, and there are two walking alongside your building again."

"What are the guys at the security door doing?" Gunny asked.

"Well, one guy looks like he is explaining something to the others. He keeps pointing at different parts of the doors, then saying something. One of the other guys looks like he's taking notes."

"Well, that can't be a good thing," Gunny Mac harrumphed. "OK, keep watching them and let me know if anything changes."

He gave the phone back to Fallgatter and moved back in line. Everyone was intently watching what they could see of the courtyard when there was a thump on the window as a pair of hands appeared on the ledge. Each American took and involuntary hop back. Slowly, a face appeared in the window, and with a lurch, the man there managed to get his elbows on the ledge. He used his hands to form a tunnel between his eyes and the window to try and see into the room.

"Can he see us?" asked Loralee.

"No ma'am," offered Sgt Chen. "This is one-way glass."

Everyone froze, though, and after a few moments, the man stopped trying to see in, and dropped out of sight. There was a collective outtake of breath.

LCpl Saad sidled up to the far side of the window and tried to look down, asking, "How did he get up here? He must have been standing on someone's shoulders."

LCpl Steptoe, PFC Ramon, and Drayton Bajinski came into the office and everyone jumped again. A nervous laugh followed, much to the three's confusion.

"Gunny?" asked Steptoe.

"LCpl Steptoe, the president wishes to speak with the vice-president now," Gunny said as he saw the beginnings of an objection form on Steptoe's broad face. "And that is a direct order."

LCpl Steptoe grabbed a hold of his objection and smothered it, saying "You've got it, Gunny."

He took the PDA out of his pocket and began the process of powering up. The president had wanted some degree of privacy, so after a search of the offices, an earbud had been found which was compatible. He held it up to his ear without actually clipping it on. A series of beeps and tone sounded, signaling when it was ready. LCpl Steptoe retrieved the number, then requested the connection.

"This is LCpl Steptoe. The president wants the vice-president." There was a pause. "Yes, we know this is early, but you need to get her now. And hurry up please, our power is getting low on this thing." He looked up at the president. "It'll be a moment, sir; they have to go get her."

Everyone except for LCpl Saad watched Steptoe expectantly. And waited. And waited.

Gunny Mac saw Mr. Dravid watching Steptoe along with everyone else.

No use taking chances, he thought.

"LCpl Kramer, please escort Mr. Dravid back to the Admin office," Gunny ordered.

Dravid started to object, but he obviously thought better of it and followed Kramer out of the room.

Finally LCpl Steptoe spoke up. "No ma'am, this is LCpl Steptoe. Here, let me give you the president."

He handed the PDA to him and stepped back. The president clipped the earbud around his right ear and held the PDA up to his mouth despite the omni-directional mic, which could clearly pick up his voice from fifteen feet away.

"Jennifer, this is the president. You know, we are rather tired of sitting around here. Tell me you have some good news for us." He put his right hand up to his ear, pushing the earbud firmer into place. He nodded a few times before his face contorted. "No, that isn't good enough! What do you mean you can't speak to any of them?" Another pause. "In case they haven't noticed, this *is* pretty much a crisis. I'm sure they want a peaceful solution, so why the stonewalling?"

He glanced at the others in the room before leaning forward in his chair, as if to exclude them.

"What does she say about that?" He pulled at the collar of his shirt. With the power out, the air conditioning wasn't working, and it was pretty warm in the office. "Really? That's pretty hard to believe, but if she says so, then I have to trust her. OK, where does that leave us? Where is the *Reagan*?"

PFC Ramon nudged MAJ Defilice at the mention of the *Reagan*, and he looked down at her and nodded. Gunny wondered what that was all about.

"And Paul Lefever and General Litz both agree about keeping the Rangers in Korea?" He looked up at the ceiling. "Well, I am not sure I agree, but unfortunately, I am sort of out–of–the–loop here, so I will defer. If their ambassador is being kept out of the loop, so be it. But keep Pitt working it so . . ." another short pause "He what? When were you going to give me that gem of information?" He stretched out his legs and let his hand drop for a moment before bringing the PDA back up to his mouth. "OK, OK, it may do some good. This is his environment, let him earn his pay today. When does he arrive?" He looked at his watch. "Will he have an audience with the PM?"

LCpl Steptoe was watching the PDA, and as a red light started flashing, he frantically tried to signal the Gunny. He

147

caught the Gunny's attention and pointed at the PDA, drawing his other hand across his throat. Gunny Mac stepped up.

"Mr. President, the power on the PDA is failing. I strongly advise you to close this call now," he said.

The president looked up at Gunny with annoyance clear on his face. Then he sighed and said, "Jennifer, I need to go now. We are running out of power for this thing. Let's skip the next scheduled call and pick it up again on the next one, OK? But if anything happens between now and then, we will initiate a call at that time."

He took the earbud off his ear and handed the PDA back to LCpl Steptoe who hurriedly powered it down. He sat there for a moment in thought.

"Well, are you going to keep us in the dark?" Loralee asked. When there wasn't an immediate response, she added "It's not like anyone here is a security risk."

At that, the president actually smiled. "I guess you're right. Well, the Indian ambassador seems to know nothing and can't speak to anyone back here. Secretary Pitt decided that he needs to come to defuse the situation. He should arrive here in another four hours or so. The *USS Reagan* will be off the coast in another ten hours as well. We have a Ranger battalion Quick Reaction Force in Korea, and I thought it was going to move to Diego Garcia, but it seems our friends in DC think that would put on a too aggressive face on us. Don't want to upset the Indians, after all." He chuckled wryly, and the others joined in. "No one of any weight is talking to any one of us, nor to the UN, nor NATO. So it looks like we wait it out for a while longer. And pray for Secretary Pitt."

He slowly got up and walked out of the office. No one followed him. They turned around to watch the line of men going back and forth between the embassy wall and the consular building, each lost in his or her own thoughts.

Chapter 30

Wednesday Morning, The White house, Washington, DC

"Well, if the president doesn't make it, do you think we can use that to leverage the Indians to open up their financial markets?" Secretary of Commerce Ron Mason asked while looking around the room.

General Mark Kantres, the Army Chief of Staff, broke his pen in half and threw it on the conference table while the Secretary for Homeland Security, Phil Mitchell, leaned forward on his elbows to stare at Mason with a look of incredulity.

"Oh come on, people! Don't tell me you haven't been thinking of what we can do if this all plays out poorly. We've been trying to get our banks into the Indian market for decades, and they keep blocking us. That means American jobs and American profits. Of course I hope things work out well, but if . . ."

Vice President Wright looked carefully around the table, noting reactions to Mason's comments. General Kantres was a man of action, so his reaction was not surprising. Same with Kai Yen Lin. She was the president's woman, after all. Phil Mitchell was somewhat of a surprise to her. She had rather thought he was not a strong supporter of the president. Paul Lefever was stoic, no expression on his face. But it was surprising that so many others were either stone-faced like Paul or actually seemed to be listening to the Commerce Secretary. Was there an opportunity here?

Ron Mason was a florid-faced man, and Jennifer Wright often thought his soft, pudgy body would be far better suited to sitting around a double-wide in his underwear, drinking beer, and complaining about how the refs stole the game on Sunday. The fat rolls around his eyes gave him a squinty look, as if he was rather dense. But his grooming and clothing were impeccable. His full head of grey hair was flowing and precise, his fingernails manicured, and his suits were superbly made and matched with the finest silk ties and gold cufflinks. Many people could not get beyond the seeming disparity between his unremarkable physical appearance and his fashion-conscious attire, and they often underestimated him. The vice-president did not. She knew that Ron Mason was an inordinately crafty, manipulative, intelligent, and possibly dangerous man. She hadn't had too much contact with him before, but as she thought about it, perhaps it was time to cultivate a somewhat closer relationship with him.

"Gentlemen! Ladies! As I just briefed you, President Eduardo is doing fine, at least as well as can be expected. And with Secretary Pitt due to arrive within a few hours, I am sure this whole situation will be defused."

The vice-president had initially balked at letting Pitt go to India, and she used his security as an excuse. But the secretary could be quite persuasive, and it occurred to her that this could be a win-win for her. If the secretary could somehow find an ending to the stalemate and get the president home, well, she was the one in charge, and she would get the credit for guiding the nation through the crises. And if things did not turn out so well for the president, well, at least she could show she was a woman of action, and she had spared nothing in her attempts. And it would discredit Pitt, one of her rivals in the game of White House power-mongering. Of course, if it came to that, she would have already won that game, and it would be now her task to lead the nation forward, forward in the right direction.

"Dr. Ryan, you had mentioned that several other nations and the Vatican have been able to get audiences with the External Affairs Minister. What have we had reported back to us from these meetings?" she asked, looking expectantly towards Kathleen Ryan, the Deputy Secretary of State.

"Yes Madam Vice-President. As you know, we haven't been able to get an audience, nor any of our principal allies, nor the UN. The Arab League evidently met with the PM, but we've heard nothing back on that yet. The assistant secretary for the league has promised to give us a report. The Vatican and a few national representatives have been able to meet with the Minister . . ."

As the good doctor droned on, the vice-president smiled inwardly while keeping her face attentive to what was being said. Yes, this was turning into being a win-win.

Chapter 31

Wednesday Afternoon, The USS Reagan, The Indian Ocean

The last Osprey was being towed to the elevator as Col Jeff Lineau shouldered his pack and started walking over to the base of the island where he could see Josh Conners waiting for him. The surprisingly stiff breeze blew across the deck with the tang of salt giving it a clean sort of smell. Sailors in various brightly colored vests ran back and forth while directing the Ospreys and the Marines. One sailor in a red vest almost ran him down as he approached his old roommate.

He rendered a crisp salute, which was returned, then put out his hand and shook the admiral's offered hand. "Good to see you Josh."

"Welcome to my little kingdom," Admiral Conners said, turning to indicate a waiting captain, a slight, trim man with only a hint of grey around his temples. "Jeff, this is Mike Carter, this tub's skipper. He's a ROTC guy," he said with a laugh, pronouncing the acronym as "rotzy," "but OK for all of that."

The captain stuck out his hand. "I don't hold it against the Admiral that he decided to go to a trade school instead of a university, so I guess I can't hold it against you," he said with a smile.

Jeff took the hand and was surprised by the particularly strong grip.

"And you went to . . . ?"

"THE Ohio State University, thank you very much," he replied, with an emphasis on the "The."

"I thought you said you went to a university? Last thing I knew, 'THE' Ohio State University was just a football trade school."

All three laughed.

"I've been telling him that for the last five months, but it doesn't seem to sink in," Conners said.

"Begging the admiral's pardon, and with utmost respect, of course," Capt Carter said with faux humility, "but at least we can field a competitive team, a national championship team at that. And I can't even bet with you during March Madness because some school I know can't even get invited to the dance."

The twinkle in his eyes and easy smile showed this was an ongoing jibe.

And without a real comeback, the admiral clapped the skipper on the shoulder and said, "Some day, Mike, some day! You just wait. Our turn will come."

Rear Admiral Conners looked out at the Marines gathering alongside the edge of the flight deck.

He turned to Col Lineau and said, "Jeff, why don't you get your men below for a few minutes and have your staff meet up in the ship's CIC conference room. We've been going over a few possible scenarios, but we really need to run these by your guys."

"Yes, sir. I'd like to get my men fed, but we really need to do some egress drills. Most of my Marines have never seen any military tactical bird, much less an Osprey."

"Sounds good. Mike, please have the Chief take care of the colonel's men. Then meet us up in the conference room," the admiral said.

"Yes, sir. I've got a boat to run."

The ship's CO moved off while Jeff motioned Norm Ricapito over.

"Admiral, this is LtCol Norm Ricapito. With my XO flying, Norm will be my second-in-command for our ground task force." The two men shook hands.

"Norm, tell the Sergeant Major to get the men below decks and fed," Col Lineau said before pausing. "No belay that. I am going to need Mike up with me. Have the Master Guns get them below deck, have a piss call, get fed, and then go to the hangar deck and practice getting on and off the Ospreys. I want this to be second nature to them. Then get my staff up to the conference room."

He looked up at the admiral as LtCol Ricapito walked off to relay the orders. "What's the situation?"

"Same as before. Basically nothing. No one is doing anything. One of your Marines has been released, I've been told. He went out with the diplomats and is on his way to

Cairo if he isn't already there."

"Are we still getting the sitreps?" he asked his old friend.

The admiral smiled and said, "Yes, your Gunny Cassel seems quite adept at making sure there are Marines providing "security" for the comms. I guess the powers that be decided to keep everything at that young man's apartment. But your Gunny seems to hear everything, and within a few minutes, she sends us a pretty detailed summary of what's happening. Then a couple hours later, we get a sanitized version of the same through DOD."

"Well, I'm glad it is Gunny Cassel there. She has a way about her. If she wasn't a Marine, I'm sure she would be doing hard time somewhere," he said as they both laughed.

Col Lineau changed tack and asked, "Any chance we're going to get an OK to do anything? An official OK?"

"Doubt it. The Army Rangers are not being allowed to play, so it looks like we'll have to wait and see."

Both men stared over the bow of the *Reagan*. There was a subtle change in the feel of the ship, almost a sense of urgency. The wind across Col Lineau's face started to pick up. He looked back, and he could begin to see a huge rooster tail in back of the mammoth vessel. The flight deck had to be seven or eight stories high, so how could he possibly see a rooster tail? The wind across the deck started to buffet him. He looked back at the Admiral.

Josh Conners leaned in so he could be heard, "This is one fast bitch when she wants to be."

"I guess so!" Jeff said in amazement.

The ready group commander turned to walk through a hatch into the bridge tower as the Commandant of the Marine Corps followed.

Chapter 32

Late Wednesday Afternoon, US Embassy, New Delhi

Sergeant Anthony Niimoto was thirsty, very, very thirsty. Drinking was pretty much all he could think about. He had even unlocked the access to the cupola and climbed down into the bell tower's base to try and find something to drink. He had found a first aid kit which had some cough syrup, and he had drunk that, but the medicine seemed to make him even thirstier. He was still searching when voices inside the tower somewhere below him made him scurry back up the ladder and securing the cupola hatch with a piece of rebar.

It came to the point that he was dreading, but finally, he took the empty cough syrup bottle and peed in it. The urine looked dark and foreboding, but with surprisingly little hesitation, he drank it. The warm, bitter liquid going down his throat did little to assuage his thirst, but the logical part of his mind told him all liquid was good for him. He was surprised that he didn't gag it right back up.

He peeked over the wall again to the huge group of Indians who seemed camped outside the wall. He wondered what would happen if he just walked down the tower and into the crowd. Would they even know who he was? Would they assume he was an American, or could he pass himself off as from an Asian country? Could he make it to the Japanese or British embassies, and would they even let him in the gates considering they were most likely on high alert as well?

He settled back and looked up, lost in his thoughts. The bell was actually quite pretty in the late afternoon sun. It had a deep burnished gold hue. He wondered for the thousandth time just what its purpose was, why it was even there. When the power was cut off to the embassy and consulate the night before, the bell tower stayed powered up, so obviously, it has its own power source. Why would a simple bell tower have its own power? It didn't make sense.

At the very apex of the tower was a small rubber-looking pulley contraption. Sgt Niimoto sat up to get a better view. From that wheel-like piece of equipment hung a cable, which came straight down to the bell. Sgt Niimoto moved over for a better look. Now he could see a small cable running from the apex down along the curved ceiling of the belfry to one of the many boxes adorning one side of the wall. He hadn't noticed this before as it was painted with the same paint as the tower walls. In bright daylight, it would have been rendered practically invisible. But in the fading afternoon light, the shadows made it stand out some.

He followed the cable down to a small box, a nondescript grey metal compartment. Alongside the box was a red-handled lever, like a large switch. He knew he should leave it alone, but curiosity overcame him. He sidled up to the box, put his hand on the lever, and slowly pulled it.

There was a click and the bell started to lower with some groans and squeaks. Sgt Niimoto slammed the handle back up and the bell stopped with a jerk, slowly swaying from side to side. He waited for some hue or cry to show that the bell's movement had been seen or heard by someone. Nothing changed. Everything remained quiet.

He grinned. Well, he had figured out one thing about the tower. If he ever got back up here with any of the other Marines, he would have fun showing them that.

He crawled back to his position and settled in for the long night.

Chapter 33

Early Wednesday Evening, US Embassy, New Delhi

"Thank you, Mr. President for taking the time for this."

It had taken a little convincing, but finally the president had agreed to rehearse a quick movement from the admin office to the vault below decks. Gunny had actually wanted to move the president there now, but he had declined to move. So at least in three tries, they had been able to rehearse a move and had gotten it down to a minute-and-a-half before the president thought that had been enough rehearsing. Gunny wanted to go through the whole thing again after dark, but he doubted the president would be up for it. Besides, there was no natural light going down the stairwell or on this level, only the emergency lighting, so doing it at night wouldn't make that much of a difference.

After the third rehearsal, the president merely grunted and walked down the passage to the stairwell going up. Gunny motioned to Sgt Chen and LCpl Steptoe, who hurried to catch up and accompany the president back to the admin office. Gunny wiped his brow. Without the air conditioning going, it was getting pretty hot and sticky in the building. He could feel his t-shirt sticking to his back. Like most of the others, he had taken off his uniform blouse and left it above decks.

PFC Ramon was another Marine who has taken off her blouse, and her sweat was soaking her t-shirt. She was still in the vault, and as what seemed to be the norm now, she was talking to MAJ Defilice. Her damp t-shirt did little to conceal her compact torso and the rather significant bra that served to support her breasts. While speaking, she absent-mindedly reached to pull at the edge of the left bra cup, pulling it out slightly while shrugging her shoulders as if to settle things better. Gunny looked away guiltily.

Gunny looked back to check on the progress of Loralee down the passageway, but Drayton had her arm and seemed in earnest conversation. He followed them and made his way up the stairwell, around the corner, and back down toward the admin office.

The president had already sat down on the couch to which he had laid claim and was making some notes on a pad of paper. Gunny slung his weapon and started to sit down when he caught eyes with PFC Van Slyke, who had been left behind in the office during the movement rehearsal and who was now standing behind LCpl Wynn. Van Slyke slowly shook his head as a lump formed in Gunny's throat. He hesitantly walked over to the desk on which Wynn lay and looked down on her. There was no doubt that she was dead. The labored look on her face while she fought for life was now relaxed and pallid. Her fight was over. Gunny reached over and took her hand.

"Gunny, shouldn't we stage some of this food in the vault? MAJ Defilice thinks it might save some time if it comes to that," PFC Ramon said, crowding up behind him.

"There isn't any air circulation in there, and it's hot, so any of this we bring down there, if it starts to spoil, it'll be pretty ripe," he responded flatly, still holding LCpl Wynn's hand.

"But what if we take some now and . . ." she came around him and saw LCpl Wynn. As she stopped talking, the others seemed to notice for the first time and approached to stand around the desk.

"Is she, you know . . . ?" the president asked after walking over and looking over PFC Van Slyke's shoulder.

"Yes sir, she's dead. She couldn't fight anymore. If we could have gotten her to a hospital, I think they could have saved her. Keeping her here, we killed her," Gunny said bitterly.

Loralee spoke up, "You know that wasn't possible, Gunny. We've been trapped in here, and we couldn't have gotten her out. They killed her, not anyone in here."

"But what if we had just taken her outside and left her there, I bet they'd have taken her and got her to a hospital," he protested.

Gunny Mac barely even knew LCpl Wynn yet. He didn't know her parents' name, if she had a boyfriend, what she liked to eat, how she felt about things. But she was in his unit, and he felt an overpowering sense of responsibility for her. She was part of his family, part of his very essence.

"Bullshit! They were the ones who shot her, after all. No telling what they might have done to her or if she'd be held hostage at another place. You did what you had to do, and any blame lies on them. Not you. You know that, and we don't need you wallowing in self-pity now. You need to do your job," Loralee said, looking at him with piercing eyes.

Gunny Mac looked back at those eyes. She was right, and his intellect knew that even if his heart did not.

"Chen, Van Slyke, go relieve McAllister and Rodriguez. Steptoe and Kramer, go relieve Saad. Mr Dravid, if you can lead the way to the reefer?"

He reached down and put his arms around LCpl Wynn's still body and lifted her up. He had always heard that dead bodies seemed heavy, but she seemed very light in his arms.

Chapter 34

Wednesday Night, US Embassy, New Delhi

Sgt Anthony Niimoto was dreaming of lemonade, ice cold, in pitchers. He could feel the cold cascade down his throat, filling his stomach. He could feel the very cells of his body swell up as the lemonade poured directly into them.

A commotion beneath him finally broke through his consciousness. He slowly dragged himself up and peered over the edge of the cupola wall to see four men dragging some sort of pressurized tank over the embassy wall as the crowd watched and buzzed in anticipation. Two men made it over and sat waiting as two others straddled the wall and slowly lowered the tank into the others' waiting arms. The receiving men grunted and almost dropped the cylinder before setting it on the deck. The other two climbed down and together, the four men walked over the main doors of the embassy, pulling the cylinder on a small, wheeled stand.

Sgt Niimoto dialed the embassy. PFC Fallgatter picked up the other end.

"Fallgatter, get me Gunny," he said.

As he waited for the Gunny, he watched three of the men point and gesture at the door while one seemed to work on the cylinder. With only the running lights providing illumination, it was hard to make things out clearly.

"This is Gunny, what do you got, Tony?"

"Gunny, there're four men with a cylinder at the main doors. It looks like some sort of welding or cutting set-up. I think you need to get over there."

"Shit! Really? Can you see what they're actually doing?" Gunny asked.

"I can't see yet, but it doesn't look good."

"OK, I'm going now. Pick me up on the Post 1 phone. Gunny, out."

Tony shifted to where he could maintain a better view. The men had brought the cylinder right up to the doors. There was a barely visible spark and then a tongue of flame shot out. He could hear the hiss all the way across the courtyard. He glanced back and could see a line of eyes peering over the wall and intent upon the men at the doors.

There was a dull glow as the flame touched the door. In the glare, Sgt Niimoto could see the man holding a piece of dark plastic or something in front of his eyes. Sgt. Niimoto guessed they didn't have real welding goggles available.

The phone flashed and Sgt Niimoto snatched up the handset.

"Tony, what's happening out there now?" Gunny asked.

"It looks like they're trying to cut through the door. But there's no one else there. Do you want me to take them out?"

There was a pause, then Gunny said, "No, they'll know then that you're there. Let's stand by and watch. These doors are pretty solid. I am going to give the phone to PFC Rodriguez. Let him know what is happening."

The flame kept going, and there was a dull glow on the metal of the right door where the flame was touching, but not much else. Sgt Niimoto kept watching. The heat of the night seemed even hotter from the direction of the doors, but he knew that had to be his imagination. After about fifteen minutes, the flame flickered then gave out. The four men examined the slowly fading glow on the door. One man leaned back and gave it a hard kick. They looked like they were talking it over, then turned and came back to the wall. One-by-one, they climbed over, and two of them went to report in to another group of men waiting outside the wall under a huge tree.

"Rodriguez, tell Gunny that they've given up. Looks like good old American workmanship has prevailed. American workers one, Indian workers, zero."

He hung up the phone and looked back into the crowd, which had grown smaller in the night. Smaller in number, maybe, but the atmosphere of those remaining seemed a little more intense, a little more focused.

Chapter 35

Wednesday Night, US Embassy, New Delhi

"Sgt Nii says they've given up," PFC Rodriguez announced to the Marines surrounding the door.

Gunny stood where he was crouching alongside Post 1 and slung his weapon. The rest of the Marines, except for PFC Van Slyke who was left with the president, and LCpl Saad who was left in the Cultural Affairs office, stood up along with MAJ Defilice from their hasty positions and moved towards the door.

LCpl Kramer reached out to the point where they had heard a dull thud a few moments before and said, "Hey, it is a little warm. I can feel it!"

Sgt Chen and PFC Ramon moved up to feel the spot too, nodding in agreement.

"Why did they try to come through the doors? Those are about the strongest things there. Why not through the embassy walls themselves?" LCpl Steptoe wondered aloud.

Gunny felt a sense of foreboding at that thought, but it was coupled with a sense of determination.

"Well, I guess they're playing their hand. And that is that," he said to the others.

Gunny considered for the umpteenth time bringing everyone back to the admin office to concentrate his resources, but Post 1 was too valuable a piece of real estate to give up. Even if the security cameras didn't work anymore, the post glass was bullet proof, and while there were no firing ports, the slots for accepting ID cards and papers could be used for outgoing fire and gave pretty good coverage down both passageways and the hatch to the stairwell.

"Sgt Chen, you and Fallgatter stay here at Post 1. The rest, we're going to back to the admin office. We need to make sure our shit is together on this."

Chapter 36

Wednesday Morning, The White House, Washington, DC

"Madame Vice-President, Director Lin is here," the vice-president's front desk secretary told her over the intercom.

The vice-president looked up from the television where she was watching Dani Craig, the press secretary, at the press conference. That woman was good, she thought. She was conveying confidence while saying absolutely nothing. That was one woman who needed to stay on in her administration.

Craig had handled the Pitt situation well. When denied landing rights, Secretary Pitt had his pilot declare an airborne emergency, so he'd been allowed land. He had not been allowed to debark his plane, though, and was still sitting on the tarmac. Craig had made it sound, without actually lying, that Pitt was in India working to diffuse the situation and bring the president home.

The vice-president leaned toward the intercom and said, "Send her in please."

David looked at her, raising one eyebrow in a question. She motioned him to keep in his seat.

She would keep Craig, to be sure, but the Director of the CIA was another story. Quite frankly, she didn't trust her. The woman had the ear of the president, and she was unnaturally smart, but her almost stilted way of speech and her obvious affection for the president did not bode well for a future working relationship. And while she may understand the technological aspects of gathering intelligence, she did not have experience in the human side of intelligence gathering. Yes, Dr. Lin would be one of the first to go.

Kai-yen Lin walked into the office and stood in front of the vice-president's desk.

"Please sit, Dr. Lin," the vice-president said, indicating a seat in front of the desk. She started to get up to join the director, but at the last second decided to stay where she was.

Dr. Lin sat on the outer edge of her seat, back straight,

a printed report in her lap, hands folded on the report. She waited patiently.

Vice-President Wright inwardly sighed before beginning, "Dr. Lin, I asked you to see me to give me your input on this. Not what you gave at the meeting, but your take. The president just asked me to ask you."

"Yes, Madam Vice-President." There was a pause.

"Well then, can you give it to me? I am due to talk with him again in fifteen minutes."

Dr. Lin cleared her throat, then started, "There has been a significant degree of increased activity in all electronic spectrums. This is to be expected, but there has been an interesting pattern of electronic activities in the wavelengths commonly associated with communications between this building," she paused to pass the vice-president a satellite photo of a large, non-descript building, "and to the area surrounding the embassy."

"And what is this building?" the vice-president asked.

"That is the Council of Ethnic Preservation. It is a pseudo-governmental organization with strong ties with the ruling party and the labor unions. Its funding comes from official government grants and private donations. We do have some ground assets outside the building now, and there has been increased traffic of persons whom we believe to be associated with both security and military agencies, albeit no one at an executive level."

She handed over some more photos of various men in civilian clothing entering the building.

The vice-president smiled. It was the same everywhere. Military men in civilian clothes always looked out of place. Even with different styles in clothing in different countries, they stood out like sore thumbs.

"It is our assessment that the Indian government is at least giving tacit support to the takeover. It certainly has not marshaled troops into any place where they could take action. In fact, two Indian army divisions, the 32nd Armor and the 5th Infantry, have been moved out over the last week for supposed previously scheduled maneuvers, and most of the aircraft at Hindon Air Force Base near New Delhi have been flown elsewhere. I have a list here of the types of aircraft that have left and what is remaining," she said as she looked up expectantly at the vice-president who waved the list off.

"The tone of the news media has been muted. There have been some outspoken critics within the parliament, such as Virag Dasmunsi, who have been publically advocating for a full response by the police, but the primary response seems to be silence. I must point out that Dasmunsi's vocal posturing may be merely a platform for the Indian Nationalist Party to damage the ruling party."

"Do you think Mr. Dasmunsi has any real power in this? Can he affect anything?" Vice-President Wright asked.

"The Indian Nationalist Party has risen in the polls since the last election, and if there was an election held today, it is possible that Mr. Dasmunsi could become the new Prime Minister. That is purely conjecture, of course. Polling data in India is notoriously unreliable."

"So for the $64,000 question, why would the current government be giving any support for this? Why risk serious repercussions within the diplomatic community?"

The vice-president folded her hands into a teepee and placed the tip of the teepee up against her mouth, tilting her head down slightly to look at the director.

Kai-yen Lin looked more uncomfortable, if that was possible.

"We do not have any ground assets at a level high enough to be in on discussions within the Party's inner circle. However, due to the current unrest, and coupled with rising anti-American sentiment within central and northern India, most of our analysts agree that this move might be intended to raise nationalistic sentiments and shift public unhappiness from the Party to the US."

"And how far will the Indian government go with this?"

"There are patterns within communications transmissions that might be indicative that the situation has gone on further that it was intended. And our ground assets at the site outside the embassy are reporting that there seems to be some degree of disagreement among the aggressors there. There has been hesitation and, until recently, no firm move forward into the embassy grounds, although there seems to be preparation for such a move. This would also support the concept that the Party does not know itself how this situation should be resolved."

The vice-president took that last bit of information in with some interest, although she hoped she hid that. Was it possible that the prime minster would let loose his dogs and let them attack?

Wanting to change tack, she leaned forward and asked, "What do you think of Dr. Ryan's assessment of the effectiveness of other nations' efforts?"

"The Arab League offers the most reasonable chance for a peaceful resolution. They have had considerable success in Africa, as you know, and in the last incident in Kashmir. It is our assessment that the League is truly trying to bring this situation to a conclusion. The Vatican is a non-player in our assessment. Of the others, perhaps Thailand might have some pull with their effort, but not much."

"Thailand? I hadn't heard about that. When and what was that?"

"The Royal Thai ambassador to India, Dr. Amarin Suphantarida, was able to get an appointment with the Minister yesterday at 16:30 local. Thailand, as you know, is heavily dependent upon Indian investment and as a customer, so there is a reasonable connection. But we don't see too much happening here."

David discreetly coughed, then said, "Madam Vice-President, we have your call to the president in five minutes. I suggest that we go into the conference room?"

"Very well."

She stood up, came around the desk, and offered her hand to Dr. Lin who awkwardly shook it.

"Thank you Dr. Lin. Please keep me posted. You can reach David here at any time."

Hand still in the grasp of the vice-president, Dr. Lin faltered before saying, "Well, Madam Vice-President, as I said, there had been no firm move into the embassy until recently. I want to report to you that about twenty minutes ago, there was some degree of activity at the embassy. At least four men with what appeared to be a propane torch approached the embassy front doors. We could not see what was being done there due to the overhang, but the light reflections we could see were consistent with an attempt to cut open the doors. That effort evidently failed as could be expected, but this signifies a significant rise in the intensity of the situation."

The vice-president kept her face neutral as her heart gave a flutter. Was the end game approaching? She dropped the director's hand.

"Well, as you say, they weren't successful. Keep me posted on anything further."

She turned and walked down the hallway, flanked by her secret service agents.

Chapter 37

Wednesday Night, The USS Reagan, The Indian Ocean

"You all know none of this is going to happen. Contingency 'A' possibly, just being a platform to whisk the president away. But all this planning for a forced entry? Never going to happen," CDR Steve Kinney said, looking at the rest of the planning group.

LtCol Saunders rubbed his eyes and glanced at the overhead before looking back at the glaring commander and saying, "You're right, it probably won't come to anything. But it sure doesn't hurt to plan it now, does it? My commandant, your admiral, the wing commander, and the ship's CO are discussing that possibility right now, but they've given us our marching orders, so I suggest we get to it. Mr. Evans, you were saying?"

Clyde Evans was the State Department rep aboard the *Reagan*. An ES1, he technically outranked everyone in the compartment, but to LtCol Saunders, he seemed to let the military-types run the tempo and direction of the meeting. At 32 years old, he was reportedly an up-and-comer, but the other officers had told Tye that Clyde didn't care for the military and hoped this stepping stone would quickly pass and he could get back to the "real" world of State.

"Well, as I said, embassies are usually considered to be the sovereign territory of that nation. There may not be an actual basis for this is most cases, but this concept has been generally honored throughout modern history."

"So you are saying that if we bomb or land troops at our embassy, then the Indians can't say anything?" CDR Shelly la Porte, the squadron OPS O asked.

Evans grimaced while bobbing his head side to side before saying, "Well, sort of. But to get there, you have to cross Indian airspace, and if you drop bombs on the embassy, what if a bomb falls outside on the street and kills someone? That could be considered an act of war."

"And that, my friends, is why we can't just go in and carpet bomb all around the place, then send in these Marines to pick up the esteemed passenger," CAPT Ted Ngata, the Battle Group G3 remarked. "OK, let's look at what we have." He held out one hand and pointed to the forefinger with his other.

"Asset Number 1: The *Honolulu* steamed ahead while we were puttering along with our 'bad' shaft and is in position about 10 miles offshore in corridor 'Santa Fe.' She's there to provide support, but she can also be used to rescue downed aircraft or even to affect an air-to-sea transfer of the president. I don't think we've ever done that between an Osprey and a sub, but it certainly should be possible."

He put out another finger and counted it off.

"Asset Number 2: Our Big Eye. I have no idea how the Old Man got her, but she is sitting in a secure hanger at Farkhor and can be on station when our own birds arrive."

The third finger came out.

"Asset Number 3: we have almost 100 Marines and four Ospreys. Certainly we can do something with them."

The fourth finger made its appearance.

"Asset Number 4: we have a damn carrier here with a full complement of aircraft, ordnance, and men and women. This is what the *Reagan* was built for. I suggest you put your heads together and come up with a viable plan to give to the old man. Even if we never use it, we need that plan. That is why they call it a 'contingency plan.' Got it?"

There was a chorus of "aye-ayes" as pubs were re-opened, discussion re-joined. After hours of work, there were still many more ahead. It was going to be a long night. LtCol Tye Saunders hoped that there was plenty of that good Navy coffee in the pot.

Chapter 38

Early Thursday Morning, US Embassy, New Delhi

Thirst was overwhelming, and Sgt Niimoto didn't know how much longer he could last. He had drunk his urine twice during the night, but still, he could think of nothing else but getting something to drink. He tried to sleep, but the fitful catnaps he grabbed hardly qualified as that. At one point, he stared over the walls at the men gathered around, and he could see bottles of beer being passed. Once again, he contemplated just walking over and asking for something to drink. If they took him, they took him. At least his thirst would be over, one way or another.

But he wasn't seriously tempted. Instead he snuck back down the ladder to try and scrounge up something, anything to drink. He found nothing. He brought up the medical kit where he had found the cough syrup and went through that. Nothing to drink. He tried taking some cotton pads and rubbing them on the surface of the bell, hoping to mop up any nighttime condensation. While the cotton seemed damp, he could not squeeze anything out. He found an oxygen cylinder in the kit and took it out of its case, hoping some dew might form on its metal surface.

As the sun's rose-colored fingers began to reach across the dawn sky, he realized that he had maybe one more day left. After that, he was either going to try and make the embassy or just lie down and fade away. He was going to tell Gunny this morning he was going for it after dusk.

There were far fewer people over the wall than there had been before, but those that were left seemed more determined, more focused. A few buses had come by and carted people off, from the looks of it to the new stadium down Sadar Patel Marg, but the stadium was too far away to be sure of that. A group of men approached the ladder on the Indian side of the wall and started over, carrying a bundle. Sgt Niimoto could not quite make out what the bundle was. They made it over the wall and began to scurry across the courtyard. Sgt Niimoto reached for the phone.

PFC Rodriguez responded, but Sgt Niimoto could not croak anything out. He tried to lick his lips, but to no avail. Finally he was able to force out his message.

"Rodriguez, there are bunch of men at the doors. I think they are going to try something. Let Gunny know."

"Sure Sergeant."

He could hear Rodriguez relay the message and Sgt McAllister's acknowledgement, then he heard fading footsteps as the PFC ran down the passage.

Sgt McAllister came on the line and asked, "How're you hanging, Korea Joe?" concern evident in her voice.

"I'm OK. Could use a little drink of something though."

"I hear you, buddy. Oh, here's Gunny," she said before handing the phone off.

"What do you got this time, Tony?"

"Well, there're three guys at the door. I can't see what they are doing." The light was getting brighter, but it was still hard to make out. "They've got a bundle that they are putting down at the base of the door, right in the middle. Now they are . . . shit they're running! Get back Gunny, I think they're trying to blow it!"

He could hear the Gunny react, yelling at everyone to get back. The seconds seemed to drag on. Sgt Niimoto crouched with just the top of his head over the edge of the cupola wall. What if he was wrong about that? He felt dizzy and lightheaded and wondered if he was thinking straight. A huge blast, felt more than seen, exploded against the embassy doors. Sgt Niimoto was flung down, a huge hand pushing on his chest. He sat stunned for a moment, then scrambled up, rifle ready to take out anyone trying to enter the embassy. As he peered through the settling dust, he could see the door standing as normal, nothing out of place. He let out a dry chuckle. He guessed that was why they called them blast doors. He crawled to other side of the tower and looked down on the angrily gesturing men who perched on the wall and seemed more than a little peeved that their entrance had not been blown.

"Better luck next time, Mowgli," he muttered with a smile on his face.

Chapter 39

Thursday Morning, US Embassy, New Delhi

The blast was a muffled thud that barely shook the security door. A little dust fell from the overhead, but that was about it. Heads began to appear from where the mad scramble to get out of the way had taken everyone. Gunny, Kramer, and Steptoe had ducked in back of Post 1, and now they stood up, along with Sgt McAllister and Rodriguez who were inside the post. LCpl Saad and Sgt Chen had made it further away and were now getting to their feet a good fifteen meters past Post 1 down the north corridor.

Gunny turned around to see PFC Ramon standing in the stairwell, putting down her hand to MAJ Defilice, who smiled and took it, standing up. Drayton was in there as well, a look of unadulterated excitement on his face. He looked like he was at some sort of amusement park.

Down the south corridor, toward the ambassador's office, PFC Fallgatter still lay prone, his arms over his head.

"Hey dipwad, you want to join us?" Kramer shouted at him as everyone gathered in front of the door.

They could hear PFC Van Slyke yell a slurred "Everything all right?" from the admin office where he had been left with the president and Loralee. Gunny stepped back to look down the passage where he could see three anxious faces peering back at him.

"Steptoe, go down and let them know everything's fine, and ask the president to get back in the office. We don't need him to start wandering around."

As LCpl Steptoe ran down the passage, they all stared at the door.

"Man, that is some damn good door," Sgt Chen exclaimed as he stepped up and gave it an experimental shake.

Gunny slung his weapon and put his hands on his hips. "Well, I guess their intent is pretty clear. I think it is time we moved the president. Major, if you wouldn't mind, would you please get him and Loralee and escort them to the vault?"

"Sure thing, Gunny," he said as he slung his weapon and started down the passage.

"And let's get SSgt Child down in the vault, too, while we have chance. Kramer and Chen, can you get him there? Wait a minute, though, before you go. LCpl Steptoe, you take Fallgatter and go into the Cultural Affairs office. I know that is a change, but it's closer to the stairwell than the ambassador's office, and you might need to beat a hasty retreat. Keep your eyes peeled and let us know what's going on. Everyone else, into the stairwell. We've got McAllister, Rodriguez, and Kramer as the fire team at the top of the well, then Chen and Saad at the bottom with Steptoe and Fallgatter when they get there. The rest of us will be in vault. OK? Just like we planned. Right?" He looked at Little Mac, still inside Post 1. "Give Korea Joe a call and let him know what we're doing."

"Uh, Gunny? Rodriguez and me, well, we've been thinking. Post 1 has the best fields of fire. We sort of think we need to stay in here," Little Mac said.

"Pat, we went over this. If anyone stays inside Post 1, well, they won't be able to retrograde to join us. They'll be cut off."

"Fifth General Order, Gunny," she reminded him.

Gunny let out an exasperated sigh and said, "I am properly relieving you."

"How about if me and Rodriguez just wait here a little longer? I mean, look. It's what, ten, twelve meters to the stairwell. If we have to get there, it'll take us a second or two, especially if the rest of the team covers us. Besides, the door is holding, so there's no rush now."

Gunny hesitated. He had made his plan, and he really wanted it to unfold as he envisioned it. But he also did not want to have any dissension now, so he decided he could adjust a little here.

"OK, stay here for now. But when you get the command, fall back to the stairwell immediately. You got that?"

"Sure Gunny. Do you think we want to get our asses shot off? Kramer, just don't you go and plunk us when we come to join your own sorry ass," she said.

"I would never do that to a Sergeant of Marines! Now a PFC, however . . ."
Kramer started.

The group broke out in laughter.

"OK, our fun meter is obviously pegged. Let's get going. We know what we have to do, and if anyone really insists on inviting themselves in for tea, well, we're just going to have to dissuade them," Gunny said before turning and starting up the passage where the president, Loralee, and Mr. Dravid were being escorted down towards him.

"Gunny, the president needs to report this escalation. Where is Steptoe?" MAJ Defilice asked.

"LCpl Steptoe, get out here!" Gunny shouted, his words echoing down the passage.

After a moment, LCpl Steptoe stuck his head out the Cultural Affairs office.

"Front and center, Steptoe. The president needs to use the com again. How's it looking?"

LCpl Steptoe grimaced, then said, "We are almost out of juice. The battery may have recharged itself a little after we last powered down, but there isn't much left."

"There is no getting around that now, soldier. I want to get back to DC now," the president said as he came up to stand beside Steptoe.

"Marine, sir, Marine," muttered Gunny.

The president obviously heard him but chose to ignore the comment as LCpl Steptoe powered up.

"I am going to give it right to you, sir. No use me wasting any juice on this," Steptoe said.

He watched the small screen for a moment and handed it to the president, who put the earbud in his ear. The rest crowded around to listen.

There was a short wait, then his eyes lit up and he started, "This is President Eduardo. Give me the vice-president." There was a very short pause, and then evidently the vice-president answered. She must have been right there. "OK, OK, wait there. I don't really care now who gave whom the OK to negotiate with anyone. None of the negotiations have worked. We've got people trying to blow up the doors here to the embassy, so I think they've made their intentions clear. Has there been any movement on the Indian government's part?" The president paused, nodding as he listened.

"Then what about the military option? What's going on with that?"

He paused again.

Suddenly he shouted into the PDA, "I don't give a good goddamn about that. This is already an act of war, or hadn't you noticed? We've got a number of people here who have to be evacuated now! I am making an executive order here, Vice-President Wright. Let me be clear. All US military forces are to take whatever action they can to rescue us immediately. Am I clear?"

The president's face was getting red as he shouted, and specks of spit flew out of his mouth. He listened for a few seconds.

"No excuses, just do it. I know the *Reagan*... the *Reagan*... hello? Hello?"

He looked at the PDA which had suddenly gone dark.

"Shit!"

LCpl Steptoe grabbed the PDA and looked at it, hitting a few buttons.

"That's it sir. It's dead."

The circle of people crowded in a little closer, staring at the PDA. Their last window to the US had just been cut off.

Chapter 40

Wednesday Evening, The White House, Washington, DC

Vice-President Wright was beside herself. Just who did this arrogant piss-ant ambassador think he was talking to? She looked around the table where no one seemed to want to catch her eye.

When she had heard that the ambassador from Thailand had initiated negotiations with the Indians, she demanded to know who had authorized that. No one seemed to have an answer for that, so she had Dr. Ryan contact the US ambassador to Thailand who told her that he had spoken to the Thai ambassador to India. Dr. Ryan reported that back to the vice-president who then demanded that the ambassador be put on the phone. She ran that into the speakers. Now, the ambassador, Case, his name was, was calmly acting like nothing was wrong.

His voice came over the speakers, "As I told you, Madam Vice-President, this was an act of a sovereign nation which was further acting on a request from the rest of ASEAN. We had nothing to do with that."

"And once again, ambassador," she said, making the word "ambassador" sound like a pejorative, "do you think the Thai government should be representing us, representing us without us even knowing he is doing so?"

"Technically, he is not representing us at all. He is representing ASEAN and the Royal Thai government," the ambassador patiently explained.

"But you spoke to him, didn't you, before he got in to see the minister?"

"Yes, Madam Vice-President, I did."

"And if this is solely an ASEAN matter, why would you speak to him first?" she asked, looking around the table in triumph.

"Madam Vice-President, according to the US-Thai Cooperation Treaty, I am bound to inform the Thai government of the presence of any operational forces in Thai territory. I merely informed Ambassador Suphantarida before he met with the minister so he would not be taken by surprise should that fact already be known."

No one could see the ambassador, but the exasperation was beginning to show in his voice.

"The Reagan Carrier Group had been cleared a month ago to pull liberty in Thailand, so I don't know why you would have to call to inform him about that," she said, genuinely looking puzzled.

"I am not talking about the *Reagan*. I am talking about the Marines who transshipped through here."

"What do you mean, the Marines?" she asked.

The vice-president looked over at General Litz who looked up with a confused expression on his face.

"The 100 or so Marines who flew in to U-Tapao and then flew off for destinations unknown, Madam Vice-President."

She reached over and hit the speaker mute.

"General Litz, what's this about?"

She thought about it and realized that there hadn't been a Marine guard outside the conference room as normal. A Secret Service agent was now taking that duty.

General Litz looked over to the three other four-stars in the room, none who seemed to have anything to say.

"I am sorry Madam Vice-President. I don't know anything about this. But I will find out," he said, motioned to one of his aides. "COL Shriver, call down to Col Lineau at Quantico and find out if any of his Marines flew into Thailand."

The vice-president turned off the mute.

"Ambassador, I'll be getting back to you. Remain accessible to this phone," she said, hanging up before there was a reply.

"I want to know what's going on. With the president out of the picture, I am in charge. Is that clear?" she demanded.

There were nods around the conference table.

"And in order to be in charge, I have to know what is going on. No half-baked cowboys doing things their way," she said as she glared at the others, slowing taking each person in, focusing her anger.

The person manning the com link to the President suddenly stood up and said, "Yes sir, Mr. President," and flipped the switch which brought the president to the speaker. "Madam Vice-President . . . ?" he looked over to her.

She quickly moved closer to the intercom on the table in front of her and spoke into the mic, "Mr. President, this is the vice-president. How are you, sir? And let me assure you that things are progressing, but we are trying to figure out who authorized the Thai government to negotiate for your release and return—"

"OK, OK, wait there," the president interrupted. "I don't really care now who gave whom the OK to negotiate with anyone. None of the negotiations have worked. We've got people trying to blow up the doors here to the embassy, so I think they have made their intentions clear. Has there been any movement on the Indian government's part?"

The president's voice sounded strained.

"We have not been able to get a meeting with anyone other than their ambassador, and he doesn't seem to be in the loop. The Arab League has been able to see the key players, but nothing concrete is getting done," she told him.

"Then what about the military option? What is going on with that?"

She looked around the room again before answering, "We have the Reagan Carrier Group close to India now. And we have our forces on alert in Korea. But we don't want to provoke anything with a rash act."

The president's voice screamed over the speaker, "I don't give a good goddamn about that. This is already an act of war, or hadn't you noticed? We have got a number of people here who have to be evacuated now! I am making an executive order here, Vice-President Wright. Let me be clear. All US military forces are to take whatever action they can to rescue us immediately. Am I clear?"

Everyone stared at the speaker as if the president was going to climb right out of it.

"Mr. President, perhaps you should rethink that. Do we want a shooting war with India now?" the vice-president asked hesitantly.

"No excuses, just do it. I know the *Reag—*"

The president's voice cut off as the speaker went silent.

The com tech jumped up and said, "We've lost the signal, the one from New Delhi to Katmandu!"

There was stunned silence in the conference room.

General Kantres broke the silence with, "Well, we heard the man. Can we move the Quick Reaction Force now? We have them standing by, and they can be in the air in thirty minutes."

The vice-president looked over at David. They had discussed this possible situation.

"General Kantres, we appreciate your Ranger's readiness. But we need to make sure the president is in the legal position to make valid orders, given his situation. I have asked the attorney general to look into this."

She looked up at the man, who seemed uncomfortable with the question. Good, if he was uncomfortable, then maybe David's assessment was correct after all.

There was a general uproar as everyone started to talk at once. The Army colonel who had left came back in and whispered to General Litz. He nodded and looked up.

"Madam Vice-President. It seems that the Marines have left. Quantico is empty."

A sense of foreboding came over her, and she wasn't quite sure why. Just what the hell was going on with the Marines?

Chapter 41

Wednesday Morning, The USS Reagan, The Indian Ocean

Rear Admiral Conners looked up at CAPT Ngata at the podium. "Thanks Ted. I think we can all see that this is a good start, a basic NEO, but we also know it needs lots of refining. So let's take this bad boy back and iron out the wrinkles we've brought up." He looked around the space. "Any saved rounds?"

Col Lineau cleared his throat before saying, "As you know, the Marines have been out of the ordnance loop for awhile, and I know I should have kept up with innovations on my own, but can someone please go over this Mk402 again? I'm still not quite sure how this is supposed to work."

CAPT Ngata pointed toward the back of the space and asked, "Commander Scali, would you like to take this?"

Lieutenant Commander Frank Scali, a 35-year mustang and the ship's ordnance officer, stepped up to the podium.

"Well sir, the Mk 402 is a weapon designed to incapacitate troops in the open with little damage to structures. Upon detonation, it attenuates in applied directions and consumes available oxygen in the fireball while creating an overpressure."

He paused to look at the colonel.

"Uh, can you repeat that so a dumb grunt can understand?" Col Lineau asked.

"Yes, sir." He paused to think. "OK, the Mk 402 is a warhead on an iron bomb. Prior to detonation, the blast can be sort of aimed to push out in most directions. When it explodes, it burns up all the oxygen in the area and creates a shock wave that can rupture eardrums or even lungs, depending on how close someone is to the point of detonation."

Colonel Lineau had a visceral image form in his mind of bodies on the ground, their lungs ruptured, a bloody froth coming out their mouths. It did not sound like a good way to go.

"As our SJA briefed, if we can limit the effect on target to only those people and structures that are within the embassy grounds, well, that is an attack on US soil, not Indian. So we think the Mk 402 is the best bet. Because of the embassy building itself, the consulate, and the embassy walls, if we can get a vertical strike in the courtyard, we can 'aim,' so-to-speak, the blast back upward, and the embassy structures should work to limit effects beyond the embassy grounds. Anyone in the courtyard or outside the buildings facing the point of impact, well, their lungs are going to burst. Some people in the building itself may lose consciousness due to oxygen deprivation, but the embassy building is pretty strong, so there should be no major damage. If the president is in the center of the building, as we have been briefed, well, the inrushing oxygen should replace the burned oxygen before any permanent damage has been done."

"And when we land 60 seconds after impact, we won't be affected?" the colonel asked.

"You shouldn't, sir. You should be fine."

" 'Shouldn't.' I like that, especially when it's our asses on the line," Col Linaeu said, eliciting a general chuckle around the space. "And what about the hostile-types who aren't in the grounds when your bomb goes off?"

"Well, sir, the attenuation won't be perfect. Anyone near the walls might become casualties. Even if they are not, they certainly won't be combat-effective for a little while, at least. They should be rather dazed."

"OK, I am going to take your word on it. I do have another saved round, though," he said, looking up at the admiral, who nodded.

"I understand the need for us to limit bystander casualties. But I'm pretty nervous on shutting off the Big Eye for two minutes only ten minutes before we hit the LZ. Isn't that going to make us pretty vulnerable?"

The Air Force liaison, Maj Godwin, jumped up and said, "I'll take that one, sir." He moved to the podium. "I am not an expert on all the black box toys, but you understand how the Big Eye is going to work, right?"

Col Lineau gave a half-hearted shrug.

"Well sir, the Big Eye is going to basically block all electromagnetic emissions along a set path. This one will be about 100 miles wide by 200 miles long and will follow you along your route as well as cover the CAP. While you're in this path, nothing can see you except eyeballs on the ground. And if eyeballs see you, what can they do about it? They can't call anyone. But the Big Bird can somewhat regulate the type of electronics it will jam. So, we are going to keep all military detection equipment jammed hard, but we'll open up the telephone frequencies. That will allow us to get a warning out for people to clear the area as well as warn the president and your Marines to get as deep in the embassy as possible."

"And you think the Indians will have stopped jamming the embassy themselves?"

"There is a good chance they will. We don't believe they know about Big Eye's capability, and they shouldn't know anything is being employed. If they lose their own signals, we think they'll assume that it is their own jamming equipment, and they are going to turn it off. They need to communicate too."

"OK. Thanks. Give me a rifle and a target. All this other stuff is magic, as far as I am concerned," he said as another laugh swept the space.

"OK people, let's get this thing refined. CAPT Ngata, how about . . ." the admiral looked at his watch, "another brief at 1100?"

"No problem, sir," the captain said as he gathered his papers, motioned to his combined planning staff, and left the space.

The two friends sat there for a moment before the admiral asked, "What do you think, Jeff?"

"Well, it isn't too refined, but a gorilla with a club is not too refined, either, and I wouldn't want to face one of them."

"Yeah," he said with a chuckle. "I guess you're right. You've got your Marines bedded down?"

"My commanders are getting briefed now, but yeah, the troops are trying to grab some z's. Hey, that Big Eye drone is something, isn't it?"

"You bet. Have you even seen it? It is not very big,

about the size of a Viking. But it can paralyze a small country, and it can stay on station forever."

"How did you get it anyhow? That's a strategic asset. You don't have them in a carrier battle group."

"Ah, it's all who you know. You remember that Air Force firstie, the wrestler, the one who caught me in the third period after I was leading him and pinned my ass? Back when we were second classmen?"

"You mean the guy who knocked you out of Nationals?" Jeff asked.

"Yes, that asshole. Well, we've kept in touch, and he is STRATCOM now."

"One year ahead of us and he is a four-star? Fucking Air Force pukes!" he said without real conviction.

"Yeah, well he's actually OK, all things considered. I called him up and told him he owed me for that match. Well, actually I just told him we needed it and not to ask questions. And he came through. Not bad for a bus driver who needs an entire airfield to land an itty-bitty plane," the admiral said.

There was a knock on the hatch, and before the admiral could respond, the Com O and SJA came rushing in and said, "Sir, we've got another message from the president. The Indians tried to blow the embassy doors, but you have to read this."

He handed the admiral a slip of paper.

Rear Admiral Conners read the paper, then passed it to Colonel Lineau. He looked back up to the SJA

"So, the President of the United States has given an executive order to the military to use all available means to affect a rescue. Am I reading this right?"

A broad smile crossed the SJA's face before answering, "Yes, Admiral, you are. And that just might be your out."

"Do you think that might hold up?" the admiral asked.

"It might, sir, it just might. Probably, in fact, if I had to bet my pension on it."

The admiral turned and said with faux formality, "Well, Colonel of Marines, it seems like the situation has escalated. Do you think we should obey this executive order?"

"Damn right I do!"

"My feelings exactly," he said.

He turned to the SJA. "Please inform Captain Ngata that no further refinement is necessary. We are going with what we have."

His tone then took a serious bent. "I want the first launch of the Ospreys and Col Lineau's Marines in 30 minutes. Make it happen."

He looked at Col Lineau and said, "It's showtime!"

Chapter 42

Thursday Morning, US Embassy, New Delhi

Since the blast, Sgt Niimoto almost forgot his thirst. He scanned the crowd below. Groups of men had come over the wall and up to the embassy building and back, some glassing the embassy through the gate or from makeshift stands that allowed them to look over the wall. Men had gone into the consular building as well.

Outside the walls, a crowd had begun to gather but were standing around watching while men in civilian clothes seemed to be organizing things. Although their clothes may have been civilian, their no-nonsense air was that of military or police.

A sudden increase in shouting below the tower caught his attention. He sidled over to the courtyard side and peaked over. His heart dropped. About fifteen men were manhandling the Marines' 106 out of the auxiliary armory.

While the Marines were re-arming after the embassy takeovers, some Army supply officer found the old mothballed M40A2 106mm recoilless rifles. These were ancient pieces, first introduced during the Vietnam War era. The rifle fired a 106 mm shell, either HEAT, high explosive plastic-tracer (HEP-T), or antipersonnel-tracer (AP-T) flechette rounds. The rifle had an effective range of about 2500 meters, but a good gunner could hit targets far beyond that.

The weapon was brought on target by a ballistically-matched parallel-mounted M-8C .50 cal. spotting rifle. The trigger was a round knob. Pulling on the knob fired the .50 cal, and when the spotter round hit the desired target, the knob was pushed to fire the 106 mm round. Theoretically, the 106mm round would impact where the .50 cal round had impacted.

The rifle was recoilless because the recoil was not stopped by the breach. Rather, the gases formed by firing the round were ejected out vents in back of the weapon. During weapons training, the instructors had put a wooden ammo case behind the rifle before firing. The backblast smashed the case into splinters.

The weapon was sort of a dinosaur, but one of the powers that be decided that an impressive piece of what looked to be artillery might someday intimidate a violent crowd. No Marines had had to use one yet, but they stayed in the inventories of some 24 embassies.

The weapons were old, but the rounds had been re-packed into plastic casings. Only the flechette rounds were deemed necessary, and each embassy was given 10 rounds.

The rifles themselves were too large to be stored inside most embassy vaults, so a secondary armory was constructed at most embassies near the entrances, and the weapon and rounds were stored there. The spotting rifles and sights were stored along with the other weapons in the main armories.

And now, right below him, the men were manhandling the beast into the courtyard. They got the rifle up on the tripod and pointed it at the door. Sgt Niimoto slowly brought his rifle up and sighted on one of the men. But then he thought that if the satchel charge hadn't damaged the doors, then a flechette round certainly would not. He lowered his weapon and waited, quietly calling in to Little Mac to tell them what was happening.

There was obviously some discussion going on. The Indians probably hadn't seen a recoilless rifle, and they were trying to figure it out. Loading the beast was fairly intuitive, and without too much trouble, a round was loaded and the breach locked into place. One man seemed pretty adamant that he had found the trigger, and he squatted beside it. Without a sight, though, aiming the weapon was problematic.

With a growing sense of disbelief, Sgt Niimoto watched as one man squatted in back of the rifle, using his eyes to take general aim on the door. He motioned right and left, up and down, as the rifle was aimed. Still squatting, he gave a thumb's up to the gunner who reached out and pressed the trigger. There was a huge explosion and dustcloud, and just like the wooden box back at Quantico, the man in back of the rifle was blown to bits. A mangled torso blew up against the embassy ground's wall. Some men who had been watching over the wall ducked back at the blast. Now they had looked back over and were pointing at the body below them. Others in the gun team walked over to look at the man.

Sgt Niimoto stifled a chuckle.

Dumbshits, he thought.

He looked over to the embassy doors, and sure enough, they seemed fine. There might have been a scuff mark high and to the right, but it was not too noticeable. At least the Indians didn't seem to notice it.

He really wished he could understand Hindi. The discussion was getting heated below him. The group of men came back to the rifle, and to Sgt Niimoto's profound amazement, they turned the rifle around so the breach faced the embassy and the muzzle pointed at the wall. They loaded one more round, and a new man stepped up to sight down the barrel and bring the breach in line with the embassy doors. Once everything was aligned, he gave the signal, and the gunner once again pushed the trigger. The blast was just as deafening, but this time the man aiming the weapon took 106 mm of flechette round right below the chin. There was a huge crash as the round continued its course unabated and smashed into the embassy ground's wall. Chips of plaster and brick flew everywhere, some flying up in the air before falling and pattering around Sgt Niimoto like small pieces of hail.

A sound almost like a donkey braying briefly echoed around the courtyard for a moment. Some men looked up trying to see the source, but in the confusion of the moment, they quickly lost interest.

Chapter 43

Thursday Morning, US Embassy, New Delhi

With a sudden click, the lights flickered on. Air began to move as the air conditioner started up. Loralee Howard groaned with pleasure. Gunny felt a moment of elation as well, but the he realized that this was probably not a good sign. Unless it signaled the end of the siege, the power was on because the Indians needed it for something. And after hearing from Sgt Niimoto about the 106 incident (which brought peals of laughter from the Marines and Major Defilice), it didn't look like the siege was over.

He rushed up the ladder and went to Post 1. The screens were flickering to life, the security cameras coming online. Both Little Mac and Rodriguez were watching them as if they could will them to stabilize quicker. Images of some feet milling about could be seen at the edge of the front entrance camera's transmission.

"Sgt McAllister, get me Niimoto," Gunny said.

She pressed the code and handed the phone through the window slot.

"Tony, we've got power now. What's happening out there?"

"Gunny, they've brought in some heavy duty stuff there. It looks like a huge cutting torch."

On the monitor, a group of men appeared, pushing a huge cylinder forward. One man put on a welder's helmet and lit a torch. A jet of fire appeared on the screen, a jet of pure white. He raised it up, but as he moved it towards the door, he went out of camera view.

"Maybe it will be as ineffective as the last attempt," the president said from the ladderwell in back of them.

"Sir, I really need to ask you to get back down below. Let's see what this situation will bring," Gunny told him.

All eyes turned toward the door. The tensions seemed to ease somewhat until a small puff of smoke appeared inside the entrance.

"Shit," someone said. Gunny wasn't sure who it was.

Gunny picked up the phone again. "Tony, what can you see?"

"I can't really see what the cutter is doing, but I can see people clapping each other in the back. It doesn't look good. Do you want me to take them out?"

"Not yet. I need you up there. And that cutter might give out. If they make an entry, we're going to engage. So wait until we tell you or you hear our shots, then engage them. Try and hit the tank and see if you can get it to blow or something."

"Aye-aye, Gunny. Can do," Niimoto said.

Gunny Mac turned around to look at his Marines, then said, "OK, it looks like they might have figured a way in. Sgt Chen, get Steptoe and Kramer. Major Defilice, can I ask you to go down to the vault and stay with the president? Van Slyke, you and Ramon go with him."

The major shrugged and went down the ladder with Van Slyke following. PFC Ramon looked daggers at the Gunny before following.

What the fuck's with her? he wondered.

Oh well, he had other things to worry about.

"Pat, you and Jesus, there, watch that monitor. We need to know how many are out there and where."

As Chen returned with the other two, he turned to them and said, "Sgt Chen, take your team and get a good angle. If they open up a hole, fire through it, take them out."

A grin spread over Chen's face. "Gotcha, Gunny!"

He began to place Steptoe and Kramer, trying to figure out the best positioning.

"Fallgatter and LCpl Saad, join me here in the ladderwell. We are the covering fire," Gunny told the two other Marines.

Everyone moved in position and slowly fell silent. The waiting began. Despite the air conditioning coming back on, sweat began to trickle down Gunny Mac's back. Another puff of smoke appeared. Then a dull orange glow began to diffuse around that spot.

Suddenly, a spark shot through the door and bounced around the deck before fading. PFC Fallgatter let out a yelp, drawing glares from the rest. He looked sheepishly down.

More sparks started shooting in, a steady stream of them. Sgt Chen looked back.

"Gunny!" he shout-whispered, "I can almost see outside. I'm going to engage!"

"That's your call," Gunny told him, tightening his grip on his weapon.

Sgt Chen crept forward. He looked at the monitor through the Post 1 window, noting the position of the men outside the door. He made a mental adjustment and moved to the left, angling his M18 toward the right. He pushed it forward and blindly fired a three-round burst through the sparks. The sparks suddenly ceased.

There was a whoop from inside Post 1. "You got one of them Chen!" shouted Little Mac. And the rest are clearing out."

There were a few shouts from within the embassy, and LCpl Kramer slapped Sgt Chen on the shoulders.

"Quiet everyone. They'll be back, so let's not get too carried away with ourselves. Nice shot, though."

Gunny wiped the sweat from his brow. He knew they would return.

Chapter 44

Wednesday Night, The White House, Washington, DC

The vice-president rubbed her gritty eyes. She felt disgusting and could really use a shower. She looked around the conference room. Empty coffee cups littered the place, and a steward was bringing in yet another tray of sandwiches. Small groups formed, broke, and formed again, like shoaling fish, discussing, yelling even, pointing at computers or printed reports. For the moment, she was a spot of calm amid the chaos.

She caught the eye of Arnold Hatch, the president's chief of staff, and nodded slightly. He was the only other person seemingly alone at the moment. David had been slowly pushing him aside as events progressed, and no one seemed to notice. No one except for Arnold and the vice-president, that is. Arnold just stared at her for a moment, then looked away.

General Litz, General Kantres, Admiral Mike Keogh, the Navy CNO, and General Stacy Johnson, the Air Force Chief of Staff, were the center of a group of mostly uniforms in the midst of an animated discussion. General Litz forcefully pointed at the CNO who shook his head, pointing at a printout. The chairman kept glancing up at her, then back at the people surrounding him. He called out to Paul Lefever, who came to join them, and handed him the printout. The secretary started to read it when a look of shock came over his face.

"*Well, this can't be good,*" the vice-president thought.

With a little hesitation, the secretary made his way to her followed by the flags. He handed the printout back to General Litz, offering him the floor.

"Madam Vice-President, we just got an op order forwarded to us from PACCOM. It seems that the Regan Battle Group has launched a NEO to rescue the president," he said, then stood quietly, waiting for her reaction.

She was stunned. "You are telling me what?"

"Ma'am, at 0730 Z, the *Reagan* launched four

Ospreys with a contingent of Marines and fighter escort to conduct a NEO."

"Marines? They don't do operations anymore. What are you . . ." she trailed off. Of course, now she knew to where all the Marines had disappeared. She looked back up. "And just who authorized this NEO?" Her eyes burned into General Litz.

"Well, according to this op order, it seems that the president did." He handed the vice-president the first page of the printout. "See here? In the Mission Statement? It says '. . . in compliance with the direct orders of President Michael Eduardo, Commander in Chief . . .'"

He looked at her for a reaction.

"And just when did the president give the Battle Group such an order?" she demanded.

The general swallowed, the hesitantly said, "Well, he did, sort of. During our last communications with him."

"That was not a legal order. We have determined that while the president is under duress such as he is now, under isolation as he is now, it's just as if he is under surgery or otherwise temporarily incapacitated, and his orders carry no legal weight. He doesn't know the big picture and cannot make a reasonable decision."

She seemed to be reciting this more to convince herself than the others.

"Besides, just how did the *Reagan* know about this?'

There were some downcast eyes among the flag officers as the general said, "Well Madam Vice-President, we don't know at this time. But we are looking into it."

"Do that. But first, we are not going to war over this. Get a hold of the *Reagan* and pull the plug on this thing."

There was some more nervous shuffling of feet, and the vice-president felt a pang of apprehension.

"Madam Vice-President, we regret to inform you that we have been out of touch with the group commander up until now." Admiral Keogh held up a satphone for her to see. "We were already going to do that, but the NEO task force itself, well it's completely out of communications. They've got a Big Eye," he looked furtively around the room, "and it has put a dead zone around them. The Big Eye can cut off all—"

"Yes, I know all about the Big Eye, General. I helped fund the prototypes. I know what it can do. General Johnson, the Big Eye is one of yours. Contact the crew and shut it off."

"There seems to be a temporary communications problem with the Big Eye." she said, looking embarrassed. "We haven't been able to raise it."

Temporary problem? So this is how this is going to be played, the vice-president thought to herself..

She began to feel control slipping away.

"According to the op order, there will be a window, at 0947 Z, that is a little over an hour from now, where the Big Eye will shut down the telecommunications jamming. They want to try and contact the president and also give out a warning to bystanders to get away because they are going to drop a Mk402. They want to minimize casualties. We can use that window to shut this off," General Litz said, looking hopeful.

"And where is this task force now?" she asked dryly.

General Litz looked back to one of his strap-hangers who whispered in his ear. The general turned back to her and said, "According to our calculations, it should be over Indian airspace at the moment. We are trying to get a visual with our satellites now."

"Who is the commander of the Battle Group?"

Admiral Keogh stepped up, satphone in hand. "Rear Admiral Joshua Conners. Do you want to talk to him? I've got him standing by."

He held out the phone helpfully.

The vice-president sat in thought for a moment. The dice had been thrown. If she picked them up from the table now, history would look on her as a weak. If the NEO could somehow work, she would be the strong vice-president who took forceful action. And if the NEO failed, well, she would be hanging her hat at 1600 Pennsylvania, and she could worry about weathering the storm from the pacifist crowd later. It was time for damage control.

"I don't know about any of you, but I am sick-and-tired about all this BS stonewalling we are getting from the Indians. It is time to put an end to this. If the *Reagan* and some Marines have found an opportunity to get this done, then we sure the hell are going to back them up."

The faces around her were stunned, to say the least. She looked at Dr. Ryan, who had pushed her way into the group once it was obvious something big was up.

"Get word to the bystanders around the embassy somehow that they need to get out of the area. But don't do it too early. Just give them enough time to move back. A Mk 402 does not have that big of an effective casualty radius. Then prepare statements to give the Indian government through our friends stressing that this is not an act of war, but merely a NEO on what is officially our sovereign soil. Oh, and get Secretary Pitt off the ground now. I don't want him still sitting at the airport when this all goes down."

She paused for a moment.

"General Kantres, maybe it's time to move the Quick Reaction Force. The barn door may already be open, but you never know.

"Come on people! Let's get going on this! What else do we need to do to ensure a successful operation? Let's go!"

There was an explosion of noise as people rushed to phones and computers.

Chapter 45

Thursday Morning, US Embassy, New Delhi

More and more men were coming into the courtyard with a sense of purpose. Sgt Niimoto watched them flank the door and take positions behind the columns. There were probably fifty or so men crowded down there. One man had picked up the torch again, lit it off, and was trying to sidle up to the small cut and enlarge it while staying out of the line of fire.

"Aye-aye, Gunny. I'll wait. I'll try for the cylinder first, and it that doesn't work, I'm going to start taking them out," he said.

He placed the phone down and raised his weapon. The last exchange had happened too fast for him to get off a shot, and he was not going to be left holding the bag this time.

The metalworker did not have a good angle for a nice clean cut, but the opening was nevertheless getting longer. Everyone was focused on the cut. A burst of muffled gunfire rang out, almost too muffled for him to hear up in the tower, but the sudden hail of return fire left little doubt as to what had happened. Sgt Niimoto didn't consider the ambient temperature, spin drift, coriolis effect, or any other of the external ballistics he was taught. He was too close for them to have much effect.   He tried to compensate for the bullet drop considering his height above the ground, focused on the cylinder, and slowly squeezed off a shot. Nothing happened. He could see chips of plaster and stone fly as rounds from inside the embassy and rounds from outside which impacted the doors ricocheted about. He sighted again and squeezed off another shot. Again, nothing. It looked as if his rounds didn't have enough penetrating power to do anything to the heavy cylinder. OK, he would shift to more lively targets.

As he acquired a target, a man with a black t-shirt crouching behind a column, the volume of fire slowed, then stopped. Men peered around at the door, and the metal worker picked himself up from where he had hit the deck, picked up the torch, and tentatively, with encouragement from the others, started his cut again. He worked a small circle, and with a big shower of sparks, that circle fell into the embassy, leaving a rough 12-inch hole in the door. Someone gave a shout, and the Indians started firing into the hole. One man, tall and rangy, approached from the side with what looked to be a grenade. Sgt Niimoto shifted his aim, and as the man reached out to throw the grenade in, he took the shot.

The round, traveling at over 1200 feet per second, impacted the man's right shoulder and entered his chest cavity. He staggered, dropping the grenade. A few men must have thought he had thrown it into the hole as they started firing again, but the shot man understood. Sgt Niimoto could clearly see the look of resignation on his face as he fell to a sitting position, staring at the grenade. There was an explosion, and Sgt Niimoto instinctively flinched. When he looked back through the scope, he could see the battered body of the man up against the embassy wall, blood welling beneath him. Another gunman, one of the ones in back of a column, was writhing in pain, clutching his leg. Sgt Niimoto could hear the man's shouts from up in the tower. There was an increased fusillade of fire as two men ran up and grabbed the wounded man by the shoulders, dragging him out of the line-of-fire from inside the embassy.

Something small and round came out the hole. One of the Marines had thrown his own grenade. With a shout, the gunmen threw themselves flat. Trying to compose himself, Sgt Niimoto took aim at a gunman, and when the grenade detonated, he pulled off a shot. He quickly re-acquired the target only to see that the man was unharmed. Tony had missed. Snapping off a shot accurately was much more difficult than squeezing off a shot. He gave a grunt and slapped himself alongside his head. He had to do better.

He looked down at his remaining rounds: eight more in the clip and ten more arrayed in front of him. He had to make these count.

As the metalworker edged his way forward again, Sgt Niimoto put the scope's crosshairs on the man's shoulder blade. Reconsidering, he moved the aiming point to the man's spine. At this elevated angle, he didn't want the round skipping along the man's scapulae. His target nervously crept forward, then reached out again and started cutting. Another man crept up along the opposite side of the cut and reached his weapon around, firing into the hole without exposing his body. Sgt Niimoto let out half a breath and squeezed the trigger this time. The rifle chuffed and kicked against his shoulder. He quickly shifted aim and squeezed again, aiming center mass at the gunman firing right into the embassy.

The first round impacted the metalworker directly on his spine, on the C7 vertebrae. The 178 grain round shattered the bone, sending shards throughout the unfortunate man's lungs and heart. He was dead before he knew he had been hit. The second round also entered its target's back, but lower and to the left. The gunman dropped, then tried to crawl out of the way. Another man rushed over to help him.

Two men crept up the grab the feet of the metalworker and drag him alongside the edge of the embassy building. A large, heavyset man met them and turned the prone body over. He seemed to notice something, then quickly tore off the dead man's shirt. Sgt Niimoto has a sinking feeling as the man checked the body for an entrance wound on the chest. He flipped the body back over, pulled the bloody shirt back, and touched the wound there. Sgt Niimoto could clearly see the confused expression on the man as he checked the dead man's chest, then understanding dawn on his face as he looked at the dead man's back. Hand still on the wound, he suddenly looked back over the courtyard and up. With one of the odd chances in combat, he happened to look directly at the tower and caught sight of Sgt Niimoto aiming down at him.

Tony brought his rifle to bear, not wanting to fire like this, to expose himself. He never really thought to drop back down out-of-sight as that would only prolong things. And he really did not want to hide anymore. He wanted to face his enemies. Through the scope, Sgt Niimoto could see the man's eyes widen, a shout beginning to form as he started to swing his own weapon around. Tony Niimoto smoothly pulled back on the trigger sending the boattail round down from the tower, across the courtyard, and into the man's throat. The man fell as if poleaxed, and Sgt Niimoto swung his weapon to take aim at one of the two men who had dragged the metalworker. To Tony's surprise, the man jumped back and started pointing back at the embassy door. Somehow, they thought the round which had taken out the man had come from inside the embassy. Sgt Niimoto sighed with relief.

Over the next 15 minutes or so, Sgt Niimoto became a machine. Pick a target, wait for fire into or out of the embassy, then squeeze off a round. He took out a replacement metalworker with a headshot, but most were other gunmen. Fifteen shots, fifteen hits. Twelve obvious kills. He had contemplated keeping the last round for himself, like they do in the movies, but he realized that that would help nobody in the embassy, so he used it to take out an automatic rifleman who was pouring fire into the hole in the door.

He had called into the embassy to let them know he was out of ammo and to ask what he should do. They were understandably a little busy, but through PFC Rodriguez, Gunny told him to hold fast and wait. So he was waiting now. Yet another metalworker was cutting away at the door now, making progress. He had at least three quarters of a large square cut out, an opening which would be large enough to let at least two men enter abreast. And Sgt Niimoto didn't have a way to stop him.

He looked back over the other side of the wall. There were a dozen or more men up on the makeshift stands, watching the progress of the men at the door. As he watched, one of the men seemed to be having problems with his phone. He kept looking at it. Then trying to call someone. He tapped a man next to him and said something. The man handed him his phone, but that one didn't seem to be much better.

Bad comms will kill you, he thought as he moved back to watch the enemy's progress.

Now that his killing mode had passed, he was thirsty again. But somehow, that didn't seem so important anymore.

Chapter 46

Thursday Morning, US Embassy, New Delhi

When the first piece of the door fell in, a small circle of about 12 inches in diameter, incoming fire had intensified, and a round skipped off the deck to hit Sgt Chen in the calf. He seemed more angry than hurt, and he returned fire, cursing up a storm. But Gunny could tell that the shock was now setting in. Chen was quieter, somewhat distant. But he refused to go below.

The first grenade to come flying in somehow took them by surprise, despite the fact that they expected it. Somehow, no one was hit. The second grenade had dinged LCpl Steptoe, though. Nothing serious, but sobering none-the-less.

And now Sgt Niimoto was out of the picture. He had probably single-handedly kept the gunmen out of the embassy for the last twenty or thirty minutes, but there was nothing he could do now. And the Marines watched, almost mesmerized, as the new cut line slowly grew along the door. LCpl Kramer had tried to get enough of an angle to take out the man on the torch, but the hole was too small, and the volume of incoming fire drove him back. It was only matter of time now before the opening was cut.

No one had thought to disable the security cameras, so they could see on the monitors the gunmen massing to storm the embassy. An increased volume of fire suddenly came in the opening.

"Mother fucker! Again!" Sgt Chen yelled, grasping his calf, right where he had been hit before.

Another round had hit him, almost in the same place. Kramer rushed over to where Chen lay in back of Post 1, helping him up.

"Chen, you OK?" asked Gunny Mac.

"Oh sure, Gunny, if you count those cocksuckers shooting me in the goddamn leg again as being OK."

He muffled some curses and Kramer bound the leg again, wrapping the bandage right over the existing one.

More rounds came to ricochet around the entrance. This position was becoming untenable.

He heard a shout from below him. "What's happening up there?" It was the president, followed by a sheepish-looking Army major.

He shouted down, "Mr. President, can you please go back to the vault? We can't do our job here if we have to worry about you. Major Defilice, can you please escort him back?"

They looked up at him, then moved back out of sight. Probably not back to the vault, Gunnye thought, but it was better than nothing.

He moved back to where he could see the front doors. The opening was getting close to being cut through. Well, he had to make some changes.

"OK, everybody listen up. We'll pull back to the ladderwell and try to secure the hatch here. When they get in, they'll probably take time to search the ground floor, and that'll give us time. We're going down to the bottom deck where we can mass our fire. You know, like the Spartans when they fought the Persians. Let them come at us in small numbers. Sgt Chen, we need to carry you. I don't want your blood to leave a trail to the ladderwell. OK? Let's move it."

"Uh, Gunny?"

It was Sgt McAlister, speaking through the voice grill of the post. He turned around with a questioning look.

She looked at PFC Rodriguez who gave a slight nod, then she said, "Well, like we told you before, me and Jesus here, well, we kind of figure we should stay here."

"No, I want you to fall back. We can't stay here."

"General Order Number 5, Gunny."

"I told you before, I'm relieving you."

"Well, we don't see it that way." She paused, taking a deep breath. "Look Gunny, we can cover that opening there, when they get it. We can fire right under the document slot and cover the whole thing. This glass here is bulletproof, so what can they do to us? You need the time, and we can give it to you." She paused again. "You know we're right."

Gunny's mind raced. He wanted to pull them back, to keep them safer. His thoughts flashed for a brief second to

Colonel Parks, trying to teach his very green driver so long ago what it meant to be a leader. Now he knew what the colonel meant.

The cut line on the door was getting close to being completed. The rest of the Marines were waiting on his decision.

"Besides, Gunny. We're all probably going to catch it today, and we'd rather go out on Post than hiding in some dark vault, probably getting shot in the ass by Fallgatter or Ramon," she said with a laugh.

He made his decision.

"Roger that, Sergeant. Man your post."

He raised up his arm in a salute. Both Little Mac and Rodriquez came to quasi-attention and returned the salute.

"You've got balls, Pat. You too Jesus."

He turned to the others and ordered, "All right, let's move it."

LCpl Kramer and PFC Fallgatter picked up Sgt Chen and carried him to the ladderwell and down below. LCpl Steptoe wiped up a few drops of blood dripped from Chen to the deck. Gunny Mac turned to look one more time at Post 1 before closing the hatch, but both Sgt MacAllister and PFC Rodriguez were attentively watching the embassy door. The hatch swung shut, cutting off his view of them.

He hurried down the ladder, a two flight set of stairs with a landing between. When at the bottom, he could see the first floor hatch by looking up the middle between the sets of steps. Gathered at the bottom was the rest of the party, everyone except for the two in Post 1. They all looked to him.

"Well, they're almost in. I don't know how long we can keep them out, but we are sure going to try. Sgt McAllister and PFC Rodriguez have volunteered to stay at Post 1." He could see Loralee quickly lower her head in prayer. "Frankly, I don't know how long they can hold out, but it's a good position."

"Well, we can keep them under observation, at least. So we know," Major Defilice said, looking at the gunny.

"What do you mean, sir? How can we do that?" Then it dawned on him "Yes! The auxiliary security closet."

He rushed down the passage almost to the vault and opened a small room full of monitors. This was a redundant monitoring station that monitored inside various embassy spaces. It was not under Marine control, so it had slipped his mind. Others following him tried to crowd inside, but the space was too small.

"Sgt Chen, take Kramer and Fallgatter and take a position at the bottom of the ladder. We need to hit them if they get that far."

Everyone else crowded the best they could to get a view of the second monitor, the one which showed inside Post 1. Both Marines were alert and ready. Sgt McAllister had her hand on Rodriguez's shoulder. Inside the space it was silent, the only sound the breathing in and out of nine sets of lungs.

Suddenly, Rodriguez pointed. The monitor had no sound, but his shout was evident. Both Marines put the muzzles of their weapons out the document slots and pulled the triggers. The reports could be heard in the distance, coming past the closed hatches, then down the ladder well and passage. They could hear the answering fire as well.

The glass of the post seemed to shudder as Rodriguez first ducked, then straightened up and reloaded before firing again. A sound of an explosion reached the watching group. A grenade must have been employed, but the Post was pretty strong.

"How long can they last?" the president asked, concern evident in his voice.

To Gunny, it seemed like the concern was actually for the two Marines, not for his own personal safety.

"I don't know, sir. It depends on what weapons they have."

"Shouldn't we go do something?" It was Ramon, who sat clutching her M18, looking oversized in her grip.

"No Ramon, we shouldn't. If we open the hatch, they'll know where we are, and that's that. Those two Marines have pretty good protection now. And they knew what they were doing. We won't John Wayne it and let their decision go to waste."

Talking ceased again as they watched the screen.

Coolly, Sgt McAllister and PFC Rodriguez took turns firing out the port. It looked like they were on the range without a care in the world.

Gunny's pocket started to vibrate, an awareness that crept up on him, so intent he was on the monitor. Puzzled, he reached into his pocket and pulled out his phone. It was ringing as if nothing was wrong. The incongruity struck him.

He flipped it open and said, "Hello?"

The woman's voice on the other end seemed frantic. "Gunny McCardle, is that you?"

"Yes it is. Who is this?"

"Hey, I've got somebody," he could hear her shout to someone else before she came back to him. "Gunny, this is Major Rogers. Is the president with you? Is he OK?"

"Yes ma'am, he is. As far as OK, well, we're under attack right now, and frankly, I don't know how long we can hold out."

He knew the major, of course. It was a small Corps. And the voice did sound like hers.

"Gunny, we don't have much time. I'm surprised we got a hold of you as it is. You've got to hold out longer. "In . . ." There was a pause, then, " . . . in twenty-two minutes, the Navy is going to drop a big-ass bomb on the embassy, danger close. This is a Mk402, and it won't destroy the embassy but it will mess up anyone outside and suck up a lot of the oxygen. Get everyone as close to the center of the building as possible. We'll be there right after that, so get ready."

He was a little confused, and he asked, "You're coming?"

"I'm out to sea, but the Colonel has every swinging dick he could find and they're coming in to get you. Look, we'll be cut off any sec. Where do you have the president?"

"On the lower level, in the vault."

"OK, I'll tell them, if I can raise them. Get in that vault and hunker down."

The line was cut.

"Who was that? I thought the phones didn't work," LCpl Steptoe asked curiously.

Gunny stared at the phone for a second. He couldn't believe it. Rescue?

"Everybody, listen up. The 'Dant is coming to get us. I don't know how. But that was Major Rogers on the phone. So all we have to do is hold on a little longer, and we're home free."

There was a sudden explosion of sound as everyone tried to talk at once.

"Quiet everyone!" he shouted. "We need to move back to the vault. They've got some sort of bomb they are going to use to prep the place."

He thought of the two Marines in Post 1. He hoped the Post would protect them from the bomb. They just had to hold out a little longer. If they could, then this was going to work. He looked back up the monitor. McAllister and Rodriguez were still calmly alternating their shots, one covering the other while that Marine reloaded.

His hopeful optimism fell as on the screen, they could see Sgt McAllister fall back, hand to her throat, then drop out of camera range to the deck. There was a collective shout in the closet. A seeing eye round must have found its way through the slot and into the post. They could see PFC Rodriguez turn around and look down at her, then they could see him shout and move to the slot and empty his clip. As he fumbled with this clip to reload, he looked up and out the post glass, yelling. Several barrels poked into view, through the document ports, and muzzle flashes filled the screen. They could faintly hear the gunfire above them as they saw PFC Rodriguez fall back.

There was muffled shouting in the deck above them, celebratory shouting.

The president seemed shocked as he said, "They're gone! Just like that!"

Gunny tried to think. He needed time, and he had to act now. He grabbed LCpl Steptoe and Saad and rushed back down the passage to the ladderwell. He looked at the three Marines there.

"Look, Post 1 just fell. But the 'Dant is coming with the rest of the Marines to get us out of here. We need time, though. In about twenty minutes, there's gonna be one mother of a bomb landing on us, but it isn't going to bring the place down. So we need a diversion."

He looked at Chen. No, Chen couldn't run.

"Kramer, Steptoe, Saad, I want you to quietly go up the ladder. Go to the second deck. If and when these yahoos open the hatch, light them up, then run like hell. Keep them chasing you. We've got three more decks up there, make them chase you. But in seventeen minutes, get into a closet or head in the middle of the building and hunker down. Keep them away from the president. You got it?"

All three nodded.

"Then go. Quietly now. Remember, they're right outside that hatch there."

The three Marines started carefully up the ladder.

"Sgt Chen, you take Fallgatter here and cover the bottom of the ladder. And keep quiet!"

"I think I'll join them here. It sounds like fun," said Drayton smiling, but his hands were trembling and his face pale.

Gunny clapped him on the shoulder. "Roger that."

He ran back down the passageway and called out, "Mr. President, I have to insist on you getting into the vault now. You too, Loralee."

"Where did those three soldiers . . . sorry, Marines go?"

"Sir, we need more time, so they'll draw anyone to the upper decks and away from you."

"So they are sacrificing themselves, too?" he asked, seemingly distraught.

"I hope not, Mr. President. I hope they buy us all enough time to get out of here."

"Gunnery Sergeant!" said Mr. Dravid.

Gunny Mac kept forgetting that he was around.

"You need these attacking men to go upstairs?" he asked, and without waiting for an answer, ran down the passage.

Gunny instinctively brought up his weapon, but realizing that fire would draw attention to them, he held off. He tried to signal Sgt Chen, but by that time, Mr. Dravid was already climbing up the ladder. Gunny rushed to look up, but Mr. Dravid passed the first deck hatch and kept on climbing. Gunny hoped that was a good sign.

He looked at his watch. They had fifteen minutes until the prep fire. He wheeled back and ran as quietly as he could back to the vault. Major Defilice and PFC Ramon were at the hatch. Inside, Loralee had taken an M18 off a table where the extra weapons had been put and was loading it. She looked up and caught the Gunny's eye.

"You think I'm just going to sit here?"

The president looked at her and said, "I think I'll take one, too."

Gunny looked to Van Slyke and told him, "Prep the president on that. Make sure he knows how to use it." He looked around the vault, thinking. "We need to be ready to pull this hatch shut. I'll get Sgt Chen to lock it."

The vault had a unique safety feature, one which made little sense to the gunny. While it had a safety release inside the vault, it could not be locked from inside. It had to be locked from the outside. So if worst came to worst, and they needed to seal the hatch of the vault, to lock it, then someone had to be outside of the vault to do that.

A flurry of movement caught Gunny's eye. It was Sgt Chen, motioning up the ladderwell. There was a burst of fire from above, and then Mr. Dravid's voice could be heard shouting something. Hindi-sounding voices responded, then there was the sound of rushing footsteps going up the stairs.

Gunny crept forward. No one seemed to be coming down. He hoped the ploy would work, and he hoped his Marines would survive their efforts. Sporadic gunfire echoed from above. At least they hadn't been caught yet. He looked at his watch. Eight minutes.

He moved back to the security closet and looked in, but not much could be seen on any of the screens. A few passing bodies, a few shadows.

He barely heard a plunk, plunk, plunk as something came down the ladder, bouncing on step after step. He looked up just as a quiet "shit" echoed down the passage. The explosion was deafening in the confined spaces. Shrapnel whined as it flew down the passage towards them. The blast stunned him for a second, then he gathered his wits and looked down towards the ladder.

Sergeant Greg Chen, Private First Class Michael

Fallgatter, and Drayton Bajinski lay shredded at the end of the passageway. PFC Fallgatter gave a moan and moved his arm when a burst of fire ripped into him.

Gunny whipped around and dived toward the vault. With Major Defilice, he pulled the hatch partway shut. As a shape came into view to inspect the bodies, both men opened fire, and the body fell. Gunny looked at his watch. Six minutes.

A rifle came around the corner and sprayed down the passage, hitting nothing before being pulled back. Gunny fired on the rifle, but missed. He knew what had to be done.

He looked around the vault, at each face there. He finally settled on Van Slyke, his face still bandaged. He was a good man.

"PFC Van Slyke. You and me. We're going to go out there and secure the hatch."

There was an explosion as another grenade was rolled down the ladder.

"Major, if I can ask you to keep the president safe here. Hopefully relief will get here soon."

He got up as Van Slyke came forward.

"No!" shouted PFC Ramon. She took a deep breath. "You've ignored me since I got here, you've ignored me for the last two days since this stuff started. I'm a Marine, dammit, and not a 'Princess.' Peter can barely see out of his eye, and Gunny, you're as bad a shot as I am. But you need to be in charge here. It's the mission that's important here. Greg and I are going."

She indicated Major Defilice, who stood there with a wry look on his face.

"No, Ivy, I want you to stay here. Van Slyke and I will go," Gunny said.

"Dammit Gunny, didn't you hear me? For once, you'll let me be a Marine!" she shouted, glaring at him.

"Gunny, I don't think I'd stand in her way," said the major. "And I think we need to go pretty quick," he added as he whipped off another shot down the passage.

She stared at Gunny for another moment, then swept her arm, clearing off files from a heavy table.

"Greg, help me with this," she told MAJ Defilice as she

bent over to push the table.

"Wait a minute," he told her.

The major walked up to Ramon and stood her up. He bent down and picked her up, her feet dangling a good eighteen inches off the ground. He looked at her for a moment, then kissed her solidly on the lips. Her arms curled in back of his neck. They stopped, and stared in each other's eyes for a moment before he put her down. Without comment, they pushed the table out the door.

Loralee's eyes glistened, and she quickly wiped them.

"Well," was all she could say.

As the door started to close, Gunny hit the side of his head with his hand.

How could I have forgotten Tony?

"Wait!" He grabbed the landline and dialed up Sgt Niimoto. "Come on, answer, answer!"

MAJ Defilice fired down the passage again. "Uh, Gunny, a little urgency?"

"Yeah?" Niimoto here."

"Tony, no time. In three minutes, the embassy is going to get hit with a Mk402. You've got to take any cover you can. Any!" The line went dead as the door of the vault was shoved shut, cutting the wire.

Chapter 47

Thursday Morning, US Embassy, New Delhi

The vault door closed with a sense of certainty. Major
Defilice put his shoulder to it and hit the keypad to lock it.
Somehow, though, PFC Ramon did not feel alone. She looked
up at the major and smiled. Well, it was time to get going.
She turned around and started pushing the heavy metal
table.

"Ivy, let me push, you cover me," he told her.

She was still hyped for standing up to Gunny, and she
bristled for a second before relenting. He was right. He could
push this easily alone. He bent down, and he pushed the
table along edgewise, so the top of it preceded them like a
bulldozer blade. It was a heavy metal table, and should stop
quite a bit of anything thrown at them.

Ivy followed, weapon at the ready, pointing over the
table. Twice, she fired as they made their way down the
passage. When they were almost there, a grenade bounced
down the steps.

"Down!" she shouted.

The impact was loud and the shock wave actually
moved the table back a few inches. They both instinctively
stuck their heads over the edge to check it, but nothing
penetrated the heavy tabletop. They smiled at each other
with relief and started moving again.

As they approached the opening, they both sidled to
the front wall. An arm came around the corner with a rifle,
and Ivy snapped off a burst, surprisingly hitting the arm.
With a shout, the arm was yanked back while the rifle it had
been holding fell to the ground, bouncing until it came to a
stop on top of Drayton. Ivy felt a little gorge rise in her throat
as she looked at the four men lying there, the three
Americans and one Indian gunman.

Greg looked at her, grabbed her hand and gave it a
squeeze. Despite the intense circumstances, she felt a wave of
affection roll over her.

He positioned the table and gave her the signal to

cover him. She stood up and fired up the ladder while he pushed the table out to block the bottom. Sgt Chen's body served to help anchor it in place. It may not have been much of an obstacle, but maybe it would stop the grenades from being rolled down on top on them.

There was a shout from above and a thud of descending feet. Greg stood, cool as a cucumber and fired. Ivy ducked under his arm and fired her own burst. Two bodies fell to the landing, just a couple feet away from them. They both ducked back as return fire peppered the ladderwell. The burst stopped and was followed by a small cascade of spent brass, which bounced down the stairs.

There were some voices from above, then the plunk, plunk, plunking of a falling grenade. They both leaned back as the grenade lodged against the table and detonated. Except for her ringing ears, Ivy was untouched.

She could feel Greg's big body lean against her, hard and powerful. This was a man. She looked at him and knew then that this was the man for her, the one who could meet her expectations. She wanted to spend the rest of her life with him.

There was another mad rush down the stairs. Again, they both popped out, one low and the other high. Again, they forced the retreat.

The major looked down at the private first class, smiled, and said, "Some fun, huh?"

They could hear discussion in Hindi going on above them. As it stopped, several grenades came bounding down the stairs, exploding against the table. As soon as they detonated, a bum's rush of steps came rushing down at them. They both struggled back up to engage, firing up the ladder. Without a sound, MAJ Defilice fell back, rifle falling from his hands. Ivy stopped and looked. A round had hit him high on the forehead. His eyes were open, but looking at nothing. Just like that, he was gone.

More men rushed down the steps firing into the major's prone and unmoving body. A sense of rage engulfed her. Even here, even now, she was being ignored. She turned and fired into the mass of men, dropping two of them.

"I am a Marine! Remember that! Private First Class

Ivy Huertas Ramon, USMC!"

One man stumbled and fell down the steps to come up against the table. Ivy leaned over and crushed his nose with a vicious swing of her rifle butt. She felt a sharp pain high in her chest and looked down in amazement at the small flower of red blossoming up over her left breast. It hurt, but not as much as she might have imagined it would, and otherwise, she felt fine. Somehow, the round had not hit anything vital, but the bright red blood welling on her white t-shirt made for a vivid image.

The man who shot her looked at her in amazement as well. Ivy swung up her weapon and put two rounds in his chest.

The next round took her low and in the stomach. She felt the mulekick and sat down, in back of the table, confused. Her breathing became difficult, and she glanced down to see a growing red stain along her belly. She looked at Greg and leaned over, head on his chest. She slowly reached over and touched his face, feeling the stubble, taking in the strong jaw, strong now even in death.

Oh, Daddy, she thought, *you'd have liked him so.*

She slowly faded away. She never felt the shock of the huge explosion that rocked the embassy.

Chapter 48

Thursday Morning, US Embassy, New Delhi

Tony Niimoto watched the battle unfolding beneath him. The cut which finally made an opening in the door had come accompanied by a cheer from the men outside the embassy. Now men were leaning in, firing, and falling back. Others reached around to throw grenades, the detonations echoing oddly across the courtyard.

He felt elation as some of the men fell. A few were pulled back alongside the edge of the wall, but three lay on the ground, across the threshold of the door, quite obviously dead. Someone in there was kicking some ass, and for every gunman hit, Sgt Niimoto felt a lift.

Those small lifts could not overcome the feeling of helplessness and despair overtaking him, though. Being able to see and hear a battle, one in which his fellow Marines were engaged, and not being able to do anything, well, that was its own kind of hell.

He had contemplated trying to sneak down to the 106, still in the courtyard below him, thinking somehow to turn it on the men assaulting the doorway. But the number of men in the courtyard and on the embassy walls covering those inside made him realize that any move there would be useless.

Three gunmen seemed to gather themselves. They shouted at each other, and in a concerted rush, ran into the opening. All three fell before even getting into the embassy. One stumbled on one of the bodies already lying there and was hit. The other two managed to get to the threshold before falling. The bodies were piling up.

A voice from on top of the wall shouted across the courtyard. One of the men cupped his ear, and the voice repeated itself. There was an acknowledgment. Then several men got prone and crept up along the edge of the wall. They reached out and began to pull the bodies back. A burst of fire challenged them, and one man was hit in the arm, but the bodies were cleared and dragged out of the way.

A group of a dozen or so men climbed over the wall and sidled forward, out of the line of fire. They joined the other gunmen and conversed for a few moments. All of them moved forward into position just to the left of the opening. Several grenades were thrown in, and upon their detonation, the men made a mad rush into the embassy. Several fell, but at least fifteen made it in. There was a furious exchange of fire for about 30 seconds, then the fire ceased. A moment later, a gunman came to the door and out onto the steps, signaling the men on the wall. There was a cheer from the men there, and another couple dozen hurried over the wall, across the courtyard, and into the embassy. Several of the men pushed in the cutting equipment that had made the breach in the door. Sgt Niimoto's heart fell.

Sick, he sat back down, back against the cupola wall. There didn't seem to be much hope. He began to wonder what he should do. He really hadn't thought he would be in this position. Surely someone would have noticed him by now. Heck, when he laughed out loud over the 106 firing, he thought he'd blown it. But he was still sitting in the tower, unnoticed and ignored.

He could hear a few bursts of gunfire from deep inside the embassy, but he didn't bother to look. He couldn't bear it. He wondered at his odds if he simply walked out and tried to act like a bystander. It was probably his best chance. He moved over and looked at the crowd outside the embassy grounds.

Well, it looked as if whatever problem there had been with the telephones was over. People were now talking on them. There were about a hundred of the military-looking men there, many peering over the edge of the wall or through the gate now that fire from inside the embassy had ceased. There were also a couple hundred people just watching from outside the walls, unable to actually see inside the embassy compound. Some were taking photos or videos, some were just chatting. One man was wheeling a cart with some sort of fried snack, not getting far as people kept stopping him to buy. Well, Tony was just going to have to try and mingle and slowly move through the crowd and to one of the other embassies.

An official-looking car came rushing up from the distance, tires squealing. Two men jumped out and began to yell at the crowd. One of the military-looking types came over to challenge the men, but one of the newcomers grabbed his arm and began gesturing with huge expansive sweeps of his arms. Bystanders began to gather around. Sgt Niimoto wondered what the heck that was about when he saw his phone flashing with a call. He picked up the receiver listlessly.

"Yeah?" Niimoto here."

It was the gunny, his voice elevated with stress. "Tony, no time. In three minutes, the embassy is going to get hit with a Mk402. You've got to take any cover you can. Any!"

The line cut off.

Sgt Niimoto started at the receiver. He really had no idea what a Mk402 was, but it couldn't be good. And only three minutes? There was no way he could get down the stairs, confront the men on the wall, and somehow get out of there. And with the access to the consulate sealed, he could not even make it there.

"Shit, shit, shit, shit, shit!"

What was he going to do? He looked about the cupola wildly. He wondered if the walls of the campamile would protect him. They were pretty strong. He crept over and crouched down against the wall. He felt awfully vulnerable.

Crouching there, his eyes caught the bell. That was a pretty strong piece of gear there. He scuttled over to the bell and crawled underneath it. There was a gap of about 18 inches between the bottom of the bell and the deck, but at least he'd be protected from overhead fire, he thought. But that gap seemed pretty big now. Awfully big. But how could he lower the bell?

He could hit the red lever on the wall, of course, but then he'd be outside. How could he do it from the inside? He climbed partway out from under the huge bell, then grabbed the first aid box, expecting the incoming bomb at any second. He quickly pulled it in and opened it. Bandages, splints, the oxygen bottle, ointments. He grabbed a roll of bandages. Would that work?

Feverishly, he unrolled the bandage. It certainly

looked long enough, but did he have enough time? How long did Gunny say? He took a deep breath and made his decision.

Scooting under the edge of the bell, he ran over to the control lever, standing upright despite being in view of those below. He tried to tie the bandage on the lever and gave it a short tug. The bandage came undone.

"Shit!"

He told himself to calm down then tied a more substantial knot. That should hold. Carefully, he unraveled the bandage as he made his way back to the bell and crawled back under. He carefully and slowly pulled the bandage. The lever moved, then held up. Taking a deep breath, Sgt Niimoto put more pressure on the bandage. He could see it start to untie, but the lever suddenly slipped into position, and the bell began to drop. Sgt Niimoto slid back to the middle of the bell as it slowly came down. Eighteen inches, twelve inches, eight inches, six inches. There was a huge pressure wave that slammed the belfry, and an outrushing of air. Sgt Niimoto felt the explosion more than heard it, then he felt nothing more.

Chapter 49

Thursday Morning, Sadar Patel Marg, New Delhi

Dr. Amarin Suphantarida felt frustrated, useless and tired. He had been in to see the minister twice, but beyond some platitudes, nothing was really said. He had an interesting meeting the evening before, though. Along with Mohammed Kalhil of the Arab League, he had been asked to meet with representatives of the Indian Nationalist Party. There, they had been told that the continuing situation was an anathema to international relations, and that they were appalled that there had yet to be a peaceful resolution. The undercurrent Pui felt was that they wanted the two of them to let the Americans know that this situation could be laid at the feet of the current administration, and should their party somehow slide into power, they would be stalwart allies of the US.

But from the current government, there was really no concrete action. So the siege at the US Embassy was still underway, and the US president may or may not even be alive. No one knew for sure what the situation at the embassy was. Both CNN and BBC, which had been broadcasting live satellite views of the embassy grounds, had been cut off in India a few hours before, and now with the phones out, he couldn't get updates from back in Thailand.

He had taken his driver to try and get closer to the embassy to see if he could get a better feel of things, but he had been stopped and told to wait by the stadium where an Indian spokesperson would supposedly brief the foreign press.

He sat sweltering in the car as the temperature slowly climbed. Even for a Thai, New Delhi sure could get hot. Much to his surprise, his phone suddenly rang. He grabbed it, almost tearing his pocket in his hurry to get it.

"Hello?"

"Pui, this is Rick. Don't ask questions, but where are you? Are you at the site?"

Surprised, he answered "At National Stadium. Why?

What . . . ?"

"Look. In about nine minutes, the US military will drop a Mk102 bomb on the embassy. Most of the blast should remain within the embassy grounds themself. Don't ask me how. But there's concern that people close to the grounds may be within the casualty radius. The bomb sucks up the oxygen, and there can be internal damage to people too close. We need someone to get over there and get as many people away from the embassy as possible. Can you do it?"

The Thai ambassador looked at his phone. If there was some sort of big bomb coming, well, quite frankly, he wanted to get as far away as possible. He was at least a thousand meters from it now, but more sounded better.

Instead, he calmly responded, "Of course, Rick. I am on it right now."

He hung up and told his driver to rush to the embassy who protested that they could not get close, so Pui took the extra fifteen seconds to explain the situation. To his credit, the Indian driver took off, and when an armed policeman tried to stop them at a roadblock, he blew right past him.

The embassy could barely be seen down the tree-lined boulevard, but people in front of it certainly were evident. He was mentally counting down the seconds as they rushed up.

A couple of hundred meters from the embassy, the driver pulled the car into a sliding stop. They both jumped out, and the driver started yelling in Hindi. For a moment, no one seemed to pay attention to him. Then slowly, people began to gather. An officious-looking man, in black paramilitary-type clothes and carrying a rifle, came up and began to shout. His driver shouted back, nonplussed. The ambassador looked at his watch.

"Look. I am the Royal Thai Ambassador to India. In less than a minute, there is going to be a huge explosion at the embassy, and anyone too close is in danger. You've got to get your men back as well as all these people," he said with as much force as he could muster.

When he mentioned an explosion, at least one of the bystanders understood English, because he shouted back to the crowd in Hindi. There was a gasp, then people started to push back. They moved slowly for a few seconds, then some people began to run. People who weren't even there looked up to see the people running, so they jumped up from what they were doing and began to run as well.

His driver continued to extort people, and it became a mass exodus. People were screaming and shouting. Some of the men dressed in black paramilitary gear began to run as well, some of them jumping off the embassy walls to do so. He looked at his watch one more time and shouted to his driver that they needed to get out of there, too. Both of them turned to run. He kept glancing at his watch as they ran, being elbowed by other panicking people. A young woman fell in front of him to be kicked by several people. His driver stooped to help her up, and the ambassador took her other arm as they managed to half-drag her along. As nothing was forthcoming, he wondered what would happen if he was being played, if he was starting a panic for no reason.

He needn't have worried. A huge explosion erupted behind him, pushing him to the ground where he landed on the woman he was helping. There was an odd sensation in his chest as if he couldn't breathe for a second, but then an inrush of air seemed to fill his lungs. He gasped and looked at the young woman who was sobbing, arms covering her head. He helped her up to a sitting position. A food cart lay on its side a few feet away, hot oil spilling onto the road. He looked back.

Near the embassy walls, he could see some people prone. But further out, closer to him, people were struggling to their feet.Pui could hear something coming, a whup-whup. He turned around again to see a huge helicopter, no, one of those hybrid plane-helicopters the Indonesians used for pirate interdiction, but with "U.S.MARINES" emblazoned on the sides, come directly over head and move off to the embassy. He could see the huge rotors tilting as the machine slowed down and began a descent into the embassy compound itself. Three more of the planes flew over to circle the embassy. There was a burst of fire from one of them into the embassy grounds.

The Ambassador had done what he could. Now he decided to sit down right there and just watch the show.

Chapter 50

Thursday Morning, 25,000 Feet Above New Delhi

LT David Littlehawk was in his element, flying his Lighting II. The warrior blood of generations flowed through his veins. The air this high seemed unnaturally bright and clear. Down below him, over the vast metropolis, a ground haze almost obscured the details of buildings, roads, parks, and all the things that make a city a city. He didn't need sight for this mission, though. He simply watched his HMDS to know that he was on target.

A military history buff, he smiled at the thought of being on an actual weapons run. He felt a kinship with the brave Dauntless pilots at Midway, diving down on the Japanese carriers. Of course, he wasn't going to be diving his big F-35C. Nowadays, with smart ammo and guided munitions, when in the attack mode, all the plane had to do was to get in the cone and the munitions would do the rest. Further, unlike the Dauntless pilots, he didn't have Zeros ready to jump his tail or a barrage of anti-aircraft trying to bring him down.

The Mk402 he carried needed to have a near vertical drop for the blast to have the desired vertical attenuation, so there had to be as little lateral drift as possible. And while air friction would essentially eliminate most of the drift if the release point was high enough, the intent here was to get that drift to zero. But with smart ordnance, the bomb itself would take care of that. All LT Littlehawk had to do was to pickle the bomb at the right time. So, it wasn't exactly like flying a Dauntless, basically using the plane to aim the bomb. His HDMS would tell him where to fly and when to release. He didn't want to admit it, but it was almost like being on autopilot. He could have been on a training run back at China Lake.

With the more experienced pilots needed to fly CAP, it was left to one of the junior pilots to take the run, and the skipper thought it ironic that having almost missed the mission, he should be the one to take it in.

His HDMS flashed, and he adjusted the heading of the big bird to match the optimum flight path as computed by his navigation system. "Cougar, this is Chickenhawk. Commencing run now."

"Roger Chickenhawk. God's speed," his CO's voice came over the comm.

He kept his Lightning II on the steady heading. His track monitor kept him honest as he approached the target. The screen on his PCD, set to maximum magnification, could pick up the target through the ground haze now, the middle of the embassy courtyard, right on one of the abandoned vehicles there. Of course he couldn't pick up the laser painting on the vehicle now, courtesy of his wingman, some thousands of feet below him and off to the side, but he knew it was there.

The numbers in his HDMS kept getting smaller, getting to the point of release. His thumb hovered over the pickle. Now! He pushed the pickle and the Mk402 detached and began its solo descent.

He immediately pulled up and started to climb. He was in no danger from his own ordnance. But now that he had released it, he wanted to get back up and do what a fighter pilot did: shoot down planes. Let anyone try something, and this warrior would knock him out of the sky.

Chapter 51

The door shut with a sense of finality, cutting the communications line. Gunny stared at the phone receiver for a moment, hoping Sgt Niimoto understood his hurried warning. He slowly placed the receiver back in its cradle and looked around the vault.

The president and Loralee Howard were looking up at him. Loralee had her M18 and seemed confident. The president looked a little lost. He could see SSgt Child's feet on the deck behind the last set of shelves where they had laid him down. Child remained unconscious, but he was still alive, his strong body unwilling to release its hold on life. PFC Van Slyke moved toward the closed door and took up a position facing it. Outside, they could hear a muffled burst of fire. They all looked at each other, wondering, hoping.

More shots rang out, then an explosion. Gunny put his hand on the door as if that could help him see how Ramon and the major were. Part of him wanted to rush out and join them, but it was too late for that. He could not leave even if he wanted to without jeopardizing those left inside the vault.

The president and Loralee came up to join them at the door. They stared uselessly at it. They could not see anything, they could not do anything, yet the four of them stood there.

Another set of explosions could be heard, fuzzy and muffled as if they were far, far away, then some shots. And incredibly, seemingly a voice yelling out. They could not quite make out what was said, but it sounded like Ramon. A few more gunfire reports, then nothing. The vault became silent, only their steady breathing sounds making their presence known.

Was it over? They looked each other in the eyes, that thought weighing heavily on each of their minds. Suddenly, a low rumble filled the air and the vault shook, items falling off the racks. Loralee fell to one knee, and Van Slyke quickly reached down to help her back up. Gunny took an involuntary breath, afraid there would be no oxygen, but the seals on the vault were good.

"That's them! We just need to hold out a little longer."

There was a palpable sense of relief among themselves.

"Van Slyke, come here. Let's clear this other table here and use it as a barricade in front of the door."

Both of them started shoving electronics and manuals and extra weapons off the table and onto the floor where it joined the items already shoved there by Major Defilice and those which had been knocked down by the explosion. They started shoving the table into place when a set of hands joined them to help. The gunny looked up into the president's eyes.

Between the three of them, they managed to jam the table around a rack and into place on one edge in front of the door.

"OK, let's see what we can pile up in front of this," Gunny said as he started rummaging through the electronics, books, and other odds and ends.

As Gunny lifted two heavy pieces of some sort of testing equipment over the edge of the table, the president asked, "Why not put those on this side of the table? That makes more sense to me."

"Well sir, if we do that, and if a round penetrates through the table, then all of this can become shrapnel. All this glass and metal and plastic, well it can just fly around. On the other side of the table, most of that should be stopped."

Loralee nervously chuckled and said, "He's got you there!"

The president almost seemed to begin to glare at that, but he suddenly relaxed and laughed. "I guess you're right. And maybe he should be making the decisions here, not this dumb California boy."

It really wasn't that funny, but all four of them broke out in laughter. In the stress of the situation, the knowledge that they may be the only ones left alive, and now the hope of a possible rescue, well there was sense of hysteria to the laughter.

"Peter, cover the left side of the door there," Gunny

said.

PFC Van Slyke merely nodded, his swollen face too mangled by now to say much.

"Loralee, if I can ask you to sit here in back of this table and cover the middle, and I'll take the right."

Still chuckling, Loralee got between the two Marines. "What about me?"

Gunny felt a tap on his shoulder.

"Sir, maybe you should just move to the back of the vault over there and get down. We'll cover you the best we can."

"Do you really think that will make any difference if they get in before our people do?" the president asked.

Gunny had to agree and shook his head.

"Then I'm going to join you here. I've got this rifle here, and Peter has shown me how to fire it."

"Roger that, sir. I guess you're right, and the more firepower we have here the better."

He moved over a space to let the president move in between him and Loralee.

"Thank you, Gunnery Sergeant," the president said sincerely.

Gunny placed his weapon butt on the deck and took the president's M18. He hit the magazine release and caught the falling magazine, checked it, and slid it back into the weapon. He pulled back the charging handle and released it before handing the weapon back. He took another full magazine out of his pocket and handed it to the president as well.

"It's on safe now, sir," he said, pointing. "Push it up, and you are hot. Pull the trigger when you have a target. You're good to go."

The president nodded and slipped between Loralee and the gunny. They stared at the door, listening for any sound.

"Why did they do that?"

The other three looked at the president. "Why who, sir?"

The major, Major Defilice, and that woman Marine, Ramon. I don't understand why they did that," he said, looking confused.

Loralee elbowed Gunny McCardle, raising her eyebrows. She was a civilian, but she understood. Perhaps it was because of her brother, or perhaps it was just her makeup.

Gunny looked over at the president and said, "Mr. President, I really don't know if there are words to explain that. It's almost something you have to feel, and in order to feel it, you have to experience the same training, the same camaraderie, the same feeling of family we have. You would do anything to protect your kids, wouldn't you?"

"Yes, but that's different. They're my flesh and blood. Any animal will protect its offspring. That is nature. But those two and the sold- . . . uh, Marines who went upstairs, and the two in the guard booth, they aren't family. They aren't flesh and blood. But none of them hesitated. And that little Ramon, she is just like some of the high school girls I remember. You were going, and she backed you down. She went. And the major went with her."

"Yes, they went. But you're wrong sir. We are flesh and blood. Maybe not by genetics, but we are family. Our bonds are greater than mere genes. And Major Defilice? OK, he isn't a Marine, but we'd be damn glad to have him as one. He understands what it's all about."

Some voices came through from the passage. Did they sound Hindi? They seemed right outside the door. Everyone froze, then relaxed somewhat as the voices seemed to fade away.

The president picked it back up, "But they must have known they were going to die, right?"

"I imagine so, Mr. President. But they both, well, all of them, Major Defilice, PFC Ramon, Sgt McAlister, PFC Rodriguez, Sgt Chen, Drayton Bajinski, and probably the three who went above decks as well, they knew they probably would not be making it. To be honest, I don't know if we are going to make it. But Marines do their duty, no matter what."

Loralee added, "My brother Ian, the one I told you about, the Marine who lost his legs in Afghanistan? You now, all he tried to do was to go back. He kept appealing his decision, trying to show that he was every bit as able as any other Marine despite his two prosthetics. He had a 70% pension, tax-free, and VA benefits, but could he stop and move on? No, he had to get back with his unit before their next deployment. It was his biggest regret that he didn't make it."

There was a small thud against the door. Then some voices. The four froze, not moving a muscle. A soft glow appeared on the door, then a puff of smoke followed by a stream of sparks. An acrid cloud of smoke came into the vault and eddied around the ceiling.

"Get down!" Gunny ordered needlessly.

All four crouched behind the table, protected from the steady stream of sparks shooting into the vault. There were four simultaneous clicks as four safeties were flipped to "fire." Sweaty hands nervously gripped the weapons.

While the vault door was a pretty heavy alloy, it was not made of the same material as the embassy security doors. The torch being used made pretty good progress. They watched the cut line get longer and longer around the lock as whoever was doing the cutting tried to isolate it. When the lock was completely cut, it still did not budge, so after a moment, the cut line started to descend between the door and the vault wall itself. As the lines of the cut met, the locking mechanism fell away, leaving a small gap in the door. PFC Van Slyke started to raise his weapon, but Gunny pulled it down and motioned for all four to get down. As they crouched behind the table, they could hear Hindi voices at the small opening as if someone was looking in.

The torch started up again, and a cut was being made at the very top of the door, cutting through the heavy steel bar there. After a moment, the bar was cut, and the torch shifted to the locking bar on the floor.

There was a shout of triumph, then gloved hands came in to grip the door at the new opening. Gunny motioned to the other three, and they came up, weapons aimed. As the door was pushed open a crack, Gunny opened fire, followed by the other three a split second later.

At least one set of hands was hit as the other two sets jerked back. There was some furious shouting down the passage and footsteps running from further down toward the other offices. They could hear an excited exchange right outside the door. A hand appeared around the edge of the partially opened door and threw in a round object.

"Down!" shouted Gunny as the four crouched behind the table.

A horrible four or five seconds followed, which stretched for an eternity. There was a deafening blast as the grenade detonated. Gunny and Van Slyke immediately sat up, weapons over the edge of the table. Three men tried to rush in, but their concerted burst dropped all three in their tracks.

Gunny looked down at the men, one in plain view, the other two partially obscured by the door. He has just killed a man, maybe more. He was glad the man in front of him was face down. He didn't want to see him, to form any feelings for him. The two other bodies jerked as they were dragged out of sight, but one in front of him stayed, a testament of some sort.

"Good shot, you two. Thanks," Loralee said, coldly looking down on the gunman.

The voices outside stopped. Gunny knew they were regrouping, ready to try and end it all right there in the bottom deck of the embassy.

"Do you despise me?"

Gunny looked to his left in surprise at the president, who had his weapon pointing up, and an almost sorrowful look on his face.

"Sir?" he paused for a few seconds, not expecting such a question at a time like this and not quite knowing how to respond. "With all due respect, I am kinda focusing on the next few minutes. I don't think this is a good time for a retrospective."

"No, I really want to know. I need to know. You've been telling me for the last two days about the Marine Corps, how important it is to you, to them," he waved his arm as if to encompass the entire embassy. "Now all of them are dead. And I'm not stupid. We can't hold out here much longer. And we can't hope for rescue. So now, I want the truth. I was the one who took away your Marine Corps. Me. Michael Antonio David Eduadro. So I am asking you, do you despise me?"

Both PFC Van Slyke and Loralee sucked in their breath. Gunny turned to look back at the small opening in the door. He thought for a second or two.

"No, sir, surprisingly I don't. Oh, I was pissed when you wouldn't let us fly the Corps colors for your honor guard two days ago. That was plain disrespect. But about our Corps, I guess you did what you thought was right at the time, and you can't fault a man for following his conscience. Not that it makes much difference now."

There was some gathering noise from out in the passage. All four turned to the opening and raised their weapons.

"Thank you, Gunny. And for the record, I think now I may have been wrong. I can see that sometimes, government is not all about dollars and cents. It's about heart and soul. And I know this may mean nothing, but if by some chance we get out of this, I'm going to bring back the Corps. I swear it."

"Mr. President, I appreciate that. But I'm afraid you just might not get that chance. Here they come!"

Loralee Howard, diplomat's wife and sister to a Marine, Private First Class Peter Van Slyke and Gunnery Sergeant Jacob McCardle, United States Marine Corps, and Michael Eduardo, President of the United States of America, lifted their weapons and faced their incoming fate.

Chapter 52

Thursday Morning, 1000 Meters From the US Embassy, New Delhi

Sitting in the jump seat, Col Jeff Lineau could see the first Osprey flare out and land in the embassy courtyard some 1000 meters ahead. There had been some discussion about FAST-roping, but he had decided that letting the embassy walls protect the debarking Marines was more important. Well, Marines and Navy. There had been some last minute additions to the mission. A SEAL team was included in the first bird. They were going to take position in the bell tower as a sniper team and cover the operation from there while Captain Kreig's 3d Team secured the courtyard.

There were some other additions as well. Each bird had a corpsman from the *Reagan* to supplement Doc Hollister, and both the Colonel's bird and Capt Mahmoud's had a flight surgeon as well. There were two Indian-American sailors with them who could speak Hindi and Urdu. Each bird had a Navy "co-pilot," pilots who had at least flown rotary wing planes before, and each door gunner was a Navy gunner's mate, freeing up four Marines to join the others entering the embassy. There were also two deck controllers or "yellow shirts." The Ospreys didn't have enough seats for all the pax, so some had sat on the deck between the sling seats for the entire trip. Hopefully, more people would have to sit that way on the way back.

Peering through the Osprey's windshield, he could see the tell-tale flashes of the door gunner engaging something, then the big bird almost disappeared behind the distant wall. He started a mental count. Five seconds, ten seconds, fifteen seconds. He wished his comms worked, but the area was back under blackout. Suddenly, the first bird rose fully back into sight and pulled away, just as the second bird, with LtCol Ricapito's team aboard, flared in from the other side of the embassy for a landing on the roof.

As they flew closer, he glanced down through the windows beside the co-pilot's feet. There were quite a few people down there on the street, many of them pointing up at them. For the hundredth time, he hoped that none of the people besieging the embassy had anti-aircraft weapons. At this height and speed, his bird, in particular, due to its approach lane, was pretty vulnerable.

As they came up to the embassy, the second bird pulled up and out. With the Osprey's flight angle, he could clearly see the newly painted "United States Marines" and US flag, which had been hastily applied to cover the Indonesian markings. His own Osprey rushed in, ramp already down.

Col Lineau quickly unbuckled and followed the rest of the Marines out, his headquarters on the heels of Major Roberto's team. As soon as his foot hit the courtyard deck, the Osprey jumped into the air to go and take its place in the orbiting station above the embassy.

The embassy grounds looked surprisingly in good condition. The various plants and trees had obviously suffered a big force, and the embassy itself looked a little scorched and had some broken windows above the first deck, but frankly, he had expected worse. There were, however, quite a few bodies, perhaps thirty or more, lying motionless around the courtyard. As he ran up to the embassy's front door, he passed several bodies that had blood froth coming out their mouths. Not a pretty way to go, he thought.

He looked up into the bell tower to see the SEALS getting in position. Capt Kreig already had most of his Marines up on the wall, weapons pointing out, but no one was firing.

The fourth and final Osprey took off after debarking Capt Mahmoud and 1stLt Hoins. Capt Mahmoud quickly moved his Marines out to the consulate building to keep anyone there from coming over to the embassy itself. Hoins just as quickly took her team up to join the colonel at the steps to the embassy.

There was a flurry of shots from inside the embassy. He rushed up to the front door itself when LCpl Neller, 1st Team's runner came bursting out the door from inside.

"Sir! We've run into some bad guys in there when we tried to clear the first deck. Major Roberto thinks we can take them, but that's gonna keep us from checking below for a few minutes. He wants to know if Colonel Ricapito can get there."

The plan had been for the Major Roberto to sweep in the embassy from the front, then rush down the main passage to check the two offices where the president was last known to have been. He was then to send a team down to the lower deck to check out the vault where there was also a possibility they had holed up. He wished he had been able to get confirmation on where they were from Major Rogers. He wasn't all that confident that the major would have even been able to reach them during the break in the jamming, though.

LtCol Ricapito's team was to land on the roof and blow an opening there, then make its way down, clearing the building and then covering the retrograde from that vantage point.

There was a rattle of fire and a few rounds pinged around them. Col Lineau swore and spun around to see most of Mahomoud's Marines and some of Kreig's firing en masse into a broken window on the consulate building.

Just then, there was a blast from somewhere above him on the embassy roof. He looked up to see a Marine leaning over the edge, waving small green flag. Colonel Ricapito was in, but how fast could he adjust? He needed to get the word, then move down five decks.

He looked to Capt Mahmuoud, but he and his Marines were engaged with somebody, and with the people he saw outside the embassy grounds, he wanted Kreig's presence on the walls keeping them back.

"Neller, tell Major Roberto that he has to get into those offices now. Whatever it takes. If they're clear, he needs to check all the others. We'll take below decks. McNair, get over there and tell Captain Mahmoud to give me ten Marines. Have them meet us below on the bottom deck."

As PFC McNair took off across the courtyard, the colonel turned to the lieutenant, saying, "It's us Stacy. Let's get your team down the ladder in there and do a search. They could be anywhere, but the vault is our best chance."

She turned to her small team and gave a quick

command, then led them into the embassy. They all knew where the ladder going down below was, but knowing on paper and in real life can sometimes be a little different. As they rushed in, they veered to the left somewhat before spotting the ladder and rushing to it, a few rounds pinging around them from the gun battle going on down the long passageway there.

Colonel Lineau was right on their heels. As he rushed in, the Sergeant Major caught his eye, sitting on the deck, back up against the bulkhead, holding his left forearm while one of the *Reagan*'s corpsmen worked on the biceps. He had chosen come in with Major Roberto's team and had evidently taken a hit. His anger was a palpable force, and as he rushed by, Col Lineau knew the Sergeant Major would not let something like that keep him back.

He rushed past the shattered Post 1, not taking the time to look in, and dashed into the ladderwell just as some rounds came bursting up. He ran through the opening, dragging LCpl Luc with him and to the steps leading up and out of the line of fire. One of the lieutenant's Marines was just standing there, rounds pinging around. He grabbed her by the body armor and swung her out of the way as well.

Leaning over the rail, he looked down to see the lieutenant, the master guns, and two Marines standing almost elbow-to-elbow on the landing below, exchanging gunfire with a handful of men standing at the bottom of the ladder. Almost in slow motion, he could see the master guns stagger, then one of the other Marines as well. But with their body armor stopping the rounds, neither went down, and the gunmen at the bottom of the fell one by one until none were firing back.

Colonel Lineau vaulted down the steps with the other two in tow. He had to leap over another Marine, Cpl Smith, who had taken a hit to the leg before he could join the other four rushing to the bottom. There were several dead gunmen there and a table blocking the way, which had to be straddled. On the other side, there were several dead Marines: Sgt Chen, PFC Ramon, and that was probably PFC Fallgatter. There was a rather large military-looking man (secret service?) and another civilian there. There was barely enough time to let all of that register. They rounded the corner and saw three gunmen, rifles in hand, at the far side of an ajar door to what had to be the vault. His heart sunk. Were they too late? His gut told him that the president and any others were in there, and from the gunmen's attitude, it did not look good.

As they came into sight, one gunman saw them and tried to scramble into the vault to get out of the line of fire, but as one, the now seven Marines opened up, and the three men had no chance. They were cut down where they stood.

Ten Marines from Capt Mahmoud's team came stumbling down the ladderwell behind them. With a tremendous sense of loss, Col Lineau moved forward with the others to look into the vault, knowing what they would see.

Chapter 53

Thursday Morning, US Embassy, New Delhi

Two rifles appeared around the edge of the door, firing wildly in. The rounds ricocheted around the vault, but no one was hit. All four of them fired on the rifles, but seemingly none of them were hit either. This happened twice more before one of the rifles dropped on the floor. Gunny didn't know which one of them had hit it.

Some fingers came around the edge of the door and started pulling it open wider, but this time, a round hit the target, sending a piece of the finger flying off to land on the deck, clearly in view of those inside. They could hear shouts of pain.

The inside of the vault was becoming full of smoke, and the bitter acrid smell was getting overwhelming. Loralee's M18 started to waver, and she finally slid down to take a knee. She looked up apologetically and coughed.

There was an increase of incoming, and PFC Van Slyke grunted, slapping the back of his butt. But he kept upright, returning the fire. His magazine emptied, and with a calm collectiveness, he slipped in another mag. It was hard to see, but it looked like several people rushed past the door to the other side. His ears were ringing so much that he didn't trust Van Slyke to respond to words, so Gunny pushed Van Slyke over to the left a bit to give him a better angle to fire at anyone coming from that direction.

There was another increase in the volume of incoming fire, and the three of them shot wildly out through the door. He didn't think he was hitting anything, but he couldn't stop. He was at his end game. Smoke obscured his vision. As he changed his magazine at the same time as the president, PFC Van Slyke held up his hand. The firing had stopped for a moment. OK, they needed to use their ammo smarter. They slowly aimed out the door, waiting for a real target.

PFC Van Slyke shifted his point of aim further to the right and fired off a double tap burst.

"Shit!" a voice rang out in English.

It was immediately followed by a different voice. "US Marines, US Marines! If you are American, we are here to rescue you. Identify yourselves!"

Gunny couldn't believe he heard right. His ears were ringing, but the words were unmistakable, and the accent sounded right. In fact, it sounded like Master Guns Chung!

"This is Gunnery Sergeant McCardle. We are holding our fire," he shouted as he put out a hand to push down the muzzle of the president's weapon.

A head peaked in. It was the master guns.

"Is the president here with . . ." he started before seeing the president standing there, unshaven, dirty t-shirt, and holding an M18. Nonplussed, he said, "Mr. President, can you come with us please? We have a flight ready to take you out of here."

Marines came in and helped the four of them out.

Colonel Lineau was there himself, and he caught the Gunny's arm, asking "Anyone else in there?"

"Just SSgt Child, sir, in back of the rack there, on the deck. He's hurt pretty bad and isn't conscious. I think that's all."

A tremendous wave of despair and fatigue washed over him. His det, his Marines. Only Van Slyke and he made it. And Child, if you could count that as "making it." How could he explain his failure to keep his Marines alive?

His mind was a blur as they were hustled down the passageway to the ladderwell. Marines were already picking up the bodies. One Marine he didn't recognize picked up PFC Ramon, her limp arms swaying lifelessly as the Marine moved. Tears came to his eyes.

"Them too," he told them, pointing out Drayton and the major.

SSgt Pierce, from the KL det, simply nodded.

In a daze, he made it up the ladder, assisted by someone who didn't register with him. They got up to the entrance, and he could see the damage inside Post 1. Two other Marines were at the glass, looking inside with somber expressions. Marines were moving about with a sense of purpose. Major Roberto came out of the passageway leading toward the ambassador's office.

Gunny Phelps from Quantico was there, and he gave Gunny McCardle a thumbs up. He saw the president then, and rushed out shouting to someone. They half-dragged the president to the opening in the door, finally getting him to release his M18.

Gunny Phelps came back and spoke to Major Roberto. "It's clear sir. I think we need to go now."

"Roger that, Gunny. Get that bird down."

Gunny Phelps turned to what looked like a sailor in a yellow jacket, like they had on carriers and said, "Petty Officer Martin, bring her in." He looked out the opening at someone else. "You two, cover him!"

Gunny Mac leaned against the bulkhead. His mind was floundering, like it was stuffed with cotton. He sat there alone despite being surrounded by Marines. He could hear a loud noise growing from outside. A Marine poked his head through the opening.

"It's landing now!"

A half-dozen Marines surrounded the president and moved him outside. Not knowing what else to do, Gunny Mac followed, but stopped as he got through the opening. A huge Osprey was landing, "US MARINES" emblazoned on its fuselage. Gunny Mac hadn't seen one of them in years. The Marines ran the president down to the bird and up the ramp. Others pretty much carried Loralee to the bird. She raised an arm and waved to him as she was carried up the ramp. Other Marines poured in. The sailor in the yellow jacket waved two ping-pong paddle-like signals, and the Osprey fairly jumped into the air. Another Osprey started to come in for a landing. Colonel Lineau stood next to him, watching the president leave.

Gunny turned to him and said, "Colonel, we've got three Marines in the reefer in the ambassador's pantry. We've got three Marines somewhere above deck. And we've got Sgt Niimoto up in that bell tower. All of them come with us. We're not leaving anyone behind."

Without pause, Colonel Lineau called up LCpl Luc and another Marine. "McNair, go tell those SEALS to bring Sgt Niimoto's body with them. Luc, tell Colonel Ricapito to bring the Marines in the reefer and whoever is above decks. He may have already found their bodies, but they come with us."

The second Osprey landed in the courtyard. Colonel Lineau looked at him. "You two get on that one. I want you out of here."

"Begging the colonel's pardon, but no sir, I need to stay until all my det has been loaded on board. I need to know that they're going back to the US for their families."

The CO put his hand on his shoulder and nodded. He gestured to PFC Van Slyke, who was being attended to by a corpsman. The two made the walk together, the corpsman still working on him as they moved, and boarded. An orderly line of Marines formed up and quickly got onboard. The yellow-jacketed sailor waved his magic wands and the Osprey took off, a small windstorm buffeting those left.

Half of the remaining Marines left their positions on the wall to begin to form again. LCpl Luc came running up to the CO.

"Sir, Colonel Ricapito has the three Marines from the reefer and will have them on the roof in three mikes. They've found the other three Marines, too. They are ready to take off as soon as your bird leaves."

"Thanks, LCpl Luc. You get ready, you and McNair. Stick on my ass. I don't need you two wandering off," the colonel said.

A third Osprey landed in the courtyard, and Gunny could see another coming in to apparently land on the roof of the embassy.

PFC McNair came running up, saying, "The SEALS, they are coming down now, but they said there are no Marine bodies up there."

Gunny looked up in confusion, then a little anger.

"Bullshit! I spoke to him just a little while ago, right before this place got hit. He is up there!"

Or could the blast have knocked him out of the tower? Or even burned his body up? He looked at the bodies lying about the courtyard. None seemed too terribly damaged from outward appearances, so no, his body had to be still around somewhere.

Master Guns Chung walked out and called to the CO. "Colonel, we've got to go. There is some movement over the wall, maybe a force coming here."

"We're not going without Tony!" Gunny shouted, running into the courtyard, around the Osprey and through Marines starting to board.

LCpl Luc ran after him. They ran into the broken hatch to the bell tower and almost collided with a group of four SEALS coming down.

"You, come with me!" gunny ordered, his tone brooking no argument.

The six of them crashed up the steps and finally through the broken hatch into the cupola. Gunny looked about in desperation.

"Uh, just what are we supposed to be doing here?" It was the SEAL lieutenant, looking perplexed.

"We've got a Marine here, and we're taking him back," Gunny said with certainty.

He looked around, then over to the edge where he could see out over the embassy wall. He couldn't see a body on the ground there.

"We told the other Marine, there's no one here. No body, nothing."

He rushed over to the other side. He could see nothing on the ground there, either. He could see an Osprey on top of the embassy, Marines boarding. He could see the Osprey below him in the courtyard, almost everyone evidently onboard, the colonel standing there looking up at him, gesturing.

"Sorry, but we're leaving," the lieutenant said, his SEALS starting to move out.

Gunny looked back into the cupola. Despair struck out at him, almost a physical blow. Then he noticed something was out of place. He couldn't figure it out for a moment, but then it struck him. The bell. It was flush on the deck. He wondered how that happened. Did the blast do that? He moved up to it. A small tangle of rolled cotton was coming out from under the bell, ragged and torn.

"Get back here! Now!" he shouted as he started to push at the bell, to tip it over, but it was too heavy. LCpl Luc started to help.

The four SEALS exchanged glances, then rushed over.

The six of them moved to one side and tried to push it up. The bell tipped, then fell back down with a thud.

"OK," one of the SEALS shouted, "on my command, heave, then you Marine," he pointed to LCpl Luc, "stick your radio under the edge. Then we can grab it. OK, HEAVE!"

The bell tilted up six inches, and LCpl Luc was able to jam his useless radio under the edge. The six men lowered it onto the radio, shifted their grips, then grasped under the edge of the bell. With one concerted heave, the bell came up and over to crash on its side up against the cupola wall.

Lying on the deck where the bell once covered, Sergeant Anthony Niimoto looked up in a daze, a small medical canister on his chest slowly feeding oxygen around his face with a soft hiss, a medical kit open beside him.

"Hey Gunny," he croaked out, "do you have anything to drink?"

Chapter 54

Saturday Morning, The White House, Washington, DC

The President of the United States of America sat in the chair in front of his desk in the Oval Office and looked at the three others there. This was the first time he had a chance to meet with them, his trusted advisors.

Well, the old Chinese curse of living in interesting times was surely upon him. The last three days had been a hectic whirlwind of activity, and only today were things sinking in. Sitting in the Oval Office right now, in some ways, it seemed like the last week had never happened, that, it had been a dream. But President Eduardo was a changed man, and that brought reality into focus.

After his hurried evacuation from the embassy, the flight back to the *Reagan* was almost anti-climatic. He found out later that the plan had been to lower him from the Osprey to a waiting sub, but the complete lack of Indian response had prompted them to return to the *Reagan* directly, and, in retrospect, much to his relief. He hadn't envisioned dangling from the bird to get on a sub. Instead, the Osprey had made a graceful landing on the *Reagan*, and he had walked off to the cheers of hundreds of sailors on the flight deck. The unreality of it was such that he actually stopped and shook hands with as many sailors as possible, as if he was back on the campaign trail.

He was taken up to the flag officer's stateroom where he called his wife, her tearful cries of relief almost overwhelming him. He made some other official calls while wolfing down a pastrami sandwich handed to him, then got a quick shower, shave, and change of clothes (he never did find out whose clothes those were) before being whisked away back down to the flight deck where a waiting C2 was there to fly him to Diego Garcia.

On the way down, he saw Gunny Mac in the mess decks and went up to him. Gunny stood up to face him. The president simply put his arms around the gunny in a bearlike hug, then stepped back. No words were exchanged. None needed to be.

He took the flight to Diego Garcia, surrounded by an escort of Navy fighters, where he met up with Secretary Pitt. Pitt's plane was re-designated Air Force 1, and together, they made the long flight back to the US. It wasn't a relaxing flight, of course. There was numerous phone calls to the US and with various heads of state, there were several briefings on what had and was still happening, a brief stopover in Hawaii for refueling, and only a few hours of sleep.

The landing at Andrews was almost festive, with music and huge numbers of officials and press. He felt like a returning hero, but in his heart, he felt that this "hero" was an imposter. He really hadn't done anything heroic. Others had done that.

A quick stop at the White House for a carefully choreographed press conference and medical check-up, then it was off to Camp David with his family for the night and next morning. As he looked around Camp David, it seemed odd not to have Marines there. Secret service agents had taken over each of the Marine details.

That afternoon, it was back to the White House for meetings and more meetings, with the vice-president and Cabinet, with the Senate and House leaders, with his staff. Then he insisted on calling the families of all those killed in the takeover and rescue. That was pretty rough, but he knew he wanted, no, he had to do it. Finally, he was able to get upstairs and to sleep.

Now, after his morning briefings, he had the Director of the CIA, his National Security Advisor, and his chief of staff sitting around him. He pondered what Bo Waters had just said.

"So that is the way it needs to be?" he asked.

The president looked over to Arnie, who nodded. He put his hands in back of his head, elbows out. He swung around a bit so he could look out the window. A Marine was there, standing at parade rest, back toward him. The president didn't know his name, but he must have just made it back from India himself. A sense of security tinged with affection washed over him. He smiled, then turned back.

"We don't hold the Indian government responsible?

At all?" he asked.

"Not quite, sir. We have gotten assurances that they will pay for all the damage to the embassy as well as make payments to the victims' families. But we cannot make the takeover out to be an overt act by the Indian government. That would be tantamount to war."

"But it was an act of war. An attack on US soil."

The National Security Advisor agreed. "Yes, it was, sir, but with the snap elections called for, well, this particular government looks like it is going to be out on its ass."

"And that looks like a pretty sure thing?" he asked, looking over at Kai-yen.

"From our projections, I would have to assume it will be a significant win for the Indian National Party. Popular backlash against the Prime Minister and the ruling part is growing, and that was most likely the tipping point for his dissolving Parliament and calling for new elections. He probably thinks this is his best chance at retaining power, i.e., before full disclosure of his party's support of the takeover."

Despite the seriousness of the conversation, the president had to smile. Kaiyen was an old, old friend, but she was perhaps the only person he knew who would actually use the phrase "i.e." in a conversation. He was actually surprised she didn't use the full Latin "*id est.*"

"I have also spoken with Viraq Dasmunsi personally. He assures us that India is and will remain a close ally, and he hinted he is willing to re-open past negotiations, such as opening up their financial markets, under his new administration. He made what I understood to be an appeal to help keep this situation as what has been described in the Indian press."

"So, we act like this was a mere group of terrorists, which acted due to Indian armed forces being elsewhere on previously scheduled exercises. This 'terrorist' group saw an opportunity and grabbed it, and the Indian government was slow to respond due to a fear of escalation and loss of life? And that they invited us to conduct the actual evacuation due to it being US soil?"

"Pretty much so, yes, sir." Arnie sat back, watching

him.

"And that will fly?"

"Well, the government did send in the police as soon as the Marines started landing. They arrested over a hundred people. But no, this won't fly with most of the world's leaders. On the other hand, it really only has to fly within India and within the general American populace. Oh, FOX, CNN, and all the rest will cry that there's a cover-up, but I've already reached across the aisle, and we'll have full cooperation on that front. And the rest of the world will just accept what we agree to say." He paused. "And that's the value of modern diplomacy. People act as if outright lies are the truth without batting an eye."

"Oh, I know we have to do this. But it really sticks in my craw. If you were there, if you had seen those young men and women die, well . . . well, that's over and done with. Arnie, I want Secretary Pitt briefed on this, and I want him to take point. I want him in bed with soon-to-be Prime Minister Dasmunsi. Let's make this fade away as soon as it possibly can. Pitt is a good guy, by the way. I want him brought in closer to the circle in the future.

"OK, I've got another meeting in a few, right Arnie? So quickly, about those other things. The awards? Do we have Congressional sponsors yet?"

"Yes sir, "Arnie nodded. "Congressman Birch requested to sponsor all of them."

"Good. I want this done quickly, not going through a couple of years of DOD approval. But push them on those other awards, too. I want these people to feel our deep appreciation. My appreciation.

"And the Marines?" the president added, looking a little apprehensive.

Arnie laughed at this one and said, "Mr. President, I have made a few calls. This one is going to sail through without a problem. The Marine Corps is pretty popular right now, and there were already a lot of people, people in Congress and out in the constituency, who rather thought the Marines should never have been down-sized. Even if you hadn't promised what you did, I think someone on the Hill would have hitched their wagon to this train."

The President looked a little relieved. Hopefully, this was a promise he could keep.

"You being a bona fide hero too isn't hurting matters. We don't have too many presidents personally fighting terrorists, you know," Arnie said, motioning over to where the M18 the president had used in India was already framed and hung on the wall.

The president felt guilty about that, posing, in his opinion, as a hero. But he also understood political capital when he saw it, and he did feel a certain pride in having stood up and traded rounds with an enemy.

"And I still want your input on the bloodletting. Lefever is gone." The president raised a hand to cut off his chief of staff's protest. "Oh, I'll wait a little bit, but that asshole is out of here within two months. I am willing to take your advice on Wright. She can stay out her term. But I want your input on who may have been acting out of their conscience and who was acting for political gain. And then, what you think we should do about it."

The president stood up and said, "Thanks for your support. You have served your nation, but I personally appreciate your loyalty."

He shook each hand in turn. As they left, he walked back to his desk. The Marine was outside, still at parade rest, his dress blues tight against his broad back.

The President of the United States smiled.

Chapter 55

Two Months Later, HQMC, Quantico

Brigadier General Jeff Lineau sat in his office, listening to the hubbub going on outside the hatch. He realized that inside the office, things had gone silent.

"Excuse me? I didn't catch that," he said.

LtCol (Col Select) Tye Saunders looked down at his notebook, then back up. "I just told you we are authorized to approach all former Marines now serving in the other branches about returning to us. We really are going to need a senior cadre to help guide this expansion, and the Chiefs of Personnel of the other branches have pledged their support."

General Lineau smiled, saying, "I guess it helps getting that support when the Commander in Chief himself asks for it."

There was a general chorus of laughter.

Tye added, "I spoke with Major General Lawrence this morning. He has decided to give up his second star to return to the Marines as our new FSSG CG. He told me one star with the Marines was much better than any number of Army stars."

There was a chorus of "Ooh-rahs" at that quote.

"That's really good news. I knew General Lawrence, back in the day when he was still a Marine. He is a great logistician, and it'll be nice to have him back and out of his Army greens. He is going to help a lot in getting us back on our feet. I'm glad he saw fit to give up his Army career and that second star," General Lineau said, feeling a big sense of relief at the news.

The Sergeant Major, arm still in a sling, spoke up, "On a related note, we are starting to interview retired Marines about coming in for temporary orders. This afternoon, I've got an interview with that Staff Sergeant, the one who lost his legs in Afghanistan, the brother of Loralee Howard. If he's fit to sit in back of a desk, I'll send him into see the XO for final approval. But, as you say, if the request comes from the Commander in Chief, I guess we're going to find that this

Marine still can serve."

Another round of laughs went around the office.

"Speaking of Ms. Howard, I haven't heard back about her move. We had Marines helping her?" Gen Lineau asked.

Major Mahmoud spoke up, "Yes, sir. The entire S-1 and S-4 sections showed up Saturday and packed her up. Her belongings should probably be half-way back to her hometown now. She said she was going to visit a sister, then head on back. She just didn't want to stay in DC anymore."

"OK, let's keep track of her. I especially want her to be here for the Birthday Ball. You know, I talked with her on the *Reagan* and then again while flying back to CONUS. That is one amazing lady."

Cpl Tyson knocked and stuck his head in the hatch. "Sir, Admiral Conners is here to see you."

"Send him in!"

He looked at the others. "Ladies and gentlemen, can you give me a few moments?"

His staff got up and started to leave when Joshua Conners walked in, looking out of place and a little lost in civilian clothes. Tye Saunders reached out to offer his hand.

"Good to see you, Admiral Conners."

Conners took the offered hand, saying, "That is just Mr. Conners now, I'm afraid."

"Begging the admiral's pardon, but no it isn't. You are Rear Admiral Joshua Conners, Friend to the Corps. You will always be an admiral to us. And we'll never forget what you did for us."

The others nodded in agreement. It couldn't be true, but it seemed like a small tear formed in the admiral's eyes, a tiny bit of moisture.

"I'll take the 'Friend to the Corps' title with pride." They looked into each other's eyes before the XO turned away and followed the others out of the office.

The tall man in civilian clothes hesitated a moment, then turned to his old classmate, hand out. "That star looks good there!"

"Well, it's only temporary. It hasn't been officially confirmed yet, and they could still come to their senses any minute now and kick my ass all the way back to North

Dakota. But the President says wear it, so I wear it."

"So what happened to 52-and-a-wake-up?"

"Bastards won't let me retire now. Something about needing me to build up the Corps again."

"Well, that's good for you. I can't see you sitting on your ranch pushing cows around. Julie would be bossing you around unmercifully," the admiral said.

"You've got that right!"

They both laughed and sat down. The silence carried on a little bit too long for comfort.

"Josh, you know how much that sucks. I can't believe they did that."

"Oh, we both knew our careers were over after this. We both went in with open minds. You came out a hero, and I'm not being funny here. You really were. And I'm happy you escaped the headman's axe. But we both knew what was going to happen, and OK, it happened. I still wouldn't change a thing."

"But we saved the president. If we hadn't acted, he'd be dead by now, and we might be at war. You were the one who did that. You made it possible," Jeff said earnestly.

"But I broke the cardinal rule in the Navy. I acted without telling my chain of command. They don't trust me. Audrey Race at PACCOM chewed my ass, and the CNO? You don't want to know what went on in his office. Oh I know," he said forestalling Jeff's protest, "I am getting the Distinguished Service Medal for the action, but the CNO left no room for interpretation. I was told to retire. So I did."

"And I told you, let me talk to the president. I think I can get his ear for this."

"And I appreciate that. You can't understand how much. But no. I'm done. I'm going home," Joshua told his Academy roommate.

The silence stretched out again.

"But now you've got your star." He brightened. "A real Commandant. So they're bringing back a whole division?"

"Yep, and the FSSG. No air wing, though, for now at least. We're in negotiations with the National Guard now to take back Camp Lejeune."

"Hey, that's great."

"We're getting back the Marine Barracks in DC from the Park Service, and General Litz says he wants me there. But I want to be in Lejeune. I can't command from DC!"

"Heavy is the crown. Well, you'll have to be a politician now, and get somebody else to do command. Just think if it, though, you should get another star. Both of us making two stars. I never would have believed it."

"Three," Jeff Lineau responded quietly.

"Three? Three what?"

"Three stars. I have to wait until the division is stood up, but I'm going to get three stars," he said, looking a bit apprehensive.

Josh Conners threw back his head and laughed, standing up and rushing over to give him a bear hug and pound his back.

"You bastard! Three stars! Who'd you blow for that?"

The Commandant of the Marine Corps gasped for breath.

"I never said they knew what they were doing! Hell, all I care is that the Marines are back. Even if we owe it to a Navy puke like you, the Marines are back!"

Chapter 56

Three Months after the Embassy Takeover,
Wisconsin Avenue, Washington, DC

First Sergeant Jacob McCardle drove the staff car up
Wisconsin Avenue, past the trendy restaurants and bars. As
the light turned red, he slowed the Ford down. Through the
side window, he saw a good lunch crowd eating at the
sidewalk tables at the Mumbai Café. Two young women were
sitting in the sun, laughing, drinking what looked to be
mango lassis. He wondered if they would like Thums Up
colas. Probably not. No one except him did. The light turned
green, and he continued north.

The ceremony had been well-organized and was
touching, he had to admit. The Rose Garden looked peaceful
and serene. The white chairs for the attendees had been
placed with care. Four placards on silver frames had stood to
the left of the podium with photos and bios of the four
honorees.

First Sergeant McCardle got there early, then stood in
the back as the dignitaries and guests filed in and took their
seats. He saw Loralee Howard, so he sat down beside her,
disregarding the name tag on the seat assigning it to
someone else. She reached out and squeezed his arm.
Finally, all were in place, and the doors to the Oval Office
opened. The President, General Lineau, the Speaker of the
House, and the immediate family members came out and
made their way to the garden.

The First Sergeant hadn't seen the family members
since the funerals, but their images were imbedded in this
mind. Some of the immediate grief present at the funerals
might be missing now, but a sense of solemnity, sadness, and
yes, pride now was evident.

The cameras rolled as people took their seats and the
president went to the podium to speak. And it was a good
speech: heartfelt, earnest, and respectful. Good politicians
could do that, but the First Sergeant thought that this was
not an act, that it really was from his heart.

Then it was time for the awards. The President called each family in turn up by the order in which they fell and presented the wreathed star with the sky blue ribbon. Sergeant Tracy Ann McAllister. Private First Class Jesus Emilio Rodriguez. Major Stanley Paul Defilice. Private First Class Haydee Huertas Ramon. All presented with the Medal of Honor.

Each family solemnly accepted their loved one's award with both sadness and pride. Little Mac's father, a sun-weathered cowboy, thanked the president and stoically accepted his hug. PFC Rodriguez's grandmother, the person who had raised the young man since he was a toddler when his mother was sent to prison, openly cried. Major Defilice's young son stepped up, clearly not understanding the importance of the ceremony, his small, innocent face looking back at his mother, the major's ex-wife, to see what he was supposed to do. And Pedro Ramon, Princess' father, took the award in his hands, looking at it for a long moment before crossing himself and looking heavenwards, quietly mouthing his pride to her, his only daughter.

Normally, a Medal of Honor took a year or two to get approved, but by having a Congressional sponsor recommend these in a special session of Congress, these four were shoved through the system in record time. Not that anyone in DoD was complaining.

The evening before, First Sergeant McCardle had gone up to Arlington to see the graves of PFC Ramon and Major Defilice. They had been buried side-by-side there, and the grass already covered any sign of the digging of the graves. But the small images of the medals were already on the tombstones. Someone had already had them emplaced. The First Sergeant had just stood there for half an hour, lost in his thoughts before leaving and going back to the hotel reserved for the ceremony guests.

He continued his drive north. He thought about all that had happened since that fateful day. The sense of despair at losing his Marines, the sense of joy when he saw LCpl Steptoe and LCpl Saad on the *Reagan*. Yes, those two had made it. LCpl Kramer hadn't. He had been shot while trying to free Mr. Dravid, who had been leading the gunmen on a wild goose chase, and when they figured that out, they held him down to execute him. LCpl Kramer wasn't going to allow that, and he rushed from a closet to save him. Eight-to-one odds might work in Hollywood, but they don't usually work in real life, and Hank Kramer was cut down, soon to be followed by Mr. Dravid. But Steptoe and Saad were able to draw the men up one more flight of stairs before the bomb hit, and both had been knocked unconscious. LCpl Steptoe had recovered enough to catch the attention of LtCol Ricapito's Marines as they came pouring in through the hole in the roof. LCpl Saad had taken some fairly serious cuts from flying glass, but he was quickly attended to and brought back to the *Reagan* without problem.

Getting back to the US was a blur to him. Then there were the debriefs, the funerals, the press interviews. He had taken a week's leave, but he felt lost back home, so he had come back to Quantico three days early. His promotion to First Sergeant was a surprise. No more "Gunny Mac." "First Sergeant Mac" did not have the same ring to it. Everyone called him "First Sergeant McCardle."

There had been another smaller ceremony at the Pentagon that morning before the Medal of Honor ceremony. The new Chairman of the Joint Chiefs, General Kantres, and the Commandant had presented the awards to the rest of the det.

Navy Crosses went to Tony Niimoto and Hank Kramer. Hank's father accepted the award for him. 2ndLt Tony Niimoto looked good in his new bars. He was reporting to OCS at Ft Benning in two weeks. Soon, the Marines would have their own OCS back, but for now, it was still the Army school for new looies.

Corporals Steptoe and Saad were both presented the Silver Star. Both had very large extended families at the ceremony. Sergeant Chen and Private First Class Fallgatter were also presented the Silver Star. It hurt the First Sergeant to see that no one was there to accept the medal for Chen. His mother had been contacted, but she refused to come, saying she had better things to do. Loralee Howard, who had become somewhat of a den mother to the Marines, took the award instead. Her brother, SSgt Cannon, looked a little old for a staff sergeant, but he stood proudly beside her in his uniform. You could not even tell that he had prosthetics under his trouser legs.

LCpl Wynn, SSgt Child, Cpl Crocker, and Cpl Ashely were awarded the Bronze Star. There had actually been some tension about that at the Department of the Navy. Some people felt that while their loss of life and injuries were deplorable, except for Wynn, they hadn't actually done anything to earn a medal. But this had taken on a political life of its own, and the medals were awarded.

Midshipman Fourth Class Peter Van Slyke also was awarded a Bronze Star. His face was still pretty disfigured, and he had already had two surgeries, but he had been appointed a midshipman at the Naval Academy. It was a presidential appointment of course. It looked like the line of Van Slyke officers in the Marines was going to continue unabated.

And First Sergeant McCardle? He was awarded the Silver Star. He looked down at it, hanging off his dress blues blouse. He couldn't decide if he felt guilty or proud for having it. He had been offered a field commission as well, but after thinking long and hard about it, he turned it down. He was enlisted and he was proud of that. That was what he knew how to do.

And he was going back to India. A First Sergeant normally did not lead a detachment, but the embassy was being repaired and would open again in two months, and he requested to go there and bring the det back. Cpl Steptoe also asked to return, and the rest of the det would come from various other posts.

He pulled in the large circular drive at Bethesda Naval hospital and off to the right where he found some official vehicle parking. Getting out of the car, he made his way to the front and walked in.

"May I help you?" the older man at the information desk asked before he took in the First Sergeant's face. He had been on the news enough lately, and with his dress blues and Silver Star hanging there, he was immediately recognized. "Oh, First Sergeant McCardle. Welcome to Bethesda Naval Hospital. Can I help you?"

"No, thanks. I know where I'm going."

He had come to visit Van Slyke and Saad while they were there, but he hadn't been to where he was going now. But he knew the way. He went down the main passageway, then to the elevators in the far back, on the right. He took one up to the third floor and walked down to the ward on the end. The nurse at the desk looked up to help, but he waved her away.

He slowly walked to the third room on the left, 3002C. He knew the number already. He stared at the number for a minute before he steeled himself and walked in.

Staff Sergeant Joseph Child lay on the bed, a respirator in his mouth. The formerly huge, impressive figure seemed shrunken and withered. A purple heart was still in the box at the small table beside the bed, and on the bed, between his feet, was the bronze star. His father must have left it. His father lived in Bethesda now, taking care of his son. He had accepted the bronze star that morning without a word, but he had not gone to the Medal of Honor ceremony.

The Physical Evaluation Board and just made a determination that SSgt Child was no longer fit for duty in the Marines. He was given a 100% disability and a retirement date of the first of next month. He would be moved to the VA Hospital in Detroit where he would live out however long he had left in a room there.

First Sergeant McCardle stood there, watching the slow rise and fall of SSgt Child's chest, listening to the wheeze of the respirator. This was the man of whom he had been, quite frankly, in awe. A better Marine than him. He wondered for the thousandth time that if their roles were reversed, would Child have brought back more of the det home?

He walked to the side of the bed and reached out, taking Child's hand in his. It was limp and cool, so unlike the man who had moved it, who had controlled that hand before.

This was why the First Sergeant hadn't been able to come up to this room before. He couldn't accept what this man had become. But now he had to face it, to say goodbye. SSgt Child was a hero, a real Marine. One of a long line of heroes. But now he had passed the torch. And Ramon, Rodriguez, and McAlister had taken him up on it. Niimoto and Kramer. Van Slyke, Saad, and Steptoe. They would take that challenge into the future, bringing that tradition of honor and courage with them to a new generation of Marines.

And yes, he admitted, so might he. That was his mission now. To prepare for the future of the Corps.

He took an envelope out from inside his blouse and opened it, taking out a photo. It was a photo of the detachment in front the Marine House, taken a week before the presidential visit. He had downloaded it on his phone, and when he got back to the US, he had printed it out. Before, the eyes of the Marines who had died seemed to look at him accusingly. But now, as he looked at it, it seemed more as if they were looking at him in support. They were family, after all.

He placed the photo neatly on Staff Sergeant Child's chest. Taking a step back, he came to attention and saluted. Holding the salute for a few moments, he brought it down sharply.

"Good bye, Joe," he whispered.

He did an about face and marched out of the room and into his future.

THE PROUD

Indian Ocean

Asad closed his eyes against the salt spray being kicked up by his small panga's prow as it raced across the waves towards the huge tanker ahead.   He glanced over to the right to the companion boat matching their speed as they chased down the behemoth.   He could see his cousin Ghedi hanging onto his panga's gunwales as it was pounded by the waves.

Finally, his first action as a *badaadinta badah*, or "saviors of the sea."   For awhile, though, he hadn't been sure it would ever happen.   Finding a position with a Habargedir crew hadn't been difficult after he and Ghedi had made the trip from Galinsoor down to the coastal city of Hobyo.   They were all of the same clan, after all.   But finding a target had not been so easy.   After being launched from the mother ship almost 10 days ago, the two pangas, nothing more than open skiffs, had been making their way across a vast expanse of nothing.   The two inland boys had suffered, much to the amusement of the more seasoned fishermen who made up the rest of the crew.   With fuel and food running out, at last, lights in the blackness caught their attention.

Now, as the morning sun came into its full glory, they were in the final sprint to the huge ship.   "Asad" means "lion," and he felt like a lion, in the final charge to bring down his prey.   He checked his AK one more time.

At a signal from Raage, his helmsman, the second boat peeled off from them.   The plan was to approach their prey from the stern, one boat to each side of it.   Their targets rarely put up a fight, but it was better safe than sorry.

Their target loomed bigger and bigger as they bounced over the waves.   Asad thought the freeboard was much higher than on the hostage ship upon which they had

1

practiced back outside of Hobyo before setting out. None of the other three crewmen seemed concerned, though, so he tried to put it out of his mind.

As they got closer, Asad picked up movement on the stern. Two crewmen seemed to be manning a fire hose. Part of Asad's anxiety washed away. If they were manning a fire hose, then they obviously had no weapons. As they came up closer, within rifle range, Asad raised his weapon to target the men. Taban, the boat leader, reached over and hit down hard on the barrel of his AK.

"You idiot! Who told you to fire on them? Haven't we told you that they are worth money to us, but only if alive!"

Asad started to protest. He hadn't been about to fire. He just felt it was prudent to be ready for anything. But with the bouncing of the boat and the looming bulk of the tanker, he let his protest die in his throat. He would clear that up later.

Just before they reached the stern, a sudden jet of water hit their companion boat. Ghedi and the others were knocked over, and their boat swerved aside to evade the blast. Asad figured they would switch sides and hit them next, but in only a moment, his panga was moving alongside the huge vessel and essentially out of reach.

As they moved up the side of the ship, the little panga bounced around in the waves created by the ship's wake. Their practice run in Hobyo was on a ship at anchor, but this was different, and he never realized it would be so severe. He had visions of being thrown overboard and being sucked down into the huge propellers and chopped up like *oodkac*. With a curse, though, Raage jerked hard on the big outboard to give them a little breathing space, not that it seemed to make that much of a difference.

They continued to move up alongside the immense length of the ship, still keeping close to give them some protection from anyone above. Finally, they reached just short of the bow, where the small curvature of the hull gave them even a bit more protection. Taban stood up, balancing himself on strong legs, grappling gun to his shoulder. Taking aim, he fired, and the hook went up into the air, line trailing. It seemed to hang suspended for a moment at the apex before falling back to the other side of the freeboard. Taban quickly pulled it tight, and immediately Hanad started scampering up, rope attached to his belt and AK strapped over his back. A white face suddenly appeared over the side, staring at Hanad as he climbed. The man above reached over to try and dislodge the line, but with Hanad's weight on it, that was going to be difficult.

A stuttering of rounds went off beside Asad's ears. Taban had picked up his Uzi and peppered the ship's sides around the man, who quickly jumped back out of sight.

Asad kept his eyes glued on Hanad. He was the key to all of this. Either he or the climber on the other boat had to get a ladder attached. The tanker had much higher freeboard than most targeted ships, so that was going to be even more difficult. But they had no choice. Besides the fact that this ship would bring in a huge payment, they would be out of fuel soon and adrift in the ocean. They had to get aboard.

The huge ship began to move away from them. Its captain obviously thought to try and crush the panga on the other side. Asad was not too concerned, though. There was no way the big ship could move quick enough to crush the agile skiff.

Hanad seemed to reach the top. Before going over the edge, though, he unlimbered his AK and pointed it forward. His rifle would precede him. This was a critical moment. A smart and brave sailor would lie in wait, then as soon as the barrel made it over the edge, grab it and use it against Hanad, who would be at a huge disadvantage hanging over the water.

It looked like the sailor was neither smart nor brave. Hanad jerked himself over the railing and disappeared from sight for a moment. In a few moments more, the rope that had been attached to his belt began to jerk upwards, pulling up the rope boarding ladder. It seemed to take forever, but finally, the ladder made it to the top and was secured.

Taban motioned to Asad to go up. He slung his AK and tentatively reached for the ladder. The small skiff bounced up and down in the waves, making that first step perilous.   If he fell between the boat and the ship, he could be crushed.   If he survived that, he would undoubtedly drown.   No one would come back from him during the takeover.   He took a deep breath and stepped onto the first rung of the ladder, which was lying on the bottom of the panga's deck.   As soon as he had one foot on it, the boat dropped away from him, leaving him dangling on one foot a meter or so above the panga.   As he struggled to get his other foot on the ladder, the boat came slamming back up, almost knocking him loose.

"Let's go, Asad.   Now!" Taban ordered.

Steeling himself, Asad took a step up.   This time, when the skiff fell away, he was more secure.   Slowly, trying not to look down and very conscious of the water beneath him, he worked his way up.   He was never so grateful when he was finally able to reach over the railing and pull himself aboard.

"It's about time, country boy.   Here, watch him," Hanad said, pointing with the muzzle of his rifle to an overweight, pale-looking man sitting in front of him, hands clasped on the top of his head.

Asad looked at the man.   He had never been this close to a *cadaan* before.   He wondered if the tinge of pink on the top of the man's balding head was his natural color or if the paler face and neck was.   The man had a defeated look in his eyes.

Hanad hurried over to the other side, presumably to tell that crew to come back over to the starboard and use their ladder to climb up.   Asad wondered where the second of the ship's crewmember was.   He could only see the one sitting in front of him.   He warily glanced around, sure that someone was going to jump out at him.

The clatter in back of him almost made him jump, instead.   But it was Taban, just getting aboard.   Taban merely nodded at him before going to join Hanad.

The foreigner didn't seem like a threat, so Asad risked a glance up to take in the length of the ship.   An incomprehensible mess of pipes and valves stretch back to the superstructure, seemingly a kilometer away.   This was

4

one huge, huge ship.

"Where's Taban?"

Raage had clamored aboard. They were truly committed now. Their small boat was undoubtedly drifting off now, unreachable. It was this huge ship or nothing.

Asad motioned towards the other side, out-of-sight due to some raised structures on the deck.

"And this is our first hostage?" Raage poked at the man with the muzzle of his ancient M14, laughing as the man jerked back, sliding along the deck on his butt. "*Kha'nis calooleey*," he snorted out, before trooping away to find the rest.

Asad looked down again at the fearful man. He agreed that the foreigner was fat, as Raage said. He wasn't too sure about the *kha'nis* part, though. His rifle wavered a bit. This man was no threat, just a sorry individual. He moved a few steps forward to the man, then used the muzzle of the rifle to lift the man's chin. He wanted to look into the *cadaan's* eyes, wondering what was going on in his mind.

"*Pleez*," the man said, looking back up at him. Asad could understand some Arabic, but whatever the man was saying was beyond him. It was obvious that the man was begging him, probably for his life. And that pissed Asad off. Did he look like some soft woman? Was he not a lion, someone to be feared? Whatever sympathy he might have had for the man washed away. He smacked the man against the side of his head with his rifle muzzle, not hard enough to stun, but still sending a message that this foreigner would understand.

"Shut up!" he yelled out.

The man cowered on the deck, arms covering his head, whimpering in fear. Asad felt a brief and sudden moment of compassion before he suppressed it. This was no place to be weak.

"Bring the *cadaan* aft," shouted Hanad, poking his head around some pipes before rushing off.

Asad felt some disappointment. Was he just a hostage guard? He shrugged and motioned with his rifle for the man to get up and move forward. The man slowly got up, and as he moved forward, kept looking fearfully back at him.

Did the idiot think he was going to shoot him?   No money to be made in that, Asad knew.

Ahead of him, Asad could see people rushing back towards the ship's superstructure.   He caught a glimpse of Ghedi ahead, and despite the distance, he could see the excitement in his cousin.   And here he was, nursemaid to a fat *cadaan*.

The man was moving slowly, and they hadn't even reached the superstructure when the huge ship began a slow, ponderous turn. He hadn't heard any shots.   Was the ship's crew trying to get away with them already aboard?   He motioned to his hostage to sit down.   The man looked at him warily as he slowly sat down on the deck.

Asad wondered what he should do.   In rehearsals he had been tasked with assaulting the ship's bridge.   Should he go there?   He was just about to do that when Ghedi came down a ladder with a big smile on his face.

"The *cadaan* abandoned the bridge.   The ship is ours," he said, excitement still evident in his voice.

"What about the crew?" Asad asked.

"Oh, we were a little slow.   The last one got into a compartment just as we rushed up.   Dalmar called it a '*panic room*,' something in their language."

"What language is that, anyway?" Asad asked his cousin.

"English.   This is an American ship, and we now own it!"

6

Chapter 1

6 weeks earlier
Naval Station Norfolk, Virginia

Staff Sergeant Burke Davidson, USMC, looked at his Table of Equipment in frustration, wondering for the hundredth time if he had made a huge mistake.   Eight months ago, he had also been a staff sergeant, but in the Army.   More specifically, he was a Ranger with a solid career ahead of him.   But after all that mess at the US embassy in India, he had accepted the offer to go back into the newly reconstituted Marines.   He still wasn't sure why he had done it.

At 17, after getting his parents' permission, he had joined the Marines, but he had only been a PFC when the bulk of the Marines had either been absorbed into the rest of the armed forces or been given their walking papers.   Burke had been lucky, being accepted for a transfer into the Army, and the Army was now what he knew.   Especially after getting scrolled into his Ranger battalion, he found acceptance and pride, and the Army was his home.   But when the request came for SNCO's and NCO's with former Marine experience to apply for transfers, he got a hair up his ass and put in the paperwork.   Maybe it was the press those Marines who fought off the mob in New Delhi received.   Maybe it was memories of his short time as a Marine.   For whatever reason, he applied, and his application was accepted.   So here he was in the temporary barracks at Little Creek, the platoon sergeant for 1st Platoon, Kilo Company, 3d Battalion, 6th Marines.

The 6th Marines was the first regiment officially reconstituted, and 3d Battalion was the first battalion to go on float.   After months of pre-deployment work-ups, it was deemed ready, given the Commandant's blessing, and given orders to mount up.   But as usual, Marines or Army, the higher ups didn't have a clue.   Anyone who thought this battalion was ready for combat was fooling himself.

Take the T/E in his hand, for example.   He had less than half of his required equipment and little hope of obtaining it.   He had brought this up with Gunny Darius 20 minutes ago.

"If we don't have it, that's because the Army hasn't thrown it out yet," was the Gunny's rote reply.

Ha ha funny, he had thought derisively, but that didn't help him get what he needed.   He was tempted to call some of his buddies down at Ft. Bragg to see what he could scrounge up, but he wasn't sure what his reception would be. Voluntarily leaving the Rangers was not something accepted very well.

To top things off, he had no lieutenant to run interference for him.   Oh, the new looie was coming, after he finished off some sort of promotional tour, and given his history, he could be a good one.   Cpl Steptoe vouched for him, too.   But he needed to be here now, getting the platoon ready.   No one could out-do a Ranger SNCO, but it would help to have some bars, even gold ones, supporting him.

SSgt Davidson sighed.   *No rest for the wicked*, he thought, as he got back to work.

Chapter 2

Same day
Naval Station Norfolk, Virginia,

Second Lieutenant Anthony Niimoto, USMC, nervously pulled on the bottom of his Summer Service Alpha jacket while standing behind the battalion XO.   Major Hansen rapped on the CO's hatch, then stuck his head in.

"Sir, Lieutenant Niimoto is here, checking in," the major informed the commanding officer.

Tony didn't know why he was nervous.   He had met the president himself and the commandant, both on more than one occasion.   Now he was sweating meeting his new commanding officer?

"Send him in, major," the CO's voice came out through the hatch.

The XO stood to the side, motioning Tony in.   Tony stepped through, marched up to the CO's desk, and came to attention.

"Second Lieutenant Niimoto reporting for duty as ordered, sir!"

He stared at a spot a foot above the CO's head. Peripherally, Tony took in the short, barrel chested man sitting in front of him.   Tony had never met LtCol Pavoni before, but he knew of him, of course.   After the downsizing of the Marine Corps, it was hard not to at least know about other Marines, and as the Alpha Company commander of the Marine Security Battalion, then Major Pavoni was well known as a pugnacious fitness freak, but one who enjoyed tipping back a beer or two.   Tony knew that the Marines in his company both respected and feared the man at the same time.   Now he had been both promoted and given command of the first battalion to deploy since the reestablishment of the Marines as a fighting force.

LtCol Pavoni came to his feet, hand out over his desk.

"Welcome aboard there, lieutenant.   Glad to finally get

you here.   You're the last of the battalion's officers to arrive, and none too soon.   We get underway next week, as I'm sure you already know."

Tony shook the CO's hand, not sure if he was still supposed to be at attention or not.

"Thank you, sir.   And I'm sorry for the delay in—"

The CO held up his hand to stop him.

"Don't worry about it.   We all know the reasons. Stand at ease, by the way."

Tony shifted to a modified parade rest.

"What we have to do now is get you to your platoon and get you up-to-speed as quickly as possible.   Normally, you would've been here for the entire work-ups, but that wasn't going to happen."

Tony started to say something, but once again, the CO held up his hand.

"I know it wasn't your fault. And if the commandant tells me to hold a boat space for you, well, I hold a boat space.   I've got you assigned to Kilo Company.   I'm not sure if the Sergeant Major or XO told you yet, but Kilo will be cross-decking on smaller fighting ships while the rest of the battalion will be on the two amphibs. Right now, we've got to get you to your company.   But you owe me a chat.   Maybe in Rota, I want you to sit down with me over a beer and give me the real scoop about Delhi, Marine-to-Marine, not what that Fox made-for-tv movie showed."

Tony reddened a bit at that.   He'd had enough of that movie already.

"First things first, though. You're out of uniform," the CO said, a scowl on his face.

Tony panicked.   *Out of uniform?*   He had been prepped hard before all the public appearances, so he should know how to get dressed.   He looked down quickly at his uniform to see what he might have missed.

The CO opened a drawer and took out a green braid. "Do you know what this is?" he asked, his scowl turning into a smile.

"Um, no sir?"

"This is the French fourragère."   He moved around the desk and started attaching the braid to Tony's left epaulette.

"The 5th and 6th Marines were awarded the fourragère after they earned the Croix de Guerre with palm leaf three times during World War I. And now, this is part of your uniform until you leave the regiment."

Tony's heart stopped pounding. It seemed as if the battalion CO was not above messing around with his Marines a bit, scaring him like that.

"So, anyway, let's get you down to Kilo. All your fun and games are over now, so get cracking."

"Aye-aye, sir," Tony replied, coming to attention, again.

The CO hadn't actually said "dismissed," but Tony took it that he was, so he about-faced and marched out of the office. The XO was still standing there, and behind him was a lance corporal.

"Lieutenant, this is Lance Corporal Upton. He'll take you over to Kilo later, but he'll be your guide for now. Captain Svenson and his headquarters are out training with the company and won't be back until this evening." He looked at LCpl Upton, for confirmation, who nodded back. "So get yourself checked into the Q, change into cammies, then draw your gear until your company gets back in."

"Aye-aye, sir!"

As they walked down the passage to the front hatch, he could see Upton surreptitiously eyeing his chest. Tony was used to it. Not too many Navy Crosses were worn by active duty Marines. First Sergeant Ames had one, back from Afghanistan. And there was a sergeant, one of the Army transfers, who had a Distinguished Service Cross. But that was about it.

"Sir, was that all true?"

"Was what true, lance corporal?"

"You know sir, what that movie said. In India."

Tony sighed. He was never going to get used to this, he knew.

"Sort of true. But they made it out to something much bigger."

There was a pause as they reached the front hatch and stepped out into the sunshine, putting on their covers before continuing.

"Cpl Steptoe, he says what they showed about you is

11

true."

Tony stopped and looked at Upton. "You know Cpl Steptoe? Is he here?" he asked excitedly.

"Oh, yes, sir! He's one of our radio operators. Didn't you know that?"

"No, I didn't," he responded, but with a bit of spring in his step.

He hadn't seen Stepchild since the President's State of the Union address, back, what, nine months ago? And now they were serving together again. That thought gave him a surprising amount of comfort as he looked forward to this deployment.

Chapter 3

Early that evening
Naval Station Norfolk, Virginia

Tony was waiting in the company office when a familiar figure ambled in. Tall and soft, he looked more like the village idiot than the genius he was.

"Stepchild!" Tony called out, rushing over to shake hands.

"Tony . . . I mean, Lieutenant, sir, glad to see you again, sir!" Cpl Steptoe told him.

Tony immediately felt a small gap widen. Even though he had been a sergeant while Stepchild had been a lance corporal, they were still enlisted together, in a very small detachment. Stepchild's reaction highlighted the gulf between them now, with him being an officer. It saddened him a bit, to be honest.

He pushed that thought away.

"And how the heck are we in the same company? Is that a coincidence?"

"Well, you know, sir, friends in high places, I guess. I begged the skipper to be one of your radio operators, and he didn't seem to think I was getting above myself."

"But I thought you would be one of those computer jocks, in a nice air-conditioned office."

"Well, technically, I'm a 2802. A radio operator. But after I went to go visit SSgt Childs up at that VA hospice in Detroit, well, I decided I needed to get out with the real Marines. You know, in the mud and the rain."

Tony was quiet for a moment. SSgt Child had been a Super-Marine. He had earned a Silver Star at La Paz, only to fall in Delhi. Steptoe had hero worshiped him, hence his "Stepchild" nickname.

"Well, it's good to see a familiar face. I'm glad you're here with me," Tony told him. "I ran into Van Slyke when I was a reviewing officer at the Naval Academy. He's doing well there, but since the State of the Union, I haven't seen

Saad or First Sergeant Mac."

"Well, you know I went with First Sergeant Mac back to Delhi before I requested field duty. He just left there for the company headquarters. Corporal Saad's at the detachment in Cairo now." He looked up at the front hatch. "Oh, here's the skipper. I guess you've got to go."

Tony looked up to see three Marines, still dirty from training, come in the hatch. He tried to read the nametags, which were partially covered by deuce gear, wondering which one was Capt Svenson.

A tall, lanky African-American Marine saw him and called out, "Ah-ha! Our long lost lieutenant, I believe. Welcome aboard! Let me drop this gear, and let's talk."

Svenson? Tony wondered. He sure didn't look like a Swedish Viking. He dutifully left Stepchild and followed his new company commander into his office, taking a seat when the captain gestured for him to do so.

Capt Svenson draped his deuce gear over a hat stand in the corner, stretched, and then held out his hand.

"I'm glad to have you here at last. We needed you here a couple of months ago, to be blunt. But I guess some things can't be helped. Although why the Marines, in their infinite wisdom, thought having you there ringside at that UFC fight in Vegas was more important than you training with your platoon is beyond me."

"You saw that, sir?"

"Once the CO told me you were mine, I watched a lot of what you were doing. After I called some of my buddies down at Benning to see how you did in school. Do you know what they told me?"

"Um, sir, well, I finished at number two at the Infantry Officer Basic Course," he answered, feeling a bit on the defensive.

"Yes, academically, you did well, and your personal fitness was good. But they also told me that you lacked a bit in leadership. And, leadership, lieutenant, is more important than book smarts. But you're young yet, still green at the gills even if you're a mustang. And SSgt Davidson, your platoon sergeant, is going to help you out there. He's pretty seasoned, a Ranger who accepted an inter-service transfer.   Listen to him, and he'll help you."

Tony had gone to Benning for his officer and infantry training as the Marines were still reconstituting their own schools back in Quantico, and it seemed that every one of his classmates professed a desire to be a Ranger. (He suspected that some of that may have been mere lip service. He had heard about how difficult the school was.)   He wasn't quite sure how much he was going to like having an ex-Ranger as his platoon sergeant, and he really didn't like the inference that he personally was somewhat lacking.   For the last year plus, he had been feted pretty much everywhere he went, and now it was hard to get this reality check.

The captain hadn't stopped talking.   "And this is really going to be important to you, 'cause you're going to be on your own.   Your platoon will be on the *Jason Dunham*. I'm putting Second and Weapons Platoon with me on the *Gaffert*, the new LPD, and we'll be the point of main effort. Third will go on the *Independence*, which was the first littoral combat ship.   Sorry you get the older platform, but frankly, your platoon is probably the least combat-ready right now.   I should tell you though, that the captain of the *Dunham* is none too pleased with you being aboard.   They fought against being assigned the entire platoon.   But they have a history of having Marine FAST teams on board going back to 2006, even if those teams were only 20 Marines. Without an embarked extra medical team, the ERSS or ERRS or whatever they call them, I guess they conceded that you can be shoehorned in someplace.   Consider yourself lucky, though, that you get your entire platoon.   Third can only embark with two squads."

"The rest of the battalion is going to be on the *Pearl Harbor*.   I'm not sure how much you've been told yet, but the main body of the battalion will be doing some showing of the flag and re-introducing the Marines to the region, but we are designated the Maritime Raid Force, and our task will be anti-piracy. That's why the company is not on one deck, and you and Third aren't even on an amphib.   We're going to cut square circles in the ocean to keep the pirates at bay, so be ready for a long, boring deployment.   And as I am sure you realize, this is pure politics. Some of your friends in high

15

places want to make sure the Marines get some press.   So no matter how the Navy complained about you and Third going on combatants, well, they weren't going to win that fight."

He got up and poured himself a cup of coffee from where it had been brewing on a bookcase.   He offered Tony one, which was accepted.

"Not everyone in the Navy is upset, though.   We're supposedly taking over this mission for now from the Navy, and the SEALs training us couldn't be happier.   They think this will free them up with their 'real' missions," he said, using his fingers to make quotation marks in the air, "so they can poop 'n snoop to their hearts' content.   To be honest, I think this is a mistake, to push us before we're ready.   But like I said, this is purely a political decision to get the Marines back in the public's eye as a fighting force.   The Marines got a huge boost from Delhi, but I think the administration needs to justify the expense of building the Marines back up as a fighting force."

Tony wondered at the heavy use of "they" and "Marines" instead of "us" and the more commonly used "Corps."   This was a temporary office, so it wasn't surprising that there were no personal mementos up on the walls.   But Tony was now fairly sure that his company commander was another Army transfer.   Not that it really mattered, he guessed.   The Corps could get former Marines in the higher enlisted and officer ranks, and new recruits and second lieutenants were no problem either, but for lower NCOs and mid-level officers, well, most of these had to come from other services.

"We've got two more days of training here in Little Creek, then a 96 for the long weekend.   Since you've just arrived, I'd like you to stay here on duty so the other platoon commanders and the XO can join the troops and go home before we set sail."

The company commander had said "troops."   That settled it.   He was Army.

Captain Svenson looked like he was going to say something else.

Here it comes, Tony thought. The *don't-expect-any-*

special-treatment lecture, which he had received several times so far.

But the captain shook his head slightly, then stood back up, offering his hand.

"I'm glad you're here now, and I look forward to having you in my command.   We're all professionals here, and that's what I expect from everyone in the company."

"Thank you, sir, and I'm glad to be here, too."

Chapter 4

The next day
Naval Station Norfolk

The Black Hawk came in fast, flaring out over the ship below. Tony pulled his heavy gloves tighter around on his hands. He was familiar with the Fast Rope Insertion Extraction System (FRIES) having fast roped at Benning, but that was over an open field.   This time, though, it was onto a deck of a mothballed freighter which was under contract to the Navy.

He felt nervous.   Sliding down a heavy woolen rope in the middle of all the things that stick up on a ship was one thing.   But this was also the first time most of his platoon would see him in action.   He knew enough not to take over from SSgt Davidson, who had led the rehearsal the morning before, but he didn't want to watch as an observer from the pier at which the target ship was berthed, so he had inserted himself with 2d Squad to observe the takedown.   He just prayed that he would land standing and not on his butt.

The Navy SEAL instructor, BM2 Alfryd, had barely acknowledged Tony before the final brief and before they boarded the Blackhawks.   Back in Delhi, Tony had been rescued by 1stSgt Mac and a SEAL team, and Tony wanted to know if the petty officer knew any of them, but the sailor's brusque manner didn't seem to offer the opportunity.   So Tony had just stood around while his platoon went through their paces.

Capt Svenson was there as well, and given his comments about Tony's supposed leadership weakness, Tony was extremely tempted to step in and take over.   But he would have had to know what was going on to do that, and the mission itself was the most important thing, so he just hung back and observed.

But he knew he was being observed as well.   Only Stepchild knew him, and now he had both his platoon trying to get a feel for him and his company commander observing him as well.   That put more pressure on him than sliding down 20 feet of rope.

The two ropes hung on either side of the helo, and the first man to fast-rope was sitting at each one, legs over the edge, hands on the rope. The helo came to a hover, and at the command of the fast rope master, the first two men hopped off and started to descend. The next two men immediately moved over and stepped out, followed by the next two. Tony has shifted his position to be ready, and without hesitating, grabbed the rope and swung out, legs wrapping around it and acting as a partial break, slowing his descent. He felt the rotor wash and had a glimpse of another Marine going down the opposite rope, but within seconds, he hit the deck and stepped back. Immediately, the Black Hawk took off, clearing the area.

Tony had been on the last bird in, so he stepped to the side of the freighter, watching his Marines move through their paces. He had to admit that they seemed pretty professional. Maybe his platoon sergeant knew what he was doing after all.

Capt Svenson was observing the operation from the ship's flying bridge. He was with the company first sergeant, who Tony hadn't officially met yet, and the two seemed to be discussing what was happening. The first sergeant looked down at Tony, then flicked a finger at him, seemingly pointing him out to the commander. Capt Svenson gave Tony a brief glance before going back to his conversation.

What does that mean? Tony wondered. *Should I be walking around? Should I be taking charge?*

He couldn't get a feel for his new boss, and that made him uncomfortable. For most of the past year, 2dLt Anthony Niimoto had been somewhat of a hero, and the admiration and even deference given to him had propped him up, had given him a bit of an inflated ego. Now, his new commander didn't seem too impressed, and that brought Tony back to earth. He knew he had to get his head on straight and prove himself worthy of his shiny new bars.

To be truthful, Tony felt a bit of a fraud. While the rest of his detachment in Delhi had fought, really fought, and many of them had died, Tony had basically sat in a bell tower and taken target practice at the rioters (which was now the "official" term used for the people who attacked the embassy.)   He had been hungry and very, very thirsty, but except for when the Navy had dropped that mother-of-all bombs, he had not really been in much danger.   Discomfort, yes, but danger, no.   Yet he had become a 15-minute celebrity, and he had been called "hero."   The thing is, he didn't feel like one.   And now, it seemed as if he had a company commander who saw through the facade.

As his platoon went through its paces and secured the ship, Tony wondered if he was up to the task.   Not just to impress Capt Svenson, not just to impress his Marines, but to prove to himself that he could be a good officer and not just some guy who could shoot a rifle.

Chapter 5

A week later
Aboard the USS Jason Dunham, at sea in the Atlantic

SSgt Burke Davidson pulled off his utilities trousers, and in his skivvies and t-shirt, slid into his bunk. He was exhausted, and despite the other two petty officers in the berthing space holding a conversation, he knew he would have no problem falling asleep.

At Little Creek, Burke had gone onboard the *Pearl Harbor*. Intellectually, he knew it wasn't as big as a carrier, but it seemed immense to him. The embarked Marines had dedicated berthing spaces, the mess decks could feed hundreds of hungry Marines and sailors at the same time, and they even had a climate-controlled gym. There were soda machines and a geedunk where you could buy snacks and small items. It was like being on a small base.

The *Dunham*, on the other hand, did not offer the same amenities. Oh, it looked like a warship, fierce and tough. But it was not designed to carry troops, and when you added the platoon and the Navy Special Boat unit, things were rather tight. Their gear had to be stashed in any available nook or cranny, and simple things such as chow and showers became an intricate dance of coordination. Nothing seemed to mesh.

The crew seemed OK, but it was obvious that the Marines were considered outsiders, a bump in the road to their mission. A few had complained to Burke that the *Dunham* was not an amphib, that it was not supposed to carry Marines at all. Burke just shrugged his shoulders at that. Orders were orders, after all, and complaining to him served no purpose. He had no power to change things,

He naturally gravitated to BM2 Doug Kaye, the Special Boat Unit petty officer in charge. Even if he was Navy, his detachment was also an add-on, not really part of the crew. Plus, he was a pretty good guy. He was an island boy, from Honolulu, and that was a far cry from Burke's home on Maryland's Eastern Shore, but they seemed to be cut from the same cloth.

And Doug had some pretty good toys.   His .50 cals were pretty awesome, and that was a language any Marine or soldier could understand and appreciate.   He had even agreed to let the platoon test the big guns off the fantail tomorrow after his unit got in their firing.

Burke glanced about the compartment.   He shared it with Doug and four other petty officers.   It barely seemed big enough for one, much less six.   At least it was dry and comfortable enough.   As a Ranger, Burke had spent many a night in the mud, getting eaten alive by mosquitoes or freezing in the snow.   The Navy was a different sort of life, and he wasn't sure he could ever spend a career doing the same routine over and over, but there were bennies to it.

He slipped on a pair of eyeshades he had taken off a United flight, turned to the outboard, and drifted off to sleep.

Chapter 6

Naval Station Rota (Base Naval de Rota)
A week after embarkation

Tony Niimoto requested permission from the duty officer to
go ashore, saluted the colors on the fantail, and hurried
down the gangplank. After a week onboard, it was good to
get off and place his feet on Mother Earth.

The trip itself hadn't been that bad—more boring than
anything else. Oh, there were things to do to keep busy, but
not much that was exciting. They had spent one afternoon
fast-roping onto the *Pearl Harbor* while it was underway,
and that was a little different than doing it on an old
freighter sitting at the dock. The highlight of the crossing
had been the .50 cal fam fire SSgt Davidson had arranged
with the Special Boat Unit. But for the most part, the
crossing was pretty bleak.

As a security detachment Marine, Tony had been
subject to numerous inspections, and like most junior
Marines, he somewhat resented when the officers kept
hovering about during the preparations. Their job was to
get lost, then come back and do the actual inspection itself.
The SNCO's could handle getting the unit ready. But now,
as a new platoon commander, he also had the urge to get
down into the berthing compartments while the men cleaned
them up or prepared for a gear inspection. It was all he
could do to keep back and let SSgt Davidson and his squad
leaders do their jobs.

With that pent up need to do something, he was finally
in a position to be grateful that his platoon sergeant could get
the men ready for base liberty. That left him without any
responsibilities, and he was the first one off the ship.

He may have been the first one off the *Dunham*, but he
was not the first Marine ashore. The three lieutenants from
the *Gaffert* were already walking down the pier. Only Rob
Kaus wasn't there yet even if Tony could see the
Independence already tied up at her berth.

THE PROUD

Leading the trio was 1stLt Stan Kremer. He was a pretty hard man to miss. Stan was a Naval Academy graduate, one of the few to get a Marine billet, although with the Marines being built back up, that should change. He had been an All-American wrestler at the Academy, placing second at the NCAA tourney at heavyweight. He was big, but not much of that was fat. Tony had met him for the first time on his second day with the company, and he immediately gravitated to the big guy. His blue eyes held a twinkle that seemed to project good humor. Company XO's were not always the "alpha" in a pack of lieutenants, but in this case, he held the others in his orbit. But it was impossible to hold that against him. If Tony was a betting man, if he had to wager on one of them becoming Commandant one day, then his money was going on Stan.

Gil Desroches was the Weapons Platoon commander. He had been born in Haiti, and although he had come to the US at a young age, he had never quite gotten rid of his French-tinged Caribbean accent. It was obvious to Tony that both Gil and Stan were tight, which made for an interesting-looking couple. Stan was big and fair, looking like a short-haired version of Marvel Comics' Thor. Gil was short, broad-shouldered and very dark. What they both had in common, though, were prominent smiles that seemed to be permanently fixed on their faces.

The third member of the group was another newbie, 2dLt Joe Hartigan. Tony didn't know what to make of him. Joe was rather quiet, but he seemed always to be listening, taking things in. Except for the Marine high and tight, he looked like any other guy with nothing to make him stand out. He looked like he could have been serving burgers at the local McDonalds, wherever his hometown was. Tony didn't even know that yet.

"I see you didn't waste any time, there. I told Gil that you'd still be onboard," Stan said with his usual smile plastered on his face as the three of them walked up.

"Told you, my man," Gil replied, punching Stan in the arm.

Tony winced at that. Gil hadn't pulled the punch, and it landed solidly. Stan didn't seem to flinch, though.

"When there's beers to be had, we mustangs don't mess around.   We know what's what, right Tony?" Gil went on.

Tony had to smile at that.   A cold beer really did sound great at the moment.   He'd grown fond of Sam Adams while at Stanford well before enlisting, though.   He hadn't needed his time as an enlisted Marine to learn to appreciate some brew, but this kind of banter was the norm in the Corps amongst friends.   He hadn't felt that camaraderie since Delhi, and it felt good to feel those bonds again.

The whole feeling of brotherhood felt strange to him since joining his platoon.   He was a Marine, and he had good, capable Marines in his platoon.   But there was a gap between his Marines and him now, even with Stepchild.   He respected his Marines; he admired them.   But this seemed more on a professional level.   He felt somewhat restrained, though, on what he could say and do.   Naturally gregarious, Tony was a joker at heart.   As a young Marine, and even as an NCO, if there was a prank being pulled, or if there was goofing off, Tony was probably at the center of it all.

Now, as a commander, he didn't feel he could do the same thing.   He still didn't know what it meant to be a lieutenant, but he was pretty sure it did not involve short-sheeting a rack.   So he was trying to be more professional in his dealings with his platoon.   He was more candid with SSgt Davidson, but that was still on a more professional level.   And although he had made Stepchild his radio operator, he still hadn't come to grips with their change of status.

That didn't seem to be a problem with Stepchild, though.   Other than calling him "Lieutenant" and adding in the obligatory "sir," he didn't seem to have changed his manner with him.

Tony wondered if he should have accepted the commission.   He enjoyed being an NCO.   He enjoyed being part of something larger than himself.   So far, being a lieutenant was just not as fun, to put it at a basic level.

But now, he was meeting up with the other lieutenants to share a beer and get some chow at the O-Club.   He felt he could relax.   He had only known these guys for a few days back at Little Creek, but they seem to accept him, and that was enough.

Tony mimed drinking a stein of beer, even shaking it as if getting out the last drop. Gil laughed and clapped him solidly on the back.

"Told you so. My man knows how to down some brew," he said with a laugh.

Stan looked over to the other pier where the *Independence* was tied up. "Do we wait for Rob?" he asked.

"Wait? You want to wait until the *Pearl Harbor* ties up and everyone else drains the taps?" Gil asked. "And you know Rob. That anal bastard is probably conducting a skivvy inspection before he lets his platoon off the ship." That elicited a laugh from the others.

Rob seemed like a great guy, but even with his short time in the company, Tony could see that Rob tended a bit to the micromanaging.

"He knows where we are. I say we go get ourselves a table and just save him a seat." Gil offered, looking to Stan for confirmation.

"Yeah, I guess you're right. OK, let's get this show on the road."

They walked across a huge parade deck towards the club. Tony didn't know what to expect about Spain, but as the ship pulled in, it seemed somewhat dry and almost desert-like. The buildings looked like the ones in Old Town San Diego—light stucco walls and orange tile roofs. To be fair, though, maybe it was San Diego that looked like Rota and not the other way around.

The Officers Club was a large building in the same design. Walking inside, though, aside from the cool blast of air, seemed to take them back in time. In reality, the building could not be that old, but it had a feeling of age. The heavy use of wood and the large collection of unit plaques on the walls added to the feeling. Tony remembered from a history class back at boot camp that the Spanish *Infantería de Marina* was the oldest existing marine corps, formed back in 1537. He doubted it, but he still wondered if any of the plaques went back that far. Now that would be impressive!

There were three Spanish officers sitting at a table in

the bar area, but they didn't seem to notice the four Marines as they entered.

"You guys grab a seat. I'm getting the first round," Stan told them.

They sat down, taking in the surroundings. Tony had been at Camp David and at the embassies in Delhi and Amman. But this felt more like the "real" military. It was only the O-Club, true, but it reeked with history, with the ghosts of countless sailors and Marines passing through.

Stan came back with two pitchers, one Budweiser and one San Miguel. Tony preferred Sam Adams, but cold beer was cold beer. The waitress came over with glasses and started to serve them, but Tony grabbed the pitcher of San Miguel poured himself a glass. He watched the bubbles for a moment before taking a long swallow.

The hoppy flavor, bubbles, and cold wetness slid down his throat. It tasted great!

The waitress left some menus. Tony knew he wanted to get some food, but for the moment, all four of them just savored their drinks.

A puzzled look slowly came over Gil's face. "Maybe it's been too long at sea, but I've had San Miguel before, and this tastes a little different."

"Two different companies," Joe told him.

"What? Stan said this was San Miguel."

"In the States, if you had San Miguel, you had the Filipino brand, which is the original brand. They opened up a brewery later in Spain, and during the war, the two companies split. So this is a different beer and a different company."

"Ah, kind of like Budweiser in the US and in the Czech Republic, right?" asked Tony

"Well, no. Bud in the US just took the name, which the Czech company used first. With San Migoo, the Spanish company was started by the Filipino one. Sort of a reverse colonization."

Tony shrugged. He had had San Miguel back at Stanford, so he supposed it must have been the Filipino kind. He wasn't sure he could recognize the taste one way or the other.

THE PROUD

The waitress came back for their food order.   Tony ordered a cheeseburger, as did Joe and Gil.   Stan elected to go for fried calamari and gazpacho.   Gil hooted at Stan's choices, but Tony was a bit curious.   He had eaten calamari before, of course, but he had only seen gazpacho prepared on television.   He didn't know what a cold vegetable soup would taste like, but he liked salads, so maybe it would be good.

They sat around, drinking their beer, talking about their upcoming several months.   Stan seemed to think that they could actually be quite busy, but Gil agreed with Capt Svenson that this would be a boring deployment for Kilo Company.   The rest of the battalion would do much more as well as hit better liberty ports.   For Kilo, it was possible that they would only see land here in Rota on the way in and again at Rota for the washdown on the way back.

"So how's life on the *Gaffert*?" Tony asked the others.

"Oh, she's a sweet ship," answered Stan.   "The chow's great, the ride smooth, and the gym's pretty amazing.   I've even got my own stateroom while these two retreads share a stateroom designed for four.   The ship's designed to carry a battalion, if it has to, and we've got a company minus."

"Damn, I wish I could say the same.   We're pretty much crammed into wherever they can stick us.   The chow's good, I guess, but getting anything done's a pain in the ass."

"Yeah, Rob pretty much said the same thing.   The *Independence* is not too happy with them aboard."

"Same with the *Dunham*.   Captain Svenson told me our skipper really fought against having us on board.   They're in the business to shoot, not carry Marines.   And us taking over their own ship's VBSS teams missions, well, I don't think they like being part of what they consider a dog and pony show.   A couple of the junior officers confirmed that to me, but I have to say, they've been nothing short of professional now that the decision's been made."

"Well, you being a hero and all couldn't hurt in that regard," put in Gil.

There was a moment of silence as everyone gauged Tony's response.   Since his arrival at Little Creek, the others had been pretty circumspect about the elephant in the room.

Nothing was mentioned about Delhi. Now the first crack in that wall had been made.

"So Tony. Why did they call you Korea Joe in that movie? I mean, your last name is Japanese, not Korean," asked Stan.

Tony looked up. He knew this was just the opening they sought. They wanted to know what really happened, but they didn't want to push. He dreaded sitting with the battalion CO later on and retelling the story, but this was different. These were his peers. He really didn't mind, and in fact, in a way, he relished the opportunity to tell someone his version of things, the good and the bad.

"Well, it's no big thing, really. I had an idiot DI who couldn't tell the difference between being a Japanese-American or a Korean-American, and the name just sort of stuck. And the movie made it seem like that was all I was called. But the movie made lots of mistakes, and that was just one."

He left it hanging, and Gil took the bait.

"So what really happened?"

They leaned forward to listen when Rob walked in. He joined them, taking grief for being late. He was poured a beer.

"So, you were about to say?" Stan prompted after Rob settled in.

Tony went on to describe what happened at the embassy, the most unlikely events leading up to the isolation of the president inside the embassy with the security guard detachment, an Army major, and old lady, and an Indian civilian. Everyone had seen the movie, of course, so they knew the players, but Tony tried to give it a reality check.

For most of the time, Tony had been in the bell tower, so he didn't really know every detail of what happened inside the embassy building other than what Stepchild, 1stSgt Mac, Saad, and Van Slyke had told him after the fact. But still, his account was from the horse's mouth, so-to-speak, and the others listened with rapt attention. At one point, the Spanish officers at the other table stopped their conversation to listen in as well, but that didn't stop Tony.

Tony focused on what he did and what he heard. He

had intended on downplaying his role a bit, but it didn't quite work out that way. He didn't embellish anything, but neither did he downplay anything.

He got a big reaction when he told them he had been so thirsty that he had drunk his own urine. The others groaned, and Gil stopped him to refill his beer for him, then holding it out for Tony to drink.

When he recounted the Indians taking the old 106 recoilless rifle out of the locker and using it, only to have one guy killed by the backblast, then turning the big rifle around and getting another guy killed by the round, the table burst out in incredulous laughter. Even the Spanish officers at the next table laughed, all pretense of not listening in gone.

"No shit?" asked Gil. "I thought that had to be pure Hollywood! That really happened just like that?"

Tony assured him that what he said was the Gospel truth. That seemed to be the highlight of his tale to Gil, at least. Rob had questions about the mechanics of shooting the attackers. Stan wanted to know how he figured out what to do when he got word of the incoming bomb, and all of them seemed interested in the publicity events he attended after the fact.

And if Tony didn't deny a fling with a certain starlet as the press had reported (by only telling them "A gentleman doesn't tell tales"), it wasn't his fault if they assumed more happened than the truth (which was nothing happened at all, much to Tony's chagrin).

As Tony went on, he could almost see the bonds of brotherhood forming, drawing them closer together. He knew these bonds would be strong, as strong as the ones he had formed with the Marines in Amman or Camp David, for that matter. Delhi was different, though. He had lost friends there, and that created stronger bonds between the survivors. He prayed that he wouldn't have his bonds with these friends, with these brothers, similarly strengthened.

Chapter 7

Aboard the USS Jason Dunham, Off the Coast of Somalia
A week later

Private First Class Jerry Masterson nervously checked his M4 for the umpteenth time.   Two hours ago, he had been about to dig into his pancakes on the mess decks.   Now, he was ready to go into action for the first time.   He wasn't sure if he was ready.

"Just like rehearsal, Jerry.   No problem, right?" asked Cpl Winsome, his fire team leader.

Jerry merely nodded.   His throat felt too dry to speak.

A year ago, he had been drifting in life, living with his parents back in Milwaukee.   When the news hit about the embassy takeover in New Delhi and what the Marine Security Guard Detachment had done, he had felt a rush of patriotic fervor.   He immediately enlisted and was lucky enough to get a quick boat space at boot camp, the first one back at the newly re-commissioned Marine Corps Recruit Depot, Paris Island.   The Marine Corps was in a state of upheaval as it rushed back to full status, but for Recruit Masterson, boot camp was enough of an upheaval in and of itself.   What was going on Corps-wide was above his event horizon.

He finished boot camp and the School of Infantry and was assigned to the battalion at Camp Lejeune.   The next six months were hectic as the battalion was formed and trying to get ready for the upcoming deployment.   Kilo Company was going to be the anti-piracy raid unit, so the company's training was a little more specific.   1st and 3d Platoons were going to be away from the company headquarters, so each had to be able to handle any mission thrown its way.   Jerry's squad was assigned as a boarding party.

2d Squad and 3d Platoon's 1st Squad left Camp Lejeune a week early for Little Creek to cross-train with the Special Boat Unit.   There would be two boats on the *Jason Dunham*, and when investigating a suspicious target, each one would have a fire team on board as a boarding party. The boarding parties had previously come from the ship's sailors, from what they called the VBSS, but this seemed like a good job for the Marines, so they got the mission.

It has all seemed rather fun and even adventurous back at Little Creek. But this was the real deal now. A patrol plane had spotted a suspicious boat, and with the ship nearby, they rushed to the scene.

The small boat bobbed off in the distance, maybe 500 yards away. It had tried to flee when the *Dunham* steamed up, but a few well-placed shots from the ship's big 5/62 gun in front of the boat stopped it in its tracks.

Despite the *Dunham's* top-of-the-line technology, it was not designed to carry Marines nor "swicks," (Special Warfare Combatant-craft Crewmen). Getting the RHIB's (Rigid Inflatable Hull Boats) off the deck and into the water was a rather old-fashion method of hoists. More specific to Jerry was the fact that once the boats were in the water, the way his fire team would board the boats was via a cargo net, just as Marines did back off the shores of Tarawa and Iwo Jima. It was one thing to do that back in Little Creek in the harbor. It was an entirely different thing to do that out in the middle of the IO.

When the boat's coxswain gave the signal, the fire team climbed over the side and down the net. Jerry tried not to look down at the water. As the ship rolled with the gentle waves, he was alternately pressed against the ship's hull and then swung out to hang in the air. Concentrating on one step at a time, he was relieved to feel hands grab his legs. He had made it.

With both boats loaded, the ship's first lieutenant saluted, and the boats cast off to head out to their target. Jerry unslung his M4 and took his position on the port side of the boat. Opposite him on the starboard side was LCpl Javon Jones with his M27 IAR. Jerry took a surreptitious look over at JJ. That IAR was a mean-looking weapon, and Jerry had really enjoyed firing it at SOI. He looked forward to the day that he could become the team's automatic rifleman.

He jerked his mind back to the task at hand. The

target was now only about 200 meters away. Jerry's RHIB was the lead boat, and so a Navy Lieutenant (JG) was with them. Jerry thought his lieutenant should be aboard, but his was not to reason why, he figured. Sgt Alvarez, his squad leader, though, was on the trailing RHIB which broke off to circle to the other side of the target to provide covering fire, if needed.

As they approached the target boat, Jerry was surprised at how old and beat-up it looked.

This was a pirate boat? he wondered.

There looked to be four skinny men on board wearing not much more than shorts and loose cotton shirts. They were standing facing the RHIB when the translator took out the bullhorn and shouted out to them. The translator was a civilian assigned to the ship. He wore Navy overalls without any insignia. He was as black as any of the African-American Marines or sailors, much darker than Jerry himself, but his features seemed more hawk-like and sharp. Jerry really didn't know what to make of him.

Whatever he said, though, had an effect. The four men raised their hands over their heads and stepped to the middle of their rickety boat.

The RHIB's coxswain, BM3 Eric Hadley, expertly brought his boat alongside, and with Jerry and the other sailor on the .50 cal covering, Cpl Winsome, JJ, and PFC Cal Rafferty, the other rifleman, jumped on board, followed by the Navy JG. Only when the others had the four men covered did Jerry and the translator cross over.

The boat was pretty small, and with six more men aboard, it was positively crowded. The wooden sides of the boat seemed almost rotten, and water sloshed around beneath their feet. Jerry glanced over the water to the *Dunham*. If he was going to be out in the middle of the ocean, he rather preferred a nice big ship like that over a claptrap boat he wouldn't even use back at home on Lake McNeil on a calm and sunny Sunday afternoon.

Jerry had no idea on what was being said, but it was obvious that the translator was accusing the four men, and it was just as obvious that they were denying whatever that accusation was.

With Jerry and Cal covering the men, the others started searching the boat.   It took only moments for JJ to pull back a tarp and uncover some rifles.   A thrill coursed through Jerry.   They were pirates, after all!

The JG picked up one of the rifles, which looked to be an old AK47.   He shook it in his hand.

"Ask them what these are," he told the translator.

Some unintelligible gibberish went back and forth before the man turned back to the Navy officer.

"They say they need those for to protect from pirates. They say they are just the simple fishermen."

"So where's their nets, huh?"

The translator went back to the men and parleyed the question, getting an answer back.

"They say they lost the nets in the storm.   Now they are only trying to go back to the home."

Just then Cpl Winsome reached down and pulled up a plastic case.   Jerry could clearly see the words "Samho Jewelry" stenciled on the side of the box.   Winsome handed it to the JG whose eyes lit up.

"And this?" he shouted, directly to the four men. "Where did they get this first aid kit?"

The translator asked, then told the JG, "They say they found it floating in the water."

"Bullshit.   The *Samho Jewelry* was hijacked last year. That was the second time that bad-luck ship has been pirated, if I remember right."

"Of course, you are most right.   These men, though, they will not admit to wrong.   They will admit they are fishermen only.   This is their way."

"Fishermen," the JG sneered.   "Right.   Well, we've got enough here to bring them in."

He got on the radio to report back to the ship and to order the other boat to tow the pirate boat back to the *Dunham*.   The pirates themselves had their hands flexi-cuffed, and two were placed in each RHIB.

Jerry felt elated.   He hadn't been sure he was ready for action, but it had gone down just like rehearsal, just as Cpl Winsome had told him.   And they had caught honest-to-goodness pirates.

As they came alongside the *Dunham*, Jerry figured that every single man and woman not on watch was there on deck to see their catch. He caught sight of Terry Miller, his best friend in the platoon. Terry and Jerry, they'd been called ever since boot camp, as if they were bonded together instead of two individuals. Terry must be green with envy. Jerry wanted to wave, but that wouldn't be too professional, so he tried to maintain his war face instead. The other Marines and sailors were watching, after all.

As they were tied alongside the big ship, the pirates were hoisted aboard like cargo. Cpl Winsome ordered Jerry to sit in the pirate boat as security, which seemed strange to him. Who was going to steal a beat-up pirate boat out in the middle of the ocean? But he did as he was told while everyone else except for a sailor on each RHIB clamored up the cargo nets back onboard the *Dunham*.

The next few hours crawled by at a snail's pace. It was pretty hot sitting there, and the *Dunham's* slow rolling was at odds with the pirate boat's bobbing. That incongruity upset his stomach. He was happy to get relieved to get some chow, although the relief had more to do with getting off the small boat than any real desire for food. He hadn't thought of the *Dunham* as a stable platform, but when compared to the pirate boat, it was almost like being on dry land.

Terry found him on the mess decks, and of course, he wanted to know every detail. With half-a-dozen Marines around him, he recounted everything. The fact that most of them had been watching through binoculars kept him from embellishing the tale too much, but he tried to make it a bit more exciting than it actually was.

After chow, he went down to the cramped berthing area to clean his weapon. The improved M4 was a pretty good weapon, but it was still a finely-machined piece of gear, and salt water could wreck havoc with it. He had to make sure it was pristine, and not only because Winsome and Alvarez would check it, but SSgt Davidson was sure to go over it with a fine-tooth comb. The platoon sergeant frankly scared Jerry, something he wasn't afraid to admit to himself.

He was just reassembling his weapon when LCpl Taylor Nguyen came rushing in.

THE PROUD

"They're letting them go!"

A chorus of "who" came from the few Marines in the space.

"The pirates, they're letting them go!   You gotta see this!"

Everyone, including Jerry, rushed out.   No way was anyone letting their first pirates go!

But they were.   Jerry watched in astonishment as the pirates were being carefully led to the cargo net and allowed to climb back down into their boat.   What looked to be food, water, and fuel was then lowered into the boat as well.   The ship's crew and embarked Marines stood in silence while this was happening.   Some had looks of confusion on their faces, but most had looks of disgust.   One sailor looked like he wanted to do something about it, but the others hustled him down below decks.

It took about 15 minutes, but the pirate boat was finally loaded.   One of the pirates tried to start the outboard motor, but it wouldn't catch.   After a few fruitless minutes, a sailor in overalls was sent over.   He took off the outboard's cover, and within a minute or two, he had the motor going.   He came back as the pirate boat was cast off and slowly pulled away.   One of the four men stood up on the bow's gunwales and waved broadly to the assembled men and women.

There were a few muttered obscenities among the crew, but most of the sailors and Marines seemed to be in shock. Jerry was amongst those numbers.   What was the use of catching pirates if they were just going to be let go?   It made no sense at all.

Chapter 8

Aboard the MV Wilmington 400 miles off the coast of Somalia
Three weeks later

Chief Mate Craig Murphy stood at the railing of the big merchant ship, sipping a coffee and watching the waves slip past as the sun peeked above the horizon.   He was ready to go home to June and their small house in Connecticut, but deep inside, he knew he would miss all of this.   But with his Navy Reserve retirement about to kick in, it was time to go. June had put up with his months and years at sea, and he promised her this was his last cruise.

Financially, he would be comfortable enough.   His Navy retirement would be almost $3,000 a month, and his pension as a merchant mariner would more than double that.   Add June's pension from the Torrington School District, and well, they would be doing OK.

June felt that he could have stopped sailing earlier, but the fact was that Craig liked being at sea.   He liked the life. The fact that his Navy retirement wouldn't kick in until he was 60 had been his excuse to keep going.   But next month, he was hitting the big six-oh.   He had no more excuses.

One more port at Capetown, then his final run to Baltimore.   It was hard to realize it was almost over.

He turned around, leaning back against the railing. He could see the captain in the bridge, silently looking out over the Indian Ocean.   Todd Iverson was younger than Craig, and he had managed to reach the position Craig couldn't quite seem to achieve.   Craig thought Todd was a bit of a jerk, but he was honest enough to himself to realize that his opinion could be colored a bit by jealousy.   It might not have been overt jealousy, but Craig often pondered on why he had never been made master of a ship, any ship.   As a Chief Mate with over 360 days at sea, he was a licensed master, but actually getting command of a ship had been something that had never materialized.

THE PROUD

Even in the Navy, he had never risen above navigator aboard a vessel. He had gotten out of the Navy too early to get command of an active duty ship, but as a reservist, not only had he never received a ship's command, he had never been to sea. Each of his reserve billets had been shore-based.

The *Wilmington* had three mates, so the captain never stood watch. But he was usually on the bridge, staring out to sea. Craig sighed and threw the last dregs of his coffee over the rails and into the water streaming past him. He should go below and get something with more sustenance than coffee before he went on watch.

He opened the hatch and made his way down to the galley. Over the years, Craig had been aboard many different ships. He had to admit, though, the *Wilmington* had a great galley, and the coffee was first-rate. He liked to blame the cooking on his ever-burgeoning girth, even if he knew a serious dearth of exercise was the more likely culprit.

He went up to the espresso machine to refill his mug before ordering his breakfast. Craig didn't know if he really liked espresso more than drip-brewed coffee, but he sure liked the process of making it. The whooshing sound of the machine alone was enough to get him going. Just as the last drops filled his cup, the PA came to life, calling the 2nd Mate and him to the bridge.

What now? He thought, glancing at his watch. He still had 20 minutes before he was on duty.

His stomach growled reminding him that he hadn't actually gotten anything to eat yet. He hoped whatever the captain wanted wouldn't take too long. He didn't want to have to get something brought up to him on the bridge as while not verboten, and while it would be normal on most ships, it was certainly frowned upon aboard the *Wilmington*, just one more thing about the captain that annoyed him.

He blew on his latte, trying to cool it down so he could take a big gulp, and grabbed a couple of doughnuts that he stuffed into his mouth as he left the galley and made his way slowly up to the bridge. The PA repeated its call.

"I'm coming, I'm coming," he muttered as walked, careful not to spill any of his brew.

He stepped into the bridge and looked around. The captain wasn't there.

"He's on the bridge wing with Mr. Harris," Randolf Fenix, the helmsman told him without being asked.

Craig nodded and opened the hatch to the flying bridge. The captain, John Harris (the Second Mate), Rolf Weiss (the Third Mate), and Bong Benedicto, one of the Filipino crewmen, were already there, looking through binos aft of the ship.

"What's up?" he asked.

The captain handed his set of binos to him and said, "Take a look back there, maybe two miles and five tenths, a few points off the port quarter."

Craig took them and looked. He couldn't see anything, so he adjusted the focus to try and compensate for aging eyes. He was about to tell the captain that he didn't see anything at all when a faint spray of white caught his attention. Looking closer, he could see one, no two small shapes trailing them. His heart fell.

"What do you think?"

Craig paused a moment, trying to pick out more details.

"Well, probably what you think. What are we, 400 miles out? And two small boats in our wake? Pirates." He paused again, then asked, "Are they gaining on us?"

"It looks like it. We only now picked them up on the radar, but it seems they may be closing the gap."

"So, do we call it in now?" John asked the captain.

Craig pulled down the binos and handed them back. He knew the captain had to make a decision. If they really were pirates, then they needed to report it. If they weren't, then crying wolf could have some repercussions.

The captain seemed lost in thought. Craig did resent the fact that Todd was captain and he wasn't. Todd was younger, and Craig had been with the line longer. But in this case, he was glad he wasn't making the decision.

"An hour ago, there was another distress call from a Liberian-flagged freighter up near the straits. So before we start pulling assets, let's make sure about this. Mr. Weiss, let's change course and see what they do. Come to 240 and hold it steady."

"Aye, Captain," came the heavily accented reply.

A ship the size of the *Wilmington* could not turn on a dime.   Even after the new course was put in, it took awhile for the huge ship to begin its ponderous turn.   Rolf came back to the bridge wing and joined the others as they watched their wake and the two boats in it.   At first, it seemed as if the boats would continue along their previous course.   Craig felt a sense of relief wash over him.

That relief turned to icy fingers of apprehension when suddenly the two boats veered to the right, back on an intercept course.   It seemed as if they were going to have company after all.   To make matters worse, by changing the *Wilmington's* course, the distance between them and their pursuers was cut.

"I guess that answers that," John remarked to no one in particular.

A blossom of anger bloomed within Craig.   This was his last trip, and he was damned if he was going to be held in some little Somali hut while negotiations went on about how much was going to be paid to release them all.

"Mr. Murphy, I want you to get the crew together. They'll be going into the panic room.   You, a helmsman, and I will stay on the bridge until the last moment, then join the others if it looks like they're coming aboard.   Mr. Harris, I want you to take charge of the panic room until I get there. I don't want any panic, though, among the crew.   If they get aboard, they get aboard.   No heroics.   We just do what we're told until the insurance company secures our release. Understand?"

They all nodded.   Craig understood that their standing orders were to do nothing in the way of defense.   That stuck in his craw, but the insurance companies had their reasons, he guessed.

He passed word on the PA for everyone to gather in the galley, then made his way back down.   When the trailing boats changed course to intercept them, he had felt a tremor of fear.   That fear was mostly subsumed, though, to be replaced by anger.   He couldn't believe this was happening on his last voyage.   And while he knew pirates had taken some pretty big ships, it was still hard for him to imagine the

Wilmington being boarded and captured by men out in little skiffs. The *Wilmington* had a crew of 19, so how could a few jumped-up fishermen take them down?

Most of the crew had gathered in the galley by the time he arrived. They knew something was up, but the looks on their faces reflected curiosity more than anything else. The last person to arrive was the Chief. Craig would have liked to be able to pull him aside beforehand and brief him, but there was no changing that now.

"Can I have your attention please?" he asked, waiting for everyone to quiet down. "We have a situation here. It looks like we are the target of a pirate attack . . ." He had to stop as the crew broke out into rumblings. New regulations allowed for more non-citizens to crew US-flagged ships, and the bulk of the *Wilmington's* able and ordinary seaman were Filipino, both naturalized US and Philippines citizens, and while all could nominally speak English, a few seemed to need the others to repeat what Craig had said, but in Tagalog.

"Quiet, please! Quiet down! There is no need for panic here. If they do come aboard, we just need to wait it out."

"But Sir Craig, what if they come to kill us?" asked Ting, one of the ordinary seaman, fear evident in his voice.

Craig never knew why the Filipinos tended to call him "Sir Craig" and John "Sir John." He asked a few and never got much of an answer. They called the captain "Captain," and the Chief "the Chief," but while the other few nationalities aboard called him Mr. Murphy or even "Chief Mate," with the Filipinos, it was almost always "Sir Craig," with the "sir" sounding more like "ser."

"They won't kill us. How can they get any money from the insurance company if they did that?"

"They've done that before," someone else interjected, with others nodding in agreement.

"And that's why the captain's ordered everyone into the panic room. And remember, most of the time, the pirates never even get aboard. We're a big ship with a real high freeboard. I've seen the two pirate boats. They look like crap, like the first decent wave is going to break them apart."

"Then why are we going to the panic room?" asked Rio, one of their few Indonesian crew members.

"It's just a safety precaution.   If they do manage to get on board, there's no way they can get into that compartment. We'll just need to wait it out for rescue or worst case basis, until our ransom gets paid.   Look, we can discuss this more later, but for now, I want everyone to move down to the panic room.   If these guys never get on board, then no harm. no foul, right?"

As the crew started slowly moving out, he grabbed the Chief Engineer.   "Can you kinda take over in there?   The captain's staying on the bridge for now, but the panic room's sorta in your scope of responsibility, right?   I mean, once the captain has given the order to go there."

"Well, I'm not so sure about that.   The captain's got full authority over safety, but sure, I'll handle things until he gets down there," replied the Chief, the only man on board with more time at sea than Craig.

Craig shook his hand and hurried back up to the bridge. The captain and Rolf Weiss were on the bridge wing, so after nodding to Randolf, who was still on the helm, he went out to join them.

He was surprised to see how close the two boats were. He didn't need the binos to see the men inside each one, looking up at them.   The *Wilmington* was supposed to be a pretty fast ship, but the little skiffs sure didn't have a problem closing the gap between them.

"Everyone's on the move towards the panic room now. The Chief's in charge down there now."

The captain frowned.   He and the Chief didn't really get along that well.   Part of that was the shipping line's policy of both of their scopes of responsibility, something a bit more muddled than in most shipping lines.   Part of it probably was the age difference.   The Chief was older and had many more years afloat.   And part of it just might have been personality differences.

"What'd the CTF say?" asked Craig.

"They didn't," was the simple reply.

"They didn't?   But that's what the CTF's for, right?"

Bong Benedicto had been watching and listening to the

interchange. Now he turned away from the two men.

"I haven't contacted them yet," the captain replied, voice calm but firm.

"Uh, Todd, in case you haven't noticed, we've got two pirate skiffs about ready to crawl up our ass. Don't you think we should let the Combined Task Force know about it? You know, in case we might need some help?" Craig's rising anger was evident in the note of sarcasm as he spoke.

"Mr. Murphy," the captain told him, the emphasis on the formal salutation indicating his displeasure at Craig's breach of decorum, "if you bothered to read up on our policies, you would know that we report to corporate. They'll contact the CTF if they deem fit."

"'If they deem fit?' What the hell? They're not out here. It's our ass on the line, not theirs." Craig was getting rather excited.

"Remember the *Fedor Varaksin*?" was the captain's response.

The mention of the Russian ship stopped Craig's blossoming tirade. Three years before, the *Fedor Varaksin* had been carrying relief supplies for Ethiopia when 12 Somali pirates took her. The Russian frigate *Yaroslav Mudryy* responded, and after the pirates would not stop, the frigate fired on the rudder, crippling the cargo ship. There was a tense 6-hour standoff with the pirates parading crew members in view of the frigate, hands tied and rifles aimed at their heads.

The Russians stormed the ship, and in the firefight, 12 of the 18 Russian crewmen were killed. The official reports were that the pirates killed the hostages, but the underground rumor was that at least 10 of them had been killed by Russian weapons.

Underground rumors also held that only five pirates were killed in the actual firefight. The rest surrendered. But where all versions of what happened converged was that shortly after the ship was secured, perhaps within 30 minutes, all 12 pirates were dead and their bodies thrown overboard.

In addition to the loss of life amongst the crew, the *Fedor Varaksin* was heavily damaged and had to be towed to the Kherson Shipyard in the Ukraine for lengthy and costly repairs.   As far as Craig knew, it hadn't even been put back out to sea yet.

"Corporate wants to find out just what CTF ships are in the area before putting out a distress call.   I think you can agree that however effective some navies might be in re-taking ships, as crew on this ship, maybe someone other than the Russians or Chinese might be in our best interests. We'll be safe in the panic room until the right rescue effort can be mounted."

Despite his frustration, Craig had to admit that made sense.   He wasn't sure whether corporate was more concerned about the crew or the damage the ship might receive, but either way, the crew was at risk.

That didn't make it any easier to take, though.   He looked back at their wake, and the two boats were only two or three tenths or so in back of them.   They looked pretty small back there, and the *Wilmington* was a pretty big ship. It wouldn't be easy for them to make it up to the deck.   He wondered if there was anything they could do to make it a bit harder for them, maybe enough to tip the balance.   A germ of an idea began to form.

"And with that, I think you and Mr. Weiss here need to get below.   I will follow in a few moments along with Mr. Fenix."

"Aye, aye, sir," Craig responded, getting back into a more formal mode of address.   He and Rolf made their way below.   Just as they came to the ladder leading to the panic room, Craig stopped.

"Hey, I've got to check on something right quick.   You go ahead."

Rolf gave a non-committal grunt and continued on.

Craig reversed direction and made his way out onto the deck at the stern of the ship.   He needed to get to the one of the high-pressure fire hoses.

"Can I help you, Sir Craig?" came a voice from in back of him.

Craig jumped, heart in this throat.   He spun around to see Able Seaman Benedicto behind him.

"You scared the shit out of me!" he gushed out.   "What

the hell are you doing here?"

"Well, Sir Craig, I wanted to see what I might do to keep the pirates off this ship. I don't want to go be a hostage for months. Irish, my wife, she's going to have a baby soon, our first. And I want to be there when our baby comes, when we do the christening. I don't want to sit there in Somalia."

He looked at Craig expectantly.

"But they might not even take the ship. And even if they do, corporate will get us out."

"No offense, Sir Craig, but the line is not as dedicated to get the crew out as quickly as you Americans."

Craig wanted to protest, but he couldn't. An American shipping line, or British, or whatever, tended to act with more vigor to rescue their own countrymen than the crews, which were usually Filipino, Indonesians, or the like. It wasn't that they were expendable, *per se*, but the priority was for the home country officers first.

"Well, Bong, I don't know what we can do. I just wanted to go aft and see if maybe one of our fire hoses could be of use."

"I was thinking the same thing, Sir Craig."

Together, they made their way to the stern. There were two fire hoses available, one on either side of the big orange rescue boat which perched on the sled, and without rhyme or reason, Craig chose the port hose. He peeked over the side. The two boats were pretty close. All the men were armed, and Craig wondered if he was doing the right thing. He glanced back at the bridge wing, but the captain had left it. He was probably down below already.

Craig took the hose nozzle off the rack and started to get in position when Bong reached over and took it from him.

"No disrespect, but when have you used a hose last? I think I should aim, and you turn it on."

Craig had to agree. As an Able Seaman, Bong had more recent experience in using a hose. Like all ships, the *Wilmington* conducted the required weekly fire drills, but as the Chief Mate, Craig never handled the equipment himself. He went to the lever that would open the flow of water.

By now, the boats had split up, each heading up a different side of the *Wilmington*. Craig could tell that they had been spotted, but no one fired. That emboldened him a bit.

"OK, Bong, I think they're almost in range. Let me know when you want the water."

Bong waited a few more moments before calling out "Now!"

Craig shoved over the lever, then rushed to look over the side. It was a long way down, and the vertical distance and the forward motion of the ship worked to dissipate the force of the water. But it was still powerful enough to knock the pirates from their squatting positions. One man almost went overboard.

As the boat swerved away, Craig rushed to the starboard side to see if he could get at the second skiff. In the intervening seconds, however, that boat had made it past the stern, and it was now protected by the bulk of the ship. He ran back to Bong, but the second skiff had skirted the reach of the hose and was also coming in to hug the ship's side.

He wasn't sure just what he could do. He knew he should get down to the panic room, but he felt that he had to do something. He couldn't just give the ship up that easily to friggin' beat-up skiffs.

Leaving Bong, he started running up the length of the ship. Perhaps "running" was too generous a phrase. Shipboard life wasn't conducive to a strict exercise regimen, and Craig was getting on in years as well as in girth. So "hurried" might have been a more accurate term to describe his efforts to get forward. He was breathing heavily by the time he made it all the way to where the pirate boat was matching them.

He had only been there a moment when a grappling hook came flying up over the rail. It was pulled back until the hook caught. Craig hesitantly approached it, then looked over the side. Below him, one of the skiffs paced the big ship. Four faces were looking up, and one man had started to climb the rope.

Craig wondered if he could dislodge the rope. This

wasn't the Middle Ages where he could send pots of boiling oil down upon those besieging the castle. Anything that could be done, he would have to do it as he was. He reached out and pulled on it, but with the man's weight on it, the rope was too solidly attached. He was about to give up when one man below raised his rifle and fired a volley of rounds.

As far as he could tell, the rounds weren't close, but he could understand the implicit warning. He jerked himself back, but he did it so suddenly that he fell and smacked his head in the *Wilmington's* unforgiving deck. He was stunned for a second. He knew he should hightail it out of there and get down to the panic room, but he needed a moment, and sitting there was the best he could do. And when a rifle muzzle was pointed over the rails, followed by two arms that pulled their attached body up and onto the ship, he knew his chance was gone.

The man pointed the rifle at Craig, yelling something that had no meaning to him. But he understood the rifle. So Craig just stayed put as his head cleared. It wasn't long before another man clambered aboard. This was a much younger man, barely more than a boy, actually. The first man told him something, then ran off, leaving the boy to watch over him. Craig wanted to say something to him, but he wasn't sure what he could say. The boy didn't look aggressive, and Craig knew the pirates would not get ransom money if he was killed, but to say he was not scared would be a pretty big lie. He really should have gone with the captain to the panic room.

The boy jumped up, and that startled Craig, too. There was another man coming aboard, this one older and seemingly more confident. Craig wondered if he was the leader. The two spoke for a few moments when yet a fourth man came over the rail and aboard. Craig had counted four men in the skiff, so with four aboard, they were pretty committed. Their skiff had to be out of reach by now.

The fourth man glared at Craig. The guy had a crazy gleam in his eyes. He wasn't that tall, maybe 5' 6" or so, and he was small, but with a wiry strength evident. He came up to Craig, looking at him, a smile coming over his face and revealing several missing teeth. He had an old, ancient rifle that Craig recognized as an M14. He pointed it at him, then poke him with the muzzle. Craig had a sudden fear that this man did not care about a ransom, that all he cared about was violence. He felt gorge rise in his throat. He was certain the man would kill him. Without thinking about it, he scooted back, his butt dragging on the deck. But surprisingly, the man just made some comment, laughed, and ran off.

The younger boy stayed, though. He moved a step forward, then put the muzzle of his AK under Craig's chin, using it to force Craig's head up.

Was this it? he wondered. *Was this how it was going to end?*

"Please," he whimpered, not knowing what to say. He just wanted to live. He wanted to get back home to June.

That seemed to anger the boy. He swung the rifle's muzzle, smashing Craig against the side of his head.

Craig fell over on his side stunned. The rush of fear tasted like vomit in his mouth. He cowered, afraid to move. Eventually, Craig risked a glance up. The boy was just looking at him, and at least he didn't seem about ready to explode into violence anymore.

Another man came back for a moment and said something to the boy before rushing back off. The boy looked down at Craig before telling him something. Motioning with his rifle got Craig's attention, though, and despite his dizziness, he managed to get up.

The boy kept trying to hurry him aft. Whatever was happening back there, Craig didn't want to be in the middle of it. Coupled with being smacked on the head, well, he wasn't pushing the pace despite the boy's evident eagerness to get back to the superstructure.

But they did make it just as yet another young man came out of the forward hatch. He excitedly spoke to Craig's captor. Craig could just make out the heavily accented words "panic room," but he couldn't miss the jubilation in either of the two boys' attitudes and speech.

It seemed as if the *Wilmington* was in the hands of pirates.

Chapter 9

Aboard the Jason Dunham
That afternoon.

Burke turned the corner on the flight deck. He was never going to get used to running on board the ship. It took about a million trips around the postage stamp-sized flight deck to make a mile, and with the other Marines and sailors trying to get in a run before chow, the "rush hour" made for a crowded work-out. In times like these, Burked missed the long, tree-shaded trails back at Bragg.

As this was not a platoon session, Burke was in his old Army shorts and black t-shirt with the gold "RANGERS" proudly emblazoned across the chest. The lieutenant had proven to be OK, trying hard to keep out of his hair, but in a tradition probably going back to the Roman legions, Burke enjoyed pulling his chain, and wearing the shirt was one way of doing this. Lieutenant Niimoto was Marine this and Marine that, always talking about forging the new Corps, but after the look on the lieutenant's face the first time he saw him in the shirt down in the berthing spaces, well, Burke knew he had that gadfly. Better yet, he knew the lieutenant would never actually say anything about it.

Running on the flight deck took coordination. It was so small that anyone who deviated from the pace could cause a traffic jam that would make LA proud. And PFC Jesus McNamara was slowing down in the afternoon heat. When Burke had first seen McNamara's name on his orders, he thought his first name was given by some sort of born-again Christians. But he was Jesus as in *Heysus*, the Latino pronunciation. He looked Latino, too, and could speak Spanish, but how that jibed with his last name, Burke wasn't sure yet. He made a mental note to ask Sgt Dailey, McNamara's squad leader. Burke was of the school that the more you knew about your men, the better able you were able to do your job.

"Come on, McNamara, pick it up. You don't want to

look like a pussy in front of all these squids, do you?" he quietly told the lagging Marine as he pulled up alongside of him.

"No staff sergeant," the PFC blurted out, with a hint of the drill field still in his voice.

He pushed forward for a few paces until they came to the end of the flight deck, and they had to slow down for the turn. Burke decided to run in back of McNamara to keep him going. It was easy to lose yourself while running. Burke thought back to his first month on board the ship. The worst thing was the boredom. As a Ranger, he had never experienced so much down time. Oh, there was that time he sat on the runway at Pope for three days, ready to fly down to Guatemala. The fact that they never actually left made that whole evolution seem like a waste even if the brass made it sound like the simple threat of the Rangers did what it had to do. But still, that was only three days. This was over a month and counting.

There had been the initial excitement of capturing the pirate boat, but that had faded when the boat was released. The sailors aboard took it better than the Marines. This wasn't the first time for them. Several of the petty officers told him later that the pirates were lucky it had been a US ship that took them. Had it been a Russian, Chinese, or even Korean ship, they would be residing at the bottom of the IO now. General consensus amongst the sailors was that maybe the Russians and Chinese had it right—the Marines quickly came to the same conclusion.

After that first bit of action, if you can call it that, the routine had fallen to boring repetition, like the old movie *Groundhog Day*. They got up for a shit, shower, and shave, held formation, went to chow, held classes, maintained gear, went to chow again, held more classes, had a bit of free time, went to chow yet again, then had movies, books, card games, or limited internet time. There were a few ship-wide drills, and the underway replenishment was interesting enough, but those were Navy-run. The Marines were mere observers.

Burke was somewhat addicted to his Kindle, and he could download books at sea, but he found an old, dog-eared copy of *Mr. Roberts* in the ship's library.   Right there, in the first paragraph, were the lines:

> *For the most part it remains on its regular run, from Tedium to Apathy and   back;   about five days each way. It makes an occasional trip to Monotony . . .*

describing the *USS Reluctant's* routine.   That pretty much described the life aboard the *Dunham*, too.

Aside for the boredom, life wasn't bad.   The food was good, the rack dry.   They had a huge selection of movies, and even the pre-season NFL games were beamed out to them.   With the first game of the season coming up in a few weeks, there was a palpable undercurrent of excitement forming.

More importantly, the platoon was gelling.   That surprised Burke.   He figured with the close quarters and lack of interesting things to do that the Marines would be at each other's throats.   But the squad leaders were actually doing a good job in keeping the Marines occupied.   Burke was still rather partial to the quality of Rangers, and when compared to his Marines, perhaps most Rangers were more skilled in the combat arts.   But of his three squad leaders, two had always been Marines, and one had been an Oregon National Guardsman.   A weekend warrior!   Grudgingly, Burke had to admit that all three would have been good Rangers.

And that thought made him feel a bit guilty.   He was a Marine now.   He had made the decision, and he had to live with it.   No second-guessing it.   But he was constantly wondering if he had made the right choice, what his friends back in Ranger-land were doing.   He was constantly tempted to say "That's not the way we did it in the Rangers."

Even though he had initially enlisted as a Marine, in his heart, he still felt more a part of the Army.   He felt like a Ranger. He knew he could do his job, and do it well, but for his own happiness and satisfaction, he knew he had to embrace his new life.   Or maybe re-embrace it.   He remembered how proud he had been at his boot camp graduation parade back in San Diego.   He remembered how proud his parents had been.   Without ignoring everything else, his service as a Ranger, he needed to not just do his job, but bring back that pride, that sense of being, of existence, which said he was a Marine. He sighed and shook his head. He wasn't unhappy.   He just felt a bit disconnected.

He looked down at his watch before sprinting up a step, telling PFC McNamara "You've got 20 minutes 'til chow. Better get below and shower up.   We don't need you spoiling the squids' delicate appetites."

McNamara gratefully nodded and pulled out of the circle of joggers.

"Delicate appetites?   Um, seems to me that there were a lot of jarheads losing their lunches on the crossing over here."

Burke looked up to see Doug pulling alongside of him.

"Well, BM2 Douglas Kaye, US Navy.   Next time we go ashore, why don't you come with us.   I'm sure I can find some extra snakes for you to try.   But wait, I forgot, you Navy guys need three squares and midrats in order to go to war."

"Ah, Staff Sergeant Burke R. Davidson, of, Uncle Sam's Misbegotten Children, at least I could keep whatever you serve down.   It seems to me I remember one certain Marine losing his dinner on the crossing."

Burke grimaced before replying, "Ah man, that's low, Doug.   I thought I was going to die.   OK, OK, you guys have the stomachs of iron here."

They both laughed as Doug slapped Burke on the shoulder.

"Don't tell anyone here, but I puked non-stop for weeks at Special Boat school before I got used to it," Doug confided.

"My lips are sealed, good buddy," Burke told him, then paused for a second before continuing, "Well speaking of puking, I'm getting hungry, and we've got pork chops tonight.   See you below."

Burke peeled off and made his way into the hangar and to the ladder leading below.   Life aboard the *Dunham* wasn't bad, but it was pretty boring.   He just wished something exciting would happen.

Chapter 10

Aboard the Jason Dunham
The next day

Tony Niimoto was admitted into the CIC. He was surprised to see the ship's captain in there as well along with several other senior officers. She saw Tony and merely tilted her head towards one of the sailors sitting at a row of electronics. Tony wondered what was up. Earlier that morning, there had been reports of a pirate action up near the straits, and the *Gaffert* was steaming post-haste to possibly take some action, but that was surely too far away for the *Dunham* to do anything about it.

The sailor looked up and gave Tony a headset.

"This is a secure line. Just key this button when you want to speak," he told him, indicating a small button on the cord connecting the headset to the console in front of him. "You are X-ray-Five-Alpha, and you are speaking with Romeo-Niner-Romeo."

He handed Tony a small piece of paper on which he had scribbled the call signs. Tony thanked him and put on the headset.

"Uh, this is X-ray-Five-Alpha, over," he hesitantly transmitted.

There was a short pause. "X-ray-Five-Alpha, this is Romeo-Niner-Romeo Actual. As I am sure you know, we're on our way to a possible hijacking now in the IRTC..."

Tony had to think for second before remembering that stood for the Internationally Recommended Transit Corridor.

"... but you've got your own confirmed hijacking now. After all this time at sea, we've got two at the same time, and I've got my own hands full. So you've got it. I've already sent you an ops order, but your ship is already working on it. They are in charge. Sorry I can't support you more now, but you've got the training. I've got full confidence in you. Look, I've got to get going here. You got anything for me now? Over."

Tony felt his heart flutter. A real pirating? And 1st Platoon was getting it? He felt a rising excitement.

"No, sir. I mean, Romeo-Nine-Romeo, I have no questions now, over."

"Roger, X-ray-Five-Alpha. If you need anything, send me a message. Romeo-Niner-Romeo, out."

Tony took off the headset and turned towards the ship's officers. The CO motioned him over.

"Well, lieutenant, considered yourself informed," the captain told him.

Physically, CDR Stetson was a little heavy, maybe even matronly. But her light blue eyes had a strength of character that brooked no nonsense. There was no doubt that she was in charge.

"We've got time to do this right. The ship was evidently taken yesterday, so it's not like we can stop the attack from happening in the first place."

And we're just finding out about this now? he thought to himself.

The captain noticed his expression and said with a shrug, "Evidently, Baltimore Shipping Lines decided that they didn't want a Russian ship in the area rushing to the rescue, given that our Cossack friends can be a little exuberant, shall we say, in their rescues. How they knew our position and the Russians', well, that's another issue altogether. So they waited until today and went through back channels to make sure it would be a US ship that responded."

She changed tack. "This is nothing different that what we've rehearsed. I want you to get your platoon preparing for a helicopter assault, but as soon as you get them started, come back here so we can give you your orders."

"Yes, ma'am," he replied. "I'll get SSgt Davidson briefed. My company commander, though, is sending over an operation order."

She picked up a small bundle of papers stapled together on the corners. "You mean this?"

"Um, maybe so, ma'am," he said hesitantly.

She dropped them on the deck.

"Well, unfortunately, your commander is not here,

lieutenant, nor is he in command here. I am. LCDR Chang here is my Ops O, and he'll give you your orders as soon as we have them done. Questions?"

Her gaze seemed to pierce deep into Tony's brain. He felt flustered.

"Um, no ma'am. I understand ma'am."

"OK, then. I suggest you go down and get your sergeant started. Then come back up here while we work out the details."

She turned back to the others, clearly dismissing him.

"Aye-aye, ma'am," he responded as he turned around and hurriedly left the CIC.

He slid down the ladder, feet on the handrails as good as the saltiest sailor aboard, excited to be seeing some action. He was ready. His platoon was ready.

He was grateful that he would be only be facing some third world pirates. The *Dunham's* captain, on the other hand, now she would be a tougher nut to crack. He laughed out loud at the thought as he hurried below, a passing sailor looking at him as if he were crazy.

Maybe he was crazy. He joined the Marines, after all!

Chapter 11

Over the Indian Ocean
5:00 AM the next morning

Sergeant Pat Dailey checked the safety on his M4 for the hundredth time.   He kept going over everything in his mind, trying to foresee any possible problems.   From everything he had read, everything others had told him, the only sure thing to happen was the unforeseen.

He glanced about the MH60 Sea Hawk, but in the darkness, his Marines were more shadows than anything else.   Up forward, he could just make out the form of SSgt Davidson.   The platoon sergeant wouldn't normally have been on the operation, but with LCpl Owens down hard with some sort of bug, he insisted on taking Owens' boat space, and the lieutenant had agreed.   At first, Pat had been put off by that.   Davidson could be a bit of an asshole, but the more he thought about it, the more he liked it.   The platoon sergeant's combat experiences in Iraq and Afghanistan could only help.

The helo was pretty crowded, though.   Normally, this version of the Sea Hawk would carry 11 combat-loaded Marines, but by pushing the envelope, and by leaving behind things like meals and full packs, they managed to stuff his entire squad of 12 (13 minus Owens) plus Doc Supchak and Davidson.   On the other bird, Aiden Stanhope had his squad, the lieutenant, and Cpl Steptoe.

This was Pat's first taste of action.   He was too junior to have served in Iraq or Afghanistan.   His duty stations had been Quantico, Camp David, and the embassies in Riga and Berlin.   He had been excited to be back in a combat-oriented Corps, but now, racing above the waves, he was having a few doubts.   He wasn't afraid of danger.   He was afraid of screwing up.

They had done three rehearsals that evening and into the night, using the *Dunham* itself as a practice target. Everything seemed straightforward.   But it was the unknown that worried him. He hoped he would make the right decisions when that happened. It was a nice security blanket to have Davidson with them, but he knew he was the squad leader, and it was on his shoulders to make sure each Marine did what he was supposed to do.

He checked his safety again.

The flight was supposed to take an hour and a half, but he was sure that they had to have been airborne longer than that already. He checked his watch. Only an hour had passed. He settled down to wait out the remainder of the flight.

When the Navy crew chief started swinging out the fast rope rigs, he knew they were close. He nudged Cpl Salazar, who in turn sent that nudge down the line. He could feel more than see everyone shift in their seat, getting ready.

He got a comm check with each fire team leader. The new Tactical Squad Radios, attached as they were inside the helmet, were pretty high speed. Even with the wind blasting in the open helo doors, he could both talk and hear without too much problem. With a flick of the switch, back, he could communicate with each member of the squad. In the middle position, it was just with the fire team leaders. Forward, it was with the other squad leaders and the platoon commander. A different-toned beep in his headset told informed him on incoming calls and from which level they were.

He couldn't communicate with the crew chief, though, unless he used one of the Sea Hawk's headsets. He chose not to use one. He figured the crew chief would motion for him to put one on if they had to speak.

Looking out the doors, he could see the faint orange line of the oncoming dawn. The idea was to hit the *Wilmington* in darkness. He doubted the pirates had night vision gear, so that made sense.

"OK, night vision goggles on," he transmitted to the others over the squad frequency.

It took a second or two for the goggles to gather in the ambient light, but soon, everything was in the spooky radiation-green hue. But he could see. And everyone was looking back at him.

The helo banked, and they were all pressed deeper into the web seats. He could feel the Sea Hawk slow down, then flare up. He could see the *Wilmington's* superstructure come into view.

The crew chief/fast rope master threw out the ropes, first one side, then the other. He gave the signal, and Jones and Torrance, the first two to descend, grabbed the ropes and were gone. There was no turning back now.

Boom, boom, boom. Each Marine left the Sea Hawk. Pat scooted up to follow Cpl Bonaventure's team. He reached out, grabbed the rope, and pushed off. The night vision goggles tended to flatten out images, making them more 2D than 3D, but they had done this enough before to be able to judge the distance down.

His feet hit the deck, and he let go, quickly moving to the side so Doc wouldn't land on his head. More feet hit the deck, then the helo lifted off. It was supposed to take a station off the *Wilmington's* starboard, ready to give fire support or to rush in and get them in case things got dicey.

Out of the backwash, Pat could suddenly hear. The wind flowing around the superstructure and the waves seemed quiet after an hour and a half in an open-doored Sea Hawk.

"Check in," he keyed over the radio to his team leaders.

All three did. Everyone was down without a problem. He could see Third Squad, which had fast roped further aft in the ship, moving out. Their mission was the panic room below. The ship's blueprints and been e-mailed to them on the *Dunham*, so they knew the quickest route to the panic room. But seeing something in a drawing was one thing. Seeing it for real and through night vision goggles was another. He wished them God's speed.

First Squad's mission was to secure the bridge and take control of the ship. The *Wilmington* was fairly automated, and the engines and rudder were actually controlled from the bridge itself. But still, the engines could also be over-ridden in engineering, so once the bridge was under control, either squad would be given the mission to secure the engineering spaces before the entire ship was cleared.

There was no sign of any opposition. Even

considering the darkness, that didn't seem reasonable. The Sea Hawks were pretty noisy, and certainly someone should have noticed.

Pat reported to the lieutenant, then rushed his team aft towards the bridge. Speed was of the essence, so they were doing a modified sort of bounding overwatch, with Third Fire Team providing cover.

A sudden volley of fire sounded in front of them, and rounds pinged around Pat and LCpl Billings from First Fire Team. The sparks caused by the rounds hitting the structures around them looked like flashbulbs through his goggles. He hit the deck and keyed his mic to call for supporting fire, but Davidson had beat him to it. The platoon sergeant had grabbed LCpl Torino, Third Fire Team's automatic rifleman, and directed his fire up to the small deck alongside the bridge. Torino laid down a heavy blanket of rounds from his M27. Pat could see the rounds pinging off the superstructure, and he didn't know if anyone had been hit up there, but the incoming fire ceased.

Pat and Billings looked at each other from where they had taken cover. Billings rolled his eyes, a huge smile on his face. Pat laughed, actually laughed, after having almost caught some rounds. He knew he should have felt frightened, nervous, angry—anything other than excited. This wasn't a game, after all. But that is just what he felt.

"OK, Billings, let's go," he told the lance corporal, still wondering about his odd reaction to being under fire.

"Let's keep it moving, First Squad," SSgt Davidson's voice came over the tactical circuit.

Pat caught the platoon sergeant's eye and raised one hand in acknowledgment. He started bounding forward again, nerves on full alert. Up ahead, he could see Third Squad disappearing inside the ship's superstructure. They would be at the panic room soon, so First Squad had to speed it up.

First Squad was to enter the ship on a hatch towards the starboard. As Third Squad had entered at a different hatch, this one had to be cleared. Consideration had been made to using the ladder that went up along the outside of the superstructure all the way to the bridge, but the officers thought this would have them too exposed to any pirate with a weapon.

He was about to remind Cpl Horton of the proper clearing techniques, but he bit that back as he could see Horton's fire team deploy up ahead, just as they had in a million rehearsals back at LeJeune and Little Creek prior to getting underway. He shifted a bit to his right and brought his M4 up so he could give cover if needed.

In one way, Pat felt like an observer. Through the night vision goggles, there was a bit of an unreal aspect to what he was seeing. That created a feeling of detachment, that he was watching a Discovery or History channel show on the military. He knew that he had to snap out of that mindset. As being fired at only a few moments before attested, this was for real. And he was the squad leader. It was up to him to make sure things went well.

As Horton's team entered the ship's superstructure, Pat moved ahead to follow. He had planned to enter along with Second Fire Team, but he decided that he could best direct the action from further up ahead.

Inside the ship, the lights were on in the passageways. Pat flipped off his night vision goggles. Cpl Horton was already at the base of the ladder they were supposed to climb, covering someone, probably PFC Dawkins, who was going up. They had four decks to go to reach the bridge level, and each level opened up the potential for an ambush.

The plan was for Horton's team to lead the way to the hatch leading into the bridge. Once there, those Marines would provide cover while Cpl Bonaventure's Second Fire Team would actually breach the bridge, taking out any opposition. Cpl Salazar's Third Fire Team would secure the way up to the bridge to keep anyone from climbing up their asses. Once the bridge was secure, Bonaventure would stay on the bridge while Salazar and Horton went below to secure the engineering spaces if needed.

"Tango-Six-Charlie, this is Uniform-Eight-Lima, what's your status, over?" came over his headset.

This was a secure frequency, so Pat didn't know why they were sticking with call signs, but the lieutenant had insisted on going by the book. With his fire teams, Pat wasn't going to do that, he had decided, as he was afraid of getting things mixed up.

"Uh, Uniform-Eight-Lima, this is, uh, Tango-Six-Charlie. We have passed Topeka and are moving towards Vegas. No opposition here yet, over."

For the purpose of this raid, things had been simplified, and "Topeka" referred to the hatch leading into the ship while "Vegas" was the bridge.

"Uniform-Eight-Lima Actual, this is Uniform-Eight-Lima-Seven. My 20 is with Tango-Six-Charlie now, and we'll be at Vegas in two mikes," came SSgt Davidson's voice over his headset.

Pat recognized his platoon sergeant's voice, but he wasn't sure what the "Seven" in "U8L7" meant. He wondered if Davidson had reverted to Army-speak.

"Roger, Uniform-Eight-Lima, uh, Seven. Copy that. I can see that on my display, even if all your icons are looking stacked up after Topeka. I just wanted to make sure there were no casualties from that burst of fire back on deck. On this side, Alpha-Three-Romeo is approaching Omaha," Lieutenant Niimoto responded, using the code name given for the panic room. No opposition—"

Just then, the sounds of muffled gunfire could be heard, a single volley of fire quickly followed by WWIII as other weapons opened up. Third Squad was probably two decks below them, so the weapon reports muddled together with their echoes within the close confines of the ship's passages. Lieutenant Niimoto's call was cut off.

Pat keyed the squad frequency. "Horton, Third's in it deep, so move it. We need to reach the bridge now!"

"Roger that," Cpl Horton responded.

Looking up the ladder, he could see a rush of activity. He hurried up after them, up four decks until they were at the hatch leading to the bridge. There were five of them standing there in the confined space, with another fire team lined up on the ladder below. Pat knew they should be disbursed, but given the reality of the ship's construction, he didn't think that was going to happen.

With four Marines covering, PFC Dawkins reached out and tried the door handle. It turned, but when Dawkins put some pressure on the door, it didn't open.   He turned back and shook his head.

Well, it figured that it would be either locked or blocked on the inside.   It would have to be blown.   Cpl Horton moved up and placed one of the new remote-controlled shape charges up against the doorjamb.   The new charges were fairly compact and when detonated, were pretty directional as to the path of the blast, but in a confined passageway, even the backblast could be deadly.

There was another passage running down the outboard starboard side a few yards from them, and another on the port side farther away.   Pat could leave Bonaventure's team on the deck below, but it might take them too long to rush up the ladder after the blast and get into the bridge.   So he called them up and told them to take cover in the starboard passageway.   That way, they'd have only a couple of yards to cover to enter the bridge.

He told two of Horton's team to take cover with them and two to go take cover on the port side.

"Remember, the reports were that two friendlies are not in the panic room with the others.   They could be on the bridge, so make sure anyone you shoot at is a pirate," Pat reminded them.

Pat knew the bridge would be darkened with only low red lights on for illumination.   When it was dark outside, it had to be dark inside the bridge for anyone to see out. However, if they went in with night vision goggles on, a pirate could simply turn on the bridge lights, and they would be temporarily blinded for a few precious seconds while their goggles adjusted.   He ordered the lights in the passage to be turned off, then had half of the Marines flip their goggles back on with the infra-red lights beaming.   If the pirates kept the lights off, then they would be able to see.   If someone turned them on, the rest of the Marines would be able to see.

"OK, when you're ready," he told Horton.

As some of the Marines were essentially blind now, without their night vision goggles, Cpl Horton gave the countdown over the squad radio.

"Five, four, three, two, one," he intoned before a huge

explosion and shockwave washed over them all.

Pat had practiced with the new breaching charge, but it was one thing do set it off on a range, another thing altogether inside a ship. His ears were ringing as he got caught up with Bonaventure's fire team as they rushed forward.

The door to the bridge was gone, completely gone. It hadn't been made to military standards, of course, but Pat was amazed that the small charge had taken the door right off its hinges.

Pat followed Torino into the bridge, pulling off his own goggles as someone had, in fact, turned the lights on inside the bridge. Outside the broad, sweeping windows of the bridge, the dawn was making its presence known with a beautiful, rosy entrance on the horizon. Why that registered with him, he wasn't sure, because right in front of him was the body of a man, most of his head and chest crushed. The exploding hatch must have caught him flush. Pat had never seen someone killed before, yet the dawn, something he had seen thousands of times, seem to register more with him.

There was an immediate staccato of fire as PFC Rivera opened up on a man trying to hide behind the captain's chair. He was holding an AK, and although the chair did not offer that much protection, it seemed enough as nothing hit him. The man seemed to be doing a sort of dance, bouncing from one foot to the other, even popping up to peer over the chair at the Marines.

All told, he probably should have dropped his weapon, because Pat, Torino, and Rivera opened up again, and this time, the captain's chair was not enough protection. The man dropped bonelessly, the rifle clattering to bounce on the deck. Blood started to flow out from underneath him, and despite the ringing in his ears, Pat clearly heard the loud exhalation of air that came out of him before the man lay still.

"There's another one!" someone shouted out.

Pat spun to see someone rushing in from the hatch leading to the railing outside. Five sets weapons opened up, and that man dropped as well, face first, his body sliding forward several feet.

The smell of cordite filled the bridge, stinging Pat's nose.   He swung the muzzle of his M4 back and forth as he searched for any other threat.   Horton's team and SSgt Davidson came in as well.

"Check them," the platoon sergeant ordered.

Pat felt a twinge of guilt.   They sure looked dead, but he needed to confirm that.   He shouldn't have had to have the platoon sergeant tell him.

He moved up to the man by the captain's chair, the one he had helped shoot.   He kicked away the man's AK, then with LCpl Torino, flipped him over.   Pat felt a little lightheaded as he looked at the man. He had just taken a human life.

The man sure didn't look Somali, though.   Pat would have guessed him to be European, to be honest.   But whatever his background, he was certainly dead.

"Sgt Dailey, I don't think this guy was armed," LCpl Hester called over.

Pat got up, wiped the blood on his hands on his trouser legs, then moved over to where Hester and Salazar were standing over the man who had been shot last.   He had been hit several times, one round right in the throat, but for whatever reason, there wasn't nearly as much blood as with the dead man by the captain's chair.

Pat looked around.   It was true.   He didn't see any weapon.   Had they shot a man trying to surrender?

"He was armed," SSgt Davidson said, his voice calm and collected.

"But, I don't see any weapon here," put in PFC Rivera, his voice raised up a notch.

"He dropped it overboard when you shot him," the platoon sergeant replied, looking at each of them in the eye as he did so.

"But, he's here inside, how could he drop it out there?" asked Rivera.

"Was he running in here?" asked Davidson.

There were nods from the others.

"Why run into a firefight without a weapon?   No, he was coming here to fight, and you did what you had to do.

All of you. He started his attack, you took him down, and his weapon went over the rail. Simple as that. Now move him over there by that guy," he told them, pointing the man who had been killed by the explosion.

SSgt Davidson looked Pat squarely in the eyes, waiting for a response. Pat wanted to believe him, but going back through his mind, he wasn't sure. Could the guy have had his hands up in the air instead of reaching forward to them? On the other hand, he felt he had to believe the platoon sergeant. And Davidson was a combat vet. He probably had his head on straighter in the excitement of a firefight.

Pat took the easy out. "You heard the platoon sergeant. Move this guy over. I've got to report in."

They rushed to comply as SSgt Davidson gave him an almost imperceptible nod of his head.

Pat switched over to the platoon freq. "Uniform-Eight-Lima, this is Tango-Six-Charlie, over."

"Tango-Six-Charlie, this is Uniform-Eight-Lima, go ahead, over."

"Uniform-Eight-Lima, Las Vegas is secure. I say again, Las Vegas is secure. We have three enemy KIA. No friendly casualties, over."

"Say again your last. How many enemy KIA, over?" the lieutenant's voice asked.

"That was three KIA. One, two three, over."

"Tango-Six-Charlie, we have secured Omaha and have released the hostages. We have one, repeat one enemy WIA. The ship's captain informed us that at least eight pirates boarded, so there are four more onboard here somewhere. Have you seen any signs of the two missing hostages, over?"

Pat looked back at the dead white guy. If he were one of the missing crewmen, he wouldn't have had the AK, would he?

"That's a negative. No hostages here, over."

"Roger that. Wait one," the lieutenant told him. There was an ensuing 20-second silence before he came back with "Tango-Six-Charlie, proceed as planned to Chicago, but take extreme care. We've got four pirates aboard here somewhere. I am keeping the crew here until those pirates are located.   And be advised that Alpha-Three-Romeo will commence a search for the missing crewmen as well as the pirates.   They will be starting forward and working their way back.   Make sure your transponders are working, and for Pete's sake, identify your target before engaging.   We don't need any friendly fire incidents, over."

"Uniform-Eight-Lima, roger that.   Will proceed to Chicago to carry out the mission.   I will coordinate with Alpha-Three-Romeo-Actual to make sure we both know where the other is, over."

"Tango-Six-Charlie, this is Uniform-Eight-Lima, roger, out."

SSgt Davidson had been listening in when he was on the radio with the lieutenant, but the team leaders were not on the same freq.   He called Salazar up, and together with Cpl's Horton and Bonaventure, briefed them on the orders. Nothing had really changed from the original ops order, but the missing four pirates was a concern.

"OK, Hank, you've got it here.   Just be ready in case those guys want to try and retake the bridge.   But remember, Third Squad's going to be conducting a search, so don't get itchy trigger fingers when they come by.   You've got to make sure you ID any target.   Got that?" he asked Cpl Bonaventure.

"No problem.   We've got it," was the expected reply.

He gave the order for Salazar to take his team and lead the way.   Getting to the engine room was a pretty direct shot down the same ladder on which they had come up: eight decks down and then a short zig-zag to the entry.   Expecting a gang of pirates at every level, the two fire teams, along with Pat and the platoon sergeant, made their way down.

At the engineering spaces hatch, made their entry, fully expecting another firefight, but the spaces were empty.   The engine room was clean.

"Uniform-Eight-Lima, this is Tango-Six-Charlie, over."

"Go ahead, over."

"Chicago is secure.   No sign of enemy nor of the missing crewmen, over."

"Roger that.   I've got Alpha-Three-Charlie sweeping

the living spaces now.   I want you to search every inch of the engineering spaces.   Our two missing crewmen could be anywhere, especially if they've been killed and stashed somewhere.   So be thorough, over."

"Roger.   We'll be looking hard, over."

"Oh, and Pat, you did good today.   I'm proud of you. This is Uniform-Eight-Lima, out."

Pat felt a rush of pride.   He looked up to catch SSgt Davidson's watching him.   The platoon sergeant gave him a thumbs up.

Damn, the lieutenant and the platoon sergeant? he thought to himself.   His first taste to combat was proving to be something special.

Chapter 12

Aboard the MV Wilmington

"Roger, this is Uniform-Eight-Tango, out," Tony said into the handset before giving It back to Cpl Steptoe. "Thanks, Stepchild."

He grimaced at that. He really needed to watch that, especially in front of the squad leaders and SSgt Davidson. He has just been so used to calling Steptoe by his nickname back at the detachment that it had become almost ingrained.

He shook it off, though. He was too excited to let that affect his mood. He turned to the others.

"The CO gave us a 'well done.' It looks like we're the only ones who had any action. That piracy they were called to? Looks like a false alarm. Seems as if the Pakistani crew were on some sort of strike due to the conditions on their ship, so the company had to stand down. So that's twice now that First Platoon has accomplished a mission while everyone else has been sitting on their asses!"

Tony's smile was infectious, and Sgts Dailey and Stanhope went so far as to high five each other. Even SSgt Davidson was smiling.

"Everyone's worried about the two missing crewmen, though. We're supposed to do another search, checking every compartment, every locker, everything. The *Dunham*'s steaming here at flank speed, but before that, we'll have the Sea Hawks back from refueling, and the helos will be bringing Third Squad and some ship's personnel as well. Our orders are to stay on board, look for the missing guys, guard the prisoner, and basically wait until the *Dunham* gets here. I'm going to leave the search to SSgt Davidson here. I want you to organize it," he said directly to the platoon sergeant before turning back to encompass the others as well. "And remember, just because we didn't run into the other pirates during our first sweep doesn't mean they're not here hiding out someplace, so be on your toes. Cpl Steptoe and I are going to go back to the bridge and brief the captain on what we're doing now. Any questions?"

There were a few shakes of heads.

"OK, then, let's get going. Oh yeah, the captain said he's going to get the galley going, too. He swears by the food on this ship, and he's going to break out the steaks for his crew and for us. So SSgt Davidson, please figure out some sort of schedule to get everyone some chow if we're not done with the sweep before it's ready."

There was a chorus of "aye-ayes" as SSgt Davidson took the two squad leaders under his wing to get the search underway.

Tony started to move up to the bridge, his big radio operator in tow. He still felt excited and hyped. In Delhi the detachment had been on the defensive, trying to hold out. This time, though, they had been in the offense, taking it to the enemy. This felt far more satisfying. Even when that lone pirate had opened up on them, instead of feeling frightened, he had felt a rush of excitement.

Of course, the fact that the pirate had only been hit once in the thigh and once in the side was a little embarrassing. How the heck five Marines could open up on a guy only 10 yards away, and in a confined passage at that, and only hit him twice was beyond Tony's imagination.

The pirate couldn't have weighed more than 130 pounds. He had passed out after being shot, and Doc Supchak had given him first aid, assuring Tony that the man would make it. Tony had assigned one of the fire teams to watch over him, which might have been overkill, but what the heck? Maybe when the translator came on the inbound Sea Hawks, the guy would come to and they could find out what happened to the missing crewmen.

Chapter 13

At Sea in the Indian Ocean

Craig tried to shift his body, to get some sort of comfort so he could fall asleep, but that seemed an impossible task. He had finally become numb to the smell of rotting fish, but the rough planks of the deck in the hold just didn't allow for comfort.

He looked over at Bong. Although it was fairly dark in the hold, the damage to Bong's face showed up like a beacon. Craig felt pretty guilty about that. Whatever Bong's intention, Craig should have ordered him to the panic room. But he'd been caught along with Craig, and when the pirates tried to get the two of them to open the panic room, Bong had been beaten unmercifully.

Craig had taken quite a few shots himself, but the pirates had shown a degree of ruthlessness as they beat the crap out of Bong. Craig wondered if the beating was more for show, to let Craig know they were powerless. But even if he had wanted to, Craig could not have gotten inside the panic room. He tried not to wonder what he would have done if he had the ability to open it up.

Bong had yet to regain full consciousness, now a full day after their capture. When the pirates had given up trying to get the panic room open the day before, both Craig and Bong had been tied up and left in the passageway. The young guy who had first watched over Craig on deck still watched them, and Craig hadn't been able to tell if he had even the slightest sympathy for what had been done to the Able Seaman. He had wanted to think he recognized the briefest flash of empathy in the young man's eyes, but Craig had known that could have been just wishful thinking.

Craig had lain beside Bong for quite awhile. Several times pirates had come back to look at the two of them, but no one had offered any water or food. Once, two men had come back and seemed to be arguing over them. That rather concerned Craig. He didn't think he was going to be executed outright, but another beating seemed a probability rather than a possibility.

Untold hours later, several of the pirates had come down and rousted Craig. He had struggled to his feet, old bones and muscles complaining about the abuse. Bong had been beyond the ability to stand, so finally two pirates had given their rifles to a third, then reached down to pull Bong upright. The third pirate was one of the other youngsters, and he had problems holding all three rifles. For a brief moment, Craig had visions of pulling a James Bond, head-knocking the young man and grabbing the weapons. But even had his hands had not been tied, that would be pretty much impossible for him to pull off anything like that. A Hollywood star he wasn't.

They had been led up the ladder and out on the deck. It had been night, about 12 hours or so since they had been taken, and the ship calmly steamed under the stars. It had been a little surreal. It had seemed so normal on one hand, steaming under the night sky, but the armed pirates left little doubt that things had been decidedly not normal.

They had been led/pushed over to the starboard side. Craig had a momentary fear that they were going to be pushed overboard, to disappear into the deep, dark sea. But as he had gotten to the edge, he could see a fishing boat steaming alongside the *Wilmington*. There had been a rope ladder leading down to it. One of the pirates had pulled a knife out, which shone wickedly in the moonlight, but with a few quick jabs, he had cut through Craig's bindings, taking off a bit of skin from his wrists in the process.

Craig had been pushed forward to the rope ladder, and with shouts and gestures, they made it clear that he needed to climb down. He had peered over the edge. The fishing boat seemed a long way down there, and while he realized they had slowed the *Wilmington* down a bit, it still had seemed like she was moving along at a pretty good clip.

Someone had jabbed the muzzle of a rifle into his back, and none too gently. Craig knew he had to go. Taking a deep breath, he clamored over the side, his feet flailing for a moment in the air before they found purchase on the rungs. Slowly, never taking more than one hand or foot off the ladder at a time, he had made his way down, eyes focused on the sides of the ship, never looking down.

He had been surprised when rough hands grabbed his legs and hustled him off the ladder. It hadn't taken nearly as long for him to climb down as he would have thought.

They had seemed to be having a problem with Bong, though. There was no way he could have climbed down on his own, half-conscious as he was. At one point, it looked like a pirate was going to go first and kind of guide him down, but they had abandoned that, and finding a rope, they tied it around his chest and under his arms before lowering him down to the boat. He banged against the side of the ship on the way down, which had caused his body to spin. As he had reached the fishing boat, he went past the grasping hands, splashing into the water for a moment while the pirates on the boat yelled back up to the ones on the ship to pull Bong back up. It took a moment, but Bong had been finally hauled back aboard.

It had only been then that Craig noticed that one man was obviously not Somali. Even in the darkness, he looked white. He had caught Craig looking at him.

"Enjoy your host's hospitality," he had said in a heavily accented English and accompanied by a laugh.

After Bong had been freed from the rope, the English-speaking man had moved to the ladder and climbed up, along with another guy who probably was Somali. Then most of the pirates who had captured the *Wilmington*, the ones who had beat Bong and him, had come down.

Craig had wanted to call out to the English-speaking guy to ask him what was going to happen to the two of them, but fear trumped his curiosity. He didn't say anything.

Craig had edged back towards the stern, trying to remain inconspicuous. He had looked up at the bulk of the *Wilmington*, wishing for the hundredth time that he had joined the others in the panic room. Down below like this, though, he had gotten a different perspective on his ship. From the bridge or the decks, the *Wilmington* was just the *Wilmington*. Nothing special. Down below like this, though, he had realized that she really was a huge vessel, one he really wished he was still aboard.

One of the pirates had walked over and roughly

grabbed Craig's shoulder, dragging him to a square hatch in the middle of the working deck. Craig had tried to peer into the dark hold, but before he could gather himself, he was pushed into it.

Panic had hit him in the split second he was falling, but he had landed on something soft, or rather somethings soft, slimy and horribly putrid. This was a real fishing vessel, he had realized, even if the fish were way past having any commercial value. He had tried to stand up, but the sliding, rotten fish bodies kept him from getting to his feet. He gagged, saliva flowing from his mouth as he tried to keep from vomiting.

Feet churning, and maybe more on his knees than anything else, he had made it to bare deck alongside the pile of fish. He lost the battle with his stomach, and his long-ago breakfast had joined the rotten fish in the hold.

A shadow had then blocked the small amount of light coming in from the open hatch, and Craig could see Bong being lowered into the hold as well. When he was down, voices yelling out let Craig know he had to get the rope off of Bong. Trying to be gentle, he had slipped the rope off of him, then pulled the barely moving body back off the fish and to the side. Even half conscious, Bong's face had twisted in disgust at the horrible miasma which pervaded the hold.

After about twenty minutes, a rope had come down with a flask of water and a plastic shopping bag with some hard bread in it. Craig hadn't needed to be told to come get it. He had rushed up and untied the two items, then carefully drank half of the water and ate half of the bread. He hadn't known how long Bong would be out, but he would need his share when he did come to.

This little fishing boat's engine had become louder as the boat picked up speed and pulled to the starboard. Craig had figured that they were parting ways with the *Wilmington*. They were off on their own.

Chapter 14

On the USS Jason Dunham
Four days later.

Squat, thrust legs back, chest to the deck, push back up, legs back under, stand up, 28.

Sweat was already pouring off of Burke as he did his 6-count squat thrusts, which were merely a normal squat trust with a push-up thrown in the middle. He had 72 more to go for this set, then three more sets of 100. These had always been one of his favorite exercises, but on the *Dunham's* flight deck, they were a little more difficult than on the dirt back at Lejeune or Bragg. It wasn't just the rough surface of the flight deck which tore up his hands and caught at the toes of his shoes as he thrust his legs and brought them back up. The rolling of the ship itself added to the process, bringing balance into play. Frankly, he loved it, although maybe he wouldn't have minded it if the sun wasn't baking the flight deck into an oven.

Part of his mind had to concentrate on each count of the exercise. It would be easy to catch a toe and fall on his face. But the rote nature of the exercise also allowed for thinking and retrospect. People had different ways to clear the mind of the extraneous—for Burke, exercise did it.

Daily shipboard life had gotten back to the routine since their return from the *Wilmington*, but there was a different mood in the air. The *Dunham*, Marines and sailors alike, had completed a successful mission. There seemed to be a sense of mutual accomplishment, a sense that the *Dunham* team had succeeded. While the Marines and the Sea Hawk crews may have been the first ones to reach and step aboard the *Wilmington*, it had taken the entire *Dunham* crew to send them off, and after the merchant ship had been secured, there had been quite a number of sailors coming over to do whatever it was that sailors do.

Most of the Marines had re-embarked aboard the *Dunham* the next day as the Navy ship arrived and stood half a mile off the beam. But the ship's captain had sent over engineers and others to make sure the *Wilmington* was sea-worthy. The captain had even gone over to take a look around and meet the merchant ship's captain.

When the platoon had returned to the ship, many of the sailors had offered their congratulations, and Burke had had to re-tell the accounts of the rescue several times to different groups.

It wasn't as if there had been bad blood between the sailors and Marines before. There had been some complaints that a DDG is not an amphib, but Burke had never felt any real animosity. It was just that there were two separate groups: the *Dunham's* crew and the Marines and Special Boat Unit. Now, that atmosphere had dissipated. They were one team.

99, 100. One set done.

Burke took a break, wiping the sweat from his eyes.

Damn, it's hot out here on the deck.

He walked over to the hangar where he had stashed a plastic bottle of water and gratefully took a long swallow. It wasn't cold anymore, but it was wet, and that was what mattered. He took some deep breaths, trying to slow his pulse rate.

PFC McNamara swung by on his way around the flight deck.

"Oo-rah, staff sergeant!" he yelled as he passed.

Burke had to smile. McNamara may not be the sharpest pencil in the pack, but he was dedicated. Ever since Burke had had to rally him the week before, McNamara had been hitting the flight deck at every opportunity. It was probably impossible that his physical condition had so dramatically improved in just a week, especially as a full day had been spent on the *Wilmington*, so Burke figured that McNamara's improvement had been mental, not physical. He had just figured out that he could do it instead of wondering if he could do it. There was a huge difference. And with his platoon sergeant there, the PFC had an additional burst of confidence.

Burke had learned that lesson back at RASP before being scrolled into the Rangers. Almost any soldier could physically make it through RASP. They weren't going to kill you, after all.   But what made soldiers drop was the mental part.   They just gave up.   They thought they couldn't do it. And if they thought they couldn't do it, that became a self-fulfilling prophecy.   When Burke was in his first RASP, he refused to acknowledge that he might fail.   He would set up barriers in his mind that wouldn't let those thoughts surface. And by knowing with no degree of uncertainty that he would make it, he did.

And with that thought, he put his water back and went back out in the middle, out of the way of the joggers, to begin his second set.

He reminded himself that he should bring some gloves next time.   He would probably forget again, though.   It was one thing to put up with pain when it was necessary, but gloves would help his hands handle the hot, rough flight deck better.   No pain, no gain, but that could be taken a bit far.

He finished that set of 100, then came back to get another swallow of water.

"Staff sergeant, you got a minute?"

Burke looked up to see Sgt Dailey standing by, a slightly troubled look on his face.   Burke really didn't have a minute.   He had two more sets, but Dailey had seemed a bit down since the mission, and Burke Knew he needed to get to the bottom of it.   The squad leader had done a good job on the *Wilmington*, so Burke was not sure what the issue was.

"Sure, Pat.   Let's move over here," he told him, indicating the long, narrow deck that ran alongside the hangar.

Burke didn't think the design made much sense as the forward end led to nowhere, but they could use it to gain a bit of privacy, something hard to get aboard the ship.

"So what's up?" he asked.

"Um, I've been thinking.   I mean, I've been wondering. You know when we took the bridge?"

"Yeah, so?"

"Well, that one guy, the one who came in, well, I know you said he was armed, but I never really saw him with anything.   I just shot.   Are you sure, I mean, I'm not doubting you, but are you sure he was armed?"

Burke laughed and said, "Buck fever, my man, buck

fever."

"Huh?"

"Back home, we call that 'buck fever.' You go out hunting, you see that big buck in front of you, and you lose focus. You get lost in that big buck. The Dallas Cowboy Cheerleaders could march by, and you wouldn't notice. You get nervous, maybe you jerk your shot. The thing is, you miss things. And when you focused on that pirate coming in, you did what you had to do. You shot him."

The thing was, the man had not been armed. Not that it mattered to Burke, but he thought it would to Pat. The guy was a pirate, and he was rushing to the bridge. If he had surrendered out there on the flying bridge, he would be alive today, but he decided to charge, and why charge in if you weren't planning to fight?

Back in Afghanistan, Burke had watched his platoon sergeant, SFC Winston Doyle, die in some dusty hellhole of a village. There had been a short firefight, but that had been over for at least 10 minutes. They had gathered up some of the people to question them when a young boy had rushed out of a house. The boy couldn't have been more than 12 or 13, and Doyle warned him to stop. The kid didn't look angry or anything. Maybe Doyle thought he was rushing to be with one of the men being questioned. But for whatever reason, Doyle let him come. And since Doyle didn't fire, the others, including Burke, withheld their fire.

Remembering it in a sense of slow motion, Burke could still see the boy smile as he came up, slow to a stop beside the platoon sergeant, then explode into a rose-colored mist. Doyle was killed immediately. Burke was hit in the cheek by shrapnel, earning his second purple heart. Hank Burns ended up losing his leg. All because no one wanted to shoot an "unarmed" kid.

That wasn't going to happen again on his watch. That pirate rushed in, and he paid the price. Burke knew he should explain that to Sgt Dailey, to drive it into his head. And maybe he would later, when things faded a bit. But for now, he thought it better for there to have been a weapon, one lost in the firing.

"I guess that could've happened. I was pretty pumped

up, so I was just reacting."

"And that reaction was the right one.   If you hadn't, you might have lost some of your squad.   Ya done good, there, partner," he said, that last line in an exaggerated drawl.

Sgt Dailey looked at him for a moment, then nodded.

"Thanks staff sergeant. I guess I knew that, but I just wanted to be sure, you know?"

"Well, now you're sure.   And you're keeping me from my last two sets.   You should join me sometime for those. It'll give you a chest that might actually attract the senoritas."

"OK, OK, next time, I'll join you.   Not that I need any help with the ladies, mind you."

Both men laughed as they moved back to the flight deck.   Sgt Dailey went below, and Burke went to attack his last two sets.

Chapter 15

The same afternoon
Aboard and unnamed fishing vessel

"Do you know what I'd like right now?" he asked Bong. "A big scoop of Coldstone chocolate, with raspberries and sprinkles."

"What's Coldstone?" asked Bong as he lay back on one of the drier stretches of the deck.

"You don't know Coldstone Creamery? It's only the best ice cream in the world! And you get to put any topping on it you want."

"Nope, we don't have any in Ilocos."

"But you've been to Manila, and they have one in Makati. And I know they have them in some of the ports we've pulled into," Craig protested.

"Nope. Never been to one. But for me, I could use beautiful *Inihaw na Bangus* right now, just like my Maravic makes."

Craig shuddered before replying, "Isn't *bangus* fish?"

"Yes, a fried fish, and this way is with tomatoes, onions, and *siling pang-sinlgang*. My Maravic makes it . . ."

He didn't complete the sentence, but brought his right hand up until the tips of his fingers touched his lips, then he swept the hand away, opening the fingers and making a smacking sound with his lips, like an overly-dramatic French chef.

"You can think of fish now, in this stinking hold full of rotting *bangus*?"

"This mess isn't *bangus*. *Bangus* is a special fish, white and sweet. And it has to be fresh, the eyes still clear before you cook it," Bong told him.

"Still, fish is fish, and I've had about my fill of it. I'm not sure I ever want to eat fish again."

Bong merely harrumphed. Actually, Craig had to admit that the horrible stench had gotten better, or more probably, his nose had just gotten more used to it. Maybe his nose had just been burned out. Instead of the gut-wrenching, nauseating stink of rotten fish, the smell was more of a pervasive miasma that hovered around—not slapping him across the face, but still a definite presence.

The slime was still pretty bad, though. Craig had found an old piece of cardboard with which he shoved part of the mess of fish aside, using the cardboard like in ice scraper. It was here where the two men lay, trying to keep out of contact with the rotting pile of fish. As the small boat rocked in the seas, though, hunks of fish would slide down the pile and invade their space.

Craig was grateful that Bong was conscious, though. He had come to their second day in the vessel. He wasn't moving much as moving hurt. But mentally, he seemed like the old Bong. Craig knew he must have some internal damage, but that would have to wait until later to be addressed. Hopefully, that was. Hopefully they would be released soon and able to get him to a doctor.

The fishing boat's engine suddenly slowed down and the boat started to rock a bit more. One of the cylinders was pretty obviously missing, so Craig didn't take too much notice until a rope ladder was thrown into the hold and two of their captors climbed down. No one else had been in the hold after the two of them had been put inside, so this was new and potentially threatening. Craig stood up, putting himself between the two men and Bong.

When they got to the bottom, their disgust at the stench was obvious. The young guy, the same one who had first watched over Craig pulled his raggedy t-shirt up and over his nose. Despite the situation, Craig had to smile. That t-shirt gas mask wasn't going to do him any good.

That smile faded as both men pulled out wicked–looking blades.

Was this the end? Now, after all this?

The older guy looked Craig right in the eyes. He held the knife up to his own throat, put his other hand over his mouth before lowering it a bit and saying the one English word, "No." He then shook the knife at Craig, pretty much ignoring Bong, who was still lying on the deck, but watching intently.

The older man told the young guy something, and the

young guy waded into the pile of fish, shoving them to each side like Moses parting the Red Sea. He seemed to be searching for something, but the tricky light evidently caused some problems. A head poked down into the hatch and a voice yelled out, but the older guy just muttered and waved his knife back towards the hatch.

Suddenly, the young guy found whatever he was looking for and called out, shifting his t-shirt off his mouth for a second to yell before pulling it back up. He almost gagged, but he reached down and pulled on a small string. To Craig's surprise the string was attached to a plank, and the plank came up revealing the bilges. The older guy motioned with the knife for Craig to join the younger guy. As Craig hesitantly took a few steps forward, the guy kicked Bong, yelling and motioning for him to move, too. Bong slowly got up and staggered forward before Craig put an arm under his arm and around his back to assist. It was only about 3 or 4 steps, but he wasn't sure Bong could make it on the slime covered deck before falling and hurting himself even more.

They got to the open deck and peered inside. If the hold itself was vile, the bilge was hell incarnate. Not only was the black water oily and as noxious as water could be after years without cleaning, but the rotting fish liquids had dripped in, making a soup that was everything evil. Craig's heart dropped.

The older guy gave Craig a small shove, motioning for him to get into the bilge. He started to protest, but the guy reversed the knife and slammed the hilt into his head, almost knocking him out. Craig had no choice but to step down, then help Bong down as well. He stood there, ankle deep in the fluid, looking hopefully up at the man as if this was far enough. The man raised the knife again as a reply.

Craig slowly kneeled before laying down in the mess. The putrid, viscous fluid felt almost alive, like it was creeping over his skin. Craig couldn't help it—he heaved into the mess. If anything, his vomit only made things better, diluting the truly horrible things in the, well, he couldn't even call it water anymore. Whatever it was, then.

To Craig's surprise, the younger guy clamored in after

them.   He motioned for Craig and Bong to lie together, asshole to belly button.   Then he got down and lay in back of Craig, reaching over him with his knife so the blade was against both his and Bong's neck at the same time.   The message was pretty clear

The older guy replaced the board, leaving them in close-to-darkness.   Craig was grateful for the chinks which let a little light in until the other guy started shoving rotten fish back over their entrance, and liquefied fish began to drip down onto his face.   He started to cough when the blade pressed deeper against his neck.   He took the hint and suppressed it.

The ship's engines cut off, and the boat began to rock in the swells. That caused the bilge water to lap back and forth in small waves, splashing as each wave hit their prone bodies.   The three of them lay together like sardines, and Craig wondered what was going on.   Had they reached port?

A thump alongside the starboard side of the boat seemed to confirm this for a moment, but then they wouldn't still be rocking.   They must be being boarded.   Heavily accented voices drifted in through the hatch to the hold confirming the boarding.   Craig could not make out much of what was being said, but he could pick out a few words of English.   Heavy footsteps pounded above them.

"What is this?" a better-defined voice reached them.

Craig knew that someone was looking into the hold. He contemplated yelling out, but the knife pressed ever-so-slightly harder against his neck.

"No ice.   No ice.   Fish bad," answered a Somali-accented voice.

The first voiced yelled out in another language, probably Eastern European, possibly asking for instructions. Craig didn't know what he wanted.   Did he want the man to come down and search the hold?   If he discovered Bong and him, would there be a firefight?   Would the two of them make it out alive?   Or should the man just leave them there, still captive, but safe for the moment?

A muffled voice seem to answer back.   There was a moment of silence, and Craig could picture a sailor, peering into the hold.   With the horrid smell and vile condition of the hold, no sane man would want to enter it. But would duty overcome disgust?

Evidently not.   Nothing more was heard coming in through the hatch.   There was more clumping about above them, but after another five or ten minutes, that stopped as well.   The fishing boat's engines picked up and the boat started moving out.   Craig still didn't know if he should have felt relief or disappointment.

The young man holding the knife relaxed, removing it from around the two captives.   He hit the board above them with the heel of one hand, but the cramped quarters kept him from putting any force into it.   He tried to shift his position so he could force the board up with his back, and in doing so, scored a cut at the base of Craig's neck and shoulder.   Craig cried out in both pain and shock.

"*Waan ka xumahay,*" or maybe "*wan ka zumahay,*" the young man cried out, dropping the knife into the filth.

He put his hands down and pushed, lifting the boards up with his back, liquefying fish sliding around and falling into the bilge.   He pulled Craig up, then looked at the blood flowing down and staining his shirt.

"*Waan ka zumahay,*" he said again, with a note of what sure sounded like regret.

Was he apologizing?   That seemed ironic to Craig. He reached up to feel the cut, which wasn't actually that deep, but burned like hell.   Craig figured that infection was a far greater risk than any actual damage made by the knife.

"Don't worry about it," he told the young pirate.

That almost made him laugh despite his situation.   He had just been cut by a, yes, by an actual cutthroat pirate, and he would probably get infected, and he was telling the kid not to worry?   He shrugged and reached down to help Bong up thinking about the strange, strange world into which he had gotten himself.

Chapter 16

Hobyo, Somalia
Two days later

Maslax Kusow sipped his *shah adays* and sighed with contentment.   This was his favorite place for drinking the spiced tea, even better than what his wife made, not that he would ever tell her that.   The shop put just the right amount of cardamom—not too much, not too little—and not enough black pepper to drown out the other flavors.

Maslax was "working."   Oh, he had never really held a normal job, one that lasted more than a week or two. Maslax scrounged, connived, sweated when he had to—anything to make a bit of money.   "Legality" was not something that overly concerned him.   His work often straddled that fine line of what was officially encouraged by the government and what was done by the many minions surviving on the streets of Hobyo.   Sometimes, those government officials who publically supported law and order were the very same ones who hired Maslax for tasks that were at odds with their public stances.

He sipped his tea and watched the bustle that always surrounded the waterfront.   Most of the people went about their daily routine in a vacuum, intent on whatever their current task was.   Maslax was always aware of what others were doing, what they might be saying.   Aside from the fact that in Maslax's line of work, he had upset more than a few people, and it made sense to watch out for anyone wishing to extract a bit of revenge from his hide, a hide of which he was really quite fond, being aware of what was going on also presented opportunities.   And finding those opportunities was something at which Maslax excelled.

The morning sun beat down on the streets, and with no breeze coming off the ocean, the temperature was climbing. Maslax debated on calling it a morning and going home. But something kept him there.   He wasn't quite sure what it was, but he had played hunches before, and his hunches usually turned out to be right.

He looked about trying to figure out just what had attracted the attention of his subconscious. Nothing really seemed to jump out at him, and that frustrated him. He prided himself on being a master of observation, but he just couldn't quite put his finger on what it was.

His gaze drifted to the fishing boats, dhows, and pangas tied up at the piers. Nothing seemed to catch his eye at first, but suddenly, there it was. Several men were escorting two women in full burkas off an old fishing boat. He broke out into a smile.

He had noted the boat pulling in earlier, but he realized now that no fish had been offloaded. Now, two Arab women were being helped off the boat, one being rather large and the other needing some assistance. Arabs were not uncommon in Hobyo, and many did wear full burkas. But why would two Arab women be on a fishing boat? And why the close escort?

Truth be known, Maslax might have crewed on pirate pangas once or twice before. He had quit once the foreign navies had stepped up operations. He had no compunction against taking a ship, *per se*, but he did have an aversion on getting shot while doing it.

But just because he might have pirated before, he felt no sense of loyalty to those who still did it. Maslax's loyalty was to himself first, his family second, and this tribe third. He didn't recognize the four men leading away the "women," so in his mind, they were fair game.

He signaled Jiinow, the shopkeeper, and got up. He had to move quickly, and Jiinow knew he would come back to pay for his tea. He pulled his beat-up Vespa back from the line of parked bikes, and got on, looking everywhere except at his targets. Out of the corner of his eye, he saw them turn right and walk down the main street fronting the water. He turned his scooter around and followed them, keeping well back.

One of the men had a firm grasp of the larger "woman's" arm. If Maslax had any doubts before, they were gone. Men, especially non-Arab men, did not touch Arab women like that. He tried to keep from smiling as he puttered along well in back of the group.

THE PROUD

The turned right on the next side street.   He took his time, not wanting to be spotted, and when he turned the corner as well, a moment of panic hit him.   They were gone!

The panic lasted only a moment, though.   As he drove past a parked SUV, he caught sight of them inside.   He kept going, then stopped ahead, pulling out a cigarette and lighting it.   The SUV started, pulled out onto the road, then passed him.   He pulled back out and followed in trace.

As long as the pirates kept inside the city, the crowded streets would keep the car slow and allow Maslax to keep up. If they got outside the city, his little Vespa did not have the oomph to follow.   Finding them then would take some effort and expense.

He was pleased, then, when after only five minutes or so, the car pulled into a courtyard.   He couldn't follow them in, but by stopping on the street outside, he could see them get out and manhandle their captives up the stairs to a second story door in the back.

Maslax carefully pulled the filter off his cigarette and placed it in his pocket.   For someone who had a flexible system of morals, he was very meticulous about littering.   A man just does not leave his trash for others.

He started his scooter back up and started to make his way to the north side of town.   Maslax made his living by knowing things, and he knew of a foreigner, a Chinese man, who would pay for what Maslax had observed.   Pay very well, in fact.

Yes, this had been a very profitable morning.

Chapter 17

Hobyo

Even if he wasn't going to admit it, Asad was glad to be back on solid ground. He was an inland boy, after all, the constant motion of the panga had been rough on him. The American ship had been better, but then they had transferred to that horrible fishing boat with the two prisoners. Asad was nominally Muslim. He prayed as required—at least when it was convenient. And he didn't eat pork, not that there were many pigs back in Galinsoor. But he was pretty fastidious and embraced that aspect of Islamic law.

That fishing boat was vile. The smell alone would make a normal man sick without even taking the constant rolling into account. And the odor! It was utterly unspeakable. How those two men could survive down there was beyond him.

He had tried to stay on deck, near the bow, on the trip to port. He only went back to lower food and water to the prisoners, wondering how they could eat in that putrid mess. But the white guy had taken the food, and on the second day, when the other guy had awakened, both seemed to be eager to eat and drink. What made matters worse was that the hold not only had piles of rotten, decaying fish, but the two men had nowhere to piss or shit. They were lying in their own body wastes. When the foreign navy ship had appeared, Taban had ordered him down into the hold.

"Make sure they keep quiet," he had told him. "If you absolutely have to kill one of them to keep them quiet, do it, but try to keep at least the other alive for the ransom. But remember that it would be better to have no ransom but be free than to let those foreigners know we have the prisoners. So if you have to . . ." he went on, pulling an extended forefinger across his throat.

So Asad had done as ordered. He had gone into the hold with Hanad. He had tried to breathe shallowly, but still, he had to fight from vomiting. He tried to pull his t-shirt over his nose, but that didn't do any good, either.

It took a bit of searching, but he found the hatch into the vile, poisonous bilge. With a degree of fortitude he hadn't known he possessed, he got down into the bilge, made even more noxious when the white guy vomited into it. His own stomach rebelled, but he managed to control it, to keep it from shaming him.

Then came the wait. He could feel the water creep into his pores. But it was heavier, more viscous than real water. He could imagine all sorts of disease-carrying organisms invading his body.

When he heard the voices, he tensed up.

Please don't make a sound, he silently implored the two foreigners.

He had never killed anything larger than a goat, and he didn't want to start now. But the men were quiet. And when the all clear was given, he hurriedly tried to push up on the hatch, not waiting for Hanad. He couldn't get the leverage, so he tried to shift and push up with his back. When he moved, he accidently cut the white man.

He was aghast at himself. He hadn't meant to do that; the man had been cooperating. He had reflexively apologized to the man several times, but the man surprisingly seemed OK about it.

Asad couldn't get out of the hold fast enough. And despite buckets and buckets of seawater, he had still felt contaminated. It wasn't until they had gotten to Hobyo and he had access to a bath that he had finally begun to feel normal.

He looked over at his two prisoners. They had both been chained around an ankle and to a metal ring on the floor, but they had a bit of movement. They had been given a bucket of water apiece with which to wash, and while the water had turned almost black with filth, they were only nominally cleaner.

The brown man was still suffering from his beating. He slept a lot, as he was doing at the moment. Asad still didn't know why he had been beaten so badly. He hadn't been resisting. And if he died, well, that was less ransom for them to split, right?

His gaze shifted to the white man.   He seemed old, like a grandfather.   What was he doing out at sea?   Shouldn't he be home with his wife, with his children, with his grandchildren?   Asad realized didn't even know his name. He wasn't that familiar with American names to begin with, but maybe Tom or Jerry?   Ronald?   George?   Osama? Michael?   Mickey?   Starbucks? That was about the extent of his knowledge of American names. The man was sitting down, leaning against the wall, head back.   The cut Asad had given him was more evident now that he had been partially cleaned up.   The expanding area of redness was also evident.   Asad recognized the first signs of infection.

He felt pretty bad about that.   If he hadn't been in such a panic to get out, he would not have cut the man.   And unless the Americans paid the ransom soon, Asad knew the man might die.   He wondered if he should have insisted on getting the man some medical care when they arrived in port, but quite frankly, he hadn't want to draw any attention to the gash.   He hadn't told anyone what had happened. Besides, it was not as if the others could not see it.   They had more experience in this kind of thing.   They would get the guy medicine if he needed it.

He began to wonder about the man.   Where was his home?   How many goats did he have there?   How many sheep?   Was his wife a good cook?   It would be easier to think of the man, of both men, as enemies, as people trying to steal Somali resources as foreigners had been doing for centuries, but as both were chained captives, well, they didn't look like enemies.   They certainly were not dangerous.

He shook his head.   Such a train of thought was dangerous, even if the two men were not.   They were his enemy, and they had come into Somali waters.   They took a chance, and now had to pay the price. And as soon as the rich Americans paid the ransom, they would be going back home to their families.

He settled back.   He had only an hour or more until Ghedi would come to relieve him, and then he could get back out of this stinking room and away from these stinking, unclean foreigners.

Chapter 18

Aboard the USS Gaffert
Four days later

Captain Terrell Svenson strode down the passage towards his stateroom in a foul mood.   He was royally pissed off.   He felt cast aside, a little kid being told to run along now while the adults took care of things
　　He had heard that the two missing crewmen from the *Wilmington* had been located even before the brief.   When the captain had begun the brief with the comment that the US government would not allow citizens to be held for ransom, a thrill had run through him.   At last, he was going to see some action.   He was going to get some vindication.   So when he found out that they were bringing in a SEAL team to be the point of main effort, well, this was just one more case of wasted potential, of close, but no cigar.
　　All his life, Terrell had dreams of being somebody.   Growing up in Chicago, of course, he had Barrack Obama's example as a local African-American who made good.   But it was his uncle who had more of an effect on the young man.   His uncle was first elected as Chicago's Cook County District Attorney and then a few years later appointed as the district's U. S. Attorney.   He was a man whose reputation was stellar.
　　His uncle had gone to school under the ROTC program, then let the Army pay for his law school as well.   He had gotten in his fighting chops as both an Army defense counsel and prosecutor, and when his obligation was up, he resigned and joined the office of the DA, quickly becoming a rising star.   He was elected as the DA at a relatively young age, and after he was appointed as the U. S. District Attorney, there were rumors of higher political aspirations.
　　If it worked for Uncle Doug, Terrell figured it could work for him, too.   So he applied for ROTC, got a scholarship, and was commissioned as a second lieutenant in the Army.   But he was not going into law.   He was going infantry, airborne specifically.   He wanted to become a general.

But while he seemed to fit the mold, from his appearance, carriage, and on-paper abilities, Terrell never seemed to excel. He was an also-ran. And despite being in the 82nd Airborne's alert battalion more times than he could count, he never went anywhere. He had never heard a shot fired in anger.

Then there was Jenny. Jennifer Lorenz. Jenny was a civilian working for the base adjutant, and he had met her at the gym. Tall, almost as tall as he was, she was a big, strong girl, just what Terrell liked. They started working out together, and one thing led to another. Soon, they were in the full throes of a passionate affair.

The only problem was Captain Henry Lorenz of the 2nd Battalion, 505th Parachute Infantry Regiment, her husband. Oh, the two had problems and were not even living together. But they were technically still married, and he was drawing married BAH. In the Army, their affair was a no-no.

Terrell had been called in before his battalion commander and read the riot act. He had been shown a letter of reprimand, already signed. He knew his career was over. But the CO had thrown him a lifeline. The Marines were being stood back up, and they needed junior and mid-level officers to fill the ranks. If Terrell would put in for an inter-service transfer, well, that letter might just make it into the "circular file."

Terrell didn't hesitate. He accepted. The Army had been merely an instrument to a goal. The Marines could serve the same purpose. He put in the paperwork, got accepted, and left for Camp Lejeune. Amazingly, he got a rifle company, one slated for deployment. He worked tirelessly to excel, to impress his new CO. He was ready to jump into the fire.

Consequently, he had been devastated when they were called forward for action only to find out it was a false alarm. To make matters worse, 2ndLt Niimoto and his platoon had conducted a successful rescue of a merchant ship. Niimoto! It wasn't as if that guy needed any more publicity. He had gotten lucky once before, and then lightening had struck a second time. As Niimoto's company commander, some of that glory would rub off on him, but still, that was reflected glory, not earned glory.

Then, word came down that they had located the two crewmen.   Surely this would be his chance at last.   But the powers that be decided no.   This was evidently too sensitive to be given to the raw Marines.   This would go to the SEALs. These were the same SEALs that were all too happy to pass over anti-piracy duty to the Marines so they could do their "real" missions.   But now they were being rushed back when there was actually something to do.

If the Marines weren't ready, then why were they deployed in the first place?   And what better proving ground than a baptism of fire?   Terrell knew if given the mission, they would succeed.

It didn't help that the SEAL lieutenant for the team they flew in was understanding and even a bit sympathetic. It might have been easier had he been an asshole.   Then Terrell could hate him and his team.

It also didn't help that the Marines would be involved, albeit in a supporting role. The fact was that they had been examined and been found wanting.   The real warriors, the ones who would get the glory, would be the SEALs.

After the brief, he had gotten on the secure comm back to LtCol Pavoni.   The CO was well aware of the situation, and Terrell got the feeling that he was pissed, too.   But he told him that this was a Navy-commanded operation and to march on.   He was going to try to send Major Conrad, the XO, down to meet them, but he stressed this was not to take away any of Terrell's authority or to take command, but merely to give Terrell a bit more horsepower in dealing with the Navy staff.

Terrell did appreciate the vote of confidence.   In his last battalion, at least, he knew that LTC Harbaugh would have probably sent his XO or OpsO to actually take command over a mere company commander.

They still had a full day's steam to get into the AO, and they needed to hook up with the *Dunham* and the *BRP Ramon Alcarez*, a Filipino frigate on anti-piracy patrol. When the Chinese government had passed on the intel on the hostages, the Philippines had demanded to be a part of the rescue as one of them was a Filipino citizen.   Terrell wasn't sure how they could contribute, and given the initial discussion, no one on the ship's staff was sure either. But orders were evidently orders, and contribute they would.

In the back of his mind, though, was a thought that made Terrell feel guilty. Somalia was the home of Black Hawk Down, the Battle of Mogadishu. The Somalis had proved that a simple operation could go awry. And if it happened again, maybe Kilo Company could serve in a little more glorified position than as a simple security element? He couldn't bring himself to out-and-out wish for trouble. But still . . .

Chapter 19

Aboard the USS Gaffert
The next day

"I thought the skipper was going to bust a gut, he was so jealous," Stan told him.

Tony had been flown to the *Gaffert* for the ops order. First Platoon was almost an afterthought in the operation, ordered to hold a blocking position to the south of the objective.   He had taken his orders and was ready to fly back to the *Dunham*, but like any good Marine with a few free minutes, he had gone into the wardroom where the mess attendants had rustled him up some food.   Chow was a commodity you took when and as often as you could.

The other lieutenants had come along, Rob to get some chow, too, but all to get a first-hand perspective of the re-taking of the *Wilmington*.   In between mouthfuls of veal cutlets, velvet cake, and bug juice, Tony gave a pretty unvarnished account of things.   He knew he already had a rep, and he didn't want to embellish anything but rather keep it low-key.   He shouldn't have worried.   None of the others seemed jealous in the least, and all were hanging on every word, even going so far as to give the occasional high-five as Tony went over a particular event.

"Well, now it's your turn.   You're the security force for the rescue, and that'll be in the thick of things."

"Speak for yourself, Kemosabe.   I'm the XO, which means I'm stuck on this tub while you guys get all the fun. Gil here, he's the one on the security force, even if the skipper is taking command of it."

Gil made a fist with his right hand and slammed it into his chest over his heart twice, nodding.

"And I'm just like you, a blocking force," added Rob, a bit of cream frosting sticking to the corner of his mouth.

"Well, whatever.   At least we're all involved.   Not like the rest of the battalion, up in the Med right now.   I bet they're jealous, at least," Tony told them.

"Yeah, I bet.   But payback's a bitch.   I got an e-mail

from Mason last week with a pic of him and Jayden on the beach in Benidorm.   Not only did they have a brew in hand, but also two topless British girls in just their teeny weeny bikini bottoms," Stan responded.

"Mason?   Jayden?"

"Ah, forgot you were a new join.   Mason is the XO and Jayden's a platoon commander in Golf Company.   And the *Pearl Harbor* had three days of libo in Benidorm.   I've never been on the coast of Spain, I mean at the resorts, not Rota, but from what they tell, me, it's pretty intense."

"Stan, Stan, Stan," put in Gil.   "You're a married man, my man.   I haven't been to Benidorm, but I've been to Marbella, and believe, me, that's not the place for married men.   Too much temptation.   But for single men, especially single, good-looking men like yours truly, well, 'heaven' is a pretty good description."

"Good looking?   Have you had your eyes checked lately?" Stan asked with a laugh.

"My man, the proof is in the pudding.   Have you ever seen the master strike out?"

"Well, yeah.   How about in Oceana, what, two weeks before we shipped out?"

"Ah, those girls only want pilots.   And none were even good-looking enough for me.   Besides, if you remember . . ."

Tony took a swig of bug juice as he listened in to the banter. He smiled as the two tried to outdo each other.   This camaraderie was something he missed, something he really hadn't had since Delhi.   It made him feel part of something bigger, something important.

On the *Dunham*, he really didn't have that.   A wall had been built between his Marines and him.   There was respect, for sure.   There was a degree of affection, even. But he was now an officer, and even with Stepchild, a Marine with whom permanent bonds had been formed, there was now a gap.   Tony often wondered if he had made the right choice in accepting his commission.

He could joke around with the junior Navy officers on the *Dunham*, to be sure, but it wasn't quite the same.   He was a temporary guest on the ship, and they had different backgrounds and different futures.   This, though, this was part of the brotherhood. He imagined the Roman legions, as they marched into northern Europe or the British Isles, joking and teasing the same way, laughing about their prowess with Egyptian or Spanish women, putting down their companions, their brothers-in-arms. It gave him a feeling of belonging.

"Hey, I hate to interrupt this love affair you two have got going, but Tony and me, we've got to get moving. We've got about five minutes to get up to the flight deck," Rob interjected.

"Don't get your panties in a bind, my man. They're not going to take off without you," Gil told him.

"Time and tide wait for no man. And neither does Navy Air. So with that, we need to get going. Come on Tony. And to you three, we bid you a fond adieu!" he said with a Three Musketeers flourish, sweeping his imaginary hat to the floor as he bowed low.

Rob stood up, grabbing one last piece of velvet cake. Tony dutifully got up as well. He looked at the others. It would have been nice if they could all have been on the same ship. The *Gaffert* was designed to carry many more Marines than just one company (-). She could handle them all easily. But the powers that be had decided that they needed more platforms, and each platform needed a FAST.

He shrugged as he followed Rob out of the wardroom. He had already sent the op order forward to SSgt Davidson, but he had a lot of work to do and not really that much time to do it. He had to get back to his platoon.

Chapter 20

Aboard the USS Jason Dunham

"Take a seat on that rack, there," Burke Davidson told the three squad leaders.

The three Marines dutifully sat down on Petty Officer Saxby's bottom rack while Burke sat down across from them on Doug Kaye's rack. Places for meetings were scarce aboard the *Dunham*, and he had to grab what he could when he could.

He took a moment to look at each one. Sgt Jerry Alvarez was a serious, somewhat quiet Marine, but from all reports, and some of those reports were from Doug Kaye, he had his squad working well with the Special Boat Team. He was pretty squared away, which was probably to be expected from a Marine who had spent his entire career on embassy duty.

Sgt Pat Dailey was also squared away, having served on embassy duty and at Camp David. He had performed well on the *Wilmington*, reacting instinctively and keeping on control of his squad. He had questioned the shooting of the unarmed pirate, but Burke took that as a sense of honor and justice. Combat could get dirty, and lines of morality could shift a bit, but Pat had acted when he had to act and left the moralizing until after. Burke could live with that, even respect that.

Dailey and Alvarez had always been Marines. Even if they had no combat experience, even if the Marines had been out of the warfighting business for the last 11 years or so, Burke still expected them, as Marines, so be able to fight and to lead. So far, neither had disappointed him.

He shifted his gaze to Sgt Aiden Stanhope. His first impression of Sgt Stanhope had not been favorable. He was a wiseass, to be frank. Getting a laugh seemed to be his prime purpose in life. To top it off, he was a transfer from the Oregon National Guard. Burke had worked with Guardsmen in Iraq and Afghanistan, and they had driven their trucks, built their installations, and even fought well.

But Burke was a Ranger, and Rangers knew they were the best. Guardsmen were, well, they didn't call them weekend warriors for nothing. They were teachers, cops, truckers, farmers, stockboys at WalMart first, soldiers second. To most active duty soldiers, if the Guardsmen were any good, they would be regular Army, right?

But Aiden Stanhope was good. By his actions, he had changed Burke's impression of him. Of the three squad leaders, Burke perhaps trusted Stanhope the most to accomplish a difficult mission. He had forged Third Squad into a tight, efficient unit. The lieutenant had been very impressed with him on the *Wilmington*, and while Stanhope didn't know it yet, the platoon commander had confided in him that he was recommending the squad leader for a Navy and Marine Corps Commendation Medal with Combat V.

Burke also had to re-think his position on the Guard and Reserves a bit. While waiting for the movie to start one evening in the mess decks, Sgt Stanhope had recounted to them about his two deployments to the 'Stan with the Guard, how that had cost him two jobs, two well-paying construction jobs that his active duty pay could not match. He had gone through his savings keeping up his mortgage during his first deployment, but when he went back only 18 months later, he couldn't manage it, and he had to sell his house. His wife and three kids moved back in with his mother-in-law.

If Burke had thought about it before, he probably thought that Guardsmen used their service for a few extra bucks without having to be a full-time soldier. He never considered that serving could be a financial hardship. And even having experienced that financial hardship, Sgt Stanhope's volunteering to get back into the active forces was pretty admirable.

All three squad leaders sat there, waiting for him to speak. Burke still felt the Rangers were the elite to the US military, but he had to admit that he had a pretty good set of NCO's under him. They could do the job.

But while they had performed well accomplishing their first two missions, both of those missions had been pretty cut-and-dried. There were obvious good guys and bad guys, and obvious course of action. Their upcoming mission might be a bit dirtier.

"You all got the lieutenant's Five Paragraph Order. We know our mission, and frankly, it could be just as easy as that. We go in. We get out after the hostages are rescued. We are back in time for lunch. And all of you have already been bloodied. You are not rank newbies in the game of war. So no problem, right?"

None of the three said anything. They knew there was more to this.

"But let me tell you something. Somalia is the land of *Black Hawk Down.* If one thing the Battle of Mogadishu taught us is that nothing there is as easy as it might seem. The people here will just as likely pick up a rifle and shoot you as help you, even if you're there to help them. And in this case, we're not going to help anyone. We are going to impose our will on them, to take back what is ours."

He paused. Although he had gotten scrolled long after the battle, the Battle of Mogadishu was now as part of Ranger history as was Iwo Jima for the Marines or Camerone was for the French Foreign Legion, where soldiers fought against huge odds. And he had served with Rangers who had been with the 3rd Battalion, 75th Ranger Regiment during the battle. He had gotten first-hand accounts of the crazy mayhem that occurred, how hordes of Somalis had taken to the streets to fight.

"We may not have anything to do with the rescue itself. In fact, we probably won't. We're just an insurance policy. But that won't keep the locals from staying away. They might just decide to make things hot for us, either just by mob mentality or because the local warlord thinks he has to show everyone he's the top dog. So, what I am trying to tell you is to keep alert, keep on your toes. Don't let anyone get separated from the rest. We may not be the point of main effort, but the Somalis don't care about that.

"We are part of a rescue force to rescue one American and one Filipino. I don't want to lose anyone from our platoon over them. Not one Marine, *capisce*?"

All three squad leaders nodded their understanding.

"We're not going to have *Black Hawk Down 2* here," he

told them.   "OK, then.   All three of you've got a lot to do, so let's get cracking. "

He got a chorus of "Aye-aye, staff sergeants" as the three Marines stood up and filed out of the berthing space. Doug came in after they left, evidently standing outside the hatch, giving Burke the time he needed.

"They all set?" the Special Boat Team detachment commander asked.

"Yeah, they're going to be fine."

"Well, kick some ass for me, OK?   I wish we were going in, too, but that's a little far for us, I guess.   So I'll just sit back here and wait for you to come back covered in glory," he said, sounding a bit wistful.

"Ah, you're not going to be missing much.   It'll all be routine, and we'll be back before you know it."

Burke wondered to himself if that would be true.

Chapter 21

Ten minutes out of Hobyo, Somalia
The next dawn

Capt Terrell Svenson was excited, no doubt about it. Not scared, not concerned, but excited. Finally, after almost 13 years in the military, he was going to see some action. The Osprey flew low over the waves, closing the distance with the approaching shoreline.

He looked around at the Marines, his Marines, alert and ready. He was still disappointed that he was not going to be the point of main effort, but he had to admit, LT Starlinger was a good guy, and he couldn't bring himself to resent him. The entire SEAL team, in fact, exuded confidence and a sense of lethality.

So what if the SEALs were going to be the actual ones to enter the building where the hostages were being held? He was going to be the one to take care of security, to fight off anyone who came up to stop them. And since Col Saunders, the MEU CO had sent down the three Ospreys from the *Pearl Harbor*, he had more than enough seats to take every Marine ashore. And since that also freed up the *Gaffert's* own Army Black Hawk detachment to supplement the Navy Sea Hawks, he could get his other two platoons ashore, too.

Not even the infighting within the command could get him down. Normally, the Amphibious Group commander, a Navy officer, would be in command during the sea stage of an operation, while the MEU commander, a Marine, would take over as they crossed the beachline, but with both of them in port in Italy, they were sort of out of the loop. Col Saunders had sent down LtCol Pavoni, the battalion (more specifically, the ground element) commander down with the Ospreys, but CAPT Dregg had put his foot down and insisted that CDR Harrelson had overall command as it was the Navy SEALs who were the point of main effort. So LtCol Pavoni was back in the CIC monitoring the operation, probably chomping at his bits.

As an Army man, he was used to Black Hawks, and in

fact, there was an Army detachment of Black Hawks aboard the *Gaffert* as the Marine Corps had yet to really re-establish their air wing. But the Ospreys, while they kind of made him a bit nervous, were a fine ride. They were booking it. The scuttlebutt was that General Lineau had insisted that there was Marine Air presence, so three of the Ospreys that had been transferred to the Navy when the Marines were gutted were transferred back to the Marines. The three birds were paid for by blue dollars rather than green, and the supply chain was still blue, but emblazoned on the fuselages of each was a proud "U. S. MARINES."

He glanced once more at his Google Maps printout of Hobyo. While it had grown quite a bit over the last 10 years after the construction of the docks (paid for by USAID, he was surprised to find out) and after drought had continued to devastate the country's interior, it was still barely 3 km long. And it still had only two major routes of egress into and out of the city. One route took off to the north, and Third Platoon would be the blocking force there. One left the town towards the southwest, and First Platoon would be the blocking force there. But neither should get any action. Whatever was going to happen would happen around the building just north of the center of town. Terrell would deploy his Marines around the building, protecting the SEALs who would be forcing entry into it and rescuing the hostages.

He had to be quick, though. The Ospreys were fairly large birds, and luckily, there was a soccer field right next to the building. But they had to get out and deploy while the SEALs fast-roped into the building and took the pirates down before they could harm the hostages. They had rehearsed on the deck of the *Gaffert*, but that was a far cry from real life in a built-up area. Terrell was concerned about the timing. Well, they would just have to do it.

He glanced at CDR Harrelson. The man was trying to look calm and in control, but Terrell knew he had to be about shitting bricks. He may be a great boat driver, but this was a bit out of his element. Terrell doubted the man was scared about life and limb, but more likely scared about failure. He wanted to tell the commander to just sit back, let the Marines and SEALs do their jobs. Then he could get the credit and a nice ribbon to adorn his chest.

The big Osprey banked hard to the left. They were getting close. Of the three-bird formation, two would take the Marines to the soccer field as the third would fast-rope the SEALs onto the target building's roof before dropping off Kilo's mortar section and two squads of the machine gun section to provide LZ security. The rest of the Weapons Platoon and Third Platoon's wayward squad that couldn't embark aboard the *Independence* would provide security to the west of the target while Second Platoon and Terrell's headquarters element would provide security to the north, east, and south of the objective.

If they were more robust to the west, well, that gave more security to their aircraft and would help to speed up their egress. Terrell didn't figure them to be there for more than 10 minutes, 15 minutes top, and he needed to get everyone back on board quickly.

The Osprey's crew chief gave them the one-minute signal. It was almost go time!

The roar of the rotors and big engines shifted. Terrell knew that the rotors were shifting from horizontal to vertical flight. As the Osprey came down, he surreptitiously reached down to unbuckle his seatbelt. He knew he was supposed to wait until the bird was actually on the ground, but he wanted to be able to move immediately.

And then, with a thump, they landed. He jumped up and followed his Marines down the cargo hold and ramp. This was just like rehearsal!

Or not!

As soon as his feet hit the dirt, he was blinded by dust. The *Gaffert's* nice clean deck had nothing to push into the air. The Osprey threw up a lot of heat, much more than a Black Hawk did, but it also threw up much more of a rotorwash. And when landing in a dusty soccer field, it seemed to pick up half of Somalia. More on instinct than anything else, Terrell simply ran, trusting his feet to keep him upright. It probably only took a few moments, but it seemed longer before he broke out of the dust and could see again. He glanced up and saw SEALs fast-roping down a hovering Osprey.   He was on track, and only 30 or 40 meters from the objective.

He motioned to Sgt Black, his radio operator.

"Tell LtCol Pavoni we are on the deck," he ordered before moving out, trusting the sergeant to keep up.   With the new personal communications system, he had easier and more direct coms with his platoon commanders and with the SEAL team, but he still needed the longer-range radios to communicate with higher headquarters, and he planned on keeping those higher headquarters well-informed of all action they had to take.   Terrell wanted to succeed, to show the world he was capable.   But an indication of that acceptance by others would be with a medal.   He didn't want to admit to himself that he could be medal hunting, but there it was.   He also knew that the Corps had a reputation on being much more parsimonious with medals than the other services, but if this all went down right, certainly there would be a Bronze Star in the making?

He glanced back.   He could see Lt Desroches organizing his Marines.   The man was good, he had to admit.   His weakest platoon commander was probably Lt Hartigan, and he had played with the thought of replacing him with the XO for the mission, but that might indicate to the CO that he could not train his lieutenants.   It was better that he rode the young officer and corrected him on the ground, if it was needed.

He had relented, though, with the XO.   With the increased boat spaces due to the unexpected arrival of the Ospreys, he had let Lt Kremer go with Desroches to manage the LZ security.

The Osprey hovering over the objective took off and swung around to land on the LZ.   The SEALs were in!   He had to move it.

He looked around, ready to kick Lt Hartigan in the ass, but to his surprise, the young second lieutenant was moving ahead, and with SSgt Pierce, his platoon sergeant, he was already beginning to encircle the objective.

"Don't hold me back, Sgt Black," he yelled.   "Keep up with me!"

If the radio operator rolled his eyes at that, Capt

Svenson didn't notice.   He rushed forward.

There was a brief staccato of fire. Was that inside the objective or outside?   He looked around.   It was morning, but not too early.   There should be people around, going about their daily routine, but he couldn't see anyone except Marines.

"Two, this is Six.   Are you under fire, over?" he keyed into his company circuit.

As the comm was secure, he didn't feel the need to use call signs, and he had told his lieutenants to use plain language to ensure there were no misunderstandings.   This might be breaking the SOP, but Terrell wasn't above that if he thought he had a better way of doing things.

"That's a negative, Six.   The fire is coming from inside the objective, over," came the response from Lt Hartigan.

"Roger that.   Keep your eyes open, though.   We may have some rats bailing ship right ricky tick.   Out."

He arrived at the south side of the objective.   This would give him control of both the east side of the security force and over the LZ security force at the same time.

He backed up against the stucco wall of a shop or something, across the dusty street from the objective, motioning for Sgt Black to join him.

"You got your SITREP format?" he asked the young Marine.   He had spent a lot of time before and during the deployment drilling the radio operator on the various reports sent to higher headquarters.   He didn't want to stop his flow of leadership to sit down and write a report, so trained his radio operator to do them instead.

"Yes, sir," came the expected reply.

"OK, go ahead and send it.   Make sure you let them know there has been hostile fire."

He wondered a bit about the last.   Had it really been hostile fire?   Or had that merely been a trigger-happy SEAL?

He could monitor the platoon frequencies, so when several messages were sent about approaching "possible hostiles," he leaned forward to peer down the road leading to the beach.   A man was in the middle of the road, leading a donkey cart.

A frigging donkey cart?   Was that what these people used?

The man had stopped, and one of the Marines stood up, motioning with his M4 to move back.   He may not have understood the English, but he certainly understood the M4.   He hurriedly turned his donkey around and moved back as fast as the little animal would pull the cart.

Idiot, he thought.   *Surely he heard the Ospreys come in.   He was lucky he wasn't shot.*

"Some 'hostile,'" he said to Sgt Black, not expecting a reply.

There was another round of automatic fire, then an increased volume, obviously coming from several weapons.   Terrell jumped, despite himself.   He wondered what was going on.   The SEALs could communicate with him, of course, but he didn't feel he should initiate a query.

The fire ceased.   He looked at Sgt Black, who raised his eyebrows and shrugged his own lack of understanding.   Black was a good kid, he realized.   He rode him hard and expected a lot out of him, but that was OK.   He was going to have to take care of him after all of this was over.

The sun had begun to warm up the streets and buildings.   A fly buzzed around, looking for someplace to land.   It seemed a little surreal to Terrell, to be sitting here in the sun in a deathly quiet town on the coast of Africa.   Whatever he expected combat to be, this wasn't it.

He settled down to wait, wondering what he should be doing.   The XO reported in that the LZ was secure and the mortars set up.   With a town as small as Hobyo, even his 60's could cover the entire area of operations.

He looked at his watch.   He thought that surely the hostages had to have been rescued by now.   Despite his expecting something, anything to happen, he jumped a bit when Sgt Black touched him with his radio handset.

"Sir, it's battalion.   He wants to speak to you."

He looked at his wrist to where he had written his assigned call sign.

"This is Foxtrot-Niner-Romeo Actual, over."

"Foxtrot-Nine-Romeo, this is Whiskey-Four-Delta Actual, over.   The assault element reports there are no friendlies at the objective.   I repeat, no friendlies.   They will continue to search, but they do not expect to find anyone.   Consolidate your position and await further orders.   Do you copy, over?"

No friendlies?   The hostages were not in there?   How could that be?   They had received good confirmation, even a satellite photo.

"Roger, Whiskey-Four-Delta.   I copy that, over."

"This is Whiskey-Four-Delta, out."

He leaned back against the wall of the shop.   *What now?*

Chapter 22

Hobyo, Somalia

Asad heard the clatter of the aircraft up to the north.   He tried to look out the small window, but he couldn't see anything.   He knew that sometimes a government official would fly in to take payments or to meet with the town leadership, but this didn't sound like the same thing.   This sounded like a number of aircraft.

He looked over at his charges.   The white man, *Craig*, the translator said his name was, was getting worse.   His neck was red and swollen, and it seemed his breathing was being affected.   Asad had managed to bring in a blanket, and it was on this that the man was laying down.   Asad was not a doctor, but he didn't think Craig would last much longer.   He felt guilty about that, and not only for the loss of a ransom.

The other man, *Bong*, wasn't even an American.   He was from the Philippines.   Asad knew that was somewhere in Asia, but just where or why someone from there was working on an American ship, he really didn't know.   At least Bong seemed to be getting better.   He was more alert, and he was trying to take care of Craig.

As the noise from the aircraft reached them, Bong looked up.   A look of hope came over his face.

Asad reached down and picked up his AK.   Could the Americans be mounting a rescue attempt?   If so, then Asad was happy they had moved.   It had all been part of the overall plan, Taban had told him.   The two men had been dressed in the burkas the Arab women wore when they were taken from the ship to the first house, but that was not intended to fool anyone, only to make sure certain eyes saw them.

The *badaadinta badah* knew there were traitors in the country, willing to sell out their brothers.   And there were only so many places to take hostages.   So the two men were taken to their first stop and hustled inside.   Then, at a specific time told to them by one of the foreigner men who supported them, they took the two hostages out to the roof, ostensibly to bathe them. Asad wasn't sure how some sort of eye-in-the-sky could spot them. Maybe they had trained birds? But he took his leaders' word for that.

Then, at night, again at a specific time, the two prisoners were placed into large barrels, and along with five empty barrels, were taken by donkey cart to their present position. Only Taban, Ghedi, Korfa, (the man who could speak English) and Asad came into the house, and their weapons stayed inside. Nothing was shown to the outside world. Aziza, an older women, stayed downstairs and fixed their food, but she never came upstairs where they kept the prisoners.

Asad thought all the subterfuge was silly. What could the Americans do? There were thousands of men in Hobyo, warriors. He couldn't believe that they would risk any more men just to rescue one of their own when only a payment would get him back. For such a rich country, such a payment was like the bite of a mosquito, nothing more.

Asad was young, but he had been taught about the *Battle of the Rangers*. It was true that over 1,000, maybe 2,000 of his people had been killed in Mogadishu on that day, but they had shown the Americans that the Somali scorpion had a fierce sting. Surely they wouldn't try anything like that again.

Some of the aircraft noise started getting louder. He could begin to make out a thwok-thowk-thowk sound. He rushed over to look out the window. He couldn't see anything at first, but then a huge shadow passed directly over his head. It was low and loud. It flew down 100 meters or so, then hovered over the intersection just barely within Asad's field of view. Ropes came out, then men started sliding down the ropes like water drops sliding down a stalk of grass. As soon as the soldiers reached the ground, they ran off and out of sight. Within moments, the Black Hawk, for Asad could not mistake the distinctive shape which had been plastered on t-shirts for years and which played a role in the movie readily available throughout the country, rose and flew away. Another Black Hawk flew in, and more soldiers came sliding down ropes. It too flew away, and suddenly, all was quiet.   People who had been on the streets below only two minutes earlier had seemingly been swallowed up by the city.

Asad was amazed.   True, any country which could make such an amazing weapon of war had some power.   He had to admit that seeing the Black Hawks in person was different from seeing the movie. And they looked much more powerful than the small helicopters used by the government. But his people had shown that they could bring them down. Why would they come again?   Wouldn't it be much easier just to pay their fine, the ransom, to get their man back? And did the Philippines have the same power?   Could they be involved, too?

He looked back at the two prisoners.   Craig was asleep, or perhaps unconscious.   Bong, though, he was smiling at him.   He seemed pretty satisfied.   Asad had an urge to go over and hit him.   Those were American soldiers, not Philippines soldiers.   So they wouldn't help him.   He wanted to smack that smug look off his face.

He sat back down, AK cradled in his lap.   He watched his two prisoners, suddenly wishing he was someplace else. If the Americans found them, what would happen to him? He didn't want to wish anything bad to Ghedi, but he wished this had happened yesterday when he was off.   But he had until nightfall until he would be relieved, and he had to stay put.

He kept jumping back up, looking out the window opening.   But he couldn't see anything.   That didn't relieve him.   He could not see the street directly below him.   But he could imagine.   And he imagined soldiers, hundreds of them gathering outside the door ready to break in and take back their countryman.

He was pretty wound up, and when the door burst open, he would have shot Taban if his safety hadn't been engaged.   Taban merely scowled.   He had brought his weapon with him, which was against their plan of no weapons on the street, so things must be getting tense.

"The Americans are down the street, only 100 meters away.   But they don't seem to be moving.   The other ones, they attacked the false house.   But now, they are all just sitting there, doing nothing.   We've got people moving around, gathering others.   We're going to get them into the street.   Once the Americans see we are serious, they will leave.   But if not, then we'll make the *Battle of the Rangers* seem like child's play."

Asad nodded.   Fighting?   He hadn't thought it would come to that.

"You need to stay here.   Watch the prisoners.   Even if we chase out the Americans, we've lost if we don't have them.   But, if the Americans come in here, you need to kill them both.   We need to show them the only way to get people back is to pay their fines like civilized people.   Let the insurance companies pay.   It is not even the shipping line's money.   But if they come in like this, well, the price they will pay will be in dead men.   Do you understand?"

"Yes, I understand."

"Can I count on you?"   He looked over at the two men.

"Yes, you can.   I will do my duty."

He slapped Asad on the back.   "Good boy.   I knew it. I need to go help gather up the people.   We've got different clans here, and we disagree often, but we need to unite against the Americans.   It won't be long until you hear our roar."

He turned and left the room.

Even with two other men in the room, Asad suddenly felt very alone.

Chapter 23

Hobyo

Private First Class Mason Shuga hunkered down with the rest of his fire team at the end of Route Denver, or Denver Road, or something like that.   At least that's what Sgt Stanhope had called it when they received their OpOrder. He wasn't sure why the Somalis would name a street after a city in America here, and he never saw a street sign with that name.   In fact, it was just a dusty, dry street, and it was getting hot as hell.

They were supposed to be on the ground for only 10 or 15 minutes, but it had already been 30 minutes, and where the streets had been abandoned as soon as they fast-roped in, there were now small signs of activity.   He had glimpses of people looking out of windows and once or twice, scurrying across the street up ahead.   One man had looked out over a roof at them, cell phone in hand.

He could tell Cpl Kim was getting antsy, too.   He had called back several times to their squad leader, trying to find out what was going on. Mason and LCpl Kropkowski, the team's automatic rifleman were on one side of the street, Cpl Kim and PFC   Rossi were on the other side, taking cover behind a box of some sort.   "Krop" was there to lay down a base of fire, if necessary, and Mason was there to keep bad guys off of him.   Both were in the shadows made by the buildings, but soon, the rising sun would have them all lit up.

He looked ahead down the street.   There weren't any crowds of chanting locals, but there was an undercurrent of movement, of tension.   It wasn't something he could put his finger on, merely a feeling.

He caught some movement about 50 meters ahead.   It was that same raghead they'd seen a few minutes earlier, the one who'd dashed into one of the buildings.   As he came out, though, this time, Mason caught the unmistakable sight of a rifle strapped to the man's back.   The man glanced down towards them, but as he was standing in the direct sunlight, he didn't seem to see the four Marines lying in the dust. The man looked back at the building for a minute, seemed to shout something, then hurried off.

"Did you see that?" he asked Krop.

"Yeah, I saw him," came the reply. "Just another idiot out for his morning constitutional."

"No, I mean, he was armed."

"No shit? Are you sure?"

"Fucking right I'm sure. I saw it."

"Damn! I could have lit him up!" He turned his head and quietly called across the street to where their fire team leader lay, "Cpl Kim, Shuga here saw a weapon on that guy who came out of the building there."

The fire team leader scooted out a bit so he could see around the box.

"That building?" he asked, pointing to the only two-story building down the road in front of them.

"That's the one," Mason replied.

"You sure about that?" came over Mason's earphone. "Remember what they told us about civilians and our ROE. "

"Positive. And he was looking back in that building as he left, maybe calling out. There's gotta be someone still inside."

Cpl Kim scooted back behind the box. He looked back over his shoulder to where the rest of the squad was deployed.

"OK," he told his team over the radio. "I'm going to send this up. It could be important, but that's for the lieutenant to decide. Good job, though, Shuga. Way to keep focused."

Chapter 24

Hobyo

2dLt Tony Niimoto peered through his binos at the nondescript building a mere 50 meters down Route Denver.

"So, do you think it's anything?" he asked his platoon sergeant.

The wooden box which had provided concealment for Cpl Kim and PFC Rossi was nowhere near big enough to do much for those two, Sgt Stanhope, SSgt Davidson, and him, so they really weren't even trying to remain hidden. They just got as close to the wall of the building beside them and hoped for the best.

"Well, sir, I don't know what it is, but my spidey sense's tingling. I think something's up there. But it's your call," was SSgt Davidson's response.

"I know what you mean. My spidey sense is tingling, too. But what if that guy was just coming back to check on his wife and kids before taking off. I mean, we just landed with well over 100 Marines. I would take precautions, too. And if we went in just to find out that a family is in there, well, harassing the civilians is out of our mission statement. We do not want to instigate anything here."

"Sir, you've seen this place. Do you really think if we break in on some Somali momma that she's gonna be calling up CNN to complain about it? But like I said, it's your call."

"Well, let's wait for the overhead view and then decide. And we've got to clear it with the skipper, too." He looked around at the five of them there. "And let's get a bit disbursed. One grenade is going to take all of us out."

The helos had taken off and were on station offshore, so Tony had called for one to fly overhead and take a look. It should only be a minute or two more. He kept his position while Sgt Stanhope and his fire team moved back a bit, clearly uncomfortable about leaving their platoon commander and sergeant forward. Tony knew that the two of them shouldn't be together up there as well. If something took him down, then he needed SSgt Davidson to take over.   But he wanted to bounce his thoughts off of someone, and the platoon sergeant was his best sounding board.

They lay there in silence, watching the heat waves radiate off the quiet street.   He wondered what the local name for it was.   "Denver" seemed too grandiose for the dusty road.   Tony was from another coastal town, Pacific Beach in San Diego, but this coastal town might as well have been on another planet.   The eerie silence contributed even more to that disjointed sense of being totally out-of-place.

The silence was finally broken, faintly at first, but then with more strength as the whup-whup of the Black Hawk approached and the huge-looking bird shot over the building of interest.

"Did you see that?" SSgt Davidson asked excitedly.

"Yeah, I saw him."

While watching through the binos, he had seen a head poke out one of the glassless windows on the second story of the building.   And with that head was the unmistakable silhouette of an AK47.   The head swerved to follow the path of the Black Hawk before disappearing back inside.

"Still think that was daddy checking on momma, sir?"

"No, I guess I don't.   What that is, though, I still don't know.   Let me call up the bird and see what they saw."

He motioned to Cpl Steptoe, who was in the doorway of a building on the other side of the street.

"Get me the air.   I want to find out what they saw," he told his radio operator as he hurried over to him.

He waited while Stepchild made the connection and handed over the handset.

"Jedi One, this is Bravo-Eight-Victor.   What'd you see, over?"

"Bravo-Eight-Victor, the house itself looks clear, but there is single rifleman on top of the building across the street, coordinates to follow.   Two-zero-zero-nine, zero-six-zero-eight.   I say again, two-zero-zero-nine, zero-six-zero-eight.   The rifleman is oriented towards your position, over."

"Roger that, I copy two-zero-zero-nine, zero-six-zero-eight, one rifleman, over."

THE PROUD

He quickly plotted it on his satellite photo of the town onto which the grid system had been superimposed.   He wished the Black Hawk crew had given a 10-digit coordinate, but with a 10m margin of error, it should still be good enough to identify the house.

"Bravo-Eight-Victor, be advised that there is movement down by the docks.   People are gathering there, and some looked to be armed, over."

"Jedi One, roger that.   Thanks for your help, over."

"We aim to please, Bravo-Eight-Victor.   This is Jedi One, out."

Tony found the building on the photo, then looked up to identify the real thing.   He wouldn't have given it a second glance.   It was rather non-descript.   Only one story, it would not give extensive fields of fire.   But one thing was evident.   It could cover the front door of the building that had attracted their attention.   That was one more nail in the coffin.   There was definitely something up with it.   He knew he had to investigate.

He keyed on the company freq on his personal communications system.

"Six, Six, this is One, over."

"Roger One, what've you got, over?" came Capt Svenson's voice over the net.

Tony had already reported that the house looked suspicious, and he knew the captain would be waiting for a report.

"I think there may be something there.   The overflight saw a rifleman covering the entrance, and I spotted an armed individual inside.   Request permission to investigate further, over."

The response was immediate.

"Roger that.   Take all precautions, but check it out. And be quick.   We expect a recall at any moment.   Report back as soon as you have any information.   This is Six, out."

That was easy, he thought.   He looked over at SSgt Davidson who merely shrugged, then gave him a thumbs up. He had obviously been keyed into the circuit as well and had heard their orders.

This could be absolutely nothing.   But something told

Tony that something big was afoot.   And there was only one way to find out.

He moved back and called his squad leaders and platoon sergeant over.   He had some awfully quick planning to do.

Chapter 25

Hobyo

Sgt Dailey motioned his squad forward, and they began to move out, hugging the north side of the street. This would keep them out of sight of the sniper up ahead, but might open them up to observation from whomever was in their objective.

SSgt Davidson might have chosen Sgt Stanhope's squad for the assault, but the lieutenant assigned First Squad that mission with Second in support. The platoon's main mission was still in effect, to conduct a blocking position at Elena, the codename for the intersection of Routes Cleveland and Denver, and Third Squad kept that mission. It made sense, leaving Sgt Stanhope in command if anyone. The alternative was for Burke to remain back at Elena, and that dog just wasn't going to hunt from the gitgo.

Instead, he was with the lead squad. He figured the lieutenant wanted some experience at the point, and that was fine with him.

He glanced over at the building across the street. He knew Cpl Winsome was already up there along with the STA team attached to the platoon. Their mission was to monitor the possible sniper and take him out if necessary. The lieutenant was concerned that Winsome's team could alert their target, but he figured that the Somalis knew they were there, so if a team was spotted, as long as they didn't seem to notice whomever was doing the spotting, things would be OK. At least that was the plan.

Burke would have felt more comfortable with a Ranger sniper, or even a genuine Marine sniper. The Surveillance and Target Acquisition sniper was a Marine with some training, and he had to have qualified expert on the range, but he hadn't attended the full-fledged sniper course. But with less than 100 meters between them and the potential sniper, even a run-of-the-mill rifleman should be able to make the shot at that range, so a STA sniper should have no problems. He hoped.

They wanted to move quietly, but speed was more of an essence. There had to be eyes on the street, and a simple phone call could alert their target. So they moved forward in a controlled jog, hugging the buildings.

On the small alley parallel with Denver, he knew the rest of Second was moving forward as well. They would cover the back of the house. He could monitor their position on his face shield display, each blue triangle representing a Marine. He knew some soldiers and Marines didn't like the displays as they could interfere with their vision, but for Burke, he was able to focus past the displays and on what was in front of him, much like he could focus past a dirty windshield when driving. He could still see them, but his attention was forward.

It seemed only a minute or so until they were at the building across the street from their objective. Burke knew the STA team was in place, but he couldn't help looking back to check them. A Marine, probably Winsome, was kneeling and pointing in the opposite direction. Burke hoped that might draw some attention away from the LCpl Issac, the STA sniper, who was looking right down the street to them.

Sgt Dailey got everyone's attention, then passed "Now!" over the squad net. Cpl Salazar's team didn't hesitate. The four Marines rushed forward, PFC Rivera hitting the door with his shoulder, smashing it open with one blow. The rest of the squad, along with Burke, immediately followed. A single shot registered, coming from down the street. Burke didn't waste time looking back, but the fact that it was only one shot was pretty indicative that Issac had been on target.

He rushed from the sunshine into the darkened room. A Somali woman was backed up against a wall, her fear almost palpable. She said nothing, merely motioned with her hands upstairs. Sgt Dailey told two Marines to guard here, then the rest rushed to the small stairway.

The stairs were only wide enough for one Marine at a time. Thoughts of Horatio at the Bridge flitted across his thoughts. He hoped the Somalis were not students of Greek history.

A door barred the way at the top of the stairs. PFC Rivera had been able to take a running start at the front

door.   Here, the cramped quarters and the incline kept the
Marines at bay for a bit.   They had to kick at the door five or
six times before the hinges gave way.

Chapter 26

Hobyo

Asad was nervous.   No, scared, to be truthful.   He couldn't understand why he was left alone, why not even one person was left to help him.   He had spent the last 30 minutes pacing the room, even climbing up to look out the window to see what he could see.   When the American Black Hawk flew by again, he looked out again and could almost touch the soldier manning a huge machine gun, a gun that seemed to be pointing right at him.

The next fifteen minutes had been almost unbearable. He kept expecting the Black Hawk to come back.   He knew his fellow Somalis had taken them down before, but after seeing one close up, he couldn't imagine how.

Were the Americans coming? he wondered for the umpteenth time.

He looked back at his prisoners.   Bong was sitting, a slight smile on his face.   The Filipino crewman was enjoying his agitation.   Craig was also awake now, silently watching him as he paced.

He pointed his AK at Bong, but the expression on the man never wavered.   He was either very brave, Asad conceded, or just very confident that the Americans would rescue him.

He had two calls come in, checking on the situation. During the second call, he had asked Taban to send someone to help.   Taban told him there would be hundreds of men there soon, so just to hold out.   He hoped he would last that long.

He had just about convinced himself that nothing would happen when he heard a commotion in the street below.   He rushed over to the window and looked out as a single shot rang out and a huge crash sounded from downstairs.   He caught a glimpse of uniforms rushing to his building, and voices rang out below him.

His heart fell.   He knew the Americans had arrived.

And he knew his duty.

THE PROUD

He slowly turned to Craig and Bong.   Who first?
Well, since it was the Americans who would kill him, he
should kill the American first.   He walked up to Craig and
raised his AK.   Bong cried out something in his language,
but Asad ignored him. His finger tightened on the trigger.

Craig merely looked him back eye-to-eye.   No fear, no
anger.   He almost had a look for forgiveness.   The muzzle
of his AK wavered.   Then the pounding of feet sounded as
the soldiers below came up the stairs.   There was a crash as
one or more of them hit the door, the door that could keep
him safe for only a few more moments.

He knew his life was over.   And he knew it was his
duty to take these two men with him, to teach the Americans
a lesson.   He was Asad the Lion.   He had the blood of
warriors in his veins.   He could do it.

With renewed determination, he raised his rifle, the
muzzle unwavering a half a meter from those unblinking
eyes.   He wished this Craig man would show some fear,
even some anger.   Not this forgiveness.   Who was he,
someone who came and took Somali resources, who kept
Somali children hungry, to forgive him?

A sense of righteous anger filled him for a moment as
his fingers tightened on the trigger once more as additional
crashes sounded against the door.   And just as quickly, that
anger dissipated like a small whirlwind in the desert dust.
He knew what he had been told about foreigners, and maybe
it was true.   But that was not Craig, not Bong.   These were
just two men trying to make a living, trying to go from one
place to another.   If some people were raping Somali
resources, Asad knew that these two were not guilty.   They
were innocent, and the Quran forbid the killing of the
innocent.   Asad was not overly religious, but some things
were just evident.

He sighed and stepped back just as the door crashed
open and soldiers rushed in.   Instinctively, he raised his AK.

Chapter 27

Hobyo

SSgt Davidson was the second one into the dark room that took up the entire top floor of the building. Almost immediately, he took in the two men chained to a bolt on the floor and the local, a young-looking man, but armed and raising his AK. Burke started to raise his own M4 as one of the chained men lunged to grab the Somali.

The stupid fool's going to get shot, he thought as he maneuvered for a shot to take out the Somali while missing the well-meaning but foolish Filipino. LCpl Torino was beside him, also trying to get in a shot.

The pirate twisted, and the Filipino, still yelling, reached the end of his chain, and the two were separated. This was his chance.

He just started to squeeze the trigger when an authoritarian voice called out "Cease fire, cease fire!"

That registered despite his excitement. Too many hours on the range made that almost instinctual. He looked about in confusion until he recognized that the command to cease fire came from PFC Rivera. The young Marine was rushing forward to impose himself between the rest of the Marines pouring into the room and the pirate, who was now cowering on the floor.

It was only then that he realized that the Filipino prisoner, Mr. Benedicto, was shouting at them as well, telling them not to shoot.

"Hold your fire," he told everyone, a little needlessly, to be sure.

He turned to the heavyset American still lying on a blanket on the floor.

"Mr. Murphy? Mr. Craig Murphy?" he asked.

The man didn't say anything, but merely nodded.

Burke switched to the squad command circuit.

"We've got them. Both of them," he told Lt Niimoto, proper radio procedures be damned.

Chapter 28

Hobyo

Maslax put down his Samsung and started calculating.   He knew his Samsung was probably a Chinese clone, but maybe that was better when going online on the Chinese-installed network.   While most of the world had been connected to the internet for years, Hobyo had only gone wireless less than a year ago.   And as Maslax worked with information, he had immediately gotten connected.

He had gotten up early this morning and was down at his favorite shop sipping *shah adays* when the American aircraft had appeared.   Everyone else had quickly disappeared, but as far as he knew, the Americans didn't want him, so he stayed at his table, sipping the tea.

He had counted six Black Hawks, their unmistakable silhouette familiar to most Somalis, and two of the wasp-like shapes of Apaches.   He hadn't recognized the three other aircraft, so he had pulled out his Samsung and done a net search.   It hadn't taken him long to discover they were called "Ospreys," and that they were used by the US Navy, Air Force, and Marines, as well as by the Indonesians, Chileans, Spanish, and Koreans.   As he didn't know of any Indonesian, Chilean, Spanish, or Korean hostages about, that left the Americans.

He got caught up in some of the technical aspects of how the plane could shift its propellers upwards to then act as a helicopter.   This looked to be a pretty technological achievement, he had to admit.   He looked up the troop-carrying capacity and did his calculations.

From what was listed online, he figured that there were anywhere from 160-180 American Rangers now in Hobyo. With more than 25,000 people in the city, it might seem that the small number of Rangers could be easily overwhelmed, but despite what some people believed, *The Battle of the Rangers* showed that they had teeth, and many more Somalis had been killed in driving the Rangers back to their camp.   Maslax figured it was better to just let the Americans get their hostages and get out so things could get back to normal.

The fact that this rescue operation was occurring was probably due to his own actions was not lost on him. He smiled as he sipped his tea, wondering what would happen if some of his more militant fellow citizens knew of his part in things. He had been well paid by the Chinese, but he was not stupid enough to flash that money around. It was hidden back in his home, and even his wife didn't know about it. He would slowly ease bits of the cash out as time went on.

One of the big Ospreys flew directly overhead as it headed back out to sea. Maslax could read the "U.S. MARINES" on the sides of the plane. That made him bring up his Samsung again. He couldn't speak English, but he could enter the letters in Google. He re-read the Somali-language Wiki article on the Osprey, and there was the mention of the Marines again. He hit on that link, then came to a long article on them.

What he read was new to him. To Maslax, as with most Somalis, American soldiers were all Rangers. That was just the generic name for them. From what he had read, the Marines were a separate service with a much longer history. They had fought all over the world and in many wars until they had been mostly disbanded and were only now being brought back up to strength. Why the Americans needed separate armies was not explained in the article, but to Maslax, it didn't really matter. Rangers, Marines, whatever. They were Americans, and they wanted to get their hostage back. It might seem like a huge waste of time, effort, and money to rescue one man, but who knows how foreigners thought?

He ordered another glass of *shah adays*. This was probably as good a spot as any to take in whatever was going to happen. There hadn't been explosions or obvious sounds of fighting, so it was probably relatively safe, and if the Americans decided to bomb Hobyo, then his small house was not going to offer any protection.

When the Americans had first flown over, people had scattered and disappeared indoors. Now, with no huge war taking place, people were starting to come out and gather in groups.   Cell phones were in open use.   He knew his wife would be calling him if she had a phone, but since she didn't, his phone remained mercifully quiet.

There was an open area directly across from the dock, about a block away from where he sat.   In the evenings, men would gather there to play *shax*, drink tea, and socialize. Now, men were gathering there.   It wasn't long before most of the men's attention seemed focused on one-armed man who seemed to be stirring them up.   They were too far from his middle-aged eyes for Maslax to recognize the speaker, but it wasn't long before the other men began to chant. Many of them had weapons, and they were thrusting them over their heads.

When the crowd, which had by then grown to maybe 100-150 men, started marching out, Maslax was torn.   He knew he should stay put.   Nothing was going to happen to him here, and he could enjoy his tea.   But Maslax was cursed with an undying sense of curiosity.   His wife told him he was worse than a cat, poking his nose into everything.

Maslax was not going to get into a fight with the Americans, but whatever was going to happen was certainly different from the routine.   Maslax could not just sit there and not know what was going on.   He paid for his tea, then got up and walked over to the mob.   It was going to be an interesting morning.

Chapter 29

Hobyo

2dLt Tony Niimoto put down the handset and looked towards his platoon sergeant.

"OK, here's what we're going to do. Captain Svenson says we've all got orders to get out of here as soon as possible and back to the ships. We're going to get the hostages out first, then we'll follow. I told them Mr. Murphy is in pretty bad shape, so they're going to take him off the roof right here. It's going to be one of the Army Black Hawks, and they don't have litters like the Navy Sea Hawks, but the Black Hawks are still here on station while the Navy ships are still 50 miles out. So the Black Hawk's going to come down to the roof, put one wheel on the edge, and we've got to get Mr. Murphy on it. I want you to go up there and make sure there're no wires or anything up there that'll cause a problem. We'll put Mr. Benedicto on it, too, along with Doc Supchak and the first of our Marines to go back."

"Aye-aye, sir, but do you think it's a good idea to put Doc Supchak on the bird first? I mean, this whole situation could still blow up in our faces."

Tony thought about that for a moment before calling over the corpsman from where he was tending to Mr. Murphy.

"Doc, how is he?"

"Not too good," he told his platoon commander, glancing back at the Chief Mate before lowering his voice. "Look sir, I don't know if he's going to make it. That infection is as nasty as I've ever seen, and it's in his system now. I've given him antibiotics, but there's not much else I can do for him. He's got to get back to the *Gaffert's* sickbay, then maybe back to Landstuhl ASAP."

"Does it make sense for you to ride back with him on the first bird?"

"Not really. I can't do anything for him now, and to be honest, I don't want to get stuck on the *Gaffert*. Who knows when I can hitch a ride back to the *Dunham*?"

"Oh, good point.   I guess I assumed that the flight would go back to the *Dunham*, but if you say Mr. Murphy's got to go back to the *Gaffert*, well, maybe I need to rethink that."

He turned back to SSgt Davidson.

"OK, I guess you were right.   We'll put the two hostages on the Black Hawk, and I'll let the skipper know it has to go back to the *Gaffert* instead.   And don't put any of our Marines on it.   I don't want them stuck on the *Gaffert*." He looked at his watch.   "We've got about 10 minutes before the pick-up, so let's get going.   After that, we'll head back to Elena and re-embark as per our original order."

"What about our prisoner?" asked SSgt Davidson.

They both looked over to where their translator was speaking to the young man.

"The skipper says keep him bound until we leave, then let him go.   He could've killed the hostages, but chose not to, and Mr. Benedicto vouches for him."

Chapter 30

Hobyo

Asad finally accepted that the Americans were not going to kill him and was starting to relax. His hands were still bound in back of him, but no one was mistreating him. No one was beating him as his own people had beat Bong. He knew, though, that without Bong's interceding, he would be a corpse right now. He wondered why the hostage had done that. Why had he saved him? It didn't make sense.

Only Bong was not a hostage now. He was.

He turned to Ali Bile, the Somali interpreter working with the Americans.

"Why do you work with them?' he asked.

Ali shrugged. "The pay's good," he simply said.

"But, they come to rape our land, to take our resources."

Ali gave him a condescending smile. "Do you really believe that?"

"Well, sure. We are the *badaadinta badah*, right?"

"'Saviors of the Sea?' Really? Those who take these ships are criminal, pirates, just as the foreigners accuse. Money is the goal, plain and simple."

"Bah. How would you know?" Asad asked the older man.

Ali let out a loud laugh, which drew the attention of the Rangers in the room.

"How do I know? Because I was a pirate. I helped take three ships. And I gladly took the ransom money."

"So how did you end up with the Rangers, then?"

"Rangers? Not all Americans are Rangers. These are what they call 'Marines.' But no matter. I realized what we were doing was wrong, against the Quran. Look, what was the ship you took doing? Was it fishing our waters? Was it taking our resources?"

"No. Not this one. But some do, right?"

"No, the Americans, the Russians, the British, the Chinese, they don't fish here. These are not Ethiopians, not even Indian who sometimes fish here.   They are just going from one place to another.   We stop them for money and money alone.   Look," he said, as he sidled a bit closer. "Why didn't you kill the two hostages.   Surely that was your orders."

Asad looked down, not able to meet the older man's eyes.

"Because, they had done nothing wrong.   I could not kill innocent men."

"So you already knew the answer.   You knew that to do so was wrong.   So why do you ask me?"

Asad didn't respond.

"These Americans are something of barbarians.   They have superb technology.   They can do many things.   But their spirit is not as strong as ours.   They are loud.   They drink.   Sometimes they allow women to boss them.   But they are also like children, easy to laugh and enjoy life.   Yes, I take their pay, but they treat me like an equal."

He waited a moment before continuing, changing tack.

"And what about you, Asad Farah?   What will you do after this?"

"After this?   If the Rangers let me?   I will go home, I think."

"And your people?   Your clan?   What will they think, what will they do now that you failed in your mission?   That you failed to kill your prisoners?"

His heart dropped.   This question had been hovering around in the back of his mind, a question he had refused to acknowledge.   But now, he was forced to confront it.

"You may be a northern man, but I think you know. I'm sure it's the same with your clan.   At best, I'll be exiled. At worst . . ." he left that unspoken.

"So, if I could get you to America, would you be interested?"

Asad was taken aback.   *America?*

"Why would I go there?   And why would they let me? I just held one of their people captive.   I cut him, and he may die."

"The Americans are a strange people.   They fight like devils, but they don't hold blood feuds like we do.   They

130

forget about the past. To them, you saved their man's life. If I can get them to understand that you could be killed for doing that, then they will feel an obligation to take you."

"But America? What would I do there?" He thought about his sweet Ayaan back in Galinsoor, the girl he had intended to marry.

"They call America 'The Land of Opportunity.' You can do anything you want there. And there are many, many Somali communities there."

"I don't know. How can a man live without his clan?"

"There are other *Hawiya* in America, even, what are you, *Degodia*?"

He waited until Asad nodded.

"I thought so, from your accent. Anyway, there will be plenty of your clan there. But in America, other Somalis become your clan. *Dir, Ishaak, Darod, Rahawein*, all become your clan."

Other *Hawiya*, sure, Asad could believe that. But the *Dir*, from the very far north? They were so different from his people.

"But you better make up your mind. I heard the Marine lieutenant. They will be leaving soon, and they plan to let you go. I don't think your crew will be happy to see you alive and the prisoners gone, so I would suggest you go with them. Go to America, make some money, and come back when time has softened emotions and you can buy your way back into your village's good graces."

Asad thought for another moment before asking, "Do you really think I should?"

"I think you would be stupid not to."

It was all too fast. He couldn't think. He had resigned himself to dying and had accepted it. But now that he was alive, he didn't want to let go of life. He didn't want to die. Ali was looking expectantly at him.

"All I ask is that once you're in America, remember me. If I need your help to go there, if I need a sponsor, you owe me that."

Ali's motive became clear, but that helped Asad. If Ali wanted to go that badly, then there had to be a viable future there. Asad did not want to die today. If America was an

THE PROUD

option, then so be it.
    "OK, I'll do it."

Chapter 31

Hobyo

"OK, cut that away. I can hear the bird inbound. We need to get all of this clear," he shouted out to the Marines helping clear the roof.

As a young Marine, before he had transferred to the Army, SSgt Davidson had seen a video of a CH-46 carrying a SEAL team trying to land on an amphib. A wheel had caught in the panic net on the sides of the ship, and the helo had tipped over and sunk into the deep Pacific Ocean. He knew it might not take much to cause disaster, so with the precarious roof-top pick-up already beyond the norm, he had to make sure all possible precautions had been taken.

The last wire was cut and fell to the street below. He looked over the edge and watched it hit the ground. Across the street, the body of a Somali lay still, face-first on the roof, a rifle still clasped in his hand. LCpl Isaac had done his job.

Cpl McClaren's fire team emerged from the small roof access, struggling to keep Mr. Murphy from being jostled as they carried him, using the blanket he had been lying on as a make-shift stretcher. They were followed by the lieutenant, Sgt Alvarez, Mr. Benedicto, Cpl Stepchild, Doc Supchak, and Ali, their interpreter.

"Corporal Bonaventure, I want some security up here, but stay away from this side of the roof. The Black Hawk's coming down here. Sergeant Alvarez, have your men put Mr. Murphy over in that corner. Wait until I give you the signal, then bring him over. Doc, you go with them."

"Hey, Bull," Sgt Alvarez shouted out to Cpl McClaren, "over here," as he moved out to follow his orders.

"Everything set?" Lt Niimoto asked.

"I think so, sir. I will handle the landing, but if Cpl Stepchild can tell them to land along the northern edge, I think that'll be best."

He could see the platoon radio operator start the call without waiting for the platoon commander to approve. The Squad Tactical Radios were great tools. They could be hands free, a dedicated radio operator was not needed, and they could be tailored for commanders only or for everyone. And if a tablet was hooked up via a simple connection, he could speak privately to individuals simply by touching their icon.   But they only went up to the company level, their range was limited, and they could not connect with outside agencies such as air.   This limited their use when calling for supporting fire or when trying to bringing a Black Hawk on the edge of a rooftop in a dusty Somali town.

"Sir," Ali was saying, trying to get the lieutenant's attention, as if he had been trying for some time.

Lt Niimoto turned to the Somali as the incoming Black Hawk began to make a wide turn to get into an approach.

"OK, what. But make it quick."

"It's about that young man, the man who saved your two hostages."

"You mean the one who held them captive, first?"

"Yes, most of course.   But he also saved them.   And because he saved them, he will die."

Burke looked up at that.   The lieutenant looked confused, too.

"Why would he die," the platoon commander asked the obvious question.

"That is because sir, he was ordered to kill them.   But his heart is pure, and he could not kill the innocent.   So he must pay.   He is most sure to be killed dead," Ali said in a matter-of-fact voice.

"I'm sorry for that.   But what can I do?" he asked.

"When others help you Americans, you must to take them back to America where they will be safe.   This is your own laws.   This is your 'J-1 Fear of Persecution Visa.'"

What? thought Burke.   *What is this, an immigration scam?*

"I don't know anything about that," the lieutenant told him.

"Then he will die.   After torture.   I am not to tell you what you must do.   But it is most right thing, and this young boy, he saved your American person's life.   Please, send him to the ship.   They can decide there."

The helo was flaring, slowly making its way over the

street.   Burke could not wait to hear the lieutenant's decision.   He had to guide the Black Hawk in.   He rushed to the edge of the building, watching the distance close.

As a Ranger, he had been taught how to guide in a helo, and as the pilots were Army, it went smoother than he expected.   In addition the pilot could see the edge of the roof.   It was not a blind landing.   It didn't take long before the helo was essentially hovering, one wheel planted firmly on the roof, the other two out over the street.   The rotorwash was significant, enough to make ripples in the blood pooling under the dead Somali sniper on the house across the street, but it wasn't too bad.

He motioned for Cpl McClaren to bring over Mr. Murphy.   Peripherally, he could see Ali still pleading his case with the lieutenant, but Burke was focused on getting Mr. Murphy on board.   The merchant crewman was a big guy, and one slip would send him crashing two stories down to the street.

They paused at the side of the bird, trying to military press the man into it, but the crew chief was having problems grasping the worn blanket and pulling him in.   LCpl Gittens jumped up into the helo, and Burke moved over to help.   It took several tries, but finally, Mr. Murphy was in the Black Hawk.   Gittens jumped out, and Burke signaled Mr. Benedicto to approach.

As the Filipino came forward, Burke saw the lieutenant nod his head towards the Black Hawk.   Ali rushed to the roof access and yelled below.   The platoon commander caught his eye.   Burke merely shrugged.   That was the lieutenant's call.

Mr. Benedicto was in much better shape than Mr. Murphy, but he had still been pretty badly used.   He had to be assisted up and into the bird.   The crewchief held his hand up to the side of his helmet, and nodded, obviously in the horn with the pilot.   He looked at Burke, hands raised in question.   Burke held up one finger. He looked back to see the prisoner being hurried forward, hands still bound.

He wasn't a big guy, so Gittens and LCpl Kihlstadius pretty much picked him up and threw the frightened-looking man into the Black Hawk.   Burke gave the crew chief a thumbs up, and the helo slowly lifted off the roof.   It seemed to hover for a minute, then the nose dipped as it began to pick up speed and altitude.   Within moments, it was moving quickly towards the sea.

"Well, that takes care of that," he said to no one in particular as they watched the helo fly away.

When the rocket hit the Black Hawk, it took everyone by surprise.   The helo was about 200 feet high, maybe 500 meters away when a trail of grayish smoke raced from the ground and struck it.   The helo immediately banked to the right, losing altitude and trailing black smoke.

"Fuck!" someone said, an emotive thought shared by pretty much everyone on the roof.

The helo was doomed, plunging down towards the white houses below.   It disappeared behind a building, and the stunned Marines waited for the inevitable crash.   To their surprise and delight, the Black Hawk limped back into sight, still trailing smoke, but flying cockeyed.

"Come on you bastard, fly!" someone, maybe Bonaventure, shouted.

Cpl Steptoe was already on the hook, reporting to higher headquarters what had happened.

As if by force of will, the pilot kept the Black Hawk aloft.   It was low and trailing smoke, obviously in distress. It looked like it made it past the beach and over the water, but that was hard to tell from their position.   Burke prayed that it could make it out to the ships.

As they watched, hoping to catch a sight of the Black Hawk, to confirm it was still in the air, Sgt Stanhope's calm voice came over the platoon.

"Six, this is three.   We've got several hundred hostiles approaching our position.   What are our orders?"

Chapter 32

Hobyo

Tony Niimoto spread the map out on the roof of the house, looking over to where Sgt Stanhope had his squad deployed some 150 meters down Route Denver. He could not see the mob approaching from his viewpoint, but there was a small undercurrent of noise just at the threshold of his hearing.

"OK," he told SSgt Davidson, Sgts Dailey and Alvarez, and Cpl Steptoe, who were gathered around him. "The skipper says to hang on, and he'll get the word upstairs for an immediate evacuation. They've already started their retrograde, but the mortar platoon is still on deck, so he's going to redeploy the 60's for some fire support until he gets some more information. He says not to engage the Somalis unless they attack, but to present a united front to see if they'll back down. The Ospreys are too big to land anywhere here, so it'll have to be Black Hawks, just as in our original plan."

"Why don't they just bring in the Apaches and send the ragheads running?" asked Sgt Alvarez.

"Well, our orders are not to engage. And no one is sure what hit that Black Hawk, so I think caution is the name of the game right now."

"Fuck caution, sir. It's our asses on the line. I don't want to be part of *Black Hawk Down* 2."

No one wanted to mention it, but it was in each of their minds. It was probably in every Marine in the platoon's mind as well.

"This isn't Mogadishu, Sgt Alvarez. And we don't know what the mob wants. Let's take this one step at a time."

Tony looked back down at the map, studying the area. He used his chin to activate his face shield display, and each of Third Squad's Marines as well as the STA team's icons came to life, showing the squad's disposition. Sgt Stanhope was in control of the intersection, ideally suited to block two avenues of approach. But could one squad hold back "hundreds" of angry Somalis?   On one hand, the position was ideal.   On the other hand, it left them hanging out there.   He flirted with the thought of rushing the rest of the platoon to join him, but there really wasn't enough room there to deploy a full platoon.

He looked about the rooftop.   The pirates had picked this building for a reason.   It was the only two-story building within a few blocks, so the fields of observation were about as good as for what could be hoped.   It was relatively solid, and the window openings were small when compared to other buildings in the area.   And as one Black Hawk had already picked up passengers from the roof, others should be able to do so as well.   That is what settled it for him.

"Three, this is Six.   I want you to pull back to our position immediately.   Do not engage the mob unless they attack.   But move back now."

"Roger that.   We are on our way.   Three, out," came the calm-sounding reply.   Tony thought they might as well have been conducting a routine training exercise back at Lejeune for all the stress that was evident in the squad leader's voice.

"OK, I don't want anyone sneaking up on us by hugging the buildings on this side of the street, and I think this house is too small for us to adequately deploy all of us, so Sgt Dailey, I want you to take your squad and clear that building," he motioned with his hand to the house across the street, the one with the dead sniper on top.   "Check to see if there is a back entrance, and cover that if there is. Otherwise, get your squad on top.   We'll cover your front door and you'll cover ours.   Got it?"

"Yes sir," came the reply.   "And when the birds come to get us?   I don't think they'll be able to set down there."

"No, when they come, be ready to come back.   You'll be flying first, then Third Squad, which I am keeping downstairs here, then First Squad.   Sgt Alvarez, you've got this roof, so move your teams to have full coverage."

"Aye-aye, sir," the Second Squad leader said before moving off the roof to gather his Marines.

Tony looked at his platoon sergeant before asking,

"Anything else?"

SSgt Davidson looked up for a moment, eyes and forehead scrunched in concentration.

"No sir. I don't think so. But our ride out of here better be quick. There're a million places for bad guys to hide here, and I think we'd be hard-pressed to defend this if push comes to shove."

Both men walked over to the roof's edge and looked back towards Elena. Third Squad was already in view, performing a quick bounding overwatch retrograde. Tony marveled at how precise, how professional they looked.

Directly below them, Cpl Horton's team was rushing across the street. Pvt Lambie lifted his size 13 boot and kicked in the door, disappearing inside. Tony's breath caught for a moment. The private hadn't cleared the room, just went right in as easy as he pleased. Cpl Horton saw that and rushed his team in as well. There was no shooting, though, so they hadn't met up with any resistance.

Sgt Dailey got his entire squad into the small house, and in a few moments, Tony could see a Marine push up through a hatch in the rear of the roof. It wasn't much longer before the entire squad was up with the squad leader deploying his teams to give them the best observation and coverage.

PFC McNamara nonchalantly picked up the legs of the dead sniper, pulling him back away from the leading corner of the building and to the roof's center to give LCpl Bouchard, the team's automatic rifleman, that preferred firing position.

Sgt Dailey looked up at Tony and gave him a thumbs up. The two were separated by only 10 meters or so, but the gap looked awfully large. Tony was already second-guessing himself for splitting up his platoon.

Below him, Third Squad had reached its position and was entering the building. SSgt Davidson touched his arm, and when Tony looked at him, the platoon sergeant merely pointed back towards Elena. There was visible movement. Tony lifted up his binos to get a better look.

Only the fringe of the mob was in view, but he could count at least 30 or 40 Somali men, most armed with rifles.

Some were AK's and some looked to be antiques. Antiques or not, a round fired from either could ruin a Marine's entire day.

"SSgt Davidson, I want you to go below and make sure Stanhope's in position to block the entry. Take Doc with you, and leave him there. Come back up here when you're done."

He looked back to the mob. If they milled around there, then this could be a headless mass of people with no set plan. If they immediately set off down Denver, well, things could be getting ugly very soon.

For a moment, it looked like they might just be that headless mob. But through the binos, Tony could clearly see on man pointing down Denver towards their position.

Shit, he thought.

Chapter 33

Hobyo

CDR Galen Harrelson looked up at the tall Marine captain looming over him. If he thought he was intimidating him, he was sadly mistaken. No Marine captain was going to be able to do that, but the situation, on the other hand, was doing an admirable job of intimidation.

"But sir, we need to reinforce First Platoon. They've got hundreds of hostile at their position. We've got to move now."

"'Hostiles' or just a mob?" he asked.

"A mob now, but their intent is clear," came the excited reply.

"I'm glad you're privy to their very thoughts, captain," he said, drawing out the rank until it was almost an insult. "But our orders are clear. We're to get everyone back on the ships without getting into a firefight. Our air is incoming, and we've got the two Apaches on station if the situation gets dangerous."

"With all due respect, sir, it is already dangerous. Look, we've already got Third Platoon embarked and airborne. Let's turn them back to reinforce First Platoon."

"And throw more fuel into the fire? I'm afraid not."

Galen knew how to handle junior officers, but ground operations were something different. He as a boat driver, for goodness sakes, not a grunt. He had won the Commander, Naval Surface Force, U.S. Atlantic Fleet Junior Officer Shiphandling Award as a mere JG, something unheard of. He had published articles in *Proceedings* and could competently discuss crossing the T with a line of 32-gun man-of-wars or anti-submarine warfare in the Gulf. His environment was the dynamic, shifting ocean, not the dusty, static streets of some Godforsaken African town.

He understood why the captain had put him ashore. He wanted to make sure that this was a Navy operation, and until that Marine O5 had shown up, it made sense. Frankly, though, Galen thought that the Marine might have been a better choice.

But the operation had succeeded in finding the hostages. After being stymied at their objective, that unexpected and thoroughly welcomed call had come in. The Marine platoon, one of the supporting forces, had somehow found and rescued them. They had even been put on a helo before all hell broke loose. First, the helo had taken a hit, and Galen didn't even know yet if they had gone down or were still airborne. Then, while they were loading back up to get the hell out, that same platoon who had found the hostages reported being approached by a mob.

He had reported back, and his orders had been clear. Get every American off the ground, and immediately.

Already, the platoon of Marines who had taken the northern blocking position had been picked up, and even if he had the authority, Galen was not about to order them back into harm's way. The SEALs were loading up as well along with some of the Marines here at the objective. He had relented in allowing Capt Svenson to change the order to keep the mortar platoon to the last bird, but that would only give them a few extra minutes.

As far as his other platoon, well, between the helos to pick them up and the others to provide support, he hoped that would be enough. That had to be enough.

He wished the power-that-be would have released the *Benjamin Franklin* to provide support, but from what he had been told, that would have been too aggressive, an act of war rather than a rescue mission. Maybe so, but a huge aircraft carrier steaming up and down the horizon had a way of quelling aggression.

"OK, I understand, sir. But request permission to remain back here until the last two Ospreys come in. I want to be able provide any support if it is needed."

Galen looked up at the lanky Marine. The man seemed earnest.

"I guess that'd be OK. Tell my chief to take you off the manifest on this flight."

He looked over at the big Osprey, waiting for him.

"And I've got to get going. We need to clear the LZ for the next one."

"Aye-aye, sir. Godspeed, sir."

Galen pushed the edge of his helmet back up for the hundredth time as he hurried off. He was sure glad to be getting off the ground and looking forward to his familiar berth aboard the *Gaffert*.

THE PROUD

Chapter 34

Hobyo

"I want everybody down and out of sight.   No use showing off our position," the lieutenant's voice came over the open platoon circuit.

PFC Jerry Masterson hunched down, but not before catching Terry's eyes down on the other building and tapping the side of his helmet.   That was Terry's and his secret signal, but he couldn't really say what it meant.   It was more like bumping fists, or something, but only for the two of them.

He still wasn't sure why Second Squad was on this mission.   They had been trained for working with the Special Boat Team, and even if they had let the pirates go later, that is what they had done on their first mission.   But now, they had gone ashore in helos and had to fast-rope in. He had done that back at Lejeune of course, but they hadn't spent as much time doing that as the other squads.

At least that got him out on a mission with Terry.   This would give them something to talk about after they got back to the States.

As a middle-class white kid from Milwaukee, he never thought that his best friend would be a short, muscular African-American sweet potato farmer from the deep south. Well, Terry's family was farmers, at least—Terry joined the Marines to flee that life.

But they had bonded at boot, and they had even been assigned to the same company and the same platoon.   And now they were closer than Jerry was to his real brother, Paul. They had plenty of free time on the *Dunham*, and the two of them spent hours planning out various business enterprise they could do together that would keep them in girls, cars, and whatever they wanted.   LCpl Nguyen told them they reminded him of the two guys, Tom Hanks and that black guy, in that old movie, *Forrest Gump,* but those two were stupid.   Jerry was smart, and Terry worked hard, so they had to succeed.

First, though, they had to get out of this place. There were hundreds, maybe more ragheads coming to them, and he had seen *Black Hawk Down*, too. He knew what could happen. He looked over to where the lieutenant and the platoon sergeant were huddled, heads together. The lieutenant was a hero, and the platoon sergeant a combat Ranger, so he figured they would get them out of this OK.

He shifted to look up at the sky. He couldn't hear a helo coming yet. But they had to be coming soon, right? Before he had been told to get down, he could see a big Osprey landing in the distance, probably picking up Second or Third Platoon. Their turn had to be next.

He could hear the rumble of the ragheads approaching. He hoped they might just march on by, but if they wanted trouble, Jerry was more than willing to give it to them. No mob of uneducated, stinking ragheads could take on the Marines.

There was a crash just on the other side of him. He turned over to see flames on the roof. They were licking JJ's legs, and he kicked out, sitting up to slap at them.

"Fire, fire" came the command.

He spun around and looked over the edge of the roof, pausing for a split second. Hundreds might have been an understatement. The filled the road all the way back to the intersection. A piece of the wall just below him exploded, and it took him a second to realize that they were shooting at him.

He lowered this M4 and emptied his magazine into the crowd. Screams and shouts echoed up from below as both rooftop squads opened fire.

Suddenly a friggin' mule kicked him right in the chest. He fell back, unable to take a breath. He was aware of the firing going on, but most of that was outside of his tunnel vision.

"Cease fire, cease fire," came the command, not that he was in any condition to be firing.

Cpl Winsome grabbed him and turned him over.

"You OK Jerry? You hit?"

Jerry nodded, but to being OK or to being hit, well, even he wasn't sure.

THE PROUD

His fire team leader called out for Doc Supchak, then opened his flak jacket.   He probed around, and when his fingers hit the upper right side of his chest, the pain lanced through him and he cried out.

"Well, shit, you big baby.   Look, you ain't hit," Winsome told him with a laugh.

Jerry looked down.   Sure enough, there was no blood. He was red, and already, bruising was starting to form, but his reactive armor had stopped the round.   Maybe it was in relief, but suddenly, he could breath freely again.   He laughed, but that brought back the pain.

"Yeah, I bet that hurts like a mother fucker, but you'll live."

"Did we win?" he asked his team leader.

"Win, well, I doubt it.   They sure ran though, when we hit their asses.   The lieutenant's on the hook with the company, and maybe we'll get some more support, but I think they'll be back."

Chapter 35

Hobyo

Terrell Svenson watched the Osprey take off. He wished he had thought of a way to keep more of his Marines ashore, but at least that prig of a commander was gone and he was the senior man there. He had a platoon in the shit, and that wasn't going to happen on his watch.

He was wondering if he should wait for the inevitable radio call or to just grab the bull by the horns when that call came in.

"Six, this is One. We are under attack. I say again, we are under attack. We have 200, I say again, two-zero-zero, enemy who have attacked us, over."

"One, this is six. What is your situation, over," he asked eagerly.

He knew this was his out, his excuse to disobey orders.

"We have beaten them back, at least temporarily. We have two WIA, zero KIA. Enemy KIA," there was a pause, and Terrell could picture Lt Niimoto surveying the field of battle. "Enemy KIA, approximately 12, I say again, One-two, over."

"Roger, I understand. Hold your position, and I will try to link up with you. I will call air on station, and the mortars in direct support. Keep this circuit open, and I will get back to you, out."

He felt a thrill almost physically rush through him. At last, he could prove the temper of his steel.

Second Platoon had already lined up in sticks to board the incoming Osprey.

"Lt Hartigan, fall back. Do not board!" he ordered his platoon commander.

The Navy chief looked over and asked "What's up? Why're you changing the embarkation order?"

"I'm not changing the order there, chief. I'm changing the mission. We're going in relief of my First Platoon."

"You can't do that! You heard the commander," he sputtered.

"Well, the situation's changed.   First Platoon's been attacked, so now, we'll go kick some ass."

"But, but . . ."

Terrell ignored the chief, calling over Lt's Kremer, Desroches, and Hartigan.

"Lt Desroaches, I know you don't have all your men, but I want our 60's ready for support.   Get them locked into Route Denver on either side of First's position.   Lt Kremer, you're in charge back here.   Take the headquarters section and anyone else left and keep the mortars safe.   If you receive any opposition, call in that Osprey," he pointed to the bird just as it came in to land on the soccer field, "or better yet, see if he'll stay right there with his rotors turning, and get the hell out of here.   Lt Hartigan, you've got two minutes to get your platoon ready."

"How're we getting there, sir," Lt Hartigan asked. "Air?"

"We're marching!"

Chapter 36

Hobyo

Tony looked down at the street below. There were maybe a dozen obviously dead Somalis on the ground. Others had been helped away from the kill zone, and two poor souls were laboriously crawling back up the road.

As with New Delhi, Tony didn't feel a bit of remorse, but rather a sense of excitement. He felt a bit guilty for that. The dead men below him hadn't woken up that morning and decide to kill a Marine today. They had gotten up, maybe kissed the wife, and gone out to earn their day's wage. And now they were dead, their blood coagulating in the dust. Well, it had been their choice to attack, and they had paid the price.

He glassed Elena. The mob hadn't disbursed. They were still within easy rifle range, but Tony was not going to engage unless being actively attacked. He wasn't sure if they were up for another attack, given what had just occurred.

He looked back at his Marines. PFC Masterson had taken a round in the chest, but other than being bruised, he was OK. Over on the other building, PFC Dawkins has taken a round in the arm. Doc Supchak was over there now, and he had reported that Dawkins was OK, too. It could have been worse, for sure.

He had gotten ammo reports, and they were still well-armed. The firing had been so quick before the Somalis had turned tail that most Marines had fired only a partial magazine, possibly a full one. He thought he could turn back several more attacks before ammo might become an issue.

"Sir, I've got a target on top of a building over there, at your two o'clock," LCpl Isaac told him.

Tony looked, taking some time before finding the man. He was hiding behind something that looked like a swamp cooler back in the US, and he was armed. He wasn't aiming his weapon, but merely observing them.

"Don't hit him, but take a shot and hit that thing he's hiding behind. Let him know we're watching him."

He watched through the binos as the STA sniper aimed and fired. The round hit about 6 inches above the man's head. The Somali quickly ducked back, sliding on his butt until he reached the edge of the roof and dropped over.

"Good shot, Isaac," he told him.

He looked at his watch. It had been about fifteen minutes since the attack. High overhead, the two Apaches had come on station, circling like birds of prey. He wasn't sure why there was the delay in getting them out of there, but he knew it couldn't be long now.

Something caught his attention back at Elena. He wished the entire intersection was in view, but because of the slight bend in Denver about 150 meters down, much of Elena was hidden. A pick-up truck was slowly being moved into position. In the back, there seemed to be a heavier gun of some sort. Something like that would most likely be able to punch through their body armor.

"Corporal Steptoe, get those Apaches and tell them we need help, now. They've got a technical."

He watched as the pickup edged closer. He could have told Isaac to take out the driver, but he wanted the truck down, not just the drivers. Better leave it to the Army Apaches.

Comm with the Apaches was not great, certainly not as good as when Marines were calling in Cobras. But a frequency had been allotted for air-to-ground calls, and in a moment, the two Apaches arched over and began a run. Somalis saw that, too, and began to scatter. Surprisingly, the truck stayed put—foolish or brave, Tony didn't know.

For added security, he brought the mortar section up on the hook and gave them a fire mission for Elena, with rounds to hit after the Apache's made their passes. It might have been his imagination, but he thought he could hear the thunk of outgoing mortars.

The Apaches screamed in, one after the other. Just as the lead bird opened up with his 30 mm chain gun, four columns of smoke streaked up, two aimed at each bird. The first Apache took a direct hit on the undercarriage. It nosed over and within seconds, smashed into the buildings below. A huge fireball erupted, to the horror of the watching Marines.

The second Apache had a split second more time, and the pilot veered his bird hard to the left. There was an explosion, and the steady whup-whup of the bird became rougher, but the pilot managed to keep her aloft. Aloft yes, but out of the fight.

Tony was in shock. This ragtag mob had managed to bring down one of the fiercest aircraft flying. He could hear cheering, and he looked back at Elena to see Somalis jumping up and down. He was about to order his platoon to open fire when the intersection erupted in explosions.

The 60 mm mortar is not the most powerful weapon in the American arsenal, but in a confined area like the intersection, the effects of the rounds were devastating. Lt Desroches and SSgt Thierry, the mortar section leader, were pinpoint accurate, dropping at least four rounds right in the intersection. At least one was a direct hit on the technical, completely destroying it.

The threat to the platoon had been taken out, but at what cost? Two soldiers had just died trying to save them. The smoke was still billowing a scant 400 meters away, marking where they had fallen.

Tony had been excited, but the deaths of the two soldiers sobered him up quickly. His thoughts drifted to those who fell in New Delhi, friends of his. It was up to him to keep his Marines alive, to let no one else die.

He wasn't sure he was up to it. People expected him to lead, to be the super Marine, all because of Delhi, all because he wore the Navy Cross on his chest. But he had just been a sniper like LCpl Isaac, never having to think about much more than windage and elevation. He had not had to lead Marines. But because he could shoot, people now thought he was a hero, the next Chesty Puller. Deep inside, Tony knew he was just a California surfer boy, an X-games kind of guy. The Marines had been an exciting ride, but did he have what it took to lead Marines in combat?

THE PROUD

Chapter 37

Hobyo

It was like rats scurrying around. You knew they were there, but you could not get a clear view of them. SSgt Burke Davidson knew the Somalis had not given up. They were massing for something.

The lieutenant was on the radio, first with the skipper, then on the air freq trying to find out when they could expect to get evacuated. With the platoon commander focused on getting them out of there, Burke was monitoring their tactical situation.

The thick column of black smoke that marked where the Apache had gone down had dissipated somewhat, but even the diminished plume was a reminder that these Somalis were not without their own capabilities. The technical in the intersection still smoldered as well, but the trade-off wasn't worth it.

There were two two-story buildings about 300 meters to the north, and these gave a pretty decent view of their position. The Somalis realized this as well, as they could catch furtive glimpses of movement on the roofs. Burke had already lain in a fire mission on the buildings, but they couldn't rain mortars on them unless the Somalis attacked again. This galled Burke, but at the same time, he knew firing might just push angry men into attacking again. He felt in his bones that they would attack again anyway, but there was a small chance that they had had enough.

Sgt Dailey was moving to each Marine, making sure everyone was OK, mentally ready to repel any further attacks. Burke felt a bit of fatherly pride in that, even if he was only five or six years older than the squad leader. The sergeant was developing into a fine combat leader.

He caught a few flashes from the two buildings and shouted "Get down!" even before he heard the reports and rounds started splattering on the wall below him. Both roofs had a small, 18-inch tall lip surrounding the edges, and his Marines instinctively hugged the northern edge of the

wall as the automatic rifle peppered their building.   The
house that Second Squad was on was lower and closer to the
enemy, but so far, the machine gun was focusing on the
Marines around him.

Within seconds, the Marines were firing back.   Three
hundred meters might seem a long way off, but when firing
over buildings, it was even closer than the 500 meters at
each Marine had qualified at the range.   Explosions of white
dust marked where their return rounds were striking.

He called in the mortar fire mission, but it would be a
good 45 seconds before the rounds would be on target.

A round pinged off a helmet beside Burke.   It shoved
the helmet cockeyed, but LCpl Bouchard merely straightened
it back up, and continued to fire.   There were some machine
guns that could penetrate the Marine Corps helmets at a
range of 300 meters, so it was a relief to know that this was
one of the lighter weapons.

The enemy gun ceased fire, whether from being the
gunner being hit or from him retreating, he didn't know.
Almost immediately, Burke could hear screaming coming
from beyond the second building.   Below him and across
the street, he could see Sgt Alvarez scrambling to direct fire
down over the far edge of his position.   Burke didn't need a
radio report to know that Second Squad was under assault.

He was just about to ask the lieutenant if he should get
Third Squad to reinforce Second when it dawned on him.

"Sgt Dailey, get some men and cover our six, now!"

While everyone's focus was on the attack on the north
side of Second Squad's position and while they had moved to
get cover from the incoming fire, no one was covering the
south side of their position.   Cpl Horton's team just started
to wheel about when an explosion sounded below them.
Burke rushed to the southern edge of the roof and caught
sight of an RPG gunner not 20 meters away, aiming to fire
another rocket down the small alley leading up to the
backside of their position.

Dust from below obscured the man somewhat, but dust
was not going to stop his 5.56 round, and with a three-round
burst, Burke took the gunner down.

Rounds started both hitting the southern lip of the roof

and zinging overhead as Burke dove down the roof opening into the second floor before hurtling down the stairs to the first.   Dust and smoke filled the big room, and Marines were scattered, most trying to get their bearings.   It was obvious that the bulk of the squad had been oriented to the front, where the door and windows were, not to the featureless back.   That had saved them from the main effects of the RPG, but pieces of the house itself had turned into shrapnel, and Burke could see a few cases of blood starting to redden the dust which covered most of the Marines.

Peripherally, he could see the woman prisoner looking quite dead below the hole which now graced the back wall. Without body armor, she hadn't stood much of a chance. Their translator had obviously been with her, but he had Marine-issue armor, and while battered, he was trying to sit up.

Rounds started coming into through the gaping hole in the wall.

"Stanhope!   Cover that!" he yelled, rushing the hole.

While all Marines seemed mobile, the blast itself must have dazed them as they seemed slow to respond.   Burke rushed to cover the new entrance.   Just as he arrived, a man rushed in, shouting.   He was within the reach of Burke's M4 before Burke could react.   But that meant he was also within the muzzle of the Somali's AK as well.

The Somali must have been prepared for fighting, but maybe he thought the Marines would be dazed, or maybe it was Burke's war cry.   Whatever the reason, he hesitated for fraction, and that was all SSgt Burke Davidson, U.S. Marine Corps, needed.   With one smooth motion, he thrust out his right hand, bringing up the butt of his M4 to crash against the Somalis' chin.   The M4 was a shorter weapon, not as effective in butt strokes and the like than even the M16, much less the old M14.   But with the force and accuracy of the strike, the Somali crumpled.   Without thinking, Burke leveled the weapon and put two rounds into the man.   He spun around and fired again, taking down the second Somali who was ducking to rush in through the hole.

He felt the kick of a round hitting him low in his reactive armor, and while it almost took his breath away, he continued to fire out into the alley. He could see several bodies falling, and not from his firing. First Squad must be taking them under fire as well.

A Molotov cocktail came flying through the air, but it splattered on the outside wall just at the edge of the hole. Another 6 inches, and it would have come inside. As it was, flames started to billow.

Sgt Stanhope pushed forward with two Marines and started to add to the outgoing fire. Burke looked over at the dust-covered squad leader. Blood was streaming down his arm, but that could not erase the smile on the man's face. He looked over at his platoon sergeant.

"Oo-rah," he shouted, stopping only to drop the empty mag and replacing it with a new one.

Through the growing smoke and flames, he caught a glimpse of another Somali rushing forward, Molotov cocktail in hand. Before he could throw it, though, he was shot down, and the bottle broke, covering the man in flames.

The house they were in was mostly stucco with a wooden frame. It wouldn't take long for the whole building to go up. There was another crash against the wall— probably another Molotov, he figured.

By bullet or burning, it was evident that they Somalis really wanted to dig them out of their hidey-hole.

THE PROUD

Chapter 38

Hobyo

"Six, we are under heavy attack. I repeat, heavy attack. I estimate 200 enemy with small arms and automatic weapons. We really need some support here, over," Tony shouted into his radio mouthpiece.

Flames were licking over the edge of the back wall, interfering with Cpl Horton's team from firing at the attackers below. Cpl Bonaventure had shifted his team over as well, but that left only Cpl Salazar's team and LCpl Isaac to hold back the Somalis who were starting to edge back down Denver to them.

"Roger, One. I read you. Hold on. We don't have air on station, but we'll be at your position soon. Make sure your Marines know we're coming. We don't need any friendly fire here, over."

"Roger. I copy. But please, get here quick. Out."

Mortar rounds continued to fall back at Elena and along Denver, but with the Somalis aware of them, the effects of the rounds were minimized. Tony had clearly seen a round land less than a meter from a prone Somali with no effect on the man. Additionally, with the narrow street, many rounds were landing on top of the adjacent buildings. Tony had forgotten what the section's combat load had been, but he knew they hadn't carried that many rounds, and they would be out soon.

"Sir," his platoon sergeant said as he rushed up from below and threw himself down at Tony's side. "I think the whole back wall is on fire. I'm not sure how long it'll last, and if this place collapses, we don't want to be up here when it does."

Tony squirmed around to look down and over at the house across the street. Incoming fire had slackened off a bit, but there was still enough not to expose oneself for any more time than necessary.

He hated to give up the high ground, but when it collapsed, it wouldn't be that high anymore, he reckoned.

Looking back at the flames and smoke, that wouldn't be too long now.

"OK, tell Alvarez we're coming over, and get Third over there now.   I want one fire team from First up here to cover, then once everyone else is over, we'll come over, too. See if you can't get some sort of dispersion over there."

"Got it," his platoon sergeant replied before scurrying back and almost throwing himself below.

Tony called up Capt Svenson again to let him know his plans.   He called in to target his current position, thinking to hit at the Somalis as they took the building, but he was told that the mortar section was flat out of rounds.   Without air, without mortars, he was out of any supporting arms. Wistfully, he thought of the *Dunham's* big 5/62, but even if the ship was in range, the flatness of the city would preclude the gun from being very effective.   It wasn't a mortar which could loft rounds up and down.

The door on the house across the street opened up, and fire team by fire team, the Marines rushed over.   One Marine, it looked like PFC Rossi, was hit in the leg as he crossed, but Cpl Kim and LCpl Kropkowski picked him up and dragged him inside.   Several other Marines looked to take hits as well, but their body armor kept them from going down.

"That's it, sir," Sgt Dailey yelled out.   "We've just got me and Third Fire Team, and you and Steptoe, too.   You ready?"

He took one more glance around.   There was no sign of Capt Svenson.   He shook his head before going down the ladder.

Smoke as already forming in the second story, but as they went down the stairway, it got thicker.   Flames were actually licking inside the hole that had been blasted inside the back wall.   LCpl Torino let out another burst with his IAR through the hole, keeping anyone out there at bay.

"She dead?" Tony asked, indicating the woman whose house this probably was.

It was pretty obvious, but if there was any life left in her, they would have to take her with them.   He needn't have worried.   Sgt Dailey assured him she was quite gone.

Tony shrugged and followed the remaining Marines to the doorway. Just inside the building on the other side, Cpl McClaren motioned them to go.

With a rush, the remaining seven Marines bolted for the other side. Tony was the fifth in line. It was only 8 or 10 meters across, but even that was too far. A searing pain struck his leg, and he buckled into the dust. His face bounced off the dirt, driving his helmet's face shield into his lip. He was jerked up by Sgt Dailey and Cpl Steptoe and dragged through the doorway and into the house.

"Doc! The lieutenant's been hit!" Stepchild shouted as the laid him down on the deck.

Tony looked down at his leg. His desert cammie trou were turning red with blood. He figured he should be feeling pain, but after the initial stab, his leg was more numb than anything.

Doc was wrapping the leg of an alert-looking LCpl Rossi. He had been hit in the same leg, the right one, as had Tony. That made sense as the enemy were back towards Elena, and their right legs were on that side as the crossed.

Doc Supchak calmly walked over, cut part of his cammie legs away, and examined the wound. He poked with his fingers a bit, which reawakened Tony's pain mechanism.

"You're lucky, Lieutenant. No real damage, just grazed. You've lost some blood, but you'll be fine," he told him, ignoring Tony's jerking as the fingers probed. "We'll have to clean it up later back on the ship, but let me wrap this up, and you'll be good to go for now."

Afraid he was going to be nauseous, he had hesitated to look at the wound. But as Doc wiped it down with Betadine, he was too curious not to look. There was a gash high across his thigh, maybe four inches long and a half-an-inch deep at the center. It was awfully close to his family jewels, he realized. Their body armor had a balls-protector, but that was for getting hit from the front. Tony had gotten hit from the side, so a round a bit higher would have entered his thigh and proceeded merrily along the way to his nutsack. He couldn't help but shudder at the thought.

A voice cried out in pain as rounds started coming right through the stucco walls. Marines dove for the ground along the side walls as return fire opened up above them.

The Somalis had evidently claimed their old position and were firing right through the thinner walls of this position. Tony, had only been half-bandaged when he had lunged for the side wall, and now he ordered that any piece of furniture be brought forward and made into a makeshift barricade.

Flames sprung up to block the window opening facing the street. They were going to try to burn them out of this building as well.

He tried to pull up his platoon disposition display, but the icons kept fading in and out. He must have knocked something loose when he had fallen on his face. His comm seemed affected as well. It was spotty, but he clearly heard a voice come over the platoon freq.

"Holy shit. Here they come!"

THE PROUD

Chapter 39

Hobyo

Captain Svenson had been monitoring First Platoon's frequency, and he heard that same radio message. He looked around at his Marines and knew he had to move.

At that moment, he felt on top of the world. This was what he had been born for. This was his purpose in life. And now he would prove it to anyone who had doubted him.

A long time ago, he had seen an old movie, *The Wind and the Lion*. He had actually forgotten most of the movie, but there was one scene that had stuck with him. In that scene, the Marine captain was leading his group of Marines to confront the prince or some such title, the guy who controlled Sean Connery, who in turn was playing the last of the Barbary pirates. He got his Marines into formation and essentially double-timed down the middle of the street, sending all the locals diving for cover and leaving the French and German military delegations slack-jawed. He ran right into the prince's palace, took on the guards, and saved the day. It was all fiction, of course, but still, the scene resonated with him.

And now, there he was, essentially doing the same thing, and with pirates, none-the-less. He knew the "book" way would be to clear each block, each building before proceeding. But he also knew that First Platoon probably did not have the time for that. The mortar section was out of rounds, and with who knows how many Somalis gathering, the platoon could not hope to hang on forever.

He had essentially run his force down Route Cleveland, Hobyo's main thoroughfare. He hadn't run in formation as in the movie, but rather in two loose columns. It had been a calculated risk. He figured the Somalis would be focused on where the hostages had been kept, not at the fake position. So far, his opinion had proven true. They had not run into anyone.

But now they were coming up to Elena, and with a hard right, they would be only 250 meters from the embattled

First Platoon.   And coming up to the intersection, they could see the back of some Somalis, men who were probably armed.

Terrell should have been in back of at least one squad. His job was to lead the Marines into battle, not be the point man.   But he had taken his place at the head of one of the two columns.   He had tried to justify it to himself by saying he had to control the formation, to know if they had to shift to a more accepted one.   But in reality, his soul was singing for action.   He may not be blood-related to the Vikings whose name he carried, but he was like-minded.   He thirsted for battle.

When the message had come over First's Platoon frequency, he swung into action.   With a "follow me" sweep of this arm worthy of any WWI NCO going over the top, he broke out into a run, his Marines quickly closing with him. This may not have been anything taught in any battle manual, in any military textbook.   This was not military science.   This was just an unstoppable force.

And sometimes the gods of war favored the audacious.

THE PROUD

Chapter 40

Hobyo

Maslax Kusow hung back, watching the final push.   He had learned his lesson before.   He had been eager to watch the trap set for the American helicopters, and he had almost been caught in the explosions that rocked the intersection a few moments later.   So now, he was as back as far as he could go and still see the action.

The Rangers, no, the Marines, he reminded himself, could not last much longer.   There had to be over 500 men gathered to take vengeance.   Most of the Americans would die, but Tablan Barre, that angry young man who claimed to be the great-grandson of the country's third president and seemed to have led the pirate mission that captured the American sailor in the first place, had stressed that they needed some of the foreigners left alive.

"How much longer do you think they'll last?" he asked Osman, an old friend who also preferred to stay back and out of harm's way.

"Look, you can see the smoke from Korfa's house now, so it won't be long.   They'll be roasted if they don't come out."

"Poor Korfa.   That guy can't get a break.   I hope he goes to Taban and gets paid for all of this when everything's over."

"Won't happen.   You remember what his father did, what, 20 years ago?   No way Korfa's getting anything from this."

"Yes, you're probably right."

Maslax vaguely heard movement behind him, but he figured it was just more people coming to the party.   He turned to Osman to say something when his friend's head erupted into a pink mist.   Maslax stared stupidly as Osman fell to lie still on the ground.

He turned around, and his heart stopped.   A mass of Americans was rushing up, death on their minds.   More shots rang out, and people began to fall.

162

As everyone's attention was focused forward, when people began to fall, the others must have thought the shots were coming from the trapped Marines, so they started running backwards. This placed them right into the path of the onrushing horde.

Maslax only hesitated a moment. He darted to the side and into the doorway of a house. He couldn't open the door, so he hugged it, trying to make himself small.

The Marines hit the mass of people like a hammer, and they began to scatter. Most of the people in the back were not armed, just there to watch the fight. They got in the way of the ones with rifles. Some in the back were even shot by people in the front who were trying to target the Americans.

Leading the Americans was a tall, black Marine. He was everywhere, shooting, hitting, yelling. Maslax was sure he saw several rounds hit the tall man, but he never paused. His soldiers were all around him, madmen. Somali after Somali fell, and within a minute, they broke and ran. That left a gap down towards the other group of Americans, and the tall Marine led his soldiers down towards them.

Maslax stepped out from the door in spite of himself. He knew he should run, but something made him watch. He had to see.

As the Marines ran down the road, Maslax was surprised to see that there were really not that many of them. There had been far, far more men attacking the Americans than both groups of Americans combined. But his countrymen had run from them. He looked about, wondering how many Americans had died. He didn't see any on the ground, but there were maybe 20 Somalis, either dead or wounded.

The men on top of Jamal's house started firing on the Americans, and at last, they started slowing down to fire back. Maslax felt elated. He knew he had caused all of this by selling the information on the hostages, and he would do it again if he had the chance. But he felt proud to see his countrymen fighting back.

The Americans weren't lying down, though. They fired their own weapons, and one soldier lifted a tube. It didn't look like an RPG, but there was something about it that had the same feel.   There was a whoosh, and a rocket flew out to hit Jamal's house.   Whether it was the American's rocket or the fire that burned fiercely, the entire house collapsed, bringing all the men who had been on the roof down into the flames.

A round hit the door a few inches from his head.   That was enough for Maslax.   It was time to get out of there.

Chapter 41

Hobyo

"Well, Lieutenant, I guess you're happy to see me," Capt Svenson told him. "But you should've seen me out there. I was awesome," he exulted.

Tony was happy to see him, of course. That last furious assault had almost broken through before the captain had come up with Second Platoon and various odds and ends to hit the backside of the Somalis. His leg was beginning to ache, and many of his Marines were hurt, but by some sort of miracle, none had been killed. Doc told him that Pvt Lambie would probably lose his left arm, but with due respect to the private, that was a small price to pay for what could have happened.

But they were not out of the woods yet.

"So when're the birds coming in?" he asked. "We've got some hurt Marines who need medical care."

"Well, the Ospreys can't land here. They're too big. And no one knows what brought down the Apache and the Black Hawk yet. Our orders are to go to the beach, just south of the docks for a pick-up. The beach is pretty broad there."

"With all due respect, sir, I think we need to get going then. If we give them enough time, the ragheads'll be coming back, and back with a vengeance," put in SSgt Davidson.

"And then we'll kick their ass again, Burke! We're Americans, and we know from an ass-whupping!"

Tony thought the skipper was looking for a "oo-rah" or something, but when they all just looked at him, he went on.

"But you're right. Lt Hartigan, I want you in the front. Lead your platoon back to Elena, then you're going to have to use the smaller alleys and such to make it to the beach. We should hit it only a few hundred meters from our pick-up point. Sgt Black," he directed to his radio operator, "Get Lieutenant Colonel Pavoni on the hook. I want to give him a first-hand account on what happened."

THE PROUD

Joe Hartigan had been standing next to Tony, and as the captain turned away, Tony asked, "What's going on with him?   I mean, I glad as shit you arrived, but what's with him?"

Joe looked up to make sure the captain was not looking.

"Well, he's turned into this fucking super hero.   It's all him this and all him that.   But you should know, he disobeyed orders to come save your ass.   And man, you should have seen him back at Elena.   Just like in a movie. He was fucking awesome. Pow! Smack!   Those guys were running in pure fear."

"That's great and all, and I appreciate it, but is he still spoiling for a fight?   Or are we going to hightail it out of here?"

"I don't know.   Your guess is as good as mine.   And with that, I gotta get going if we're going to move.   You OK, though?" he asked pointing to Tony's leg.

"Don't worry about me," he replied.

Truth-be-told, his leg was stiffening up.   But he had only 600 meters or so to go, and nothing was going to stop him.

Although it seemed longer, it probably only took 10 minutes to have everyone down and ready to go.   Second Platoon had already moved out, and First fell in to follow in trace.   Tony kept waiting for an attack, but nothing was happening.

From their last position to Elena, bodies and blood trails littered the area.   Elena itself was even worse.   There was a torched body inside the destroyed technical, and at least 15 bodies lay in crumbled heaps on the ground.   Tony was not big into body counts, but he estimated that at least 40-50 Somalis had died.   And two Americans.

He looked to the left where the smoke from the downed Apache still rose.   From their planned path, the Apache could not be more than 100 meters out-of-the-way.

The captain was walking up and down the formation, stopping to slap Marines on the shoulder or share a laugh. Tony tried to raise him on his radio, but it was still acting squirrely. As Capt Svenson came closer, Tony waved him over.

"Whadaya got?" the company commander asked as he got there.

"Well, sir, that Apache.   Look, it can't be more than 100 meters off our path, two or three of these little city blocks.   We need to go there and pick up the bodies."

The captain looked surprised, as if wondering why he hadn't realized that.

"Of course, of course."

He looked up at the back of Second Platoon ahead. The lead element of the platoon was probably past the point that was even with the Apache, and turning them around could cause problems.   The captain seemed to realize this, too.

"OK, I want you to take your platoon up and over and recover the bodies.   Then move parallel with Second to the beach.   You should come out right at the pick-up point. And that provides flank security to each other."

He started to move forward, then seem to think better of it.

"In fact, I think I'm going with you, too."

Tony turned to Cpl Steptoe and had him relay the change.   He limped forward to make sure Sgt Alvarez didn't get lost in the maze of small alleys and roads.   He needn't have worried.   The Apache called to them as its parts pinged and crackled as they cooled.   They came around one corner, and partially buried in a small house, the Apache looked huge.   Two men were looking at it, but they ran as soon as the Marines came into view.

The Apache was burnt pretty badly, and the rotors had snapped right off, but it was surprisingly intact.   Cpl Winsome's team made their way into the rubble of the building and to the crumpled nose of the helo.   After a few moments, the team leader came back out.

"Sir, there's only one body in the bird, burnt to shit.   I think it's the pilot, the one in the back."

Tony looked at his commander.   He could see the captain had the same thought.   The Somalis had captured the other pilot.

Well, nothing to do about now, he thought.

"OK, we need to get him out of there.   Sgt Alvarez, take

who you need to get it done."

"Uh, there's also another body there," Winsome added.

"The co-pilot?" Tony asked.

"No sir.   I think it's a kid.   I think the Apache crushed her, you know, when it crashed.   But the fire, well, it burned the girl, too."

There was nothing he could do about that either, so Tony told Sgt Alvarez to recover the pilot's body.   He passed to the other Marines to be watchful as they waited. The longer they waited, the more time the Somalis had to re-group, but they had to recover the soldier.   No one would be left behind.

He leaned against the wall of a shop.   His leg was throbbing now, and he felt sick to his stomach.   Looking at the map once again, nothing had changed.   200, maybe 250 meters to the beach.   Two football fields.   A thirty second run. He could do it.

At last, Alvarez came out, Cpl White and LCpl Nguyen carrying the burnt body of an American, someone whose name Tony didn't even know.   The body was still in the sitting position—its burnt flesh unable to move.   They had evidently discussed how to carry the body back, because as soon as they got out, LCpl Nguyen turned around and dropped his pack.   Sgt Alvarez and Cpl White tied the body to his back.   Burning a body made it much lighter, but still, this had to be a heavy burden.   But Nguyen gave a thumbs up, and so Tony gave the order to move out.

They barely much more than stepped out when the point man, Pvt Rafferty, came to a stop, pointing his rifle at a pile of garbage bags.   Everyone moved to the side, weapons at the ready.   Rafferty took a cautious step forward, then dropped his weapon, franticly throwing trash bags aside.

"Come here, come here!" he shouted to no one in particular.

Tony rushed forward with the rest, and through the milling Marines, he saw a blackened, broken man lying on the ground behind the scattered bags.   An American.   The co-pilot.

Somehow, he had not only survived the crash, but he had gotten out and dragged himself out of sight.   It had been, what almost an hour since the crash?   He must have been in agony, and he had barely enough strength to call out to Rafferty as he walked by.

Doc Supchak rushed up and made a quick examination. Doc was competent, but his bedside manner could use some improvement.

"He's pretty fucked up," he told Tony.   "His back's broken, and maybe his skull, too, at the very least.   And the burns are pretty extensive.   I don't know if he's going to make it."

Tony looked at the soldier.   The man was conscious, and Tony could see he understood what was being said.

He turned back to Doc, but the Navy corpsman was slipping out of his flak jacket.

"I need one more," he shouted out.

Immediately, three or four more were thrust at him. He took LCpl Gittens'.   He pointed over to where two wooden poles were holding up some sort of striped awning, and they were retrieved.   He closed the jackets and placed them bottom to bottom.   Sliding the poles through the arm holes, he ran the poles down the length of one, up the bottom of the other, and out that one's armholes.   Doing this on the other side with the other pole resulted in a makeshift stretcher.

Working quickly and professionally, he directed the Marines to shift the soldier onto the stretcher, keeping his neck straight.   The pilot groaned, but other than that, made no sound.

"What about you?" Tony asked the doc, touching his own flak jacket to indicate what was on his mind.

Many of the Marines had already been hit by enemy fire or shrapnel, and only the high effectiveness of their reactive body armor had kept them alive.   Without the body armor, Doc and Gittens were at serious risk.

"I guess we just gotta get down to the beach and outta here real quick, right lieutenant?" he replied with a smile before moving off to walk with the stretcher bearers.

"Good job, Tony," the captain told him as they started to move out.   "I have to admit, I completely forgot about retrieving the bodies, so, well, I guess you saved his life.

You kept me from making a huge mistake."

"Well sir, I guess I owe you."

Captain Svenson laughed.

"I guess you do at that," he said, slapping Tony on the shoulder.

That pushed him off balance, tweaking his leg, but the captain was already moving off.

The sun was overhead now, beating down on their heads in the small, hot alleys.   First Squad now had point as Second carried the pilot, and Third was bringing up the rear. First was probably 100 meters or less from the beach when all hell broke loose.   Tony should have changed helmets with someone, he realized.   He needed to be able to communicate.   But it was too late as he rushed back, Steptoe in tow.

Third Squad had only then passed the Apache when they had been hit from the rear.   The Marines were trying to take cover and return fire, but the incoming was fierce.

"Steptoe, tell the other two squads to get to the beach and join up with Second Platoon.   Third's going to do a slow retrograde to give them time.   As soon as they've hooked up with Second Platoon, let us know and we're going to break contact and get out as fast as we can.   They need to be ready to support us.

A round hit Tony high on the shoulder, spinning him half-way around.   He knew it would hurt tomorrow, but he didn't have time for that now as long as his armor protected him.

The captain was running around like a crazy man, extolling the Marines to fight.   He didn't take cover, but remained in the open.   He had been hit once in the arm, which now flopped loosely at his side, but that didn't seem to faze him.

The Marines' outgoing fire seemed to have stopped the pursuing Somalis, but Tony knew they were probably being flanked.   He also knew they had to occupy the Somalis until Second Squad, burdened by the pilot, had made it.

SSgt Davidson was giving the fire teams their retrograde order, that is, what fire team would go first, to drop back and then provide cover for the next, which would then provide cover for the third to move back, and so on. This had to be a choreographed dance, keeping rounds going downrange while not hitting each other.

At last, Steptoe told him that Second Squad had performed the link-up. Tony gave the order, and immediately, Cpl Horton got his team up and rushed back 20 meters before stopping and kneeling. Then it was the turn of Cpl Bonaventure's team, that had been firing in support, to get up and move in back of Horton's team before turning and kneeling again. Finally it was Cpl Salazar's team, although Tony and Steptoe, the captain, and SSgt Davidson waited until the last moment to go with that team.

There was a bend in the alley ahead, which would make it easier to defend. With Cpl Salazar's team parked right at the front of the bend, both of the other two teams would be covered from incoming fire. At that point Tony figured they had to be only 60, 70 meters from the beach. They could sprint it.

Cpl Steptoe gave a grunt in pain, but when Tony looked at him, he got the OK signal.

Cpl Horton got his team up and moving around the corner. It was working like clockwork. Then it was Second fire team's turn again. Cpl Bonaventure jumped up, followed by his team. Just as they were passing the last Salazar's team, Pvt Miller went down hard. Capt Svenson and SSgt Davidson jumped up to grab the private and drag him around the corner, and then Salazar's team got up to bound back. Tony nodded at Cpl Steptoe who stumbled as he got up. Tony steadied him, and when he turned, saw the blasted radio on his back. Pieces of broken radio had peppered his neck, but nothing looked serious. He was just a bit dazed. Tony gave him a shove, then started to follow.

He risked a quick look back and saw the Somali, standing as calm as you please, taking aim with an ancient rifle. Tony tried to wheel and dive for safety when the lights went out.

THE PROUD

Chapter 42

Hobyo

"Can we switch sides?" the captain asked him.

SSgt Davidson had Pvt Miller's right arm while the captain had the left as they dragged his limp body down towards the beach.   But with the captain's left arm dangling uselessly, that meant he had to essentially walk backwards.

"Oh, sure, sir," he responded.   They laid Miller back, then switched positions.   The private's eyes were slightly open, but the pupils were rolled back, and he was unresponsive.   Burke knew he was gone.   It looked like a round had hit him under the arm where there was no body armor and then penetrated into his chest cavity.   Grabbing him under his arms, they picked his upper body back up and moved off, letting his heels drag in the dust.

Ahead of them, Cpl Horton started to get his team down, to provide covering fire again.

"Just keep going!" Burke shouted.

The alley ended just ahead, maybe 30 meters, and Burke could already see the expanse of beach and the deep blue sea beyond.   He wanted to take advantage of the bend in the alley and get the Marines out of the maze of passages and to link up with the rest of the company.

A couple of silhouettes rose up where the alley opened up to the beach, and Burke heart jumped before he realized that those silhouettes belonged to Marines, Marines who were covering them.

"Move it, people!   Move it!" he yelled out.

Even carrying Pvt Miller, it took only moments until the two Marines burst into the open, the bright sunlight almost blinding them.   Both platoons had linked up, and most of the Marines were down taking cover behind the natural berm made by tides.

Burke scanned the skies, but there was no sight of Ospreys coming for the pick-up.   A sense of anger struck him.   He knew the Somalis had some sort of anti-aircraft weapon, but no matter, the company needed to be picked up.

It was only then that he noticed the huge shape making its way onshore, still maybe 600 or 700 meters out. A sense of relief swept over him. It was one of the *Gaffert's* LCACs, the huge air-cushion landing craft. Burke wasn't sure how he could have missed it at first. The LCAC kicked up a good amount of spray as it came racing over the water.

He realized that the LCAC was a good choice, better than a helo. It would be able to ride right up on the beach, and it would take some pretty powerful weapons to knock one out, much bigger than the Somalis had heretofore shown that the possessed.

Burke looked around at the Marines gathered on the beach. The LCAC had a huge weight payload, but the deck was not that big for 80+ Marines. He didn't think, though, that too many Marines would bitch if they had to pack it in asshole to belly button.

The captain and he had slowed down as soon as they hit the sand of the beach, and several other Marines had rushed up to help.

As several sets of hands reached out, one voice simply told them all, "I've got him."

It was PFC Masterson. Terry and Jerry.

The others backed off as the young Marine reached down and hoisted his buddy onto his shoulders. He stumbled a bit, and someone reached over to help, but he held up a hand to stop him. He was going to do this alone.

The poignancy of the situation might hit him later, but Burke had work to do. The LCAC would be ashore in a minute or so. Already, he could see Ian Pierce from Second Platoon moving to the waterline to act as a beach master in guiding in the big beast.

"Squad leaders, give me a head count," he passed on the platoon freq.

Doc met Masterson to look at Miller, but the shake of his head confirmed to Burke that the private was dead. Doc then came up to the captain, but the company commander waved him off.

All three squad counts came back. Everyone had made it to the beach. The LCAC was slowing down to move up onto the beach, so he told Second and Third to get ready to board and told First to cover them.   Once the first two squads were onboard, then First would rush onboard and the LCAC's ramp would close.

He tried to report to the lieutenant before remembering that the platoon commander's radio was down. He took off his helmet to get a better view and looked around, but couldn't see him.   The captain was standing, looking back into the town, so Burke trudged up to ask him if he'd seen Lt Niimoto.

Just as he reached the captain, he saw Cpl Steptoe stagger out of the alley.   The radio operator stumbled and took a knee in the sand.

Burke immediately realized his mistake.   He had gotten a head count, but of the squads.   He had neglected to account for the platoon headquarters and for the STA team. He had just seen LCpls Isaac and Hyde of the STA team, but he hadn't accounted for Steptoe and the lieutenant.

He took a step to go help Cpl Steptoe when his blood ran cold.   Several Somalis burst out of the building closest to the beach and grabbed Cpl Steptoe, yanking the Marine back into the alley.   Burke started to raise his weapon, but firing would endanger the Marine as well, so he pulled his weapon back down and started to run.   In the back of his mind, he knew he should have support, but instinctively, he just ran.   If they got Steptoe out of sight, they would never be able to find him again.

As he ran, the long legs of the captain passed him, sand flying.   The captain had his 9 mm out, waving it in his good hand as he ran.

It took only seconds, but they closed the gap and flew into the alley, this time, their eyes needing a moment to adjust to the shadows.   Another Marine ran alongside of him.   Burke glanced to the side to see that of all people, it was PFC McNamara.

A burst of fire sounded in front of them, and the captain stumbled, but didn't go down.   Two Somalis held Cpl Steptoe between them, while a third was standing, firing back at them as they ran up.

Captain Svenson fired off two shots, but Burke couldn't see if he had hit anyone.   The Somali gunman seemed ready to break and run, but he fired off another burst. Burke heard the captain grunt, but with an inarticulate war cry, the Marine covered the last 10 meters and physically crashed into the three Somalis and Cpl Steptoe.

When the captain crashed into the group, they all went down. One Somali had already been hit, but the other two were scrambling to get back up when Burke fired two shots into each one. Both went down immediately.

Burke pulled Steptoe back, away from the others. The radio operator was dazed, but conscious.

"Captain, we've got him. Let's get the hell out of here," he shouted at the prone company commander.

Capt Svenson didn't move. Burke moved over and turned the Marine over. Blood pulsed out of his throat. His eyes were open, and they struggled to focus on the platoon sergeant.

"I guess I did OK, huh?" he asked, the words gurgling as blood fought with air.

"You sure did, sir. Hang on, we'll get you back."

The captain seemed to shrug as his eyes closed. He breathing became labored.

"I've got him, Staff Sergeant."

PFC McNamara leaned over and picked up the lanky Marine, slinging him over his shoulders.

"OK, get out of here."

He motioned back to the beach. He could see other Marines beginning to approach the alley, more cautiously, though, more by-the-book. McNamara reached them, and the other Marines rushed to help him with the company commander. Burke turned to Cpl Steptoe, who was still somewhat dazed.

"Where's the lieutenant?" he asked urgently.

"He didn't make it," came the reply. "He got shot back there."

"Bullshit! You saw him get killed?"

"He, he pushed me back, then I heard the rounds hit him. I saw all the blood. I couldn't go out there to get him."

Burke stood up. He looked back to the beach. Sgt Dailey was there at the end of the alley with several Marines.

The drone of the LCAC was clearly audible, and he knew they needed to load it and get out of there.

"Staff sergeant?" came the question over the platoon freq.

"Pat, get these Marines on that LCAC. Give me 5 minutes, and if I'm not back by then, tell whoever is in charge to get underway."

"Where are you going, over?"

"I'm getting the lieutenant, so you get going. That's an order."

He looked back at Cpl Steptoe.

"Can you stand?" When the radio operator nodded, he went on, "Go back and join the others."

He turned away, then cautiously stepped over the three dead Somalis. Keeping to the shadows, he felt hundreds of eyes on him, and he expected to be jumped at any second.

As he approached the bend in the alley, he hugged the near side. He could see some blood splatter that reached from beyond the bend, and he heard the low murmur of voices.

He quietly reached into his buttpack, feeling around for his signaling mirror. He brought it out and oh so carefully pushed it around the edge of the bend, taking in what was on the other side.

Three armed Somali men stood around the motionless body of Lt Niimoto while a fourth was going through the lieutenant's pockets. Blood covered the lieutenant's face.

Burke looked down at the magazine sticking out of his M4. It was his last mag, and frankly, he didn't know how many rounds were in it.

Well, it is what it is, he thought.

He flipped his M4 off safe. Taking a deep breath, he charged around the corner, firing at the standing men. Two went down immediately before they could register the attacking madman, and the third looked up in panic, raising his own weapon.

He took aim and pulled the trigger again, only to hear an empty click. He was out of ammo. Closing the gap in only a second, the kicked the man who had been searching the lieutenant's pockets as he tried to stand and thrust the muzzle of his rifle as hard as he could deep into the other's throat just as the man fired his rifle, rounds blasting past his ear, deafening him.

He could feel the muzzle of his M4 hit bone, and the man fell down, clutching his throat. Hands grabbed him from below, knocking him down, and as he fell, he twisted, trying to bring the barrel of his M4 down on the fourth man's head.

Instead of hitting him squarely, the rifle seemed to roll over the man's back, and Burke lost his grip. The M4 went skittering across the alley. Burk hit the ground hard as he fell, knocking the wind out of him. He tried to roll over, but strong hands held him down and started to move up his body, raining blows that thankfully, his body armor absorbed.

Burke tried to buck the man off, but the Somali was unbearably strong. He evidently realized that his blows were having no effect because the stopped hitting and pinned one of Burke's arms with his knee as hands sought his throat. Burke looked up into eyes that already registered victory.

Back at RASP, Burke had been taught hand-to-hand combat, of course. His mind raced as to his options. But while Burke was in great shape, this man was a monster. Panic almost took over when we remembered one of his instructors stressing that no one was defeated until he was cold and dead, that anything could be used as a weapon.

As the big hands closed around Burke's throat, and with his left arm trapped, Burke reached over with his right, unclasped his helmet, and with one smooth motion, swung it around, connecting with the side of the Somali's head. The man faltered, but the pressure he was putting on Burke's throat didn't cease. Burke brought his arm back again and swung, connecting once more. The man slumped over for a moment, then looked down at the helmet with wariness. Burke thought he would protect himself, but evidently this was a war of endurance. Would Burke be choked unconscious before he could beat the man into senselessness?

He brought his arm back one more time as spots began to form in front of his eyes. Putting everything into it, he started to swing.   The man on top of him evidently decided that he needed to protect himself as he let go of Burke's throat to bring up his arms, but it was too late.   The helmet connected with a solid crack, and the big man collapsed.

Burke pushed the man over, mounted him, and began to rain blows down on the man's head.   The helmet was uniquely designed to protect a head, but in this case, it was a deadly weapon.   Burke literally crushed the man's skull, turning it into a blood-splattered mass of mush and brain matter.

Burke knew the man was dead, but adrenaline kept him going for a few more blows.   It wasn't until he shifted position to get in a better shot and his leg touched the body of Lt. Niimoto that he got control of his berserker rage.   He put down his battered helmet and slid off the body of the Somali.   Down the alley, the other Somali, the one he had hit in the throat, was slowly crawling off.   Burke ignored him.

He lifted the lieutenant's arm and turned him over. Much to his surprise, bubbles were forming over the platoon commander's nose.   He was still alive!   He looked around—he had to get his commander back to the beach.

A noise in back of him caused him to jump up.

"Is he still alive?" Cpl Steptoe asked him.

"What the fuck are you doing here?   I told you to evacuate."

"I know, Staff Sergeant, but me and the lieutenant, we go back a long way, and the more I thought about it, as my head cleared up a bit, the more I wasn't sure he was dead. And if you were going to see, well, I figured maybe I would help."

Burke let that go for the moment.

"Well, he's pretty fucked up, and I can see you're still fucked up.   But let's get going . . . "

They were interrupted by shouts coming from further down the alleyway.

"Oh shit!   More company.   We don't need that."

He looked around.   He stepped up to a door on the right and tried the doorknob.   It was locked.   He rushed to the next one and tried it.   To his surprise, it opened.   He looked inside, but it seemed as if no one was home.

"OK, we need to get the lieutenant in there.   But he's bleeding like a stuck pig, and we can't advertise that we're inside."

"Use that awning there.   It won't stop the bleeding, but maybe it can sop up enough so we don't leave a trail," Steptoe told him, pointing to one of the ubiquitous awnings which graced many of the city's buildings.

Burke ripped it down as the voices got closer.   They didn't have much time.   He bundled the lieutenant up, regardless of what damage he might be causing, and before the blood could seep through, he rushed the lieutenant into the dark interior of the house.   Cpl Steptoe pulled one of the dead Somalis over closer to the door and left him face first there, hoping to cover up or at least disguise and blood they might had left.

Cpl Steptoe just managed to get inside and the door closed when the voices outside raised in pitch.   They had found the scene of the fight, and they sounded none too happy.

Burke and Steptoe froze, afraid to make a sound.   An eon later, the voices proceeded down the alley towards the beach.

"Now they're between us and the rest of the company," Cpl Steptoe whispered.

"Doesn't really matter," Burke told him.   "The company shoved off 5 minutes after I took off for the lieutenant.   We are well and truly alone now."

"Well, fuck," came the simple reply.

Burke tried to call into the platoon, but now his radio was not working.   Pounding a Somali's head into a pulp with the helmet was probably not conducive to the electronics, he figured.   He looked to Steptoe and the PRC 92 he was still humping, but that had already been turned into a pile of parts, mostly broken parts.   It was ironic that in this age of communications, when everyone had a cell phone, they couldn't speak to anybody.

They sat silently for awhile, listening for returning voices.   Lt Niimoto hung on, soft gurgling noises rising from him at times.   Burke tipped him on his side so he wouldn't

179

drown in his own blood.

Eventually, he got up and looked about the house for something he could use as a weapon. He found a few kitchen utensils, but frankly, his K-Bar was much better suited for a fight.

The small house had a sleeping loft up a ladder in the back. Figuring it was better to be even partially out of sight, he and Steptoe maneuvered the lieutenant up the ladder and laid him on the wooden floor of the loft. Burke tried to clean up the blood which now stained the floor of the main room below, but that was not going to happen.

As they waited out the afternoon, he was amazed that the lieutenant was still hanging on. The man had a will to live.

After a few hours, his bladder was screaming for attention, so he crept down the ladder and back into the main room, looking for something in which he could piss. When he heard voices outside, he quickly moved to the door and froze, K-Bar out.

The voices trailed off, and he started to relax when he heard a door open. A few moments later, it closed, then he could distinctly hear footsteps coming back across the small alley. Another door opened, this one right next door. Someone was checking the homes.

He considered trying to hold the door closed, but that would undoubtedly bring unwanted attention. He looked around. The room was dark, and it was possible that someone looking in from the daylight outside might not see everything.

He hugged the wall by the door and waited. The steps approached, and the door swung open, the open door itself blocking Burke from view. The door stopped for a moment, and started to swing back shut when it was suddenly thrust back open and a man rushed forward, looking at the blood stains in the middle of the floor.

He should have paid attention to what else might be in the room as Burke gave him no chance. He rushed the man, his left arm grabbing the man's forehead, pulling it back, while the right drove the tip of the K-Bar into the side of his neck, then forced it forward, ripping through flesh, arteries, and veins.

The man was dead before Burke could lower him to the ground. Cpl Steptoe came down the ladder, and between the two of them, the manhandled the dripping body up to the loft and lay it down beside the lieutenant. There was nothing they could do about the blood, though. It looked like a slaughterhouse.

Burke realized that if he had been back in the loft when the man had come in, things could have been much worse. That was a mistake alleviated only because he had had to take a piss. For the rest of the afternoon, he sat on the floor by the door, leaving Cpl Steptoe to watch over the lieutenant. Nothing much happened as they sat in silence, watching the flies come and gather to sample the bloody bounty on the floor.

It wasn't until he was sitting there that he realized he had been bleeding himself. It might have been a round, it might have been during his fight with the big Somali. But the back of his arm had contributed to the sanguineous mess on the floor.

As the sun started going down, there was more activity in the alley outside. He heard the call to prayers, then people walking about and talking. People had most likely been in hiding, and now, with the fighting stopped, they came out to take joy in their continued living and to find out what happened.

Not everyone was joyful, though. A woman's wailing erupted from down the alley. Burke wondered who her husband or son had been. Had he perhaps even killed him? As a rule, Burke did not think too much about who he may have shot. But sitting on the floor, alone with his thoughts, it seemed a bit different.

He was almost caught off guard when the door opened once again. A woman with a baby in her arms walked in. She stepped in the blood, looked down at it in horror, and opened her mouth to scream when Burke was able to jump up and clamp his hand over her mouth. His K-Bar was ready to strike, but he couldn't. He wrestled the woman to the ground as the baby started crying. Holding the knife to the woman's throat, he put his forefinger over his lips. She nodded her acquiescence, even if obviously frightened out of her wits.

Cpl Steptoe came down to help, and they ended up tearing a sheet to bind the woman and cover her mouth. The baby kept crying, though, and Burke was worried that that might attract some attention, but he was at a loss at what to do.

Cpl Steptoe came to the rescue. The woman was bound, hand and foot, and they had put the baby in her lap. Steptoe picked up the baby, the reached over to pull the woman's robe off her shoulder. Her eyes widened in panic, whether for fear for her baby or for fear of rape, Burke didn't know. But when Steptoe held the child to her breast and the baby started suckling, she relaxed. He guessed she figured no one would take care of a baby's feeding if he planned to kill them.

Despite their situation, Burke had to smile. Cpl Steptoe was a big man, and here he was standing, bent over, holding a tiny child to a woman's breast so it could drink. They couldn't untie the woman's arms, so he had to stand there for a good ten minutes before the child was satisfied. Then, instead of putting the baby back down, he held the child against his chest. Steptoe's body armor couldn't have been comfortable, but the baby soon fell asleep against it.

They all sat there: Cpl Steptoe, the woman, and Burke, staring at each other, waiting it out. Things got quieter outside. Burke risked opening the door a crack, and only a few lights were on. Together with Steptoe, they brought the lieutenant down to the main room. He was still hanging on, but his breathing was feeble.

Burke rummaged through a wardrobe, but nothing there would fit over their uniforms and body armor. He had wanted to break up their silhouette so they wouldn't stand out so much from a distance, but everything was too small. There were men's clothes in evidence, and that changed Burke's time schedule. He had planned on moving out well after midnight, but if this woman's husband was out discussing the day's events with others, well, he would be coming back. Burke wished he could talk to the woman, so see if maybe her husband was off fishing or something, but even if he could speak Somali, could he trust what she told him?

So it was dark, but not too terribly late when Burke and Cpl Steptoe slipped out of the house, carrying the lieutenant. They had left the woman alone, figuring that with them gone, she would eventually dislodge or even chew through her gag and call for help.

Burke had taken Steptoe's M4 and was leading the way, but his arms were still burdened by Lt Niimoto's legs. If it came to a fight, he would have to drop the lieutenant before being able to fire.

They passed several house in which oil lamps burned and voices emanated. They both jumped when a door opened behind them, but whoever it was didn't look in their direction and merely walked back towards the center of town.

It actually took only a few minutes to make it to the end of the alley. But this revealed another problem. While the houses in the alley seemed to lack electricity, the beach area did have it, and there were many more lights on there. The docks themselves were also well lit. Burke had toyed with the idea of stealing a boat, but he could see now that this wasn't going to happen.

To make matters worse, there was an open café just 20 or 30 meters away, and the place was packed with men. They were drinking tea or coffee or whatever people drank in Somalia, but most of them seemed armed.

Burke knew that just because he could see them clearly didn't mean they could see the three Marines. They were in the darkness looking out, and the Somalis were in the light. Still, he was far from confident.

"OK, Steptoe. What do they call you, anyway? Surely not Harrington?"

"Uh, just Steptoe's OK."

"No nickname? Well, no matter for now. Look, a boat's out of the question now. We're just going to have to swim for it."

"Swim?" came the worried-sounding response.

"No, not fucking swimming to the USA. Just to get out there. Then we have to wait until we get spotted. We've got to have the area under surveillance, right?

"Well, yeah, I guess so, but . . ."

"But what?" he interrupted.

"Um, I'm not that strong a swimmer."

Oh shit, Burke thought.   *Lord, don't put this on me, too.*

"Well, you're just going to have to make do.   You had survival training.   We can make floats out of your trou. Some sailor once did that here in the IO for five days before a Pakistani fishing boat picked him up.   Look, as soon as we're chest deep, just drop your radio in the water.   Drop everything except your M4. I'll help you."

"How're we going to get down to the beach?" Cpl Steptoe asked, using his head to indicate the men at the café.

"They can't see us, so we're just going to walk. Taking our drunk friend with us.   No running, no calling for attention."

"OK," he replied, uncertainty evident in his voice.

Burke wanted to move before Steptoe, or he, for that matter, had second thoughts.   He started to move, still holding onto the lieutenant's legs, so Steptoe was force to follow.

As he trudged down the beach, he was waiting for the shouts, for the shots.   He was ready to dash.   He wanted to dash right then.   Every instinct cried out for it.   Hearing Cpl Steptoe muttering under his breath what sounded like a prayer didn't help him.

He let out a huge breath as his feet hit the water.   He knew they weren't safe yet.   They had to get out into the deep, out where no one could see them even if it was daylight.   The sea was calm, and while that would make it easier to swim, it would also make it easier to spot them.

Once they got to about four feet of water, he had Cpl Steptoe dump his radio.   A little further out, he had the Marine remove his trousers and tie off the ends.   With the legs closed off, a person could blow into them, inflating them with air until they worked as camouflaged water wings. They didn't hold air well and had to be re-inflated every few minutes, but what he had told Steptoe about that sailor had been true.   It did work.

As the salt water hit the lieutenant's neck, he moaned in pain, but that was the only sign of life he made. Burke struggled to keep the lieutenant's face above water as he towed him and Cpl Steptoe out further from shore. Several times, the lieutenant's face became completely submerged.

Telling Steptoe to hold the lieutenant, he slipped off his own trousers and made a float, but this time to make a pillow to keep the lieutenant's face out of the water.

Leaning back, he pulled the two other Marines out. Water splashed over his own face, and he swallowed more than a fair share of the Indian Ocean, but he kept kicking. Just as he would get into a rhythm, he would have to stop and re-inflate the lieutenant's float, or he would have to stop as Steptoe struggled to get air back into his.

He just concentrated on kicking, kicking. He was doing a modified sort of elementary back stroke, using only one arm as the other held the lieutenant's collar and one leg, but he had to lower his legs some as they would kick the other Marine if he let them rise back up to a more normal, more efficient position.

He had to stop every half an hour or so to rest and drink water. He tried to get some down Lt Niimoto's throat, but he wasn't sure that any got down. To be honest, he thought the lieutenant was probably dead. He couldn't discern any sign of life as they bobbed in the ocean. But he wasn't about to let him drift away.

Steptoe was having a hard time. As he swallowed sea water, he tended to choke and panic. And panicking was a sure way to drown. Burke kept trying to calm him down.

The effort was getting to Burke as well. He just kept on concentrating on kicking, kept concentrating on moving the three of them further and further away from the shore. He didn't know to where he was going. Despite what he had told Steptoe back on the beach, he knew any UAV's or other surveillance means was not going to be searching the ocean. If they were being used, they would be watching the city itself. Their best hope would be to be spotted by some fisherman, hopefully fishermen who were not pirates themselves. But in the big IO, the chances of that were small. The sailor had managed it, to be sure. But Burke knew he couldn't do the same with the two other Marines. He just didn't have it in him to stay afloat for five days.

Something bumped against his legs, and he kicked out. It was probably just the lieutenant's legs, but thoughts of sharks started to fill his mind. All three of them were bleeding, and didn't blood trails call all sharks from hundreds of miles around? He kept tilting his head, trying to see an approaching fin in the darkness.

When the light hit them, he was taken by surprise. He hadn't seen an approaching boat. And he was completely deflated. All of this, and for nothing. He tried to unlimber Cpl Steptoe's M4, but it slipped between his nerveless and waterlogged fingers to sink into the deep.

The boat came up alongside of them, the searchlight blinding them.

"Well, umm, you boys want a ride back, or are you Marines bound and determined to make it on your own."

BM2 Doug Kaye, the Special Boat Team commander, reached down to offer them an arm up and into the RHIB.

Chapter 43

Hobyo
Three weeks later

Maslax leaned over to tie his shoe.   He was just one more citizen out on his daily business, coming home after a hard day's work, after all.   But his attention was focused on a certain nondescript house.

He really didn't have to be there.   His Chinese contact would pay him if things went well, and in this case, the payment would keep him solvent for a long, long time.   But his inquisitiveness forced him to be there.   It was like an addiction.

There!   That donkey cart.   It looked normal, but the four men with it did not.   Oh, they could be Somali.   They could be American, for all he knew.   But they had a sense of purpose that the other people still out and about lacked. These were competent men, dangerous men, men you did not want to cross.

As they approached the house, the cart stopped, and two of the men got out to look at one of the wheels.

Nicely done, Maslax thought.

The men seemed to converse for a few moments, then two men went up to knock on the door.   Not everyone in Hobyo knocked on doors, and the critic in Maslax's mind gave them an X in that box, but still, some did, so it seemed to work.   The door opened, and the target looked out.   One man pointed to the cart, and as Taban looked, all four men rushed him, pushing the surprised man inside before closing the door.   A few moments later, two men came out, then took two barrels off the back of the cart and made as if delivering them to the house.

Only two barrels, he noted.   *Well, that means there are still a few others out there.   More opportunity for me.*

No one seemed to notice when the four men came out, rolling what were now obviously full barrels instead of empty ones.   They heaved the barrels up into the cart, then went along their way.

THE PROUD

Maslax was still rather upset at the carnage that the Americans had caused. Some 87 people had been killed, the best he was able to figure. The Americans had answered with too heavy a hand. But business was business. He had no sympathy for Taban and the others, the ones who brought this on top of them.

He had no idea what would happen to the pirate, nor did he really care. He would watch the internet, but he doubted he would find anything out. Maybe he would ask the Chinese man. Maybe not. But he would certainly keep his eyes and ears open. There was more money to be made.

Chapter 44

Aboard the USS Jason Dunham
November 10

"Happy birthday, Marine!" was called out several times as SSgt Davidson made his way to the mess decks.

He thanked the sailors and waved. The ship was pretty tight now. Even if it was the Marines who had gone ashore, it had been a team effort. And personally, Burke figured he owed his life to a certain Navy boat team.

There was also the fact that someone leaked the word that he was being recommended for a Congressional Medal of Honor. The fact that this very ship was named for a Marine Medal of Honor recipient was not lost on the crew.

Burke didn't know what he felt about that. He knew he may not even get the medal. Not every, even perhaps not most, medals were approved. And he wasn't sure how it would affect his life. He had begun to understand how Lt Niimoto must have felt.

He knew how Capt Svenson would have felt though. It would only be the natural progression of what he deserved. The guy certainly had had an ego, but if he talked the talk, he absolutely walked the walk. He had been put in for a Navy Cross, posthumously.

The man might have been ambitious, he might have been egocentric, but Burke had to give him mad props.

He entered the mess decks. The platoon was already there, as was a good portion of the ship's crew. The Navy cooks had done a great job. The cake was a perfect eagle, globe and anchor. Burke didn't think that even the chefs on those cooking shows on the Food Channel could match the cooks' skill.

"Happy birthday, Marine," Doug Kaye wished him.

BM1 Kaye, he reminded himself. Doug had been promoted ten days before.

"Thanks Doug."

"What, no snappy comeback?" he asked.

"No, I think today, well, no, no snappy comeback."

THE PROUD

The mess decks were called to attention as the captain, her officers, and Lt Kremer came in.   The company commander had just flown in for the birthday ceremony, and Burke knew he had to leave for the *Independence* right after this for Third Platoon's birthday celebration.

The ship's captain put everyone at ease and made the usual remarks about the Navy Marine Corps Team, and the history of the Corps.

Lt Kremer nodded at Burke.   Before the reading of the Commandant's letter, he had asked to read two others, and the company commander agreed.

Burke pulled one out of his pocket, and without preamble, began to read:

To the Marines of First Platoon, Kilo Company, 3d Battalion, Sixth Marines.

> *First, I want to wish you a Happy 256th Birthday.   I now have first-hand experience on why the Marines are what they are, and that is the finest fighting force in the world.   Without you, I would not be here to celebrate this birthday with you.   But because of you, I am home safe with my wife June, and today, we will open a bottle of champagne and toast to your continued success.*
>
> *My health is much improved.   Recovery will be long, but I'm a fighter, you can count on that. Bong Benedicto e-mails me every day, and he gives his wishes, too.   And Asad, our erstwhile captor, he's living with a Somali family in Minneapolis, taking English as a Second Language courses.   We still keep in touch.*
>
> *To all of you, I want to give you my deepest thanks, especially to those who gave the ultimate sacrifice.   I don't deserve that honor.*

With deepest respect,
Craig Murphy
Lieutenant Commander, US Navy Reserve, (Ret)

He folded the letter and put it back in his pocket. He thought back to when he found out that the pilot of the stricken Black Hawk had somehow managed to keep it in the air and back to the *Gaffert*. Even then, Craig's survival had been no sure thing. His heart had stopped three times before the infection had been gotten under control.

Losing Craig would have been a blow. Sure, the political statement would have been made. But for the Marines, it would have seemed as if their losses had been for naught.

He took out the second letter, an e-mail he had printed out that morning.

"OK, this is from the lieutenant, so listen up." There was a stir as attention was focused on him.

> *To First Platoon,*
>
> *I wish I could be with you for our birthday. Some of you celebrated it last year, but this would have been my first time with the platoon.*
>
> *I am doing better. Bethesda is much better than Landstuhl. I had gotten used to living with the squids on the Dunham, so this is more like home. (Joke)*
>
> *They say I need some more surgeries, but I think I might pass. I think the scars might make me look tougher. Regardless, I think I'll be discharged soon, so no matter what, I'll be there at Little Creek when you pull in next month. You can't get rid of me that easily.*
>
> *Mike Lambie's here at Bethesda, too. They're going to fit him with one of those bionic arms, and he's pretty psyched.*
>
> *But really, on a serious note. I can't begin to write just how proud I am of you, each and every one of you. I know I wouldn't be here without SSgt Davidson and Cpl Steptoe, but I would never have even gotten that far if it wasn't for all of you.*
>
> *I've spoken with Terry Miller's family, and they send their best, too. He was a good Marine,*

and he'll be missed.

    Well, I don't want to keep you from your cake, so Happy Birthday!

2dLt Tony Niimoto

There was a round of applause. Burke had been happy to hear that the lieutenant would be coming back. How he had even survived was a miracle. The doctors had said that he had lost too much blood to live, but the guy had fought back and made it.

When Lt Kremer had briefed him after the op, he had told him that he was the new platoon commander. But Burke had declined the title. As long as the lieutenant was fighting, he was the commander. Burke liked his current job just fine.

He nodded to the company commander, then took his place by the cake.

Lt Kremer stepped forward, then called out, "Attention to orders!"

After everyone came to attention, he began:

From the Commandant.

Two hundred and fifty-six years ago, our Marine Corps was formed. Since then, we have fought "in every clime and place," doing our duty to God and country. From the Revolutionary War to the Barbary Pirates, from The Halls of Montezuma, to Haiti, from the trenches of WWI and islands to WWII, to the Frozen Chosin, from Vietnam to Iraq and Afghanistan, we have always answered the call. Even when we were tasked with reducing our size, we saluted smartly and march off. But you can't keep the Corps down. As events in New Delhi proved, our nation cannot exist without a robust, capable Marine Corps.

And now we are back at the tip of the spear, as recent our actions in Somalia have proven. Make no doubt about it.   The Marines are back.

So to all Marines and Sailors, those deployed overseas, to those training and preparing for their next deployment, and to the warriors who no longer wear our uniform, I honor your selfless service to our country.   And to our loved ones, those who endure the many hardships that come with service in the Corps, I want to extend my most sincere thanks for all you have done

Happy 256th Birthday, Marines!

Semper Fidelis,

Jeffrey Lineau

General, United States Marine Corps

Lt Kremer turned to the ship's CO.

"Commander Stetson, I want to personally thank you for allowing us to celebrate this ceremony and for the lovely cake your cooks baked.   This is important to our very being, and I appreciate your support."

The captain nodded.

"Will the oldest and youngest Marines please step forward."

"As is our custom, the first piece of cake will be presented to our guest of honor, Commander Cynthia Stetson."

Sgt Dailey, using Burke's sword, had cut one piece, which was put on a plate that Sgt Alvarez took to the CO. She graciously accepted it.   Burke was glad he had thought to bring his sword, given that he would have thought that they would have used Lt Niimoto's for the birthday ceremony.

"By tradition, the second piece of cake is presented to the oldest Marine present."

"Ladies and Gentlemen, the oldest Marine present is Staff Sergeant Burke Davidson.   As of our birthday, Staff Sergeant Davidson is 31 years and 141 days old."

THE PROUD

Burke took the piece offered by Sgt Alvarez and took a bite.   He was surprised at how good it tasted.

"The third piece of cake is presented to the youngest Marine present."

"Ladies and Gentlemen, the youngest Marine present is Private First Class Jerry Masterson.   As of our birthday, Private First Class Masterson is 19 years and 12 days old."

PFC Masterson gravely took his piece of cake.   Burke glanced over to see a tear form and roll down the young Marine's cheek.   Pvt Miller had been one week younger than Masterson.

It was another miracle that only one Marine in the platoon had been lost.   Second Platoon had lost two Marines, and then there had been the company commander and that Army pilot.   But even thought they had been in the thick of it, only Miller had been killed. Still, that was an important loss to his family and loved ones.

"Ladies and gentlemen, this concludes our ceremony. Please join us for a piece of cake and a glass of bug juice to help us celebrate.   Thank you for your support."

People milled about, congratulating each other, grabbing pieces of cake.   When Burke saw there would be enough, he grabbed another piece.   The Marine Corps birthday was about the Corps, not really the cake.   It had been celebrated in the past with the old C-Rat pound cake. But damn, the mess specialists had outdone themselves on this one.

It was hard to believe that he was the oldest Marine on the ship.   He was only 31, for goodness sake.

This had been an eventful deployment, and he was still trying to sort things out.   He wondered if the Rangers would have done a better job in Hobyo.   Before the deployment, he would have put money on it.   After-the-fact, well, he wasn't sure.

He walked out of the mess decks and to the rail, watching the water rush past.   Sometimes, he had felt that he had made a mistake in coming back to the Corps.   There was no getting around the fact that he was proud of his accomplishments while a Ranger.   But the birthday ceremony also highlighted something that made a Marine a

Marine.   Back in the US, there would be balls as well, and for some families, this was the highlight of the year.   The simple pride in being part of history, being part of an organization that transcended self was perhaps more celebrated in the Corps than in anywhere else.

Burke was still perhaps more proud as an individual of getting scrolled as a Ranger, but the overall unit pride, well, the Marines excelled at that.

"Happy Birthday, Staff Sergeant."

Burke turned around to see PFC McNamara joining him at the rail.

"Happy birthday to you to, Jesus."

They stood there for a few moments, just watching the water.

"Jesus, I've wanted to ask you this for awhile, but back there in Hobyo, why did you follow me when I went back into the city?   No one told you to go, so why do that?   You were in the clear.   You were about to be evacuated.   Why follow me back into the fight?"

"Why did you go?" he asked back.

"Well, it was my responsibility.   I'm the platoon sergeant."

"And it was my responsibility, too.   You're my platoon sergeant, and I'd follow you anywhere.   If you need to get in the thick of it, I've got your back.   I don't have to ask or wonder why.   I know you're going to do the right thing, so if I stick with you, I'm going to do the right thing."

Burke harrumphed.

"Now you're just kissing my ass," he said, but he was moved.

"I'd rather kick your ass, all due respect, on the flight deck.   What say we have a birthday run before evening chow?"

"You?   You think you can take me on?"

"Sure do, Staff Sergeant.   I wanna see if the oldest Marine can stick with one of the youngest."

"You're on, there P-F-C," he said, emphasis on each letter.   "See you back on the flight deck in five."

He rushed below to his berthing space.   Maybe a run was what he needed.   He whipped off his uniform and threw on his shorts.   He sniffed his socks, and while a little ripe, he figured they'd do.   On they went, followed by his shoes.

He grabbed his black Ranger shirt, and just before he pulled it over his head, he hesitated.   He put it back down on his rack, smoothing out the arched gold letters with the gold frame.   He was proud of being a Ranger, and he wouldn't change that for anything.   But now, he was a Marine again.

Burke folded the shirt up and placed it back in his locker.   Rooting around, he found the new shirt, the one the lieutenant had gotten made up in Germany and had sent down to the platoon.

The green shirt was nothing amazing to look at, the art a little amateurish.   But over a caricature of a bulldog were the words "First Platoon, Kilo 3/6."   Below the dog were the words, "Pirate Posse."

Burke thought the lieutenant could have come up with something better, but like the C-Rat birthday cake, it wasn't the item, it was the meaning.   And this shirt had meaning.

Sliding the shirt on over his head, he pulled it down. He wished he had a mirror, but it was what it was. He ran over to the ladder leading above decks.   He had a certain   PFC's   ass   to   kick.

THE PROUD

THE MARINES

Chapter 1

Pagasa Island, The Spratly Islands
Two days earlier

"OK, *padir*.   I got to go.   Give *madir* my love."
　　Analiza's father kissed his hand, then held it up to the cam on his side as she clicked off the connection.   While she was glad that SMART provided a free connection for residents of Pagasa, it was not the same thing as being home. She missed her family.   She looked forward to December when she could go home for three whole weeks, three weeks of family and friends, of seeing strangers, for goodness sakes. With only 300 residents in Kalayaan town, everyone knew everyone else.   Everybody and everything was the same. Sometimes Analiza prayed that something, anything, would happen to break the monotony.
　　Staring at the now dark computer monitor, she wondered yet once again if the separation from family and friends was worth it.   It wasn't the job itself, which she actually enjoyed.   The pay was certainly good, more than she could ever earn anywhere else in the Philippines as a teacher.   Most of all, even as a civilian, Analiza was proud to be serving her country.   But like all residents, she knew she was on the island merely to stake the country's claim to it, and more importantly, to the huge gas reserves and rich fishing grounds surrounding this region of the Spratlys.
　　She got up, nodded to Bong, the young café clerk, then stepped out into the night.   As usual, the pollution-free air was clear, and the stars were bright.   Yes, a few things were better here than in Manila, or even her hometown of Cebu. She could never see so many stars at night back in Manila. And traffic?   A traffic jam here was when two people bumped into each other while walking into the grocery store.

1

Even though it was quite late, Analiza wasn't concerned about walking to her small apartment.   That was another thing that was better here.   It was safe.   This wasn't just because of the garrison of 40 soldiers on the island.   Since every civilian was screened and the population was limited, crime was almost unheard of.

A breeze kicked up, blowing her long brown hair across her face.   Pushing it back, she glanced across the runway at the small dock on the east side.   It was rare when they had a boat there, especially a foreign boat.   Almost everything on the island arrived by air, and except for a few small privately owned bangkas, the small boats belonging to residents and used to go to the reef to fish, larger boats rarely pulled into port on the island.

Gossip was one of the island residents' Olympic sports, so there was no such thing as a secret.   The boat at the dock was a fishing boat from Taiwan that had developed serious engine problems and needed to make an emergency docking in order to effect repairs.   Why the boat was in Filipino waters was not explained, but the Republic of China and the Philippines, along with Vietnam and Malaysia, had an uneasy alliance with regards to the Spratlys.   With The People's Republic of China claiming the entire group, it made sense for the smaller players to support one another.   So even though the mayor had been suspicious regarding in which waters the boat had been fishing, it was granted docking rights.

The runway itself was dark, but a lone light illuminated the guard watching over the boat.   It was too far away to see who it was, though.   Analiza wondered if it might be Alan; whoever it was, he had the right build to be him.

Analiza had just turned twenty-four, still young, by Filipina standards, but in a country in which the family held such primacy, she was anxious to start her own family.   Her mother, after all, had married at sixteen.   But with a father who worked as a merchant marine, her family had the cash to send both her and her brother to school, and so boys and dating were out of the question while she was still studying.   Now, however, she was out of school with a well-paying job.   And Alan, well, he might not be the one, but Analiza thought it might be fun finding out if he was.   The pickings might be slim on the island, but with 40 soldiers, most young and fit, these just might be the best odds she would ever face.

She laughed at the thought, and that emboldened her. Why not just saunter over there, a girl just taking a walk, right?   "Good" girls, she knew might not be so open, but what could it hurt?

She made her way across the runway to the water's edge, then turned left and continued on as if taking a stroll. She kept looking ahead to see who had guard duty.   With fifteen soldiers off the island tonight on their weekly check/resupply/changing-of-the-guard of Likas, she knew the chances were at least decent that the guard was Alan. Only the junior soldiers would be assigned to the duty, and Alan wouldn't be going to Likas until the following week.

When she got to about a hundred yards out, the soldier turned his head, and a little thrill ran through her.   It was Alan.   He stood the bright light and couldn't see her yet, so she brushed her hair back with her hands and looked down at her clothes.   She hadn't dressed to kill when she left for the internet café: brown shorts, a loose, ratty t-shirt that didn't quite meet the top of her shorts, and flip-flops.   The gap between the shorts and shirt was her style.   She was quite slender and tended to dress to keep attention on her waist rather than her less-than-generous breasts.   But she wished she were wearing something nicer.

"Hi Alan, is that you?" she asked innocently as she came up.

Alan jumped, then wheeled around, only relaxing as Analiza walked into the circle of light.

"What are you doing here?" he asked, a smile creasing his face.

"Oh, I couldn't sleep, so I decided to take a walk.   I didn't realize you had guard duty," she said, trying to keep her voice innocent.

"Someone has to...."

Analiza stared, not quite understanding as shadows seemed to jump out at Alan, cutting the words off in his throat.   The shadows materialized into three men, one in back of Alan with his arm around the Filipino soldier's neck

3

and the other two rushing in front of him.

The three men moved with dangerous, violent grace, but Alan wasn't a pushover. The soldiers stationed in the Spratlys were among the country's best, and one reason Alan had caught Analiza's eye was that he was so, well, so much a man. Alan reached back to gouge his attacker's eyes and somehow grabbed enough of the man's ears to bring his attacker up and over his back as he jerked himself forward. The assailant landed hard on his back on the ground, and Alan lunged forward, striking at the man's exposed neck.

The blow never got there. There was a soft chuff, almost insignificant, as one man pointed a handgun at Alan and fired. Alan fell on top of the prone man, limp and lifeless.

Analiza was having a difficult time understanding what was going on. Why were Taiwanese fishermen attacking Alan? Then their uniforms registered. They were soldiers, too. Pagasa was being attacked!

While The Republic of China technically claimed all of the Spratlys, the two countries had an understanding, what with the People's Republic of China being their strategic adversary over the island group. So why attack?

The two upright soldiers pushed Alan's body off the third man, pulling him upright, voices jabbering in what she recognized as Chinese. With the way his body flopped, she knew for certain that Alan was dead. She gasped and stepped back.

Three sets of eyes swiveled to her. It was as if they had forgotten she was standing there. It was only then that something else registered. Instead of Taiwan's red flag with the blue and yellow star thingy in the middle, over the boat now flew the red flag with the yellow star of the People's Republic. This wasn't a Taiwan attack. This was China invading them!

The garrison had to be warned. She wheeled around and started to run. For a moment she thought they might let her go, just a helpless girl in the darkness. In seconds, however, she heard the heavy footfalls of someone chasing her.

Her left flip-flop tore and fell off, the hard coral runway

digging into her foot with each step, but she couldn't stop. She had to warn them. She could see the lights ahead, but they were a long way off, and the footsteps were right behind her. She opened her mouth to scream, knowing no one could hear her yet, when the heavy body crashed into her from behind, driving her face onto the runway and sending her into blackness.

Chapter 2

Pattaya, Thailand

1st Lt Peter Van Slyke walked into the Fantasy Sports Bar on Walking Street, peering around to find his group.   It was quite late, but the street was well-lit with garish neon signs, so with the low light levels inside, it took a few moments for his eyes to adjust.

"Welcome, sir!" a petite waitress almost sang in a high, lilting voice as she came over to greet him.

This was a sports bar, complete with three pool tables and a number of televisions currently showing various sports, ranging from what looked, at first glance, to be soccer, billiards, and badminton.   He shifted his attention to the waitress.   She was cute, no doubt about that.   She might have come head-high to his chest, and she might weigh 90 pounds soaking wet, but in her cheerleader-looking outfit, well, Pete hoped she was a good omen on what might happen later on in the night.   He had heard enough about the surplus of women in Pattaya on the ship before pulling in, and though he was normally somewhat shy around the fairer sex, he figured that here, his wallet might trump his appearance, and he was looking forward to that.   But first, he had to attend to a tradition.

He was just about to tell her he was meeting a group when a voice called out, "Glad you decided to join us, there, lieutenant of Marines.   Why don't you get your scarred ass over here and buy us a round."

He looked to the right to see Capt Niimoto, along with the rest of his old security guard detachment, sitting at a table, bottles of Chang already in evidence.   Pete was normally quite conscious of the huge scar that distorted the entire left side of his face, but the captain had an equally impressive one on his neck and face, courtesy of his Somalia adventure.   So from him, he didn't mind the barb.

"Sorry sir," he said as he pulled out a chair.   "The

colonel wanted me to finish my gear inspection before libo, and I only now got it done."

"You know what they say there, lieutenant. 'Excuses are like assholes. Everybody has one, and they all stink.' I thought I trained you better than that," SgtMaj Jacob McCardle told him, Chang in hand.

"Well, now that Ricky Recon has chosen to grace us with his presence, as soon as he gets his drink, we can get to the matter at hand," the captain said, motioning over for a waitress.

Pete looked at the gathered Marines, all of them from his old security guard detachment in New Delhi. There was Captain Anthony Niimoto, then a sergeant, but now the senior Marine in this elite group. Next to him was SgtMaj McCardle, who had been a gunny and the detachment commander at the time. Gunny Mac had been a good guy, but not the most aggressive Marine around. SgtMaj Mac had seemingly grown into his rank, and he seemed more assured than Pete remembered him.

Stepchild was there, too. Sgt Harrington Steptoe, the tall, soft-looking Marine who was now the captain's company comm chief. Next to him sat GySgt Ian Harwood. Ian had gotten out with the embassy staff and guests and hadn't taken part in the fight, but he had still been part of the detachment. Only Mahmoud Saad was missing, doing whatever he was doing back as Ft. Meade. A lance corporal at the time, he was already a staff sergeant and doing some sort of secret squirrel stuff at NSA.

These were the men with whom Pete had formed an unbreakable bond. They were all well-known throughout the Corps, of course, being largely responsible for not only keeping the president alive but in bringing back the Corps as a viable combat unit. But their bond was on a more personal level, that of men who had fought together and lost friends. Each year, on the anniversary of the takeover of the embassy, those who could got together to toast their fallen comrades. A few times it had been over the internet, and several times, the commandant had joined them, given honorary status as the man who had led the rescue mission. But this, their eighth ceremony, was the first time that they were meeting overseas.

And this was the first time that they would be saluting Joseph Child. SSgt Child had passed away a few months earlier at his Detroit VA hospice.

Pete's Chang arrived, and now that they were all charged, SgtMaj Mac took over.

"To Joseph Child!" he declared, raising up his bottle of Chang.

"To Joseph Child!" the rest of the New Delhi vets chorused, raising their own bottles of beer.

Pete looked over at Stepchild. He had been devoted to Child, hence his "Stepchild" nickname. The big Marine tilted up his bottle, but a tear could be seen rolling down his cheek.

One by one, SgtMaj Mac went down the list. Seth Croker. Tracy " Little Mac" McAllister. Jesus Rodriguez. Samantha Ashely. Ivy "Princess" Ramon. Mike Fallgatter. Greg Chen. Shareetha Wynn. Each one got an individual toast.

Then they went to the others. MAJ Defilice, the assistant Army attaché. Drayton Bajinski, the USAID officer. Capt Leon-Guerro, their company XO who had been there at the time. And Mr. Dravid, the old Indian man who was treated as little more than a servant, but whose sacrifice might have kept the president alive long enough for the rescue.

Pete couldn't help but feel a lump in his throat. And, as usual, he felt a bit of guilt that he had survived when so many others hadn't. If he hadn't been shot in the face at the very beginning of the siege, he probably wouldn't have survived. But as he was badly injured, the others had to take the more dangerous missions, and most of them didn't make it.

With the roll call finished, each of them sat back, quiet. No one had to speak. Their presence alone gave each other support.

For the thousandth time, Peter Van Slyke wondered about his position in life, in the Corps. He was the sixth generation of Van Slykes to serve as a Marine. His grand-father had earned a Medal of Honor in Vietnam. His father had been killed in Iraq.   There had been little doubt that Pete would become a Marine, even when the Marines had been cut back to little more than a ceremonial guard.   And then, as a PFC, he was thrust into the embassy takeover.   As a result, he had been given a presidential appointment to the Naval Academy, despite his horribly disfigured face that had still required several surgeries and therapy while he was a midshipman.

His notoriety at the Academy helped him, and despite the fact that his grades, while good, were not at the top of the class, he was appointed as the second set brigade commander.   Taking his commission, he excelled at The Basic School, then at the Infantry Officers Course.   All of this forced him to put up a front, to act like he was confident when he was actually self-conscious about his face almost to the point of not being able to function.   He knew that eyes were on him, staring at him.   And that made him want to freeze up, to put a hood over his head *a la* the elephant man.

Being assigned to B 1/7 as a platoon commander, though, had given him at least a degree of confidence.   His Marines seemed to like him, even to be proud of the fact that their commander had seen combat.   And he loved Thursdays, when, if they were not in the field, their PT was sports.   It was like he had his own private football team.

He had made an uneventful pump, doing exercises with the Japanese, Koreans, and Filipinos, but he had never pulled into one of the "good" liberty ports like Pattaya. After getting back to Pendleton, he went to one of the semi-annual tryouts for recon, and not surprisingly, he was selected, not having too much difficulty with the RIP and BRC or dive school after that.   This was now his first deployment as a recon platoon commander, assigned to the 15th MEU.

The other four Marines were all with the BLT, with Mac as the battalion sergeant major, Capt Niimoto and Stepchild with Kilo Company, and Ian Harwood as the supply chief. Pete's presence with the MEU was a coincidence, but he knew that SgtMaj Mac or Capt Niimoto had pulled strings to get the rest of them assigned together.   The captain even had his old platoon sergeant, Burke Davidson, the guy who was awarded the Medal of Honor in Somalia for saving his ass, assigned back to him as his company first sergeant.

Slowly, they started talking again, enjoying the camaraderie. New Delhi was not mentioned, but life in general was. Capt Niimoto brought out his tablet to show photos of Amalyn, his new daughter. She was his fourth kid. When Pete was with him in New Delhi, the then Sgt Niimoto was a goof ball, a laughing surfer dude from San Diego. It was odd seeing him now as such a proud family man.

The captain had been good for Pete, though. Shortly after getting underway, the two had a long discussion, catching up on old times. When Pete had asked him about surgeries, the captain had told him he had none after he was stabilized. He didn't want surgery for purely cosmetic reasons. He called his own disfigurements his "Heidelberg scars." Pete even thought that the captain might be more proud of this scars than his Navy Cross or Silver Star, if that made sense. At that moment, Pete vowed that he'd have no more surgery on his own face. It was what it was.

Gunny Harwood was getting a few sheets to the wind. If he got too far gone, Pete knew SgtMaj Mac would get him back to the ship. The MEU commanding officer's prime directive for the three days of liberty was that there were to be no, repeat no liberty incidents. As no one wanted any liberty curtailed, it was "watch out for each other time."

The waitress brought Pete another bottle of Chang. It was only his second, but as he watched her walk away with a nice wiggle in her butt, he reminded himself of what he wanted to do later, and he didn't want to be drunk while doing it.

He was wondering how he would make his escape and go to one of the more adult-oriented bars when 1stSgt Davidson walked up. Pete had not talked to him yet, but he recognized the only active duty Marine with the Medal of Honor.

"Skipper," he said, leaning in to Capt Niimoto. "You need to get back. The SP's are going to be rounding up everyone for a recall, but you need to get back and meet with the CO ASAP."

10

Capt Niimoto looked up with a confused look on his face.   "Why, what's up?"
The 1stSgt looked around the bar, then leaned closer and said so only those at the table could hear, "It looks like the Chinese may have invaded the Spratlys."

Chapter 3

Beijing, China

General Li Zhiyuan, Deputy Chief of Staff of the People's Liberation Army, left the tall General Staff Headquarters, his driver wending his way through the bustling traffic. The architect had designed the headquarters to look like it was seemingly balanced on a point, like a reverse pyramid. To General Li, it had always seemed to him that it symbolized the PLA, precariously balancing itself and the needs of the nation against the political types from the Central Military Commission, the party and state officials who controlled China's vast and powerful armed forces. General Li was a party member, of course. He could not have attained his present rank had he not been. But he always thought the military and the defense of the country should be left to those in the military, not the politicians, especially the politicians who openly embraced western culture and economic growth.

And now, he was the one doing the balancing. He knew the way forward for China, and with a few like-minded individuals and the support of loyal subordinates, and with the push from the still unknown person or persons higher in the power structure of the country, he had taken action, action that would vault China into its proper position as the world's premier superpower.

He had been pleased though, that in the early morning briefing for General Chen Jun, the PLA chief of staff, no word had yet leaked out of the operation. He knew it would get out soon, but he wanted the operation presented as a *fait accompli*, not something still in process.

His fingers drummed on his knee as they slowly made their way through the morning commuter traffic to the nondescript white building that was the actual nerve center for the operation. He hated wasting time even when things were routine; with the operation in full swing, it was even worse. If there had been any way to control the operation from the headquarters, he would have done it. But there was no way that could be kept secret, and he could not afford the CMC getting wind of it and closing the operation down before it could succeed.

The driver finally pulled in front of their destination. No one rushed forward to open his door—General Li did not need nor allow for such symbols of subservience. He stepped out of the car and walked into the building. The lone soldier at the simple desk came to attention and saluted before taking a key and opening the door behind him, a door that looked like tens of thousands of other doors into the city, leading into shops, homes, and offices.

General Li had thought to get some counter-terrorism experts to maintain security, but the Intermediate Action Unit personnel were all technically part of the police force, not the Army, and thinking that hiding in plain sight was a better option, he had elected to go with a single PLA soldier manning the entrance.

While the hallway of the building looked like every other building, the room into which he strode would have made the National Space Administration proud. It was bright, almost blindingly white, and spotless. Various computer hubs buzzed with activity with about 30 people engrossed with their stations. It was hard to believe that this was the heart of the action that was thrusting China forward into the future.

The target of his attention was looking over the shoulder of another technician, focused on whatever information was being gathered on that man's computer. Sung Wenyan was in his mid-30's and looked like a shopkeeper. At about 180 cm, he probably weighed 80 kg and had a continual smile cemented to his face. That smile might fool others into thinking he was a nice, congenial fellow, but Li knew that it hid a pretty cold and calculating mind. "Wenyan" might mean refined and virtuous, but the man himself was anything but that.

He was brilliant, though, to give credit where credit was due. His problem was in not using his brilliance for the good of the people but rather for his own gain. A master programmer, Wenyan had bedeviled companies and government agencies for several years by hacking into their systems.   Initially, he never caused much damage nor received material gain from his escapades, but he left calling cards to announce his success.   As time went on and he became bolder, however, he did manage to siphon several million yuan into an off-shore bank account from the Department of Interior's accounting department.   His downfall came when he hacked into the PLA's most secure system, playing a pornographic video of him and a woman on a loop that took the PLA's best computer minds almost three hours to stop.   Both he and the woman had worn hoods, but like many criminals, Wenyan couldn't keep a secret, and when he bragged to a friend, that friend had turned him in.

Sung Wenyan had been quickly tried and sentenced to a bullet in the back of the head—only, he hadn't been killed. He had been stashed in Qincheng Prison, where mostly political prisoners were kept.

An anonymous phone call had led General Li to Sung. It was the nature of Chinese politics that such calls were best not ignored, so he had taken a trip to the prison to meet the hacker.   It was immediately clear to him that Sung was an asset that was too valuable to waste.   He made an offer that Sung could not refuse, and by pulling his own strings, got him transferred into Army custody.

Sung was still a prisoner, albeit a prisoner with authority, one whom General Li kept plied with good-looking and accommodating women (all loyal PLA soldiers, of course) and Jack Daniels, Sung's beverage of choice.   Li didn't trust Sung, pure and simple.   He didn't mind the womanizing and drinking.   While General Li chose not to poison his own body with alcohol, in his opinion, one of a man's duties in life was to give pleasure to women, to take a woman, any woman, and reduce her to a grateful, if quivering, exhausted state.   General Li's secret hubris was his ability to do this, something that he had undertaken to achieve with as much single-mindedness as he undertook most tasks.   So he understood this need, even if the reports he was given by the soldiers assigned to this task were that Wenyan was perhaps more interested in his own gratification than that of the women's.

That Wenyan had this weakness was perhaps not surprising.   As one of the 40 million or so "bare branches," men who had little hope of finding a wife due to the long years of illegal abortions of female fetuses, he was just one man who contributed to the growing social ills of the country.   He may not have the courage to have joined one of the *New Nien* gangs, those groups of desperate young men who controlled prostitution, smuggling of sex slaves from neighboring countries, drugs, kidnapping, rape, and all sorts of other crimes.   But he took out his frustration in his own way, trying to obtain wealth and women, and with his weaknesses, the general could control him.

General Li had a disdain for the bare branches and what they were doing to the nation.   Just as the original *Nien* gangs had contributed to the fall of the Qing Dynasty, so the *New Nien* were tearing down China.   It was not lost on him, though, that what he was doing could be a relief valve, not only providing China with much needed resources, but starting the country down a path that could lead to new territory, territory that needed young Chinese men to administer.

Despite his disdain for the *New Nien* and other bare branches, he was more than willing to use any of them to further the nation's causes.   It wasn't that he trusted any of them.   What specifically rendered Wenyan as someone who could not be trusted was that he used his gifts for his own ends, either for money or fame.   He did not use them to better the Chinese people.   For that, General Li could not forgive him nor trust him.   Use him, however, that he could do.

And General Li Zhiyuan, Deputy Chief of Staff of the PLA, was perhaps in a better position to use Wenyan than most anyone else.   Because of his position, Li was one of the few people in the country to know one closely held state secret: China had back doors into most of the world's satellites, communications systems, and even military software.

Over the years China had been taking over more and more manufacturing from other countries, and this included in electronics.   Part of this was because of price and quality, part of it was because China had long ago taken over the production of rare earths from the USA, those critical elements needed for most high tech applications.

Chinese wizards had developed components that would pass the most rigorous inspections.   They would function as designed by the customers, but when subjected to a very tight and specific frequency, the housings of the components would act as simple on-off switches, allowing Chinese programming to enter and hijack various functions.

This was a huge leap from August 30, 2007 when the Chinese had caused a B-52 at Minot Air Force Base to be loaded with six nuclear cruise missiles and take off.   It took three hours for the Americans to realize what had happened and divert the plane to land at Barksdale AFB in Louisiana. This in itself was a significant step forward from earlier in the year when Chinese hackers caused Vice President Cheney's 757 to land at Singapore.

It took both hackers and American corporations sub-contracting out vital components to Chinese companies for them to be able to do this.   After these two incidents, some politicians in the US, Japan, the EU, and other countries objected to vital parts in communications, military equipment, and defense-related satellites being "Wal-Marted," as the term became known, but the bottom line ruled the roost, especially as any part could be supposedly tested.   And if Chinese-made components were not ordered, then they could be slipped in and substituted through bribery, or on one case, by a brilliant act of subterfuge, something right out of a Hollywood movie.

With this ability to open up windows into satellites and communications hubs, someone like Sung Wenyan could essentially take control over them.   And this was the final piece of the puzzle.   For years, General Li had chaffed at the handcuffs placed on his country when dealing with the rest of the world.   The bowed and scraped to the African savages in order to get their raw materials.   They paid exorbitant prices from Australia, the US, and Russia for more raw materials.   They had the power to take what they wanted, but the politicians would rather play diplomatic games.

But someone, someone probably as high as a member of the Central Committee, had given him the information about Sung Wenyan.   Someone had sent him a link to a study that had advocated China's taking control of the Wanli Shitang, what the rest of the world called The Spratlys.   That someone or *someones* had to be like-minded with him.   Someone wanted him to take action.

He had taken the hint.   For him, the new China would start with the Wanli Shitang.   Chinese had been in these islands for over 2,500 years, and it wasn't right that a collection of small, weak countries could keep China from the much needed gas and oil reserves, much less the rich fishing grounds that could help feed China's billion-and-a-half people.

Last night, it had started.   Thitu Island had fallen quickly, the special forces unit from The Sword of Southern China getting on the island on a Taiwan-flagged fishing boat.   There were no friendly casualties and only a handful of Filipino soldiers killed before the rest, as well as the civilians, were captured.

Things had not gone so well on Taiping, where the Taiwan Marines had not been taken by surprise.   Even though the electronic measures had functioned as planned, Marines with rifles, 120mm mortars, and 40mm autocannons did not need advanced electronics.   The larger Sword of Southern China special forces team assigned to take the island had been wiped out before they could even land.

Taiping was still cut off from all means of communications, but now, General Li had to give the order to divert the *Changbai Shan* and the *Jinggan Shan*, two of the PLA Navy's Type 071 Amphibious Transport Docks, along with their embarked 1,800 Marines, to the stubborn island.

The longer this took, the more likely it was that word would get out.   General Li needed the Wanli Shitang completely in Chinese hands before the world realized what had happened.   The Central Committee couldn't back down then.

"So, Mr. Sung, what's your report?" he simply asked the

hacker.

Sung Wenyan turned around, then nodded his head respectfully, something the general knew was an act.

"General Li, by all accounts, we are still cloaked in secrecy. The enemy satellites are all showing what we want them to show, and there has been no alarm from anywhere."

"Sir, what about the outgoing burst from Taiping?" asked the computer operator at whose station they stood.

"What was that?" demanded the general.

"Ah, nothing to be concerned about, sir," put in Sung hurriedly. "There might have been a short burst of static from Taiping before we gained control of the communications nexus. But there has been no response from the Taiwan renegades, so there is no reason to be concerned."

General Li looked into Sung Wenyan's eyes. There was something more going on there, he thought. But what was done was done.

"What about Thitu Island? What are the reports?"

"Sir, the glorious soldiers of the Sword of Southern China bask in their accomplishments in taking back our land from the Filipinos. However, the water and electricity have been sabotaged, and well, the exalted soldiers need engineers to fix those. Communications are well and truly down there, so we have to rely on the special forces team's internal communications."

With all the "gloriouses" and "exalteds," Sung was spouting perfect revolutionary rhetoric, but Li was not fooled. The man had a pretty high opinion of himself, and the remark about the soldiers not being able to fix the water production was a jab at what he thought of their mental capabilities.

He wished for the hundredth time that this command center was back at headquarters, or that he could even use his cell phone to get updates. He had to get back for another inane meeting on procurement when all he wanted to do was to sit there, leading the operation. He had good men out at sea and in the attack, but here, at the heartbeat, he had a criminal in charge. That didn't sit well with him. Perhaps he should have brought in someone else, like Col

Lian, maybe, to camp out in the control center until they could bring everything out into the open.

"Mr. Sung, I have to be back at headquarters. I will return in two hours. If anything happens that needs my attention, have someone go across the street and give me a missed call, and I will get back here immediately," he instructed the hacker.

Just a little bit longer, he thought to himself as he left the building. *Then I can stop this sneaking around and let the world know what we've done.*

Chapter 4

Aboard the USS Makin Island

1stLt Peter Van Slyke edged forward a bit to get a better view. It was packed pretty tight. All the senior Marines and the available Navy officers and chiefs were crowded into the briefing room while LCDR Grace Sullivan, the Task Force intelligence officer went on with her brief.

"So, as you can see from this timeline, at 2315 local time, an ROC Army comm tech received what started as an emergency message over his system. It cut off immediately as if a switch was turned off. He tried to re-establish the link, but nothing was going through. A few moments later, a call on another circuit gave a routine message that normal communications would be interrupted for a short period while some repairs were being made.

"Normally, that might make sense, but the tech was worried that there was some sort of emergency unknown to the garrison at large, so he tried to contact two ROC ships in the area, but all comm was down, not just to the Marine garrison.

"At 2322, this was reported up the chain of command, and a routine scan of satellite photos was ordered."

She flashed up on the screen a photo of the lights of an island surrounded by darkness.

"This was taken by an ROC satellite at 2320."

She then put up another photo so that both were side-by-side.

"The one on the right was taken at 2305. Note the cloud cover, cover that is not present on the one on the left. This raised some immediate flags, so the ROC armed forces command contacted the Pentagon to ask for their help in figuring out what was wrong. As it turned out, it wasn't only the ROC satellites that were affected. Each US and, as we found out later, UK and Japanese satellites were also affected in the same way. Running our data through analysis, we quickly determined that what we were seeing, real time, was an exact duplicate of what had happened one month before. Our satellites were being spoofed."

She paused for effect, noting the concerned looks around the room as the significance of that sunk in.

"There was also an anomaly concerning two PLA Navy ships in the region, the *Changbai Shan* and the *Jinggan Shan*, which are Type 071 Amphibious Transport Docks. "

She pulled up another satellite photo.

"We track all major combatants, as you know. Well, the computers back at DIA pulled up a small glitch, an anomaly on their track.

"We also contacted the Philippines Armed Forces to ask about their forces in the region, and they informed us that they were in the middle of a communications interruption. So that makes comm problems for both the ROC and the Philippines?" she said, her rising voice making it more of a question than a statement.

"Given all of this put together, the Pentagon issued orders for us to get underway, for the *Gerald R. Ford* Battle Group to steam south from the Sea of Japan, and for the 13th Air Force at Anderson AFB on Guam to go on alert. As the commander told you earlier, at the time, it was better to be prepared even if we didn't know what was going on.

"But now, this is new information. At 0730 local time, the *USS Mississippi*, one of our attack subs, was able to come in close to Thitu Island and take photos through its periscope. Initially, the island seemed deserted. However, the *Mississippi* eventually took this photo."

The photo came on the screen. It was clearly taken from long distance, but just as clearly, a soldier in uniform could be seen smoking a cigarette outside a building.

"This is a soldier in the PLA, in fact, a special forces soldier from what is known as 'The Sword of Southern China.' And this confirms that whatever is happening, the People's Republic of China is behind it.

"I should point out, though, that while the *Mississippi* took the photo at 0730, they could not get it to us until almost four hours later. Whatever is affecting communications over the Spratlys, it can even keep a nuke sub from communicating while it is in its range. It can get out simple text messages using its Extremely Low Frequency antenna, but as most of you know, a sub cannot send images nor receive via the ELF, and we needed NSA to confirm the photo before we could now act on it.'

There were more murmurs as this sunk in.   If the Chinese were in back of this, and if they could take over satellites and knock out communications, what else could they do?

"I will be updating everything we know on a continuous basis.   And now, I'm going to turn it over to Commander Belling, the Ops Officer."

Pete leaned back to take it all in.   Before the float he wondered if they might have a contingency somewhere.   He never imagined that he could be staring at the brink of WWIII.

Chapter 5

Over the South China Sea

Major Camino "Ting" Opena looked over to his wingman, Lieutenant Senior Grade Joseph Acacio, as they hurtled over the water towards Pagasa Island in their Saab Gripens. Both pilots were assigned to the 570th Tactical Composite Wing at Puerto Princesa, the unit responsible for not only Palawan, but also for defense of Philippines' assets in the Spratlys.

Ting really didn't know what to expect on this reconnaissance mission. He had been briefed, of course. With communications down over Pagasa and Likas, it made sense that a recon overflight be made, but if the Americans were right, there might be a Chinese threat right now on the islands. Ting's mission was to get eyeballs on the target to see if there was anything different from what the Filipino weather satellite was currently showing.

He checked the gauges on his old Gripen. The Gripen was a reliable plane, but this one had been purchased back in 2014, and it was feeling its age. For the thousandth time, he wished the Air Force had bought the American F-16 back then, but the bean counters back in Manila objected to the upkeep costs of the Fighting Falcon, and the Swedes promised a much cheaper supply chain for the Gripens. So the serviceable Gripen became the Air Force fighter, replacing the even more ancient F5. If there were Chinese on the island, though, Ting didn't look forward to any sort of confrontation with any of the top-of-the-line Chinese fighters.

The flight from Puerto Princesa to Pagasa was only 240 miles, a little over 30 minutes in his Gripen, so he knew he should be coming up on the island soon. The plan was for both aircraft to make a pass from south to north, then bear west before looping around and passing over the runway from west to east.

Although not in his orders, he and Joseph had decided to keep off the radio unless it was absolutely necessary. If there were Chinese there, it would do no good to let them know they were coming.

Ting looked out of his canopy and signaled to Joseph that they needed to begin their descent. Joseph gave him a thumbs up, and so Ting started bringing his Gripen down, knowing Joseph would stay on his wing.

It was low tide, so he could see Half Moon Shoal below him as he passed over. It wouldn't be long now.

He brought his Gripen down to 5,000 feet, low enough to get a good view of the island as he flew over. Bringing his plane to a heading of 3-3-2, he only had to keep in a straight line to fly right over it.

Suddenly, his entire cockpit control went dark. Panic swept through him. This had never happened to him before. He cursed the choice of the politicians who had decided the Gripen was "good enough," and he went through his restart procedures while his plane began an ungainly glide down towards the sea. Nothing seemed to work. He tried again, but his cockpit panel remained ominously dark. Looking out, he could see that he was perhaps 1,000 feet up, although it was harder to tell than if he had been over land.

He knew he had to punch out. He spared a glance up to find Joseph, knowing the mission was now up to him, but he couldn't spot his wingman. There was no time. He reached down and pulled on the ejection seat release. This was essentially an explosive charge, not connected to the plane's power. The explosion slammed Ting into the seat, or rather slammed the seat up into his butt. It felt like he had been hit with a club, and he was thrown into the air at something like 500 miles per hour, he figured, based on the plane slowing down a bit with the engines shut off.

He was stunned, and his right arm was numb, but when he felt the opening shock of his chute opening, he let out a breath he hadn't even realized he was holding. He was going to get wet, but at least he should make it.

He looked back up to try and catch sight of Joseph's plane, hoping he went on with the mission and was not coming back to see what happened. He could report back to base, and they would send a Huey out to get him.

He was surprised, then, to see the bright orange and

white parachute of another ejection seat about a mile away, making its own descent into the water. That parachute came from a Gripen, he knew, so Joseph had also suffered the same catastrophic cockpit failure.

Their Gripens might be old, but they were reliable, and two of them didn't fail like that at the same time. A sense of foreboding rushed through him as he drifted down closer to the water. If this was a deliberate attack of some sort, then what was going on?

Chapter 6

Beijing

General Chen Jun, the Chief of Staff for the People's Liberation Army, strode back to his office.   To say he was angry would be an understatement.   The general was a powerful man in China, and he was not used to being called before the Central Military Commission like a student called before the school principal.   Especially when the accusations were groundless.

China invading the Wanli Shitang?   It was preposterous.   This was clearly a political move by the Americans, the Taiwan government, and the Filipinos.   To what end, he wasn't sure, but they had manufactured some inconclusive "evidence" that the American ambassador had presented to the general secretary.   What made matters worse was that the general secretary, in his additional position of chairman of the CMC, seemed to give the accusations some credence.

His aide rushed in front of him, opening doors and getting people out of his way.   The aide was used to the general's famed temper, and he was trying to keep a lid on any potential explosions.

General Chen burst through the double doors to his outer office.

"Where's General Li," he asked, handing his cap to a waiting aide.

"Sir, he left the headquarters on a family emergency, and he isn't answering his phone," Captain Lin Shi Wei, told him, her eyes downcast, waiting for the outburst.

"And so you stopped at that?   I told you I wanted him now.   Send a driver to his house, and I don't care if his wife or his daughter is on her deathbed, I want him here now." He looked around the office.   "Senior Colonel Wang, I'm going to want the entire general officer staff in my conference room in fifteen minutes.   I trust that you can get that done?"

"Yes sir," his junior military aide shouted before

rushing to his side office to make the calls.

General Chen went into his inner office and sat down. He would get to the bottom of this and then personally shove the accusations up the American ambassador's ass.

Chapter 7

Over the South China Sea

Lieutenant Colonel Marco Salcedo looked about the big C-130 as it made its way to Pagasa Island. He had almost 160 soldiers crammed into the big bird, far more than its official capacity of 92 combat-ready troops, but by packing the soldiers in like sardines, they managed to shove them in for the 45-minute flight.

They had been on alert since this morning, and when the two Gripens had disappeared, it looked like things were on hold. But when the OV-10 that had taken off at the same time as the Gripens had stood 20 miles off Pagasa and had taken photos of the island, and when the Hueys had rescued both downed pilots without incident, the powers that be decided that whatever took down the Gripens had to be only aimed at fast movers. So the president himself had ordered the mission.

And with only 15-20 Chinese soldiers on Pagasa, the best they could tell, the 160 soldiers from his battalion would be an overwhelming force, more than enough for the PLA soldiers to just give up without loss of life. Marco got the feeling that perhaps an even more robust option had been considered, but with only one working C-130 available at Puerto Princesa, either waiting for another plane to arrive or perhaps that the response shouldn't be too big as to start an all-out war made this option the best one.

If the PLA soldiers did give up, Marco was under strict orders to ensure none were hurt. The Chinese would have made their statement, and the ball would be then in the politician's court.

Marco had been in combat before, fighting against Abu Sayyaf as a lieutenant and captain. But no one currently serving in the Philippines armed forces had been in full-scale combat. The Navy had had some clashes around Scarborough Shoal and in the Spratlys, and the Air Force had that one dog fight with the Malaysian Air Force a few years back, but the ground forces hadn't really been called upon to defend the country against a foreign enemy.

Part of him wanted the Chinese to fight back. Even with only a part of his battalion, Marco was sure his men would prevail, and against the Chinese? Well, his future would be assured, either in the Army or in politics. On the other hand, he knew the Philippines could not risk a real war with China, a war that the country could not hope to win.

He knew that actual combat was not likely. But the Philippines was making a statement that it would not be pushed around, and that they would not relinquish their claim to their portion of the islands, the ones in their own territorial waters. And if nothing else, then this operation would be a success.

The big plane banked to the left, ready to make the loop that would bring it aligned with the runway, landing west to east. With the ramp down, his troops would rush out the back and present an overwhelming force to the Chinese who seemed to be centered around Kalayaan town itself. As the C-130 rolled slowly down the airstrip while the troops disembarked, his unit would be essentially on line, able to circle around the town, surrounding it. The line might have some gaps considering the numbers he had with him, but against such a small number of Chinese, it shouldn't matter.

No, the Chinese would have to surrender and without harming any of the civilians or the garrison soldiers they must have surprised and captured.

Marco moved up to the hatch leading up to the cockpit. He wanted an aerial view as they came in. Captain Ibasco was an outstanding officer and would be one of the first out of the plane, and he could be counted upon to get the attack formation going, so Marco felt confident taking the time to get a better view of things as they landed.

As with the OV-10 that did the recon, the C-130's radios quit working as they approached the area. But the plane flew fine.

As he sat down on the small jump seat, the co-pilot leaned over and yelled into his ear, "That's Pagasa Island, sir, right over there."

Marco had been on the island before, but this view was new to him. Ahead, in the distance, the island was clearly visible despite the slight haze.   The C-130 was lined up on the runway, slowly making its descent.   Off on either wing, two OV-10s flew alongside.   The OV-10's were not heavily armed, but their four M60C machine guns and two pods each of 2.75 inch Folding Fin Aerial Rockets still gave him a stronger sense of security.

He looked back into the cargo bay.   The ramp was being lowered.   The troops were packed in tight, and Marco prayed that the plane didn't hit any turbulence, possibly throwing one of his soldiers out.

He looked back forward, a nervous sense of excitement building.   This was where he would make his mark on history, he knew.   This was where all of his training, all of his hard work, would come to fruition.

They were only two hundred feet up and possibly half a mile out when there seemed to be an explosion on the island and smoke billowed into the air.   But it didn't billow straight up—four fingers of smoke seemed to reach out to them.

It took the pilot's "Oh, shit" to register what was happening.   He then knew this wasn't some giant hand reaching out to them, although it might as well have been. He only had time to clutch the silver cross he wore around his neck before his world erupted into heat and flames before going dark.

Chapter 8

Aboard the USS Makin Island

"Pete, you've got to take down the anti-air or we're well and truly fucked," Capt Niimoto told him as he gathered his notes.

"Don't worry, sir, we'll do it," he replied.

Peter Van Slyke was pretty confident about his platoon's capabilities, but he hoped his bravado was not misplaced.   Going in without normal comm was worrisome, but the Marines prided themselves on making do.

This mission would be tricky even in optimum conditions.   Taking off from the *Makin Island* in an Osprey, they would link up with the *USS Mississippi*, fast rope down to the submarine, then use that platform to insert onto Thitu Island before daylight took away their cover of darkness. The photos they had received from the Philippines Air Force were not the clearest, so it was difficult to make out exactly what kind of anti-aircraft missile battery the Chinese had, but whatever it was, it had to be taken out or Kilo Company would be blown out of the sky like the Filipino C-130 had been.

While his platoon was being inserted, the amphibious group would continue at flank speed towards the Spratlys, and tomorrow, Kilo Company would land and seize control of Thitu while the rest of the MEU would proceed to Taiping to reinforce the ROC Marines who had managed to hold back the first Chinese attempt to take the island.

That was based on the last known intel, of course. The Philippines had been asked to send an OV-10 over Taiping, and it looked to still be in ROC hands.   But somewhere out there, two PLA Navy Amphibious Transport Docks were unaccounted for, and if they arrived and took the beleaguered island first, then all bets were off.   A single MEU probably could not take the island back from up to 1,800 PLA troops, so the MEU's orders were to stand off if that happened and let the politicians try to defuse the situation. No one knew if the Chinese would feel the same way with an American MEU on the island, though. Would they back off rather than risk WWIII, or would they forge ahead and try to take it?

India Company was set to take off within 30 minutes to try and get some feet on the ground on Taiping, but the danger zone was after the first Marines hit the ground but before enough forces could be built up to offer a serious opposition to the Chinese. To further complicate things, they still had no comm with the ROC Marines on the island, so there was the threat of friendly fire. The ROC had managed to obtain communications with one patrol boat outside of the blackout area, and it was supposed to precede them and let the garrison know that help was coming, but no one knew what the PLA Navy had in between the island and the boat. So the Philippines Air Force had agreed to send an OV-10 in first and land, letting the ROC Marines know that the Ospreys were friendlies.

The entire communications, satellite, and aircraft issue was causing panic right up to the White House. The MEU S-2 had briefed them that there was a full-court press to get to the bottom of what was happening. All US and allied forces had been put on the highest alert and techs were going over every piece of electronic equipment as well as software to determine just how deep the issue went. Currently, the effect seemed to be limited to around the Spratlys, but if the Chinese could do it there, the feeling was that they could reach anywhere.

The Chinese were denying everything, of course. Their non-involvement had to be considered, but all the evidence, meager as it was, pointed to them. From the anomalies in some of the recorded data to the Filipino overflights, the Chinese were the most likely aggressors. The S2 reported that NOAA had managed to re-power an old weather satellite and was getting it back online, and the initial reports were that it was sending back real-time data, but it would take awhile before it could be re-programmed to acquire militarily useful information.

And if it was not the Chinese, then who? The Spratlys were claimed as a whole or in part by China, Taiwan, the Philippines, Malaysia, Vietnam, and Brunei. Although what had attacked the US systems seemed beyond any current capabilities, the only nation that could possibly have developed those capabilities was the People's Republic of China.

The fact that it was all modern systems that were compromised was not lost on Pete.   Older systems had been unaffected.   OV-10's and C-130's could fly, even if not communicate.   The ancient radar installation on Palawan had been able to track aircraft over much of the Spratlys. And now, a 30-year-old weather satellite seemed to be up and running again.

The Marine Corps was no different from any other organization—it relied on high tech for just about everything. Pete felt naked knowing that all the gadgets and weapons that helped make the US military unsurpassed in the world probably would not work on this mission.   They probably no longer had that technological edge.   When it got down to it, this might be one US Marine against one PLA soldier, man-to-man, on an even playing field.

He had less than an hour before his platoon was to take off, so he took his leave of Capt Niimoto and left the briefing room.   High tech or low, his Marines had to be ready.

Chapter 9

Beijing

General Li took the handset and spoke.

"Senior Captain Chou, I gave the order over 10 hours ago for you to proceed to the objective and take it. Now, I am told that you are still hours away. I put you in command there to ensure there were no foul-ups, yet I see that there are. Can you please explain yourself?"

"General, the *Changbai Shan* has suffered a breakdown of one of its Pielstick engines, and that has seized up one shaft. We are proceeding forward at 12 knots."

General Li did the quick calculation in his head, going from the archaic knots to kilometers before responding, "And the *Jinggan Shan*? Is it also down?"

"No General. It is functioning as normal."

The general tried to control his temper. His authority was stretched further than was legal as it was, and the entire fate of his country was on a precarious perch. He could not afford alienate the idiot of a commander.

"Senior Captain Chou," he said calmly, "The Americans are sending a task force to the islands now. They are still out of range for their tilt-rotor troop transports, but they will be in range sometime in the morning. If their plan is to reinforce Taiping, then you do not have the firepower to evict them. So I think it is in all of our best interests if you send the *Jinggan Shan* forward and take that island by morning. Is that understood?"

"Yes, General. I understand and will comply."

General Li handed the handset back to the tech. He would rather have had someone more aggressive in command of the two ships, but Chou was reliable and trustworthy. He would follow orders without question.

He moved back to the plastic chair he had commandeered. It looked like he would be in the command post for the duration. His cell and tablet had been screaming for his attention, so he had finally just turned them off. Evidently, something had leaked out, but if he wasn't at headquarters, he couldn't be questioned.

"General Li, sir," Air Non-commissioned Officer 3rd Class Yan interrupted, calling from his station, "we have some activity from the American task force."

"The carrier group?" he asked as he stood up and walked over to him.

"No General, from the amphibious group."

He pointed to the screen where icons seemed to be lifting off the main icon for the amphibious group.

"These are their Osprey aircraft, General."

General Li looked at their position and calculated distances. They were still too far out, he thought. The tilt-rotor Marine planes had a range of about 1,600 km, and that meant that the planes could not fly to the islands, disembark troops, then return. He wondered if they were only going one way, to land on the island and then stay there. But that would mean that with the three planes that lifted off, there would be somewhere between 72 and about 100 troops sent to Taiping Island, a nuisance, to be sure, but nothing that even the one battalion on the *Jinggan Shan* couldn't handle. He really didn't want the US to get involved with any fighting, but he had always known that the risk of that happening was significant. The Americans had a habit of not considering their best interests before getting involved in the business of others.

He thanked Yan and went back to give Senior Captain Chou the new information. It wouldn't change his mission, but he had to take into account the added US Marines to the ROC Marine forces on the island.

Chapter 10

Over the South China Sea

Major Hayden Cannon looked down at his calculations for the thousandth time.   The numbers seemed correct, but as he looked out, he couldn't see any sign of the KC-46 refueler.

They had taken off from the *Makin Island* knowing the distance was too far to take the infantry to Taiping Island and make it back to the ship.   And with the comm all screwed up, a normal refueling link-up was out of the question.   Mechanically, his Osprey flew fine—it was just that he couldn't communicate with anyone else.

Without satellite navigation he had to use seat-of-the-pants flying, just like pilots back in WWI.   At least he could get windspeed from his instruments, so his calculations should be fairly accurate.   As a midshipman back at the Academy, he had to learn about set and drift, never in a million years believing that would ever come in handy.   But the calculations for flying were essentially the same thing.

He was fairly sure that his flight of four planes was in the right area, but without the tanker, he was going to have to turn back.   He could still reach the objective, but he wouldn't have the legs to return.   His orders gave him another 15 or 20 minutes to link up with the tanker before he had to abort.   Then it would be back to the *Makin Island* to link up with the Osprey that had inserted the recon platoon and wait until the ship got close enough to the objective that they could make the round trip without refueling.

The sun was getting lower on the horizon.   Visibility was still good, but it was getting darker.   Aerial refueling an Osprey was not particularly difficult, but all things considered, Hayden would rather get the planes refueled while it was still light.

He glanced down one more time at his knee board. Yes, the numbers were correct.

A small red light reflected off of his canopy, just like the movies when a sniper has his victim targeted. He looked off to his left.   Off his wing, 1stLt Gravure, the co-pilot for

Eight-Seven-Eight, was gesturing, making an exaggerated motion pointing to his left. He had the laser the Navy had given them all, something like a bulked-up laser pointer used for simple lectures and meetings. It had proven pretty effective for catching each other's attention, and they had even been able to send a few simple messages via Morse Code.

Hayden didn't need any Morse Code to know that he and Capt Kranovich had to have spotted the tanker. He pulled his own Osprey up a bit, and sure enough, in the distance, he could see the lights of a large plane.

He began a slow turn to meet the distant plane, the other two Ospreys guiding off of him. He knew the plane had to be the KC-46, but still, he was relieved when they got close enough to confirm that. The tanker had flown from Kadena AFB, so it had to reverse course once the linkup had been made so they would refuel while still closing the distance to the objective.

Although navigating like this was theoretically possible, he hadn't been too confident that they could pull it off, the Ospreys and the tankers coming in from opposite directions and linking up. It had been worth a shot, though, and now it looked that taking that chance would pay off dividends. He would be able to get his PAX on the objective in another hour.

Chapter 11

Beijing

"You tell her that her *Gong Gong* is sorry he missed her party, but that he will bring her something special when he sees her," General Chen told his wife over the phone.

The fact that he missed his granddaughter's birthday party, while not a disaster on a national level, was just one more nail in the coffin of this horrible day. From the opening salvo, he had been scrambling to find answers and assuage everyone from the Politburo on down. To top it off, General Li was still missing, and he needed his deputy chief of staff as a sounding board. Too many of his subordinates told him what they thought he wanted to hear. Li Zhiyuan did not do that. He could be counted on to give an honest and thoughtful opinion.

The Americans, now joined by the Japanese, the Filipinos, and the Russians, were pressing the issue. It was not surprising that the Americans, Japanese, and Filipinos would cooperate in whatever game they were playing. All three were constantly maneuvering to diminish China's power in the region. But now that the Russians were playing, that added a new wrinkle. Either they had been taken in by the American game, or they had their own game in play as well.

General Chen had assured the general secretary no less than four times now that there was no basis to the claims. He was still sure of that even if a few naval units were still out of any communications. That in itself was odd, but it wasn't anything about which to worry.

His secretary announced Major General Guo, head of the Fourth Department, who had called a few minutes ago to say he needed to see him. He told his wife goodbye, assuring her that he would return home when he could, then looked up as Guo centered himself on his desk and saluted. He had a young Air Force captain in tow. The captain looked nervous as he shuffled a folder and his tablet.

"General Chen, I think you need to see something. I

didn't want to tell you over the phone, though. This has to be face-to-face."

"Go on," he told Guo calmly, but with a sense of foreboding building up inside of him.

"I would like to turn this over to Captain Xu Da Wu. He is the man who identified this possible anomaly."

General Chen merely nodded as the young man stepped forward. He was clearly nervous, but he spoke with a surprisingly firm and confident voice.

"General Chen Jun, I want to report a problem with our communications systems..." he began before being cut off by the chief of staff.

"A problem with our communications? You are from the Fourth Department. Your mission scope covers enemy communications, not our own."

The captain looked up at his immediate boss, who was avoiding eye contact with anyone.

"Yes General Chen, that is our mission, of course. However, in order to determine if any enemy has penetrated our own systems, we do examine and test them. This is akin to you scanning your home computer or tablet for worms or viruses."

"OK, go on," the general prompted him, not liking the direction in which this conversation was going.

Capt Xu took a deep breath before continuing, "Nothing was evident at first, but I noticed a few anomalies. It's hard to describe them even now, but they were like little dust balls, innocuous, but out of place. That made me look deeper and with more care, and I found what I believe to be some serious breaches in our systems."

"And what do you mean by 'breaches,'" the general asked.

"Sir, I can't say just yet what they are and how they act, but I can say with all certainty that they are there. There are tracks, if I can call them that, all over the place. They have to be doing something, but I just can't tell you what yet."

General Chen felt a rise of elation.

"I knew it! The Americans are behind all of this. I've got to let the general secretary know about this!"

He started to get up when the captain held up a hand to stop him.

"General Chen, I have to inform you that these tracks were not made by the Americans," Xu said quietly.

"Not the Americans?   Then who?" he asked in a confused voice.

"I am ashamed to tell you, General, that they were made by us.   By the People's Republic of China."

General Chen flopped back into his seat, stunned. Someone in China had manipulated the PLA's computer systems?   Was this in-house, possibly a coup?   But surely he would be aware if the Army was planning the first coup in the PRC's history.   It couldn't be the PLA.

If not the PLA itself, then who?

Then his heart dropped.   If it wasn't the PLA, then it had to be the party or the state, not that it mattered as they were one and the same.

He asked Captain Xu to show him the data.   He was sure that the captain was correct, though.   What he had to figure out now was what to do about it.   If this was a party plot of some kind, he needed to determine who were the players and who stood to benefit.   Once he knew that, he would then decide what to do to protect the PLA.   If that also served to protect him, all the better, but his priorities were to the PLA and to the nation as a whole.

Chapter 12

Aboard the USS Mississippi in the South China Sea

Sergeant Jesus "Jay" McNamara did a final equipment check of his team. They would be the second team to lock out. SSgt Lesean Tolbert's team was already in the lock-out chamber with the lieutenant, and his team was waiting for it to cycle through.

The *Mississippi* was a *Virginia*-class attack sub, and as such, it had the integral lock-out trunk, capable of letting eight divers exit the sub. This was the first time Jay would lock out of an actual trunk. In training he had locked out through a torpedo tube, which was claustrophobic, to say the least. From what he saw in the walkthrough, though, this looked pretty high-speed-low-drag.

The last few hours had been hectic, to say the least. Not just the last few hours, the last day. It was only about 30 hours ago that he had been sitting down at a Pattaya bar to grab a beer and ogle the dancers that the recall had been made. From there the amphibious group had made its mad dash to the South China Sea with the Marines and sailors in frantic planning mode. When the lieutenant had finally given them their op order, they had almost no time to fine-tune anything. They would have to execute and adjust as necessary.

First team was assigned to go with India Company to the Taiwan-held island, leaving Tolbert's Second Team and his own Third Team to go with the lieutenant to the Filipino Thitu Island, what they called Pagasa Island.

Sergeant McNamara was a boot sergeant, perhaps still a little green to be a team leader, but when the shit hit the fan, he was still a Marine and expected to perform like one.

Getting to the sub had been a mission in and of itself. They had boarded one of the Ospreys in the late afternoon, then flew over the water for a couple of hours before somehow finding the *Mississippi* in the middle of nowhere. With the Osprey hovering, they fast-roped down to the rolling deck of the sub. A submarine on the surface is not the most stable platform in the world, and the target portion of the deck was pretty small.   One Marine, LCpl Mater actually missed the small flat area and hit the sloping sides of the sub as it rolled, falling into the water.   He was immediately fished out by the Navy crew, but it was a reminder that this was the real shit.

Somehow, they all made it aboard along with their gear. The *Mississippi* didn't have a Special Operations Forces Stowage Container, so they had to bring all their own tanks as well as the gear needed for the mission.

While the *Mississippi* steamed (Jay didn't know if "steaming" was the correct term for a nuclear attack sub) to the objective, both teams went over their gear, making sure everything was in top working order.   When locking out of a submarine at 70 feet below the surface, it didn't pay to have anything malfunction.   They also made good use of the galley.   The food was surprisingly good, and they even had ice cream.

The lieutenant and the gunny went over the plan several more times, making some minor modifications.   Jay wasn't sure the changes would make any difference given their lack of accurate intel, but they couldn't hurt, he figured. Jay's team was assigned to the main buildings to try and gather information as well as to protect the civilians in case the Chinese decided to take retribution on them once Kilo arrived.   SSgt Tolbert's team was assigned to take out the Chinese anti-aircraft battery.

This would not be Jay's first action with some of the members of Kilo.   Jay had been with then Lt Niimoto's platoon on the hostage rescue in Somalia, so he had worked with Captain Niimoto, 1stSgt Davidson, Gunny Dailey, Sgt Steptoe, and Sgt Isaac.   To bring the web even tighter, his platoon commander, Lt Van Slyke, had been with the captain when the skipper won his Navy Cross at New Delhi.

Coincidences were one thing, but from what he had heard, Captain Niimoto liked to surround himself with people he trusted, and he had the pull to get people assigned to him.   Jay's own assignment to the recon unit supporting the BLT, though, was most certainly a coincidence.

Jay felt much closer to the first sergeant though, than to

the captain.   It was the first sergeant, back when he was a staff sergeant, who had run up behind him while out on the *Jason Dunham's* tiny flight deck, urging him to run faster. Jay was a pretty big guy, and it was hot that day.   He was about to quit when Davidson, in his black Ranger t-shirt, basically shamed him into pushing it.   It wasn't until afterwards that he realized he had it in him to push it, that it felt no worse after pushing it than when he just plodded along.

That had made him run each day he had free time, anxious to see his platoon sergeant, wanting to show him that he was improving.   And he felt Davidson had taken him under his wing, almost like a big brother.   So when SSgt Davidson had bolted off with Cpl Steptoe back into Hobyo, the Somali city where they had rescued the two hostages, Jay didn't know why he was leaving the safety of the beach, but he knew he had to follow him.

The platoon sergeant had ordered Jay to take back the body of Capt Svenson, so Jay wasn't with him when he found Lt Niimoto and rescued him.   But his intent had been to cover Davidson's back, no matter what, and he still felt that way today.   There was no expiration date on loyalty.

Without Davidson, Jay probably would not be in recon. It was the enjoyment of running that his platoon sergeant had awakened in him that turned him from a big soft Marine to a big hard Marine, one who naturally gravitated to recon. He had always been at home in the water, and now he had the physical and mental endurance to excel in the unit.

That would probably surprise any of his homeboys back in Flagstaff.   Back there, he was still Jesus, the slightly pudgy goth boy.   Oh, he had been on his school football team ("Go Eagles!"), but that had been mostly due to his size. He was more at home helping his mother with the taqueria and playing his video games.

If he got his coloring from his mother, he got his size from his father, and it was his father who convinced him to join the Marines.   Not that his father liked the military—in fact it was the complete opposite.   To say that Colin McNamara was not the best father around was an understatement. He disappeared for months at a time, showing up for awhile, promising that things would be different this time, and getting a few dollars from his mom before proving that this time was no different.

During the last time he was home, while somewhat drunk, he went on a rant about the military and how it was the tool of an imperialistic and dictatorial government. That perked up his ears. If his dad was against the military, well, maybe that was something for him. So after graduation, with his mom's blessing, he had joined, only expecting to serve one enlistment, then using the GI Bill to get his degree. He never expected that he would like it so much.

And now, here he was, onboard a nuclear submarine, getting ready to walk out of it while it was still 70 feet down. His friends back home would never believe it.

The signal light on the walkout trunk turned green. The first group had already exited and the trunk was ready for them. He sent in LCpl Maus first, then they passed in the tanks before he entered the chamber, to be followed by the rest of his team, the gunny, and Doc Swanson. The trunks were designed for nine men, and with the eight of them and the Navy diver who would work the chamber, it was a tight fit.

The diver (Jay couldn't remember his name) went over the procedures yet again, but Jay was going over the mission again in his mind. He couldn't screw this up.

Everyone put his tanks on and checked his equipment. When each Marine and the doc gave his thumbs up, a sailor outside the trunk closed and locked the hatch. The diver started letting the water in from the outside. Immediately the trunk began to fill and the pressure began to build. This was different than diving down and clearing your ears and sinuses. When diving, you could stop for a moment if you were having a problem clearing. In the trunk, as long as the Navy diver was letting water in, you had to clear on his schedule. But he watched everyone closely. If anyone held out his hand, thumb down, he would stop until that person could clear.

When the water was chest deep, the diver turned off the white lights and turned on the red lights. The top of the sub was 70 feet below the surface, but no use showing any lights to prying eyes.

It was only a minute or two until the trunk was completely flooded. The diver signaled the OK with his forefinger and thumb, then swam up the big metal tube that dominated the top of the trunk. Maus, who was going to be the navigator, followed him. When his fins disappeared, the rest followed in their designated order.

Jay took his turn, swimming up the tube, which looked like nothing more than a cheap chimney. It was big enough, though, to easily fit him, his pack, his weapon, and his tanks. As he exited the hatch, he automatically looked back at the sub, the huge bulk a dark shadow beneath him.

When the gunny joined them, the Navy diver gave them another thumbs up and re-entered the trunk. They were on their own now. Divers are used to hand-and-arm signals, so without too much fanfare, they formed up and began to swim off, LCpl Maus leading the way with his dive board, LCpl Brugal swimming directly over him, scanning the water in front of him.

The water was clear, and in the darkness, plankton lit their passage with an eerie, radioactive-looking glow. Jay held up his hand, watching it become outlined as he disturbed the water with his passage, exciting the plankton. Despite the decent visibility, though, each Marine had a buddy rope connecting him to his swim buddy.

The waters around the Spratlys were pretty deep, especially near the Manila Trench. But most of the islands themselves were protected by coral reefs. Within 30 minutes, they had reached the reef just to the west of the island. He couldn't see it, but Jay knew there was a sunken Filipino Navy ship near them, a victim of that reef.

They eased themselves over the reef, careful not to break the surface of the water and possibly be spotted from shore. Once over, the water deepened a bit, but they could now see the bottom. Jay halted the team, then with PFC Wellington dangling below him on the other end of his buddy line, he and Maus slowly came to the surface. Scanning the beach ahead, he caught sight of a small, faint glow. That was their target. Maus took a bearing on it, and the two slowly sank back down.

With their new bearing, it was only about five minutes before they were more crawling than swimming as they eased ashore.   LCpl Mater met them, pocketing the small glowstick he had used as a signal, and led them into the low but dense trees to where the lieutenant was waiting.

First Platoon, Bravo Company, First Reconnaissance Battalion was on enemy-held territory.

Chapter 13

Beijing

General Li looked at the screen, willing somehow that the icons were a glitch, a bug.   But he knew they were accurate. There had been three lifts of planes to land on Taiping, and now a fourth was taking off from their amphibious carrier, now less than 300 km away.   The first lift had only three planes, with one going off to the south before turning back, but the next two lifts had four planes each.   So that meant there could be as many as 360 US Marines on the island to complement the 80 Taiwan Marines already there.   That was up to 450 troops to defend it.

He could order the assault now that his own two ships were waiting within an hour's steam of the island.   He certainly had enough soldiers to take it in an all-out fight. But the problem was their ability to quickly build up forces. Even though each ship had LCACs, and each ship had helos, none of these were in large enough numbers to be able to get forces ashore quickly enough to overwhelm the defending forces.   He thought he could still prevail, but the cost would be high.   And with the American planes returning to their task force, they might be able to land even more troops before that bleating lamb of a Senior Captain Chou could get his troops in the assault.

For the hundredth time during the night, he wished he had taken in the Air Force on the plan.   One J11 fighter could have quickly knocked the US planes out of the air. But General Li frankly did not have anyone high enough in the Air Force hierarchy that he could trust, and secrecy was paramount until after the islands had been seized.   The Air Force tended to be pretty "progressive," a term that merely meant "out-for-oneself" to him, more concerned with economic factors than with national security.   So in order to keep the circle of leadership smaller, he had bypassed the Air Force.   Only five people currently knew the true scope of the operation and its reason, not including whomever on the Politburo had been pulling his strings.   The rest of the actual fighters, from private to senior captain, thought that the Americans were the aggressors and that the entire party and military leadership were coordinating their response. Now, the general was wishing he had brought in at least one more person, someone wearing Air Force blue.

He had to admire the pure balls of the Americans, though. To fly those tilt-rotor aircraft blindly to a refueling point was an ambitious move. He had watched the screen with dismay as the three planes had hooked up with the larger one coming from their base in Okinawa. There was nothing else it could be rather than a refueling link, and when the planes had not only landed but then took off again, it was confirmed.

He wondered if it was time to brief General Chen and the politicians. He had really wanted to already have Taiping in Chinese hands before he did that, but with Thitu Island, maybe that was enough to goad the leadership into taking action. It wasn't as if the Americans were going to meekly slip away. China was going to have to take them down a notch.

On the other hand, maybe he could bring in one Air Force general, one person who could control a few assets. One J11 earlier would have done it, but now, perhaps a few more assets would be required. He hadn't wanted to damage any of the structures on the island, but that might not be an option at this point. At least there weren't any civilians on Taiping, unlike on Thitu. It just all boiled down to timing.

"Mr. Sung, you are positive that enemy communications are still down?"

"Yes, General Li. We remain in full control of all satellites, and there are no sea-cables between the two islands and anywhere else. Of course, as I informed you before, while we are also jamming the immediate area, we do not know if there is an older system available that can be used to slip through our coverage. I can think of three methods myself that could be used to communicate with either ships outside our coverage or with the mainlands of Vietnam or the Philippines."

"And we have no indication that they are certain on

what is happening?"

"Other than the fact that they have sent a task force? Well, no, we have collected no SIGINT to that fact, but as you know, we are not fully staffed for that."

The general chose to ignore the slight tinge of sarcasm in Sung's reply. He looked back at the opposition forces screen. The *Gerald R. Ford* battle group had stopped off the coast of Okinawa and was now making square circles in the ocean. It was imperative that they stayed out of any fight-- even if he had the entire resources of the PLA in his hands, he knew that if they waded in, he would have a very difficult time defeating them.

He wasn't sure if it was uncertainty on what was actually happening that kept the battle group away or concern over what had happened to the two Filipino Gripens. General Li thanked his lucky stars that it had been fairly easy for the Second Department to infiltrate Saab, and in routine upgrades, a simple kill switch had been installed in the planes. If it had been the Malaysians who had responded with one of their Russian-made SU-30's, well, despite their nominal efforts to date, those planes were secure from Chinese actions (the Malaysians were just not as high a priority to their efforts.) They might not have been able to communicate, but they could have flown and fought.

The Americans, on the other hand, were perhaps the highest priority. But even with their forces, there were gaps. On the carrier off Okinawa, while the F-35's were all compromised, the older F-18's that had gone through their most recent upgrade were pretty much secure. But as they wouldn't know that, he thought that would keep even the F-18's grounded for the time being.

Based on what he knew, he thought it would take the Americans at least a week or more to analyze their aircraft and take remedial action. He had no doubt that they would figure it out, though, so his window of opportunity was limited.

He yawned and looked at his watch. The city would be coming alive as people started stirring and getting to work. He needed a shower, he knew, and he could use a few hours sleep, but he wondered if he should try and make contact with Lieutenant General Li, the most likely Air Force candidate to go along with the plan. He knew, though, that time was of an essence. He couldn't keep the operation under wraps for much longer—he was somewhat surprised that the veil of secrecy had lasted as long as it had, to be honest.

He stood up to get a cup of tea when the operator on the opposing forces screen motioned to Sung. The general walked back over to see what had caught his attention. Sung saw him come up and stepped aside so the general could see.

The recent flight of aircraft to take off of the American ship was not headed to Taiping. It was heading to Thitu. They were going to try to take it back, it seemed.

The general was glad that he had diverted what was supposed to be the second wave to go to Taiping down to Thitu. It was only another 40 men on the two fishing boats, but when the Taiwan Marines had stood off the first wave, he had not wanted to waste the smaller second wave, so he had sent them to Thitu, mostly just to wait until they were needed. Now, it looked like they might be needed right where they were.

But this was upping the ante. While the Americans might suspect the attack on Taiping was conducted by the Chinese, they couldn't be sure. If somehow they landed their planes on Thitu, and they were not all shot down, confirmation of that would be there.

And confirmation was not what his guardian angel on the Politburo needed. General Li was astute enough to realize that whatever political firestorms were raging, the simple fact that no one on the Politburo "knew" what was happening let them deny, argue, and create doubt amongst their enemies. This is what the Americans termed "plausible deniability," one of the few English phrases he remembered from his classes at the National Defense Academy. The time spent arguing and denying gave him time to complete the mission before presenting it to the world at large.

He wished he had better communications with the small group on Thitu. Communications with the two big ships were fine, but the same cyber-jamming of the opposing communications seemed to be affecting their smaller unit radios. Sung had given him some half-ass excuse as to why there were problems, but the bottom line was that communications were intermittent at best the further any unit went south.

He looked up to Commander Hung, his Navy representative, a man personally picked by his father, Admiral Hung, to assist him.

"Commander, I want you to order Senior Captain Chou to send the *Jinggan Shan* south to Thitu Island and prepare for a landing. Keep the *Changbai Shan* at its present position and await further orders. And keep trying to raise Major Ching on Thitu. He needs to be warned about the incoming assault."

The young commander hurried to comply as General Li Zhiyuan went to the toilet to shave and straighten himself up before going back to the headquarters. He knew he was at a nexus, and he had to take action. Complete secrecy was gone, and now he had to get the other key players in the military and the country at large to not only accept, but embrace the new China era.

Chapter 14

Pagasa Island

"You, empty the bucket," the Chinese soldier told her, pointing at the white paint bucket that was now full of urine.

Analiza sighed inwardly, but let nothing show on her face. This wasn't the first time she had been called to latrine duty.

Just as the Chinese soldiers began their attack, Rayner Umberto, the assistant public works engineer, had shut down the power plant. This wasn't just a simple on and off switch, although such a switch did exist. This was a disguised kill switch that he had shown her once, used to disable the generator in just such an emergency. He had then used an old M16 to fire on the generator, destroying a few cables as a red herring before stashing the weapon and sneaking away to be taken prisoner with the rest of them.

The fighting had been over quickly, but the Filipino soldiers had just given him enough time to get this done. This was not without cost, of course. Taken by surprise with most of them asleep in the barracks, six soldiers had been killed, not including Alan, five had been seriously wounded, and the rest captured. Only one Chinese soldier had been killed in the fighting, although another two seemed to be wounded pretty seriously.

Without power, neither the water pumps nor the desalination station worked. So they had no lights, no running water, no anything. The Chinese had taken Rayner and Val Williams, the chief engineer for the town, to try and fix the generator, but after making a good show of replacing wires and cables, they "failed" in their efforts to get it working. Analiza had been concerned that the Chinese might use more violent ways of getting them to fix it, and she knew that Val would break under the slightest of coercion methods, but the Chinese basically left them alone after they had supposedly tried.

After taking over the island, the Chinese had gathered them all into the community center, posting several armed guards with them at all times. While the surviving soldiers were handcuffed, the civilians were not.

Without working toilets, a large bucket that had been a plaster bucket in a previous life had been surrounded by a sheet to become a makeshift toilet for excrement, and two smaller buckets were for urine. But over two hundred people created a lot of body waste, and the smell could get pretty ripe. So the buckets had to be emptied regularly.

Analiza lifted the bucket, careful to avoid spilling any on either the floor or her legs. The ammonia-smelling vapor made her eyes water, but she made her way to the main door. The soldier who had told her to empty the bucket opened the door for her.

"Not close this time. You take it far, to the trees," he told her, pointing out into the darkness.

He gave her a flashlight, but she wasn't sure how to hold it and the bucket at the same time as it took both hands to heft her load.

Another soldier stood on guard outside the door, and he pointed to the trees as well. None of the soldiers could speak Tagalog or Visaya, as far as she could tell, although she realized that could be a bit of subterfuge. But several did speak English, a few surprisingly well. She nodded to the second soldier, then carefully took the three steps down to the ground.

The bucket handle was digging into her hands, so she put it down for a moment, straightening back up and stretching. Four soldiers were in position around the two sides of the community center that she could see. Another group of half a dozen or so was sitting in front of the general store, seemingly relaxing and chatting. Several broke out into a laugh at something another must have said. She couldn't see any of the rest, but she knew some must be over at the missile launcher they had erected down close to the runway. The starlight and waxing moon was bright enough to let her see what was around her, but the launcher was too far away for that.

Bending back over, she lifted the bucket, splashing a bit over the side and onto her foot. She was tempted to just dump the rest right there on the sparse grass, but she didn't know if the soldier was still watching her.

Overall, the Chinese were treating them as well as could be expected, even letting the town doctor treat the wounded soldiers and Gracie Belvedere, who had somehow taken a round into her thigh during the fighting. But she didn't want to openly defy any of them, giving them the excuse to erupt into the orgy of violence she still expected at any moment.

The open area around the buildings seemed larger when carrying a full bucket of urine. She turned on the flashlight and held it while holding the bucket handle at the same time, sort of straddling the bucket while she duck-walked to the trees. The flashlight helped a bit, but she could not aim it right to where she needed it to see where she would be stepping. She was afraid she would step into a hole, spilling everything over her.

She finally made it to the small, densely packed scrubs they called trees, not that they would deserve that title anywhere back home on Cebu. They were barely 10 feet high this close to town.

Picking the bucket up, she half poured, half threw the contents into the brush. There was something odd about the sound of it though. She did not get the expected splashing sound of urine hitting the leaves both still in the bushes and as ground litter but rather a more subdued sound. She put down the bucket and lifted up the flashlight to look.

At first she could not comprehend what she was seeing. The leaves looked weird, the pattern and color a bit off. And with urine soaking everything, there were dark spots. Then, like a camera coming into focus, her brain registered what she was seeing. A man was lying on the ground. A soldier man, dressed in soldier clothes, goggles over his eyes, and holding a rifle pointing right at her.

Surprisingly, she wasn't frightened. While his face was painted up, this man was not Chinese, nor was he Filipino. In a flash, she realized he had to be an American. The man slowly brought up a finger to his lips, indicating she needed to be quiet.

"But, ... what...?" she started before shutting her mouth.

He had asked her to be quiet, and here she was talking? She quickly flipped off the flashlight, and he disappeared from her sight.   She knew he was in that pool of darkness just a few feet from her, but she could see nothing.

When she heard nothing else, she picked up her bucket and turned back.   As she walked her pulse raced.   She expected to hear shouts, shots, anything.   But there was nothing.

As she climbed back up the stairs and into the community center, she looked around, wishing she could tell someone, anyone what she had seen.   But she was wary, not trusting one of the Chinese soldiers to not be able to understand one of the local languages.   She felt like she had to do something, though.

She brought back the empty bucket, and on a sudden whim, grabbed the other, even if it was only half full.   She picked it up and began to take it outside. The guard looked at her with his eyebrows raised, but said nothing.

As it was only half full, she could carry it across the grass with only one hand.   She looked ahead, trying to see just where she had dumped the previous bucket. The tree line was basically featureless.

She got to the trees, trying to perhaps smell the urine, but with the other bucket beside her, she wasn't sure if she was smelling that or the previous load. She couldn't tarry, though, so she bent over and slowly emptied the bucket on the ground.

"There are 206 civilian prisoners in the community center.   That's the building that I came out of.   There are 15 Filipino soldiers held prisoner there, too, but they are handcuffed.   Five are hurt pretty bad.   There are close to 60 Chinese soldiers here, all armed with rifles, some kind of small rocket launchers, and a missile launcher down by the runway.   At the community center, there are about 15 of the soldiers.   I don't know where the rest are.   God be with you," she said in a measured, forced whisper.

She was about to straighten up when a voice whispered out from about 5 yards to her right.

"Did you say 60 soldiers?   Six-zero?   Not 20?"

She paused, before answering back into the bushes,

"Sixty.   Six-zero.   There were about 20 at first, but another 40 arrived yesterday."

She waited for another question, but when none came, she straightened back up and turned around.

As she stepped off to return to the center, a voice whispered out, "Thank you, miss.   And God be with you, too."

Chapter 15

Pagasa Island

1stLt Pete Van Slyke motioned to Sgt McNamara to come to him, then waited, feeling the slosh of cold urine soaking through his clothes.   None had hit his face, thank goodness, but his utilities and flak jacket had gotten a pretty good soaking.

He had watched the young Filipina make her way right to him, lugging the heavy bucket.   They had observed a couple of other buckets being emptied before, but whether that was dishwater, food, or what, they couldn't tell, and the buckets had been dumped much closer to the community center.   The girl had been struggling, so the bucket had to have been heavy.   She had a flashlight, but the beam was bouncing all over the place, not giving her a good path.

She had kept on walking, getting closer and closer. Night vision goggles were great, but they washed out color and depth.   Still, he could tell she was rather attractive and quite petite.   Her long hair had kept falling in front of her face, but with two hands holding the bucket and flashlight, she couldn't brush it back.   He had a sudden urge to jump out and help her.

She had walked right up to where he was lying.   He hadn't wanted to move, but he couldn't help but to shrink back a bit.   Then, she had picked up the bucket and threw it into the bushes, most landing right on him.   It was piss.

He had automatically raised his rifle, and when she had shone the flashlight on him, he had to will himself to remain calm.   The chances were that she was not aligned with the Chinese.   She was pretty obviously a Filipina civilian.   So he had taken a deep breath, trying not to cough on the ammonia fumes, and had motioned her to be quiet.

She had looked startled and started to say something, but then she had gathered herself and walked back.   Pete had hoped she would stay calm and quiet, but he had watched the community center closely for any sign of alarm.

He had glanced over to his right where LCpl Maus was

lying.   Maus had a smirk visible under his goggles.   Pete had to smile, too.   He guessed it was pretty funny.

When the girl had appeared again, with another bucket, Pete had perked back up.   She had made it back almost to the same spot, then had whispered her message.   That had taken him by surprise.   There were 60 Chinese on the island, not 20?

He had spotted about 14, and he had figured that there were a few down at the launcher, but where were the other 40?   Cpl Holleran and LCpl Brugal were somewhere on the other side of the town, getting eyes on that side, but without comm, they had to make their way back before he would know what they had spotted.

Sgt McNamara crept up to lay beside him.

"Man, sir, that's just not right," he whispered, sniffing at him.   "I wondered what she threw at you, and I had my suspicions, but wow!"

"Yea, yea, I know.   I know I'll hear about it later, but now, we've got to get a message back to Capt Niimoto.   That young lady told me there are 60 Chinese soldiers here, not 20."

"Sixty?   Shit!" was the sergeant's response.

"I want you to send two men back to the insertion point and hold up the light board with '60 enemy' on it."

"Aye-aye, sir, but you came through this crap.   It's pretty thick, and it'll take them awhile to get there.   And if the sub's watching, well, I hope they can relay the message."

"Look, we didn't run across anyone in the bush.   It doesn't look like they are running patrols.   Probably too secure with whatever cyber-warfare things they've got going. So tell them to stand up and move when they get out of earshot.   Grab Pags. He's got the light board.   And send someone with him.   Tell them to stop back on the other side of town and do what they deem best when the shit hits the fan."

"I'll send Destafney with him," Sgt McNamara whispered back, then started crawling away.

Pete thought that was a good choice.   Cpl Pagano was his comm NCO, a competent Marine in his own right, but Cpl Destafney was one of the top Marines in the platoon.

Before they left the sub, one of the petty officers had given him a black metal board he had fabricated. After plugging in a keyboard, they could input letters or numbers, 15 characters in all, that lit up on the board. The petty officer assured them it was waterproof, and the boat's XO told him that they would keep a periscope trained on the beach. At their high magnification, they should be able to see any messages.

How they would be able to pass that message on to the MEU was another question. But Pete had to try. Kilo Company needed to know what they faced.

Chapter 16

Pagasa Island

Sgt McNamara looked at his watch for the umpteenth time. Only a minute had passed since the last time he had checked. He grimaced, knowing he needed to calm down.

He was nervous, though. With Destafney on the other side of the town (he hoped), there were only the five left from his team, Doc Swanson, and the lieutenant here. Their mission was not to take out the Chinese forces—that was the job of Kilo Company. Their mission was to protect the civilians while SSgt Tolbert's team was to take out the missile battery. But with over 60 Chinese soldiers in a defensive posture, that would be a tougher nut to crack for Capt Niimoto.

At least Holleran had located the bulk of the Chinese. He had gotten back only 30 minutes before and reported that the soldiers had seemed to be bedding down at what was designated as the mayor's house on their map.

While their mission was protecting the civilians, the lieutenant, still stinking of piss, had told him that given the opportunity, they would help even the odds somewhat for Kilo. Of course, that left them up shit creek without a paddle if things went south. So the more they did for Kilo, the faster Kilo could take back the island and keep the Chinese off of the platoon's ass.

He looked at his watch one more time. *Crap! Only another minute gone.*

As the sun started making its presence known in the east, there had been a small degree of stirring around the town. One soldier had walked out towards the runway, smoking a cigarette. He stopped before reaching it, though, and stood there in the open area, scratching his balls with one hand and controlling the cigarette with the other. He wasn't that far from Jay, so he could clearly see the soldier holding the butt with his thumb and forefinger, the other three fingers splayed up, in an OK-kind of position.

Jay wasn't sure why the assault wasn't going to be done

in the wee hours of the morning under the cover of darkness. It didn't seem like a good idea to let the Chinese wake up and get their heads on straight before the attack.

Jay was more nervous now than he had been in Somalia, even if that had been his first taste of combat. In Somalia, he had been a PFC, just following orders. He had been a bit scared, but in his heart, he really didn't think he could actually die. Carrying Capt Svenson's body back had made it sink home a bit, but he had been off the beach shortly after that.

Now, as a sergeant, he felt the responsibility for his team. It wasn't just Joe-grunt Jesus McNamara worrying about what he had to do, it was Recon Team Leader Jay McNamara worrying about what everyone was supposed to do. He was afraid of failure more than of personal injury.

He looked at his watch again. At last! Within a minute, SSgt Tolbert would take out the missile battery. And if all went according to plan, about four minutes later, Kilo would land.

Jay crossed himself, then took out the small wooden crucifix that hung around his neck and kissed it. He felt more than saw a stirring as the other Marines around him got ready for action.

Even though he was expecting it, when he heard the firing open up not 400 meters away, he flinched. He couldn't see the missile battery through the trees on the other side of the opening leading to the runway, but he could see the smoker who startled, swung around to look in the direction of the battery, then started running back. He hadn't even brought his weapon with him.

They withheld their fire as the soldier ran back into town. There was no use in firing on him and giving out their position just yet. The gunfire at the battery intensified for a moment, then there was an explosion. Smoke started to rise over the trees. First Team had connected.

The guards at the community center ran to the south side of the building to look. This was poor tactics. If the Marines had wanted to attack the building, having the guards now all on one side left three sides undefended. Evidently another Chinese soldier saw that, too, because he came running up, yelling at the bunched-up guards. The guards split up, going back to their previous posts.

The firing stopped. Jay wondered if that signaled success or if Tolbert's team had been taken out. As Chinese soldiers rushed into view, a much larger blast echoed, and Jay could see a huge metal part from the battery rise up 100 or 150 feet, tumbling end over end. That pretty much sealed the deal. Green smoke puffed up to join the black billowing skyward—green was the color to signal the Ospreys. That done, SSgt Tolbert would be moving back towards the town, keeping in the trees, though, so they wouldn't be able to move quickly.

Jay strained to hear the sounds of the approaching Ospreys. They could not afford to have been close enough to be within range of the battery before it was taken out, but now, it was imperative that they land before the alerted Chinese could better prepare for them.

About a dozen soldiers rushed from the direction of the mayor's house and ran into the community center. Jay tensed up. If the Chinese blamed the Filipinos for some home-grown sabotage, then they would have to move quickly to keep them from suffering reprisals.

Several of the soldiers came back out with one of the Filipino men and seemed to be questioning him. Jay sighted in on the soldier who looked like he was in charge, waiting to take the shot if need be. But while the Filipino looked uncomfortable, he didn't seem to be being threatened, merely questioned.

Then he heard it. The Osprey was a big bird, but it could move quickly, so from the time that it could be heard until it arrived was generally somewhat short. Away from the town, back towards the north end of the island, the Osprey was rapidly making its approach.

Jay couldn't see it, and neither could the soldiers on the front porch to the community center, but they could all hear the plane. The plan was for the first plane to come in low and fast-rope its Marines right into the dense tropical scrub about 600 meters north of the town. This would keep the bird out of direct fire from anyone on the ground except for possibly from the far southern end of the island, but that would be a pretty long shot, and hopefully, SSgt Tolbert's team would have eliminated that threat.

This insertion should focus the Chinese attention towards the north when the next three birds would come in at wave height, essentially dropping their ramps right on the runway, doing a slow taxi while the Marines jumped out. With the Chinese attention towards the north and the three Ospreys using the trees along the north side of the runway as cover, hopefully, the Marines could debark and the Ospreys could get back into the air to provide supporting fire.

One of the problems with the Osprey was that it was faster and had longer legs than anything else in the MEU. Cobra II's could not provide air support, and with the fast movers grounded, the Ospreys had to provide their own support.

There was a mad flurry of activity as officers or NCO's started giving orders and the rush of Chinese soldiers started to organize into recognizable tactics. Jay was disappointed, though, when a good dozen or so soldiers who were in view oriented to the south, and among them was a heavy machine gun. Whoever was in charge there was not an idiot.

Jay looked over at PFC Wellington, pointing to the machine gun, maybe 300 meters away. Wellington nodded. That would be their target.

The Osprey to the north could still be heard when the faint addition of the ones coming in to the south became noticeable. Jay was listening for it, so he heard it first, but after only a few moments, the Chinese became more focused. They had picked up on it, too.

With the southern part of the island so flat, visibility was limited anywhere through the trees, so neither Jay nor the Chinese could see the incoming birds. It looked like the Chinese were orienting down the open area towards the runway, which made sense as the brush was so dense as to make passage extremely difficult.

But the Ospreys never broke past the edge of the trees. If the runway was the top of a T, the open area leading to the town was the lower stem of the T. The Ospreys went down the west end of the T, then did a U-turn and took off again, never coming into the heavy machine gun's sights. But the Marines who had been on those Ospreys would be in view momentarily.

As the six recon Marines and Doc were on the east side of the open area, they would be able to see the Marines just before the Chinese could. And the moment Jay saw that first Marine bounding forward, he opened fire on the machine gun. Within seconds, the rest of them opened up as well.

Three hundred meters across an open, flat area was not particularly far, but it seemed as if their rounds were bouncing everywhere except on target. The Chinese soldiers wheeled around to fire at them, and the machine gunner started to turn his gun around when he slumped. Another soldier pushed him out of the way and started firing, the heavy rounds cutting through the bushes just a foot or so above the recon Marines' heads.

It looked like two rounds impacted the soldier simultaneously, and the heavy gun went quiet. The other soldiers backed away taking cover behind a small white building. Five of them were left motionless on the ground where they had been hit.

Kilo Company Marines were pouring around the edge of the corner in the tree line, rushing forward, covering each other. They were in a kill zone, and the best way to get through it was to move quickly. One of the Ospreys made a long turn out over the sea and started a run in. With the civilians intermixed with the Chinese, it might be limited in where it could fire, but any added support was welcomed.

Recon had taken out the missile battery and a machine gun. Now Kilo Company was in the attack.

Chapter 17

Pagasa Island

Sgt Harrington Steptoe followed in trace of Capt Niimoto. As soon as they had landed, he had tried the comm, but as expected, whatever was jamming them still worked.   So he was down to Plan B.   Three junior Marines, PFC's Bouchard and Toti and Pvt Sullivan, in turn followed him in trace.

As the company comm chief, he had to ensure there were some means of communications.   With normal comm being jammed, he had to reach back to WWI tactics and employ runners and wire.   As runners, the young Marines would carry messages back and forth as the skipper required. Once they got in a static position, then the wire would come into play.   The *Makin Island* and provided the wire as well as the hand-held phones.

"Come on, Toti, keep it tight," he admonished the slightly-built Marine.

Toti seemed to jump each time rounds went off, and Steptoe wondered if he was the right man for the job.   There was nothing that could be done about that at the moment, though.

This was Steptoe's third taste of combat.   He had been with the skipper back in New Delhi, then with him again in Somalia.   This was his first experience against an actual professional foe, but as before, he had a surprising lack of fear. He wasn't sure why this was.   A rational man would have a degree of fear, or at least apprehension.   Steptoe really didn't have any.

No one who knew the young Harrington Steptoe would ever have guessed he would end up being a Marine, much less an NCO.   While tall for his age, he had always had a degree of softness about him.   His father, an accountant, had moved the family when Steptoe was a young boy from Philly to Winsted, Connecticut where they were the only African-American family in the neighborhood and one of the few in the entire town.

On his first day at school, Mr. Martin, the PE teacher

had made him one of the captains of that day's basketball teams, and rather obvious case of racial profiling, but Steptoe was able to immediately dispel the idea that all blacks were somehow experts in b-ball with an extraordinary display of a lack of coordination. Steptoe was not a jock. However, the lack of physical coordination he displayed in sports did not follow through on a Wii or PlayStation. As a gamer, Steptoe became quite skilled and even took a second place finish at an All-New England Battlefield 4 tournament.

Steptoe was not sure what made him sign up for the Marines. He had seen an old advertisement for the Corps on YouTube, one that made the subject Marine look like he was in a video game, and that had caught his interest. But while on a trip to New York for a tournament (in which he bombed out early), he wandered into the recruiting station and at the spur of the moment, signed up.

At boot camp, he had done quite well in the course work, even if he wasn't the fastest runner or the quickest over the obstacle course. With a first name of Harrington, he was ripe for a nickname. He wasn't happy with the one he received: "Cracker." With his lighter skin and splash of freckles across his nose, his partiality to country western music, and his love of gaming, the other African-Americans had jerked his chain about him not really being black. That hurt him more than he let on, but thankfully, that nickname had fallen out of use by the time he was with his second duty station, New Delhi. There, because of his rather obvious hero-worship of SSgt Child, he gained the new nickname of Stepchild.

That nickname was only used by a few people now, those who had survived the embassy takeover. No new nickname had stuck, and with his formal-sounding first name, he was either Steptoe or Sgt Steptoe, depending on who was addressing him.

Captain Niimoto got up from his kneeling position and ran 10 or 15 meters down the edge of the tree line, so Steptoe got up to follow, motioning for his shadows to get up and move as well. Up ahead, 2d Platoon was in contact, but with the dense brush and trees alongside the opening leading into town, the headquarters element had to stay at the edge of the open area as well, out of direct sight from a good portion of the buildings in the town. This still left them vulnerable to fire, either aimed at them or that aimed at the Marines in Second.

One of the Ospreys flew overhead, its Gau-17 minigun letting loose a burst. It swung back to return to the runway area, probably to make another run.

One of the machine gun teams attached to Second was laying a base of fire into the town itself. Steptoe was only a hundred meters or so back, but he couldn't yet see the target. From the return fire, though, it sure seemed like there were more than just 20 Chinese soldiers on the island. They had seen five dead soldiers around the destroyed anti-aircraft battery, so that would have left only 15 or 16 in the town.

He could see firing coming out of the tree line on the east side of the open area, but the small yellow ribbon tied to the top of one of the stunted trees was the signal that this was the recon unit. Steptoe wanted to send a runner over to them to find out what they knew about the enemy, but ordering one of his runners to go across 200 meters of open area while it was under fire was asking a bit much.

A Marine from Second, Cpl Ayala, it looked like, was hugging the tree line, leading a recon Marine. They spotted the skipper and made a last sprint to flop down beside him. Steptoe edged forward.

"Sir, Cpl Kinney from recon here. We took some friendly fire from your platoon coming in through the trees. We popped the smoke to get them to quit firing us up, but I think that gave away your position to the Chinks... oh sorry sir, I mean the Chinese."

"Shit," the skipper replied, seemingly oblivious to the slur. "Anyone hit?"

"Yes sir, LCpl Mater. He's pretty fucked up, but one of your docs is hooking him up now," came the reply.

A flurry of rounds hit the dirt not 2 meters to their right.

"Here, get in here for a moment," Capt Niimoto ordered, and the two Marines, Steptoe, and the three runners wormed their way into the dense brush where they could at least sit up and look each other in the eyes.

Steptoe knew what the skipper was thinking. With 1st Platoon out to the north, making themselves a target of sorts, he had hoped that the Chinese in the town wouldn't know which way to turn when Second began its rush to get into position. But if smoke was popped in the dense brush, that would give away 3d Platoon's position, coming in from the southwest. The Chinese would now know from where their point of main effort was assaulting.

"OK, we're still on track. There were five dead soldiers back on that battery. Your work, I presume?" he asked the recon Marine, who nodded back. "OK, good job on that. Cpl Ayala, what were you able to see in front of you?"

"Well, sir, there were another five KIA's around a machine gun, but they were dead by the time we got up there. And we've been firing back at some others, but I don't know if we hit anyone yet."

"Well, that means there can only be 10 or so soldiers left. We're OK."

"Sir, didn't you get the message?" asked the recon corporal.

"What message?"

He looked to Steptoe out of habit, but without any working comm, Steptoe was just as much in the dark as he was.

"There're around 60 Chinese on the island. We signaled that back to the sub."

"We never got that," the skipper told him as he leaned back, eyes not focusing on anything as he thought.

He came to a decision.

"Where's your lieutenant?" he asked Cpl Kinney.

"Over there, sir," he replied, pointing across the open area to the east tree line.

"OK, who's your team leader?"

"That would be Staff Sergeant Tolbert, sir. But we've also got Gunny Sloan with us."

"You do? OK, then, I want to see the gunny here. Stepchild," he said, turning towards his comm chief.

Capt Niimoto rarely called him by that nickname in public, but old habits had a way of surfacing when stress levels were high.

"I want your runners to get me the platoon commanders for Second and Third, the XO, and Weapons. I don't know if we can get to 1st Platoon and the first sergeant, but I want to try. Then, can you run wire around the perimeter of the town? Inside the tree line?"

Sgt Steptoe looked down at the aerial photo he had been carrying, slowly calculating. It would be close.

"I think I can sir, but it'll take awhile. We have to make our way through this stuff here," he told him, indicating the dense vegetation.

"OK, get on it then. Shanghai whomever you need. Just get it done. And tell the runner you're sending to First that feints and subterfuge are over. They know where we are now. I want that platoon up and in position on the north side. Don't engage unless they're fired upon, but I want to coordinate this better.

"Gunny," he said to GySgt Dailey, who had crept up to join him. "Get some bodies in here and clear this out a bit. I need to be able to talk to everyone. But be subtle. The Chinese have to be watching, so let's not give us away.

"OK, then, let's get to it."

Chapter 18

Beijing

General Li stopped inside the rest room to check himself in the mirror.   He looked liked he had been up all night, which was pretty much the case.   His meeting with General Li Huang-fu, the Air Force chief of staff, had not gone well. The Air Force General Li had flatly turned him down.

General Li didn't know if that was because the other General Li truly didn't have the vision to see how important this was to China, if he just didn't have the balls to do anything on his own, or if this was part of the growing rivalry between the two branches of the PLA.   For years, the Air Force had been the weaker sister in the armed forces, but over the last decade or so, it had been increasing in political clout.   The Air Force General Li might be seeing this as an opportunity to further his service's position, putting politics above the needs of the country.

At least that meeting had forced the general's hand. He now had to bring General Chen into the loop.   He wished he knew who exactly on the Politburo was in back of all of this.   That would help with Chen.   But regardless, he needed more assets to bring the plan to fruition, and at this stage of the game, that meant getting more people involved.

While he had considered the possibility that the Americans would get involved, he was still surprised at the speed in which they had gotten troops on Taiping and were actually assaulting Thitu.   He had hopes that Major Ching could hold out, even if the Americans got a foothold on the island.   That would give him more leverage.

He had thought the Americans would not risk an all-out war over the islands.   Their politicians were no different from those in China, afraid to take action and more inclined to talk, talk, talk.   And they hadn't committed their carrier battle group nor their Air Force assets, whether because of fear of the cyber-infection that pervaded their war machines or because doing so could trigger a full-scale war neither country wanted, Li didn't know.   But the troops they had committed were bad enough, and before he could order another assault on Taiping, he had to have some air assets.

He straightened his tunic, then turned around and walked out.   It was time.   He knew his presence back at the headquarters would have been reported back to General Chen, so there was no use delaying.   Besides, he wasn't a man who waited.   He was a man of action.

"General Li," shouted one of Chen's aides, waiting outside the chief of staff's office, "General Chen wants to see you right away!   Please come with me."

The general didn't respond to the aide, but he did follow the man.   Normally, the general took pains to acknowledge subordinates, but in this case, he needed to project himself in a position of power, of authority.

The bustle of activity in the outer office stopped momentarily as he walked through, all eyes on him.   No one there could really know what was going on, but his absence for the last two days had to have created a stir.

General Chen's secretary jumped up, choosing to announce Li's arrival in person rather than over the intercom.

"General Chen, General Li is here to see you," she said as she opened the door to Chen's office.

General Li didn't wait for a response but brushed past her and entered the large and well-appointed office. General Chen had been meeting with Colonel Ho, one of his protégés. The chief of staff looked up with an expression that showed both annoyance and relief.

"General Li, where have you been?   I have needed you here, but you disappeared and have been out of communications.   I assume you know what's been happening?"

Li inclined his head towards the colonel.   General Chen shrugged his shoulders and dismissed him, leaving only the two generals in the room.

Once they were alone, General Chen asked, "You have heard that the Americans, Japanese, Filipinos--just about everybody has accused us of launching an invasion of the Wanli Shitang?"

Li nodded.

"Well, what you don't know, since you have absented yourself, is that this might be true.   I have seen evidence that someone has manipulated our own communications and data records.   I have the Fourth Department working to unravel it, but evidence points to the possibility that units within the PLA might have taken the opportunity to seize Taiping Island."

"Yes, I am aware of all of that, and you are correct."

Emotions warred on General Chen's face as he digested that.   Li could see anger rising, but being pushed back down, if with an effort.

"Your attitude confirms what I feared.   At first your absence was an annoyance.   I needed you here.   But when it stretched through to today, I wondered if you might have some inside knowledge.   It had to be you or General Hing. Only you two were really in position to pull something like this off."

Hing? He thought.   The commander of the Southern District didn't have the fortitude to act with this degree of conviction.

"So tell, me, why I should not have you arrested right now."

"I think you know why.   I am merely a tool in this.   I am not acting alone."

"So this is not a coup?" General Chen asked, relief obvious in his voice.

"A coup?   Against my own country?   Against the party leadership?   I think you underestimate my loyalty," was the measured response.

"So if not a coup, then who ordered this?"

"At the moment, I am not at liberty to reveal that."

He would have revealed it, had he only known just who he or they were.   Instead, he had to bluff.

General Chen looked down at his desk for a moment before looking back up at the still standing Li.

"So this is being kept from me?"

General Li had anticipated the question, so he had a ready answer.

"It has been decided to keep you clean, in case events did not work out as planned.   Someone would have to take the fall, of course, and you were deemed too valuable to the nation.   You would be left with cleaning up the mess."

He could see the emotions warring on the chief of staff's face.   For someone who had risen to the top of the Chinese military, he sure lacked a poker face.   General Chen obviously wanted to believe what he had told him. Anything else meant that he was merely a figurehead, something Li knew to be unpalatable to him.

The chief of staff was silent for a moment before responding.

"And now?" came the unspoken question.

"Now, General Chen, events have transpired so that more resources will be needed to finish the task at hand. What you may not know is that not only have the Americans been going through diplomatic channels to address this, but they have landed troops in opposition to us."

Once again, the chief of staff was silent for a moment as he digested this.

"We are at war with the Americans now?"

"'War' is a very strong term, general.   We have come into 'contact' with the Americans, just as we have come into 'contact' with the renegade Chinese on Taiwan, with Japan, India, South Korea, Vietnam...I don't need to lecture you, more than anyone else, of our PLA's glorious history."

"So what is the situation now?   How involved is our 'contact?'" he asked.

"The renegade Chinese put up a spirited defense of Taiping.   Our assault force never made it to the island. The Americans were able to reinforce it with what is probably a company-size unit.   On Thitu, our assault force was able to take the island easily and is in control; however, we believe another American company-size unit may have landed on the island."

"You 'believe?'"

"Unfortunately, the same measures we took to blanket the area has had unforeseen effects on our own communications."

"And how could the Taiwanese troops repel our forces there?   They don't have more than 80 Marines or so on the island, if I recall correctly."

"A decision had been made that the assault forces remain limited to ensure secrecy."

He didn't mention that that decision had been his.

"On Thitu, only 20 soldiers took the island, although they have been reinforced with another 40. We had 100 in the assault on Taiping, and 20 took West York Island from the Filipinos. We have another 1,800 afloat and getting in position."

"And...?" General Chen prompted.

"We believe now is the time to dedicate more assets to the assault. We need air assets most of all. The Americans seem to be withholding their carrier battle group and their long-range assets from their air base in Guam. Their opposition looks to be a surgical attempt to get their troops committed, to make us pause."

"Well, maybe we should 'pause,' as you put it."

General Li was afraid of this. The chief of staff was a canny player. He had to be in order to have risen to the top. He would want to get more details before committing himself. He had to see the possibility of glory, but also failure was an option that no military leader, no government or party leader, for that matter, would want to contemplate.

"I am a military man, general. My job, as is yours, it to ensure the People's Liberation Army succeeds in all tasks. As far as pausing, that is up to those on the Politburo who are pulling our strings. But until they should so decide, it is our duty to strive for success. And to achieve success, I believe we need air assets. We have the ground troops in place."

General Chen stood up and walked to the window, looking out over the bustling city. He clasped his hands behind him, then rocked up and down on his heels.

Turning around, he asked, "And why are you coming to me? Why not your superiors, our superiors, on the Politburo and the CMC?"

"I can't answer that. They have their own agenda with aspects far beyond the mere military perspective."

General Li watched the emotions play over the chief of staff's face again. The man was an open book!

Finally, he walked back to his desk, hitting the

intercom.

"I want a general staff meeting in 30 minutes," he abruptly instructed his secretary.

To General Li he said, "Before they come, I want a more detailed brief on the situation.   If we are going to jump in, then we need to do this right."

General Li felt a rush of relief replacing the tension he hadn't really realized he was feeling.   The chief of staff had not committed anything, but neither had he ordered his arrest.   All of this could still be salvaged.

Chapter 19

Pagasa Island

There was a sharp crack of shattered leaves followed by the almost simultaneous deadened thud of the round hitting flesh. LCpl Kenny shouted out, sitting up and grabbing his thigh. Sgt Steptoe lunged forward and pulled him back prone.

The Chinese soldiers had taken to putting random shots into the foliage. They had to know something was up as no all-out assault had materialized. And as the amount of wire they had was limited, he could not go too deep into the jungle, so the firing had forced his small group to basically low crawl through the bushes. He had been grateful for this flak jacket, but the various branches had already cut up his hands, his neck, and his legs.

But now a random round had impacted on Kenny's thigh, and blood was spurting out. He kept trying to sit up, but that would expose him to more fire, so Steptoe physically laid on him, hands trying to apply pressure to the thigh.

"Sullivan," he told the private, "go deeper into this by five yards, then get up and get the doc. He needs to get here quick."

Pvt Sullivan nodded, then moved off. Sgt Steptoe looked back at LCpl Kenny, who had gotten pale and was obviously going into shock.

"OK Kenny, hang in there. Doc's coming now. You're going to be fine."

LCpl Kenny stopped trying to sit up, his breath becoming shallow. Blood was pooling under him despite the pressure Sgt Steptoe was putting directly over the wound. He tried to put more pressure, knowing he had to stop the bleeding. Another round cracked through the foliage, but it barely registered on him as Kenny's blood continued to flow between his fingers.

"Toti, help me put pressure here!" he called out.

Pvt Toti looked pale as he crawled up, then hesitantly put his hands on LCpl Kenny's leg.

"Harder, Toti! We need to stop the bleeding!"

LCpl Kenny stopped his mumbling. Steptoe looked up to see him staring upwards, mouth open, small gasps the only sign that he was still breathing.

If doc was there, he knew he could reach inside and clamp or stop the femoral artery from bleeding, but Steptoe didn't know if he could do that. He took pressure off for a moment to see if he could even see the artery, but the bleeding increased, so he pushed back down.

He looked back over his shoulder. *What was keeping Sullivan and the doc?*

Time dragged on. He wanted to look at his watch, to check the time, but he didn't want to let up on the pressure. His arms started to ache with the effort, and Toto was tiring, but they had to keep Kenny alive until doc got there.

"Hey, I think its working!" he exclaimed as the bleeding finally seemed to stop.

He looked up to Kenny's face, and his heart sank. There was no movement, no rise and fall of his chest. LCpl Kenny had bled out.

"OK, Toti, that's enough," he said, bitterness in his voice.

He didn't really know LCpl Kenny very well. He had just grabbed him, "Shanghaied" him, as the skipper had directed him. And because of that, Kenny was dead. Because of his choice. Not the skipper. Not Lt Gaines, Kenny's platoon commander. Sgt Harrison Steptoe. His decision.

He looked at his watch. He had 20 more minutes to get the wire laid.

"OK, let's move out. We need to get this done, but keep your heads down!" he told his small working party.

"What about him?" Pvt Toti asked.

"Leave him here for now. We'll recover him later. Now, we need to get this wire laid."

He couldn't help but to look back and LCpl Kenny's still form as they crawled further into the bush, dragging the wire behind.

Chapter 20

Pagasa Island

Joselito toddled up to Analiza, hands out, offering her his plastic action figure.

"You can play with him, if you want," he told her.

Analiza laughed and gave him a hug despite the situation. Joselito had obviously felt the tension, and this was his way of trying to deal with it. She took the beat up toy.

"Why thank you, Joselito. Maybe you can show me how to play with him?"

She looked around the room as the young boy happily went over the various functions of the plastic figure. All of the Filipinos were there in the middle of the community center, sitting on the floor. Four Chinese soldiers where in there as well, but none of them had made any aggressive moves.

An hour earlier, rounds had hit the center, shattering one of the windows and sending people screaming as they dove for the floor. Since then, however, the firing had died off, although they could still hear some shots being fired sporadically. Analiza wondered what was happening. The four soldiers didn't seem too concerned. It seemed to her that if the Americans were going to rescue them, they would have already done so. Was it possible that the American she had seen was only part of a small force, merely sent to see what was going on?

After the initial firing broke out, a few of the men had been surreptitiously gathering in small groups, whispering together. Whatever it was that they planned, it had to be obvious that the guards could see what was going on. Only four guards or not, they were armed and none of the Filipinos were. Analiza hoped that no one was planning anything foolish.

She glanced up as another burst of fire sounded off in the distance. Whatever was going to happen, she just wished it would happen soon.

THE MARINES

Chapter 21

Pagasa Island

"Roger that," 1stLt Peter Van Slyke said over the hand-held phone. "Most of the Chinese seem to be concentrated in the government building in the north and in the adjoining buildings. There're only a couple of soldiers back in the community center with the hostages. My take on it is that they don't want the hostages caught in a crossfire, over."

Peter had been surprised when a Marine had come through the undergrowth with the phone and trailing wire. With all the modern comm gear available to them, it seemed odd speaking into what was essentially an old fashion telephone. It was set up as a party line, for all practical purposes, so getting walked on was a problem. Proper radio procedures were a must.

"Any numbers and disposition of the Chinese, over?" Capt Niimoto's voice came over the phone.

"Movement has been limited, and we can see signs that they're fortifying their positions. But as far as numbers go, it's hard to tell. I'd say at least 25, two-five, soldiers in the government building, maybe 10 or so in the house directly to the east of that, and several more groups of 4 to 5 in the surrounding buildings. On top of the public works building, we think there is either an observation team or a sniper team, over."

"Can you take the sniper team under fire when we begin the assault, over?"

"I'm not sure. If they orient to the north, they will be in defilade towards us. If they orient to the south, then we should be able to take them under fire. I would suggest using the 60's. We're pretty sure there're no friendlies at the location, over."

"Roger, wait one..." the captain said.

Pete raised his binos again to glass the area. Captain Niimoto wanted him to provide a base of fire from the east to help cover the main assault from the north and west. The main base of fire would come from his Second Platoon from the south, but Pete's platoon would be more judicious, taking out whatever target of opportunity presented itself. His Marines would have to be more careful as Third Platoon would be in their line of fire as they moved in on the assault.

He reached down to scratch the welt that was forming on his thigh. Something had crawled in while he was laying there and taken a bite off of him, and the itch was getting maddening. He had been in the same spot for close to eight hours, and what with the bugs and a bucket of piss being thrown on him, comfort was pretty much out the window. He would be glad when things kicked off and he could at least move from this position.

The lack of activity seemed surreal to him. There were five dead soldiers in sight, lying in the sun. There was sporadic harassment fire coming from the Chinese. But after that first flurry of fighting, things went into a hiatus, sort of a Mexican standoff. Pete might not have stalled the attack had he been in charge, but he guessed Capt Niimoto wanted to make sure the assault hit with maximum power. Pete understood that, but the delay also gave the Chinese time to prepare better.

"Second, I want you to send a runner back to the 60's. I want rounds on the roof of the utility building in exactly 25 minutes from my mark. I want an Osprey in the air to follow up with anyone left on the roof. When the mortar rounds impact, that will be the signal to commence the assault. We will stick with white smoke to cease fire as previously planned. Now, I want confirmation, starting with First, over," Capt Niimoto said over the landline.

Pete hadn't seen any sign of an Osprey for at least 30 minutes, so he had assumed they were refueling or something. It was a nice security blanket to know that at least one was on hand.

"First, roger, over."

"Second Platoon, roger, over," was followed by Third Platoon's acknowledgment.

"Recon, roger, over," Pete transmitted.

It seemed odd not to have call signs, but without real comm, things were being kept simple. Of course with wire, it was possible that the Chinese had somehow discovered it, spliced into it, and were now listening in.

"Roger, so everyone's on board. Let's get this thing done. On my mark—five, four, three, two one, mark!"

Pete set his watch, then slowly moved over to Sgt McNamara.

"OK, here it is. In 25 minutes, the 60's will hit the utilities building. That will signal the attack. We're providing the base of fire, but for God's sake, we've got Kilo's Third Platoon right in our line of fire. We need to make sure we target each shot, no un-aimed rounds downrange. And we need to keep our heads low. We don't need any friendly-fire casualties here, either. I want Brugal to target the team on the roof. If the mortars don't get them, if the Osprey doesn't get them, he needs to take them out."

"He'll take them, no problem, sir. What about Gunny Sloan and Staff Sergeant Tolbert? Are they coming back here?" the team leader asked.

"No, it's just us here. Tolbert's team is joining Second Platoon for the base of fire and to act as a reaction force, if needed."

Sgt McNamara nodded, then crawled off to tell the others.

Pete resisted the urge to shout as another creepy crawler decided to sample his thigh, this time dangerously close to his balls. He reached in, felt the little bugger, then pulled it out. His fingers had partially crushed it, but a reddish ant seemed to stare defiantly at him. He flicked it away.

Pete realized that they could be at the brink of WWIII. The Marines were about to conduct an all-out assault on Chinese soldiers. Yet the world went on. Ants scurried in the brush, looking for food, living life as they had done for millions of years. They had bitten dinosaurs, and now they had bitten him. If this was WWIII, they probably would outlast humans, too.

He looked at his watch. It would all kick off in about 15 minutes. This is what he had been trained for, what the US taxpayers paid him to do. The situation might be different than anyone would have guessed. They had none of the modern technology with which he had been trained, none of the comm, not even the heads-up displays in their helmet face shields.   But when you got down to it, combat was combat, man against man.   It had been this way since humans first stood upright on the plains of Africa.

He could feel his pulse pounding.   He wasn't going to be kicking in doors.   He and his team were probably pretty safe as a base of fire unless there were more Chinese on the island than they thought.   But he still had a degree of nervousness.   He wiped the sweaty palms of his hands on his trousers.

A soldier looked out the door of the government building, then ran full out, changing direction several times as he made it to the adjoining building.   No one fired on him, letting him make it safely.   Pete wondered what was his mission, why he had to go to the other building.   He wondered if the Chinese had the same comm problems that the Marines had.   He wondered what the Chinese had done to prepare for the coming fight.

Wondering, though, was not doing any good.   He would find out soon enough.

He tried to control his breathing, to calm himself.   He had a job to do, and he was going to get it done right.

Time seemed to crawl, yet when he finally heard the soft thunk in the distance of outgoing mortar rounds, it suddenly seemed as if it was too soon, that it should take longer.   He counted down the seconds, waiting for the impact.

Even though he was expecting them, he still jumped when the six mortar rounds, two rounds for each tube, impacted all around the utilities building.   None landed on top of the building, though, best he could tell.   But as firing commenced all around them, an Osprey made its run, its minigun opening up on the rooftop.   Dust and pieces of the building went flying.   The big bird continued to the north and out of sight.

Marines came into view from the north, rushing out of the tree line.   Fire started coming out to greet them, but scan as he might, Pete could not acquire a target.   He wasn't sure if Second Platoon had targets in sight, but they were opening up with their small arms, and chips were flying off the southern walls of the buildings.

The muzzle of a machine gun poked out of a window opening and started to fire in the direction of Second, so Pete fired at it. His angle was wrong, though, and he couldn't get at the shooter. More American rounds impacted around the window, and the machine gun disappeared.

A Marine rushing from the north went down, and the single crack of the Chinese rifle seemed clear over the rest of the cacophony of firing. Despite the Osprey, at least one of the Chinese sniper team must have survived.

"Brugal! Take out the sniper!" he shouted, the time for stealth gone.

"Can't see him, sir!" LCpl Brugal shouted back.

"Get to where you can see him, then!"

To his right, a Marine got up and rushed out of the comparative safety of the tree line. It was Sgt McNamara, rushing over the 150 meters or so to the building. Rounds started whistling into the trees as he ran—their fellow Marines were firing on him!

Pete jumped up, waving his arms, yelling "Marines! Marines! Quit firing!"

A round zipped past his ear, but the firing stopped. Somebody over there had recognized they were friendlies. Of course, now that made him a target for the Chinese, but they seemed to be occupied with more immediately threatening Marines.

Pete flopped back down as Sgt McNamara somehow made it up to the building, back up against the wall. He took a grenade, pulled the pin, then stepped out a pace before lobbing it up to the roof. A second grenade followed before the first one detonated. Both explosions sounded muted, almost inconsequential, but the firing from the rooftop ceased.

Sgt McNamara looked back at Pete, then shrugged. He was committed now, and running back was probably more dangerous than staying where he was.

Chapter 22

Pagasa Island

When the explosions sounded, screams filled the rec center and people dove to lay flat.   Not everyone dove down, though.   As the Chinese soldiers spun around to look out, groups of men jumped up to take them on.

Analiza was trampled by one man as he joined the rush to get to the nearest soldier.   Either through complacency or because he was focusing on the fighting that had broken out outside, the soldier didn't see the group that gang-tackled him.

A shot rang out inside the community center, then another.   One of the soldiers was not so complacent, and he fired into the men rushing him.   It didn't stop the wave of angry men, but two went down before the soldier disappeared beneath the mass.

Analiza jumped up.   Three Chinese soldiers were down.   But the planning had not been enough.   One soldier had not been rushed, and now he faced the 200 + people in the center, weapon pointing at them.   They could take him down, but at what cost?

Almost with a communal mind, the growing mass of people took a step closer to him.   Analiza expected his weapon to open up, spewing death.

Suddenly, the soldier placed his weapon on the floor and said "*Ako ang iyong bilanggo*" in perfect, if accented, Tagalog.   "I am your prisoner."

Several men rushed him, dragging him up against the wall.   One man, Philip Ramos, grabbed the man's rifle, and thrust it under the soldier's chin.

"I'm going to blow your head off," he threatened.

"Stop that," Analiza shouted, bulling her way up and pushing the muzzle of the rifle down.

"He could have fired upon us.   But he chose not to. We are not animals here."

"They took our island.   They killed our soldiers.   I'll fucking kill him if I want," Philip yelled back.

"That's not for you to decide," she yelled, the strength of her will forcing Philip to take a step back.   "For all they've done, they have treated us as well as could be hoped for. They haven't abused us.   No rape, no murder.   We are Christian people.   We are God-fearing.   And this is how you want to act?   This is how you want your children to see us?"

That seemed to back down the crowd.   The fierce firing outside seemed to fade a bit as the adrenaline faded back a notch.

"OK, tie him up, along with the other two," Val Williams said.

Analiza looked around.   Two other soldiers, looking worse for wear, were also being held by groups of men.   She then spotted the fourth soldier.   He had been the one who had gotten off two shots, and he had paid the price for that. His bloody body lay still on the floor.

Analiza backed down as Val began to organize.   Their own soldiers were released, then the four Chinese rifles given to them.   Without knowing just who was fighting outside, the decision was made for everyone to stay put.   The Filipino soldiers would protect them but not leave to join the fighting going on outside in the town.

Chapter 23

Pagasa Island

Sgt Jay McNamara stood with his back alongside the building.   He wasn't sure what had made him jump up and make the run.   It had been instinct, not conscious thought.   He trembled a bit at the thought.   He wasn't sure how he had made it through the friendly fire to make it to the relative safety of the building.

He had thrown the two grenades blindly, but at least one of them seemed to have taken effect.   The sniper seemed to be out of commission.

He looked back at Lt Van Slyke, who was now flopped down in the open, and shrugged.   He wasn't sure what he was supposed to do next.   Running back seemed to invite more fire.   If he moved to the north side of the building, then First Platoon might mistake him for a Chinese and take him under fire.   Then there were the Chinese.   He could hear them shouting inside.   If they realized he was there, they could simply shoot through the walls and probably hit him.

The building he was up against was the one on the far west side of the community, which seemed logical as a building with noisy pumps and generators would be located further from the living areas.   Most of First Platoon would be focused on the government building, but he had to assume that someone would be assigned to this one. It sucked not having comm.   He should be able to contact the other units and coordinate something.

He got down low and began to creep forward.   He wanted to peek around the front of the building and see what was happening.   Just as he was passing beneath a window, a rifle came poking out.   He froze, not moving a muscle.   If the rifleman came forward just a bit and looked down, he would be spotted.

His team must have seen that as well as they opened up on the window, splinters of wood raining down on him. The rifleman opened up, spraying rounds back into the tree line.   This soldier was not a coward, Jay had to admit.

He felt down into his pocket.   Two more grenades left. Rolling over, he took one, pulled the pin, and motioned back to his team to cease fire.   Once they did, he took a deep breath, then stood up, hand grabbing the rifle barrel, forcing it up as the soldier continued to fire a few rounds. With his left hand still grabbing the barrel, he threw the grenade into the room, just getting it past the startled face of the Chinese soldier.   In one more motion, he reached down, grabbed his Colt, and fired two rounds into the base of the soldier's neck. The man dropped, and he could see motion as two or three other soldiers shouted and started to swing their own weapons toward him.

Rounds came through the window and the walls themselves as Jay dropped to the ground.   As the grenade exploded, shrapnel also went through the wooden walls.   If he had remained standing, his own grenade might have taken him out.

A chattering of an automatic weapon opened up, sounding like it was coming from the far side of the building. There was still at least someone left alive in there, someone firing at their fellow Marines.   Whoever it was had to be stopped.

He glanced back towards his team, and he was surprised to see Cpl Holleran and LCpl Maus pelting towards him.   They had moved forward, and by doing so, when they left the tree line to join him, the building itself had masked them from Third Platoon, keeping them out of sight.   Jay realized that he should have done the same thing.

It only took a few moments until both flopped down beside him.

"The lieutenant sent us to join you," Holleran breathlessly told him. "We need to clear this building, then hold it until Kilo can link up with us."

Another burst of the automatic weapon inside was an exclamation mark on the need to clear the building.

"OK, wait a sec."

Jay popped up, glanced inside the window opening, then fell back immediately.

"I think there're three inside here, but they look to be

down.   Give me a boost, and I'm going in.   Then you, Maus, you're smaller.   You can cover me while I pull you in, Holleran.

"OK, push hard.   I want to fly through the window," he told them.

The two Marines took him as his word, almost bodily lifting the big sergeant and throwing him inside the building. Jay hit the dead body of the soldier he had killed, then rolled on the floor, bringing his M4 to bear.

Another soldier lay facedown, motionless, blood pooling underneath him.   The third soldier in the room was sitting, but he was obviously in bad shape.   Part of his jaw was gone, and below his flak jacket, his thighs were bloody. His rifle was out of a few feet from him, and he was feebly trying to reach it.   Jay started to pull his trigger, but something stopped him.   He stood up and kicked the soldier's weapon away.   The man let his hand fall, then looked up, resignation in his eyes.

Jay simply turned away, then reached out the window to help LCpl Maus in.

"Watch him," was all he told the younger Marine as he helped the bigger Cpl Holleran in through the window.

Cpl Holleran raised his eyebrows when he saw the still-living Chinese soldier.

Jay picked up all three Chinese weapons and tossed them out the window.

"If he makes it, he makes it.   He's no threat to us now. Come on, we've got to put that machine gun out of commission."

The room they were in looked to be some sort of store room. Going right by the book, the three of them might as well have been training back at combat town, clearing the building step-by-step.   They made their way quickly through the machine shop, through the generator room. The machine gun sounded up ahead in what was probably the building's office.

There was a loud explosion that seemed to shut down the automatic weapon, but after a pause, it opened up again. Whatever their fellow Marines had just tried, it hadn't worked.

They got up to the door of the office. The Chinese soldiers were counting on their fellow soldiers to cover their rear, but they would still be on the alert for an attack from that direction. The three Marines needed to hit them hard and fast. Cpl Holleran sidled to the far side of the door. Jay was going in high, Maus low.

He held up one hand, then signaled a countdown: three . . . two . . . one.

On one, both he and Holleran moved forward, kicking in the door. All three Marines opened up, taking the two Chinese soldiers under their sights, likely before the soldiers' brains even registered what was happening. The two Chinese soldiers probably never realized that they were under fire before three bursts cut their lives short.

They stood there for a moment, staring at the two soldiers. Two men, who a moment ago, and been breathing, hearts beating. Now they were just meat.

"Well, fuck them, too." Holleran said.

Jay didn't quite know exactly what that meant, but he never-the-less wholeheartedly agreed with the corporal.

A few rounds came in through the window, sending them scrambling back out the door.

"Maus, go find a white sheet or something. We need to let the rest of the Marines know this building is secure."

It wasn't until he said it that it hit home. The building was secure. It was no longer in Chinese hands. It was now in the hands of the US Marine Corps.

Chapter 24

Beijing

"So where is the *Jinggan Shan now"* asked General Chen.

"This is the ship, General," the technician responded, pointing to an icon on the screen. "It should arrive off of Thitu in approximately two hours."

"And when will the repairs be made on the *Changbai Shan*?"

"Senior Captain Chou reports that it will be at least 24 more hours" interjected Commander Hung.

General Li tried to look calm, but inside, his anxiety was rising. General Chen had decided he wanted to see the command center and had brought along with him Major General Guo from the Fourth Department and Admiral Ding, the Chief of Staff of the PLA Navy. Li had no issue with Admiral Ding, but he knew that his actions with regards to cyber-warfare and communications would have rubbed the major general the wrong way, causing a loss of face. His little operation, after all, had made the Fourth Department look like fools, a price he had been willing to pay at the time, but that he now hoped wouldn't come back to bite him.

General Chen looked at the screen for a moment, then turned to Li and ordered, "I want the *Jinggan Shan* to hold in place for the moment while I absorb the entire situation. I don't like making a piecemeal assault, and I would rather have both ships able to assault in unison to keep the enemy from focusing their forces. I have already ordered General Li to begin preparing the air assets should I give the OK, but before I do that, I must ensure that your plan will not only work, but work with a minimal loss of life."

General Li inwardly groaned, but he let none of that show. The stupid chief of staff was going to waste the opportunity with his cautious approach. He thought to Sun Tzu's dictum:

> *Those who arrive early at the place of conflict will be in a position to take initiative.*

Those who arrive late must hasten into action troubled.

*Thus, those are skilled in conflicts will make the first move
to
prevent others from taking initiative.*

General Chen was going to let the Americans become entrenched, and that could essentially end the operation before it really got started.   He wished he knew what the situation was on Thitu, but he hadn't the opportunity to ask Sung Wenyan for an update, something he wanted to receive in private.

"So with the *Jinggan Shan* holding for the time being and the *Changbai Shan* making repairs, we have a moment to use all our assets to bring about a positive solution. Major General Guo, I want you to leave some of your best soldiers here at this command center to ensure we do not waste our superior cyber-warfare capabilities.   Admiral Ding, please have someone assist Commander Hung here in the command center.   He is doing a fine job, of course, but the better staffed we are, the better our chances at success."

General Li noticed the deft handling of that.   General Chen obviously wanted his own men present in the command center, but he also knew who Hung's father was, and if things didn't go well, he didn't want to be at odds with any of the high-ranking PLA generals and admirals if it came to finger-pointing time.   Chen might be too cautious now, but the man was the quintessential politician.

As General Chen looked back at the screen, Li sidled aside, motioning with a quick nod of his head for Sung Wenyan to join him.

Without looking directly at him, he asked in a low voice, "Mr. Sung, what is the situation on Thitu now?"

Sung glanced at his boss before looking straight ahead and responded, "Communications remain spotty, but the island has fallen to the Americans."

"Fallen?   Completely?" he whispered, surprise making it hard to keep his voice down.

"Yes, General.   Our forces have been neutralized."

General Li was shocked.   Major Ching was one of the

best young field officers in the entire PLA. Even if he was outnumbered, he could have kept the fight going for days in the dense jungle on the island. It was inconceivable that the man would surrender or be defeated in such a short amount of time. This made the situation even more desperate. The entire operation was slipping away. They could not afford to waste any more time.

"Mr. Sung. Order Senior Captain Chou to commence the assault on Thitu. The island will be taken, and taken now."

Sung Wenyan said nothing. Li could feel the anger begin to build. He knew exactly what Sung was doing. He was weighing his options, wondering with whom he should hitch his wagon. And even if he decided to go along with his orders, Sung wanted him to realize that he had options.

"And General Chen's orders?" Sung asked, his voice a whisper.

"With our current communications problems, General Chen's most recent orders could not be received, I believe, when we most assuredly tried to relay them."

"But we have no communications problems with the ships, only with Major Ching's forces, general."

"You are a bright man, Sung Wenyan. You have capabilities, for which you have been rewarded. I am sure you will find a reasonable solution for this issue."

"Yes, I have been rewarded, to an extent, that is..."

Li felt filthy bargaining like this. Duty and patriotism brooked no question, no grasping for personal rewards. But he would do what he had to do to ensure the mission's success.

"Yes, and many more will come to you, Sung Wenyan. Remember, I answer to higher authority on this, and they have much more leeway in expressing their gratitude for services rendered."

They stood there, side-by-side, neither looking at the other while General Chen spoke with Major General Chou and a young captain, gesturing at the status of forces screen.

Finally, he heard the words he wanted to hear.

"I believe that the communications problems have spread to our capital ships, general. I will ensure that they receive the correct and most worthy orders."

General Li did not let the relief he felt show in his face or posture.   He wished he could have those air assets now, but it would be better to launch immediately before the Americans could get more assets to the island.   This operation had to be completed, and completed now. Taiping may be out of the question at the moment, but Thitu could be back in Chinese hands by the end of the day.

Chapter 25

Pagasa Island

Sergeant Harrington Steptoe sat to the side, along with Lt Van Slyke and 1stLt Landon Gaines, the Third Platoon commander, while the skipper, the XO, and the first sergeant spoke with the Chinese captain.   One of the Marines from Second Platoon spoke Chinese, but only to an extent, so it was a relief to discover that the captain spoke excellent English. His arm had been bandaged, and he didn't seem too reluctant to talk.   He seemed more surprised than anything that the Americans had gotten involved.   From his point of view, the Filipinos had instigated the conflict by arresting and holding Chinese fishermen, and their orders had been to finally take back territory that had been Chinese for hundreds of years.

Captain Dan something-or-other had been the second-in-command, but on the first pass of the Osprey, their commanding officer had taken a round that had shattered his helmet and killed him.

Capt Niimoto had remarked that he was surprised that the Chinese had chosen to defend the buildings, something that fixed them in place.   So Steptoe wondered if that lucky volley from the Osprey had changed the course of the fight. Perhaps a more seasoned commander would have retreated into the dense vegetation that covered the northern 2/3's of the island.

Gunny Dailey came up and interrupted, telling the skipper that the water and electricity had been turned back on.   The Chinese captain's eyes widened at that.   Steptoe knew that the Filipinos had turned off both, telling the Chinese that the generator had been taken out in the initial Chinese assault.

A wry smile came over the captain's face as he took that in.   It had to be a tough position for him.   He had lost over half of his men in the fight, and the rest had been taken prisoner.

The Marines had not gotten away unscathed, either.

95

LCpl Kenny had only been the first to fall.   Seven other Marines had been KIA with another 15 and one Navy corpsman wounded in the assault.   With the other recon Marine who had been hit by friendly fire, that was 25 Marine and Navy casualties, more casualties in one single assault than in any attack back in Afghanistan and Iraq, maybe more than anything going back to Vietnam or even Korea.

When the count had reached the skipper, it looked like someone had punched him in the gut.   But to Steptoe, he was surprised the number had been so that low.   When the Chinese had opened up with their automatic weapons, Steptoe had been sure that First Platoon would be mowed down as they rushed from the tree line into the built-up area. If it hadn't been for the initial supporting fire coming from the Second Platoon from the south and fixing the Chinese attention in that direction, and then for the intense supporting fire throughout the assault, he was sure the casualties would have been even higher. He knew Tony, as he still privately thought of him, would be second-guessing himself, but the Chinese, even fighting from buildings, had taken even more casualties.   And these were professional, competent soldiers, not jumped-up farmers with rifles.

The Chinese captain was friendly, even talkative, but he wasn't offering much of value.   He didn't seem too taken aback by his surrender, although he wasn't too happy that three of his seriously wounded soldiers had been medivac'd back to the *Makin Island* along with 1stLt Ayers, Cpl Finnegan, and PFC Stuckey, all seriously wounded in the assault.   He kept asking when his soldiers would be returned to him.   When it seemed as if he had nothing more to say other than ask to see to his men, the skipper had him escorted back inside the community center where his surviving soldiers were being kept and having their wounds treated.

"I think he's pretty complacent for someone who just had his butt kicked," First Sergeant Davidson growled as the Chinese captain left.

"You're right," added the skipper.   "I have the feeling that the Chinese have got something else up their sleeves.   I don't want to lose the Osprey we have here now for a recon, but as soon as the medivac bird or the other one returns and we have two on deck, I want one to do a thorough recon of the northern part of this island as well as the little islands surrounding us.   I don't know what the CO has for us now, and I won't know until an Osprey gets back with our orders, but I want Second and Third to stay on full alert.   First," he directed at SSgt Willis, the new acting platoon commander, "keep assisting the Filipino civilians, but don't let them wander off.   They're not our prisoners, but I don't want a gaggle here until we've a better grasp of the situation."

"Aye-aye, sir," the bulky staff sergeant responded with a firm voice.

SSgt Willis was a gym rat, a Harlem boy who had taken to the Marines like the proverbial duck to water.   Steptoe had caught a few glimpses of him rallying his Marines when Lt Ayers had gone down, fearless in the heavy Chinese fire as he got his Marines into the buildings almost by his force of will alone.

"Lt Van Slyke, I'd like you to take the higher buildings, maybe the government building there and the control tower and just keep an eye on things.   Until our comm is back, it'll be your Mark-one eyeballs that'll be our early warning.

"Other than that, we've already got our orders.   Let's get everyone fed and watered.   When the Osprey gets back, we'll know what battalion wants us to do, so until then, just keep on the alert."

There was a chorus of 'aye-aye's' as the platoon commanders and the XO moved off.

"That means you there, lieutenant," Steptoe couldn't resist telling Lt Van Slyke before he was able to head off.

"Huh?"

"The skipper said 'watered.' That means you.   You stink like, well, like piss.   You need to get hosed down!"

Van Slyke tried to glare as Steptoe burst into laughter, but he couldn't keep it up and broke out into a laugh himself.

"So you heard about that?" he asked.

"Lieutenant, everybody's heard about it."

"Oh, just fucking great!   That's all I need now," he muttered as he strode away.

Sgt Steptoe merely laughed again.

Chapter 26

Pagasa Island

1st Lt Peter Van Slyke gave a quiet chuckle as he turned on the faucet.   He had given Gunny Sloan the orders before excusing himself to find a hose.   Stepchild giving him grief was a bit hard to take, especially when it was warranted. He'd have to get back at him later, but at least two-fold.

It had taken the Filipino engineer literally only minutes to get the island's generator going again, and with power, the pumps were working as well.   But with the water flowing, the Filipino civilians had eagerly crowded all the available showers and faucets, forcing the pumps to labor to provide enough pressure for all the demanding thirsty and ripe-smelling people.

With his Marines being positioned, enough time had elapsed that Pete had access to a faucet alone.   He pulled off his helmet and body armor before turning the water over his head.   He had actually gotten used to the smell of the urine, but once the water hit him, it was almost as if it was reconstituting it, bringing forth that harsh, ammonia smell.

He pulled off his utilities top, letting the water splash against his body, letting it carry away not only the piss, but the grime, the sweat, the ants—everything that had taken a place on his skin.   He closed his eyes and luxuriated in the feeling.

"Excuse me," a soft voice broke through his reverie.

He glanced in back of him to see a slender Filipina with huge doe eyes staring at him.   Half naked, there was nothing to hide the scars that had ravaged his face.   With his fellow Marines, he had gotten to the point that he rarely thought of the scars.   But with women he became much more self-conscious.

He reflexively jerked the hose he was holding, sending some water towards the girl, making her dance a step to the right to avoid getting wet.

"Oh, sorry!   I didn't mean that," he stammered out.

"Oh, don't worry!   You didn't get me, but after the last

few days, it wouldn't matter.   I don't think I'll ever complain about getting wet again."

"Oh...yeah, I guess so.   I mean, I know what you mean, I guess."

They stood there looking at each other, water still flowing from the hose, making an arc as it fell to the ground.

"So, um, can I help you?" he asked, trying to maneuver a bit so that the scarred side of his face was away from her.

"Are you Lieutenant Slyke?" she asked.

"Um, Lieutenant Van Slyke, yes."

"Oh, I'm sorry.   I thought he said 'Lieutenant Slyke.' But it is 'Van Slyke.'"

"And you're looking for me?" he asked her.

"Oh, yes.   This is so embarrassing.   I just came to apologize, but now I'm embarrassed to say so."

Then it dawned on Pete.   With her hair newly washed and brushed back, with clean clothes, and in the daylight, she looked different, but this was the same girl who had thrown the bucket of piss on him, the one who had then come back out and warned him.

"Ah," he exclaimed, "That was you!"

"Yes, it was," she said, obviously knowing that he now recognized her, "and I am so sorry!"

"Sorry?   For what?"

She looked at him in surprise, as if trying to see if he was serious.

"For throwing the pee on you.   If I had seen you, I would never have done it!"

Pete couldn't help it, and he broke out into a laugh. She looked at him like he was crazy.

"That's nothing, um, miss.   I was so amazed when you came back out, when you gave me the information on the enemy.   That was brave."

"But, but, I still, I mean … it's an insult to do that, right?"

"Don't worry about it, Miss...?" he prompted.

"Oh, sorry.   I don't know my manners.   I'm Analiza Reyes.   Pleased to meet you, Lieutenant Van Slyke."

She held out her hand, which Pete took and solemnly shook.   She spoke excellent English, but Pete liked the way her accent handled his name.

"You can call me Pete.   Can I call you Analiza?"

Pete could swear she blushed as she looked down.

"Of course, uh, Pete."

"Analiza, what you did was very brave, to risk yourself like that."

She said nothing, and he realized he was still holding her hand.   He dropped it.   Suddenly, he felt awkward.

"Well, I'm glad we were able to meet in better conditions," he said as he couldn't come up with anything more astute or clever.   "But I need to finish cleaning, then get back to my men."

"Oh, of course. Sorry to disturb you.   I will leave you now," she said hurriedly.

"Oh, you didn't disturb me.   I'm glad to meet you, and I hope we have a chance to speak again."

"Of course.   If you want.   Well, I'll let you finish your bath."

She immediately turned and strode off.   Pete just stood there and watched her leave.   She was petite, but he appreciated her figure as she walked.   It was only as she went around the corner of the building and was out of sight that he realized that for a few moments, he had forgotten his scars and had actually spoken to her as guys normally spoke to girls.

It was a nice feeling while it lasted, but then the awkwardness kicked in, and he knew it would never go anywhere anyway.   He would be off the island soon, on to his next mission.   And while she hadn't seemed to focus on his face, he knew that was merely because she had been embarrassed about the bucket of piss.   In another setting, she would be rather turned off by his appearance.

It didn't really bother him that much.   He was used to it.   He pulled the hose back and let the water hit his face. It was going to be good to feel clean again.

Chapter 27

Pagasa Island

"And that's basically it," Major Cannon told the skipper. "You're to hold your position here while the diplomats do what diplomats do. The word we're getting from DoD is that by holding Thitu and Taiping, we're giving our side a big advantage while they hit the Chinese at the UN and at the various embassies. It's all above my pay grade. Yours too. We don't want war, but we have to think that the Chinese don't either."

"With all due respect sir, I've got nine Marines dead. I kinda call that war," Capt Niimoto replied, bitterness evident in his voice.

Sgt Steptoe knew the feeling. LCpl Kenny's death had hit him pretty hard, too, more so now that he had a couple of hours to dwell on it.

"No one's going to deny that, captain. But in the big picture, war with China is something neither of us can afford. The world can't afford it.

"So now, just hold fast. You're going to have one plane here on station at all times. We'll have one on Taiping, too, and the other two will be working as couriers. When the *Makin Island* gets a little closer, we'll be augmented with the helos, but until then, it's our four Ospreys."

"What about Likas Island?" the skipper asked.

"OK, I'm a little confused again. Likas Island is which one?" the major asked.

"We call it West York Island, but the Filipinos call it Likas. Just like Thitu is called Pagasa Island by the Filipinos. The Filipinos had a small detachment on Likas-slash-West-York that the Chinese here told them they took."

"I think we've done what we were supposed to do, and the two big prizes here are in American hands. I'll pass this back to the MEU, and I'm sure they'll pass it up, but I doubt we'll take any action on it. Let the Chinese hold it for now. We've put the diplomats in a position of power, so hopefully, all of this'll be over soon. We'll scold the Chinese, slap their wrists, then it'll be business as usual."

"Don't you think that sucks, sir?" Lt Hosseini, the XO asked.

"Ours is not to reason why, there, lieutenant.   But think of it this way.   The Chinese are the biggest holder of American debt.   The Americans are the biggest buyers of Chinese products.   If we went to all-out war, think of the effects on not only our two economies, but the world's economy.   I'm not saying it doesn't suck.   I'm just being practical.   If there's any way to avoid war, then we're going to avoid it.   Kilo Company has done your duty, at a heavy price, to make sure we not only avoid war, but we do it in a way to our best advantage."

The company headquarters was silent as they all digested this.   Steptoe knew the major was right, but that didn't make it any more palatable.

"What about the prisoners?" Capt Niimoto asked the major.

"Well, as to that, I don't know.   I left you the Navy intel team," he said, referring to the three sailors and one Marine who were now busy interviewing the prisoners, "but other than that, I guess it's the status quo.   Just keep them under wraps for now.   I'll pass your concerns to the MEU CO when I get back.

"OK, if there's nothing else, I need to take off.   You've got Captain Nance here for the moment.   You got anything else for me?"

"Doc Ski wants two more Marines medivac'd, if you could. But no, other than that, that's about it," the skipper told him.

"No problem," was the reply.   "Get them loaded up, and as soon as they're aboard, I'm outa here."

They watched the major walk back to his Osprey. Steptoe knew he was only the messenger, but he still felt a degree of anger towards what he had said.   Somehow, it seemed to diminish what they had sacrificed.

"OK, gunny, let's get the ammo and chow distributed," the skipper ordered, pointing to the supply drop the major had brought with his flight.   "And let the mayor or whatever you call him know I would like to see him."

Steptoe looked around as people bustled about, all with jobs to do. As the company comm chief, he felt a bit out of place. Comm was still out, and after re-laying the wire, there wasn't much for him to do.

As he thought about it, though, maybe that was a good thing. If he had nothing to do until the ambassadors and all the higher-ups could get all of this straightened out, all the better.

Chapter 28

Pagasa Island

"Come on, eat up, Joselito," Analiza said, holding another spoon of soup for the small boy to take in his mouth.

He seemed to be interested in just about everything else other than eating. The big American plane getting ready to take off seemed to be particularly interesting to him.

From the terror of the fighting only a couple of hours ago, things had calmed down quickly. The Americans had asked that they stick together, so communal dining had become the choice for a late lunch. It was almost a festival atmosphere despite the presence of the 25 or so Chinese prisoners being kept in one corner of the community center and guarded by four Americans and six of their recently freed Filipino soldiers. Another handful of Americans kept coming over and taking one of the Chinese soldiers over to the front office before returning him and getting another.

"Analiza, there's your boyfriend," Satin remarked, eliciting a fit of giggles from the others.

"He's not my boyfriend," she protested before looking up to catch sight of the young lieutenant walking up to the city offices.

"How did you know who I was talking about, then?" Satin asked laughingly.

"I don't have a boyfriend, thank you very much, so whoever you meant couldn't have been mine," she replied.

She watched Lt Van Slyke, no, Pete, as he walked. He had an assured gait, full of confidence. Even from this distance, she could see the scar which marred his face. It had taken her aback a bit when she had first seen it, but she thought it gave him character and hinted at experiences perhaps better left unmentioned. Her imagination couldn't help but wonder how he had gotten the scars, though.

"Methinks she doth protest too much," quoted Honey, causing her own share of giggles.

"You know," Satin went on, "I don't know how you do it in Cebu, but in parts of the Philippines, throwing pee on a man is a proposal of marriage."

"Oh, that's not true," Analiza exclaimed as the others broke out into peals of laughter.

"How do you know? I think they do that in the north of Luzon. I mean, they smoke their dead ancestors and leave them in caves. So who's to say they don't use pee as a marriage proposal?"

By now, everyone was laughing, even the youngsters who might not quite have understood what the laughing was about but simply got caught up in the overall merriment.

"Satin, you know that's not true," she said even if she was smiling as she said it.

It was good to laugh. They had been under so much pressure, and friends had lost their lives. Now, with the arrival of the Americans, they felt the worst was over, and the simple act of laughter was really the best medicine.

She realized that Satin and the others were teasing, and she didn't mind. They were all friends. But she couldn't help but to wonder as she watched Pete enter the building and disappear from view just what he was really like. She'd only had a few words with him, really, but still . . . .

Chapter 29

\
Pagasa Island

Sgt Jay McNamara leaned back on one of the two rickety chairs, sipping at the warm coke.   The remains of some fried chicken and rice were on the paper plate he put on the built-in wooden work station that fronted the windows of the control tower.

Cpl Holleran was in the other chair while the rest of the team was sitting on the floor, eating the chow the Filipinos had given them.   Rank had its privileges, and as the two senior Marines, he and Holleran had proper chairs.

Of course, "proper" was all subjective, just as calling this a control tower was perhaps a little generous.   Oh, it had a radio for communications with incoming flights, and it was the tallest structure on the island and so had views down to the runway, but without any sort of radar or other more modern equipment, it seemed like some kid's treehouse, more than anything else.   Even the rusted, flimsy ladder they had to climb up to get into the structure at the top seemed less-than-permanent.

At least the windows that gave the tower a 360 view were in good shape and nominally clean.   Jay took another sip from the coke as he glanced around the waters surrounding the island.   As soon as the others finished eating, they would take over the watch.

In back of him, away from the runway, the heavy jungle that covered the northern 2/3's of the island looked inviting, like some sort of resort.   That was a far cry from reality, though.   The dense brush was almost impenetrable, and Jay still had gouges where the branches had stabbed him as he had made his way through it.

LCpl Maus burped, then got up and went out the back door to the metal grill platform that connected to the ladder. He stood at the low rail, then casually started to unbutton his trousers.

"What the fuck do you think you're doing, Maus?" Jay called out.

The lance corporal spun around, confusion on his face.

"I'm taking a piss, sergeant," he told him, stating the obvious.

"Not here you're not.   Those are civilians down there, and they don't need to look up and see your dick flapping in the breeze.   Besides, you'd probably splatter all over the ladder, and I ain't going to be putting my hand on that when I climb down.   Get your ass down the ladder and go use one of the heads."

Maus had the grace to look sheepish as he buttoned back up.   He went to the ladder and started making his way down.   Cpl Holleran caught Jay's eyes and shrugged his shoulders.   Mighty Maus was actually a gung ho Marine, but sometimes, he just didn't think.

"Police up your trash," Holleran told the others, handing out a plastic bag.

LCpl Brugal dumped his trash in the bag, then stepped out to the railing, stretching.   He stood there, taking a smoke break.   Jay wasn't a smoker and didn't understand why someone would smoke right after eating, but better on the railing than inside the tower proper.

Jay looked back down to the runway.   There was a fishing boat tied up at the pier on the far eastern side of the runway, the same boat the Chinese had used to first get on the island.   A few smaller boats were there as well.   In the middle of the runway, right where the open area and the lone road had been cut to lead from it to the town, the Osprey sat like some sort of huge insect.   The back ramp was down, and Jay could see the figures of two Marines lying back on it, out of the sun.

"Hey, what kind of ship is that?" Brugal asked to no one in particular.

Jay turned around, looking to the waters surrounding the north side of the island.   He didn't see anything, so he got up and stepped outside.

"Where?" he asked.

"Look, over there," LCpl Brugal responded, pointing to the west.

Jay refocused his line of sight, and there, in the distance, he could make out the large grey shape of a ship.

107

It wasn't a merchant ship, that was for sure.

"Is that the *Makin Island*?" asked Cpl Destafney, stepping beside the two of them.

It was hard to see, but it kind of had the same general shape. But it couldn't be.

"No, the *Makin Island* won't be here until sometime tomorrow, and I don't think the Filipinos have anything like that," Jay responded.

It seemed to register with all of them at the same time.

"Shit, I bet it's Chinese," Destafney said for all of them.

Jay stepped back into the tower, then grabbed the landline they had installed, picking up the phone Sgt Steptoe had given them. He keyed the handset twice, then listened. He keyed it again. Nothing.

Stepping back out, he turned towards the rest of the buildings and screamed out, "Steptoe, get on the hook now!"

Chapter 30

Pagasa Island

Sgt Steptoe was leaning back, almost drowsing.   The fried chicken the Filipinos had given them hit the spot, and the lack of sleep lately was catching up to him.   The skipper and the first sergeant were conferring, so it didn't seem like his services were in high demand at the moment.

"Steptoe, that recon sergeant's yelling for you," Sgt Isaac's voice woke him up.

"What?" he asked stupidly.

"Up there, in the control tower.   That recon team leader.   He's yelling for you to get on the phone."

Steptoe shook his head, and only then faintly heard the buzzing of someone wanting to be heard on the phone.   He got up and went to the table where he had set up his phone handset.

"Yeah, this is headquarters, over."

"It's about time.   I think we've got company.   There's a big ship coming, and I think it's Chinese, over."

"Are you sure?" Steptoe asked, forgetting the "over."

"No, I'm not sure.   I don't have Wiki imbedded in my brain.   But it ain't American, and I don't think it's Filipino. That leaves Chinese, over."

"OK, let me get the skipper.   Wait one, over."

He put down the handset and rushed out the door. Capt Niimoto was with 1stSgt Davidson, deep in discussion. Steptoe ran up to them.

"Skipper, I think you need to talk to McNamara.   He says there's a Chinese ship coming."

Sgt Steptoe expected the captain to come back to the phone.   Instead, he took off for the control tower, the first sergeant with him.   Steptoe had to agree that made more sense, so he took off in trace.

The skipper was already halfway up the ladder by the time Sgt Steptoe got to the base of the tower.   He climbed up, wishing he had some gloves.   The rust bit into his hands as he climbed.

The railing alongside the back of the control tower was crowded by the time Steptoe made it up. The skipper was looking through a pair of binos off to the west.

He slowly brought the binos down before saying, "Yea, it's Chinese. I can make out the flag. We have to assume it's not coming to apologize. First Sergeant Davidson, let's get all the actuals together right now. I would guess we've got 40 minutes, maybe more until it gets here. I want to make sure we all understand our missions."

He spun around, pushing past Steptoe to head on back down the ladder. Steptoe turned to follow him as the 1stSgt clapped McNamara on the shoulder.

"Good job, Jesus. Keep an eye on him and let us know what he's up to," he told him.

Sgt Steptoe knew that the 1stSgt and McNamara went back to their time on the *Dunham*, but it still sounded weird to hear McNamara called "Jesus." He was "Jay" to pretty much everyone else. Jay or Sgt McNamara.

Steptoe got to the ground and ran after the skipper, who was shouting for all the principles.

"I want the mayor, too," he added, trusting someone to get the man.

Steptoe was puffing by the time he reached the city offices. The building had been pretty shot up, but it was still solid and offered some degree of shelter.

The skipper was already giving orders, or more specifically, reiterating what he had previously ordered. He was not going to get caught in the same trap as the Chinese had. The buildings in the town had no strategic value. There was no reason to stay in them, becoming known targets. He was going to use the jungle to defend the island, to make it difficult for anyone to pry them out.

They weren't going to give up a toehold, either, like the Japanese did on so many islands during WWII. Second Platoon would occupy the tree line on the east half of the runway, Third Platoon the west side. First Platoon and Weapons would occupy the tree line to the south of the town, providing cover and support as the two platoons pulled back or to reinforce either of the other two platoons in the offense. No one mentioned that this was an awfully large frontage for the company.

"Mr. Mayor," he said, as that worthy came up. "It looks like the Chinese are not done with us. An amphibious ship is bearing down on us, and they could have between 1,000 and maybe up to 2,000 soldiers on board. I want you to evacuate as many of the women and children as possible on that fishing boat. That boat can easily make it to the mainland. I want your Filipino soldiers to escort them, " he said, nodding to the Filipino lieutenant who had just arrived. "and for those who can't fit in the boat, they need to get into the jungle, as far north as possible."

"That's not going to happen, captain," the Filipino lieutenant told him.

"What do you mean?"

"We've got twelve of us who are ready to fight. This is our land, and we're not leaving."

Capt Niimoto looked at the defiant lieutenant. Sgt Steptoe knew he was weighing his options. The skipper knew what his Marines could do, how they would fight together. These Filipinos were an unknown factor, and if they could free up Marines by escorting the civilians, then all the better.

"I think that you would serve best by protecting your fellow citizens, and as the commanding officer here, I think …" the skipper started before being interrupted.

"With all due respect, sir, you hold no authority over me. This is the Philippines, and you are here are our guests. Welcome guests, but still guests. Technically, I'm in charge here, not you, not Mayor Lopez. So no matter what you're saying, we're staying. We can fight together or separately, I don't care. But fight we will."

Steptoe knew the skipper was a pragmatic man. So he was not surprised that he accepted the lieutenant's ultimatum.

"Fine, we're happy to have you with us. If you can augment Second Platoon in the initial defense, I would appreciate it."

The lieutenant nodded, then saluted. Marines don't normally salute indoors, but Capt Niimoto returned the salute.

"Pete, in that case, I want you to escort the civilians down to that boat and get them underway.   But this has to be done now.   There isn't a reason to think that the Chinese will fire upon a fishing boat, but we don't know what're their orders.   The island should mask the boat from the Chinese, but for how long, I don't know.   So get it done now," he told Lt Van Slyke.

The recon lieutenant nodded, then hurried out the door and in the direction of the community center.

"We're pretty sure the ship can't approach from the west, right?" he directed the question to the mayor.

"Yes sir, that is right.   We still have wreckage there of one of our Navy ships.   If it's a big ship, that leaves only the south and the southeast corner."

"Then again, sir, just because the ship can't approach doesn't mean its landing craft and air can't hit us from anywhere," the first sergeant put in.

"Landing craft, and any kind of boat, would have to come in from the runway areas," the mayor responded.   The reefs and jungle would be almost impossible for anything to land anywhere else."

"OK, good point, but the first sergeant's got a good point, too.   We cannot assume anything.   We're oriented to the south now, but we need to be flexible and to keep our eyes open.

"Captain Nance, I don't want your Osprey a sitting duck.   Can you get up and around, off the runway?"

"No problem.   I don't want to be a sitting duck, either. I think we can fit right in the boat basin.   It'll be tight, but I've already had a look there" the pilot answered. "Between the trees and the drop into the basin, that should keep us out of sight until we take off."

"Look, I don't know how much time we have.   And I don't know how many Chinese are coming.   But we know our mission, and we've been trained well.   Let's show them what the Marines can do!" the captain extolled them.

A chorus of "oorah's" greeted him.   They were all ready for whatever was coming.

Chapter 31

Pagasa Island

Pete Van Slyke had already passed the word to the Filipinos, and he was surprised at how quickly the people had dropped what they were doing and were getting organized.   One man had run off to get one of the island's trucks, another had volunteered to pilot the boat and had taken off on a small motorcycle to get it started up, and the rest were prioritizing just who would be leaving.   It was women and children first, of course, but still, people were being quickly given numbers.

Pete had told them they had ten minutes, something he hadn't dreamed could happen, but as the old truck pulled up, children were already being loaded into the bed.   Capt Niimoto came in along with the mayor to check on the progress.

"Sir, what about them?" the XO asked, tilting his head to indicate the prisoners.

Pete had actually forgotten about them, despite the fact that they were sitting in plain sight in the back of the community center.   Some of them looked nervous, aware by the bustle of activity that something was up.   Their captain didn't look nervous, but concerned might fit.

Captain Niimoto walked over to the seated prisoners and thought for a bit.

'Leave them here.   Keep them restrained, but just leave them."

"Sir?" the XO asked.   "But they know about us," the XO persisted.

"If it gets to that, then I think the folks on that ship are already going to know what they need to know," the skipper replied, mind made up.

"Captain, if I may," the Chinese captain asked from his sitting position.   "I appreciate your treatment, but I would hate for there to be an accident, shall we say.   I am sure you have taken our national flag as a trophy, but perhaps you could see to raise it over this building?   I don't want our own forces to cause unnecessary casualties."

Pete thought that the Chinese captain had a lot of gall to ask that. His own side was about to attack, to try and kill Marines, and he wanted this favor?

"Captain, as one Asian to another, I ask this of you."

Capt Niimoto actually took a step forward.

"If we want to bring in race, your people tried to invade my ancestor's home more than once, only to be turned back by divine intervention," he said with some force. "And now, I am a fourth-generation US citizen, born and raised. So don't presume to think my racial background gives you and me any degree of kinship."

The Chinese captain blanched, obviously knowing he had overstepped.

"However, as an American Marine, it is my duty to protect my prisoners. When we prevail, I can come back and retrieve the flag. If by chance we don't prevail, well, I guess won't matter much then, will it?"

The captain looked relieved, and he nodded his understanding.

"Thank you, sir, ..." he started, but Capt Niimoto had already turned away.

"Gunny, get the flag out and put in on top of the building. Do it quick, though, then get out of here."

He turned to Pete.

"You've got to get going. I don't know how much time we have, but it can't be much. Get these civilians out of here."

"Aye-aye, sir," he replied as he rushed outside.

The truck was packed, and Gunny Sloan had commandeered a pick-up. Pete jumped in and told the gunny to take off, motioning the bigger truck to follow. They had to keep the speed down. The truck behind them was overloaded, and an accident would be catastrophic.

Still, it only took a minute or so before they reached the runway, then it was a straight shot down to the boat basin.

He looked to the west as they drove. The Chinese ship was much closer, but still quite a ways out. Pete could just make out the red Chinese ensign, though, with his naked eyes.

They pulled up to the pier, jumping out to help the

civilians get off the truck.   The children were essentially manhandled onboard.   Some of the children were laughing at the new game, but others started to cry.   Women tried to hush them.

The boat didn't look that big, but all the children managed to get on board and almost all of the women as well.   One middle-aged woman refused to leave her husband, insisting that they stay together.   Pete didn't argue.

The Filipino on the helm called out, saying that they shouldn't take any more, that they would be dangerously overloaded.   Pete called to stop the loading and told the man at the helm to pull out.

He was surprised then when one person jumped off the boat and back onto the pier.   That surprise turned to concern when he realized it was Analiza.   He rushed up to her.

"Why'd you get off?" he asked.

She looked flushed, but her reply was calm and collected.   "I only wanted to help the kids get settled.   And there're others who really needed to be on that boat, mothers of the kids, you know."

The boat was already pulling away, so nothing could be done about that. Some of the men, though, were going down to the small fishing boats that were tied up in the basin. They were going to head out, not to the mainland, but to some of the neighboring islets until it would be safe for them to come back.

"OK, but go with one of them, then," he implored.

"Sorry, Pete, but I don't like small *bangkas*. They make me sick.   So I'm staying here," she firmly told him.

One of the aircrew came riding up on a very small, beat-up motorcycle.

"Get these boats out of here, now!" he shouted.

Coming down the runway, hugging the trees, but not airborne, the Osprey was making its way to the basin. There was a flurry of activity as the small fishing boats cast off and got underway.

Pete looked around.   There were about 15 Filipinos left, and he knew there were another 30 or so still back in the town.   He was supposed to take them into the jungle and out of harm's way.

"Gunny, let's get these people back.   Load them back up."

As gunny shouted out orders, he took Analiza by the arm, pulling and pushing her up into the pickup's cab.   He jumped in as it took off, pulling the door shut as gunny swung the truck around.   They rocketed down the runway, the Chinese ship looking huge as it moved closer, but still a couple of miles out.

They turned and took the road into the town, which was already almost deserted.   Of the Marines, only Gunny Dailey was in sight, along with a small Filipino working party, filling up some plastic bottles with water.   A few other Filipinos were taking the filled bottles, then milling around.

As the trucks stopped and Pete jumped out, the gunny called out, "Sir, the skipper wants you out of here ASAP. Have everyone take some water, then you're supposed to go."

Gunny Sloan didn't wait for orders, but started directing their passengers to get the water.   It took only a few minutes before everyone had at least one bottle of water and were looking at Pete for directions.   Some had small backpacks on, others carried plastic shopping bags stuffed with what Pete hoped was food and not personal belongings. One older man had a roller bag.   How he expected to take that into the jungle, well, Pete didn't have a clue.

He looked back over his shoulder.   The Chinese ship was just clearing the tree line and coming into view.   It was still a long ways out, but Pete knew they had to hurry.

"OK folks," he called out.

A few people looked to him, but others still milled about.

"Can I have your attention, please?" he called out again.

"Listen up!" bellowed Gunny Dailey.

All eyes, turned towards him, voices stilled.

"Thank you, gunny.   OK, we don't really know what's going to happen, or if there's any danger.   But better safe than sorry, so Captain Niimoto and Mayor Lopez have decided that we all need to fade into the jungle.   I guess you've already got someone to lead the way?" he asked.

A middle-aged man stepped forward, touching his forefinger to the brim of the floppy hat he wore.

"In that case, lead on. Let's keep it tight, no straggling," he told them.

The guide and two others lead the group off.   Cpl Schmidt and LCpl Viejes followed, weapons at the ready. As Pete fell in behind them, Analiza rushed up to join him. She gave a tentative smile as Pete looked back.   He simply nodded.   It wouldn't be any less dangerous up there with him than anywhere else.   Pete hoped it wouldn't be dangerous at all, in fact.

The guide led them into the trees, entering the jungle on a small, barely noticed path.   Pete took a glance behind him before he was swallowed up by the foliage.   He had seven Marines and about 45 Filipinos with him.   He hoped this was merely a precaution, that it was unnecessary.

They had gone into the jungle by about 100 meters when a soft, but distinct report sounded off in the distance. Only moments later, an explosion sounded behind them, coming from right about where the town would be.

Everyone stopped and turned around to look even if they were unable to see anything through the trees.   The Second Battle for Pagasa Island had begun.

Chapter 32

Pagasa Island

Sgt Jay McNamara had watched his platoon commander and SSgt Tolbert's team lead the Filipinos into the woods. That left only his team and the mortar section still in the town. It was like the rest of the people, Marines and Filipinos alike, had simply disappeared.

The fishing boat evacuating some of the Filipinos had been visible, only a short way off the east side of the island and steaming north, and he could make out a scattering of small fishing boats fleeing. He knew the reasoning behind that, but it still had made him feel a bit abandoned.

When the ship had fired, it was almost anti-climatic. This was not the huge broadsides from battleships he had seen on The History Channel. There had been a flash, then a sharp retort. Moments later, he had actually heard the incoming round whistle through the air before it impacted on the city government building.

The explosion, while significant, was also less than he had expected. A hole had been blown out of one section of the second-story wall, but the building remained pretty much intact.

"That all they got?" LCpl Brugal asked.

"That's about it as far as guns. The biggest thing they have is a 3 incher," Cpl Holleran answered matter-of-factly.

Jay stopped to stare at his corporal.

How had he known that? he wondered.

If comm had been up, a quick search would have given him the same information, but somehow Holleran had that information at his beck and call.

"Well, shit, that ain't much," Brugal muttered.

"It bigger than anything we've got here, and you don't want to be on the receiving end of it. Besides, it'll be the soldiers inside that ship, their helos and landing craft, not to mention their tanks, that'll be their main weapons," Holleran told him.

Another round was fired, this time evidently missing the building as an explosion was heard beyond the town and from the jungle to the north.

"Uh, how many landing craft do they have, Holleran?" Jay asked, eyes snapped onto the distant ship.

"I think four of the LCACs. Maybe more of some smaller boats."

"I think I see all four of them, then," he told him, watching four separate hovercraft disgorge from the back of the ship.

"I think their LCACs are smaller than ours, so each one might carry 25 or 30 troops, less if they are carrying any armor. Can you see if there are tanks on them?"

"No, not yet. LCpl Maus, report this to Capt Niimoto. Let him know what's coming, if he can't see for himself," Jay ordered.

He could hear Maus in the background, reporting the LCACs, but his attention was focused on the landing craft as they wheeled around for a moment before oriented towards the shore. It was only then that he could see that two of the landing craft had tanks on board.

"Maus, let them know that there are two tanks inbound, on the first and the third LCAC, the first being the one on the eastern end of their line."

He could see a couple more conventional boats take to the water, but they would be some time to make it ashore. He barely registered another round whistling by the control tower to impact once again on the city office building.

The LCACs were picking up speed, heading towards the shore. It looked like they were going to hit the low seawall that made up the southern edge of the island. It made sense, given the dense jungle and rocks that protected the rest of the island, but that also meant that if the air cushion landing craft could clear the seawall, they would have to cross the runway out in the open. If they didn't have the clearance to make it over the seawall and up on land, they would have to debark their pax right there, and the Chinese soldiers would have to rush over close to 175 meters of open ground to close with the Marines in the tree line.

The 60mm mortars below him and up against the tree

line were zeroed in on the seawall, so Jay asked Holleran to shout down to them to get ready. He would have the corporal adjust fire as he could, but hitting a moving target when the rounds were in the air for 45 seconds was a difficult proposition. They had a wire running down to the mortar section, but using that could block someone else who needed it, and it was just as easy, if not easier, to simply shout out the adjustments.

As the LCACs were about halfway to the shore, three large helos lifted off the flight deck of the ship. The Chinese ship was not like the *Makin Island* with a large flight deck. It was more like an older American LPD, but with a smaller flight deck and from the way the ship had been angled towards the shore, Jay hadn't seen the three helos. There was no mistaking them now, though. They looked something like the Marines' Sea Stallions, so they probably had a good-sized troop-carrying capacity.

"Maus," he shouted out, "Let them know we've got three large helos inbound!"

He tried to remember just what weapons the rifle company had that could bring down a helo. He knew they didn't have any anti-aircraft missiles. The one anti-aircraft team with the MEU had gone to Taiping Island. A SMAW II Serpent could bring one down, and the Weapons Platoon Assault Section had three Serpent teams. Hitting a fast-moving helo with one would be difficult, though.

They didn't have any Javelins, the longer-range anti-armor missile, due to a manufacturer backlog, but the lighter Predator SRAW, which Jay had seen with least one team of gunners, would take down a tank, much less a helo.

Two helos pulled off to the west, making a long loop away from the southern side of the island. One helo came right towards the beach, following the LCACs in trace.

Something caught the corner of Jay's eyes to the right, not through his bino's lenses, and for a moment, he thought the Chinese had gotten a helo in without anyone noticing it. He pulled back the binos to see the Osprey taking off down from the boat basin. It looked good to see it, but the Chinese must have seen it too while it was moving into position. The next round from the ship's gun almost immediately impacted down in that direction, so that answered that question.

The Osprey quickly moved from helo to plane configuration, turned away from the line of incoming LCACs, the started to loop back, getting itself in line for a run. All of the LCACs immediately opened up with some sort of machine gun fire, but the Osprey was moving quickly into the attack. Its minigun opened up, firing on each of the Chinese landing craft which had been conveniently in a line.

Jay could see the rounds impacting on the LCAC's, now about 700 to 800 meters offshore, and sending up geysers of water in between each vessel. The second LCAC from the east suddenly swerved, whether because of damage or to try and avoid the Osprey's withering fire, Jay wasn't sure, and it almost collided with the first LCAC in line.

The Osprey reached the end of the line and started banking hard. It was still airborne despite all the rounds thrown its way. It looked like it was going to come back for another run.

The Chinese helo, though, jumped forward like a hornet, flashes from a large gun spitting fire out its side. In a moment, Jay could hear the reports. It had to be at least a 20mm cannon. One round could bring down the Marine plane.

The Osprey reversed the bank, pulling it away from the line of tracer fire reaching out to it. The pilot came back towards the beach, then kept banking until he had his plane facing back out. He went back into the attack, the LCACs starting to commence firing again as he got close.

Jay couldn't believe it. He had heard of troops in the trenches of WWI stopping to watch the dogfights, but a dogfight between an Osprey and a Chinese transport helo? It was pretty surreal.

There was a boom coming from the runway. Two Marines had run out and had launched a Predator SRAW out towards the LCACs. The missile quickly closed the distance and impacted on one of the LCACs. Jay expected to see a huge explosion, but the LCAC kept advancing.

The Chinese helo, though, evidently only had one cannon, and it was window-mounted. It had gotten itself out of position to use it and had slowed down to pivot, to get its gun facing the Osprey that was zooming in, its own minigun ablaze.

That was its fatal error. The Osprey's minigun was not designed for air-to-air fighting, but by slowing down, the Chinese helo made it an easy target for the Marine plane, and the minigun found its mark. The helo exploded into flames and plunged into the water 300 meters below.

Cheers erupted in the control tower as they high-fived each other. Jay couldn't believe what he had just seen. That captain had just managed to do something amazing.

The Osprey pulled back and started to bank again. But that exposed its belly to the Chinese ship, maybe 2 klicks further out. It was only then that Jay noticed the flashes that indicated the ship was firing with some sort of heavy automatic weapon. When the Osprey suddenly lurched, he knew the Chinese gunners on the ship had hit their mark as well.

The big bird faltered in the air, then began to lose altitude quickly. Jay could just make out the propellers starting to rotate into helo-mode. Maybe the pilot was trying to get the plane to auto-rotate. There wasn't any time, though. With a splash, the Osprey hit the water hard, parts breaking off and flying back up through the air.

His team fell silent. From the heights of joy, they had plummeted into the depths. No one said a word.

Jay looked back out to take in the whole scene. One LCAC, the first one, was on fire and evidently sinking. But the other three were continuing on, one slower than the other two, but still advancing. Explosions were sounding in the trees below as the ship's 3 incher opened up, but it would not be having any effect on the Marines in the tree line. The ship was overshooting them.

Off to the west, in the distance, the other two helos were mere specks. Jay wasn't sure what they were up to.

"OK, that's that. Let's get back to work, guys," he said. "Cpl Holleran, tell the mortars to prepare for targets 15 and 17. We'll give the order to fire. If the LCACs shift and land to the side of where they are lining up now, they have to be ready to shift, too."

The Marines below him were holding their fire. Seeing that the Predator SRAW had little effect on the LCAC, he doubted they would waste any more of the precious missiles. They would probably wait until they had a more appropriate target.

He looked around. The control tower was a little crowded, and there was no reason to put everyone in such a vulnerable position.

"Wellington, Brugal, and Cpl Destafney, I want you to climb on down. Cpl Destafney, if anything happens here, I want you to get to where you can observe the best you can and keep reporting."

He needed Cpl Holleran, but he was tempted to send LCpl Maus down as well. However, he knew he might need a runner, so he kept him. With the others climbing down the ladder, that left the three of them in the tower. That was enough to do the job.

"OK, Mark, fire off the mortars."

Cpl Holleran yelled down to the mortar section where Marines were at the ready. They released the rounds, then quickly picked up the next round and sent them after the first. Six rounds were now in the air.

One of the approaching LCACs actually picked up speed as it tried to flow over the seawall. It didn't make it. With a crash, it shuddered to a stop. Jay hadn't been sure if the wall was high enough to form a barrier, but evidently it was beyond the smaller Chinese LCACs' capabilities. Another LCAC slowed down to a stop, then let its ramp down. Jay was blocked from seeing how well the ramp reached onto the land, but a puff of black smoke from the tank onboard indicated it was good enough. He could just see the top of the tank begin to move when the mortar rounds hit.

Four rounds hit on the runway. As the runway was seven or eight feet above the low tide, they had no effect on the Chinese. Another round probably hit the water as Jay never saw an impact. The sixth round, though, somehow hit inside the LCAC that had tried to breach the seawall.

A 60mm mortar round is not the most devastating round in the world, but in the confines of a cargo bay, the effect was magnified. Jay could imagine the carnage inside.

Cpl Holleran was already giving corrections to the mortar section when the damaged LCAC pulled back, then slowly turned around.   It didn't look like any troops had gotten off.   A mortar would have a hard time putting an LCAC out of commission, but it could certainly take out its passengers.

Two landing craft, though, had been able to debark their passengers, and there was a tank on shore.   Firing began to come from the Marines, forcing the Chinese to hug the small area between the seawall and the edge of the runway, but some of them began to fire back.

"Mark, let's get some rounds on deck.   Maus, let Kilo know that there are approximately 50 Chinese ashore and one tank.   I think they've got two heavy machine guns as well."

The familiar incoming whistle and explosion made him jump.   *Why had they shifted their fire?* he wondered.

The increasing louder whup-whup-whup of an incoming helo answered that question.   Spinning around, he could see one of the Chinese helos bearing down on them from the north.   Another one was further to the north, looking like it was doing the Chinese version of a fast-rope insertion, but the one bearing down on him took his undivided attention.

"Incoming!" he shouted down to the mortar team and the lone machine gun team with them.

"Incoming" might be more appropriate for incoming rounds, not helos, but it got the point across.

The machine gunner spun around and started firing, but only got off a burst of maybe six or seven rounds when his weapon jammed.   Jay stepped out the back hatch and onto the railing, firing his M4.   He could see the rounds impacting on the canopy of the helo, now only 40 meters away and a bit higher, but they were having no effect.   His small caliber rounds could not penetrate the glass.

The pilot pointed straight at him, and Jay could clearly see him turn his head and say something to the co-pilot. He knew if that bird had a belly-mounted gun, he would have been toast.

He quit firing, pulling down Maus' weapon as well.

No use wasting ammo.   They were going to need all their rounds when the helo disgorged 25 or 30 angry Chinese soldiers.

He looked back to see if the machine gun team had cleared their weapon.   They were fervently working on it, it seemed, but Jay didn't have much hope that they could get it working in time.

One Marine, though, was running up to the helo, not away from it.   He carried a mortar tube and baseplate, holding it in front of him like some sort of personal weapon. The mortar could be fired in the handheld mode, but what he expected to do with it, Jay wasn't sure.   The mortar was not made to be a direct fire weapon.   If he managed to fire it directly at ground troops and not hit the ground first, Jay wasn't even sure the round would arm.

As he got closer, Jay recognized the Marine, LCpl Francisco Diaz.   He and Diaz had spoken a few times on the ship.   Diaz wanted to go recon, and Jay had given him what he needed to do to prepare himself.

LCpl Diaz stopped about 30 meters to the west of the control tower.   He calmly knelt, using his hands to hold the mortar in place.   His hand reached down to the trigger, and all became clear.   The M224 mortar was usually fired by dropping a round down the chamber.   The firing pin would set off the propellant, and the round would take off. However, the mortar also had a trigger.   A round could be placed in the tube, and when the trigger was pulled, the round would then launch.

One hand on the tube to aim it, the other on the trigger, Diaz intended to put a round into the helo.   Jay glanced back for a moment, and he could see the co-pilot had obviously realized the same thing.   But Diaz was at the forward quarter of the helo, and he was effectively masked from any of its weapons.   The pilots began to rotate the helo just as ropes fell out the back, probably trying to get their side-door cannon to bear.

The cannon started firing, explosions beginning to walk their way to Diaz as the helo came about.   As the bird rotated, Jay saw a Chinese soldier on one of the ropes, but holding on as the bird moved.

Come on, shoot! Jay silently implored as Diaz just knelt there, slightly adjusting the angle of the tube.

A cannon round exploded about 10 meters from him. Then, with what looked to be a nod, LCpl Diaz squeezed the trigger.

There was the familiar soft, hollow-sounding chuff as the round took off, and Jay was sure he could actually see the round as it flew past the control tower and impacted into the side of the helo, penetrating it before detonating.   An explosion literally tore out the side of the bird, parts flying, some of those parts even impacting on the side of the control tower.

Almost in slow motion, the bird turned over and fell, slamming into the ground on its side.   The props tried to turn a few more times, but they flew into pieces as the ground broke them up.   The helo bounced once, then broke apart into two huge chunks, the front section on fire.

The soldier who had been on the rope had somehow escaped intact.   He jumped off the ground and began to run, but right at the mortar section instead of away from it.   Jay didn't even have to fire as the soldier was quickly cut down. A few more soldiers stumbled out the back of the helo, collapsing on the ground.   One soldier crawled, or tried, to, that is.   He fell still, whether from being shot or from the crash, Jay wasn't sure.

Another incoming round from the ship bounced off the roof of the control tower, somehow not detonating.   He didn't know if the pilots had comm with their ship and had requested the fire, or if it was just their turn on the firing list.

"Mark, Maus, get the hell off of here!"

LCpl Maus had just put his feet on the ladder when another round came in, hitting the base of the tower.   The explosion threw shrapnel up, one piece hitting Jay in the cheek.   He reached up to see how badly he had been hit when the tower began to lean.

"Oh, shit," he heard LCpl Maus say as the tower began its long fall to the ground.

Jay watched the ground rush up before all went dark.

Chapter 33

Pagasa Island

When the first round exploded in the trees about 50 meters off to the left, most of the Filipinos hit the deck. The trees were dense enough so that no shrapnel made it that far, but it was still disconcerting.

Pete didn't think they were being targeted by the Chinese. There was no reason to do so as they had a much bigger threat with Kilo Company. The island was pretty flat, and with naval gunfire, errors in range would be the norm. Still, rounds that were overshot or on target had the same effect if they fell among you.

When under indirect fire, the rule of thumb was to disperse, but Pete feared losing control if they did that in the dense jungle. The matter was taken out of his hands, though, when a voice in back of him shouted out something in Tagalog, and people started scrambling up and pushing into the trees on either side of the path. Pete was losing control whether he wanted to or not.

He started to call everyone back when another round hit off to the left, closer this time. People started crashing forward, eager to get to the north and to the rendezvous point, a large rock on the shore that had enough deep water on the sea side of it that boats could come alongside.

Instead of trying to round everyone back to the path, he motioned to his Marines to spread out and try and cover what was now essentially a mass of people on line and moving forward. He stayed on the path himself, along with Analiza and two other Filipinos, trying to maintain contact with the people on either side of him. He didn't like the arrangement and felt somewhat helpless, but they knew where they were going. This was virgin territory to him.

Analiza touched his shoulder, catching his attention, and said, "Don't worry. We've all been to Bird Rock. We know the way. Everyone'll get there."

"I don't know. What if we run into the Chinese? I can't protect everyone when they're spread out like this."

"If they come, they come. But I don't think they'll be anxious to go digging around in the bush. Do you?"

"I guess that's a good point," he conceded.

He continued to move north with his three charges. He could see a few people on either side of him and could hear more crashing through the vegetation and occasionally calling out.

The path, such as it was, got even smaller and less distinct. If the townspeople knew how to get to Bird Rock, they certainly did not make the trip often, if the path was any indication. Branches tore at him, one raising a stinging welt on his face. He brought his visor down. None of the electronics worked, so he couldn't see his display, and while with it down he was hotter, at least his face was protected from the braches and vines.

As he trudged forward, he heard the whup-whup of a helo. For a moment, he thought the *Makin Island* was finally within range and had sent its helos to evacuate the civilians, but when he caught a quick glimpse of the helo through the low trees, he knew it wasn't American. Olive grey, the yellow-outlined red star and bar at the base of the tail assembly gave it away. It was Chinese.

Pete should have figured that the Chinese were not going to simply rely on a frontal assault, attacking on the Marines' terms. Like anyone else, they would want to adjust the battlefield to give them an advantage. What they probably didn't realize was just how thick the jungle was. As the helo was flying north, the more distance it put between wherever troops would be inserted and Kilo Company, the longer it would take for them to be an influence in the battle.

Of course, as the helo was north of his position, if the Chinese were going to move south to join the battle, they would have to go through his Marines and the Filipinos. He wished he could inform Kilo of what was happening. Sgt McNamara, though, was in the control tower, and surely he could see the Chinese helo. He would get the word to Tony.

The sound of the helo was not receding, and Pete realized that it must be hovering up ahead, possibly debarking troops, either by rappelling or fast-rope, if the

Chinese even had that capability. Pete wished he had studied the Chinese PLA in more detail. Knowing what they could and couldn't do would be a help.

If Chinese troops were being inserted 100 or 150 meter ahead, then he wanted the Filipinos out of the way. He ran off to the left first, then back across the path and to the right, telling those on either side of him to move further away from the path, then to hunker down and stay out-of-sight. He now wished he had kept everyone better under his control, but it was too late for that. He asked those nearest the path to pass the word to those further out, and to pass the word that he wanted Gunny Sloan.

He could hear the word going further out. The good thing was that in this vegetation, someone could pass within five feet of someone else and not see him or her. That was great for the Filipinos, but he had seven Marines with him, and he wasn't sure whether simply protecting the Filipinos as he was ordered trumped doing something about the Chinese soldiers who were probably ahead of him.

He had to see what was happening. He probably should wait for the gunny, but waiting could take the initiative out of his hand.

Turning to Analiza, he told her, "Stay here. When my gunny gets here, tell him to wait. I'll be back in a moment."

She looked like she wanted to argue, but she seemed to accept it and nodded, kneeling down under a gnarled tree of some sort.

Pete slowly pushed forward along the path, senses on high alert. It sounded like if there even were Chinese soldiers on that helo, they had been inserted only a short distance away. If they were there, he didn't know what their mission was, which way they were going, or how many there were. On the plus side, they probably wouldn't be expecting anyone to be out here in the middle of the jungle, a good 500 meters from the northern shoreline.

He looked back along the path. He was probably only 30 meters from where he had left Analiza and the others, but it felt like he was completely alone. He knew he should get back, or at least wait for the rest of his team, but he wanted to get just a bit further in order to see if in fact there was anyone in their path.

Stepping carefully, he moved forward another 10 meters to where a dense stand of some sort of tall, bamboo-like grass formed a barrier just off the path. Although it was only about a dozen feet high or so, it was a good four feet wide and so tightly packed as to act as sort of a pseudo-tree trunk. He had no idea what would cause it to grow that way, but it would give him some cover from which he could try and see if there was anyone in front of them.

In back of him, he could hear nothing. His charges were either silent or the jungle too dense for sound to travel far. In front of him was also silent. Even the sounds of explosions off in the distance seemed muted in the humid, oppressive heat.

He really should not be alone, and he knew he needed to get back. But first, he wanted to look down the path to see if there was any sign of the Chinese. He pulled out his K-Bar, then very slowly, he moved to the edge of the stand of tropical grass and carefully cut a few loose leaves that came off the main stalks and were blocking the view forward. The leaves fell silently to the ground, and he carefully peered around the big stalks.

The kick caught him right across the face. His helmet shield was designed as a both a screen on which his tactical information could be displayed as well as to protect him from fire and offer some degree of protection from shrapnel. It was not designed to absorb the full impact of a kick.

The face shield was driven back into his face, smashing his nose, but the force of the kick was spread out over a larger area than had the PLA soldier's kick directly contacted him across his face. Pete was knocked to the ground, and his weapon went flying back into the bushes.

Surprised, his nose aflame, but not really stunned, he grabbed the K-Bar, which had fallen beside him, and jumped up. The PLA soldier was in mid-jump doing some sort of flying back kick.

Pete had received not only the normal Marine MCMAP hand-to-hand combat training but also advanced training as a member of Recon. However, in the split second when he saw that booted foot coming his way, none of that training came into play, and instinct simply took over. He ducked while raising his hand, the one with the knife in it.

Instead of impacting on Pete's head, the soldier's leg impacted on the knife at the lower calf, just above his boot. While the kick was jarring, most of the force of the kick drove the knife deeper into the soldier's flesh where it essentially rode up his fibula, slicing his calf as clean as if a butcher might have done. The K-Bar rode up to the soldier's knee where his momentum knocked the knife out of Pete's hand.

The soldier fell to the ground, grasping at his leg which was spouting a bright crimson fountain. It was then that Pete saw the rifle slung across the soldier's back. Why the soldier had decided to go Kung Fu on him or why he was out on the path alone were questions that flashed through Pete's mind as he reached down to draw his Colt. His right hand was numb from the kick, so he had to transfer the .45 to his left hand. But at this range, which hand he used didn't matter. The soldier was in bad shape and had only a moment to try and reach around to his rifle when Pete fired two rounds into his chest. Without body armor, the rounds made a messy work of him.

With the two rounds breaking the silence, shouts sounded in front of him, foreign shouts. A burst of rounds came flying from down the path. Pete would swear later that the rounds sounded like bees going past his ear as he dove back behind the stand of grass, scrambling to get his rifle. His right hand was still numb, but he needed that M4.

He could hear the several sets of footsteps running as his left hand closed on his rifle and he struggled to swing around and face his enemies. He knew he wasn't going to make it, but he had to try.

Another burst of fire in back of him opened up, and he turned to see one PLA soldier fall on the path, the upper part of his body flopping past the stand of grass to lie just two feet from him. Pete looked back to see Gunny Sloan and LCpl Viejes charging down the path, rifles a blazing.

"Come on, sir!" his gunny shouted, pulling him up.

Pete didn't need any encouragement. Together, the three Marines sprinted back down the path.

When they saw Cpl Schmidt at the side of the path,

weapon at the ready, they dived off the path and into the jungle.

"Are you an idiot, Lieutenant?   That was a pretty fucking stupid thing to do!" Gunny Sloan shouted, his anger evident.

1stLt Peter Van Slyke didn't have a comeback to his platoon sergeant.   The gunny was absolutely right.

Chapter 34

Pagasa Island

Sgt Steptoe felt the pressure of the explosion, his breath knocked out of him. The Chinese rocket had been their most deadly weapon, killing and wounding wherever it was on target. This one, thankfully, had detonated in back of their lines, so he didn't think anyone had been taken out by it.

The fight, so far, was not like anything that he would have imagined. Both of his prior experiences in combat had been more fast-paced, more frantic action at times. Here, faced with a professional army, things had bogged down. He still wasn't sure how many Chinese soldiers were on the back side of the runway, a mere 175 meters away from him, but the LCACs and a few smaller boats had made several trips from the offshore ship.

About 20 minutes after the first Chinese landed, they had attempted an assault, spearheaded by their lone light tank. The blue tank was almost immediately taken out by a Predator SRAW fired from somewhere to his right, and with a heavy pounding of machine gun fire and mortars, the assault quickly fizzled out, sending the soldiers, in their odd blue-toned camouflaged uniforms, fleeing back to their side of the battlefield, leaving the burning hulk and four bodies on the runway.

Since then, the ship continued to fire its lone gun, but its effect was minimal. The rounds either hit on the runway, some actually skipping back up into the air, or hit long. The Chinese had some sort of grenade launcher, and they fired the occasional harassing fire, but these two caused only minor injuries to legs or arms, nothing life-threatening so far.

One sniper had tried to stick his head up above the edge of the seawall, but a quick burst from an IAR sent him flying back in a haze of blood.

The rockets, though, were a different story. The Chinese soldiers weren't even aiming the shoulder-launched weapon.   A soldier would pop up and fire, the rocket blasting across the runway to explode in the air above the Marines.   The rocket housed a fuel-air warhead, and the blast, while not huge, was deadly.   It blew down the short trees that gave them cover and killed and maimed the Marines in its blast radius.   Already, four rounds had been on target, killing 9 Marines and seriously wounding another seven.   What surprised Steptoe was that one rocket had exploded at the far left of the Marine's line where it married up with the Filipino soldiers.   The Filipinos, without body armor, fared better than the Marines.   Two Marines, Pvt Dexter and LCpl Alaman, had been killed while the Filipinos next to them had only been injured.

Luckily, the Chinese didn't seem to have too many of them.   Or at least, they had not fired too many.   Steptoe hoped that was because of supply, not because they were saving them for an all-out assault.

Meanwhile, the mortar section continued to rain down rounds on the Chinese positions.   They were quite low on ammo, so the tempo had slowed, but hopefully, the firing was enough to keep the Chinese occupied.

Steptoe was still amazed that someone had managed to take down a Chinese helo with a mortar round.   That was one for the books.

There was still one helo in operation.   It had tried to make a gun run on their position, but a Predator SRAW fired at it made it pull off, even if the shot had missed.   They could barely make out the helo on the flight deck of the Chinese ship.

The Filipino soldiers had made one mini-assault. Positioned at the far left of the Marine line at the boat basin, they had maneuvered forward in the rocks and in knee deep water to the very edge of the southeast corner of the runway, popping out to fire down the line of Chinese before pulling back.   The Filipino lieutenant reported killing at least 15 Chinese, but Capt Niimoto thought that was probably more hopeful than fact.   The assault, though, forced the Chinese to spend manpower to refuse that flank.

The skipper and the XO had discussed the possibility of assaulting the Chinese and throwing them off the island, but the same runway that kept the Chinese from successfully assaulting would prove devastating to them as well. Steptoe could see the skipper was frustrated. He didn't want to sit there as targets for the shoulder-launched rockets, but to attack would be foolhardy. Their best bets were either to egg the Chinese into a frontal assault that they could beat back or just hang on until the *Makin Island* was within range. Just one Cobra II run down the Chinese line would be devastating. Of course, a strike from the carrier group would be appreciated as well.

The best the skipper could figure was that they could expect something in another three hours or so—that is, if things were quiet on Taiping and they received all available support.

Sgt Steptoe took a deep breath. That last blast had been a little close for comfort. Whatever the Chinese were using as a fuze was less than 100% accurate, something for which he was eternally grateful. If it had detonated another 25 or 30 meters closer, that might have been all she wrote for Mrs. Steptoe's favorite son.

Over his ringing ears, he heard the land line, which was still somehow functioning, buzz. He picked up the handset.

"This is Three. We've got an incoming Osprey, over."

"Wait one, over," Steptoe told him.

"Hey skipper, Third Platoon's got an Osprey inbound," he shouted over the five meters to where the company commander was prone and talking with the first sergeant.

"Tell them to pop the red smoke. We don't him landing in the middle of this. He won't have a chance. With the smoke and that big target out there, he should get the message and get back to the MEU. Hopefully, he'll get back with a few of his friends," the captain told him.

"Three, pop a red smoke. We don't want him to try to land, over," Steptoe spoke into his handset.

"Roger. I think he's already figured it out. He's circling well off shore, but we are popping smoke, out."

There was a short delay, then down the runway, a good 500 meters away, red smoke started to form, to be wisped away in the slight breeze. Steptoe looked at his watch. If the Osprey could get back to the *Makin Island* in, say 45 minutes, and reported what was happening, then maybe they could have some help here in about 2 to 3 hours, just like the skipper said.

"Stand by," came a shout from down the line.

The Chinese must have seen the Osprey as there was a flurry of activity. A puff of black smoke indicated where the light tank had started back up. They could hear shouts as the Chinese got organized for something.

When nothing happened for a few minutes, Steptoe started to relax a bit. That was premature.

Two tanks, not just the one Steptoe knew was there, crested the edge of the runway as five separate rockets were fired into the Marine lines and what looked to be 100 soldiers came "over the top," firing as they came. Three SMAW II Serpents and one Predator SRAW reached out to the armor, two rounds hitting one tank and stopping it cold. The other tank kept coming as the Chinese rockets exploded over the Marines.

Captain Niimoto was on the handset, yelling out orders, so Steptoe kept watch forward, acting as the skipper's security. The headquarters element might normally have been back further, but with the dense vegetation, that would have kept them in the dark as to what was going on, so they were right up on the line.

Just to his right, LCpl Hanks stood up with his SMAW, trying to get a better shot at the tank that was spraying fire at the Marines. He calmly lined up his sights, then sent a spotting round downrange.

Shoot the rocket! Steptoe silently implored.

But Hanks took too long. The tank had spotted him, and with one round, hit him dead on. Steptoe was watching as the Marine simply came apart.

The blast knocked Steptoe, rolling him over onto his back. His hearing was gone, blasted away. Blood was running down his left arm, but he flexed it without problem. He rolled back over, and the tank was now only 40 meters or so from the tree line.

A frontal assault over a runway seemed stupid, but if they could keep the heads of the Marines down, Steptoe knew it could work. They could penetrate the line, then roll up the sides.   First Platoon had been sent back once firing had been heard to the north of the town to protect their rear, and they couldn't get back in time to support the other two platoons if things got dire.

Right in front of him, a few feet into the open, LCpl Hanks' arm lay, the hand looking normal.   Steptoe's attention was drawn to the fingernails and the half-moon of dirt under each one.   In his daze, he found himself thinking that Hanks should have kept them clean.

Beyond Hanks' arm, the SMAW lay, looking basically whole.   Steptoe was dazed, but he knew he should get the weapon.   He got to his knees and crawled out, stopping to carefully move Hanks' arm aside, then continuing to the SMAW.   He sat down and cradled the weapon.

Sgt Steptoe was not a SMAW gunner.   He was a communicator.   But as the saying went, "Every Marine is a rifleman."   He knew how to operate a SMAW, even if he had never fired a real one, only a simulator.   His thinking wasn't clear, but rote training took over.

He checked the optics.   If they were smashed, the weapon would be essentially useless.   But the SMAW II Serpent was designed with a roll cage over the optics, and in this case, the roll cage had done as it was designed, protecting them.

Sgt Steptoe swung his legs around, still sitting, going through the steps in firing the weapon, just like he was on the range back at Pendleton.   Place the safety on fire. Check, Hanks had already done that.   Pull the charging handle.   Check.   Hanks had done that, too.   He inspected the spotting rifle magazine, which looked dented.   He decided to skip using it.   The range was minimal, after all. He checked the sights one more time.   They were set for "HE" and 100 meters.   He hoped the round was something a little more effective against armor, but it was too late to worry about that.

Turning the range drum to 50 meters, he looked back and yelled out "Back blast area clear!"

Whether it actually was clear or not, he wasn't exactly sure given his foggy brain.   He sighted in on the tank, which was traversing both its machine gun and main gun along the tree line.   It was a light tank, but it looked huge in his sights. He was close enough that the patchwork light blue digital camouflage squares made it stand out more, giving him a specific point of aim.   He calmly depressed the launch lever and pulled the trigger, sending the rocket straight into the side of the tank.

Evidently, the round had not been HE but either HEDP or HEAA, probably the later as the resultant explosion sent the turret of the tank spinning end over end and at least 30 feet into the air.   Steptoe stared at the burning tank until something slammed into his chest.   Gasping for breath seemed to clear his head.   He had been hit, but a quick check showed that his armor had stopped the round.   He might have a broken rib, but that was a small price to pay. He scrambled back into the tree line and into the shallow fighting position he had scraped out earlier.

The skipper was still yelling over the handset, but he gave Steptoe a thumbs up. His head clearing and his hearing coming back, he felt a tremor coming over him.   He couldn't believe he had just taken on a tank and survived.

He tried to take a deep breath, but that brought on a spasm of pain from his bruised or broken ribs.   Looking out over the killing field, the Chinese attack had petered out. With both tanks gone, the infantry had retreated, but not without leaving bodies scattered on the crushed coral runway.   One soldier was only 20 meters in front of him, slowly and painfully trying to crawl back, leaving a bright red trail of blood.   He was in full sight of the Marines, but they were content to let him go.   If he managed the long crawl back, dragging useless legs, well, he was no longer a threat to anyone, and an able-bodied soldier would have to take the time to give him aid.

As the firing died down, reports started coming in. The Chinese attack, although beaten back, had been devastating.   Third Platoon had taken the brunt of the attack, and they had lost 8 Marines killed, including 1stLt Gaines.   Another 11 had been wounded.   Second Platoon had lost four Marines with eight wounded.   Doc Parker had been one of those killed, so the skipper sent Doc Sanjay, the senior corpsman, to take care of them.   The Filipinos had been the only ones to escape serious injury.

Technically, this was a victory.   But another such victory might be their last.   They just didn't have the manpower to stand up to another major assault.

Chapter 35

Aboard the Jinggan Shan

Captain Teng Huang-fu was livid.   That idiot, Major Lim, had actually gone into the attack, spooked by the American tilt-rotor that had made a brief appearance.   He had obviously been concerned that it would make a gun run on his troops, but couldn't he see that the plane had turned back?

Communications with the PLA Marines on the ground was still spotty, but he had watched the attack through his big eyes on his bridge wing.   Now, instead of three tanks on shore, he had none.   He had no armored personnel carriers, no artillery.   He had possibly 70 effectives on the beachhead and another 800 still onboard his ship.   The main issue was getting those 800 onshore where they could roll over the American soldiers.

From the beginning, this operation had been plagued with mismanagement and bad luck.   Initially, the two ships had set out with a half a brigade of Marines for a scheduled exercise.   When this contingency had come up, instead of pulling back into port to better prepare, they had been sent as is to dislodge the American invaders.

So instead of being combat-loaded, they didn't have enough ammunition and even the right types, they only had the ship's three Z-8 helos with no attack helos, and they had only 6 light amphibious tanks and 6 armored personnel carriers.

Even the ship's 3-inch gun was less than effective. Thitu was very flat, and while the gun was accurate in deflection, the slightest error in aiming or roll of the ship could send the round quite short or quite long.   The gun was quite effective in protection from smaller ships or in sinking a Somali or Malayan pirate, but against troops, it was only minimally useful.

Then the cursed American tilt-rotor had taken out not only one of his LCACs but one of his Z-8s as well.   Another LCAC had been damaged and was being hurriedly repaired, and a second Z-8 had been destroyed somehow back near the island's town.

The only good thing was that they had more than the normal 750-man Marine battalion on board. With budget concerns and shortages of bunker oil, their training cruise had been expanded to get more Marines trained instead of just the normal single battalion.

Of course, the Marines could not fight from the ship. They had to get ashore. And for all the lip service the PLA gave to amphibious operations, they just didn't have the capability to put large numbers of Marines or soldiers ashore quickly.

He raised the big eyes a bit to take in the roofs of the town towards the middle of the island. On one building, the red flag of the People's Republic had been spread out on the roof. He wondered if this was a ruse, but he had to go on the assumption that the missing Chinese citizens were inside. As such, he had ordered the building not be targeted.

There was one other undercurrent that was weighing on Captain Teng's mind that increased his anger. When Senior Captain Chou had sent him on this mission, he had made certain comments, purposely, Teng was sure, that lead him to believe that this operation was not the simple rescue and retaliation operation he had been told it was, that this was part of a larger strategy.

Captain Teng would never question orders. If the command sent him to invade Los Angeles or Sydney, he would do it without question. But Captain Teng hated incompetence. And if this was a planned operation, why would they be sent in half-assed and half-armed? Why not provide air support? Why not go in so robust that nothing could stand in their way? It just didn't make sense.

"Sublieutenant Chin, how long for high tide?" he asked over his shoulder, eyes still glued to the beach.

"Two hours and 18 minutes," came back the immediate reply.

He didn't let it show, but he was pleased with Chin. The young officer was extremely competent and would go far in the PLA Navy.

He slowly backed away from the big eyes and looked at Lieutenant Colonel Huang, the Marine battalion commanding officer. He had left the Marine standing at attention for the last few minutes.

"Well, Lieutenant Colonel Huang, I hope you understand my orders," he said, keeping a steel edge to his voice.

"Yes, Captain Teng. I understand."

"No more glory-seeking? No more impromptu deviations from orders?"

"No Captain. We will follow your plan exactly."

Teng looked the Marine over. The PLA Marine Corps was the newest branch of the PLA, only reformed back in 1980 after being disbanded for almost 30 years. They were tough, he had to admit, in superb physical shape and used to extreme conditions. But sometimes their macho self-image got in the way of modern warfare. All PLA Marines were expert martial artists, for example, spending untold hours in hand-to-hand combat training. How that helped a tanker or an artilleryman, well, Captain Teng didn't know. Even an infantryman would be better served becoming an expert with his Type 95 Assault Rifle than learning how to break a brick with his hand.

This debacle was not totally the Marine commander's fault, though, he realized. It was the Navy, his own ship, that couldn't project the Marines' full force ashore. Well, that was going to change.

"I will allow you to lead the attack from the front, as you requested. I trust that you will succeed in your mission."

The Marine's chest actually swelled as he shouted out, "Thank you, captain. I will not fail you."

"It is not me you would be failing, but China. Now, go, get your troops ready."

Lieutenant Colonel Huang saluted, then did a perfect military about face before racing off.

One of the problems with the island was that the only reasonable place to conduct a landing was at the runway, and the seawall and foundation for the runway were just high enough that the LCACs could not clear the lip and get up on the land itself. Elsewhere, the rocks and jungle were too thick to enable any vessel to get ashore. However, to the west, over the same reef that still held the rusting hulk of a Filipino Navy ship that had run aground years ago, the vegetation near the shore was not quite as thick, certainly not thick enough to stop an LCAC from at least making it up to dry land. At high tide, there would be enough clearance for his remaining three LCACs and a few of his smaller boats to breach the outer reef and make it to shore. The vegetation was still too thick there to try and land tanks or armored personnel carriers, but it was feasible for the infantry Marines.

In addition to about 90 Marines in various launches and small boats available to him, and with the LCACs overloaded, he was going to land almost another 200 Marines in the LCACs on the west side of the island where they could roll up the American's flank. Supported by his remaining three tanks, which were already being ferried ashore to the south side of the runway, another 120 Marines already ashore and still arriving, and his lone helo, this would be more than enough to overwhelm the Americans. There wasn't any way they could resist.

Chapter 36

Zongnaihai, Beijing

General Chen Jun, Chief of Staff for the People's Liberation Army, walked down the hall of the party headquarters, his mind racing. He had just left the general secretary's office. When he had been summoned, he had assumed he was going to be sacked at best, at worst, well, that was better left unmentioned.

Instead, he had been ushered in with respect by the general secretary's staff and brought to the great man without delay. The general secretary even poured him tea.

Yu Deijang, the third-ranked vice premier was also there, smiling and asking about his wife and family. He asked General Chen to give his regards to his granddaughter on her birthday. Idle pleasantries took only a minute or so before the *raison d'être* for the meeting became clear. They wanted to know what he had planned to do about Taiping and Thitu.

This floored him. The People's Republic had made great pains to separate the PLA from any avenue of power. The PLA was an instrument of the Party, controlled by the Central Military Commission. Both men sipping tea with him were on that commission. For them to ask him with the deference they were showing was unusual, to say the least. In all the history of the nation, the CMC ordered, the PLA obeyed.

Not sure what they expected, he had spouted familiar party themes. They seemed to agree with him, but before he left, they made it clear that victory in the Wanli Shitang was vital to Chinese interests.

At least he now knew which way he was expected to jump. With this in mind, he was on his way out to return to PLA headquarters and give the order to General Li to use what resources he needed to finish the job at hand. Before he could get to security, though, Wang Jinping, the second-ranked vice premier personally stopped him in the hall.

"General Chen. It is good to see you here. I was

about to call you, but as you are already here, perhaps we can go to my office and chat?"

"I would be honored, vice premier. Be assured, though, that the general secretary has already spoken to me about my duty."

"Ah, yes, the general secretary. Well, please humor me, if you will." The second-ranked vice premier held an arm out as if to escort the general.

General Chen shrugged. He wanted to get back and give the orders. Who knew what the Americans would do the longer this dragged out? But when the third most powerful man in the country asked for your presence, then who was he to say no?

Vice Premier Wang also asked about his granddaughter and her birthday. *Did the entire CMC keep tabs on his granddaughter?* he wondered.

They walked into the vice premier's spacious office. Sitting there, evidently waiting for them, were two more members of the CMC and another five members of the Politburo. This was a heavy meeting. General Chen wanted to assure them that he knew his duty, but years climbing the ranks in the PLA had given him a degree of political savvy. Sometimes, being astute meant keeping silent.

This group didn't waste time. As soon as the tea had been served, the vice premier got to business.

"General Chen, do you think the standard of living is better for our people now than it was, say 50 years ago?" the vice premier asked.

"Why certainly, sir, thanks to the Party and its leadership," came the rote answer.

"And why is that, general?"

"Well, because, well, … the Party has led the people into prosperity."

"But how? What tools did they use?"

"We built up our manufacturing, our power."

"And who do we sell to, general? Who gets all those cars, machines, tools, electronics—all those things we make?"

"Why, the world does, vice premier," he replied.

"And who is our biggest trading partner?"

"The Americans are. They buy all our products."

"You are correct, General Chen. The Americans buy 22% of all Chinese exports. So I want to ask you, if we were at war with the Americans, how much of that 22% would they still buy?"

"Trade would be cut off, vice premier. They wouldn't buy anything."

"Exactly," Vice Premier Wang said, as if lecturing an undergraduate class. "And if the Japanese, the EU, the Russians, if they joined in a war, what would that do to trade?"

"I don't know the numbers, sir. But it would cut our trade."

"It would cut our trade by 76%, General Chen. That would plunge the country into recession. Inflation would take over, and that, as I am sure you are aware, would lead to civil unrest," he said, leaning back as if his point had been made.

"But Africa wouldn't join in a war, nor India," General Chen pointed out.

"We get raw materials from Africa, but as far as hard goods, they still do not buy much from us," Liang Chen-du, a younger member of the Politburo interjected, leaning forward in his seat, his round, soft face eager to make his point known.

General Chen sat back, his tea cooling and forgotten. He had thought his way forward was clear, but it was evident to him that this group of men did not want the conflict to continue. But why make their case to him? They needed to get together and decide amongst themselves, then just tell him what to do. This was not a military decision, after all. The military was merely the tool to implement the decision, whatever that may be.

"How would your granddaughter fare, general, if you could not provide for her, to buy her the things she wants in life?" the vice premier asked.

Was that an implied threat? he wondered. If so, that was not a smart thing to do. He was not without some power himself.

And then it hit him.   Not only did he have *some* power, for the first time in the history of the nation, he had *the* power.   With a united Party, with a united CMC, the PLA had no power.   But the CMC, even the Party as a whole, was not united.   There were two distinct factions, neither strong enough to overwhelm the other faction.   The PLA, which had long been kept subservient to eliminate the chance of a coup, had the ability to shift the landscape, to put the power into one faction or the other.   It could even take over, he realized, leading the way forward for the nation.

He settled back into his chair.

"Vice Premier Wang, my granddaughter would understand if she had to sacrifice.   She would do what is right for China."

"Just as I am sure you will do the right thing for the nation, for our people.   They have put their trust in you," the vice premier said, rising to shake his hand.

General Chen rose as well, and the two men shook.

What is right for China, Second-ranked Vice Premier Wang, may not match what you think is right, though, he thought before nodding at the others and leaving the office.

Chapter 37

Pagasa Island

Sergeant Harrington Steptoe had a wicked headache, and
that bothered him much more than his aching ribs. He
realized he probably had a concussion, but he didn't want to
bother Doc Sanjay, who had some much more serious cases
to attend. With Doc Parker among the dead, Doc Sanjay
had his hands full trying to stabilize the seriously wounded.
Some of them weren't going to make it unless help arrived
right ricky-tick.

The skipper was trying to consolidate his forces. He
had pulled two squads back from First Platoon, leaving only
one squad and the mortar section to cover their rear. The
odd bursts of fire from the north were proof enough that
something was going on up there, and they could not afford
to be surprised from that direction. With only five mortar
rounds left, only one team was left as mortarmen—the other
two teams became riflemen.

The two squads from First supplemented the decimated
Third, but even then, the line was thin. The east side of the
line, with Second and the Filipinos, was a little better off, but
still, the distance between fighting positions was greater than
what was recommended.

The ammo counts were trickling in, and the numbers
weren't good. After redistribution, each Marine had about
9 rounds left. There was one SRAW Predator round, and
the machine guns had less than 20 rounds apiece. The
Chinese assaults had been turned back, but at a huge cost in
ammunition, not even considering the more serious loss of
life and limb. One more concerted effort by the Chinese
and they would quickly be hand-to-hand.

Steptoe listened in to the skipper as the company
headquarters and the platoon commanders discussed the
situation. He and Doc Sanjay were part of the
headquarters, but Doc was off treating the wounded, and
Steptoe was still somewhat dazed, so he was content to
merely observe. The comm was pretty much set, anyway,

with the wire and his three runners.

"Maybe we need to hit them first," the first sergeant said, straightening up a bit to glance over the runway.

"And cross that killing field?" the skipper asked. "That didn't serve them too well," he continued, pointing to the Chinese bodies that were beginning to bloat in the afternoon sun.

One tank was still on fire, the black smoke rising high into the air. The other two merely seemed abandoned as if they could be fired up and brought back into the attack. The one still on fire was the tank that Steptoe had taken out. It was close enough that he could smell the diesel and scorched hulk. It still seemed strange to think that he had somehow managed to kill the blue beast.

"You know we can't hold up much longer. And they keep bringing in more. If we can catch them on their offload, maybe we can knock out those damn LCACs," First Sergeant Davidson continued.

"I agree with you, Burke, but what're we going to knock them out with? A few grenades? And how're we going to get to them?" Capt Niimoto countered.

"What about around the end, like the Filipinos did?" he asked.

"I think they've got that covered now, First Sergeant," Lt Blumenthal put in. "Lieutenant Jones says the Chinese have a pretty strong force covering that flank now."

"Jones" did not sound like a typical Filipino name, but the Filipino lieutenant proved to be pretty competent, so Steptoe would be inclined to take his word on that. The skipper evidently shared the same opinion.

"I would love to take it to them. Just sitting here doesn't seem right, but in the defense, that's where we have the best chance at success. We just need to hold out until the MEU can reinforce us," the skipper said, glancing at his watch. "I think that can be as early as maybe 45 minutes?"

"I wish we could see what they're doing now," the XO said, peering through the trees and across the runway. "We think they have three tanks, right?"

"Yes, sir," Gunny Dailey responded.

"And we have only one SRAW, right?"

The gunny and the skipper nodded.

"So maybe we take out one tank, if we're lucky. That means there're two more. And that's when you want us to retreat, sir?"

The XO could be hot-blooded, to say the least. Steptoe never knew where he stood with the tall Wyoming Marine. He'd never been able to peg the man. And now he looked pretty upset.

"I wouldn't call it a retreat, Chael. The tanks can't follow us into the jungle, so by pulling back, we're going to force the Chinese to come after us on foot. And I don't think infantry to infantry that they can defeat us. Do you?" the skipper asked.

"Oh no, sir," the XO hurriedly responded. "It's just that, well, it just seems wrong to fall back in front of Chinese soldiers, sir."

"Falling back doesn't mean retreat," the first sergeant said. A moment ago, First Sergeant Davidson had been advocating an attack, but now he was onboard with pulling back. Steptoe didn't know if he had really embraced the skipper's plan or if he merely wanted to confront the XO. Neither man had ever seemed to fully accept the other, often vying for the skipper's attention. Steptoe thought it rather immature that they still brought that competition here when lives depended on professionalism.

Steptoe looked again to the Chinese position. They were less than 200 meters away, less than what every Marine fired on the rifle range. They could see the very tops of the three tanks, and there were furtive movements and quick glimpses of Chinese soldiers and they scurried about. It was surreal that they were so close, yet for the last 30 minutes or so, they seemed to be ignoring the Marines. Of course, it only seemed like they were ignoring them. They were building up their forces, and Steptoe was not looking forward to when they kicked off whatever it was they were planning. This was only the calm before the storm.

"November-Six-Tango, this is Sierra-Two-Whiskey, do you read me, over?"

It took a moment for Sgt Steptoe to realize that someone was trying to reach him over his radio. He had taken the radio off his back and stowed it in his fighting hole, just a piece of useless gear. He scrambled back to his hole, gasping from what that did to his ribs as he dove to reach the handset that he had wrapped around the harness.

"Kilo Company, come on, answer!" came another attempt, the operator throwing radio procedures out the window.

"This November-Six, um, this is Kilo Company, over!" he shouted into the handset.

"I've got them!" the voice came over, a little quieter as the operator--Sgt Bigby, it sounded like to Steptoe--spoke to someone else back on his end. "Kilo, look, you've got two Chinese cruise missiles inbound, impact in 90 seconds. These are the real thing. Take whatever cover you can, over."

Steptoe looked up to the others, but they had heard the message. All looked stunned.

"Uh, roger, over," he replied, routine taking over.

"Kilo Company, God be with you," came the simple response.

"Take cover, take cover!" the shout went out, making its way down the Marines' line.

Lt Blumenthal jumped up and rushed towards his platoon, echoing the warning.

"Well, I guess it was too good to be true, that this would be an infantry fight," the skipper said bitterly. "If they are committing cruise missiles, well, expect air strikes next if any of us survive."

"What do we do now, sir?" asked the XO, the edge of panic starting to creep into his voice.

"Not much we can do, lieutenant," the first sergeant answered calmly. "The Chinese cruise missiles pack a hell of a punch, enough to take out a carrier or an entire city block, and we're better off here and low, closer to their own troops." He craned his neck to look across the runway. "I wonder if they know they're screwed, too. No way they're going to be untouched."

Sgt Steptoe's ears were still ringing, but he became aware of a low rumbling from the north. He tried to look through the trees.

"Yea, that's them," the skipper confirmed.

He looked around at his headquarters. "It's been an honor, Marines, to serve with you. Semper fi."

There was no overt panic as the Marines came to grip with their fate. With their lines well over a kilometer long, some Marines would survive the strike, and maybe the mortar section and recon would escape unscathed, but any survivors would be easy pickings for the overwhelming might of the entire Chinese assault force. Even if some of those Chinese already ashore were casualties as well, they could already see the rotors of the helo on the far off ship turning on the deck while an LCAC started to emerge from the ship's well deck. Those would be the main landing force.

The approaching rumble became louder. Steptoe didn't realize you could hear your approaching death. He thought it would be more like the sequences shown on CNN or online, with death coming in silently. He guessed cruise missiles were either louder or slower than other forms of killing machines.

"Good work on that tank, Stepchild," Tony told him as the missiles began their final targeting.

They'd gone through a lot together. They'd both survived New Delhi when so many others hadn't. They both survived Somalia. Now, it looked like they would be going out together. It somehow seemed fitting.

Stepchild closed his eyes as the missiles reached them . . . then opened them again as both missiles continued on, out over the water.

He could clearly see the red star on both of them as the huge weapons flew on—they were definitely Chinese. He wondered for a second if they were going to turn back to get at them from a different angle, but the missiles ran true, right to the Chinese ship.

The twin explosions sent huge gouts of fire and smoke into the air. A moment later, the shock wave hit them. At more than three kilometers away, they witnessed the death of a ship.

Chapter 38

Pagasa Island

Pete took a deep drink of water, watching the Chinese Marines, he now knew them to be, load up on the big Chinese transport.   It was hard to grasp that only the day before, they had been at each other's throats.   Now, the disarmed Marines were calmly getting on board their aircraft to get out of there, guarded by only a dozen or so Filipino soldiers.

Pete had spent most of yesterday afternoon playing hide-and-seek with the Chinese Marines, the jungle too dense for real fighting.   Other than the Chinese Marine he had killed, only one other Chinese Marine had been even hit, and on the American side, only Cpl Gutenev had been slightly injured, that from a branch going through a chunk of his thigh.   None of the Filipinos had been injured.

When the Chinese cruise missiles had flown overhead, he hadn't known what was going on.   Then Gunny Sloan's helmet comm had come to life, and in the resultant mish-mash of messages, he found out the Chinese ship had been destroyed.   Pete had figured that the American forces had finally arrived, or maybe the *Mississippi* had discovered what was going on and had taken out the Chinese ship.

He was shocked to find out that the two missiles were Chinese.   They had taken out their own ship.

The Chinese Marines on the island had received orders to surrender.   Chael Shelton had told him later that evening that an angry Chinese major had followed a Chinese Marine carrying a white rag tied to a pole across the runway to be led to Tony Niimoto.   With terse words, his eyes blazing, he had surrendered his Marines to the skipper, despite his greater numbers and three tanks.

Those three tanks, in their odd-looking blue digital camouflage, stood parked at the east end of the runway. Two Chinese crewmembers stood by each one, waiting for a Chinese transport to pick them up as well.   Something was obviously up, but Pete didn't understand why the Chinese were being cut so much slack.   They were the enemies, weren't they?

It had taken much longer for the 26 Chinese Marines facing him to surrender.   They could hear the crackle of their radios, and even some yelling, but evidently, the Chinese were cautious.   When Pete had been given the message from Kilo that the Chinese were surrendering, he had risked calling out into the jungle that he would accept their surrender.   A few minutes later, a voice called out in broken English that they would be coming out, to hold their fire.

Pete had kept most of his Marines hidden, meeting the Chinese with only SSgt Tolbert and Cpl Schmidt.   He had each Chinese Marine put his weapon on the deck before the moving further back to his Marines.   They didn't have any plastic wrist ties, so there was no way to restrain them.   He had to trust that they really had surrendered.

The Chinese lieutenant had seemed upset when he saw the number of Marines Pete had, but he also seemed resigned.   With some of the Filipinos picking up the Chinese weapons, he had a few more guards to escort the prisoners back to the town, and the Chinese sullenly, but without incident, let themselves be escorted out of the jungle.

The town was pretty damaged, the control tower down, and a still smoking hulk of a crashed helo lay on the ground. Pete's heart fell when he saw the tower, but he could not leave his prisoners to check on what happened to McNamara's team.

He marched the prisoners to the runway and handed them over, then rushed back to the town, not bothering to check in with the skipper.   There were no bodies in the tower, so he ran over to the mortar section asking about McNamara.   They pointed him to the community center, which had escaped unscathed.

Inside, he found McNamara and Maus being tended by one of Kilo's corpsmen.   McNamara was conscious, but his back was probably broken.   Maus had broken legs and an arm at the minimum.   It was then that he learned that Cpl Holleran had not made it. He had been in the control tower when it had been hit, and he had not survived the fall.

This was the first of his Marines to die. He had seen other Marines die, even friends, and that had hit him, but this was different. Mark Holleran was one of HIS Marines. He had trained with him, he had lived with him. It hit him hard, and it took several minutes for him to gather himself.

The sounds of an aircraft made him jump, but it was an American Osprey, which made several passes and got confirmation over the radio that all was secure before landing. The most seriously wounded were lifted off the island and back to the *Makin Island* which had first gone to Taiping Island before being diverted to Thitu, or Pagasa Island, as the Filipinos kept telling him. An hour later, the first of the American helos arrived, bringing in supplies, more Marines, and taking off more of the wounded and dead. One of the helos brought in an MP team and the MEU XO, and they quickly took over the prisoners, allowing most of Kilo to get some rest.

By then, the Chinese ship had disappeared beneath the waves. When the *Makin Island* arrived offshore, there was no visible evidence that the Chinese ship had even been there.

An hour later, a Filipino C-130 landed, and about 100 Filipino soldiers ran out, looking ready for bear. They were commanded by a full colonel, and he wasted no time in taking charge of the island. He insisted on searching each Chinese Marine and soldier again, the PLA Army soldiers being the ones who had made the initial assault and who had been previously taken prisoner, but when he wanted to truss each prisoner like a turkey, the MEU XO, LtCol Ramsey, had intervened. Evidently, word had been passed down on how to treat the prisoners, and after some heated radio calls, probably back to the Filipino Army headquarters, the prisoners were left as they were and were fed and watered. The dead were treated with respect and covered with either white tarps or placed inside body bags.

When Pete saw how many Chinese had died, he had been surprised. There had to have been 200 bodies there waiting to be repatriated back to China. He knew Kilo Company had suffered pretty badly as well, but nowhere near that badly.

He had wondered which one of those covered bodies had been the Marine he had killed.   He knew it could have been him, maybe should have been him.   Why that young man had chosen to go hand-to-hand was beyond him.   That decision had cost him his life.   And that was why he was in a body bag, laying out on the runway, instead of himself.

While relieved that he had made it, even if banged up a bit, he didn't know what to feel.   He was still angry about Cpl Holleran, angry that none of this had been necessary. And yes, he was confused as to why the Chinese were being treated so well.   Oh, he wasn't advocating torture or retaliation, but why were they going home, even before the Marines were to be evacuated, was beyond him.   He knew this was coming from on high, but it still rankled him. Those "on high" hadn't fought in this stinking jungle.

Getting a good meal and a good night's sleep had done wonders for his mood, though.   Now, he was a little more detached as he watched the Chinese load the big transport.

"So . . ." a soft voice said beside him.

He turned to see Analiza stepping up beside him.

"So," he responded, realizing how dumb that sounded.

"It seems strange to see them just leaving like this, like they are going home from a tour."

"I know what you mean," he replied.

They stood together for awhile, neither saying anything.

"How's your nose?" she asked, obviously searching for something to say.

He reached up to gingerly touch it before answering, "It hurts, and Doc says its probably broken, but there's no serious damage.   They're going to look at it back on the ship."

With his other scars, a crooked nose, courtesy of the kick to his face by the now dead Chinese Marine, was the least of his worries.

"So, you'll be going back soon?" she asked.

Did he hear a hint of regret in the question?

"Yeah," he looked at his watch before continuing, "in about two hours."

They were quiet for a moment before they both blurted out "You know, the Philippines..." and "Can I . . ."

"Oh, sorry, you go first," he told her.

"Well, pardon me if I'm a little forward, but the Philippines is a lovely place, not like here on Pagasa. If you ever want to come visit, well, I would be happy to be your tour guide," she said in a rush, as if afraid she wouldn't get it all out.

He realized that he would like that.

"I don't know when I could," he said, seeing her eyes fall in disappointment before he hurriedly added, "but I would be happy to come visit. Maybe when this deployment is over next year."

She smiled in relief and moved closer to him as they turned their attention to the last of the Chinese to board the plane. He wondered if he should put his arm around her, but it didn't seem right. Too much had happened here. He would keep in contact, and if things worked out, he would give it a shot. Until then, he still had his platoon to lead.

Chapter 39

Beijing

Things moved quickly in the Chinese government. This was not like the West where things could drag out over years of indecision. General Chen looked at the document he was carrying. He folded it back up and slid it into his uniform jacket. He felt it was his duty to deliver it.

Had it only been 6 days, he wondered?

The PLA Chief of Staff had to admit that he had been more than tempted to choose a different path last week, when the fate of the nation rested solely on his shoulders. He could have sided with the general secretary, the man who had just two days ago turned in his resignation for "health reasons." He could have given General Li what he needed to succeed, and the People's Republic might now be the premier power in the world. But at what cost? The Americans held that unenviable position at the moment, and look what it has done to their economy. They still spent more on defense than the rest of the world combined.

And he had been tempted to do what the members of the Politburo likely feared, to stage a coup. As a military man, he held a degree of contempt for his seniors, those who made the decisions for soldiers to follow but never once having worn a uniform. That temptation was quickly squashed, though. He didn't want to become one of those whom he held in such low regard. And he knew he probably would be a poor leader. He knew the military, not agriculture, not diplomacy, not manufacturing and all the other things that made a country run.

In the end, despite his dislike of the politicians who wanted all of this to end, he knew what he had to do. He knew the Americans, NATO, and Russia feared the growing might of China, and they would not let this stand, especially the Americans. The cost to China would just be too high. Could they prevail? Possibly, but if they did, they would have destroyed their markets, the very people they needed to make China prosper.

The order to fire upon the *Jinggan Shan* had been perhaps the most difficult order he had ever given. Those were China's brave sons, men who were doing their patriotic duty. They had been blameless in everything.

But the ever increasingly aggressive American rhetoric required a dramatic action to assure the Americans that this was a mistake. That ended up being the party line, that this was all a tragic mistake instigated by others. This had been an action against both China and the US. Muslim terrorists, probably based in the southern Philippines, had hacked into Chinese systems and given the wrong information, leading the Chinese to believe that the US had planned the entire thing out and were in fact the aggressors. It had all been part of a plan to pit the two super powers against each other.

Aided by a few Chinese criminals in high places, out for financial gain, they had taken control of a small number of Chinese assets, namely two ships. It had taken a particularly astute and dedicated PLA Air Force captain to uncover the truth.

Had the Americans bought the story? Most likely not. But they didn't want war, either, and this gave them an out. The sinking of the *Jinggan Shan* provided the "punishment" to China, as would the coming announcement at the UN that the People's Republic ceded any claims, now and in the future, to the Wanli Shitang.

Of course, there were the survivors of the force to be considered as well. The crew of the *Changbai Shan* had been fairly easy. They had never closed with the Americans nor the Taiwan Chinese. It was easy to give them the concocted account of events. For the soldiers and Marines on Thitu, however, this was a bit problematic. They had fought both the Filipinos and the Americans. To convince them that this was all a big mistake, that "terrorists" had created the situation, was a little more difficult, especially as the unit that had fired the Long Sword cruise missiles had neglected to remove the red star that showed to anyone who saw it whose missile it was. Without that, it could have been a terrorist missile that had sunk the ship. All the surviving soldiers and Marines had been transferred to a base in Xinjiang for "debriefing." General Chen was confident that the new version of events would in fact soon become the ground truth.

The Politburo had authorized payments for all the Filipinos killed, most of them being in the C-130 that had been shot down, and to rebuild their town on Thitu... that is, Pagasa Island.   But that was peanuts compared to perhaps the biggest loss of this entire debacle, that the Americans now knew of the Chinese ability to hack and even shut down systems.   The entire American military was now undergoing "routine maintenance," ferreting out every piece of equipment and every program where the Chinese had gained control.   This was a huge loss, but as the largest exporter of military hardware, a loss that the Americans did not want to advertise that had happened.   They would clean their own systems first, then slowly clean the systems of all their client states.

This loss was the reason why Sung Wenyan was still among the breathing.   He was scum, to be sure, but scum with a talent.   He would help the task force that would design new ways to hack the Americans and other nations. They had lost one avenue, so a new avenue would have to be built.

He reached the locked door, guarded by a lone soldier. The soldier snapped to attention, then turned to unlock the door.   General Chen took off his cover and stepped inside.

General Li was sitting at the bare desk in the middle of the room, writing.   A perfectly made bed was in back of him. At least his discipline hadn't faltered.

General Li looked up at his entrance, then stood, coming to attention and saluting.

General Chen said nothing, but took the paper out of his pocket and handed it to him.   General Li read it, no change of expression coming over his face.   That was about what Chen had expected.

The paper was a simple receipt—for one round of ammunition.   It was made out to General Li's family.   They owed the Chinese government five yuan, payable upon receipt.

General Li folded the paper and handed it back to the chief of staff.

"Thank you for being the one to let me know. Do I have time to finish the letter to my family?" he calmly asked as if nothing much was wrong.

"Yes, you have another hour or so. I will personally deliver any letters you write."

"And the others?"

"Senior Captain Chou has received the same sentence, as has Commander Hung. No decision has been made yet for Admiral Hung. Your command center staff has been sentenced to prison for various lengths of time, excepting Sung Wenyan."

That brought a rise to Li's eyebrows. "Sung Wenyan? But..." he paused until understanding dawned on him. "Ah, his unique skills are probably needed."

General Chen merely nodded.

"It is sad that someone like him will thrive, when the patriots receive a different future, or lack thereof, I should say."

This was the closest General Li would come to a complaint, General Chen knew.

"And . . . ?" the question was left unsaid.

General Chen chose to respond to it. "The general secretary has decided to resign due to health concerns. The third-ranked vice deputy has also decided to resign. All signs point to Second-ranked Vice Premier Wang Jinping being appointed as the new general secretary."

"Ah, the general secretary? I wasn't sure if this all went that high."

"Yes, well, the ex-general secretary. I'll leave you now to finish your letters."

General Li saluted his chief of staff, who returned the salute and turned to leave. General Li's question stopped him, though.

"Why, General Chen? We could have succeeded."

General Chen hesitated. He could just walk out, his duty done. Li had chosen, and chosen wrong. Now he would pay the price for that failure.

Without turning around, he simply said, "China will succeed. But this was not the way to do it. The cost would have been too high. China is bigger than you, than me, than the Politburo.   It will last much longer than any of us, which will be evident to you personally in about an hour."

With that, he knocked on the door, walking out after the guard opened it.

Ben dan, he thought as he started walking down the hallway.

Normally, when someone called someone else a "dumb egg," it was with disdain.   But this time, he used the term with a degree of sympathy.   General Li was a good man. Good, but dumb.   To think he could play politics with the masters was idiocy.   He never should have assumed anything.   Without direct, specific orders, he should never have planned even one move.   He let his ego and nationalistic righteousness overcome common sense.   As a general consequence, the nation had been harmed.   As a personal consequence, his family received a bill for five yuan, the cost of one 7.62 mm round.

Chapter 40

Cebu, The Philippines

1st Lieutenant Peter Van Slyke watched the carousel, waiting for his bag to appear.   He wasn't sure what to expect.   He had arrived in Manila the evening before, and the frantic pace of that mega-metropolis had beaten him down.   He had been told by others to take only the official airport taxis, and as he got to his hotel near the US embassy in Ermita, he had been astonished at the filth and poverty that surrounded the Best Western.   Inside, though, the hotel had been much nicer, so he never left, eating in the hotel restaurant before trying to get some sleep.

He had gotten up early, then taken the hotel car back to the airport where he caught the 8:05 Cebu Pacific flight to Cebu.   The flight was different, to say the least.   At one point, all the flight attendants had broken out into song and dance.

The plane reached Cebu in an hour, and Pete took in the blue, blue ocean as it came in to land on the small island just off the main island of Cebu itself.   The plane landed with barely a jar and quickly taxied to the terminal.

Things seemed much more laid back in Cebu, and he immediately felt at ease.   The weather was pleasantly warm, but he wished he had worn shorts instead of his Levis which were sticking a bit.   He was just happy to be out of his uniform.   He knew his haircut labeled him as a Marine, as the Filipino ticket checker back in Manila had greeted him with a "semper fi," but with jeans and a polo shirt, he still felt the stress of the deployment slough away.

He had twelve more days of leave left to get rid of all the stress.   He had visited Sgt McNamara back at the Wounded Warrior battalion on the first day of his post-deployment leave, marveling at how far he had come in his rehabilitation.   The doctors gave the sergeant a good chance at a complete recovery.   The second day of his leave had been taking the flight from San Diego to Manila.   Now, his real leave was about to begin.

He had just spotted his seabag when he felt a light touch on his arm.   He turned to see Analiza standing there, simply lovely in her white cotton blouse and tan shorts.   He felt his heart miss a beat.

"Hi Peter, welcome to Cebu," she told him, her face radiant.

Pete didn't know what would come of his week-and-a-half in Cebu, but he was sure going to enjoy finding out.

Thank you for reading the three books of *The Return of the Marines*. I hope you enjoyed it. I would love to get your feedback, either in a review or through the website http://www.returnofthemarines.com.

If you would like updates on new books releases, news, or special offers, please consider signing up for my mailing list. Your email will not be sold, rented, or in any other way disseminated. If you are interested, please sign up at the link below:

http://eepurl.com/bnFSHH

Other Books by Jonathan Brazee

The Return of the Marines Trilogy
The Few
The Proud
The Marines

The Al Anbar Chronicles: First Marine Expeditionary Force--Iraq
Prisoner of Fallujah
Combat Corpsman
Sniper

The United Federation Marine Corps
Recruit
Sergeant
Lieutenant
Captain
Major
(Coming soon: Lieutenant Colonel)

JONATHAN P. BRAZEE

Rebel
(Set in the UFMC universe)

Werewolf of Marines
Werewolf of Marines: Semper Lycanus
Werewolf of Marines: Patria Lycanus

To The Shores of Tripoli

Wererat

Darwin's Quest: The Search for the Ultimate Survivor

Venus: A Paleolithic Short Story

Non-Fiction

Exercise for a Longer Life

Author Website
http://www.returnofthemarines.com

GLOSSARY

AO:	Area of Operations
BAH:	Basic Allowance for Housing
BM2:	Boatswain's Mate, 2nd Class
CDR:	Commander
CO:	Commanding Officer
CMC	Central Military Commission (China)
Cpl:	Corporal
CTF:	Combined Task Force
ERSS:	Expeditionary Resuscitative Surgical System
FAST:	Fleet Antiterrorism Security Team
HE	High Explosive
HEAA	High Explosive Anti-Armor
HEDP	High Explosive Dual Purpose (warhead)
IAR:	Infantry Automatic Rifle
IO:	Indian Ocean
LCAC:	Landing Craft Air Cushion
LCDR:	Lieutenant Commander
LCpl:	Lance Corporal
LTC:	Lieutenant Colonel (Army)
LtCol:	Lieutenant Colonel (USMC)
LZ:	Landing Zone
MCMAP	Marine Corps Martial Arts Program
MEU:	Marine Expeditionary Unit
NCO:	Non-Commissioned Officer
O-Club:	Officers' Club
OpsO:	Operations Officer
PFC:	Private First Class
PLA	People's Liberation Army (China)
Pvt:	Private
RASP:	Ranger Assessment & Selection Program
RHIB:	Rigid Hull Inflatable Boat
ROC	Republic of China (Taiwan)
ROE:	Rules of Engagement
RPG:	Rocket-propelled Grenade
Sgt:	Sergeant

SIGINT	Signal Intelligence
SMAW	Shoulder-Launched Multipurpose Assault Weapon
SNCO:	Staff Non-Commissioned Officer
SP	Shore Patrol
SRAW	Short-Range Assault Weapon
SOI:	School of Infantry
SSgt:	Staff Sergeant
STA:	Surveillance and Target Acquisition
T/E:	Table of Equipment
USAID:	United States Agency for International Development
VA	Veterans Administration
VBSS:	Visit, board, search, and seizure
XO:	Executive Officer

Made in the USA
Coppell, TX
11 November 2019